Ab

Cindy Myers becan̶̶̶̶̶̶̶̶̶̶̶̶̶̶̶̶̶̶̶̶
in eighth grade when̶̶̶̶̶̶̶̶̶̶̶̶̶̶̶̶̶̶
torrid historical rom̶̶̶̶̶̶̶̶̶̶̶̶̶̶̶̶
around among friend̶̶̶̶̶̶̶̶̶̶̶̶̶̶̶̶
English teacher confi̶̶̶̶̶̶̶̶̶̶ manuscript. Since then,
Cindy has written more than fifty published novels. Her
historical and contemporary romances and women's
fiction have garnered praise from reviewers and readers
alike.

Award-winning author **Amelia Autin** is an inveterate
reader who can't bear to put a good book down...or part
with it. Her bookshelves are crammed with books her
husband periodically threatens to donate to a good
cause, but he always relents...eventually. Amelia
currently resides with her Ph.D. engineer husband in
quiet Vail, AZ, where they can see the stars at night and
have a 'million dollar view' of the Rincon Mountains
from their back yard.

Carol Ericson lives in southern California, home of
state-of–the-art cosmetic surgery, wild freeway chases,
and a million amazing stories. These stories, along
with hordes of virile men and feisty women clamour
for release from Carol's head until she sets them free to
fulfil their destinies and her readers' fantasies. To find
out more about Carol and her current books, please
visit her website at www.carolericson.com, 'where
romance flirts with danger.'

Heroes in Hot Pursuit

Heroes in Hot Pursuit:
Love Under Fire

CINDI MYERS

AMELIA AUTIN

CAROL ERICSON

MILLS & BOON

First Published in Great Britain 2021
By Mills & Boon, an imprint of HarperCollins*Publishers*, Ltd
1 London Bridge Street, London, SE1 9GF

www.harpercollins.co.uk

HarperCollins*Publishers*
1st Floor, Watermarque Building,
Ringsend Road, Dublin 4, Ireland

HEROES IN HOT PURSUIT: LOVE UNDER FIRE
© 2021 Harlequin Books S.A.

Murder in Black Canyon © 2017 Cynthia Myers
Her Colton P.I. © 2016 Harlequin Books S.A.
Under Fire © 2015 Carol Ericson

Special thanks and acknowledgement to Amelia Autin Lam for her contribution to *The Coltons of Texas* series.

ISBN: 978-0-263-30259-2

MIX
Paper from
responsible sources
FSC™ C007454

MURDER IN BLACK CANYON

CINDI MYERS

Chapter One

As jobs went, this one paid more than most, Kayla reminded herself as she parked her battered Subaru at the mouth of the canyon a few miles from the Gunnison River. A private investigator in the small town of Montrose, Colorado, couldn't be overly picky if she wanted to keep putting food on the table and paying rent, though interceding in family squabbles had to be right up there with photographing philanderers on her list of least-favorite jobs.

Still, this assignment gave her an excuse to get out into the beautiful backcountry near Black Canyon of the Gunnison National Park called Dead Horse Canyon. She retrieved a small day pack from the backseat of the car and slipped it on, then added a ball cap to shade her face from the intense summer sun. A faint dirt trail marked the way into the canyon, through a windswept landscape of dark green piñon and juniper, and the earth tones of sand and gravel and scattered boulders.

A bird called from somewhere in the canyon ahead, the high, trilling call echoing off the rock and sending a shiver up Kayla's spine. Maybe she should have brought a weapon with her, but she didn't like to carry the handgun, even though she was licensed to do so. Her work as a private investigator seldom brought her into contact with anyone really threatening. She spent most of her time surveilling cheating spouses, doing background checks for businesses and serving the occasional subpoena. Talking to a twenty-four-year-old woman who had decided to camp out in the desert with a bunch of wandering hippies hadn't struck Kayla as particularly threatening.

But that was before she had visited this place, so isolated and desolate, far from any kind of help or authority. Someone holed up out here could probably get away with almost anything and not be caught. The thought unnerved her more than she liked to admit.

Shaking her head, she hit the button to lock her car and pocketed her keys. The hard part of the job was over—she had tracked down Andi Matheson, wayward adult daughter of Senator Peter Matheson. Now all she had to do was deliver the senator's message to the young woman. Whether Andi decided to mend fences with her father was none of Kayla's business.

Her boots crunched on fine gravel as she set out walking on the well-defined path. Clearly, a lot of feet had trod this trail recently. The group that referred to themselves as simply "the Family" had a permit to camp on this stretch of public land outside the national park boundaries. They had the area to themselves. No one else wanted to be so far away from things like electricity, running water and paved roads. Her investigation hadn't turned up much information about the group—only some blog posts by the leader, a young man whose real name was Daniel Metwater, but who went by the title of Prophet. He preached a touchy-feely brand of peace, love and living off the land that reminded Kayla of stuff she'd seen in movies about sixties-era flower children. Misguided and irresponsible, maybe, but probably harmless.

"Halt. You're not authorized to enter this area."

Heart in her throat, Kayla stared at the large man who blocked the path ahead. He had seemingly appeared out of nowhere, but he must have been waiting in the cluster of car-sized boulders to the left of the path. He wore baggy camouflage trousers and a green-and-black camouflage-patterned T-shirt stretched over broad shoulders. His full beard and long brown hair made him look like a cross between a biker and an old-testament patriarch. He wasn't armed, unless you counted the bulging muscles of his biceps, and what might have been a knife in the sheath on his belt. She forced herself to stand tall and look him in the eye. "This is public land," she said. "Anyone can hike here."

"We have permission to camp here," Camo-man said. "You'll need to walk around our camp. We don't welcome gawkers."

What are you hiding that you don't want me to see? Kayla thought, every sense sharpened. "I'm not here to gawk," she said. "I came to visit one of your—" What exactly did she call Andi—a disciple? A member? "A woman who's with you," she decided. "Andi Matheson."

"No one is here by that name." The man's eyes

revealed as much as a mannequin's, blank as an un-plugged television screen.

"I have information that she is. Or she was until as recently as yesterday, when I saw her with some other members of your group in Montrose." The three women, including Andi, had been leaving a coin op-erated Laundromat when Kayla had spotted them, but they had ignored her cries to wait and driven off. She had been on foot and unable to follow them.

"We do not have anyone here by that name," the man repeated.

So maybe she had changed her name and went by Moon Flower or something equally charming and silly. "I don't know what she's calling herself this week, but she's here and I want to talk to her," Kayla said. "Or satisfy myself that she isn't here." She spread her hands wide in a universal gesture of harmless-ness. "All I want to do is talk to her. Then I'll leave, I promise. What you do out here is your business— though I'm pretty sure blocking access to public land, whether you have a permit or not, is illegal. It might even get your permit revoked." She gave him a hard look to go with her soft words, letting him know she was perfectly willing to make trouble if she needed to.

He hesitated a moment, then nodded. "I'll need to search you for weapons. We don't allow instruments of destruction into our haven of peace."

She was impressed he could deliver such a line with a straight face. "So that knife on your belt doesn't count?"

He put a hand to the sheath at his side. "This is a ceremonial piece, not a weapon."

Uh-huh. And she had a "ceremonial" Smith & Wesson back at her home office. But no point arguing with him. "I'm not armed," she said. "And you'll just have to take my word for it, because I'm not in the habit of allowing strange men to grope me, and if you lay a hand on me I promise I *will* file assault charges." Not to mention she knew a few self-defense moves that would put him in the dirt on his butt.

A little more life came into the man's face at her words, but instead of arguing with her, he turned and walked down the trail. She followed him, curious as to what kind of compound the group had managed to erect in the wilderness.

The man turned into what looked like a dry wash, circled a dense line of trees and emerged in a clearing where a motley collection of travel trailers, RVs, pickup trucks, cars, tents, tarps and other makeshift shelters spread out over about an acre. To Kayla, it looked like a cross between the Girl Scout Jamboree she had attended as a child and the homeless encampments she had seen in Denver.

No one paid any attention to her arrival. A dozen or more men and women, and half as many children, wandered among the vehicles and shelters, tending campfires, carrying babies and talking. One man sat cross-legged in front of a van, playing a wooden flute, while two others kicked a soccer ball back and forth.

Kayla spotted Andi with a group of other women by a campfire. She looked just like the picture the senator had given her—straight blond hair to the middle of her back, heart-shaped face, upturned nose and brilliant blue eyes. She wore a long gauze skirt and a tank top, her slim arms tanned golden from the sun, and she was smiling. Not the picture of the troubled young woman the senator had painted. Rather, she looked like a model in an advertisement for a line of breezy summer fashions, or for a particularly refreshing wine.

Kayla started across the compound toward the young woman. Camo-man stepped forward as if to intercept her, but her hard stare stopped him. "Andi?" she called. "Andi Matheson?"

The young woman turned toward Kayla, her smile never faltering. "I'm sorry, but I don't go by that name anymore," she said. "I'm Asteria now."

Asteria? Kayla congratulated herself on not wincing. "My name's Kayla," she said.

"Do I know you?" Andi/Asteria wrinkled her perfect forehead a fraction of an inch.

"No. Your father asked me to check on you." Kayla stopped in front of the woman and scrutinized her more closely, already mentally composing her report to the senator. No bruises. Clear eyes and skin. No weight loss. If anything, she looked a little plumper than in the photos the senator had provided. In fact... her gaze settled on the rounded bump at the waistband of the skirt. "You're pregnant," she blurted.

Andi rubbed one hand across her belly. "My father didn't tell you? I'm not surprised, but he did know. It's one of the reasons I left. I didn't want to raise my child in his corrupt world."

Interesting that the senator had left out this little detail about his daughter. "He was concerned enough about you to hire me to find you and ask you to get in touch with him," Kayla said.

Andi's smile was gone now. "He just wants to try to talk me into getting rid of the baby." She turned to the two women with her. "My father can't understand the happiness and contentment I've found here with the Prophet and the Family. He's too mired in his materialistic, power-hungry world to see the truth."

Dressed similarly to Andi, the other two women stared at Kayla with open hostility. So much for peace and love, Kayla thought.

Andi turned back to Kayla. "How did you find me? I didn't tell anyone in my old life where I was going."

"I talked to your friend Tessa Madigan. She told me about attending a speech Daniel Metwater gave in Denver, and how taken you were with him and his followers. From there it wasn't that difficult to confirm you had joined the group."

"I only want to be left alone," Andi said. "I'm not harming anyone here."

Kayla looked around the compound, aware that pretty much everyone else there had stopped what they were doing to focus on the little exchange around the campfire. Even the flute player had lowered his instrument. Camo-man, however, had disappeared, perhaps slunk back to guard duty on the trail. "This isn't exactly a garden spot." She turned back to Andi. "What about the Family attracted you so much?" Senator Matheson was a wealthy man, and his only daughter had been a big part of his lavish lifestyle until a few months ago. Kayla had found dozens of pictures online of Andi and her father at celebrity parties and charity benefits, always dressed in designer gowns and dripping with jewels.

"The Family is a real family," Andi said. "We truly care for one another. The Prophet reminds us all to focus on the things in life that are really important and fulfilling and meaningful. Satisfaction isn't to be found in material wealth, but in living in harmony with nature and focusing on our spiritual well-being."

"You can't live on air and spiritual thoughts," Kayla said. "How do you all support yourselves?"

"We don't need a lot of money," Andi said. "The Prophet provides for us."

Camping on public land was free and they didn't have any utility bills, but they weren't living on wild game and desert plants, either—not judging by the smell of onions and celery emanating from a pot over the fire. "You're telling me your Prophet is footing the bill to feed and clothe all of you?"

"I am blessed to be able to share my worldly goods with my followers."

The voice that spoke was deep, smooth as chocolate and commanding as any Shakespearean actor. Kayla turned slowly and studied the man striding toward them. Sunlight haloed his figure like a spotlight, burnishing his muscular, bare chest and glinting on his loose, white linen trousers. He had brown curly hair glinting with gold, dark brows, lively eyes, a straight nose and sensuous lips. Kayla swore one of the women behind her sighed, and though she had been fully prepared to dislike this so-called "prophet" on sight, she wasn't immune to his masculine charms.

The man was flat-out gorgeous and potentially

lethally sexy. No wonder some women followed him around like puppies. "Daniel Metwater, I presume?" Kayla asked.

"I prefer the humble title of Prophet."

Since when was a prophet humble? But Kayla decided not to argue the point. "I'm Kayla Larimer." She offered her hand.

He took it, then bent and pressed his mouth to her palm—a warm, and decidedly unnerving, gesture. Some women might even think it was sexy, but Kayla thought the move too calculated and more than a little creepy. She jerked her hand away and her anger rose. "What's the idea of stationing a guard to challenge visitors to your camp?" she asked. "After all, you are on public land. Land anyone is free to roam."

"We've had trouble with curiosity seekers and a few people who want to harass us," Metwater said. "We have a right to protect ourselves."

"That defense won't get you very far in court if anything goes south," she said.

The smile finally faded. "Our policy is to leave other people alone and we ask that they show us the same courtesy."

One of the few sensible pieces of advice that Kayla's mother had ever given her was to keep her mouth shut, but Kayla found the temptation to poke at this particularly charming snake to be too much. "If you really are having trouble with people harassing you, you should ask for help from local law enforcement," she said.

"We prefer to solve our own problems, without help from outsiders."

The Mafia probably thought that way, too, but that didn't make them innocent bystanders who never caused a stink, did it?

"I'm not here to stir up trouble," she said. "Andi's father asked me to stop by and make sure she was all right."

"As you can see, Asteria is fine."

Kayla turned back to the young woman, who was gazing at Metwater, all limpid-eyed and adoring. "I assume you have a doctor in town?" she asked. "That you're getting good prenatal care."

"I'm being well cared for," she said, her eyes still locked to Metwater's.

"Asteria is an adult and has a right to live as she chooses," Metwater said. "No one who comes to us is held against his or her will."

Nothing Kayla saw contradicted that, but she just didn't understand the attraction. The place, and this man, gave her the creeps. "Your father would love to hear from you," she told Andi. "And if you need anything, call me." She held out one of her business cards. When the young woman didn't reach for it, Andi shoved it into her hand. "Goodbye," she said, and turned to walk away.

She passed Metwater without looking at him, though the goose bumps that stood out on her skin made her pretty sure he was giving her the evil eye— or a pacifist prophet's version of one. She had made it all the way to the edge of the encampment when raised voices froze her in her tracks. The hue and cry rose not from the camp behind her, but from the trail ahead.

Camo-man appeared around the corner, red-faced

and breathless. Behind him came two other men, dragging something heavy between them. Kayla took a few steps toward them and stared in horror at the object on a litter fashioned from a tarp and cut branches. Part of the face was gone, and she was pretty sure all the black stuff with the sticky sheen was blood—but she knew the body of a man when she saw one.

A dead man. And she didn't think he had been dead for very long.

Chapter Two

After ten years away, Lieutenant Dylan Holt had come home. When he had left his family ranch outside Montrose to pursue a career on Colorado's Front Range with the Colorado State Patrol, he had embraced life in the big city, sure he would never look back. Funny how a few years away could change a person's perspective. He hadn't realized how much he had missed the wide-open spaces and more deliberate pace of rural life until he had had the chance to transfer back to his hometown.

It didn't hurt that he was transferring to a multi-agency task force focused on preventing and solving crimes on public lands promised to be the kind of interesting and varied work he had longed for. "For our newer team members, plan on spending a lot of time behind the wheel or even hiking into the backcountry," FBI Captain Graham Ellison, the leader of the Ranger Brigade, addressed the conference room full of officers. "Despite any impression you might have gotten from the media, the majority of our work is routine and boring. You're much more likely to bust a poacher or deal with illegal campers than to encounter a terrorist."

"Don't tell Congress that. They'll take away our increased funding." This quip came from an athletic younger guy with tattooed forearms, Randall Knightbridge. He was one of the Brigade veterans who had been part of a raid that brought down a terrorism organization that had been operating in the area. The case had been very high profile and had resulted in a grant from Homeland Security that allowed the group to expand—and to hire Dylan and two other new recruits, Walt Riley and Ethan Reynolds.

Next to Randall sat Lieutenant Michael Dance, with the Bureau of Land Management, and DEA Agent Marco Cruz. Behind them, Deputy Lance Carpenter from the Montrose Police Department, Simon Woolridge, a computer specialist with Immigration and Customs Enforcement, and Carmen Redhorse, with the Colorado Bureau of Investigation, listened attentively. The veterans had welcomed the rookies to the team with a minimum of good-natured ribbing.

"We do have a couple of areas of special concern," Captain Ellison continued. He picked up a pointer and indicated a spot on a map of the Rangers' territory— the more than thirty thousand acres of Black Canyon of the Gunnison National Park, plus more than 106,000 acres in adjacent Curecanti National Recreation Area and Gunnison Gorge National Conservation Area. "We've got a group camping in Dead Horse Canyon, some sort of back-to-the-land group. Not affiliated with any organized movement that we can identify. They have a legal permit and may be harmless, but let's keep an eye on them."

One of the other new hires, Ethan Reynolds, stuck up his hand. Ellison acknowledged him. "Agent Reynolds has some special training in cults, militia groups and terrorist cells," the captain said. "What can you tell us about this bunch?"

"They call themselves the Family and their leader is Daniel Metwater, son of a man who made a pile in manufacturing plastic bags. He calls himself the Prophet, though he doesn't identify with any organized religion. There are a lot of women and children out at that camp, so it wouldn't hurt to keep an eye open for signs of abuse or neglect. But so far, they've lived up to their reputation as peace-loving isolationists."

"Right." Ellison eyed the rest of them. "We don't have any reason to harass these people, but keep your eyes and ears open. On to other areas of concern…"

The captain continued with a discussion of off-road vehicles trespassing in a roadless area, reports of poaching activity in another area and suspicion of hazardous chemical dumping in a remote watershed.

"Randall, you and Walt check out the chemical dump," the captain ordered. "Carmen, take Ethan with you to look into the roadless violation. Dylan, you go with—"

The door burst open, letting in a gust of hot wind that stirred the papers on the table. "I want to report a body," a woman said.

She was dressed like a hiker, in jeans and boots, a day pack on her back. Her shoulder-length brown hair was in a windblown tangle about her head and her eyes were wide with horror, her face chalk-white. "A dead man," she continued, her voice quavering, but her expression determined. "I think he was shot.

Part of his face was gone and there was a lot of blood and—"

"Why don't you sit over here and tell us about it." Carmen Redhorse, the only female on the Ranger team, stepped forward and took the woman's hand. "Let's start with your name."

"Kayla Larimer." The woman accepted the glass of water Carmen pushed into her hands and drained half of it. When she lowered the glass, some of the terror had gone out of her eyes. Hazel eyes, Dylan noted. Gold and green, like some exotic cat's.

"All right, Kayla," Carmen said. "Where did you see this body?"

"I can show you. It's in a canyon on Bureau of Land Management, or BLM, land. The Family is camping there."

"Your family is camping there?"

"Not my family." She gave an impatient shake of her head. "That hippie group or whatever you want to call them."

"The peace-loving isolationists," Dylan said.

Kayla looked at him. She wasn't desperate or hysterical or any of the other emotions he might have expected. She looked—angry. At the injustice of the man's death? At being forced to witness the scene? He felt a definite *zing* of attraction. He had always liked puzzles and figuring things out. He wanted to figure out this not-so-typical woman.

"Are you a member of the Family?" Ethan asked.

"No!" The disdain in her tone dropped the temperature in the room a couple degrees. She slid a hand into the pocket of her jeans and pulled out a business card. "I'm a private detective."

"What were you doing in Dead Horse Canyon?" Graham Ellison asked.

She took another drink of water, then set the glass aside. "A client of mine has a daughter who cut off contact with him. He hired me to find her, and I located her living with the group. Then he asked me to check on her and make sure she was okay, and to ask her to get in touch with him."

"He had to hire a PI for that?" Dylan asked.

That hot, angry gaze again. "He hired me to find her, first. He didn't know where she was. After I located her, he thought she might listen to me if I approached her initially."

"Most parents wouldn't be too thrilled about their kid running off to join a group some people might see as a cult," Ethan said.

"Exactly." Kayla nodded. "Anyway, I found the young woman, gave her the message from her father and was leaving when three men rushed into the camp, shouting. Two of them were dragging a body behind them. The body of a man. He was covered in blood and…" Her lips trembled, but she pressed them together, her nostrils flaring as she inhaled. "Part of his head was gone."

"What were they shouting?" Graham asked.

"They said they were walking out in the desert and saw him lying there."

"Saw him lying where?" Carmen asked.

Kayla shook her head. "I don't know. And before you ask, I don't know why they thought they needed to bring him back to the camp. I told the leader—some guy who calls himself the Prophet—that his men shouldn't have touched the body, and that they needed to call the police, but he ignored me and ordered the men to take the dead man back to where they had found him, then report to him for a cleansing ritual."

"He refused to report the incident?" Graham's voice was calm, but his expression was one of outrage.

"He said they didn't have cell phones. Maybe they don't believe in them."

"Phones don't work in that area, anyway." Simon Woolridge, the team's tech expert, spoke for the first time. "They don't work on most of the public land around here. No towers."

"That's why I didn't call you, either," Kayla said. "By the time I got a signal on my phone, I was almost here."

"Did anyone say anything about who the dead man might be?" Graham asked. "Did you recognize him?"

"No. Everyone looked as horrified as I did."

"Did the men do as the Prophet asked and take the body away?" Dylan asked.

"I don't know. I left before they did anything. No one tried to stop me. I wanted to get away from there and I headed straight here."

"What time was this?" Graham asked.

"I don't know. But it's a long drive. So…maybe an hour ago?"

"More like an hour and a half," Carmen said. "Dead Horse Canyon is pretty remote."

"Lieutenant Holt, I want you and Simon to check this out," Captain Ellison said. "Ms. Larimer, you ride with Lieutenant Holt and show him exactly where you were."

"We know where Dead Horse Canyon is," Simon protested.

"The canyon is seven miles long," the captain said. "She can show you the location more quickly."

Silently, Kayla followed Dylan to his Cruiser. He opened the passenger door for her and she slid in without looking at him. He caught the scent of her floral shampoo as she moved past him, and he noticed the three tiny silver hoops she wore in each ear. By the time he made it around to the driver's side, she was buckled in and staring out the windshield.

"You holding up okay?" he asked.

"I'm fine." Her clipped tone didn't invite sympathy or further conversation, so he started the Cruiser and followed Simon out of the parking lot. They followed the paved road through the national park for the first five miles, past a series of pull-offs that provided over-looks into the Black Canyon, a half-mile-deep gorge that was the reason for the park's existence. Every stop was crowded with RVs, vans and passenger cars full of tourists who had come to enjoy the wild beauty of the high desert of western Colorado.

"How long have you been a private detective?" he asked.

She was silent so long he thought she had decided not to talk to him, but when he glanced her way she said, "Two years."

"Do you have a law enforcement background?" A lot of PIs he knew started out with police or sheriff's departments before hanging their shingle to do investigations, but Kayla hardly looked old enough to have had many years on the force under her belt.

"No."

"How did you get into the work?"

She let out a sigh and half turned to face him. "Why do you care?"

"I'm making conversation. Why are you so hostile?"

She ducked her head and massaged the bridge of her nose. "Sorry. I think I've just had an overdose of arrogant, good-looking men today."

She thought he was good-looking? He filed the information away for future reference. "I'm not trying to be arrogant," he said. "Cops are trained to get the facts of a situation as quickly as possible. That can come across as brusque sometimes."

She nodded. "I get that. It's just been a tough day. A tough week, really." She glanced at him, her expression a little less guarded. "I thought I was applying for a secretarial position when I answered the ad for the job," she said. "My boss got sick and trained me to take over the business. When he died from cancer last year, he left the business to me."

"And you like it enough to keep at it."

Another sigh. "Yeah, I like it. Most of the time. I mean, it beats a job in a cube farm. I like it when I can help people, even if it's just finding a lost pet or helping a woman locate her deadbeat ex so that she can collect child support. But you see the ugly side of people a lot."

"What you saw today wasn't very pretty."

"No."

She fell silent again, and he was sure she was back at the camp, picturing that bloody body again. He wanted to pull her away from the image, to keep her focused on him. "Who are the handsome, arrogant men who rubbed you the wrong way?" he asked.

"Daniel Metwater, for one."

"The Prophet of this so-called Family?"

"Yeah. Have you met him?"

Dylan slowed for the turn onto a faintly marked dirt track that veered away from the canyon and the park. "No. What's he like?"

"He talks a good game of peace and love and spirituality, or at least, that's what he writes in his blog. But it all sounds like a con game to me, especially considering he preaches about the futility of cell phones and technology, yet he has a website he updates often when he's away from the camp. Maybe I'm too cynical, but I wanted to shake all those women who were making cow eyes at him and tell them he didn't really care about any of them. He's the kind of guy who looks out for himself and his image first."

"What makes you think that?"

He halfway expected her to slap him down again. Instead, she relaxed back into the seat. "My dad was a charming swindler like Metwater—good-looking, silver-tongued and scary intelligent. His game was as a traveling preacher. I spent most of my childhood moving from town to town while he conned people out of whatever they would give him." She ran a hand through her hair, pushing it back from her face. "I guess that experience has come in handy in my work. I can usually spot a grifter as soon as he opens his mouth. Daniel Metwater may be preaching peace, love and communing with nature, but I think he's hiding something."

"Do you think he killed the guy you saw?"

"I don't know. It depends on when the guy died, I think. Metwater was standing with me for a good while before his followers dragged the body into camp. He was wearing white linen trousers and there wasn't a speck of blood or dirt on him, so he didn't strike me as a man who had just come from a murder."

"So you think the man was murdered."

"I think he had been shot. Whether the wound was self-inflicted or not is up to you people to determine." She shuddered. "I'm going to spend my time trying to live down the sight of him. The only dead people I've seen before were peacefully in their coffins, carefully made up and dressed in their Sunday best."

"Violence leaves an ugly mark on everything."

"Yeah, well, I guess you could say reality does that, too."

She turned away, staring out the side window, as unreachable as if she had walked into another room and closed the door. Dylan focused on the landscape around him—the low growth of piñon and scrub oak, and formations of red and gray rock that rose up against an achingly blue sky. He had grown up surrounded by this scenery. The country here didn't look desolate and hostile to him, as it did to some, but free and unspoiled.

Simon's brake lights glowed and he stuck his arm out the open driver's-side window, gesturing toward a gravel wash to their left. He stopped and the passenger window slid down as Dylan pulled alongside him. "That's the south entrance to Dead Horse Canyon," Simon said. "Where do we go from here?"

"Turn in here," Kayla said. "There's a trailhead about a quarter mile farther on. I parked there, but apparently the campers have been driving right into the camp."

"I'll follow you," Simon said, and waited for Dylan to pull ahead of him.

As camping spots went, this one lacked water, much shade or access, Dylan thought, as the FJ Cruiser bumped over the washboard gravel road into the canyon. But it did offer concealment and a good defensive position. No one would be able to approach without the campers knowing about it.

As if to prove his point, a bearded man in camouflage pants and shirt stepped into the road and signaled for them to stop. Dylan braked and waited for the man to approach the driver's side of the Cruiser. "You can't drive back here," the man said, his eyes darting nervously to the Ranger Brigade emblem on the side of the Cruiser. The words *Law Enforcement* were clearly visible.

"We're here to talk to Daniel Metwater," Dylan said. "Officers Woolridge and Holt."

"I'm not supposed to let anyone drive into the camp," the man said. He was sweating now, jittery as an addict in need of a fix.

"What's your name?" Dylan asked.

"Kiram."

Dylan waited for more, but Kiram had pressed his lips tightly together. "Well, Kiram, we're here on official business and you don't have the authority to stop us. We don't want trouble, but you need to step out of the way."

Kiram ducked his head and peered into the car. "Hey, what are you doing back here?" he asked Kayla.

"I brought them to see your dead body," she said, giving Kiram a chilly stare.

Dylan let off the brake and the Cruiser eased forward. Kiram jumped back. The two vehicles proceeded at a crawl up the wash, around the knot of trees and into the side canyon the Family had chosen as their home in the wilderness.

Dylan shut off the engine, but remained in the car, assessing the situation. The motley cluster of campers, tents and vehicles shimmered like a mirage in the midday heat. A child's ball rolled a few feet, stirred by the wind, which made the only sound in the area. "The place looks deserted," Kayla said. "Do you think they left?"

"Not without all their stuff. Do you notice anything missing?"

She studied the scene for a moment, then shook her head. "Only the people."

"Stay in the vehicle." With one hand hovering near his weapon, Dylan eased open his door, ready to dive for cover if anyone fired on them. But the camp remained silent and still.

"Daniel Metwater!" he called. "We need to ask you a few questions."

No answer came but the echo of his own words. Simon joined Dylan beside his car. "What do you think?" Dylan asked.

"They could have all headed for the hills, or they could be lying low inside these tents and trailers," Simon said.

"Come out by the time I count to ten or we'll start taking this place apart," Dylan shouted. "One!"

At the count of five, the door to the largest RV, a thirty-foot bus with solar panels on the roof, eased open. A slim but muscular man, naked except for a pair of white loose trousers, moved onto the steps. "I wasn't aware we had company," he said. "We adhere to the custom of an afternoon siesta."

"Are you Daniel Metwater?" Dylan asked.

Sharp eyes scrutinized the three of them. "Yes," he said at last.

"Call your people out here," Simon said. "We have some questions about an incident that happened here this afternoon."

Metwater shifted his gaze past the two cops. Dylan turned to see Kayla standing beside the car. "You had no cause to bring these people here," Metwater said to her.

"We're here because we understand you found a dead body this morning," Dylan said. "Why didn't you report it to the police?"

"We don't have cell phones, and since nothing we could do or say could bring the man back to life, I made the decision to report the incident the next time I was in town." Metwater spoke as if he was talking about a minor mechanical problem, not a dead man.

"Where is the body?" Simon asked.

"I ordered the men who brought him here to take him back where they found him," Metwater said. "They never should have defiled our home with such violence."

"We'll need to talk to these men."

"They are undergoing a purification ritual at the moment."

"Bring them out here." Simon wasn't a big man, but he could put a lot of menace and command in his voice. "Now."

Metwater said something over his shoulder to someone inside the RV. A woman with long dark hair slipped past him and hurried away. "She'll bring the men to you," Metwater said, and turned as if to go back inside.

"Wait," Dylan said. "Who was the man?"

"I don't know. I'd never seen him before in my life. But I believe he's one of yours."

"What do you mean, one of ours?" Dylan asked.

Metwater's lips quirked up in a smirk. "I checked his pockets for identification. He's a cop."

Chapter Three

Kayla watched Dylan as Metwater dropped his bomb-shell. His was a face full of strong lines and planes, not classically handsome, but honest—the face of a man who didn't have any patience with lies or weakness. Anger quickly replaced the brief flash of confusion in his eyes as he absorbed this new wrinkle in the case. The dead man wasn't a stranger anymore—he was a fellow lawman. "Take me to him," he ordered.

"The men who found him will—" Metwater began.

"No. *You* take me." Dylan's fists clenched at his sides, and Kayla tensed, expecting him to punch the smirk off the Prophet's face. But he remained still, only one muscle in his jaw twitching.

Instead of answering, Metwater looked away, toward a flurry of movement to their right. Kiram and another burly man escorted two other men to them. "These are the two who found the body," Metwater said. "They can answer your questions."

Dylan pulled a small notebook and pen from his shirt pocket and shifted his focus to the new arrivals. Kayla thought they looked young, scarcely out of their teens, with wispy beards and thin bodies. Dylan pointed to the taller of the two, who stared back from behind black-framed glasses. "What's your name?"

"Abelard," the young man whispered.

"Your real name," Dylan said.

Abelard blinked. "That is my real name. Abelard Phillips."

"His mom was a literature professor," the other young man said. "You know, Abelard and Heloise—supposed to be a classic love story or something."

Abelard nodded. "Most people call me Abe."

Dylan wrote down the name, then turned to the second man. "Who are you?"

He swallowed, his Adam's apple bobbing. "Zach. Zach Crenshaw."

"I want the two of you to show me this body you found this morning."

Their heads moved in unison, like bobblehead dolls. Metwater started to turn back to his trailer, but Simon took his arm. "You're coming, too."

Kayla trailed along after them, sure that if Dylan remembered she was here he would order her to wait at the camp. But curiosity won out over her squeamishness about seeing the body again—that, and a reluctance to spend any time alone with the rest of the "family."

Single file, the six of them followed a narrow path out of camp, out of the canyon and into the open scrubland beyond, following drag marks in the dirt Kayla was sure had been made by the makeshift travois Abe and Zach had used to transport the body. She estimated they had walked about a mile when Abe halted and gestured toward a grouping of large boulders. "He's behind those rocks over there," he said. "We put him back just like the Prophet told us to."

"And you're sure that's where you found him?" Simon asked.

Zach nodded. "You can tell because of all the blood."

"Show me," Dylan said.

The two young men led the way around the boulders. Kayla hung back, but she still had a view of the dead man's feet, wearing new-looking hiking boots, the soles barely scuffed. Had he bought them especially for his visit to the Black Canyon area?

Dylan and Simon stood back, surveying the scene, the wind stirring the branches of the piñons nearby the only sound. The sour-sweet stench of death stung her nostrils, but she forced herself to remain still, to wait for whatever came next. "Was he lying like this when you found him?" Dylan asked. "On his back?"

"Yeah," Zach said.

"Why did you move him?" Simon asked. "Were you trying to hide something? Did you realize you were tampering with evidence?"

"We weren't trying to hide anything!" Abe protested. "We just came around the rocks and almost stepped on him. There was blood everywhere and it was awful. Like something out of a movie or something. Too horrible to be real."

"Once we realized it was a man, we couldn't just leave him there," Zach said. "There were already buzzards circling. And I thought I heard him groan, like maybe he was still alive. We thought if we got him back to camp, someone could go for help, or take him to the hospital or something."

"We couldn't just leave him," Abe echoed.

"All right." Dylan put a hand on Abe's arm. "Tell me exactly what happened. Start at the beginning. What were you doing out here?"

"We were hunting rabbits," Abe said. "We thought we saw one run over here so we headed this way to check it out."

"What were you hunting with?" Simon asked. "Where is your weapon now?"

The two young men exchanged glances, then Zach walked over to the grouping of piñons. He reached into the tangle of branches and pulled out a couple crude bows and a handful of homemade arrows. "The Prophet only allows us to buy meat for one meal a week, so we thought if we could catch some rabbits the women could make them into stew or something," he said.

"And maybe they'd be impressed that we were providing for the Family," Abe added. He looked even more forlorn. "We weren't having any luck, though."

"Why were you hunting with bows and arrows?" Simon asked. "Why not guns?"

"The Prophet doesn't allow firearms," Zach said.

"We're a nonviolent people." Metwater spoke for the first time since they had left camp. "Guns only cause trouble."

"They certainly caused trouble for this man." Dylan looked at Metwater. "You said you checked his identification?"

"The wallet is inside his jacket," Metwater said. "Front left side."

Dylan knelt, out of Kayla's view. When he stood again, he held a slim brown wallet. He read from the

ID. "Special Agent Frank Asher, FBI." He fixed Metwater with an icy glare. "What was the FBI doing
snooping around your camp, Mr. Metwater? And what
did he do that got him killed?"

AS EXPECTED, THE Family's Prophet claimed to have
no knowledge of Agent Frank Asher or what had happened to him. None of the three men had heard any
gunshots or vehicles or seen anything unusual in the
hour leading up to the discovery of the body. They
were like the three bronze monkeys Dylan's dad had
on a shelf in his home office—see no evil, hear no
evil, speak no evil. Dylan and Simon would bring
them all in for questioning, but he doubted the interviews would yield anything useful.

With no cell phone coverage in the area, Dylan was
forced to leave Simon with the body and the Family
members while he drove to an area with coverage.

"I'm coming with you," Kayla said, falling into
step beside him as he strode back toward the camp.

He'd been so intent on his job that for a while he
had forgotten about her. She was one more complica-
tion he didn't need right now. "Why didn't you stay
in the car like I told you?" he asked.

"This place gives me the creeps. I'm not staying
anywhere alone around these people." She rubbed her
hands up and down her arms. "Do you think one of
them killed that FBI agent?"

"I don't know what to think. I need the medical
examiner's report on when he died, and what kind of
weapon killed him." He glanced toward the motley
collection of RVs and tents. "I'm not buying that all
of these people are unarmed."

"The agent will have a vehicle around here some-place close," Kayla said. "Those boots he was wearing weren't worn enough for him to have walked very far, and I didn't see a pack anywhere near him."

Dylan stopped and considered her more closely. She had regained her color and no longer looked frag-ile and shaken. "I'll get someone to look for the car right away. Maybe something in there will tell us why he was out here. That was a good observation," he added. "Did you see anything else?"

"I think the two kids are telling the truth." She glanced back in the direction they had come. "When they said that about not wanting to leave him for the buzzards—I believed them."

"Maybe." He had learned not to trust anyone when it came to crime, but his instincts made him want to focus on Metwater more than the two kids. "Them moving the body makes our investigation tougher. They may have destroyed a lot of evidence."

"For a man who sees himself as a leader, Metwater is a cold fish," she said. "He seemed more annoyed by the inconvenience than anything else."

"He's going to be a lot more inconvenienced be-fore this is over. I'm going to get a warrant to take this camp apart. If the murder weapon is here, we'll find it."

"If it was ever here, they had plenty of time to get rid of it before we got here," she said. "It could be stashed in a cave or buried in an old mine or broken into a million pieces on the rocks."

"Maybe," he conceded. "But we might find some-thing else incriminating."

They walked through the camp, which was as

empty and silent as a ghost town, but he sensed people watching him from the windows of trailers and open flaps of tents. "Who did you come here to see?" he asked Kayla. "I know you said a client's daughter, but who?"

"I don't see how that relates to your case." The frost was back in her voice.

"You're the one who reported the body. You were the only non-Family member present when it was discovered. Some people might think that was an interesting coincidence."

She turned on him, cheeks flushed. "You don't think I killed that man!"

"My job is to rule out everyone. Do you own a gun?"

"I have a Smith & Wesson 40 back at my office. I have a permit for it."

"But you didn't have it with you today? Why not?"

"I don't like to carry a gun. I didn't think this was a particularly dangerous situation."

"Who did you come to see?" he asked again. "I can subpoena your files to find out. Save us both some hassle and just tell me."

She hesitated, a deep crease between her brows as she weighed her options. "I came to see Andi Matheson. She calls herself Asteria now. But she doesn't have anything to do with your case."

"You said her father hired you. Who is he?"

She glared at him.

"I'll bet I can find the answer in five minutes or less online."

She continued to glare at him, and the intensity of her gaze sent a thrill of awareness through him. Oh, he liked her, all right. Maybe a little too much, considering her involvement in this case.

"Her father is Senator Peter Matheson," she said. "I imagine you've heard of him."

Dylan had heard of the senator, all right. Until recently, he had been in the news primarily for his campaign to disband the Ranger Brigade. He had claimed the task force of federal agents was intrusive, expensive and ineffective. He had succeeded in having the group defunded, only to wind up looking like a fool when the Rangers had brought down a major terrorist group that had been operating in the area. Congress had responded by expanding the group, and Matheson had mostly kept a low profile ever since.

And now the senator was mixed up with Metwater and his bunch of wanderers. Dylan scanned the silent camp. "How did you track her down here? You said her father didn't know where she was."

"I talked to her friends. Her best friend told me she and Andi had attended a presentation given by Daniel Metwater and Andi had been very attracted to him, and to the ideas he preached. I did some more digging and verified that she had indeed joined up with Metwater and his group."

Dylan nodded. Textbook solid detective work. "Let's have a word with Ms. Matheson. Maybe she knows something she's not telling about all this."

"I really don't think—" Kayla began.

But Dylan had already moved to the nearest camper, a battered aqua-and-silver trailer wedged beneath a clump of stunted evergreens. He pounded on the door, shaking the whole structure. "Police! Open up!" he called.

A woman with a deeply tanned face and bleached hair eased open the door and peered out at them. "I'm looking for Andi Matheson," Dylan said.

The woman shook her head. "I don't know anyone by that name," she said, and started to close the door.

"What about Asteria?" Kayla asked. "Where does she live?"

"Over there." The woman pointed to a large white tent next to the Prophet's trailer.

The tent was the kind used by hunting outfitters as a mess tent or gathering area, with a tall frame and roll-up canvas sides. One of the sides was open to let in the hot breeze. Dylan moved around to the opening and peered in. A blonde woman sat cross-legged on a rug on the floor, eyes closed, hands outstretched.

"Ms. Matheson?" Dylan asked. "Asteria?"

She opened her eyes, which were a deep blue. "I was meditating," she said.

"Sorry to interrupt, but I have to ask you a few questions." He took a step toward her. "I'm Lieutenant Dylan Holt, with the Ranger Brigade task force. I wanted to ask you about the body that was brought to your camp earlier today."

Andi looked away. "I didn't see anything. I didn't want to look. It was horrible."

Kayla moved up beside Dylan, her voice gentle. "We don't want to upset you, Andi," she said. "We just have a few questions and then we'll leave you alone."

"All right." She motioned toward the rug across from her. "You might as well sit down."

The room was furnished with a cot and several folding camp chairs, but Dylan lowered himself to the rug. The coolness of the earth seeped up through the rug's pile. Kayla sat beside him. "Tell me what you saw this morning," he said.

Andi shrugged. "I didn't see much. There was shouting, and Abe and Zach came in, dragging something on a tarp. I thought they had killed an animal at first—there was so much blood. Then I saw it was a man and I looked away. I ran back here and hid." She rubbed her hand across her stomach. "I didn't want to see any more."

"Do you know a man named Frank Asher?" he asked. "He works for the FBI."

"Frank?" She stared at him, eyes wide. "What about Frank?"

"Did you know him?" Dylan asked.

"No!" She shook her head, hands clutching her skirt. "No," she repeated in a whisper, even as tears ran down her face.

"I think you did know him," Dylan said. "Frank Asher is the man who was killed—the body Zach and Abe found this morning."

Andi covered her mouth with her hand. "I told him not to come here," she said, the words muffled. "I told him not to come and now look what happened." She collapsed onto the rug and began to sob, the mournful wailing filling the tent and making Dylan's chest hurt.

Chapter Four

Kayla knelt beside Andi, alarmed by the speed at which the beautiful, defiant young woman had dissolved into this wailing heap of grief. "I'm so sorry," she said, rubbing Andi's back. "Please sit up and try to calm down." She looked back over her shoulder at Dylan, who looked as if he wanted to be anyplace but here at this moment. "Would you get her some water?" She pointed toward a large jug that sat on a stand at the back of the tent.

He retrieved the water and brought it to her. "What was your relationship to Frank Asher?" he asked. "When was the last time you were in contact with him?"

The questions brought a fresh wave of sobs. Kayla glared at him. Did he have to act like such a cop right now, firing official-sounding questions at this obviously distraught woman? "You're not helping," she said.

Frowning, he backed away.

"Drink this." Kayla put the cup of water into Andi's hands. "Take a deep breath. You've had a shock."

"What's going on in here? What are you doing to her?"

The outraged questions came from one of the women Kayla had seen with Andi earlier—a slight figure with a mane of brown curly hair and a slightly crooked nose. She rushed over and inserted herself between Andi and Kayla. "Asteria, honey, what have they done to you?"

"What's your name?" Dylan joined them again.

The brown-haired woman glared at him. "Who are you, and why are you upsetting my friend?"

"Lieutenant Holt." Dylan showed his badge. "I'm investigating the death of the man whose body was brought into the camp earlier today. What's your name?"

"Starfall."

Kayla thought Dylan was about to demand she tell him her real name, but he apparently thought better of it. "Were you here when Abe and Zach brought him in?" he asked.

Starfall wrinkled her nose. "They should have known better than to pull a stunt like that. It was awful."

"What do you mean, 'a stunt like that'?" Dylan asked.

"The man was dead. I mean, half his head was gone. We couldn't do anything for him. They should have left him where they found him and not involved us in whatever happened to him."

Andi began keening again, rocking back and forth. Starfall wrapped her arms around her friend. "You need to go," she said. "You've upset her enough."

"Do you know a man named Frank Asher?" Dylan asked.

"No. Now go. You have no right to harass us this way."

Kayla touched Dylan's arm. "Give her a chance to calm down a little," she said softly. "You can question her later."

He nodded and led the way out of the tent.

The camp was just as deserted as it had been before. "Looks like nobody wants to take a chance on running into a cop," Dylan observed.

"Or maybe they really are taking a siesta." She pulled the front of her shirt away from her chest, hoping for a cool breeze. "It's baking out here."

He glanced back at her. "You should wear a hat." He touched the brim of the fawn-colored Stetson that was part of his uniform.

They left the camp, back on the trail to the parking area. "What are you going to do next?" Kayla asked.

"There's so much that feels wrong here it's hard to know where to start." He gave her a hard look. "What's Andi Matheson's relationship to Frank Asher?"

"How should I know?"

"Her father hired you to find her. You must have looked into her background, talked to her friends and people who knew her."

"I did, but none of them ever mentioned a Frank Asher." No one had mentioned any men in Andi's life, outside of her father and a few very casual acquaintances. None of the photos and articles Kayla had viewed online linked Andi with a man. At the time, Kayla had thought it was a little unusual that a woman as attractive and seemingly outgoing as Andi didn't have a boyfriend, or at least an ex-boyfriend.

"Maybe he wasn't a friend of hers then," Dylan said. "Maybe her father knew him. It's not unreasonable to think a senator would know an FBI agent. Maybe you weren't the only person the senator had tailing his daughter. Maybe he sent the Fed after her, too."

"Or maybe Asher is the father of Andi's baby."

Dylan stopped so abruptly she almost plowed into him. "She has a baby?"

"She's pregnant. Didn't you notice?" Kayla gestured toward her own stomach.

He flushed. "I thought maybe she was just a little too fond of cheeseburgers or beer or something." He patted his own flat belly.

She stared at him. "I can't believe you said that."

"What did you expect? I'm a cop and a rancher—two professions known for plain speaking." He started walking again, long strides covering ground quickly so that she had to trot to catch up with him.

"You're a rancher?" she asked.

"My family has a ranch near here. In Ouray County." He pulled out his keys and hit the button to unlock the FJ Cruiser.

That explained a lot—from the way he seemed so at home in this rugged landscape, to the swagger in his walk that was more cowboy than cop.

He climbed in and started the engine even before she had her door closed. "If Asher is the father of Andi's baby, it would explain why she was so torn up over the news of his death," he said as he put the vehicle in gear and guided it onto the washboard road. "But why would she have told him to stay away from the camp?"

"I thought she joined the Family to get away from her father and his lifestyle," Kayla said. "But maybe she was trying to get away from Asher. Maybe he was the one who wanted her to get rid of the baby. Or maybe he was abusive."

"Would she carry on like that over a man who had abused her?"

"I don't know. Love can make people do crazy things, I guess." After all, her own mother had followed Kayla's father across the United States and back, sticking with him even when he cheated on her and lied to her.

"Are you speaking from personal experience?"

The question jolted her. "Why would you even ask something like that?"

"I'm just curious." He kept his gaze focused on the road, but she sensed most of his attention was fixed on her. "Something in the way you said that made me think you don't have too high an opinion of love."

She hugged her arms across her chest. This was *not* a conversation she wanted to be having. "I'm no expert on the subject. Are you?"

"Far from it. I've managed to avoid falling in love—serious love—so far."

"You make it sound like an accomplishment."

"I don't know. Some people might consider it a failing. My job doesn't really leave a lot of room for close relationships."

"Yet you have time to help run your family's ranch."

"Family is important to me. Which is why I don't get why Andi Matheson wanted to leave hers to live out in the wilderness with a bunch of people she hardly knows."

"Not everyone has a family they care to be close to—and yes, I say that from personal experience."

"Right—your con-artist dad. What about your mom? Brothers and sisters?"

"My mom is dead. I didn't have any siblings."

"I'm sorry to hear that."

"I don't want your pity."

He glanced at her, surprising warmth in his brown eyes. "Sympathy and pity aren't the same things."

She turned away, conversation over. She didn't like not being in control of a conversation. One of the advantages of being a private investigator was that she usually got to ask all the questions. Situations like this one always made her feel like a freak. She didn't do relationships. Not close ones. She couldn't relate to people like Dylan, with his warm family feelings and determination to figure her out.

He apparently got the message and stopped talking. She focused on breathing deeply and getting her emotions under control. They passed through a brown sea of sagebrush and rock, beneath an achingly blue sky, unbroken by a single cloud. She would never get used to how vast the emptiness was out here. The wilderness made her feel small, lost even when she knew where she was.

He stopped the Cruiser and shifted into Park. "Why are you stopping?" she asked.

"I've got a phone signal." He dragged his finger across the screen on his phone. "I'm going to call in to headquarters."

He gave whoever answered the particulars of the

situation at the camp and asked them to send crime scene techs and a medical examiner, along with more Rangers to interview people at the camp. "Simon is waiting," Dylan said. "I'm going to see if I can locate Asher's vehicle."

He ended the call and pocketed the phone, then put the Cruiser in gear once more. Neither of them said anything for several minutes as they bumped over increasingly rugged terrain. Finally, Dylan spoke. "I apologize if my questions were out of line," he said. "It's another cop thing. I want to know everything about people I'm with. I didn't mean to upset you."

His words touched her, and made her feel a little vulnerable. In her experience, people rarely apologized. "I didn't mean to snap," she said. "I'm just—on edge. Seeing that body, and then Andi falling apart like that—I guess it hit me harder than I realized."

"You're a very empathetic person," he said. "You feel other people's pain. You absorb their emotions. It probably makes you a good investigator, but it's tough."

"I guess so." She didn't really think of herself that way. If anything, she would have said she was too cynical most of the time.

He braked and pointed ahead of them. "What's that, up there?"

She caught the glint of sunlight off metal. "Maybe it's a car."

Dylan shut off the engine. "We'll walk from here."

He led the way toward the white sedan, which was partially hidden behind a clump of scrub oak. A small sticker on the bumper identified it as a rental car. When they were approximately ten feet away, Dylan held out his arm. "Stay here while I check it out," he ordered.

She waited while he approached the car. He peered in the front driver's-side window, which had been left open a few inches. Then he pulled a pair of latex gloves from his pocket and put them on. He opened the driver's-side door, which wasn't locked, and peered into the car. Then he withdrew his head and looked back toward Kayla. "You can come up here if you promise not to touch anything."

She joined him beside the car. He had leaned in and was looking through a handful of papers on the front passenger seat. "There's a couple of maps here and a Montrose visitor's guide," he said.

"The parking pass on the dash is from a motel in Montrose," she said. "That's probably where he was staying."

Dylan examined the pass, then pulled out his notebook and began making notes. "I don't see anything out of the ordinary, do you?" he asked.

The only other thing in the car was a half-empty water bottle in the cup holder between the seats. "It doesn't look like he planned to be out here long," she said. "There are no snacks or lunch, no pack or change of clothes."

"So he either figured on a quick trip or he headed out here on impulse, not taking the time to prepare." Dylan opened the glove box, which was empty except for registration papers and the vehicle service manual. He flipped down both visors. The passenger side revealed nothing, but next to the mirror on the driver's side was a photograph.

Or rather, half a photograph. A tear was evident on

the left side of the picture, a color snapshot of a man in jeans and a button-down shirt. Daniel Metwater's smiling face stared out at them.

"Maybe Andi wasn't the person Agent Asher came here to see," Dylan said.

Chapter Five

Dylan retrieved an evidence envelope from his Cruiser and sealed the photograph of Metwater in it. He took a few pictures of the vehicle and wrote down the plate number and the GPS location. "Let's go," he told Kayla as he pocketed his notebook. "I'll take you back to your car. You'll need to give us a statement about what happened at the camp this morning, then you can go. I'll probably have more questions for you later." He wanted to dig deeper into what she knew about Andi Matheson and the Family. And he wanted to see her again. Her mix of cold distance and warm empathy intrigued him.

"Do you do this kind of thing often?" he asked.

"What kind of thing?"

"Finding missing persons. Tracking down wayward children."

"Andi wasn't a lot of trouble to find. She just didn't want to talk to her father. Senator Matheson thought I might be able to get through to her."

"Seems an uncomfortable position to be in—caught in the middle of a family quarrel."

He wondered if she looked at everyone so intently, as if trying to decipher the hidden meaning behind every word he said. He wanted to protest that he didn't have an ulterior motive in talking with her, but that wasn't exactly true. He was trying to figure out what made her tick. Maybe she was doing the same to him. "A lot of my work involves dealing with people in one kind of pain or another," she said. "Whether it's a divorce or estranged families, or investigating some kind of fraud. Isn't it the same for cops?"

"Yeah." Too much pain sometimes. "You learn pretty quickly to distance yourself."

"My father made his living by preying on people's emotions. He was an expert at making people afraid of something and then offering himself as the way out of their trouble—for a price. I think seeing him in action made me wary of letting others get too close." Her eyes met his, dark and searching.

"Is that a warning?" he asked.

"Take it however you like."

Neither of them said anything on the rest of the drive back to Ranger headquarters. Carmen met them at the door to the offices. "A crime scene team is on its way out to meet Simon," she said.

"I found the victim's car, parked not too far away." Dylan read off the plate number and location.

"I'll call it in," Carmen said. "Some of the team might still be in cell phone range."

"I'll call them," he said. "I'd like you to take Kayla's statement."

"All right." Carmen sent him a questioning look. He knew she wondered why he didn't take Kayla's statement himself. He wasn't ready to admit that the dynamic between him and the pretty private detective was too charged. He couldn't be as objective about her as he liked and that bothered him. He wasn't one to let a woman get under his skin. "I'll be in touch later," he told Kayla, and turned away.

KAYLA WATCHED DYLAN leave the room, annoyed that his dismissal of her bothered her so much. So much for the detachment she'd bragged about. This cowboy cop, with his probing questions and dogged pursuit of information, drew her in.

"There's an empty office back here we can use." Officer Redhorse led the way to a room crowded with two desks and a filing cabinet. She sat behind one desk and indicated that Kayla should sit across from her. "Have you been a private investigator long?" Carmen asked.

"A couple of years."

Carmen opened up a file on the computer, then set a recorder between them. "Why don't you tell me everything that happened, from the time you arrived at the Family's camp this morning," she said. "I'll ask questions if I need you to clarify anything for me."

Kayla nodded, and took a moment to organize her thoughts. Then she told her story, about approaching the camp, and the two men bringing in the body. Carmen asked a couple questions, then typed for a few minutes more. "I'll print this out and you can read it over and sign it," she said, and swiveled away from the computer. "What happened when you and Dylan went back out there?" she asked.

"Are you going to compare my story to his?" Kayla asked.

"I'm curious to get your take on things," she replied. "Women sometimes notice things men don't— emotions and details men don't always pick up on."

"I don't think Lieutenant Holt misses much," Kayla said.

"He's new here, so I don't know him well," Carmen said. "Though he must be good at his job or he wouldn't have been assigned to the task force."

"He told me his family has a ranch in the area."

"The Holt Cattle Company. It's a big spread south of town. Knowing the country and the people here could be an advantage in this kind of work. Are you from the area?"

Kayla nodded. "But not knowing everyone can be an advantage, too. You don't come into a job with any preconceived notions."

"So what's your impression of the lieutenant?"

Kayla stiffened. "Why are you asking me?"

"I thought I sensed a few sparks between the two of you—though maybe not the good kind. Did you two have some kind of disagreement?"

"No disagreement." The two of them had worked well together, even though he sometimes made her feel prickly and on edge—too aware of him as a man who read her a little too well for comfort.

Carmen stood. "I'll get your statement off the printer and you can read through it."

When she was alone in the room, Kayla sagged back against the chair. Only a little longer and she would be free to leave. She wanted to do some investigating of her own, to try to make sense of what had happened this afternoon.

"I WANT A warrant to search Asher's hotel room," Dylan told Captain Ellison. The two stood outside Graham's office, Dylan having filled him in on his findings at the camp. "That might give us a clue what he was doing out there."

Graham nodded. "What about this PI? Kayla Larimer? Does she have any connection to Asher?"

"I don't think so. I'll talk to Senator Matheson to verify her story, but I think she was doing what she said—delivering a message to the senator's daughter."

"Did you learn anything else from her while you were at the camp?" Graham asked.

He had learned a lot—mainly that Kayla Larimer wasn't the type of woman to get close to anyone very easily. "She's good at her job, I think," he said. "Observant. She pointed out right away that Asher had to have a car nearby, after noting that his boots were new, the soles barely scuffed. And she was good with the women at the camp. She thinks Andi Matheson was so distraught over Asher's death because they had a close relationship. He may even be the father of her baby."

"What do you think?" Graham asked.

"Maybe. But Andi might have been distraught because of what she'd seen when the body was dragged into camp. It was enough to upset anyone. And the picture I found in Asher's car was of Metwater, not Andi. Asher may have had something on the Prophet that got him into trouble."

"I've got a call in to the Bureau, asking if Asher was here working on a case," Graham said. "Meanwhile, maybe his hotel room will turn up something."

"Are you going to Agent Asher's hotel?" Kayla asked.

Dylan turned to find the private detective, followed by Carmen, emerging from an office at the back of the building. "I want to go with you to the hotel," Kayla said, joining him and the captain.

"This is a police matter," he said. "You don't have any business being there. You know that."

She opened her mouth as if to argue, but apparently changed her mind. "Fine. Obviously, you don't have a need for me any longer, so I'll say goodbye." She nodded to Carmen and the captain, but didn't look at Dylan.

The snub irritated him. "I might have more questions for you later," he said.

"Maybe I'll have answers." She left, closing the door a little more forcefully than necessary behind her.

"I don't think she likes you too much," Graham observed.

"Oh, I don't know about that," Carmen said.

"What's that supposed to mean?" Dylan snapped.

"If she really didn't care what you thought, she wouldn't react so strongly." Carmen shrugged.

Dylan turned to Graham, and was surprised to find the captain grinning at him. "What are you smiling about?"

"My wife acted as if she hated my guts the first time we met," he said. "Carmen may be on to something."

Dylan turned away. "I'm going to file for that warrant." And he would do his best to forget all about

Kayla Larimer. The last thing he needed was a woman who wanted to play mind games.

KAYLA SCARCELY NOTICED her surroundings as she drove toward town after leaving Ranger headquarters. She had to find a way to see what was in Frank Asher's hotel room. Lieutenant Holt might believe she had no right to get involved in this case, but he had made her a part of it when he took her back to the camp. She couldn't drop the matter now, with so many unanswered questions. And it wasn't such a stretch to see the FBI agent's death as linked to the assignment she had taken on for Senator Matheson. Agent Asher's murder had definitely upset Andi, and Kayla needed to know why.

Even if she had never met Dylan Holt and overheard him discussing searching Asher's hotel room, visiting the hotel would have been the next logical step in her own investigation. She didn't have the authority of a law enforcement agency behind her, but part of being a good private investigator was using other means to gain information. She might be able to charm a hotel clerk into letting her see the room, or to persuade a maid to open the door for her.

She wouldn't interfere with the Rangers' work. But she'd find a way to make Dylan share his information with her. She could even prove useful to him—another set of eyes and ears with a different perspective on the case.

She flipped on her blinker to turn onto the highway and headed toward the Mesa Inn—the name on the parking pass in Asher's car. She found a parking place in a side lot that provided a good view of the hotel's front entrance and settled in to wait.

She didn't have to wait long. Less than half an hour passed before two Ranger Cruisers parked under the hotel's front portico. Dylan and Carmen climbed out of the first one, while two officers she didn't recognize exited the second vehicle. As soon as the four were inside, Kayla left her car and headed toward the hotel's side entrance.

As she had hoped, it opened into a hallway that wound around past the hotel's restaurant and gift shop, to the front lobby. A large rack of brochures shielded Kayla from the Rangers' view, but allowed her to spy on them as they spoke first to the front desk clerk, then to a woman in a suit who was probably the manager. She wasn't close enough to hear their conversation, but after a few minutes the manager handed over a key card and the four officers headed for the elevator.

Kayla put aside the brochure for a Jeep rental company she had been pretending to study and walked quickly to the elevator. She hit the call button. The car the agents had entered stopped on the fifth floor before descending again. Smiling to herself, Kayla found the entrance for the stairs and began to climb.

On the fifth floor, she eased open the door to the hallway a scant inch and listened. The rumble of men's voices reached her. She was sure one of them was Dylan's. Risking a glance, she opened the door wider, in time to see the four officers enter a room in the middle of the hall. Kayla stepped into the hall and checked the number on the room—535.

Now what? She couldn't just barge in—that was a

good way to get arrested. And she didn't want to interfere, but she wanted information.

A loud squeak made her flinch. She turned to see a maid pushing a cleaning cart down the hall. Kayla moved toward her. "Excuse me," she said. "I wonder if you could answer a few questions about the man who was renting room 535." She opened her wallet and the maid, who looked like a student from the nearby university, stared at the badge. It clearly identified Kayla as a private investigator, not a cop, but most people didn't bother to read the fine print.

"Why do you want to know about him?" the woman—her name tag identified her as Mindy—asked.

"He's part of a case I'm working on."

Mindy bit her lower lip. "I don't know if I'm allowed to talk to anyone about the guests."

"Any information you provide could be very helpful," Kayla said.

Mindy pulled a cell phone from the pocket of her uniform top. "I'd better check with my manager."

Kayla held her breath while Mindy put through the call. If the worst happened, she could make a break for the stairs, or bluff her way out of this. But when Mindy explained there was a woman cop who wanted to question her, the manager apparently told her to cooperate. Good thing Carmen was along on this job. The manager probably assumed Kayla was her. "What do you want to know?" Mindy asked, as she slipped the phone back into her pocket.

"Did you see the man who rented that room? Did you speak to him?"

"I saw him," Mindy said. "But we didn't talk or

anything. I saw him when he left the room yesterday morning."

"How did he act when you saw him? What kind of
a mood was he in?"

Mindy shrugged. "I only saw him for a few seconds. He just looked, you know, ordinary."

"Did you clean his room? Did you notice anything
unusual about it?"

"No. I mean, it's not like I spend that much time
in the rooms. I clean them and get out."

"So nothing about this guy stood out for you?"

Mindy rearranged the bottles of cleaning solution
in the tray at the top of her cart. "Not really." She
avoided looking at Kayla.

"What is it, Mindy? Anything you remember—
even a little detail—might be helpful."

"It's nothing, really."

"Even if you don't think it's important, it could be."

"Promise you won't tell my boss? We're not supposed to spy on the clients, you know? I could get in
a lot of trouble."

"I won't tell." Kayla would probably never even
see the manager.

"I was cleaning the room next door yesterday." She
nodded to room 533. "And I overheard the guy in 535.
I think he must have been on the telephone, because I
only heard one side of the conversation."

"What was he talking about?" Kayla asked.

"I don't know. I couldn't make out the words or
anything, but he sounded angry or upset. He was
shouting, you know?"

Kayla nodded. "That's very helpful. Could you make out any words at all?"

"Well...I think he said something like 'You can't do this' or something like that."

"Anything else?"

"No. I felt bad about eavesdropping that way, so I turned on the vacuum and went back to work. Did he do something bad?"

"No, he didn't. Thank you. You've been very helpful."

Mindy resumed pushing her cart down the hallway. She had scarcely passed 535 when the door opened and Dylan stepped out. He spotted Kayla before she could duck out of the way. "What are you doing here?" he demanded.

Chapter Six

"Hello, Lieutenant." Kayla gave him a cool look. "I've been waiting for you."

He moved closer, crowding her a little, frankly trying to intimidate her. "What are you doing here?" he asked again, his voice low, but not hiding his anger.

"I'm conducting my own investigation," she said. "I've been talking to the maid and she gave me some interesting information about Agent Asher." Her eyes met his and his heart beat a little faster. She wasn't the prettiest woman he had ever met, but those eyes, so changeable and expressive…

He mentally shook himself. "You shouldn't be here. You're not part of the investigation." Not entirely true. But she wasn't an official part of his team.

"I am. I won't get in the way, but I need to see."

"To see what?"

"I need to see what kind of man he was. To figure out his relationship with Andi. Her father is going to want to know."

"I could charge you with interfering with our investigation."

"I'm not interfering. Senator Matheson hired me because he's concerned about his daughter's safety.

It's possible Agent Asher was a threat to that safety, or that he knew of a threat." She raised her chin, defiant.

He took a step closer and lowered his voice. "You're not going to back down, are you?"

"Did you really think I would?"

No. Part of him—the part that wasn't a cop—would have been disappointed if she had. "I could put you in cuffs and escort you out of here."

"Oh, you'd like that, wouldn't you?" Her voice took on a throaty purr, sending a jolt of pure lust through him.

He struggled to regain control of the situation, and of himself. "I can't let you into Asher's room," he said.

"I know, but you can tell me what you find in there."

"No, I can't."

"Tell me if you find anything to do with Andi and I'll tell you what I learned from the maid."

"I can interview the maid myself."

"Come by my place when you're done here and we can talk."

He shook his head. "No."

"I'll feed you dinner."

"I'm not going to tell you anything."

"I'll still feed you."

Spending an evening alone with Kayla wouldn't be the smartest move he had ever made. She was a witness in his case and a big distraction he didn't need.

She was also the most intriguing woman he had met in a long while. "All right."

The door to Asher's room opened again and Ethan and Carmen emerged, carrying stacks of evidence bags. Ethan glanced at Kayla. "What's she doing here?"

Dylan ignored the question. "Did you get everything?" he asked.

"I think we're done here," Ethan said.

"I'll meet you downstairs," Dylan said. "I want to take one more look."

Ethan looked at Kayla again, then shrugged and headed toward the elevator.

Kayla followed Dylan to the door of the room. "You can't come in," he said.

"I know."

She was smiling when he closed the door in her face. He tried to figure out what the smile meant. Did she think she had got the better of him? They were supposed to be on the same side here—both interested in solving a murder and upholding the law. But he didn't trust her. If her father was a con artist, maybe she had learned a few tricks from him.

KAYLA LEANED AGAINST the wall, arms crossed over her chest. Why had she invited Dylan to dinner at her place? It wasn't as if her cooking was going to work as a bribe. Maybe he thought she intended to seduce information out of him. The idea sent heat curling through her belly. She had walked a little too close to the edge with that remark about the handcuffs, but she hadn't been able to resist. Seeing the cowboy cop angry had been intimidating, but also a big turn-on. There was something about him that got to her, and she wasn't sure if she liked it or not.

Which was probably why she had issued her invitation. She needed to figure out where things were going with them and what it meant. The fact that he had agreed to come by her place probably meant he was curious, too.

The elevator doors opened and Kayla straightened. Two men dressed in jeans and denim work shirts, one carrying a tool bag, emerged. They slowed when they spotted her, and exchanged a look she couldn't read, but the younger one, with brown eyes and olive skin, nodded at her as they passed. They walked to the end of the hall and passed through the door marked Stairs.

Kayla went back to watching the door to Asher's room. What was taking Dylan so long? The other cop had said they were finished, but Dylan must have found something else. Something to do with Andi? She couldn't shake the idea that Asher and the young woman were connected somehow.

She pulled out her phone. If someone came along, she'd look like she was waiting for a friend, or had stopped to make a call. She pulled up an internet browser and typed in Asher's and Andi's names, curious to see what might pop up. She watched the spinning icon as the site loaded, then let out a screech as the phone was wrenched from her fingers.

A hand clamped over her mouth, while strong arms crushed her in a painful grip. She kicked out at her captor, but a second man moved in front of her and cuffed her on the side of the head. She stared at the workman who had passed her earlier—the one with the olive skin and brown eyes.

He glared at her, then grabbed hold of her feet and held them tightly, preventing her from kicking. Together, the two men dragged her down the hall toward the stairwell.

DYLAN STOOD BY the window in the hotel room and surveyed the stripped bed and open drawers. The team had taken the clothes from the closet and a laptop computer from the safe, as well as the sheets and personal items to analyze for any evidence. If Asher had entertained anyone in the room before going to the Family's camp, they would find evidence of that. Dylan hoped the files would reveal the agent's purpose for being in Colorado.

Kayla thought the FBI agent was here because of Andi Matheson, but Dylan saw Daniel Metwater as the key to this case. Asher had Metwater's picture in his car, and the so-called Prophet had been entirely too cool about the sudden appearance of the dead man in his camp.

Dylan moved toward the door. He couldn't waste any more time pondering this. He had to get back to headquarters and start sorting through evidence. He expected to find Kayla waiting for him in the hallway. She had acted as if she intended to stay around, but maybe he had misread her. They had agreed to meet tonight, and he could get her address from the statement she had given Carmen. Still, it bothered him that she hadn't said goodbye.

He started toward the elevator, but a flash of light near the floor caught his eye. He stopped and scooped up a phone. The screen showed a browser open to a search for Frank Asher and Andi Matheson. An icicle of fear stabbed Dylan. This was Kayla's phone. He was sure he had seen her with it earlier.

He glanced up and down the hallway, which was empty and silent. Kayla wouldn't have carelessly dropped her phone. And she wouldn't have left without having a last word with him. Something had happened to force her to leave in a rush—without her phone.

He tucked the device into his pocket and called the front desk from his own cell phone. "This is Lieutenant Holt," he said. "Did a young woman with shoulder-length brown hair, about five-six, dressed in jeans and a button-down shirt, come through the lobby within the last five minutes?"

"No, sir," the clerk said. "No one has been in the lobby since your officers came through here."

"Thanks." He hung up the phone and returned to the hall. If Kayla hadn't passed through the lobby, she must have taken the stairs. He spotted the exit sign at the end of the hallway and sprinted toward it.

When he pushed open the door he caught the faint floral scent that lingered in the air—Kayla. Adrenaline pumping, he pounded down the steps. Below, he heard the sound of a door opening and closing.

He sped up, propelling himself down the stairs, bracing both hands on the railing and vaulting toward the ground floor. If he was wrong, he was going to look pretty foolish, barreling after her like this, but after a decade as a cop, he didn't think he was jumping to the wrong conclusion. Kayla was in trouble, and he couldn't afford to waste a minute. The ground-floor exit opened onto a concrete pad that faced a parking lot. A row of Dumpsters sat at the edge of the lot.

He spotted his quarry right away—two men dressed in denim pants and shirts, carrying Kayla between them. He started toward them just as one of them—the one carrying Kayla's feet—raised a gun and fired. The bullet pinged off metal and Dylan dived for cover behind the nearest Dumpster, the smell of old garbage washing over him in a foul blanket.

He drew his weapon and peered out from between two garbage receptacles. Kayla's kidnappers had positioned her in front of them now, using her as a shield. He couldn't risk a shot. He drew out his phone and dialed 911. "Two men have kidnapped a woman from the hotel by the airport," he said. "There's a state patrol officer there but he needs help." Then he hung up and immediately hit the button for his office. "I'm at the Mesa Inn in Montrose. Two men have kidnapped Kayla Larimer. Send everybody you can spare."

Only half a dozen cars were parked in this back lot. The kidnappers angled toward a dun-colored van, the kind that might have been used by a plumber. A few more yards and they would have Kayla in that van. He couldn't let them get away.

Ignoring the questions from the admin on the other end of the line, he stuffed the phone in his pocket and took aim at the van. The shot was painfully loud, echoing off the metal Dumpsters, but satisfaction surged through him as he watched the windshield of the vehicle explode into a million shards of glass.

The two men with Kayla froze. They shouted curses, though whether at Dylan or at each other, he didn't care. Kayla took advantage of their inattention to kick and flail. The larger of the two, who had hold of her shoulders, punched her savagely in the face. Dylan forced himself to look away, and fired another shot at the van, aiming for the front grille, hoping to hit the engine and disable the vehicle.

His ears were still ringing from the gunfire when the wail of a fast-approaching siren reached him. This brought a renewed wave of curses from the two men. The one holding Kayla's feet had dropped her and was firing at Dylan from behind a parked car, while the first man struggled to hold on to the woman.

Dylan squeezed off a barrage of shots that sent the shooter diving behind the car's bumper. Seeing his chance, he rushed forward and took cover behind another vehicle. He had the shooter in his sights now, and took careful aim.

The shooter's scream when he was hit sent his partner into a panic. The man shoved Kayla away from him, sending her sprawling on the pavement. Then he dived into the van. As a trio of police cars sped into the lot, he took off, tires screeching, heading in the opposite direction.

One of the black-and-whites took off after the van, while the other two skidded to a halt near Kayla and the downed man. Dylan pulled out his badge and stood, holding his gun at his side and his badge up. "I'm Lieutenant Dylan Holt with Colorado State Patrol," he called.

"What happened, Lieutenant Holt?" A trim, graying man who identified himself as Sergeant Connor moved toward Dylan while a second officer helped Kayla to sit. Two other officers knelt beside the shooter, who lay still on the pavement.

Dylan ignored his questioner and knelt beside Kayla. "Are you okay?" he asked.

She was bleeding from her lip, and a purpling bruise was swelling on the side of her face, but she nodded. "I'm okay." She touched a finger to the corner of her mouth and winced. "Or I will be."

"What happened?" Sergeant Connor asked again.

"I was waiting for Dylan—Lieutenant Holt—in the hotel hallway and those two men grabbed me from behind and dragged me down the stairs and out here." Kayla looked at Dylan intently. "Who were they?" she asked. "What did they want with me?"

He shook his head. "I have no idea."

Her gaze shifted to the man on the pavement. "Is he...?"

"He's dead," Sergeant Connor said, and took a step to one side to block Kayla's view of the body.

A Ranger Brigade Cruiser joined the other vehicles in the lot. Graham Ellison climbed out as Ethan Reynolds came running from the lobby. They silently assessed the situation, then strode over to join the others. "Graham Ellison. I'm the captain of the public lands task force." He offered his hand to Sergeant Connor.

"I've heard about you guys. The Ranger Brigade." Connor shook his hand. "We've got an ambulance on the way for the young lady."

"I don't need an ambulance." Kayla struggled to her feet. Dylan reached out to steady her as she swayed. "I'm just a little banged up," she protested, but didn't push him away. "I'll be fine."

"When you're able, we'll need you to come in and make a statement," Connor said.

"I'll tell you what little I know," she said. "But it all happened so fast I can't provide a lot of details."

"Did you recognize either of the men who grabbed you?" Dylan asked.

"No."

Connor's radio crackled and he turned away from them to answer it. But the rest of them clearly heard the message. "We have the suspect in custody," a man's voice said.

"We'll want to question him as soon as possible," Graham said. "He may be connected with a murder we're investigating."

Connor studied Dylan. "Tell me about this investigation," he said. "How does a crime on public lands connect to an attempted kidnapping in Montrose city limits?"

"There may be no connection," Dylan said. "But why would someone try to kidnap Kayla outside a room where the murder victim was staying?"

"Who was the murder victim?" Connor asked.

"A federal agent," Graham said. "Frank Asher. Did you know him?"

Connor shook his head. "Never heard of him. What was he doing in Montrose?"

"That's what we're trying to find out," Graham said. He turned to Kayla. "Let the EMTs check you out, then we'll get someone to take you home."

"I have my car here," she said. "I can drive myself."

"Someone can drop it by your place later," Graham said. "Until we know more about these men and why they grabbed you, we're going to keep a close eye on you."

She bristled. That was really the only way to describe it. She drew herself up straight and her hair all but stood on end. "I can look after myself."

"Nevertheless, we'll be checking in regularly," Graham said. "And if you spot anything out of the ordinary, call us."

"Or call *us*," Connor said.

The ambulance turned into the lot and stopped

alongside them. Dylan left Kayla in the care of the EMTs and joined Graham and Ethan as they walked toward the hotel. "What was she doing here?" Graham asked.

"She followed me," Dylan said. "She thinks Asher is connected with Andi Matheson and she wanted to find out how."

"What did you tell her?" Graham asked.

"I told her she had no business being here and if she didn't leave I could have her arrested for interfering in our investigation."

"I take it she didn't leave," Ethan said.

"I left her in the hallway while I went back into the room." No way was he going to reveal he had agreed to have dinner with her. "When I came out, she was gone, but I found her phone where she had dropped it on the floor. I checked the stairs and saw those two dragging her away."

"How did they know you and Kayla were here at the hotel?" Graham asked.

"They could have followed us. Or maybe the desk clerk tipped them off."

"Or maybe it was bad timing," Ethan said. "They showed up to get something from Asher's room, saw Kayla waiting there and decided they had to get rid of her."

"It's a big risk to take," Dylan said.

"Maybe what they were after was that important," Graham said.

"We got everything from the room, so if there was something there, we'll find it," Dylan said.

"He wasn't on a case," Graham said. "His supervisors said he took two weeks' vacation, starting three days ago. They swear whatever he was doing down here was his personal business."

"Personal business that got him killed," Ethan said.

And almost got Kayla killed, Dylan thought. The idea chilled him.

"Agent Ellison!"

The trio turned to see Sergeant Connor hurrying toward them. "Something just came in I thought you'd want to know about," he said when he reached them. "We ran the plates on the vehicle the shooter was driving and it's registered to Senator Pete Matheson."

"Was it stolen?" Dylan asked.

"That's what we wondered," Connor said. "But when we ran a search for stolen vehicle reports, what we came up with instead was a missing person's report."

"Who's missing?" Graham asked.

"Senator Matheson. No one has seen or heard from him since Friday."

Chapter Seven

Kayla persuaded the Montrose police deputy who drove her home that she didn't want or need a bodyguard. She suggested—and the officer's supervisor agreed—that an occasional drive-by to verify all was peaceful in her neighborhood would be sufficient. She would lock herself in the house and keep both her gun and her phone close at hand.

When she was alone at last, she tried to do as the EMTs had recommended and rest, but every time she closed her eyes her mind replayed the morning's events, from the appearance of Agent Asher's body to Andi's anguished tears to those moments of terror when her kidnappers had held her and bullets whined past.

And Dylan—he disturbed her rest, as well. The man intrigued and aggravated her in equal parts. She told herself she wanted to know what he could tell her only so that she could help Andi and the senator, but deep down she knew she wanted to see Dylan again because she wanted the thrill she felt in his presence— a physical craving coupled with the sense that here was a man who might be worth opening up to.

Unable to sleep, she gave up and went to her computer and once more typed Andi's and Agent Asher's names into the search engine. She found plenty of articles about Andi, mostly mentions of her attendance at various society parties or fund-raisers, with and without her father. But the only mention she found of Asher was a talk he once gave to a neighborhood watch group in Denver. The Fed definitely kept a low profile.

The chime of her doorbell interrupted her thoughts. She started to the door, but froze as she caught a glimpse of herself in the mirror over the small table in the foyer. An ugly purple bruise spread across her left cheek and a black half-moon showed beneath her left eye. She put a hand to the bruising and winced. Apparently, she looked even worse than she felt.

The doorbell rang again. Sighing, she checked the peephole and spotted Dylan Holt rocking back and forth on his heels, staring back at her. She pulled away from the peephole. She didn't really want to see Dylan right now. Not looking like this. Not with her feelings so confused. What did you say to a man who had saved your life? She really wasn't good at this sort of thing. Not that it had ever come up before, but still...

The bell chimed again.

She undid the locks and pulled open the door. "If you came to check up on me, I'm fine," she said.

"I came for dinner." He pushed past her, a shopping bag in one hand.

She'd forgotten all about their dinner date, which felt as if it had been made in an alternate reality, before she'd been manhandled, dragged across a parking lot and shot at—or, at least, shot around. "I'll have to take a rain check," she said. "I don't exactly feel like cooking."

"You don't have to cook." He set the shopping bag on her dining table and began taking out cardboard to-go containers. "I hope you like Chinese."

The aroma of sesame chicken made her mouth water, and she realized she was hungry. Starving. She hurried to the cabinet and pulled out plates. Neither of them said anything else until they were seated across from each other at her small kitchen table with full plates. After a few bites of chicken and rice she paused and grinned at him. "Thanks," she said. "You may have just saved my life. Again."

His expression sobered. "I didn't come here just to feed you."

She put down her fork. "Did you find out anything about the men who attacked me?"

"The truck they were driving was registered to Senator Matheson."

"You mean it was stolen?"

"We don't know. When was the last time you spoke to Senator Matheson?" he asked.

"Friday afternoon. I told him I planned to visit the Family's camp and hoped to speak with Andi."

"How did he take the news?"

"He was pleased. He wanted me to try to persuade her to leave with me and return to his home. I told him all I could do was give her the message, but he seemed optimistic. He told me to call him as soon as I returned from talking with her, to let him know how she's doing."

"Did you call him?"

"Not yet. So much has been going on I haven't had time."

"Would you mind calling him now?"

"Why? What's going on?"

"Call him and then I'll tell you." Dylan softened his expression. "Please."

"All right." She reached into her pocket, then froze. "I can't find my phone."

He pulled the phone from his own pocket. "You must have dropped it when those two thugs grabbed you," he said.

"Thanks." That showed how rattled she had been— she hadn't even realized her phone was missing. She scrolled through her contacts and found the number for Senator Matheson. The phone buzzed a couple times, then a message came on that informed her the mailbox of the person she was trying to reach was full.

"That's odd," she said after she had ended the call. "He's usually good about checking his messages. But his mailbox is full."

"Is that his office number or a private line?" Dylan asked.

"It's his private cell phone, I think. Dylan, what is going on?"

"The senator's administrative assistant reported him missing this morning. He left his office Friday afternoon and was scheduled to attend a Senate hearing on finance today. No has seen him since then. You may be the last person who spoke with him. I expect it will be on the news any minute now."

"I haven't had the TV on. And I was doing research online, so I didn't notice the headlines. So what's the connection between the guys who attacked me and

Senator Matheson? Did they steal the truck and kidnap him? And then they came to Asher's hotel to look for something?"

"To look for what?"

"I don't know—something incriminating? Something that linked them to both Asher and the senator?"

"You're linked to Asher and the senator. The senator hired you to track down his daughter at the camp and while you were there, Asher's body was found."

"So you think, what—that they followed me to the hotel? Why?"

"Maybe they think you saw something you shouldn't have."

"I didn't see anything."

"Then why did they kidnap you? Did they say anything to you?"

"They didn't say a word."

He scowled and bit down hard on a fried wonton. "I can't know you're safe until I figure out why those men grabbed you," he said.

"You don't have to worry about me." His concern unsettled her. "Besides, they're in custody, aren't they? I mean, the one who lived is." She wasn't likely to forget the sight of the man sprawled on the pavement— the second body she had seen that day. "I don't have anything to worry about."

"He's in the hospital," Dylan said. "With a police guard posted at his door. We haven't had a chance to question him yet. What if the attack wasn't their idea? What if someone hired them? He could hire someone else." He looked around the room. "Do you have a security system?"

"No. I don't need a security system."

"Maybe you shouldn't stay here tonight. At least until we get to the bottom of this."

"Lieutenant, I'll be fine. I have good locks, and a weapon if I need to use it. And I can always dial 911. The police station is only a few blocks away."

"I still don't like it." He attacked another wonton. "I'd think you'd be afraid to stay here alone after what happened to you today."

"I was fine until you came along with all these dire predictions of peril. Honestly, you're blowing everything out of proportion."

"Am I? You could have died today. I don't like the idea of someone trying again."

"I don't like that idea, either, but it's not going to do anyone any good for me to run around wringing my hands and fretting about it. I think I'm as safe here in my own home as I would be anywhere else. And I still think the attack on me was random—I was in the wrong place at the wrong time. Those two wanted me out of the way so they could get into the hotel room. They were even dressed like workmen."

"What did you find out when you talked to the maid?" Dylan asked.

"Not much," she admitted. "She said she overheard Asher on the phone with someone. He was arguing, but she didn't know what the argument was about."

"Maybe Asher was arguing with his killer."

"Maybe." She spooned more fried rice onto her plate. "What did your search of Asher's room turn up?"

He hesitated.

"Just tell me if you found anything to link him to Andi," she said.

"We don't know yet. He has files on his computer, but they're all encrypted. We've got people working on it." He dipped an egg roll in plum sauce and took a bite.

"Check his phone, too."

He swallowed. "Thanks. I hadn't thought of that."

She fought the urge to stick her tongue out at him. But perhaps they hadn't descended into such juvenile sparring yet. "I'm going to keep digging," she said.

"What did you learn about Andi and Asher?"

"How did you know I was researching them?"

"I saw the web page on your phone browser. Did you learn anything?"

She shook her head. "Asher has definitely kept a low profile, but maybe that's usual for a federal agent. All the mentions I found about Andi had to do with her father, or some society do she attended. She's certainly living a very different kind of life now."

"I'm going back out to the camp tomorrow to talk to Andi," he said. "I need to tell her about her father and find out if she's heard anything, and I intend to ask her about Asher."

"Let me go with you."

"No."

"She'll talk to me. You just frighten her."

"You make me sound like some kind of bully."

"Let's just say you can be pretty intimidating when you want to be."

"Do I intimidate you?" His eyes met hers and she felt that jolt of attraction again. She wasn't afraid of him, only of where these wild feelings she had for him might take her.

She wet her suddenly dry lips. "I don't know, Lieutenant—do *I* intimidate *you?*"

"*Intimidate* isn't the word I'd use." He leaned across the table toward her and cupped his hand along the side of her injured cheek, not touching her, but close enough that she could feel the heat of him. "You're a puzzle I want to figure out," he said.

She wanted to lean into him, to press her lips to his and learn if he would respond with the same boldness with which he questioned a suspect or faced down danger. But once she crossed that barrier with him, there wouldn't be any going back. Neither of them was the type to back down from a challenge.

The loud strains of Fergie sounded from her phone, making her jump. Dylan sat back, arms crossed on his chest. She avoided his gaze, checking the phone's screen instead. Not a number she recognized, but it could always be a new client—someone wanting her to spy on a cheating spouse or track down a long-lost relative. "Larimer Investigations," she answered.

"Is this Kayla Larimer?" a woman's voice asked.

"Yes."

"I have a message for you from Andi Matheson."

Kayla sat up straighter. "What is it?"

"She needs to talk to you. Can you meet her at the parking area for the Dead Horse Canyon Trail tomorrow afternoon at one?"

"What is this about?" Kayla asked. "Who is this?"

"I'm just a friend. I promised to call and give you this message. Can you meet her?"

"Yes, of course. But—"

The line went dead before she could ask any more

questions. Kayla looked up and met Dylan's eyes. "Andi wants to meet me in the morning," she said.

"I'll go with you," he said.

"She said she wanted to talk to me—not you."

"I'll go with you." His expression was grim. "I don't trust these people. I'm not going to let you go alone."

DYLAN PICKED UP Kayla from her house the next afternoon. He had been tempted to insist on staying with her overnight—on her couch, though he wouldn't have turned her down if she had invited him into her bed. He didn't trust whoever was responsible for the attack on her not to make another try. But in the end he had decided alienating her by pushing to get his way wasn't worth the trouble. He had made her show him her gun and her locks, and he was satisfied both were adequate. Then he had touched base with the Montrose PD and impressed upon them the need to make a few extra passes by her house during the night.

He showed up a half hour early the next afternoon, since he didn't entirely trust her not to slip off by herself. While he admired independence in a woman, she seemed to want to take it too far. He still got chills when he thought about how close she had come to dying yesterday.

She met him in her driveway, her purse slung over one shoulder, a steaming mug in her hand. "I could have driven myself," she said.

Did he know her or what? "Good afternoon to you, too." He opened the passenger door for her. "Look at it this way—you're saving gas and wear and tear on your car."

She slid into the seat and reached for the seat belt. "Just remember, Andi wants to talk to *me*."

"I have to give her the news about her father and try to find out if she's been in contact with him since he disappeared." The FBI had handed that job off to the Rangers.

"So the senator is still missing?" she asked.

"Yes. Apparently, there's no sign of a struggle at his home or office, and no one has seen or heard from him since he left work Thursday." Dylan put the Cruiser in gear and backed out of her driveway.

"What about the man who attacked me? You said the van he was driving belonged to Senator Matheson? Does he know anything?"

"The senator used the van as a campaign vehicle when he ran for reelection two years ago, and some of his staff workers have used it occasionally since then," Dylan said. "We still haven't been able to interview the suspect, but our research hasn't turned up a connection." He glanced at her. "So we're agreed that I'll talk to Andi?"

"Fine. But let me talk to her first. I don't want you scaring her off before I find out what she wants."

"I thought we established last night that I'm not that scary."

She flushed. Was she remembering that moment when he had almost kissed her? His fingertips tingled at the memory, remembering the heat of her against his skin, and the almost overwhelming need he had had to touch her.

"You don't frighten me," she said. "But Andi may be another story."

He pulled to the stop sign at the end of her street.

"Fine. You take the lead, but then I get to ask my questions."

"I think we've already established that you're good at questions." The amused glint in her eyes took the sting out of her words.

"That's right," he said. "When I was a kid my dad threatened to gag me with my own bandanna when we were out working and I'd pester him with too many questions."

He turned onto the highway and she settled back into the seat and sipped from her mug. "Do you like ranching?" she asked after a moment.

"I like being out-of-doors. I like working with the animals. But it can be frustrating. There's so much you can't control, from weather to cattle prices. And sometimes it's just a lot of hard work. I had to go away for a while to appreciate it."

"Where did you go?"

"To Denver. I was in law enforcement there for ten years after college. But I missed all this." He indicated the sweep of land out the windshield. "And my dad had some health problems and needed more help. When the opening for this job came up, I was glad to take it."

She didn't say anything and he wondered what she was thinking. From what little she had said about her past, he gathered she had never had a place she felt rooted to—a real home. She had come to Montrose almost by chance and had no ties here other than her job.

"This work must be different from what you did in the city," she said. "This isn't exactly a high-crime area."

"More goes on here than you might think," he said.

"But a lot of it goes on behind the scene—drugs, theft of artifacts, smuggling. And a lot of people see public lands as a good place to hide out."

"People like Daniel Metwater."

"Yeah. How much do you know about him?"

"Not a lot," she said. "He started calling himself a prophet and recruiting followers a little over a year ago. I take it he comes from money."

"His father was an industrialist named Oscar Metwater. When he died, Daniel and his twin brother, David, inherited the family fortune. David was killed a few months later in what was likely a mob hit. He had a gambling habit and had embezzled money from the family firm and apparently borrowed from the wrong people."

"In one of his official bios Daniel says something about his brother—about how his death made him see the futility of the life he had been leading and made him seek a better way."

"I guess some people would see having a slew of followers turn over all their possessions to you and do your bidding as a better way of life," Dylan said. "And from what I saw, the majority of those followers are beautiful young women."

"While some religions teach the importance of caring for the poor and afflicted, I'm guessing Daniel Metwater isn't one of them," she said.

"What about your father?" he asked. "Was he like Metwater?"

"Oh, he could quote scripture about widows and orphans when he thought it would encourage people to put more in the collection plate," she said. "But the only person he was really interested in looking out

for was himself. Metwater strikes me as the same."
She shifted toward Dylan. "Do you know why Agent
Asher had Metwater's picture in his car?"

"We haven't come up with anything yet. The computer forensics may take a while. Or we might find
out something from Andi."

She fell silent and Dylan didn't try to engage her
further. Maybe he shouldn't have brought up her father. Clearly, it wasn't a pleasant topic for her.

After a dusty ride on a rugged dirt track, they
reached the parking area for the trail, marked only by
a bullet-riddled brown sign. The Ranger Cruiser was
the only vehicle in sight. Dylan pulled into the lot and
shut off the engine, and silence closed around them.
He scanned the outcropping of rocks and clumps of
scrubby piñons and sagebrush for any signs of life.
"This would be a good place for an ambush," he said.

His plan was to wait in the Cruiser until someone approached, but before he could say so, Kayla
opened her door and got out. Almost immediately,
Andi emerged from behind a large boulder, her long
hair blown sideways in a gust of hot wind. She wore
the same prairie skirt and tank top she had had on
yesterday, a blue cotton shawl around her shoulders.

She eyed Dylan warily as he climbed out of the
vehicle and came to stand behind Kayla. "What is
he doing here?" Andi asked. "I wanted you to come
alone."

"The person who called me didn't say anything
about that," Kayla said. "I thought it would be a good
idea for him to come along for protection. You can't
blame me for being nervous, after what happened to
Frank Asher."

At the mention of Asher, Andi's lips trembled, but she brought her emotions under control. "Can I trust him?" she asked.

"Trust me with what?" Dylan said, ignoring the annoyed look from Kayla.

"Can I trust you to keep my confidences?" Andi asked. She wrapped her hands in the ends of the shawl. "I don't want certain people knowing about what I'm going to tell you."

"What people?" Kayla asked.

Andi shook her head and began walking away from them, toward the road. Kayla and Dylan fell into step alongside her, gravel crunching under their feet. "Do you mean Daniel Metwater?" Kayla asked. "Is that why you wanted to meet us away from the camp—so the Prophet wouldn't know you were meeting me?"

"Everyone in the camp is busy preparing for the ceremony this evening," Andi said.

"What kind of ceremony?" Kayla asked.

"We have a new member joining the Family. That's why I couldn't call you myself yesterday. I had to stay and help with the preparations. The woman who called was one of the ones chosen to go into town to buy food for tonight's celebration."

She fell silent again, and Dylan fought the urge to fire more questions at her. Maybe Kayla was right and he needed to let her take the lead here, at least until Andi was more comfortable with him. She was calmer today, though an air of sadness clung to her. The skirt she wore was faded, with a tear in the hem at the back, and the pink polish on her toes was chipped. As the daughter of a prominent senator, she was probably used to designer fashions and spa treatments. Was she growing disillusioned with life in the wilderness with the so-called prophet?

"How are you doing?" Kayla asked when they had walked another hundred yards or so. "You were pretty upset when I saw you yesterday."

"It was the shock of learning about Frank's death." She swept a lock of hair out of her eyes and tucked it behind one ear.

"You knew him, then," Kayla said.

"Oh, yes." She drew in a deep breath. "We were lovers. He's the father of my baby."

So Kayla had been right, Dylan thought.

"Was he coming here to see you?" Kayla asked.

"I don't know." Andi pulled the shawl more tightly around her shoulders. "I told him not to come—that I had nothing to say to him. We ceased being close months ago, before I even learned I was pregnant."

"Why did you break up?" Kayla asked.

She looked away, lips pressed tightly together.

"You probably think the answer to that question is none of our business," Dylan said. "But if there's the slightest chance that the reason the two of you split up could have anything to do with his death, we need to know."

She shook her head, still not looking at them. "I'm sure it doesn't have anything to do with his death."

"We're in a better position to determine that," Dylan said.

"Frank was my father's friend before he was mine, and in the end, he had the same mindset. He was of that world. Isn't that enough?"

"So Frank Asher and your father knew each other?" Dylan asked. He kept his eyes on Andi, though he was aware of Kayla's frown. She wasn't pleased he was asking so many questions, but that was his job.

"Frank worked for my father," Andi said. "That's how we met."

"I thought he was an FBI agent," Kayla said.

"He took a year's leave from the Bureau to work as my father's private security agent. But when my father found out we were lovers, he and Frank argued and Frank went back to work for the Bureau." Andi turned and began walking again.

"When was the last time you saw Frank?" Kayla asked.

"Last week. He must have found out I was here and he stopped me in town and said we had to talk. I was with some of the other women and I told him I had nothing to say to him. He said he would come to the camp to talk to me. I told him not to, but he didn't listen. Men don't, do they? Not when it's a woman talking."

She didn't look at Dylan when she said the words, but he felt their impact.

"Do you know anything about what happened to him?" Kayla asked, her voice gentle.

Andi shook her head. "I was so shocked when you told me it was him." She hugged her arms across her chest. "That's why I wanted to talk to you today. I knew you would wonder why I was so upset over his death. Even though I haven't loved him for a while, at one time he meant something to me, so I grieve. And it saddens me to think my child will never know its father."

Kayla put a hand on Andi's shoulder. "I'm sorry for your loss. I'm sure it was a great shock."

Andi straightened. "Of course, the Prophet will be the child's father, as he is father to all of us."

"Is that how you see him?" Dylan asked. "As a father? You and he are close to the same age."

Andi glanced back at him. "Well, perhaps not a father. But he is our leader. Our guide." She brought the shawl up to cover her head. "We should go back now. I've said what I needed to say."

She led the way ahead, then faltered, stumbling. Dylan reached out to steady her, then froze as a man stepped from the brush alongside the road. Sunlight glinted off the lenses of his mirrored sunglasses, and off the pistol in his hand.

"If you want to know more about me, Lieutenant, you ought to talk to me," Daniel Metwater said.

Chapter Eight

Kayla stood very still, more fascinated than fearful, as Daniel Metwater strode toward them. Though not a large man, he exuded power, a kind of magnetic vitality radiating from him. He moved with a swagger, a gleam in his eyes that told her he was confident of the admiration of all who observed him. As much as she loathed his attitude, she could admit to being compelled by him. She understood why so many young women fell under his charismatic spell. The promise of being the focus of such raw energy and sex appeal could be intoxicating.

When he was a few feet away, he tucked the gun into a holster on his right hip. "Are you all right, Asteria?" he asked.

She nodded, her gaze focused on the ground.

Metwater turned his attention to Kayla and Dylan. "If you want to talk to me or one of my followers, it isn't necessary to sneak around outside the camp," he said. "We have nothing to hide."

"What are you doing with that gun?" Dylan asked. "I thought you preached nonviolence."

"As the unfortunate events of yesterday prove, the wilderness is not as safe a place as it would seem," he said. "And before you ask, we've had hordes of officers swarming over the camp searching for weapons. They have already examined this particular gun and determined it isn't the same caliber as the one that killed Agent Asher. And they haven't found any other guns among my followers."

"Why do you need a gun if you don't allow your followers to be armed?" Dylan asked.

"It is my job to protect my people."

"Have you been threatened in any way?" Dylan asked. "Have there been other incidents you haven't reported to the police?"

"No." He took Andi's arm and pulled her toward him. "Come back to camp now," he said. "You must be tired. You need to rest."

Kayla's skin crawled as she watched any hint of the young woman's personality vanish in Metwater's shadow. "Andi, you don't have to go with him if you don't want," she said.

"No, it's fine," Andi said. "My place is with him. With the Family."

Metwater fixed his gaze on Kayla, an intense scrutiny that made her feel naked and exposed. "You fear us because you don't understand us," he said. "You don't understand the security and refuge I offer my followers. We are having a special ceremony this evening to welcome a new Family member. I'm inviting you both to attend. It will help you to understand us better."

"All right, we'll be there." Dylan took Kayla's arm and squeezed it, cutting off her protest. She had no desire to spend any more time than necessary with Metwater and his followers, but if Dylan thought attending the ceremony would help in the investigation, she was willing to play along.

"Come along, Asteria." Metwater prepared to lead Andi away.

"Ms. Matheson, when was the last time you spoke to your father?" Dylan asked.

Andi stumbled. Only Metwater's grasp on her arm kept her from falling. She looked over her shoulder at Dylan. "My father?"

"Yes. When was the last time you were in contact with him?"

"Months ago," she said. "We haven't spoken since I joined the Family."

"You haven't heard from him recently, in the past few days?"

"She told you she hasn't," Metwater said. "We're leaving now. We'll see you both this evening. Come at dusk and someone will be waiting to escort you to the ceremony."

"Andi, have you heard from your father in the past few days?" Dylan asked again.

She shook her head. "No."

"I'm sorry to have to tell you he's missing."

Andi's expression didn't change. "I don't know anything about that." Then she turned and, holding Metwater's hand, walked away.

Kayla frowned after her. Dylan nudged her. "Let's get out of here."

Neither of them spoke as they made their way back to Dylan's Cruiser, but once they were inside the vehicle, he turned to her. "Does it strike you as cold that Andi didn't react to news of her father's disappearance? She certainly cried buckets over Frank Asher."

Kayla nodded. "Something was off about her reaction—maybe because Metwater was there."

"But we're talking about her father. Her only living parent."

"I wouldn't necessarily have much of a reaction if you told me my father was missing," she said. Her father had been missing from her life—or at least, the fatherly part of him had—for as long as she could remember. "I don't think that makes me a horrible person."

"No, it doesn't." He started the Cruiser and pulled out of the parking area, his face grim. Kayla turned away, staring at the stark landscape. She didn't think of her father much these days, or of any of her family, really. She was sure they seldom thought of her. Since she had refused to work with them in their con games, she had ceased to be useful to them.

Dylan guided the vehicle over the rutted BLM road to the highway, but instead of turning toward Ranger headquarters or town, he took another road that led south. "Where are you going?" Kayla asked.

"We have a few hours to kill before we have to be back at the camp for their ceremony," he said. "Do you have somewhere you need to be?"

She always had work to do, but it was nothing that wouldn't wait. "No."

"Then there's someone I want you to meet."

THE BLEAKNESS IN Kayla's voice when she spoke of her father made Dylan want to punch something. All his life he had known he could count on his family to be there for him. He knew they loved him as surely as he knew the sun would rise tomorrow, and if he needed anything at all, his parents and siblings would move heaven and earth to help him. Kayla didn't have that kind of reassurance, and knowing that made him sick at heart.

"Where are we going?" she asked again, when he turned onto the narrow county road that formed one boundary of his family's ranch.

"I'm taking you home," he said.

"To your home?"

"Yeah. This is my family's ranch." He gestured to his left, and the rolling pastureland dotted with Angus heifers and calves. They rounded a curve in the road and the main house came into view—a two-story log cabin with a green metal roof. A deep porch stretched across the front of the house, and assorted log-sided sheds and other outbuildings dotted the land around it.

Kayla sat up straighter, her back pressed against the seat as if she was trying to put as much distance as possible between herself and the house. "I don't think we should barge in like this without calling first," she said.

"This is my home. I don't have to call before I show up." He guided the Cruiser under the iron archway that proclaimed Holt Cattle Company, and over the cattle guard, to the parking area under a trio of tall spruce.

"You live here?" She stared at the house.

He laughed. "I live in a smaller cabin on another part of the property. But I grew up here. My parents live here."

They exited the car and a pair of Border collies shot across the yard to greet them. Kayla bent to run her hands over their wriggling bodies. "Oh, aren't you a pretty pair!"

"Their names are Lucy and Desi," Dylan said.

"They're beautiful." She grinned as both dogs fought for her attention.

"I see you've met our vicious guard dogs!"

They looked up from the dogs as Dylan's parents approached. As was his habit now, Dylan found himself assessing the older couple. Dad was thinner than he had been before his heart attack three months ago, and he had a little more gray in his reddish-blond hair, but he looked good. So much better than he had when Dylan had first seen him in the hospital.

The ordeal had aged his mom, too, added a few more lines to her face, but she, too, looked stronger than she had when Dylan first came home. "Mom, Dad, I'd like you to meet Kayla Larimer. Kayla, this is my mom and dad, Nancy and Bud Holt."

Kayla straightened. "It's nice to meet you," she said.

"Good to meet you." Bud offered his hand.

"So nice of Dylan to bring you to see us," his mom added. Dylan could read the unasked question in her eyes. He wasn't one for bringing women around to meet the family.

"I wanted Kayla to see the ranch," he said, an answer he knew wouldn't really satisfy his mother, but she was too polite to demand more information in Kayla's hearing.

"Well, come on in." Bud took Kayla's arm and escorted her toward the house. "Are you from around here?" he asked.

"I live in Montrose. I'm a private detective. Dylan and I are working a case together."

"Are you now?" His dad's sharp, assessing gaze

made Dylan feel like the kid who had been caught sneaking out of the house his freshman year of high school.

"Where are you from originally?" Nancy asked.

"Oh, my family moved around a lot when I was growing up," Kayla said. "I love your dogs." She gestured toward the two pups, which had run ahead. "I've always heard how intelligent Border collies are."

"Oh, they're smart, all right," Bud said. "Smart enough to get into all kinds of trouble if you don't keep them busy."

The four of them mounted the porch. At the top of the steps, Kayla turned to look out across the yard, and at the snow-capped mountains beyond. "What a gorgeous view," she said.

"Yes. I never get tired of the view," Bud said. "This country has a way of growing on people, I think. Pulling them back when they try to leave."

This last comment was for Dylan's benefit, he knew. "I missed all of this while I was in Denver," he said. "I'm glad to be back."

"And we're glad to have you back," his mother said. "Now come, sit down." She gestured toward the grouping of chairs on the porch. "Can I get you something to drink?"

"No, thank you." Kayla perched on the edge of one of the oak rockers lined up against the front wall of the house. Dylan took the chair next to her, while his parents chose the adjacent swing that hung from the porch beams.

"What kind of case are you working on?" Bud asked. "Or can't you say?"

"We're investigating some goings-on that might

be related to a group that's been camping in the
Curecanti Wilderness Area," Dylan said. "Followers
of a man who calls himself the Prophet."

Bud nodded. "I heard a little about them. Sam Wilson ran into a bunch of the women at the farmers'
market last Friday. They bought a lot of his produce.
He said they seemed nice. Are they causing trouble?"

"We're not sure. Let's just say some things have
aroused our suspicions."

Bud rested his arm along the back of the swing
and gave it a gentle nudge with the toe of his boot.
"There's always a few of these types who take to the
wilderness," he said. "Back-to-the-landers or survivalists or religious zealots looking for a better way. Most
of them peter out after a while when people find out
how tough it really is to live without modern conveniences like indoor plumbing, refrigeration and heat."

"There was a group that passed through here in
the seventies," Nancy said. "The rainbow people, or
something like that. A bunch of hippies who said they
were all for peace and love, but all they really did was
sponge off anyone they could, do drugs and leave a
mess behind. Bart Tillaman had to take his front-end
loader out to the campsite after they left and haul off
two or three Dumpsters full of garbage."

"We won't let things go that far," Dylan said.
"That's why we're keeping an eye on them."

"And you're helping the Rangers with their investigations?" Nancy asked Kayla.

She looked up from petting the dogs, who had settled on either side of her. "A client hired me to find
his daughter," she said. "She's living with this group."

"Those poor parents." Nancy shook her head. "I

can't imagine having one of my children run off like that, having to hire a private investigator to track them down."

"You don't have to worry about that," Dylan said.

"No. Especially now that all three of you are living on the ranch." She smiled at Kayla. "Do your parents live near here?"

"I don't have any close family anymore," Kayla said. She shot Dylan a warning look. As if she had to warn him not to air her private business for his parents.

"I'm sorry to hear that," Nancy said. "But a small town can be a good place to be when you're alone in the world. Stay here long enough and people will be treating you like family."

"Which is another way of saying they'll want to know all your business," Dylan said, but he winked to let his mom know he was only teasing—sort of.

"Speaking of family business…" Bud put his hands on his knees and leaned toward Dylan. "I hope you plan on being at the Cattleman's Club meeting next week."

"I don't know, Dad. Work is taking a lot of my time." The monthly meetings of representatives from all the local ranches had never struck him as very productive.

"The board is really trying to get some of the younger members of local ranching families involved," Bud said. "And you could learn a lot about the way the cattle business works in this part of the state."

"All right. I'll be there if I can." One of the reasons he had returned to the ranch was to take on more of the responsibility of running cattle operations, to ease the burden on his parents. And he knew his dad got a kick out of showing off his son, the cop.

"Private investigation must be interesting work," Nancy said, once more including Kayla in the conversation. "I would think a woman would have an advantage in that field."

"Why do you say that?" Bud asked. "Because women are nosier than men?"

Nancy gave her husband a scolding look. "No. Because criminals would be less likely to suspect a woman—especially one who is so young and pretty."

Kayla shifted, clearly uncomfortable. "I've always enjoyed solving puzzles," she said. "And I like working alone and being my own boss."

"I'd love to hear more about it," Nancy said. She turned to Dylan. "I hope you're planning to stay for dinner."

"Oh, I don't know—" Kayla began.

"We don't have to be back at the camp until dusk," Dylan interrupted. "Might as well not go on an empty stomach."

"We'll grill steaks," Bud said. "Some of our own beef."

"And a salad from the garden," Nancy said.

"Right. The doctor says I've got to eat my vegetables." Bud grinned. "Say you'll stay."

Kayla nodded, and even managed a small smile of her own. "All right."

Nancy stood, and the others rose also. "While I'm cooking, Dylan can give you a tour of the ranch," she said.

Chapter Nine

Kayla eyed the horse, swallowing her trepidation. The animal was considerably taller than her, with a lot more teeth. "I've never ridden a horse before," she said.

"Sunset is an easy mount." Dylan moved alongside her, so close she could feel the heat of him, which sent a corresponding warmth through her. "I'll be right with you, so you don't have anything to worry about."

"Couldn't we drive? Or take an ATV?" She looked longingly toward a trio of all-terrain vehicles parked outside the barn.

"Horseback is the best way to see the place," he said. "Besides, my horse, Bravo, needs exercise. It's been a few days since I rode him. We won't go far, I promise."

The horse snorted and tossed his head. "I don't think he agrees with you," she said. She took a step back, which sent her stumbling into Dylan. His arms encircled her, steadying her. The hard planes and bunched muscles that defined him as so very male stirred something deep in her female core and she stared up at him, lips parted, breathing grown shallow, bracing herself against the flood of longing that weakened her knees.

His eyes locked onto hers, then darkened, and his arms tightened around her. He bent his head, hesitating a fraction of a second with his mouth near hers. Impatient, she slid her hand to the back of his neck and pulled him down.

His mouth was warm and agile, caressing her lips and sending liquid heat through her. He angled his head to deepen the kiss, the brim of his Stetson brushing the top of her hair, the faint afternoon shadow of his beard a pleasant friction against her skin.

When at last he raised his head, she blinked up at him, trying to clear away the fog of lust. "Wh-why did you do that?" she stammered.

"Because you wanted me to. And because I wanted to." He patted the horse's neck. "It stopped you from being afraid of Sunset, didn't it?"

Wishing to deny both the accusation that she had wanted him to kiss her and that she had been afraid of the horse, but knowing she wasn't that accomplished a liar, she turned away him and stuck her foot in the stirrup. "Let's get go—"

Before she could complete the sentence, he had moved to boost her onto the horse, the feel of his hand against the seat of her jeans staying with her even when she was settled in the saddle. He handed her the reins. "Don't jerk on them," he said. "Mostly, Sunset will follow Bravo. You just relax and enjoy the scenery."

That scenery included Dylan on horseback as he rode ahead of her down a trail that led away from the house. He sat relaxed in the saddle, tall and broad-shouldered, his Stetson cocked just-so on his head. What had possessed her to kiss the man like that?

The move was unprofessional and impulsive and probably a lot of other things that in no way described her.

For the next half hour she followed him down the trail. He pointed out various outbuildings and pastures, and talked about some of the livestock and the history of the ranch. "My great-grandfather bought the land during the Depression, when it cost next to nothing. He worked for years adding to it and building it up to make it what it is today." Kayla heard the pride in Dylan's voice and felt a stab of jealousy. What would it be like to feel so connected to a place? To the land?

He stopped at the top of a hill that afforded a vista of a sweeping river valley. "Our place extends to the base of those hills over there," he said, pointing.

"It's beautiful." Unlike the almost barren terrain near the national park, this valley was green, and dotted with small herds of cattle that grazed in the knee-high grass. She glanced at Dylan. He was looking out across the landscape, fine lines spreading at the corners of his eyes as he squinted in the brightness, his lips curved in a half smile. "Did you enjoy growing up here?" she asked.

"I did. I liked to ride and shoot and fish, and being outdoors." He shifted, the saddle creaking as he half turned toward her. "But when I got to be a teenager, I grew restless. I was interested in a career in law enforcement and I didn't see much chance for advancement here. It's a pretty small police department, and there wasn't anything like the Ranger Brigade back then."

"So you went to Denver."

"Yes. And I liked it. The city is a good place to be if you're a single, twentysomething guy. And it was good for my career."

"But you came back."

"My folks needed me. And it was time. As much as I enjoyed Denver, it wasn't the kind of place I could picture myself raising a family."

"You really think about things like that—raising a family?"

"Don't you?"

She shook her head. "No." The idea unsettled her a little. She was happy being responsible for herself, but she didn't need to be responsible for anyone else.

"Maybe that's why Andi Matheson hooked up with Metwater's group," Dylan said. "Maybe she thought that kind of makeshift family would be a good place to raise a kid."

"It sounds like a terrible idea." Kayla's own childhood had been defined by constantly moving around with an ever-shifting group of her father's followers. "What I can't figure is what Daniel Metwater gets out of it."

"A power trip? A bunch of devoted, beautiful women? Or maybe he's looking for a family of his own." Dylan turned his horse and led the way back down the hill. At the bottom the trail widened, so they could ride side by side.

True to Dylan's word, Sunset was an easygoing mount that was content to follow Dylan's horse's lead. Kayla was able to relax and focus away from her own fears and annoyances to the case. "From what I've read, he comes from money," she said. "Why give that up to live in the desert?"

"He thinks he's a prophet. It's his calling."

"Or he's running away from something."

"Or that." Dylan glanced at her. "Anything in particular make you think so?"

"When my father ran into trouble and needed to leave a place, he would always announce that he had had a vision—God leading him to take his message to new, more fertile fields."

Dylan nodded. "You've given me an idea."

"What's that?"

"I'm going to dig a little deeper into Metwater's background. Maybe I'll find something there that will help in this investigation. Some secret he's not keen to have revealed."

THE SUN WAS sinking behind the distant hills when Dylan and Kayla finally left the ranch. Dinner had been a leisurely affair on the back deck of his parents' home—steaks grilled outdoors, served with roasted corn and an enormous salad of fresh greens and tomatoes from his mother's garden.

Kayla had seemed to enjoy herself and Dylan had enjoyed watching her. His lips still warmed at the memory of that impulsive kiss. Maybe not the most professional move he had ever pulled, but he'd been thinking about kissing her practically since they met. When she had pulled his mouth down to hers he hadn't been about to resist. He had enjoyed the kiss very much, and he enjoyed knowing that he'd been able to breach her reserve. She had made it clear she didn't trust anyone—and maybe she had good reason for that, given what little he knew of her upbringing. But that kiss told him that maybe she was beginning to have more faith in him, at least a bit.

He braked to avoid a deer that darted across the road in the graying light. "It's going to be dark by the time we get to the camp," Kayla said.

"Probably." He switched on the Cruiser's headlights. "Maybe they'll think we skipped out on their invitation. I don't mind catching them off guard."

She crossed her arms over her chest. "Nothing about this feels right. Why do you think Metwater invited us to this ceremony?"

"He said it was to help us understand the Family more."

"I don't believe him."

"I'm not sure I do, either, but I want to know what he's up to. Why don't you believe him?"

"Because people like him aren't altruistic. I doubt he cares if we understand him and his group or not. He thrives on manipulating people. I can't help but think he's trying to manipulate *us*."

"We're not going to let him do that, are we?"

"Nobody manipulates me."

When he glanced over, she had her gaze fixed on him. Dylan wondered if her words were a not-so-subtle warning. He could have protested that he wasn't the manipulative type, but better she learn that fact for herself.

Light from an almost full moon bathed the wilderness landscape in silver, highlighting the rocky hoodoos and cliffs, and sending long shadows across the sparse grass. A coyote trotted down the road ahead, turning to regard them with golden eyes before darting into the underbrush. "I can't believe anyone would want to live out here," Kayla said. "It's so…desolate."

"It would be a tough place to live," Dylan agreed. "But it's a good place to hide." He found the parking area and pulled in and shut off the engine. Silence closed around them like a muffling blanket, the only sound the faint ticking of the cooling motor. Though the moon provided plenty of illumination, Dylan tucked a mini Maglite into his pocket just in case. They climbed out of the Cruiser and looked around.

"Metwater said he would have someone waiting for us, but I don't see anyone," Kayla said.

"Maybe he thinks we're not going to show." Dylan touched her arm. "Come on. Let's slip in quietly and see what they're up to."

They moved up the path toward the camp, placing their footsteps carefully, trying not to disturb the night's silence. As they rounded the outcropping of rock that guarded the entrance to the camp, they heard a low murmuring. Dylan stopped to listen and Kayla moved up beside him. "What's that?" he whispered.

"Sounds like some kind of chanting or something," she said.

He nodded, and led the way around the outcropping. No guards watched over the entrance to the camp—apparently everyone was gathered around the bonfire in the center of the circle of trailers and tents. The faces of everyone—men, women and children— were fixed on the leaping flames, and voices rose in unison. "In unity is power. Power is unity."

Power to do what? "Doesn't sound like a peaceful manifesto to me," Dylan muttered. "And there's a burn ban on. Want to bet they don't have a permit for that fire?"

Kayla shushed him as Daniel Metwater stepped from the crowd and stood in front of the blaze, his profile to Dylan and Kayla. The crowd fell silent as he waited. He was naked except for a loincloth, his body gleaming in the firelight as if it had been oiled. He was thin but muscular, and wore the expression of a man who was confident he was right.

Two women moved from the crowd to join him. They were dressed only in loincloths also, their breasts painted with red and black concentric circles, their eyes ringed in black, lips outlined in red. Dylan didn't recognize either of them, but they fit the profile of twentysomething beauties predominant among Metwater's followers.

A drum began a slow, steady beat, gradually increasing in tempo. Metwater extended his arms and the women took his hands. The three began a slow, hypnotic dance, swaying and writhing around each other. Beside him, Kayla shifted. "Do you think he invited us to watch an orgy?" she asked.

"Maybe he wanted us to join in."

She sent him a sour look and he bit back a grin. Then he had a sudden image of her dressed in only a loincloth and he had to look away. He forced his mind back to the business at hand. "Let's wait a bit more and see what happens before we announce ourselves," he said.

The drums stopped and the two women took seats on either side of the circle. Metwater held up his hands to silence the crowd. "Tonight marks a very special night." His voice carried easily in the still night air, with the rounded tones and precise diction of an experienced orator. Those gathered around the fire listened raptly, eyes glowing, some with lips slightly parted.

"We gather under the light of the full moon to welcome a new member to our family." He continued with a flowery speech about the sacredness of family, the importance of connection and generally how superior they all were for having made the decision to join up with the Prophet. "Ours is a sacred bond of mind, body and spirit," he proclaimed. "We are united mentally, physically and in our souls. It is a union of our most sacred natures, and of our blood."

At this last, he pulled a large dagger from a sheath at his side and sliced the blade across his own palm. Kayla gasped, and Dylan put out a hand to restrain her.

Metwater turned away from them, toward the far side of the circle. "We begin, as always, with the sacrifice," he said.

Two men—Dylan thought he recognized Abe and Zach beneath the black-and-white greasepaint that streaked their faces—escorted a young woman to the center of the circle. She wore a long white robe, and her dark hair fell almost to her waist. Her face was ivory white in the moonlight, the flames reflecting in her glassy eyes.

Metwater kissed each of her cheeks in turn, then motioned for her to kneel. He held the dagger over his head, the blade still wet with his own blood, firelight glinting off the steel. "Persephone, you have agreed to sacrifice what is necessary to make our family whole," he intoned. Then he brought the blade down to rest at her throat.

Dylan didn't have to see any more. He drew his weapon and charged forward, Kayla at his heels. "Stop!" he shouted. "Drop the knife and step back with your hands up."

Chapter Ten

Kayla's heart pounded in rhythm with her racing feet as she followed Dylan toward the macabre scene around the fire. Daniel Metwater, blood dripping from the palm of one hand as he gripped the dagger with the other, turned toward them as the girl slumped to the ground beside him. The crowd of followers around the blaze stared, but none made a move as Dylan stopped and trained his gun on Metwater. "Drop the knife," he ordered.

Metwater opened his hand and let the knife fall. Kayla moved to the young woman and checked her pulse, which was strong. She moaned a little and stirred, and Kayla helped her sit up. "It's okay," she soothed. "You're okay."

"Put that gun away now, Officer!" Metwater's face glowed red in the firelight. "I invited you here tonight to witness the ceremony, not to disrupt it."

Dylan didn't waver. "Put your hands behind your back and turn around," he said. "You're under arrest."

"On what charge?" Metwater continued to glare at Dylan.

"For the attempted murder of that young woman." He nodded toward the woman who sat beside Kayla.

Metwater's laughter was loud and raucous. Others in the crowd joined him in the mocking mirth. Anger tightened Kayla's throat, and she read the same rage in Dylan's eyes. Keeping his gaze fixed on Metwater, Dylan addressed the young woman. "Ma'am, are you all right?"

"I'm fine." Now that she had recovered consciousness, Persephone—or whatever her real name was—seemed fine, a little pale maybe, but perfectly calm.

"Of course she's fine," Metwater said. "This was a ceremony, not a murder. Haven't you heard of symbolism, Lieutenant?" He moved to the young woman's side and helped her to her feet. Kayla could smell the sweat and blood on him, odors that made him seem even more primitive and wild. "Persephone and I were acting out the symbolic death of her old self. In the next phase, you would have seen her reborn into her new life with the Family."

Kayla became aware of others in the crowd moving closer. Out of the corner of her eyes, she spotted the two men who had served as Persephone's escorts moving around to flank her.

"Tell your guards to move back," Dylan said.

Metwater flicked his gaze toward the men. "Put away your gun. Your threat of violence has tainted our sacred proceedings."

Dylan holstered his weapon. Kayla joined him, anxious to put more distance between herself and Metwater. "You're one to talk of violence," she told him. "Considering you're bleeding all over the place."

Metwater studied his bleeding palm. "Every member of the Family has some of my blood mixed in their veins," he said. "Symbolizing that I am the father and protector of all."

Kayla wrinkled her nose, but said nothing.

"The ceremony is over." Dylan raised his voice to be heard by the crowd. "Go on back to your camps."

"The ceremony isn't over until I say it's over." Metwater handed Persephone off to one of the half-naked women he had danced with and started toward Dylan.

Kayla stiffened, and wished she'd brought her gun with her. If Dylan needed backup, she wasn't going to be of much use.

"Don't argue with me, Metwater," Dylan said. "I could still take you in for questioning."

"Questioning about what?"

"The murder of Special Agent Frank Asher, for one," Dylan said.

"I told you, I had nothing to do with Agent Asher's death."

"You and your followers are the only ones around," Dylan said. "Asher came here, probably to talk to Andi Matheson, possibly to try to talk her into leaving your group. Maybe you shot him in order to prevent that. Or maybe Asher had uncovered your secret, and you couldn't risk him exposing you."

"What secret? I don't have a secret." But fear flashed in Metwater's dark eyes, though the rest of his expression remained stony.

"Don't you?" Dylan turned to the young woman. "What's your real name?" he asked.

"P-Priscilla," she said. "Priscilla Ortega."

"How old are you, Priscilla?"

"I'm nineteen."

"Enough questions." Metwater stepped between

them. "Persephone has done nothing wrong." He motioned for the dancer to take the younger woman away and she did so. "You need to leave now also, Officer." He glanced at Kayla. "You may stay if you like, Miss Larimer."

Kayla didn't try to hide her disgust at the invitation. "I'm not one of your brainwashed devotees," she said.

"I'm going to remind you again that you're on public land," Dylan said.

Metwater folded his arms across his muscular chest and met Dylan's stern gaze. "This is our home, Officer. And you're not welcome here." With that, he turned his back on Dylan and stalked toward his trailer.

"Somebody put out this fire," Dylan called after him. "There's a burn ban on for the county."

Metwater raised one hand to indicate he had heard.

"I'm going to find out your secret," Dylan called. "And when I do, I'm going to tell all your followers the kind of man you really are."

Metwater stumbled, then caught himself and kept walking. But Kayla knew Dylan's words had gotten to the man. Daniel Metwater was definitely guilty of something. Whether his crime was murder or something else, Kayla intended to help expose him sooner rather than later.

KAYLA SHIVERED AND wrapped her arms around her shoulders, then leaned forward to punch up the blower on the heater in Dylan's Cruiser as they left the wilderness area and turned onto the paved highway leading back to Montrose. "I can't get that girl's face out of my mind," she said. "When Metwater held that knife to her throat, she was absolutely terrified. She believed he was going to kill her, no matter what he told us."

Dylan said nothing, but continued to stare out the windshield, both hands gripping the steering wheel, his body tense. "Well?" she prompted. "What do you think? Do you think he was really going to slit her throat?"

"I've been thinking about what you said earlier," he said.

"What I said?" She blinked. "What did I say?"

"That Metwater is trying to manipulate us."

"Of course he is. That's how people like him operate—how they keep control of any group of people or situation. He— Oh?" Dylan's meaning hit her. "Are you saying he staged that whole business with the knife and the so-called sacrifice for our benefit? That he wanted us to see it?"

"I don't know. But replaying everything in my mind, I think he knew we were standing there from the moment we arrived. And he must have ordered his bodyguards not to make a move, or they would have been on us like a shot."

"But why? So we would think he was capable of murder?" She shook her head. "That's twisted even for a guy who calls himself a prophet."

"Maybe he wanted us to look like a couple of idiots in front of his followers," Dylan said. "Or maybe it's sleight of hand—get us to focus on the perceived human sacrifice so we don't notice something else that's going on."

"So, what else is going on?" She turned down the heater, warmer at last as anger replaced some of her earlier shock. "I can't believe he didn't have something to do with Frank Asher's murder, but he's got a whole camp full of followers who will no doubt swear he was with all of them the morning Frank was shot."

"He could have ordered the hit."

"He could have. But good luck proving that."

"I'm going to do some more digging into his background and see what I come up with."

"Will you let me know what you find?" She leaned toward him, cutting off the objection she was sure he was about to make. "I'm in this with you right up to my ears," she said. "You can't cut me off now. And until Senator Matheson tells me otherwise, I'm still concerned about Andi. I have to figure out how involved she is in all of this."

"When I checked in with headquarters earlier, there was still no sign of the senator," Dylan said.

"How could a man in the public eye like the senator just disappear?" she asked. "Do the police think he was kidnapped—or killed?"

"There weren't any signs of foul play," Dylan said. "Maybe he just decided to take a break from public life. There isn't a law against that."

"Except that Senator Matheson thrives on being in the public eye. I read an article that listed him as one of the most media-savvy politicians."

"So maybe this is some kind of publicity stunt—disappear for a while to get people talking, then show up again."

"And say what—'surprise, I fooled you'?"

"He could say he'd been on a secret fact-finding mission or something. For all we know, he's in Mexico or the Caribbean right now, relaxing on the beach while we waste resources searching for him. Metwater isn't the only manipulator we're dealing with here, I think."

"Maybe." But something about that scenario bothered her. She searched for the words to voice her impressions of the senator. "He was waiting for me to give him my report about Andi. When he hired me, he seemed very anxious to know that she was all right. If he did plan to disappear as some kind of publicity stunt or ploy for attention, it doesn't make sense that he would do so before he heard back from me."

"Was he really concerned, or was he only pretending for your benefit?" Dylan asked.

"I think his worry was genuine." But how could she be sure? She shifted in her seat. "I haven't had that much personal experience with genuine parental devotion, but I'm pretty good at spotting fake emotions. All his pomposity and bombast softened when Senator Matheson spoke about his daughter. He talked a lot about how he had tried all his life to protect her and do what was best for her. How if only she would come back to him, he could give her everything she needed and deserved."

"That kind of love can be smothering to some people—especially a person Andi's age, who is trying to exert her independence."

Kayla nodded. "He said it would be enough to know she was safe, but I had the feeling that once I located her, he would try everything in his power to persuade her to return to him. Which is another reason I can't believe he would voluntarily disappear before he was sure of her safety."

"That investigation is out of our hands," Dylan said. "We have to worry about things closer to home. I'm going to do more digging into Frank Asher's and Daniel Metwater's backgrounds tomorrow."

"Hmm." She'd be doing the same, but there was no point telling him and hearing a lecture about not interfering in police business.

"If you find out anything interesting about either of them, I hope you'll share it with me," Dylan said.

She felt her face heat, and was grateful he couldn't see the flush in the darkness. "I might. If you'll do the same with me."

"Even twelve hours ago I probably would have said no, but I'm beginning to think the two of us make a great team and we'll accomplish more working together than at cross purposes."

This admission surprised her. "What changed your mind?"

"You did great back at the camp just now—and earlier today when we spoke with Andi and Metwater. You've got a cool head and good instincts, and I trust you to watch my back."

She fought back the surge of emotion that tightened her throat. Dylan didn't strike her as the type of person to throw around words like that casually. "Thank you," she managed to squeeze out.

"I hope you'll come to trust me," he said.

She rubbed a hand up and down her thigh. "I'm used to working alone." Depending on other people was too risky.

"I think the two of us make a good team," he said again. He cleared his throat. "I'd like to see more of you."

"I'll stay in touch. I want to know what you find out about Metwater and the rest."

"I meant after this case is resolved. I liked kissing you this afternoon. I'd like to do it again."

Her breath caught and her heart pounded, the memory of his lips on hers and his arms around her leaving her with the same warm, weak-kneed sensation that had overwhelmed her in the barn. "That was a mistake," she said.

"Why do you say that? I got the impression you enjoyed it, too," he said.

Yes, she had enjoyed kissing Dylan. More than she had enjoyed anything in a long while. But letting him get that close to her would only bring trouble. "I don't do relationships," she said. "I'm not good at them." No matter how promising things started, other people always let you down. Maybe that was part of being human, but she couldn't risk any more betrayals. Other people might be good at forgiving, but she wasn't.

"I think you underestimate yourself," he said. "Or maybe you underestimate me. I'm willing to take things slow."

She shook her head, then realized he might not be able to see her. "No. You're a great guy, but I prefer to keep things between us professional."

"So no more kisses?"

"No more." She had to hold back a sigh. The kiss really had been great, but kissing Dylan again would only lead to more kissing and hugging and caressing and… She shoved the thoughts away and sat up straighter. They were almost to the turnoff for her house. She wouldn't have to see Dylan again for a couple of days at least, and that time would allow her emotions to cool off and settle. When he had time to think about it, he would see the sense in keeping his distance from her, as well.

He switched on his blinker to make the left turn, waiting for an approaching car to pass. Behind them, headlights glowed in the distance. Kayla squinted and shielded her eyes from the glare in the side mirror. What was the guy behind them doing with his brights up? And he was driving awfully fast, wasn't he?

The car approaching in the opposite lane passed and Dylan took his foot off the brake, prepared to make the turn. But before he could act, the car behind them slammed into them, clipping the back bumper and sending the Cruiser spinning off the road and into the ditch. The air bags exploded, pressing Kayla back against the seat. Then she heard another sound—the metallic pop of bullets striking metal as someone fired into their vehicle.

Chapter Eleven

Dylan woke to flashing lights and the distant wail of a siren. Pain stabbed at his skull and he realized he was tilted at an odd angle. He blinked, trying to get his bearings. Something about asking Kayla to kiss him. Or telling her he wanted to kiss her... No, that wasn't it.

"Dylan? Dylan, are you okay?" Kayla's voice, strained with anxiety, cut through the fog in his head.

"I'm okay." He tried to shift his body and realized he was sandwiched between the expanded air bag and the back of his seat. "What happened?"

"A car, or maybe a truck, plowed into us from behind. I think they did it deliberately. And I thought I heard gunshots. Are you sure you're okay?"

He felt his head. No blood there, though he must have hit it against the side of the car when they crashed. "I'm fine. What about you? Are you all right?"

"A little banged up, but nothing broken. My door is wedged into the ditch, so I can't open it."

He felt at his side for his phone and dragged it out of its holster. "I'll call for help."

"I think someone's coming. I hear a siren."

The sound was getting closer, but the flashing lights were his own. He must have bumped the control during the crash.

Moments later, two emergency vehicles arrived, followed by a third. Red-and-blue lights strobed across the darkness, and moments later the beam of a flashlight played across Dylan's face. He winced and shielded his eyes from the light as someone yanked open his door.

"Don't try to move," the responding officer said. "Not until the paramedic has checked you out."

"I think I just have a bump on the head." Dylan shoved his phone back into its holster. There would be time enough later to call the captain.

"You part of the Ranger Brigade?" the officer asked, glancing at the logo on the side of the Cruiser.

"Yes. Lieutenant Dylan Holt with the Colorado State Patrol."

A paramedic, young with a dark goatee, joined the officer, directing his flashlight beam over Dylan and Kayla. "How are you doing, miss?" he asked.

"I'm okay," she said. "Just a little shaken up, and I can't get out of the car."

"We'll help you in just a minute." The paramedic turned to Dylan. "Any pain or obvious injuries?"

"Just my head." He touched the knot on his forehead. "Nothing broken."

"You climb out then, and we'll see about getting to your passenger."

Dylan climbed out of the car, the officer and a second paramedic helping. They led him to an ambulance, where he submitted to an examination.

"What happened?" the officer, a middle-aged African American whose badge identified him as Officer Lejeune, asked.

Dylan took a moment to organize his thoughts, though most of his initial fog had cleared. "I was stopped, waiting to make a left turn, when a vehicle plowed into me from behind," he said. He kept his gaze on the Cruiser, where the first paramedic and another officer were helping Kayla climb out. "The other vehicle clipped my back bumper and we spun out of control. I hit my head and must have been out for a minute. Maybe a little longer."

"So whoever hit you fled the scene?" Officer Lejeune asked.

"I guess so." He thought about what Kayla had said—about hearing shots fired. If that was true, why hadn't whoever had targeted them stayed around to finish the job?

"Another driver called it in," Lejeune said. "She said the other vehicle was speeding and plowed right into you, then sped away."

"Did she mention any gunshots?" Dylan asked.

Lejeune and the paramedic exchanged glances. "Gunshots?"

"Someone was firing at us. I'm sure that's what I heard." Kayla limped toward them, moving ahead of the men supporting her.

Dylan shoved aside the paramedic, who was trying to apply an ice pack to the knot on his head, and hurried to her. "You're hurt," he said.

"I just banged my knee. I'll be fine." But she didn't push him away and leaned into him when he put his arm around her.

"I'll take a look at the car," Lejeune said, and strode off.

Dylan escorted Kayla to the ambulance and sat beside her as the paramedic bent to examine her knee. "Did you get a good look at the vehicle that hit us?" he asked.

"No. The brights were on—though I had the impression it was big. Maybe a pickup truck or a big SUV?" She shook her head. "It happened so fast."

The two police officers returned. "We found what could be bullet holes in the driver's-side door," Lejeune said. "Small caliber."

"You're lucky whoever ran you down didn't have a bigger gun or wasn't a better shot," the second officer, Raybourn, said.

"Whoever it was, I don't think they were trying to kill us," Dylan said. "They wanted to scare us."

"They scared me," Kayla admitted. "But they also made me mad. I never have liked bullies."

"You think this has to do with a case you're investigating?" Lejeune asked.

"Maybe." Dylan pulled out his phone again. "I'm going to get someone from my team to check out the Cruiser, see what we can find."

He stepped away to make his call while the paramedics finished checking Kayla. His stomach churned as he stared at the car on its side in the ditch, the back end smashed.

Graham answered on the fourth ring. "Hello, Lieutenant," he said, as calm and alert as if the call had come at midday, instead of after ten at night.

"Kayla Larimer and I were on our way back to town from Daniel Metwater's camp and someone ran us off the road," Dylan said. "They took a couple of shots at us, too."

"Are you all right?" Graham asked, his voice sharper. "Is Kayla all right?"

"We're a little banged up, but okay. I'd like a team to come check out the Cruiser and the area, see if we can come up with any clues."

"We'll send someone. Did you get a look at who did this?"

"No. A woman called in the accident, but it doesn't sound like she got a good look, either, though we'll want to talk to her."

"Do you think it was one of Metwater's followers?"

"Maybe." The hit-and-run was the kind of impulsive lashing out he might expect from the mostly young members of the group, but Metwater himself didn't strike him as that sloppy.

"What were you doing at his camp?" Graham asked.

"He invited us, actually, to observe some kind of ceremony." Dylan rubbed his throbbing head. "I'll give you my report later. Right now, I need to see about getting Kayla home. Then I'll wait here with the Cruiser."

"I'll have someone out there as soon as I can. If we find anything that links this to Metwater's group, you can be sure we'll be hauling them all in for questioning."

Dylan ended the call and stowed the phone, then walked back to Kayla. "I'll find someone to give you a ride home," he said. "I need to wait here."

"Officer Raybourn has already offered me a ride." She rested her hand on Dylan's arm. "Are you sure you're okay? That knot on your head looks like it hurts."

He gingerly touched the swelling. "I'll be okay. My dad always did say I had a hard head."

"I liked your parents," she said. "I forgot to thank you for taking me to meet them. I really enjoyed it."

"I enjoyed it, too." He rested his palm on her shoulder, giving her the chance to pull away, but hoping she wouldn't. "You're welcome to visit anytime."

"Hmm." She looked down, but didn't shift away or remove her hand from his arm. "I'm glad you weren't seriously hurt," she said. "When I first called your name and you didn't answer..." She let her voice trail away.

"I know. I'm glad you're not hurt, too." He brought his hand up to cup the side of her face, then bent and kissed her—just a gentle brush of his lips across hers. She let out a sigh and leaned into him, returning the kiss for a brief moment before pulling away.

"I'm not sure how to handle you," she said. "I'd better go." She turned away and hurried toward where Raybourn and Lejeune waited.

"You're doing a fine job so far," Dylan said softly.

EVERYTHING ACHED WHEN Kayla woke the next morning. She dragged herself into a hot shower, then chased two ibuprofen with a cup of strong tea. She was still sore, but felt able to get to work. She headed to the spare room that served as her home office and flipped through the mail that had accumulated in the last few days. She had been so busy dealing with Senator Matheson and Andi that she hadn't gotten around to reading it.

An envelope from the Colorado Private Investigators Society caught her attention and she slit it open, then unfolded the single sheet of heavy cream-colored paper inside.

Dear Ms. Larimer,
We are pleased to inform you that you have been selected as this year's Western Slope Private Investigator of the Year. You will be one of the honorees at the Colorado Western Region Honors Banquet in Grand Junction on August 23.
Please RSVP to the email address below and indicate if you will be bringing a guest.

Congratulations on your honor,
Madeline Zimeski, President

Kayla stared at the letter, annoyed. She hadn't even known there was a Western Slope Private Investigator of the Year. Who had nominated her? And she had to attend a banquet. Did this mean she'd have to buy a fancy dress? And shoes?

She put the letter aside and forced herself to work on a background check for a legal firm she did small jobs for, then started on a report on some surveillance she'd done on a straying husband the week before. But her mind kept straying back to Andi Matheson, the missing senator and enigmatic Daniel Metwater.

The image of him, almost naked and gleaming in the firelight, blood dripping from his hands as he held the dagger to that young woman's throat, would stay with her for a long time, she imagined. Being around him put her on edge, maybe because he reminded her too much of her own father—handsome and charismatic, good at reading people and promising them what they wanted, or exploiting their weaknesses.

What weakness had he exploited in Andi? Maybe he had painted a picture of the Family as a safe refuge in which she could raise her baby. On his side, he had a recruit with money. At twenty-four, Andi had her own funds. Had she signed them over to Metwater? Or maybe the Prophet merely liked having a senator's daughter in his retinue. Could Metwater be linked to the senator's disappearance?

She jotted these questions into a notebook she kept open on her desk, then pulled out her phone. Time to do a little more digging.

"Hello?" The young woman on the other end of the line sounded sleepy.

"Tessa? It's Kayla Larimer—the private detective who was trying to find Andi Matheson."

"Oh, uh, hi." Tessa sounded more awake, but wary. "Did you find her?"

"I did. You were right in thinking she'd hooked up with that spiritual group you mentioned—the Family."

"The one with that hot guy, right?" Tessa snorted. "I knew it. That night we met I could tell he was really into her. That was the problem with going anywhere with Andi. All the men ended up looking at her. I might as well have been invisible."

"The hot guy is Daniel Metwater, the leader of the group. He calls himself the Prophet."

Tessa yawned. "I remember now. He talked a lot about personal freedom and connecting with nature and building a true family—Andi ate it all up. I figured he just wanted to get into her pants."

"So Daniel Metwater didn't impress you?" Kayla asked.

"He was really hot, but he knew it. I mean, he had all these women fawning over him and he acted like that was just the way it should be. And all his talk about family and connection and everything didn't do anything for me. I already have a family, and the whole reason people build houses is to keep nature at a distance, right?"

Kayla smiled. She supposed that was one way to look at it. "Why do you think Andi was so interested in what he had to say?" she asked. "She had a family, too, and what looked like a pretty nice life."

"She had a nice life, but lately she and her dad were on the outs."

"Do you know why she and her father weren't getting along?"

"Oh, the usual—he still treated her like a child, always trying to tell her what to do and how to act and how to live her life. She hated that. But that wasn't really anything new. The senator was always a little...I'd call it overprotective. I think she even liked it sometimes, how she could crook her little finger and Daddy would come running. I saw on the news about her dad disappearing. Even though they weren't getting along, I'll bet Andi's pretty upset about that."

She hadn't appeared to be, but Kayla didn't bother going into that. "You said Andi and her dad not getting along wasn't anything new, so what was different this time? What made her want to break ties with her father altogether?"

"I'm really not sure. I think it might have had something to do with the guy she was seeing last year."

Kayla sat up straighter. "Who was that?"

"I never met him. Andi said he was an older man, and he worked for her father. It was all very mysterious. I told her I bet he was married, since he never wanted to be seen in public with her. She said it was because her father wouldn't approve, but it turned out I was right."

"You mean the man *was* married?" Kayla asked. No one had mentioned Agent Asher having a wife.

"Kayla told me he had a wife and three kids right here in Denver. She was furious when she found out—but not half as furious as her father. He fired the guy and lit into Andi. She decided she didn't want to have anything to do with either one of them. I think that's one reason this Daniel guy's spiel about getting away from it all and starting over appealed to her. Did she tell you she was pregnant?"

"Yes, she told me."

"So you can't blame her for wanting a better life for her baby—something more peaceful. Is she doing okay with Daniel and his group?"

"She's healthy and she seems content." No sense going into the news of Frank Asher's death.

"I'm glad. If you see her again, tell her I said hi. And thanks for letting me know you found her."

"Sure." That wasn't the reason she had called, but it was okay with her if Tessa thought so.

They said their goodbyes and Kayla ended the call.

So Andi hadn't told her and Dylan the whole story about her relationship with Frank Asher. He wasn't just her former lover and the father of her child, but a man who had betrayed her, in a big way. Had he hurt her enough to make her want to hurt him in return?

She stared at her phone, then scrolled to Dylan's number. He answered right away. "Hey," he said. "How are you feeling this morning?"

"Like I've been run over by a truck. How about you?"

"The same. And you're right about it being a truck, or at least we're pretty sure." Wind noise and the muffled rumble of traffic told her he was outside. She pictured him standing on the side of the road by the damaged Cruiser—or maybe back at Ranger Brigade headquarters in the park. "We found some paint scrapes on the Cruiser and they match up to the height of a pickup—probably with one of those heavy-duty brush guards on the front."

"Any idea who was driving?"

"Not yet. But we're going to keep digging. Have you given your statement to the Montrose Police yet?"

"It's on my list for this morning. I told Officers Raybourn and Lejeune I'd stop by."

"It would be good if you could swing by here and give us a formal statement, too. Just in case this turns out to be connected to Metwater and the Family."

"Sure. I could do that." She fought the urge to ask if he would be there. She wanted to see him again, but didn't want to appear too eager. "I've found something else for you to dig into," she said instead.

"Oh? Hang on a minute. Let me get where I can

hear you better." She waited while he walked somewhere. She heard a door open and close, then everything was quieter. "Okay, what's up?"

"I talked to Tessa Madigan this morning—Andi's friend who told me about their meeting with Metwater and the Family."

"I remember. You said a friend of hers told you about Andi's interest in Metwater."

"Right. I asked her why Andi wanted to join the group—what had made her so upset she would leave her comfortable life behind. Tessa said she thought it had something to do with the man she had been dating before."

"Frank Asher?"

"Tessa didn't know his name. She said the relationship was very secretive. Turns out there was a good reason for that."

"And are you going to tell me the reason or make me play a game of twenty questions?"

"Patience, Lieutenant. Tessa said the reason Andi and this guy split was because Andi found out he had a wife and three kids in Denver."

Dylan let out a low whistle. "I guess that made her furious. But if that man was Asher, was she angry enough to shoot him and leave him lying in the desert?"

"I have a hard time believing it, considering how big a shock the news seemed to be to her."

"Maybe she's a good actress," Dylan said.

"Or maybe there's another woman you should consider."

He was silent for a moment, then said, "The wife."

"If I found out my husband and the father of our

three children was sneaking around with another woman I might want to put an end to the relationship," Kayla said.

"And maybe a permanent end to him," Dylan agreed.

Chapter Twelve

Dylan stepped out to where the techs were finishing their examination of his Cruiser, which they had towed to headquarters from the scene of the accident. Simon walked over to meet him. "We got some chips of the paint," he said, and held out an evidence bag with three black contact-lens-sized fragments. "But they're going to be tough to match without a suspect vehicle."

"I'm thinking we should drive out to Metwater's camp and look for a black truck with a brush guard on the front," Dylan said.

"We will," Simon said. "But before we do, I have something else to show you."

Dylan fell into step with him as they crossed the parking lot toward Ranger Brigade headquarters. Graham met them at the door. "I was finally able to pry some more information from the FBI about Special Agent Asher and what he might have been doing here," he said.

"I thought he took personal time to come here," Dylan said.

"He did, but apparently before that he was looking into David Metwater's mob connections," Graham said.

"The twin brother, right?" Simon said.

"Right. Maybe the picture in Asher's car wasn't of Daniel Metwater, but of David."

"So you think Asher came here to talk to Metwater about his dead brother?" Dylan asked.

"Or his investigation of David turned up some dirt on Daniel." Simon strode across the room and snatched a folder off the corner of his desk. "I've been digging into the files on Asher's laptop," he said. "Pulling off as much as I can before the Feds take it away."

"Anything that will help us?" Dylan asked.

Simon flipped through the papers in the file folder. "Mostly they're notes about the Metwater brothers— everything from bank account information to some surveillance footage of either Daniel or David. I haven't figured out what it all means yet, but I will."

"So Asher may have been coming to the camp to talk to Daniel about his brother, or because he had learned something about Daniel himself, or was just generally snooping around," Dylan said. "Or he wanted to see Andi. He told her when he saw her in town that he had to talk to her."

"Maybe Asher wanted to warn her about Metwater," Graham said. "Maybe he thought she was in danger."

"Turned out Asher was the one in danger." Simon closed the folder. "Metwater may have decided to shut him up."

"Where do the two guys who attacked Kayla outside Asher's hotel room come in?" Dylan asked.

"We don't know," Graham said. "The guy who lived—Bob Casetti—is still in the hospital. He's apparently lawyered up and not talking."

Simon grunted. "When do we get to talk to him?"

"As soon as his doctor gives the okay. Meanwhile, Montrose PD is keeping a guard on his room."

"Does this Casetti have a record?" Dylan asked.

"He's been in and out of prison since he was eighteen, with sealed juvenile records before that. But mostly property crimes and drugs. No kidnapping or rape or even assault. This definitely breaks the pattern for him."

"So we ought to be able to put some pressure on him and make him talk," Simon said.

"Do you think the attack on me and Kayla last night was connected to Casetti and his dead pal kidnapping Kayla at the hotel?" Dylan asked. Getting roughed up twice in two days was too much for coincidence. "Maybe it wasn't me who was the target last night at all, but Kayla."

"It's possible," Graham said.

"Then it's not safe for her to be alone." Pushing back the icy fear that threatened to overtake him, Dylan pulled his phone from his pocket. "I'll call and tell her I'm on my way to pick her up. We've got a vehicle I can borrow, right?"

Graham put a steadying hand on Dylan's arm. "I'll send Carmen to get her and bring her here. She can give us a statement about what happened last night, and you can take over evening guard duty if you want. But right now I want you and Simon out at the camp looking for the truck that ran you off the road."

"They've probably ditched it in the desert by now," Simon said.

"Maybe, but maybe not." Graham squeezed Dylan's shoulder, then released him. "Keep digging. If we can find a motive for Metwater to want Asher dead, we can bring him in for questioning. And let's take a closer look at Andi Matheson, too. Maybe she did meet with Asher and the conversation didn't go well."

"Did you know that Frank Asher was married?" Dylan asked.

"Why is that important?" Simon asked. "The FBI is taking care of notifying his next of kin."

"It's important because, apparently, Asher is the father of Andi Matheson's unborn child," Dylan said. "When Andi found out he was married, she broke off the relationship."

"So she might have been angry enough to shoot him when he came around to see her," Graham said.

"Maybe," Dylan said. "Though we have a lot of witnesses who place her in the camp at the time he was probably shot. And she seemed genuinely shocked when she found out he had been killed."

"We should take a closer look at her alibi," Graham said.

"We will," Dylan agreed. "But I want to question Asher's widow, too. I'd like to drive over to Denver tomorrow and find out if she—or someone she might have hired—decided to take a trip to the park about the time her late husband was killed."

"Do it." Graham shook his head. "Usually with a murder you have trouble coming up with one likely suspect. Frank Asher had any number of people who might have good reasons for wanting him dead."

"ARE YOU AS sick as I am of making the drive out here?" Simon asked as he steered his Cruiser onto the rough BLM two-track.

"Yeah." Dylan slumped in his seat and tugged the brim of his hat lower to block the midday sun glaring off the rocks that lined the road. "And I hate being out of phone range if anything happens." Before leaving Ranger headquarters, he'd called Kayla to tell her to stay put, but she had cut off his explanation, telling him she didn't have time to talk, as she was just arriving at the Montrose Police Station. Rather than argue with her, he'd called a buddy at the PD and asked them to keep Kayla there until Carmen could show up to escort her to Ranger Headquarters.

"The captain mentioned something about you and that detective driving out here last night," Simon said as they jounced along the road. "What was she doing with you?"

"Andi had asked to see Kayla yesterday afternoon, and I went with her to tell Andi that her father was missing. When Metwater discovered us, he invited us to the induction ceremony later that night."

"Why involve a civilian?" Simon asked.

"Andi knows Kayla and they seem to have established a rapport. And she knows how to handle herself. She doesn't interfere."

"She's still a civilian."

"A civilian who is helping with our investigation."

"That's one way to look at it, I guess."

They passed the rest of the drive in silence. Dylan stared out the window of the Cruiser, nursing his anger and annoyance, not to mention a headache from where he had hit his head in the crash last night. By the time Simon parked outside the camp, Dylan was more than ready to lash out at someone for all the trouble he'd been through.

"What do you think? Look around, or talk to Metwater first?" Simon asked.

"Look around." Dylan led the way down the trail into the canyon. Kiram wasn't on guard duty today. The skinny youth who was took one look at the two grim-faced officers and melted back into the rocks.

"He probably went to tell Metwater we're here," Simon said.

"Saves us the trouble," Dylan said.

The camp was quiet, the heat shimmering off the rocks oppressive. The few people Dylan spotted were lying in hammocks in the shade or lounging in tents or makeshift brush-covered shelters. The two officers walked the length of the camp to the narrowest part of the canyon, where a few rattier tents and a lean-to made of old wooden produce crates were crowded among a collection of dilapidated cars and trucks. The intense sun had faded most of the paper labels on the flattened crates, but Dylan could still make out images of plump red tomatoes and green peppers.

A clank of metal on metal drew them around a tarp-covered shed to where two men dressed only in dirty khaki shorts leaned under the open hood of a black pickup truck with a heavy brush guard attached to the front bumper.

"Something wrong with the truck?" Dylan asked.

Zach Crenshaw jerked his head up, eyes wide, mouth open. Across from him, Abe Phillips held up the wrench. "What do you want with us, man?" he asked, his voice a nasal whine that set Dylan's teeth on edge.

"I want to know why you tried to run me down last night." Dylan took a step closer, backing the young man up against the truck and blocking his escape.

"We don't know what you're talking about." Zach had shut his mouth and regained some of his color. He motioned to the truck. "We were just trying to get this old thing running again."

"It was running fine last night when it forced my Cruiser off the road," Dylan said.

"This truck hasn't moved from this spot in a month!" Abe declared. "It doesn't even run. See for yourself." He beckoned them closer and Dylan looked under the hood at a tangle of wires and hoses, and what looked like handfuls of straw and other debris. "A pack rat built a nest in here." Abe pulled out a wad of dried grass. "Ate the wiring harness and made a mess. I haven't had a chance to get it fixed."

"Is that so?" Simon pulled out a multitool and began scraping at the brush guard, a welded pipe cage around the front grill that seemed to have more rust than paint.

"Hey, what are you doing?" Zach asked.

"I'm collecting a sample of this paint to match with the chips we took from Lieutenant Holt's Cruiser after someone ran him off the road night before last."

"It wasn't me," Abe said. "I told you, this truck hasn't moved."

"Then you don't have anything to worry about." Simon slipped the paint chips into an evidence bag and sealed it, while Dylan walked around the vehicle and took photographs from every angle.

"Why do you people always want to hassle us?" Zach asked. "We aren't doing anything but trying to live in peace."

"I wouldn't say you're doing a very good job of that so far," Dylan said. He stowed the camera. "Did Metwater put you up to going after us last night, or was that your own idea?"

Zach swore and turned away. Abe flushed. "I told you, it wasn't us," he said. "The truck's been out of commission for weeks. I'm trying to get it running again so I can go into town."

"And do what?" Dylan asked.

"I don't know. Buy a burger and a beer. See a movie." He looked around. "Anything's better than being stuck here in the desert all the time."

"I thought this place was the Family's version of paradise," Dylan said. He kicked the front tire of the truck. "Funny that there's what looks like fresh mud and gravel in the treads of these tires, if it's just been sitting here for weeks." He sent Abe a warning look, then turned away.

"Where are you going?" Zach asked.

"To talk to Metwater."

"Don't worry, we'll be back," Simon said.

The two officers made their way toward Metwater's trailer. "So, is that the truck?" Simon asked.

"It fits the profile," Dylan said. "Though the engine did look pretty shot."

"Anyone could yank out a bunch of wires and throw in some grass and trash," Simon said.

"Even a paint match isn't going to prove anything," Dylan said. "Not if they stick to their story."

"They'll cave," Simon said. "Pointing out that fresh

gravel was a nice touch. We'll lean on them some more after we talk to Metwater and we'll be hauling them back to headquarters before you know it."

"I'd rather have Metwater in handcuffs than his two flunkies," Dylan said.

"Get them into an interview room and maybe they'll spill something incriminating." They mounted the steps to Metwater's trailer and Simon knocked. No answer. He knocked again. "Metwater, this is the police. Open up!"

Silence. And no sound of movement within. Dylan moved to the tent next door. "Andi! Andi, it's Dylan Holt. Could I talk to you a minute?"

The tent flap lifted, but instead of Andi, Starfall stood in the opening. "Andi isn't here," she said.

"Where is she?"

"She said she was going for a walk." She scowled at them. "Why can't you leave her alone? She hasn't done anything to hurt anyone."

"Are you sure about that?" Simon asked.

Starfall only scowled harder.

"Do you know where Daniel Metwater is?" Dylan asked. "Did he go walking with Andi?"

"The Prophet left early this morning," she said. "If you want to talk to him, you'll have to wait until he gets back."

"Where did he go?" Simon asked.

"He speaks at gatherings around the country. I don't know where he went this time. It's not my business to know."

"When will he return?" Dylan asked.

"I don't know. It could be this evening or tomorrow or a week from now."

"Maybe he skipped out on you," Simon said.

Her eyes widened. "The Prophet would never desert us," she said.

Dylan could tell Simon was prepared to argue the point, but he cut in. "Do you know anything about Zach and Abe taking their truck out last night after the ceremony?"

She took a step back. "I don't know anything."

"You didn't see them?" Simon asked. "They ran Lieutenant Holt and the woman he was with off the road. Trashed a government vehicle and injured a law officer and a civilian. They could have been killed. If your Prophet thinks this is a good way to get us to leave him alone, he's not even half as smart as he looks."

"I don't know what you're talking about." Starfall let the tent flap fall closed.

Simon reached for it, but Dylan stayed his hand. "That's enough. We've given everyone here a lot to think about. We'll come back later when we can talk to Metwater."

"What about the truck?" Simon asked as they retraced their steps to the car.

"You heard them—it hasn't run in months."

"They might take off in it and try to run."

"They won't get far."

Simon unlocked the Cruiser and they climbed in. "Do you think Metwater was feeling the heat and skipped town? Maybe with Andi Matheson?"

Dylan fastened his seat belt. "Anything's possible, but I don't think so. Maybe it's like she said—he's off speaking somewhere. That's one of the ways he recruits followers."

"I read some of his blog and the stuff on his website." Simon started the engine. "All about family and peace and harmony. I guess that appeals to some people."

Dylan almost laughed. "But not you?"

Simon scowled. "I live in the real world. I don't need a fantasy like that."

"Careful, Simon. You might be turning into a stereotype of a jaded cop."

"Bite me, Holt."

"I'll pass." He settled back in the seat. "We'll check in with Andi and Metwater tomorrow. If they're not around then, we can start a search. Until then, I think all we can do is wait."

Chapter Thirteen

When Kayla emerged from the Montrose Police Station after giving her statement about the previous night's hit-and-run, she was surprised to find a Ranger Brigade Cruiser snugged in beside her Subaru. Her heart beat a little faster and she quickened her pace, faltering when Carmen Redhorse emerged from the driver's seat. Then her elation edged toward panic. "What are you doing here?" she asked. "Is Dylan okay?"

"Dylan's fine." Carmen's smile was warm. "I'm here to give you a ride to Ranger headquarters so you can give us your statement. I know all this paperwork is a pain, but it's important in helping us build a case."

"I can drive myself." She started toward her car, but Carmen stepped in front of her.

"You can, but this is easier. We can swing by your place and you can drop off your car. How are you feeling? That's a nasty bruise on your face."

Kayla touched the bruise she had received two days before in her struggle with the kidnappers. It was only a little tender now. "I'm okay. What is this really about? Did Dylan send you here?" And if he had, why?

"I take my orders from Captain Ellison, not the lieutenant. Considering you've been attacked twice in the past two days, he thought it would be a good idea to keep an eye on you."

"Why?"

Carmen wasn't smiling anymore—she looked pained. "I don't want to frighten you, but you might be in danger."

Kayla wanted to scoff at the idea, but the full meaning of Carmen's words was beginning to sink in. "Wait a minute. Do you—or the captain—think *I* was the target last night? I thought whoever hit us was going after the Cruiser. Did you find the driver? Did he tell you he was after me?"

"We don't know anything yet. We're just being careful."

"I can be careful at home." She started for her car again and this time Carmen let her open the door and slide into the driver's seat.

But when she tried to shut the door, the other woman put a hand out to stop her. "We need you to make a statement, anyway, so you might as well hang out with me for a few hours," she said.

"And then what?" Kayla asked.

The smile returned. "And then I think the captain is assigning Dylan to the night shift."

The words sent a tickle of pleasure up her spine. "I get the idea I don't really have a choice in the matter."

"We're not forcing you, but everyone would feel better if you'd come with us."

Kayla blew out a breath. If she did go home, she'd only sit there and stew. At least at Ranger headquarters she might find out more about what was going on. "All right. You can follow me to my place."

She left her car in the driveway, then joined Carmen in her Cruiser. "I really don't need a bodyguard," she said as she slid into the passenger seat.

Carmen shifted into gear and backed into the street. "Hey, I'm a tough cop and even I think it would be nice sometime to have a good-looking man worried about me," she said.

"You don't have a boyfriend?" Kayla asked, then immediately wished she could take the words back. She hated when people asked her that kind of question. "Sorry, none of my business."

"That's okay. It's a natural question. Let's just say the badge gets in the way of relationships for a lot of men. And even though I'm around men all day, it's not a good idea to get involved with anyone on the job. So that leaves, what—suspects? A few witnesses?" She shook her head. "I'm young. Someone will come along."

"I like being single," Kayla said. "I like making my own decisions and looking after myself."

"Oh, I agree," Carmen said. "It's lonely sometimes, though."

Yes, it was lonely sometimes. She hadn't often felt that way, but since she had let Dylan into her life, his absence left a space she hadn't noticed being empty before.

Ranger Brigade headquarters was a bustle of activity, though Dylan was nowhere in sight. Carmen led Kayla to her desk, where she coached her through her statement about the previous day's activities, beginning with that morning's encounters with Andi Matheson and Daniel Metwater, up to the moment of the crash. "I don't know how much good any of that will be for you," Kayla said when they were done. "I only had an impression of a fairly large vehicle, and that the driver didn't slow down, but hit us deliberately, then sped away."

"It's all part of the record," Carmen said. "Another piece in the puzzle."

The door opened and Simon entered, followed by Dylan. He spotted her right away and nodded, before turning to address Captain Ellison. "We found the truck," he said. "Can we get a warrant to impound it?"

"We can try," Ellison said. "Where is it?"

"At the camp. The two guys who were with it, Abelard Phillips and Zach Crenshaw, say it hasn't run in weeks, but I found fresh mud in the tire treads, and the color and profile fit what we're looking for. Simon got some paint samples."

"I'll get started on the warrant request," Simon said, and headed for his desk.

Dylan joined the two women. "How are you doing?" he asked Kayla. He brushed the tips of his fingers lightly over her bruised cheek.

"I'm fine." She tried to ignore the tremor of awareness his touch sent through her. "I don't need babysitting."

"Maybe not. But it will make me feel better."

She was trying to come up with a snappy retort when the door to headquarters burst open and two young men in dirty shorts and T-shirts, their faces sunburned, their hair windblown, burst in. "We want to confess," the taller of the two said. "And then we need your help."

ZACH AND ABE looked more pitiful than dangerous as Dylan and Ethan patted them down and led them to separate desks to give their statements. Dylan ended up with Abe, who limped to the chair Dylan offered and dropped into it with a groan. "We had to walk most of the way from camp before somebody gave us a ride," he said. "I think my blisters have blisters."

"Why didn't you drive your truck?" Dylan asked, taking his own seat behind the desk.

"That's why we need your help," Abe said. "The Prophet stole it. He can't do that, right? It's my truck. My name's on the title and everything, but he says it belongs to the Family now—along with everything else we brought with us, except what we could carry out with us."

"You talked to Daniel Metwater?" Dylan asked. "I thought he was out of town."

"He came back right after you left. Him and Asteria. I guess they only went up to Grand Junction or something. Anyway, Starfall must have blabbed that you were there and why, and he kicked us out. Told us to get whatever we could carry—but nothing else—and hit the road." He leaned toward Dylan. "That's stealing, right? We can file charges, can't we?"

"Why don't we start at the beginning," Dylan said. "You said you wanted to confess to something?"

Abe sank back in his chair. "Yeah, that." He

glanced around nervously. "Promise you're not going to beat me up or anything?"

"Just tell me what happened." Dylan had no intention of hurting the kid, but a little fear might persuade him to be more cooperative.

"After you interrupted the ceremony last night we were really ticked off that you kept hassling everybody. We're just out here trying to live in peace and you keep poking your nose where it doesn't belong."

"So you decided to teach us a lesson."

"Well…" He looked away.

"Did Daniel Metwater know what you intended?"

"We told him someone needed to do something, and he agreed."

"Did he tell you to follow us?"

"No. But we thought he approved. We thought it would be a good way to impress him." Abe looked glum. "I guess we should have known better."

"What happened?"

"Zach and I got in my truck and followed you out onto the highway. Then we rammed you and sent you into the ditch. We just wanted to shake you up and make you think twice about hassling us. We didn't mean to hurt anyone or anything."

"Why did you shoot at us?"

Abe flushed. "I was trying to shoot out the tires, but I guess I'm not a very good shot."

"You told me before that you didn't have a gun. That the Prophet didn't allow it."

"Yeah, well, last time we went into town I bought one, anyway. He's got a gun, and I was tired of eating so much tofu and vegetables. Not when the place is crawling with rabbits."

"Where is the gun now?"

"The Prophet made me hand it over to him. I mean, we were trying to help him and he raked us over the coals."

"You said he kicked you out?"

"Yeah. He said we were troublemakers. First with that guy who died, then this."

"What about the guy who died? Why did Metwater blame you for what happened to him?"

"Not for what happened to him, but for bringing him into camp. He said it caused bad juju and that was the reason the cops were around all the time. But we couldn't have just left him in the desert for the buzzards. That's just cold."

"What was Metwater doing this afternoon, while he was away from the camp?" Dylan asked.

"I don't know. Only those in his inner circle—his favorites—ever know what he's up to." Abe gave a snorting laugh. "We don't have the right chromosomes for that, if you know what I mean."

"You're not women."

"Right. He needs guys around for security and heavy lifting, but it's really the chicks he likes. We thought when we joined up we'd have access to all these hot women, but the Prophet keeps them all for himself."

"You say he was with Andi Matheson this afternoon?"

"Who?"

"Asteria."

"Oh, yeah. They were all cozy and laughing. She's definitely one of the inner circle. So can you help us get our stuff back? I mean, he can't just take it, can he?"

Dylan gave him a hard look. "You're confessing to attacking a law enforcement officer and you expect us to help you get your stuff back?"

He squirmed. "Well, yeah. We're pleading guilty in exchange for a deal."

"What kind of deal?"

He leaned forward again and lowered his voice. "We know a lot of dirt on the Prophet. We tell you what we know in exchange for...what do you call it—like a flu shot?"

"Immunity?"

"Right, immunity."

"What do you know about the Prophet?"

"Good stuff, I promise. The guy might look snowy white outside, but he's definitely not."

"You're going to have to be more specific than that if you want to avoid going to jail."

Abe went pale under his sunburn at the word *jail*. "Well, like, everybody who joins the Family has to sign a contract that says all the property you have belongs to the group, but what it really means is that it belongs to the Prophet. But that can't be legal, right?"

"If you signed the contract willingly, it might."

"People only sign it because he promises all this stuff—eternal riches and joy and peace, things like that. And then you end up living in the middle of nowhere on tofu, sleeping in tents, and the hot girls won't even give you the time of day."

"I'm going to need more than that if I'm going to persuade the district attorney to cut you a deal," Dylan said.

"Aww, man! We don't have to get attorneys involved, do we?"

Dylan remained silent, arms crossed over his chest.

Abe sighed. "All right. How about this? His name isn't even Daniel Metwater."

"No?" Dylan raised one eyebrow.

"No. I was in his RV one time and I saw a bunch of papers and his driver's license, in a folder on his desk. They all said *David* Metwater. Not Daniel, see? Maybe if you run that name through your computers, you'll find out he has a criminal record or something."

"He had a twin brother named David. The brother died. It wouldn't be that unusual for him to have kept his brother's papers."

Abe looked crestfallen.

"Where was Metwater the morning you and Zach found that man's body?" Dylan asked.

"He was in the camp."

"You saw him?"

"Yeah. Right before we went hunting. He was eating breakfast with Asteria and Starfall and a bunch of others."

"What was he doing before that?"

Zach scowled. "We all had to get up early for this sunrise ceremony. He's big into that kind of thing. I mean, the middle of the night, practically, he expects us all to get up and dance around and chant, and then he delivers a 'message.' After a while it's just the same stuff over and over."

"Sounds like you were getting pretty disillusioned by the whole experience," Dylan said.

"Well, yeah. I mean, I like some of his ideas, and I really don't mind the camping out and stuff, but I thought it would be more fun. And that there would be more women—or at least women who would give me the time of day."

Dylan slid back his chair and rose. "I'll see what I can do, Abe, but I'm not making any promises."

He left to confer with Graham, but on his way he stopped by Carmen's desk to speak with Kayla. "Anything interesting?" she asked, nodding toward Abe.

"I think he found out being part of Metwater's 'family' isn't the laid-back paradise he was picturing when he signed up. He gives Metwater a solid alibi for the morning Asher was killed, though. Apparently he was in plain sight of most of the Family members from sunrise on." Dylan leaned over, one hand on the back of her chair. "I need to stay and interview him and Zach some more, and talk with some other people. I'll find someone to take you home and stay with you at your place."

"I don't need anyone to stay with me," she said. "I mean, you have the guys who hit us in custody now."

"They weren't specifically after you, anyway," he said. "Just dumb and ticked off, trying to scare us a little."

"They succeeded there." She stood and he walked with her to the door. "Do you think they'll give you any useful information?"

"I don't know. But we have to try." He squeezed her shoulder. "You're sure you'll be okay alone?"

"I can look after myself. I've been doing it a long time."

"I'll probably be here late, and in the morning I have to go to Denver. It may be a while before I see you again."

A hint of a smile touched the corners of her mouth. "I can wait."

Maybe she only meant the words politely, but he took them as a promise of more. A promise he intended to collect on when he returned.

Chapter Fourteen

Midnight had come and gone by the time Dylan and the other Rangers sent Abe and Zach to cool their heels overnight in the Montrose County Jail. Ethan and Simon were going to continue the interviews the next morning in hopes of getting something more useful out of them, but beyond a hint at some questionable financial practices, the two had so far produced no evidence of a serious crime.

Dylan sent Kayla a text before he left town. Have a good day and be careful, he typed.

You, too.

As romantic words went, they weren't much, but she wasn't resisting him the way she once had, so he took that as a good sign. He checked out a new Cruiser from the Ranger Brigade fleet and made the drive to Denver in a good mood despite a short night's sleep, and a little after noon he found the house in the Denver suburb of Highlands Ranch the Ashers called home.

Veronica Asher was a tall, curvy woman with dark skin who wore her black hair in dozens of long braids that hung past her shoulder blades. She answered the door of the stone-and-cedar home with a toddler on one hip and two other children peeking from around her legs. "Yes?" She eyed Dylan skeptically.

"Mrs. Asher? Dylan Holt, Colorado State Patrol." He held up his credentials. "I'm sorry to bother you, but I'm investigating your husband's death and I need to ask you some questions."

She held the door open wider, then shifted the baby. "Frankie, you take your sisters to the kitchen and tell MeMaw I said you could have ice cream."

"Okay, Mama." The boy eyed Dylan warily, but took the baby from his mother and left the room.

Mrs. Asher watched them go, then turned back to Dylan. "The FBI has already been to see me," she said.

"They may be conducting their own investigation, but I'm part of a task force charged with dealing with crimes on public land. Since your husband was killed in the Curecanti Wilderness Area, a federal preserve, we're looking into his murder."

She sat on the sofa and smoothed her skirt across her knees. Her beautiful face bore the marks of grief in her haunted eyes and drawn expression. "I'll tell you the same thing I told the Feds," she said. "I don't have any idea what Frank was doing out there in the middle of nowhere. He told me he had to work on a case—for his job. But the FBI tells me he was on personal leave."

"So he lied to you," Dylan said.

"It wasn't the first time."

He studied her—a beautiful, weary woman who had been betrayed by the man who had promised to love and care for her. Was that enough for her to have left those children and driven five hours across the state to murder him? "Mrs. Asher, you say you don't know what your husband was doing out there in the wilderness area, but do you have an idea? Any suspicions?"

"Maybe he went to see that girl he was sneaking around with."

"What girl?"

"I don't think you made it to lieutenant without being a better investigator than that," she said.

"What girl, Mrs. Asher?"

She looked away, her body rigid, as if it took everything in her to hold back the rage—or the tears. "Frank was having an affair with a girl young enough to be his daughter. Senator Pete Matheson's daughter, Andi."

"So you think Frank arranged to meet Andi in the wilderness area?"

"No, I think he arranged to meet her in a hotel. That's what he usually did. I have no idea how he ended up in the desert with his head blown off. Maybe he had another side dish I didn't know about and she had a jealous husband or boyfriend who followed Frank out there and did him in." She looked at him again. "If you find out who did it, be sure and let me know so I can shake his hand."

"Mrs. Asher, where were you on August 14?"

"I was right here. I took my older children to school and my baby to the pediatrician. I had lunch with my mother and bought groceries in the afternoon, and after the children went to bed I drank half a bottle of wine and cried myself to sleep, trying to decide whether it was worth putting my children through losing their father in order to divorce my cheating husband. What I was not doing was driving halfway across the state to shoot him."

"I have to ask," Dylan said.

"I know. But while you're at it, you ought to ask Andi Matheson what she was up to on August 14."

"I've already spoken to Ms. Matheson. Why do you think she could have killed your husband?"

"Maybe he cheated on her, too. Maybe she got tired of his lies."

"Did your husband lie to you about other things— things besides other women?"

"Haven't you been paying attention? The man worked for the FBI. His whole job was telling lies— deceiving people and pretending to be someone he wasn't in order to gather information. Too bad it got to be a habit he couldn't break."

"Do you know anyone else who might have disliked Frank enough to murder him?" Dylan asked.

"I imagine Frank made plenty of enemies, but I can't tell you who they are."

"Have you scheduled any kind of funeral service for your husband?"

"Why? Do you think all his enemies will want to come and gloat?" She looked away again. "I'm sorry. That was uncalled for. The service is Thursday. Grace Memorial Chapel, 6:00 p.m."

An older woman appeared in the archway between the living room where they sat and the hall. "It's time for Kendra's nap," she said, ignoring Dylan. "You know she always goes down better for you."

"It would be better if you left now." Veronica stood.

"If we learn any more about your husband's death,

we'll pass the information along to you," Dylan said. "I'm sorry for your loss."

"Oh, yeah, we're all real sorry." She ushered him to the door. "If you find out who did this, send me a report. I don't promise to read it, but I can at least save it for the children. I'm sure they'll have questions one day. Maybe it would be good to have some answers."

Dylan sat in the Ranger Cruiser in the Ashers' driveway and studied the neat suburban home. He couldn't understand what would compel a man like Frank to betray his family the way he had. Dylan's own father would have cut off his arm rather than hurt his wife and children. Dylan intended to live his life the same way.

He pulled out his phone and scrolled to Kayla's number. "Hi," he said when she answered. "How's your day going?"

"Okay." She sounded suspicious as always. He wanted to remind her that she could trust him, but trust wasn't something you could persuade people to do with words. Kayla would have to learn to trust him in her own time. "Are you in Denver?" she asked.

"Yes. I just talked to Frank Asher's widow."

"And?"

He glanced toward the house and thought he saw a curtain twitch. Mrs. Asher and her mother were probably wondering when he was going to leave. "I don't think she killed her husband," he said. "We'll check her alibi, but I'm betting it holds."

"Which leaves who—one of Daniel Metwater's disciples?"

"Or Andi Matheson."

"I'm not buying it," Kayla said. "You know it could

be some other person we haven't even zeroed in on yet."

"It could be. But what were they doing out in the desert that morning, so near Metwater's camp?"

"I guess if you can figure that out, you'll know who did it."

"There's a memorial service for Frank Asher Thursday. Want to come with me and see if anyone interesting shows up?"

"Is this your idea of a hot date?"

Was she flirting with him? That was a good sign, wasn't it? "If you agree to come with me, I'm sure I could make it worth your while."

"Are you expecting Frank's killer?" she said. "I think criminals watch enough TV these days not to fall for that trap."

"You never can tell. Do you want to come?"

"Sorry, I can't."

"What if I throw in dinner and a movie after the services?"

"You're really tempting me, but I have somewhere else I have to be."

"Somewhere more important than the funeral of a man you didn't know?"

She laughed. "It's just a meeting of the Western Slope private investigators, but I have to go."

"They can't have the meeting without you? Are you on the board? The guest speaker?"

"You're going to make me tell you, aren't you?"

"I'm very persistent."

She sighed. "I'm getting an award."

"Congratulations. What award?"

"It's stupid. Western Slope Private Investigator of

the Year. I'm sure it will just be some cheesy certificate or something."

"It sounds like a big deal to me. I can't believe you didn't want to tell me."

"Honestly, I don't even want to go. I'd rather attend Frank's funeral. But I don't think I can get out of it without causing a fuss."

"Go. Get your honor and celebrate. Congratulations."

"Think of me while you're at Frank's service," she said. "And let me know if anyone mysterious shows up."

He ended the call and left the Asher house. He couldn't believe Kayla had won this honor and hadn't even told him. She probably hadn't told anyone. She acted almost embarrassed at the thought of anyone making a fuss over her. Maybe her family hadn't been one to celebrate accomplishments the way his had. His mom had even baked a cake to celebrate Dylan's first touchdown on the high school football team.

His phone rang and he punched the button on the steering wheel to answer it. "Dylan, it's Carmen." The voice of his fellow Ranger sounded clear over the speaker. "Did you get anything from Frank Asher's widow?"

"We'll need to check her alibi, but it sounds like she was busy here all day with the family. As much as she feels betrayed by Frank, I don't think she would have killed her children's father."

"Are you on your way back to Montrose?"

"I am."

"Good. We've had a new development. Andi

Matheson showed up here a few minutes ago. She's pretty distraught. She says her father's dead."

"LARIMER INVESTIGATIONS. How may I help you?"

"This is Simon Woolridge with the Ranger Brigade."

The familiar clipped voice set Kayla's heart to pounding. She gripped the phone more tightly. "Is something wrong?" she asked.

"Andi Matheson is here at Ranger headquarters and she's asking for you. I tried to tell her you're a private detective, not law enforcement, but she's emotional. Can you get over here and see if you can calm her down?"

"I'm on my way." She shut down her computer and gathered her purse and car keys. Andi must be really upset if Snooty Simon had resorted to calling her. Had something happened at the camp? Or to her baby?

When she arrived at Ranger Brigade headquarters, she found Simon and a handsome BLM agent, who introduced himself as Michael Dance, clustered around a wailing Andi Matheson, who sat slumped in a chair. "Kayla!" she screamed when she saw her enter the room.

Kayla rushed to the young woman and bent to wrap her arms around her. "Andi, what's wrong?"

Michael brought Kayla a chair and she slid into it. Andi clung to her, her whole body shaking with sobs. "She's been this way for the last half hour," Michael said softly. "Ever since she got here."

"Andi, honey, calm down." Kayla pushed damp hair away from the young woman's tear-swollen eyes. "It's not good for the baby for you to be so upset. Tell me what's wrong and I'll do everything I can to help you."

"It's Daddy. He's dead!"

Kayla looked at Simon. He shook his head. "We don't know any more than you do," he said.

"Daddy's dead!" Andi wailed.

"Andi, look at me." Kayla grasped the woman's chin and turned it toward her. "How do you know your father is dead? Have you seen him?"

"Daniel told me he's dead. Daniel would never lie to me." A fresh wave of sobs engulfed her.

"Somebody get her some water, please," Kayla said.

Simon filled a paper cup at the watercooler by the door and brought it to her. "Drink this," Kayla ordered, and held it to the young woman's lips.

Andi obediently took a sip. "I can't stand it," she whispered. "I always thought I'd have time to see him again. I said such awful things the last time we were together." She rested her head on Kayla's shoulder and sobbed.

Kayla shook her gently. "Pull yourself together, Andi. Tell me exactly what Daniel said to you that has you so upset."

Andi sniffed and sat up a little straighter, wiping at her eyes with the back of her hand.

"Here, ma'am." Simon handed her several tissues from a box that sat near the cooler.

"Thank you." Andi blew her nose, then took a deep breath and turned to Kayla. "Daniel called me into his RV this afternoon and told me he had some sad news for me, but that I needed to be strong for the baby's sake."

"You are strong, Andi." Kayla squeezed her arm. "Strong enough to tell me everything that happened." She noticed Simon had grabbed a notebook from a nearby desk and was prepared to write everything down. "What did Daniel say?"

"He told me my father was dead. That I shouldn't be sad because he was in a better place now."

"Did Metwater say how he knew this?" Simon asked.

Kayla glared at him, but Andi didn't seem to notice. "He said he saw Daddy's body in a dream," she said, her voice choked with tears. "He said there was blood all over him, and that he knew that meant he was dead."

"Think very carefully," Kayla said. "This is really important. Did Daniel say he saw your father in a dream, or just that he saw your father?"

"He said he saw him in a dream." She looked at Kayla, her blue eyes as wide and innocent as a child's. "He's a prophet. He knows these things. If he saw Daddy dead, it must be true."

Kayla held her close, trying to comfort her. Someone needed to strangle Daniel Metwater and tell him to keep his phony prophecies to himself. What had he hoped to accomplish by upsetting Andi this way?

At last Andi's sobs subsided. She sat up and pushed her hair out of her eyes. "I have to get back to camp," she said. "It's almost time for dinner and I have to help cook." She squeezed Kayla's hand. "I just wanted someone else to know. A friend."

Kayla's eyes stung, she was so touched by these words. "I'm glad you came to me," she said.

"We'll drive you back," Simon said. "And while we're there we can have a word with Daniel."

"How did you get here?" Kayla asked.

"I hiked to the road and hitched a ride with a tourist," Andi said. She stood and Kayla rose also.

"I'll ride with you to the camp," Kayla said.

"That won't be necessary," Simon said.

"Please let Kayla come with me." Andi grabbed her hand and squeezed so hard she winced.

Simon scowled at her, then turned away. "Come on, then."

Chapter Fifteen

Andi remained subdued on the ride back to the camp. She stared out the window in the backseat of Simon's Cruiser. Kayla thought she might even have fallen asleep for a little while.

Up front, Simon and Michael didn't speak, either. Kayla knew Simon resented her presence, but she didn't care. Andi wanted her company, so she would do what she could to comfort her. Besides, she wasn't going to miss the chance to see what Daniel Metwater had to say for himself. Had he really seen Peter Matheson in a dream, or did he know the senator was dead because he'd killed him?

They arrived at the parking area for the camp and Andi opened her door before the Cruiser had come to a full stop. "Thanks for the ride," she said. "I have to hurry and help with dinner."

Simon reached to pull her back, but Kayla grabbed his arm. "Let her go," she said. "You'll have better luck with Metwater without her there, getting worked up again."

He pulled his arm away. "Don't tell me how to do my job."

"She's right," Michael said. "Metwater might be

more candid without one of his pretty followers to impress."

Simon said nothing, but turned and led the way up the path to the camp, Michael and Kayla walking single file behind him. The camp seemed busier than usual, with at least a dozen people moving about among the collection of tents and trailers. An older woman supervised two men who were unloading supplies from a battered blue Volkswagen bus. A trio of children played with a black dog, throwing a stick and laughing as he retrieved it. Other women milled around the cooking fire in the center of the camp, while a group of men and women worked to construct a kind of brush arbor in front of one of the trailers.

Several of the campers stopped to stare as the trio made their way across the compound, the utility belts of the two officers rattling with each step. They climbed the steps to Metwater's RV and Simon knocked.

No answer. Simon pounded harder. "Maybe he's not in," Kayla said.

Simon looked around. "Where's Metwater?" he called to a passing woman.

She stared at him, then shook her head and fled.

Simon beat on the door again. "Metwater, if you don't open up in three I'm going to break the door down."

"Can he do that?" Kayla whispered to Michael.

"He's concerned for the occupant's welfare," Michael said, stone-faced.

"One. Two."

The door opened and Daniel Metwater, in jeans and a loose shirt, glared at them. "You have no right to intrude on my home," he said.

Simon shouldered past him and the others followed. "If you prefer we can take you back to headquarters for questioning," Simon said. "Your choice." He turned to the young woman who sat on the black leather sectional that filled most of the RV's living room. "You can leave now, miss."

She hurried away, not even pausing to say goodbye to Metwater. After the door had closed behind her, Simon addressed Metwater again. "Do you want to come with us, or answer our questions here?"

"I don't have anything to say to you." He flopped onto the couch, one arm stretched along the back, the casualness of the pose a sharp contrast to Simon's rigid posture.

Kayla sat on the other end of the sectional. Metwater's eyes followed her, but he said nothing. "Andi came to see me and she was very upset by some things you had told her," she said.

"There was no need for that," Metwater said. "She would have found all the comfort she needed here, with her brothers and sisters."

"She said you told her her father, Senator Matheson, was dead." Simon, still standing, moved between Kayla and Metwater. "How did you know that?"

"I have prophetic dreams," Metwater said. "I don't expect you to understand."

"Then you must have known as soon as we heard about this particular prophecy we'd be here to question you," Simon said.

"Prophecy doesn't work that way. I only receive the messages my higher power wants me to have."

"So your higher power told you the senator was dead."

Simon's snide tone probably wasn't helping the situation any, but Kayla kept quiet, shifting to the right so she could watch Daniel as he spoke. "I saw Senator Matheson's body in a dream," he said. "He was covered in blood. Too much blood to be alive."

"Or maybe you saw his body in real life," Simon said. "When you killed him."

"I didn't kill the senator." Metwater's expression remained indifferent. "I've never even met him."

"How did he die?" Michael, who had remained standing near the door, spoke for the first time.

"I don't know," Metwater said.

"Where is he now?" Michael asked.

"I don't know that, either. All I saw was his body in a dream."

"And that was enough for you to decide to upset Ms. Matheson by telling her her father was dead?" Simon demanded. Kayla thought she detected real anger in his expression.

"What is upsetting for her now will be better for her in the long run."

"And who are you to decide that?" Simon loomed over him. "The poor woman was devastated. Did you enjoy that? Did you enjoy deliberately causing her pain?"

Metwater straightened. "Now she can grieve and get on with her life. She can finally cut her last ties with her old life and move into a brighter future."

"Was that your plan all along?" Simon asked. "Get rid of her lover, Frank Asher. Then get rid of her father. What about the child? Do you plan to do away with it, too?"

Metwater shoved himself to his feet, so that he was nose to nose with him. "Get out!"

"I could arrest you," Simon said.

"For what? For having a dream?"

The two men stared at each other for a long, tense moment. Kayla glanced at Michael and saw that he had moved closer, his right hand hovering over the gun at his side, ready to defend his fellow officer if Metwater attacked.

Simon took a step back. "If I find out what you saw was more than a dream, I'll be back," he said. He strode out of the RV and the others followed.

"Kayla." Metwater stopped her at the door.

Startled, she turned. "Yes?"

"Is Asteria—Andi—going to be all right?" he asked. "I thought knowing her father was at peace would be better than the uncertainty of not knowing what had happened to him. Then she left here, so upset, and I heard she had left the camp altogether. I sent people after her, but they couldn't find her. I didn't think she would go to the Rangers."

His concern seemed genuine. "Have you ever lost someone you were close to?" Kayla asked.

His expression darkened. "My father and I were not close. I was always a disappointment to him."

"What about your brother? Didn't I read he died last year?"

"Yes." He looked away. "Yes, David and I were close."

"Then you know a little of what Andi is going through right now. If her father really is dead—and she can't be sure until the body is found—it will take her time to process what has happened and heal. You can help by letting her take things at her own pace. Be there for her, but don't press her to behave any certain way."

"I'll keep that in mind. And thank you—for being a friend to Asteria, and for not judging me so harshly."

Simon and Michael were waiting at the bottom of the steps when Kayla emerged from Metwater's trailer. They said nothing on the walk back to the Cruiser, but once they were all buckled in, Simon turned to her. "What did Metwater have to say to you after we left?" he asked.

"He wanted to know if I thought Andi would be all right."

Simon grunted and started the car. The ride back to Ranger headquarters was as silent as the journey there had been, until they turned onto the highway. "What's your impression of Metwater?" Simon asked.

Kayla looked up and met his eyes in the rearview mirror. "I'm surprised my opinion matters to you," she said.

"Dylan said you were a good observer, and a good judge of character."

This information pleased her more than she cared to admit. She considered her impression of Metwater. "I think a man would have to be arrogant beyond belief to kill a man, then describe seeing the body and try to pass it off as a dream," she said.

"Metwater is pretty arrogant," Michael pointed out.

"Yes, but he's also very smart," she said.

"So you're saying you think he really had a dream where he saw Pete Matheson's body covered in blood?" Simon asked.

"Maybe. I mean, it doesn't sound logical, but I

guess stranger things have happened." Her father liked to claim he had prophetic dreams, too—usually as a way of providing "evidence" to support whatever decision he had already made. But a few times his dreams had been eerily prescient. Kayla had always dismissed this as coincidence, but still...

"Peter Matheson is missing," she said. "When someone goes missing, death is always a possibility, so Metwater may be manipulating that possibility to make himself look good."

"How so?" Michael turned to look over the seat at her.

"He says he saw the senator dead. If we find a body, he can say he foretold it, and show how powerful he is. He impresses his current followers and makes them even more loyal, and maybe he recruits a few new ones. If the senator turns up all right, Matheson can say what he saw in his dream was the senator injured—either physically or psychically—and he merely misinterpreted the image. He'll manage to talk his followers into seeing this as another example of how tuned in he is with a higher power."

"You've given a lot of thought to this," Simon said. "I'm impressed. And I agree—Metwater is up to something. And we're going to find out what."

The sun was setting by the time Dylan pulled into Ranger Brigade headquarters, and his shoulders ached from so many hours behind the wheel. Michael Dance looked up from his desk when Dylan entered. "How was Denver?" he asked.

"It's a big city with too much traffic." He glanced

around the empty office. "What happened with Andi Metwater? Did they really find the senator?"

"Pull up a chair and I'll fill you in."

A half hour later Dylan sat back and shook his head. "And Peter Matheson still hasn't turned up—dead or alive?"

"We checked and there's been no sign of him, nor any indication of foul play. The Feds checked out his house and his office. He's vanished. But Metwater sure convinced Andi that her father is dead."

"And we don't have any proof Metwater killed him."

"None." Michael drummed on his desk with a pencil. "And why admit knowledge of the crime if he did do it? He had to know it would focus all our attention on him as suspect number one."

"What about Zach and Abe? Did you get anything more out of them?"

"Not really. The district attorney agreed to a lesser charge of leaving the scene of an accident and reckless driving. They both have clean records, so they'll probably get off with a fine and probation. And they've agreed to remain available if we have any more questions."

"They're lucky to get off so lightly."

"Except they're still crying about Metwater taking their stuff. We told them that was a civil matter they needed to take up with a lawyer. After all, they did voluntarily sign everything over to the Prophet."

"I'm beginning to think that whole bunch over there are crazy," Dylan said.

"Crazy like a fox," Michael said. "Kayla thinks Metwater is using this so-called prophecy to manipulate his followers to think he has special powers. If the senator really is dead, he predicted it. If Matheson turns up safe and sound he can offer a different interpretation of his dream and still make himself look right."

Dylan nodded. "I guess it makes sense in a twisted way."

"She's pretty smart—Kayla, I mean." Michael gave him a long look.

"What?" Dylan asked.

"Are you two, you know, together?"

"I'm not sleeping with her, if that's what you're asking."

"No, that's not what I was asking. Relax. I just thought you seemed interested in her. And you've been spending a lot of time together."

Dylan shoved himself out of his chair. "Yeah, I'm interested in her. But I'm not sure she feels the same way about me."

"Has she told you to back off?"

"No."

"Then she's interested." Michael grinned.

"Who made you an expert?" Dylan asked. "They told me you were still a newlywed."

"Yep. And I met my wife while working on a case. She found a body in the wilderness, too. And she wasn't that crazy about me the first time we met, but I won her over." He stood also. "I'm calling it a night."

"Yeah, me, too." They left together, headed in the same direction out of the parking lot. But when Michael turned off toward the duplex he and his wife, Abbie, rented near the park, Dylan continued into town.

It was almost eight o'clock when he parked in front

of Kayla's house. Light glowed from the front windows and he caught the scent of jasmine from the vine that wound up the porch post. Maybe it was too late to drop in. He sat in the Cruiser, debating, until the front door opened. "Do you want to come in, or are you staking out the place?" Kayla called.

He climbed out of the car and went to her. He didn't even wait for her to say anything, but pulled her close and kissed her—long and hard, not holding back how much he wanted her. She went very still at first, then melted against him, her arms around his back, letting him take what he wanted.

When at last he released her, she took a step back, her cheeks flushed. "What was that for?" she asked, searching his face.

"I had a hard day and I needed to kiss you." He walked past her into the house.

She closed the door and followed him into the kitchen, where he was leaning into the open refrigerator. "I'm starved," he said. "I could use a sandwich, and a beer."

She grabbed his arm and tugged him away from the fridge. "Sit down. I'll fix you something to eat. Tell me about your day."

"You first," he said, settling into a chair. "I want to know about Andi Matheson. I hear she showed up at the office, distraught."

"Did you also hear why? That Daniel Metwater had a dream about her father?"

"Yeah. Ethan filled me in. Is she going to be okay?"

"I think so." Kayla took a bottle of beer from the refrigerator, opened it and handed it to him. "In a way, her faith in Metwater, or in whatever he represents for her, will help her in her grief, though I wanted to shake him for being an idiot."

Dylan took a long pull of the beer and felt more of the day's tension drain away. "Ethan said you thought Metwater cooked the whole thing up to make himself look good," he said.

"Probably." She pulled out bread, meat and cheese and began assembling a sandwich.

He watched her work, smooth and competent, her brow creased in thought. "Did your father do that kind of thing?" he asked. "Make predictions to manipulate people?"

"Oh, yes. He was a master at it. Even I believed him, when I was too young to know better." She turned to face Dylan. "When I was seven, more than anything I wanted this particular doll that was popular at the time. One of those dolls that come with a storybook and matching outfits and furniture and everything. My father told me that if I prayed and had enough faith, I would get the doll for Christmas. I spent hours on my knees that November and December. By the time Christmas came I was absolutely certain that doll would be mine."

"And you didn't get it." He could read the pain in her eyes, a wound that lingered even after all these years.

"No. I was heartbroken. When I started crying, my father told me it was my own fault, because I didn't have enough faith." She turned back to the sandwich. "I think that was when I stopped believing at all."

Dylan's fingers tightened around his beer. What kind of person treated a child that way? "Where was your mother?" he asked.

"Oh, she always went along with whatever my father said. She was an obedient servant, like we were all supposed to be. But I couldn't do it. I couldn't be good and follow orders only on his say-so. I had to see a reason behind his commands, and too often there wasn't any logic, just what he had decided he wanted, or what would make the best impressions on others."

"I wish I had known you then," Dylan said. "I would have told you you were better and smarter than any of them."

She set the sandwich in front of him. "Don't fret over it. I don't. Or not usually."

"That's right," he said. "After all, you're the private investigator of the year."

"On the Western Slope of Colorado. There aren't that many of us." She took another beer from the refrigerator, opened it and sat across from him. "There are also awards for rookie of the year for a brand-new PI, awards for senior investigators and heroism on the job and who knows what else. Apparently, when the current president took over, she was determined to wring as much publicity as possible out of what had been a fairly sedate dinner."

"So have you picked out a new dress to wear, and practiced your acceptance speech?" he asked.

She rolled her eyes. "I don't even want to think about it." She sipped from her beer. "Tell me about your day. You saw Frank Asher's widow. What else?"

"That was enough." He took a bite of sandwich, chewed and swallowed. "It isn't the violence of this job that gets to me," he said. "I expected that. And the danger—well, most cops will admit that can be a rush. But what grinds me down sometimes is all the ways people can be mean to each other. I sat there with Veronica Asher and all I saw was a beautiful woman, a devoted mother and daughter, who was worn out with grief and hurt. Her husband made a promise to be there for her and then he broke it. And Andi Matheson was hurt, too—by Frank Asher's lies and by Daniel Metwater's manipulation. You were hurt by your parents, and hearing about it makes me want to do something to make it right, but I know there's nothing I can do—for any of you."

She stood and came around the table and put her hand on his shoulder. "Move your chair back."

He scooted it back and she sat in his lap. "Being with you makes me feel better," she said. "Isn't that enough?" She kissed his cheek, then his lips.

He wrapped his arms around her and pulled her closer still, her breasts soft against his chest, her mouth warm and fervent, her tongue tangling with his, tasting of ale and promising a hundred ways to make him forget pain and worry and stress.

He caressed her thigh and moved from her mouth to feather kisses along her jaw. "If you're trying to distract me, it's working."

"Don't mind me." She began to unbutton his khaki uniform shirt. "Finish your sandwich."

"What sandwich?" He slid his hand beneath her T-shirt, the flesh of her torso soft and cool beneath his fingers. He skimmed over her bra, dragging his thumb across her pebbled nipple, and smiled at the way her breath caught. She squirmed, and it was his turn to gasp as she rubbed against his growing erection. She had most of the buttons on his shirt undone now, and bent to trace her tongue along his breastbone.

He nudged his thumb beneath her chin until she raised her head and met his gaze. "Not that this isn't fun, but where are we going with it?" he asked.

"I was thinking eventually we could go into the bedroom," she said. "Though I have a nice sofa, too, if that's more your speed. I wouldn't recommend the kitchen table, though."

"The bedroom sounds good." He rose, and she slid from his lap, though he steadied her with his arm. "You lead the way."

She glanced back at the table. "Are you sure you don't want to finish your sandwich?"

"Later." He nudged her bottom.

Kayla's bedroom turned out to be down a short hall, a small, comfortable room decorated in shades of blue, with a faded flowered quilt on the bed. The air smelled like her—soft and faintly floral. Fresh. In the doorway, she drew him to her once more and undid the final button on his shirt.

He went to work on the zipper of her jeans. "This is the nicest surprise I've had all day," he said.

"Why is it a surprise?" she asked. "You must have known I was attracted to you."

"I hoped, but you weren't sending the clearest signals. Or maybe I just wasn't good at interpreting them."

She shoved the shirt off his shoulders. "Is this a clear enough signal for you?"

"Oh, yeah." He slid out of the shirt, then pushed up the hem of hers. "Loud and clear."

He liked that she wasn't shy about undressing. And she didn't seem to mind that he waited until she was naked before he finished shedding his own clothes.

She had a slim, athletic body, with small breasts and rounded hips. Her skin was so soft, and touching her sent a thrill of desire through him. He cupped her breast and she arched to him, and when he bent to take her nipple in his mouth, she let out a long sigh that pierced him.

She urged him toward the bed, paused to fold back the covers, then pulled him on top of her. When her lips found his he closed his eyes and lost himself in her embrace, forgetting time and place and everything but the feel of her body beneath his roaming hands and lips. She responded with a fervor to match his own, kissing and caressing until he was half-mad with wanting her.

"Tell me you have a condom somewhere in this house," he murmured into the side of her neck.

"Bedside table."

He shoved himself up, reached for the drawer on the little table and pulled out a gold box. "These aren't even open," he said, frowning at the plastic wrapping.

"I bought a new box just for you." She laughed and snatched the package from him. "Go back to what you were doing. I wouldn't want to slow you dow—" The last word died on her lips as he slid down the length of her body to the juncture of her thighs.

"Don't let me slow you down," he said, his attention focused on her sex.

"Don't you dare stop," she said, and he heard the plastic on the box rip.

He slid his hands up to caress her hips, and lost himself in pleasuring her. Her soft moans and breathy gasps encouraged him, as he worked to bring her close to the edge, but not over. She let out a cry of frustration when he slid back up her body to lie beside her. "There's more where that came from," he said.

"Promise?" She pushed him onto his back and climbed on top of him, then took the unwrapped condom from the bedside table. "Ready to get dressed?" she asked.

"Ready."

Kayla kept her gaze focused on Dylan's face as she rolled on the condom. She'd fantasized about being with him, but the reality was so much better. He approached lovemaking with the perfect combination of humor and seriousness that kept her from feeling awkward, and his obvious eagerness for her bolstered her confidence and fueled her own desire.

His eyes lost focus as she squeezed his shaft, and she felt a sharpened pull of desire deep within her. Maybe she had wanted a man this much before, but she didn't think so. With Dylan she felt less wary, freer to be herself, than with any other man, and that freedom was a powerful aphrodisiac. He grasped her hips and guided her over him, and she let out a long sigh as he filled her. Yes, this was definitely one of the best decisions she had made in a while.

She set the pace, rocking slowly, then sliding up and down the length of him, enjoying the sensation, drawing out the pleasure, until he thrust up more firmly and dragged her down to press his lips to hers. The mood shifted to one of greater urgency, and she let herself ride the sensation, closing her eyes as he reached down to stroke her, building the tension, coiling tighter and tighter until her vision blurred and she lost her breath, a voice that didn't even sound like hers calling out his name.

His fingers raked her back as he increased the tempo, and then his own climax overtook him and he crushed her to him, pumping hard, leaving her breathless and exhilarated. He held her tightly for a long moment, his breath harsh in her ears, then rolled to his side, taking her with him, his arms securely around her.

"How's your day now?" she asked, when she had caught her breath. She traced one finger down his cheek, enjoying the roughness of his unshaved face.

"The best." He laid his head on her shoulder and closed his eyes. "The best."

"DYLAN, WAKE UP. Your phone is ringing."

Dylan opened his eyes and stared into Kayla's worried face. Still half asleep, he smiled and reached for her, but she pushed him away. "Your phone," she said. "Whoever it is has called back twice. You'd better answer it."

He struggled to sit, and wiped his hand over his eyes. He'd been deeply asleep, after an evening that had included the sandwich, a shower and another bout of lovemaking with Kayla before surrendering to slumber.

"Answer the phone." She nudged him.

He followed the sound of his ringtone to his trousers, which were on the floor atop his shirt and shoes. "Hello?" he croaked, then cleared his throat and tried again. "Hello?"

"There's been a development in the Matheson disappearance," Graham Ellison said. "Grand Junction Police found his car half submerged in an abandoned gravel pit. There was a bundle of bloody clothes shoved under the front seat. It looks like Daniel Metwater's prophecy might be true, after all."

Chapter Sixteen

Dylan met Graham and Simon at the Grand Junction impoundment yard a little after four in the morning. A forensics team was already at work on Matheson's car. Floodlights on tall stands illuminated the area around the vehicle, where technicians in white paper coveralls and booties combed the interior for hair and fibers, fingerprints, blood and any other evidence. Another man worked on the exterior, examining the body for recent dents and scratches, and collecting samples of soil from the tire treads.

"No good prints but a few of Matheson's own," Simon reported, after consulting with one of the techs. "They're sending the clothing to be tested to determine if the blood is Matheson's or someone else's."

"A dive team will search the gravel pit as soon as it's light," Graham said. "A second search team with cadaver dogs will comb the area around the pit."

"Any theories on what happened?" Dylan asked.

Graham shook his head. "A couple of kids apparently drove out here to make out and noticed the top of the car in the moonlight," he said. "The girl mentioned it to her older sister when she got home, the sister told the dad and the dad called the police. They got a wrecker out here to haul it out of the water and when they ran the plate they knew they had something big."

"I think we should bring Metwater in for questioning," Simon said. "Maybe with this new development we can sweat a confession out of him."

"He's not going to break that easy," Dylan said. "And we don't have enough evidence to hold him. Until we have Matheson's body, we can't even charge him with murder. And he'll have a dozen followers who will swear he hasn't been anywhere near Grand Junction in months."

"Except Abe and Zach said they thought that's where he was for a big chunk of yesterday," Simon said.

"Which I'll admit makes him suspicious," Dylan said. "Except he supposedly had Andi Matheson with him, and considering her reaction to news that her father was dead, I can't imagine her conspiring with Metwater to kill the senator."

"Stranger things have happened," Simon said. "And if we don't detain him he's liable to disappear."

"We'll wait until we have a body," Graham said. "By then we may have enough evidence to make something stick. In the meantime, Michael and Marco are watching the camp. There's only one way into that canyon. The Prophet won't leave without our knowing it."

Simon pressed his lips together. Dylan knew he wasn't happy with this decision, but he wouldn't argue with their captain. Dylan sympathized with Simon's point of view. "Have you come up with anything in Metwater's background that we can use?" he asked. "I tried doing a little digging on my own, but you're better at background forensics than I am."

Simon shook his head. "We've got nothing. He's

the blue blood heir to his family's manufacturing fortune. His dad died last year—apparently he'd had a heart condition for years and died on the operating table, so we can't blame that on the son. Metwater inherited equally with his twin brother, David, who was apparently the family screwup. He embezzled money from the family firm, got crosswise with some Mafia types and ended up dead. His body was found dumped in a river. He'd been shot in the head. A month later, Daniel declares he's had a spiritual revelation, sells the family business and takes his evangelical show on the road, recruiting followers to join his Family. And a few weeks ago they end up in our jurisdiction." He made a face. "Aren't we lucky?"

"So, no ties to the brother's death?"

"The local cops say he's clean. And it was pretty common knowledge that the brother was in over his head with organized crime."

"Maybe Daniel's religious conversion had more to do with fear the mob would come after him than a spiritual revelation," Graham said.

Simon shrugged. "If it did, he's taking it to extremes. If I had the fortune he has, I wouldn't be living in an RV in the middle of nowhere, without running water and electricity."

"When does their camping permit expire?" Dylan asked.

"Next week," Graham said. "But they can move to another spot in the wilderness area and renew the permit. For now, I would just as soon they stay put, where we can keep an eye on them."

They split up, Dylan and Simon in separate vehicles to head back to the Ranger Brigade offices,

Graham to a meeting with FBI agents in the Bureau's Western Slope division. Dylan turned down his radio and contemplated the barren hills and red dirt washes that filled the landscape between Grand Junction and Montrose. He debated calling Kayla, to hear her voice and see how she was doing. Was she having any second thoughts about spending the night with him? Could he say anything to make her feel more comfortable with the decision?

Better to hold off on calling her. Right now it would be too easy for him to betray his own feelings and frighten her off. The truth was, he was falling in love with Kayla. Yes, it was happening fast, but he was as sure of his feelings as he had ever been sure of anything. He wouldn't take things too fast or try to push her, but he would find a way to gain her trust—to show her he was nothing like her father and the others who had let her down before.

He was almost to Montrose when his phone rang. "Lieutenant Holt?" a woman's voice asked hesitantly.

"Yes? Who is this?"

"This is Veronica Asher."

Dylan signaled and pulled to the side of the road. "How can I help you, Mrs. Asher?"

"I received something very strange in the mail this morning. I should probably call the Bureau, but frankly, I feel more comfortable talking to you."

"What did you receive?" he asked.

"It was a plain white envelope, addressed to Mrs. Frank Asher, with no return address, though the postmark is Grand Junction. Inside were a bunch of money cards—you know, the credit card things you can put a cash balance on. I called the number on the back of the cards and each one of them is worth twenty-five hundred dollars. Twenty-five thousand dollars in all."

"Twenty-five thousand dollars?" Dylan repeated. "Does that amount have any significance for you?"

"No. Except it's a crazy amount of money to get in the mail."

"Was there anything else in the envelope? A note?"

"There was a sympathy card, the kind you could buy in any store. No signature or anything."

"Do you know anyone in Grand Junction who might have sent you the money?" Dylan asked. "Maybe a charity or an organization that thought you needed the funds?"

"I don't know anyone in Grand Junction," she said. "And whatever his other faults, Frank left us well provided for. I don't know what to think about this except…" Her voice trailed away.

"Except what?"

"Do you think the money might be from Frank's killer? A kind of guilt payment or something?"

"That's definitely worth looking into. What have you done with the money cards?"

"Nothing. They're right here in the envelope they came in. But I wasn't being very careful at first. They'll have my fingerprints on them."

"Leave them there and call Frank's supervisor at the Bureau. They'll have the best resources to investigate this. Or I can contact them for you if you like."

"Would you? Every time I have to deal with them, all I can think is that they knew what Frank was up to and none of them bothered to tell me. That may be an unfair assessment, but it's how I feel."

"I'll call them and ask them to send over an agent—maybe someone who didn't work with Frank."

"Thank you."

She ended the call and Dylan mulled over the information she had given him. Daniel Metwater had a fortune at his disposal. It would have been easy enough for him to send one of his followers to one or more locations around Grand Junction to purchase the money cards with cash. He and Andi might even have purchased the cards themselves when they came to town yesterday. Even if Metwater hadn't personally pulled the trigger to kill Asher, he might have ordered one of his followers to do so. Maybe he had decided to alleviate some of his guilt by paying off Asher's widow.

Dylan put the Cruiser into gear and pulled back onto the highway. He would do as he had promised and notify the FBI of this latest development. But he would tell Graham first, and the Rangers would conduct an investigation of their own, one focused on Daniel Metwater and his followers.

KAYLA DRIFTED IN and out of sleep after Dylan left, her slumber disturbed by replays of their time together. While he had been with her, she had been sure a relationship with him was the best decision she had made in years. But away from his magnetic presence she felt less certain. She had been honest with him when she told him she didn't do relationships. She didn't have the emotional tools to be comfortable relying on someone else, and she had managed fine alone for years. He, on the other hand, was close to his family and more than comfortable with the idea of settling down with a wife and kids and the whole storybook setting. She didn't know how she would fit into that kind of life. Trying to make things work when they were so different was probably setting them both up for disappointment.

At seven she rose and made coffee, then switched on the television to the local morning program. "Very early today Grand Junction police recovered a vehicle belonging to missing senator Peter Matheson from an area gravel pit," the news anchor announced. "Divers are scheduled to search the pit for the body of the senator, who has been missing since last Friday." Video footage showed a late-model sedan being pulled from the water, the scene lit by floodlights. Superimposed on these images was a still photo of Senator Matheson, one Kayla recognized from his campaign posters.

Though Dylan had shared the news of the discovery before he had left for Ranger headquarters, seeing the footage on television somehow made it more real, Kayla found. She switched off the TV and returned to her bedroom to dress. She should have known news of the discovery of the senator's car would spread quickly. It was probably the top story on every channel. Even cut off from communication the way they were, Andi and the other Family members were bound to hear about this sooner rather than later. Dylan hadn't said, but Kayla suspected he or someone else from the Ranger Brigade would show up at the camp to question Daniel Metwater once more. Andi would be upset all over again. Kayla needed to be there for her.

She was on her way out the door when her phone

rang. Hoping it was Dylan, she hurried to answer it, not even bothering to look at the screen.

"Hello, is this Kayla Larimer?"

"Yes." Kayla checked her phone. *Caller Unknown.* Had someone from the press gotten hold of her number?

"This is Madeline Zimeski, with the Colorado Private Investigators Society. I noticed we hadn't received your confirmation for the awards banquet this Thursday."

"I've been a little busy."

"So I can put down that you're coming? And how many guests?"

"Just me." She shifted her water bottle, digging in her purse for her car keys.

"You don't have someone you'd like to invite to see you receive your award?"

She thought of Dylan, then pushed the idea away. Why would he want to sit through a boring awards banquet? Besides, he had to attend Frank Asher's funeral. "Just me," she repeated. "And I really have to go now."

"I'll put you down for one then. Let me know if you change your mind about bringing a guest. I look forward to seeing you there. And congrat—"

Kayla ended the call and headed out the door to her car. With luck she could make it to the camp before either Dylan or someone who had seen the television reports got there. She could break the news of this latest development to Andi gently and avoid sending the girl into tears yet again.

Traffic was light and she pushed the speed limit on her way out of town. She had just cleared the city limits when her phone rang again. A check of the screen showed an unknown number once more. If Madeline Zimeski had called back about that stupid awards banquet, she was going to get an earful.

Kayla was tempted not to answer, but what if it was Andi, calling from a pay phone? With one eye on the road, she took the call. "Hello?"

"Kayla? It's Pete Matheson. I need your help."

Chapter Seventeen

Kayla's car swerved and she almost dropped her phone. Heart pounding, she pulled over to the side of the road, leaving the engine idling. "Senator? Are you all right? Where are you? Are you hurt?"

"I'm not physically injured, but I need your help."

"Of course. Do you want me to call someone for you? Do you need money or someone to come get you?"

"Promise me you won't go to the authorities. Promise me now or I'll hang up and you'll never hear from me again."

"Of course. I promise. Don't hang up." Was someone there with him, telling him to say that? Did he have a gun to his head? What were the chances of Dylan and his team tracing this call?

"How is my daughter?"

The question was so conversational and unexpected that for a moment Kayla couldn't find the words to answer.

"You've seen her, haven't you?" the senator asked. "You told me you were going to see her."

"Uh, yes, I've seen her. She's well. Though she's very worried about you."

"Is she? I thought she might be glad to be rid of me."

"No! That isn't true. She was beside herself when she thought you were hurt. She loves you very much." The truth of those words made Kayla's chest hurt. Andi did love her father, no matter their differences.

He was silent for so long she thought he might have ended the call. "Senator? Are you still there?"

"I'm still here." He cleared his throat, and when he spoke his voice was rough with emotion. "I never meant to hurt her. You must believe that. Nothing I have is worth as much to me as my child."

"I believe Andi knows that. All she wants is for you to be safe."

"I need you to help me."

"To help you do what?"

"Can you take me to see Andi? Without anyone else knowing?"

"Why don't you want anyone else to know?" she asked. "So many people have been looking for you."

"No." His voice was sharp. "It's too dangerous at this point. When the time comes, I will notify the police. But not yet. Not until I've spoken with Andi."

"All right. I can do that." He wasn't really giving her a choice.

"I have an address for you, where you can pick me up. If you show up with any law enforcement, I'll go away and you won't hear from me again."

"I'll come alone, I promise," she said. "And I won't tell anyone where I'm going."

"Then get something to write this down. It will take you a while to get here, but I'll be waiting."

DYLAN TRIED TO reach Kayla, but her phone went straight to voice mail. Was she deliberately avoiding his calls? "Hey, Kayla, it's Dylan. I'm going to be out of touch for a while, on a stakeout. I'll call you when I'm back in cell range and maybe we can get together for dinner or something. Take care." He wanted to add something else—I miss you? I love you? But maybe it was too soon for that. He didn't want to scare her off. He settled for a simple "Bye" and stowed the phone once more.

Veronica Asher had scanned the money cards she had received and emailed the file to Simon, who was back at Ranger headquarters, combing through the identification numbers on the cards, trying to determine where they had originated from. Graham had made some calls to the FBI and the Bureau had promised to send a sympathetic agent to collect the cards from Mrs. Asher. They had agreed to work with the Rangers on canvassing Grand Junction area gas stations, convenience stores and grocery stores with pictures of as many of the Family members as they could obtain, in hopes of getting a positive ID on the purchaser of the cards. Once they had nailed that individual, they could use him or her to get to Daniel Metwater, or whoever had sent the cards.

The Rangers were also trying to get a warrant to access Metwater's bank records. A withdrawal in the amount of the payment to Mrs. Asher would be another strong indication of guilt. He might say he was only doing an anonymous good deed for the widow of the man who had been killed near his camp, but a prosecutor was likely to see things differently.

For now, Dylan was taking his shift watching the camp for any suspicious activity. He parked his Cruiser out of sight about a mile from Dead Horse

Canyon and hiked to the rocky overlook DEA Agent
Marco Cruz had selected as the best vantage point to
survey the action in the compound without being seen.

"Anything going on?" Dylan asked Marco after the
two had exchanged greetings.

"That big RV is Metwater's, right?" He handed
over the high-powered binoculars he'd been using to
surveil the camp. "He's had a lot of people going in
and out of there—mostly women, but a few men. But
I haven't seen him come out."

"How do we know he's still in there?" Dylan asked.

"No vehicles have left the camp, and Randall is
watching the road. If Metwater tried to climb out over
the rocks we'd see."

Dylan settled more comfortably among the boulders and raised the binoculars. "Any sign of Andi
Matheson?"

"She visited Metwater about an hour ago. When
she came out it looked like she'd been crying. Any
news on the senator?"

"Nothing yet. The FBI is canvassing the neighborhood near where they found the car, hoping to find a
witness who saw something."

"It will be interesting to see whose blood is on
those clothes," Marco said.

Dylan lowered the binoculars. "You don't think
it's the senator's?"

Marco shrugged. "Who knows? It will just be interesting. One more piece of the puzzle." He stood and
picked up his backpack. "I'm outta here."

"Hot date?"

He grinned. "You know it. Lauren is flying in from
filming a documentary in Texas."

Dylan had forgotten that Cruz was married to television newscaster Lauren Starling. The two had met when she'd been kidnapped last summer and he'd been involved in her rescue. "I'm looking forward to meeting her soon," Dylan said. "Tell her I'm a fan."

"When I see her again, you are going to be the last thing on my mind."

Marco left, moving soundlessly down the rocks, and Dylan settled back to watch. The summer days were growing shorter and here in the canyon the sun set quickly, plunging the area into darkness. As the air cooled and stars began to appear, activity increased in the camp. Dylan trained the binoculars on the center area, where two men were building a bonfire while a third man swept the dirt around the fire pit. About eight o'clock Metwater emerged from his trailer and walked over to supervise the preparations. Even at this distance, Dylan had a sense that something important was about to happen down there. Were they initiating another new member? Celebrating some religious rite he wasn't aware of? Throwing a birthday party?

He had a hard time picturing Metwater involved in something as innocent as a birthday party, but that was the kind of thing families did, wasn't it?

Metwater must have heard the news about Peter Matheson by now. Had Andi's tears when she left his trailer been because he had told her her father's car had been found in the quarry? Could whatever ceremony the group was preparing for have anything to do with the senator?

Carefully, Dylan moved a few feet farther down the slope, hoping for a better view of the action. He had no way of calling headquarters or summoning help without leaving his observation post and traveling back to the road. Better to see if he could figure out what was going on before he did that.

ANDI DROVE SLOWLY in the fading light, craning her head to read the addresses on the ramshackle buildings she passed. Her shoulders ached with tension, and her gun lay on the console beside her, loaded and ready. Everything about this setup felt like a trap to her. She wished now she had disobeyed the senator's orders and had at least let Dylan know where she was. He had tried to reach her shortly after she pulled onto the highway after talking with the senator, and she had let the call go to voice mail, knowing if she spoke to him directly she would give in to the temptation to share the news that Senator Matheson was alive and here in Montrose.

She hit the brakes as she spotted the address she wanted. She double-checked the number against the notes she had made, but this was the place. A faded sign identified the collection of boarded up buildings as the Shady Rest Motel. Judging by the prices on the gas pumps out front, this place hadn't been in business for at least a decade. Was someone holding the senator hostage here? She picked up the gun and climbed out of the car. "Senator Matheson!" she called, keeping her voice low.

"Hush. I'm right here."

She turned and saw him climbing into the passenger seat of her car. She might not have recognized him if she had passed him on the street. Instead of his usual tailored suit and tie, he wore a faded Hawaiian shirt and baggy khaki pants with a rip in the knee. He was unshaven and his hair needed combing. He looked more like a homeless person than a United States senator.

"Don't just stand there. Get in the car," he ordered.

The voice was the same at least, and the imperious tone. She slid back into the driver's seat, but kept her weapon at her side. "Senator, what happened to you?" she asked. "Are you all right?"

"I'm fine," he snapped, and fastened his seat belt.

"Do you need something to eat? Some water? Medical care?" She should have thought to bring him some food. She had a bottle of water and a first-aid kit, but if he needed more...

"I told you, I'm fine."

"The police found your car last night," she said.

"I heard on the news. I was hoping they wouldn't discover it for a while yet—that I'd have more time. Does Andi know?"

"I imagine she does by now." Surely someone would have reached the camp with the news.

"You said she was upset before. I imagine this won't calm her fears any."

"Daniel Metwater told her you were dead. He said he had a dream in which he saw your body covered in blood."

Matheson snorted. "Maybe he really is a prophet, after all." He leaned closer, studying her more intently. "What happened to your face?"

The bruises from her kidnappers' attack had faded to a sickly yellow-purple and most of the swelling had subsided, though she still wouldn't win any beauty contests. "I was attacked while working a case," she said. Not exactly a lie.

"What case? Who hit you?"

She started to tell him that was none of his business, but she wanted to keep him talking. Eventually, she would work the conversation around to where he'd been and what he had been doing. "Two men attacked me outside Frank Asher's hotel room," she said. "They tried to kidnap me, but law enforcement intervened. One of the kidnappers was killed and the other one is in the hospital." Memory of the senator's connection with the event surfaced and it was her turn to scrutinize him. "Oddly enough, they were driving a van that was registered to you," she said. "A vehicle you used in your last campaign."

"None of that was supposed to happen," he said. "They were supposed to grab the laptop and any papers and leave. They weren't supposed to interfere with anyone or anything else."

She blinked, letting his words sink in. "Senator, are you saying those men were working for you? Under your orders?"

"I should have known better than to hire two petty criminals," he said. "I'm sorry you were injured. That should never have happened."

"Why did you hire them to steal Agent Asher's things?" she asked.

"I take protecting my daughter very seriously. I had to insure he didn't have anything incriminating in his possession."

"But, Senator—"

"Start the car." He motioned to the ignition. "We need to get out of here."

She turned the key. "Where are we going?"

"I want to see my daughter. I want you to take me to her."

"Do you want to stop and get something to eat first? Maybe a change of clothes?" Seeing her father like this was going to be a shock for Andi.

"No. I know what I look like. Now get going. We don't have any time to lose."

THE FAINT SCRAPE of a boot on the rocks above alerted Dylan that he wasn't alone. He turned to see Ethan Reynolds making his way toward him. "I came to relieve you," Ethan said. "Anything happening down there?" He jutted his chin toward the camp.

"They're building up the bonfire," Dylan said. "They're into rituals. I think they're getting ready for something like that."

"Cults use ritual to bond the members together," Ethan said. "They can also be useful in reinforcing the leader's message, applying peer pressure, even brainwashing."

"I forgot you were the cult expert."

Ethan settled more comfortably onto the rocks. "I'm not sure this group qualifies as a full-fledged cult. The members seem to have autonomy, and the freedom to come and go."

"Yet none of them are leaving," Dylan said.

"Some of them may have nowhere else to go," Ethan said. "Groups like this tend to attract the disenfranchised."

"Andi Matheson has somewhere else to go, yet she's staying."

"She's found something she's looking for here."

"So what's your opinion of Metwater—twisted murderer or charismatic creep?"

Ethan shrugged. "Maybe neither. Maybe he's a sincere spiritual follower who rubs you the wrong way."

"Is that really what you think?"

"No. I'm voting for charismatic creep. He's slippery and manipulative and I think he's probably hiding something, but I can't see him pulling a trigger and blowing Agent Asher's head off. That's too emotional and visceral for him. He's a plotter, not a hothead."

"What about the money someone sent Asher's widow?"

"Maybe the money came from somewhere else."

"Where?"

"Maybe someone who read about the murder in the paper and felt sorry for the widow and three kids. Someone who wanted to remain anonymous."

"For the sake of our case, I hope it's not something that innocent."

"What about Andi Matheson?" Ethan asked. "Maybe she killed Asher because he left her high and dry with a baby."

"Maybe. But she seems even less likely than Metwater to kill a man in cold blood."

The fire below blazed up and Dylan shifted to look through the binoculars again. "Something happening?" Ethan asked.

A group of people had gathered around the fire, men and women in various stages of undress, their bodies painted, colored ribbons in their hair. As the flames leaped higher, they began to chant, the sound drifting up with the scent of piñon smoke in the clear night air.

"What are they saying?" Dylan asked. "I can't make it out."

"I think it's Latin," Ethan said.

Dylan lowered the binoculars. "You know Latin?"

He grinned. "I was a Catholic altar boy—but I've forgotten pretty much everything." He listened a moment. "I think it's something about sin. And maybe redemption or penance." He nodded. "Definitely penance in there."

Dylan raised the binoculars again. The door to the RV opened and Metwater emerged, dressed in the loincloth again, symbols traced in red and black and white paint on his chest and arms—circles and stars and arrows. They looked, Dylan decided, like a poor attempt at Native American imagery.

"Is that a dagger in that sheath at his waist?" Ethan had pulled out a second pair of binoculars and was focused on the scene below.

"It looks like the one I saw him with before," Dylan said.

"Maybe he's going to finish the ceremony you and Kayla interrupted the other night," Ethan said.

"Maybe." Or was he up to something more sinister?

Metwater clapped his hands over his head and the chanting ended midsyllable. When all eyes were on him he spoke, his voice loud and clear enough that Dylan could make out most of what he was saying. "We are assembled tonight to address the sin in our midst. We must break the chains of iniquity that bind us and purify our souls going forward."

"I'm not liking the sound of this," Dylan muttered. He could still picture the dark-haired girl with the blade to her throat, her eyes wide and terrified. Metwater could talk all he wanted about symbolic sacrifices, but it had all looked pretty real to Dylan.

Metwater motioned two men forward. They carried shovels and at his direction began shoveling coals from the fire and spreading them out in a wide path that led from the fire to Metwater's feet, some three yards away. Someone began drumming, a deep, steady rhythm like a heartbeat. Metwater addressed the crowd again, but the drumming made it impossible for Dylan to make out his words.

"I think he's telling them they're going to walk on the hot coals," Ethan said.

Dylan lowered the glasses once more to stare at him. "Seriously?"

"Fire walking has been practiced for thousands of years as a religious rite and a team-building exercise."

Dylan looked back to the camp. Metwater was motioning to the coals, while two women set basins of water at either end of the glowing path. "Now I know they're crazy," he said.

Ethan moved in beside him. "I've heard of this, but I've never seen it done before," he said. "Supposedly, the risk of injury is fairly minor, because the cool bottom of the foot does a good job of spreading out the heat, and the embers themselves actually don't conduct that much heat."

"That still doesn't make me want to walk barefoot over a bunch of hot coals," Dylan said.

"Who will be the first?" Metwater asked, his voice raised to carry over the drumming.

The silence from the group gathered around the fire was almost eerie.

"Asteria!" Metwater called. "Asteria, you shall be the first, to show us the way."

Andi stumbled forward, as if she had been pushed from behind. Dylan tensed. "What does he think he's doing?" he asked. "She's pregnant."

Smiling, Metwater took Andi's hand and led her to the start of the fiery path, the coals glowing red against the darkness. "Don't do it," Dylan muttered.

Metwater knelt beside Andi and began to tie up her long skirts. She was trembling, the vibrations visible through Dylan's binoculars. He swore and stood. "I'm not going to let this happen," he said, and prepared to climb down the rocks. All he had to do was get within firing range.

With a loud cry, Andi whirled and fled into the darkness, leaving Metwater—and Dylan—staring after her.

Chapter Eighteen

Kayla let out the breath she'd been holding as Andi fled the fire-walking scene. Some of the tension went out of the senator's shoulders, too. "Thank God she hasn't lost all her senses," Matheson said. He turned away. "Come on, let's go find her. Now will be a good chance to talk to her without the others around."

He led the way around the camp. "You act as if you've been here before," Kayla said as she followed him.

"Only once. But I've got a good memory for details. Comes in handy in my job. Now if we keep traveling in this direction, we should be able to come up on the back of the camp. I'm guessing Andi would have fled to her quarters."

He sounded so sane and competent. A businessman with a job to do—such a contrast to his downtrodden appearance. On the drive over he had refused to answer Kayla's questions about what had happened to him and what he had been doing. He wouldn't deny or confirm that he had been kidnapped, and refused to discuss anything about his car or the clothes that had been found in it. "None of that is my concern right now," he said, in answer to all Kayla's queries.

As he had promised, the path they navigated led to the back of the camp. They could still hear chanting and shouts from the bonfire, but the noise was muffled by distance. Kayla wondered if anyone had taken Metwater up on his invitation to walk on hot coals. She noticed the Prophet hadn't volunteered to demonstrate how it was done.

"You'll have to show me which shelter is hers," Matheson said.

"The big tent, next to Metwater's RV." Kayla pointed to it. A lantern hung by the door, and a fainter glow emanated from within.

Matheson paused to draw himself up to his full height. "I'm ready," he said.

Before Kayla had time to react, he left the shadows where they had been hiding and strode the short distance to the tent. He entered without knocking or otherwise announcing himself. Kayla hurried after him and ducked inside in time to see Andi turn toward them, one hand to her throat. The young woman stared, mouth open, face ghostly pale.

Kayla hurried forward, afraid Andi would faint. "It's okay," she said, helping her to a low stool. "Your father wanted to see you."

"Daniel told me you were dead," Andi said, her gaze fixed on her father.

"Daniel was wrong." Matheson pulled another stool alongside his daughter. "I had to make sure you were okay," he said.

"I'm okay." She clutched his hands. "Better now that you're here. What happened, Daddy? I don't understand. Daniel said you were dead, and then we heard the police found your car, with bloody clothes inside."

"I had to go away for a while. And I will have to go away again soon." Matheson smoothed the hair back from her face. "I'm sorry I hurt you. The last thing I wanted to do was hurt you."

"You didn't hurt me," she said. "I'm okay, really."

"Frank Asher hurt you." Matheson grimaced. "I'm sorry I ever hired the man."

"Frank's gone now, Daddy. He's dead." Andi's lip trembled, but she regained her composure. "It doesn't matter. All that matters is that you're okay. I'm sorry. I'm sorry for all those terrible things I said to you. I just...I needed to live life my way, not your way."

"I know, honey, but you need to leave this place." He patted her hand. "That man—Daniel Metwater— he isn't good for you. What kind of man expects a pregnant woman to walk over hot coals? What is he trying to prove?"

"He wanted to free me from myself," Andi said. "He told me walking over the coals would burn away all my guilt and pain. But I wasn't brave enough. I didn't have enough faith."

It's not about faith, Kayla wanted to say. *It's about control.* But she bit back the words, not wanting to interrupt this moment between father and daughter.

"Come back home, Andi," Matheson said. "You'll be safe there. You can have your baby there and you'll never lack for anything. I have plenty of money put aside to make sure of that."

"My baby." She cradled her belly and her voice took on a crooning quality. "Poor baby. Her daddy's dead."

"Frank can't hurt you anymore," Matheson said. "I made sure of that."

Kayla started and moved closer. Andi stared at her father. "What do you mean?" she asked. "Someone killed Frank."

"I killed him," the senator said. "He told me he was coming here to see you again, to ask you not to make trouble for him over the baby. He wanted you to pretend he wasn't the father. He thought the affair would be bad for his career."

"You killed Frank?" Andi asked.

"I only intended to warn him off—to tell him to leave you alone. But he wouldn't listen. He was determined to see you. He'd already hurt you so much. I couldn't stand the thought of him hurting you again. I only meant to threaten him with the gun, but he wouldn't back down. I had to show him that I wouldn't back down, either. I had to protect you."

Kayla gasped. She hadn't even realized she'd made the noise until Matheson turned on her. "You weren't supposed to hear that," he said. "I was having a private conversation with my daughter."

"We all heard you, Senator." The tent flap lifted and Dylan stepped inside, followed by Ethan Reynolds. "Put your hands up and stand slowly," Dylan said. "Peter Matheson, I'm arresting you for the murder of Frank Asher."

"No." Matheson stood and backed up, until he bumped into Kayla. She was groping for her weapon when he grabbed her, his grip surprisingly strong. He wrenched the gun from her grasp and held it to her throat. "Don't come any closer or I'll kill her," he said. "You know I'll do it. I don't have anything to lose."

THE SIGHT OF that gun at Kayla's throat turned Dylan's blood to ice. He met her gaze, and the courage he saw behind her fear strengthened him. He holstered his weapon and took a step back, his hands out at his sides. "Take it easy," he told Matheson. "No one wants any trouble."

Ethan already had Andi and was ushering her out of the tent. Dylan trusted he would go for backup. Meanwhile, he had to find a way to deal with Matheson and save Kayla.

"You need to leave, too," Matheson said, one arm across Kayla's chest, the barrel of the gun pressed to her throat. "We're going to go away and you'll never see me again."

"You can go," Dylan said. "But leave Kayla behind. She hasn't done anything to hurt you."

"I'll let her go when I'm safely away from here."

"Where are you going to go?" Dylan asked. "You know if you leave, every cop in the country will be looking for you. If you give yourself up now, the courts will go easy on you. Any jury would understand a father wanting to protect his daughter."

"That's right. All I wanted to do was protect her. Asher laughed at me when I told him he didn't deserve her. Laughed!"

"He *didn't* deserve her," Dylan agreed. "And Kayla doesn't deserve to be involved in this. Let her go, Senator."

"I'm not a bad person," Matheson said. "I sent money to Asher's wife and kids, to try to make up for their loss. They're better off without him, too, I think."

"We know you're not a bad person," Dylan said. "Prove it by letting Kayla go."

"I won't hurt her," Matheson said. "I don't want to hurt anyone."

"I know you don't. Let her go."

Matheson no longer looked like the confident, determined man who had walked into the camp. He looked old and confused. Lost. "Where is Andi?" he asked. "Where's my girl?"

"She's safe, Senator," Dylan said. "But she's worried about you. She needs to know that you're safe, too. Haven't you put her through enough?"

"I only wanted to protect her." The barrel of the gun slid down, no longer pointed at Kayla's throat, though a shot at that close range would still be lethal. Kayla stiffened, and Dylan read the determination in her eyes.

Matheson seemed to gather himself also. "I'm leaving now," he said, some of the fog cleared from his expression. He took a step forward, tugging Kayla after him.

Kayla lunged forward, throwing all her weight into Matheson's back. He lost his balance and stumbled, and the gun went off, the bullet burying itself in the rug at his feet. Dylan pulled Kayla clear and shoved her behind him, then trained his gun on the senator, who lay sprawled on the floor. "Put your hands behind your head and don't move," Dylan ordered.

Matheson groaned, but did as commanded, and Ethan stepped in to cuff him. Once he was secure, Dylan holstered his weapon and turned to Kayla. "Are you all right?" he asked.

"I'm fine." She was pale and her voice shook, but her eyes were clear and steady. "You showed up just in time."

He pulled her close and cradled her face against his chest, shaky with relief now that the danger was past. "We were doing surveillance on the camp and saw you arrive with Matheson," he said.

"Did you know he had killed Agent Asher?"

"No. But I imagine the lab reports on Matheson's clothes will show the blood is Frank Asher's," Dylan said. "He must have sunk the car himself to hide that evidence."

"When I picked him up this evening he told me he had hoped it would take police longer to find the car— that he'd have more time. Time for what?"

"To figure out how to get out of the country? To prepare to turn himself in?" Dylan shook his head. "Who knows?"

Kayla turned to watch Ethan lead Matheson away. "I feel sorry for him," she said. "I think he blamed Asher for his own estrangement from Andi."

"Killing the man didn't solve anything."

"I know, but love can make people do the wrong thing for the right reasons."

Dylan pulled her more tightly against him. "I think my heart stopped for a second when I saw you with that gun to your throat," he said. "All I could think of was that if I couldn't stop him from hurting you, I wouldn't be able to live with myself."

She looked up at him. "I don't need a man to rescue me. Just one to be there alongside me."

"I'm starting to figure that out."

"Then you're starting to understand me," she said.

"I don't have to understand you," he said. "I just want to be with you."

"That's a good place to start." She slid one hand

to the back of his head and pulled his mouth down to hers. The kiss, more than her words, told him everything was going to be all right between them. They'd found Frank Asher's killer. Kayla was safe. And they would figure out a way to meld her need for independence with his need to protect. Life wasn't a fairy tale, but he still believed in happy endings.

Epilogue

"Do I look all right?" Kayla tugged at the skirt of the dress she had chosen for the awards banquet and frowned at her reflection in the mirror. "I hate this stuff. You know that, don't you?"

Madeline Zimeski, president of the Colorado Private Investigators Society, patted Kayla's back. "You look lovely, dear. I'm only sorry your family couldn't be here to see you receive your award."

"They live out of state," Kayla said. It was easier than explaining the truth—that she didn't have any family who cared enough about her to walk across the street, much less attend an awards banquet.

Madeline checked her cell phone. "It's almost time for the awards," she said. "We'd better get back." Kayla had been hiding in the ladies' room when Madeline had come in search of her. Clearly, the president wasn't going to let even one honoree escape her moment in the spotlight.

Reluctantly, Kayla followed her back to the front table where she had been seated, her back to most of the crowd. She'd managed to choke down a few bites of dinner and make polite small talk with the board members and other honorees at her table, and was counting the minutes until she'd be free to leave.

Madeline strode to the podium and made a show of adjusting the microphone. "Now is the point in the program I know we've all been waiting for," she said. "Our annual awards. Each year we honor those of our members we feel are the finest representatives of our craft." She droned on about the voting process, the history of the organization and some other things Kayla couldn't focus on. She squirmed in her chair and wished she had opted for a drink from the bar.

"And first up, our senior private detective of the year, Malcolm Stack."

A tall man with a shock of white hair walked to the podium to accept the plaque Madeline handed him. Kayla stared at her water glass, mentally rehearsing the brief thank-you she planned to deliver.

"And for our Western Slope PI of the year, Kayla Larimer."

She had expected Madeline to draw out the ceremony more, so the announcement of her name caught her off guard. Awkwardly, she shoved back her chair and stood as a smattering of applause rose around her. As she started toward the podium a chorus of shouts and whistles echoed from the back of the room. Startled, she whirled to see Dylan standing at a table near the back. Beside him, his mother and father stood also, both clapping wildly.

"Kayla?" Madeline prompted from the podium.

Flustered, Kayla made her way to the stage. Madeline shoved the plaque into her hand, and a flash almost blinded her. "Say something," Madeline hissed, and nudged her toward the microphone.

"Umm…" Kayla stared at the plaque. Nervous laughter rose from a few people near the front. She cleared her throat and fought for composure. "Thank you for this honor," she said. She looked out across the room and caught Dylan's eyes. He was grinning like a fool, and gave her a thumbs-up. She couldn't help but smile. "And thank you to all the people who have helped me along the way. And to those who continue to support me now."

She managed to make it down the steps from the dais without tripping, but instead of returning to her chair, she walked the length of the room to join Dylan and his parents.

"Congratulations," Bud Holt said, and pumped her hand.

"We're so proud of you," Nancy added, and patted her arm.

Kayla looked at Dylan. "What are you doing here?" she asked. "Aren't you supposed to be at a funeral?"

"You didn't think I was going to pass up the chance to see you honored like this, did you?" He hugged her to him.

"I guess you don't really need to go to Frank Asher's funeral now that the case is closed," she said.

"Even if it was still open, I wouldn't miss your big night," he said.

She held out the plaque and read the text, which proclaimed her as the Western Slope Private Investigator of the Year. "It's not such a big deal."

"It is to me." He kissed the top of her head. "I'm proud of you," he said. "You deserve this."

She turned to his parents. "I can't believe you came," she said. "Thank you so much."

"You're special to Dylan, so you're special to us, too," Nancy said. "Congratulations." She nudged her husband. "Now, I think we should leave these two alone."

They left and Dylan led Kayla into the hallway. "Senator Matheson agreed to a plea deal today," he said.

"I guess that's for the best," she said. "How much time will he serve?"

"He pleaded involuntary manslaughter. He could be out as soon as eighteen months."

"What about Andi?"

"She wants to stay with Metwater and his bunch. She says she feels at home there."

"I guess Daniel Metwater was innocent, after all."

"Of murder. I still think he's up to something." Dylan pushed open the door to the parking lot. "We'll be keeping a close eye on him, as long as he's in our jurisdiction."

"I plan to stay in touch with Andi, too," Kayla said. "It's funny, when you think about it, how the two of us hit it off."

"Not so strange, really. You both are independent women and felt you didn't fit in with your family's lifestyle."

"I guess that's one way to look at it."

"Were you surprised to see us tonight?" he asked.

"I can't think of when I've been more surprised." She stopped at the edge of the covered walkway that led up to the building and turned to him. "Am I really special to you?"

"You didn't know that already?"

She pressed her palm against his chest. "I guess I did, but I wanted to be sure."

"I love you," he said. "Did you know that?"

"I love you, too. And it scares me. I've never allowed myself to love this much before."

"Don't be afraid." He pulled her to him. "You can count on me, Kayla Larimer. I'm promising here and now that I'm always going to protect you and care for you and do my best for you."

"You know the best thing about all of that?" she asked.

"What?"

"I believe you. And I'm going to do the same for you, Dylan Holt."

"That's what matters most, isn't it?" he said. "Knowing we can count on each other."

"Mmm." She pulled his face down to hers. "Less talking, more kissing."

"Yes, ma—mmm."

* * * * *

HER COLTON P.I.

AMELIA AUTIN

For my stepmother, Mary Dorothy Callen Autin, who makes the world a special place for everyone who knows her. For my stepsister, Patti Padgett Mouton Fagan, who made my father immensely proud of the woman she became.
And for Vincent…always.

Chapter 1

She's not going to get away with it. That was all Chris Colton could think as he listened to the tearful story Angus and Evalinda McCay unfolded before him. Holly McCay wasn't going to get away with keeping her in-laws from their beloved twin grandsons, all they had left of their son after he died.

Chris leaned back in his chair in his northwest Fort Worth, Texas, office and glanced at the pictures the McCays had handed him. One was of blond-haired, brown-eyed Holly McCay and her now-deceased husband, Grant. The other was of the McCay twins, Ian and Jamie.

"But they don't look like that anymore," Evalinda McCay said sadly. "Our grandsons weren't even a year old when that picture was taken, and that was more than six months ago. Holly won't even let us see them.

She's been like that ever since Grant…" She dabbed a tissue at her eyes.

"Don't worry, Mrs. McCay," Chris said, steel in his voice. "I'll take this job myself—I won't hand it off to an associate. I'll find your grandsons for you. And your daughter-in-law, too."

Angus McCay cleared his throat. "I don't like to speak ill of my son, Mr. Colton, because he's gone and can't defend himself. But he was blind to what his wife was really like. She trapped him into marriage—"

"They hadn't even been married seven months when Ian and Jamie were born," Evalinda McCay clarified in a shocked tone.

"Grant's will made her the trustee for their boys," Angus McCay continued, as if he hadn't been interrupted. "And…well…"

"The money is all she cares about," his wife threw in. She put her hand on her husband's arm. "I know you don't like to put it so bluntly, Angus, but you know it's true." Her gaze moved to Chris. "Holly took the boys and left town three weeks before Christmas. Right before *Christmas*…" She choked up for a moment before continuing. "Grant's fortune is tied up in a trust for Ian and Jamie, but Holly is the sole trustee. Which means she can spend the money any way she sees fit, without any real oversight."

Angus McCay added, "And since she won't tell us where she is…won't even let us *see* them…" He sighed heavily. "We don't even know if they're alive, much less healthy and happy."

"We tried to get custody of the boys through the courts right after Grant died," Evalinda McCay said, her wrinkled face lined with worry. "But grandparents don't seem to have any legal rights these days. Our lawyer said he's not optimistic—not even to force Holly to let us have some kind of visitation with Ian and Jamie."

"The police won't help us, because Holly hasn't done anything wrong," Angus McCay said gruffly.

"Except break our hearts, and Ian's and Jamie's, too, for that matter—but there's no law against that," Evalinda McCay put in.

"You don't have to say any more." Determination grew in Chris. If it was the last thing he did, he'd find Holly McCay and her eighteen-month-old sons for Mr. and Mrs. McCay. Not just because no one had the right to deprive good and decent grandparents like the McCays access to their grandchildren. But because the children deserved to know their grandparents. That was the real bottom line.

Not to mention it made him sick to think of Holly McCay isolating her children from their relatives for money. His foster parents hadn't abused him, but he'd known ever since he was placed with them when he was eleven that they were in it only for the money the state gave them.

"We tracked Holly here to Fort Worth, but then the trail went cold. That's why we decided to hire you, Mr. Colton," Angus McCay said now. "You know this part of the state—we don't." He glanced at his wife, who cleared her throat as if to remind him of something. "And there's another thing. It's all over the news here in Fort Worth about the Alphabet Killer in Granite Gulch."

Chris stiffened, wondering if the McCays knew about his family's connection to the serial killer. But Angus McCay continued without a pause and Chris relaxed. "We know Granite Gulch is forty miles away, and we know all the targets so far are women with long dark hair. But who knows? That could change at any time. And Holly...well...despite everything, she *is* our daughter-in-law. If anything happened to her..."

He trailed off and his wife picked up the thread of the story. "We heard on the news the last victim was Gwendolyn Johnson, which means the killer is up to the *H*s now. And Holly's name begins with *H*. No matter what she's done to *us*, Mr. Colton, she's Ian and Jamie's mother. They've already lost their father before they ever had a chance to know him. I shudder to think of those two innocent babies orphaned at such a young age." She turned to her husband and nodded for him to continue.

"We don't know what it will cost," Angus McCay said, "but we have some money saved. Whatever your fees are, we'll double them if you make this job your top priority. And we'll give you a bonus if you find Holly within a month. We *have* to find her, Mr. Colton. And the boys," he added hastily.

"That won't be necessary," Chris said, thinking to himself that Holly McCay didn't deserve in-laws as caring as the McCays obviously were. "I won't even take a fee for this one—just cover the expenses and we'll be square. But I'll find your daughter-in-law and your grandsons for you, Mr. and Mrs. McCay. You can take that to the bank."

Evalinda McCay unbent enough to smile at Chris with approval. "You're a good man, Mr. Colton. I knew we were doing the right thing contacting you." Her smile faded. "When you find Holly, please don't tell her anything. She might take the boys and disappear. Again.

No, I think it's better if you just let us know where she is and we'll take it from there. If we can just see her... talk to her...if she can see us with our grandsons...she can't be that hard-hearted to keep us away when she knows how much Grant's boys mean to us."

Chris nodded. "Yes, ma'am." He wasn't convinced Mrs. McCay was right, but he wasn't going to say so. If Holly McCay had fled right before Christmas, taking her twins—and their money—with her, she definitely *could* be hard-hearted enough to prevent the McCays from being a part of her sons' lives. *It's all about the money for her*, he thought cynically. *Just like my foster parents. It's all about the money.*

Holly McCay pulled up in front of her friend Peg Merrill's house, parked and turned off the engine. But she didn't get out right away. She adjusted the rearview mirror of her small Ford SUV with one hand and tugged her dark-haired pixie-cut wig more securely into place with the other. She hated the wig, even though she'd repeatedly told herself it was a necessity. It was already too warm for comfort, and it was only the first day of May. What would she do when the north Texas heat and humidity blasted her in July?

Ian and Jamie hated the wig, too, because it confused them. Just like the other disguises she'd donned had confused them before they came to Rosewood. Her eighteen-month-old twin toddlers were too young to put their emotions into words, but Ian had started acting out recently, refusing to put away his toys or eat the food on his plate without coaxing. Even his favorite mashed potatoes—which he called "smashed 'tatoes"—didn't seem to tempt him.

And Jamie had begun clinging in a way he never had before. Almost as if he was afraid his mother would disappear from his life. He didn't even want her to leave him with Ian to play with Peg Merrill's kids while she went grocery shopping in nearby Granite Gulch—and Jamie loved playing with Peg's children. Until a month ago he'd never been the clinging type.

Holly sighed softly. *If only*, she told herself for the umpteenth time. If only Grant hadn't died. If only he hadn't left *all* his money to their twin boys in an unbreakable trust, but instead had made provision for his parents. If only Grant's parents weren't so…so mercenary.

Not just mercenary, Holly reminded herself, shivering a little even though it was a warm spring day. *Deadly.*

She gave herself a little shake. "Don't think about that now," she muttered under her breath, doing her best Scarlett O'Hara imitation. She pasted a smile on her face and glanced at the mirror again to reassure herself she presented a normal appearance. Ian and Jamie didn't need a mother who was always looking over one shoulder. Who was paranoid that somehow the McCays had tracked her down to— *Stop that!* she insisted. *You're not going to worry about that itch between your shoulder blades… Not today.*

She was going to have to worry about it soon, though. And make some hard choices. If she packed up Ian and Jamie and everything they owned—which wasn't all that much, just what would fit into her small SUV—and moved away from their temporary home in Rosewood, she'd be on her own again. No Peg to help her by watching the twins while she ran errands, like grocery shopping or driving the forty miles into Fort Worth—or the seventy-plus miles into Dallas—to withdraw cash from one of the branch banks there.

But it wasn't just Peg's help with Ian and Jamie she'd miss. Peg was like the older sister Holly had always dreamed of, and she would miss that…a lot. Besides, what would she tell Peg? She couldn't just disappear without a word, could she? Peg would worry, and it wouldn't be right to do that to her friend. Especially since the Alphabet Killer had everyone in Granite Gulch and the surrounding towns terrified.

Holly sighed deeply, gave one last tug to her wig, then scooped up her purse and headed for Peg's house.

Down the street, Chris sat slumped in the seat of his white Ford F-150 pickup truck, parked two houses away beneath the shade of a flowering catalpa tree. He watched Holly McCay walk up the driveway, skirt Peg's SUV parked there and make for the front door. The male in him noted her slender but shapely figure in jeans that lovingly hugged her curves, and her graceful, swaying walk. The PI in him ignored both—or tried to.

He shook his head softly, forcing himself to think of something other than the way Holly McCay looked. *It's a good thing she isn't a professional criminal*, he thought instead, *because she's lousy at it.*

Oh, she'd done her best to avoid detection, he'd give her that. The short dark-haired wig she was wearing was an effective disguise of sorts. And she'd paid cash for everything—there'd been no paper trail of credit or debit purchases to follow. No checks written, either. But she'd transferred a large sum of money from her bank in Clear Lake City south of Houston to the Cattleman's Bank of Fort Worth, where she'd opened a new account when she moved to the Dallas–Fort Worth area. *That* had left a paper trail she hadn't been able to avoid, since she'd used her own driver's license and social security number. That was how the McCays had tracked her this far.

True, she'd varied the bank branches she'd used to withdraw funds, so no one could stake out one branch and wait for her to show up. That showed she was smart. But she'd slipped up by withdrawing cash from the Granite Gulch branch. Yeah, she'd done it only once, but it stood out in neon letters, since it was out of the pattern—all the other branches had been in Fort Worth or Dallas. And once Chris had known that, he'd searched Granite Gulch and the surrounding area for a woman with twin toddlers who'd recently moved in. No matter what color her hair was, no matter how much she tried to fade into obscurity, everyone remembered the twins. Especially eighteen-month-old identical twin boys as cute as buttons.

And Holly McCay was still driving her Ford Escape with its original Texas license plate tags registered in her name. *Duh!* Once he'd located a woman with twins in Rosewood, the next town over from Granite Gulch, he'd staked out the Rosewood Rooming House, where by all accounts she lived, and bingo! There was her Ford SUV with those incriminating tags.

She was registered at the rooming house using her real name, too, which had made confirmation a piece of cake. He'd almost picked up the phone to call the McCays and tell them he'd located their daughter-in-law…but he hadn't. He wasn't sure why. Was it because a warning light had started blinking that very first day when they turned over everything they knew about Holly's banking transactions? Information they shouldn't have had access to...but somehow had?

Or maybe it was the self-satisfied expression on Evalinda McCay's face when she thought Chris wouldn't see it, when he'd been perusing the financial reports they'd handed him and he'd glanced up unexpectedly. The expression had been wiped away almost instantly, replaced with the look of worried concern she'd worn earlier. But Chris's instincts—which he trusted—had gone on the alert.

He'd been a private investigator for nine years, ever since he'd received his bachelor of arts degree in criminology and criminal justice from the University of Texas at Arlington. From day one he'd trusted his instincts, and they'd never steered him wrong. Only an idiot would go against his instincts in his line of work, and for all his laid-back, seemingly good-old-Texas-boy persona, Chris wasn't an idiot.

He'd also run a credit check on the McCays the same day they'd come to see him—standard procedure for all his clients these days. He never took anyone's word they had the wherewithal to pay him—he'd been burned once early in his career and had learned a hard lesson. The credit report on the McCays had come back with some troubling red flags. They were living beyond their means. Way beyond their means, and had done so for years, despite Angus McCay's well-paying job as a bank president down in Houston. Even though Chris was taking this case pro bono and wouldn't be paid except for expenses, that credit report had given him pause.

Now he was glad he hadn't called the McCays for several reasons, not the least of which was that he knew

Peg Merrill, had known her all his life. If she and Holly were friends, then Holly *couldn't* be the woman the Mc-Cays had made her out to be. Peg had an unerring BS meter—she'd nailed Chris on a few things over the years—which meant Holly couldn't have fooled Peg about the kind of woman she was. To top it off, Peg reigned supreme in one area in particular—motherhood. The worst insult in her book was to call someone a bad mother. No way would she be friends with a woman who was a bad mother.

Besides, Peg was his sister-in-law. Former sister-in-law, really, since Laura was dead. But he wasn't going there. Not now. Sister-in-law or not, Chris didn't want to be on Peg's bad side. Especially not on a pro bono case he'd already been having second thoughts about.

Chris waited until Holly McCay strapped her twins into their car seats and drove away before he got out of his truck. He shrugged on his blazer to hide his shoulder holster, then settled his black Stetson on his head and ambled toward Peg's house, determined to find out whatever he could about Holly McCay from Peg.

"Chris!" Peg exclaimed when she opened the door. "This is a surprise. Come on in."

"Unca Chris!" Peg's two-year-old daughter, Susan, made a beeline for Chris when he stepped inside, and he bent over to swing her up into his arms. A cacophony of barking from three dogs—one of which had been Chris's gift to Laura not long before she died—prevented anyone from being heard for a couple of minutes, but eventually Peg's two dogs subsided back to their rug in front of the fireplace in the family room.

Chris settled into one of the oversize recliners, still

cuddling Susan against his shoulder while his other hand ruffled Wally's fur. "Hey, boy," he murmured, gazing down at the golden retriever Laura had adored. If his heart hadn't already been broken when Laura died, it would have broken at losing Wally, too. Chris had given Laura the puppy thinking they'd soon be moving from their apartment into a house with a large fenced yard. But that dream house sat vacant now— Chris couldn't bear to live there without Laura. And an apartment was no place for a growing dog, especially since Chris was rarely home. So when Peg and her husband, Joe, volunteered to adopt Wally, Chris had reluctantly accepted their offer. At least he'd still get to see Wally, he'd reasoned at the time—he was always welcome at the Merrill house.

Chris and Peg chatted about nothing much for a few minutes. About Bobby, Peg's napping one-year-old son, who was already starting to walk. About Joe's thriving gardening center in Granite Gulch, the Green and Grow. About Chris's highly successful private investigation business—which he'd thrown himself into even more thoroughly after Laura's death—and the fourth office he'd nearly decided to add in Arlington.

When Susan's eyelids began fluttering, Peg reached to take her daughter from Chris, but he forestalled her. "I'll put her down for her nap," he told Peg, doing just that. When he came back, Peg handed him a frosty glass of iced tea prepared the way he preferred it, with two lemon wedges, not just one.

They'd just settled back into their spots in the family room, Wally at Chris's feet, when Peg put her own glass of iced tea down on a coaster on the end table and said, "So what's wrong?" She didn't give Chris a chance to answer before she continued, "I didn't want to say anything in front of Susan—you would *not* believe how much she understands already. I told Joe he needed to watch his language now that Susan is so aware—and she mimics everything he says... *especially* the bad words." Chris laughed, and Peg said, "But something's up. You wouldn't be here in the middle of the week, in the middle of the afternoon, if something wasn't wrong."

Chris shook his head and smiled wryly. "You must have second sight or something." He hesitated, considering and then discarding his original idea of pumping Peg for info about Holly McCay on the sly. "The woman who was here a little while ago—"

"Holly?" Peg's surprise was obvious.

"Yeah. Holly McCay. I've been hired by her in-laws to find her."

Chapter 2

Two days later Holly drove away from Peg's house with her vision blurred from unshed tears. She'd left the twins in her friend's care one last time, but that wasn't why she was practically crying. She hadn't told Peg—she'd chickened out at the last minute—but she wasn't going to do errands. She'd wanted Ian and Jamie to have one last opportunity to play with Susan and Bobby...while she packed up the contents of their room in the Rosewood Rooming House and loaded everything into her SUV. Then she would pick up her boys, hand Peg the note she was trying to compose in her mind so Peg wouldn't worry about them...and they'd be gone.

Chris followed Holly away from Peg's house, keeping enough distance between his truck and her little

SUV so she wouldn't spot the tail. He was surprised when she didn't stop at any of the stores in Granite Gulch but kept driving. She kept driving even after she reached the state highway that was the boundary between Granite Gulch and Rosewood. Puzzled but not really worried, Chris let the distance between their two vehicles increase, because there weren't any cars out this way to hide the fact that he was following her.

When Holly pulled into the Rosewood Rooming House parking lot, Chris was faced with a dilemma. He drove past, then doubled back as soon as he could, just in time to see Holly entering the rooming house's front door.

"What the hell is she doing?" he muttered to himself, wondering if she'd forgotten something and would be back outside soon. He made a U-turn a hundred yards down, parked close enough so he could watch the front door and Holly's SUV, but far enough away from the rooming house so he wouldn't be spotted, and waited. And waited.

A fleeting thought crossed his mind that the Rosewood Rooming House wasn't really the safest place for a woman on her own with two young children. Not only was the rooming house full of transients, but Regina Willard—whom law enforcement had pretty much identified as the Alphabet Killer—was known to have roomed here not that long ago. *Not* his baby sister, Josie, thank God. The Alphabet Killer hadn't been caught yet, but at least now everyone in town knew it wasn't Josie.

Thoughts of Josie reminded Chris that she was still missing, even after all these years he'd been searching for her. His two most spectacular failures as a PI both had their roots in his family history—Josie…and his mother's burial place. He touched his heart in an automatic gesture. The pain he felt over those failures ranked right up there with Laura's death and his guilt over that.

If his serial-killer father could be believed, however, his mother's burial place might at last be discovered, something all the Colton children devoutly wished for. When their father had killed their mother, he'd hidden her body. She'd never been found, not in twenty years. But Matthew Colton had provided four clues to where Saralee Colton's body was buried. Not that the clues made any real sense…so far. But they were clues. He'd promised one clue for every child who visited him in prison. Annabel had been the last to visit their father, and her clue—Peaches—had been just as enigmatic as the first three: Texas, Hill and *B*. The siblings had theorized that maybe—*maybe*—the clues were pointing to their maternal grandparents' home in Bearson, Texas. But that house sat on acres of land. Even if their mother was buried somewhere on her parents' property, they weren't really much better off than they'd been when they started this sorry mess.

Chris sighed. This month was his turn to visit their father in prison. He didn't know why Matthew was putting his children through this torture—other than the fact that he could because they were all desperate to locate their mother's body and give her a decent burial—but it almost seemed as if their father was getting a perverse pleasure out of it. "The serial killer's last revenge," he murmured. Matthew Colton was dying. Everyone knew it, especially Matthew himself. "It would be just like that bastard to torture us with these disparate clues…then die. Taking his secret to the grave." He relieved his anger and frustration with a few choice curse words...until he remembered he was supposed to be giving them up. He'd resolved two days earlier that he was going to clean up his language for Susan Merrill's sake, and Bobby's, just as Joe Merrill was supposed to do.

"Heck and damnation," Chris said now. It didn't have the same impact.

Regina Willard groaned as she rolled out of her uncomfortable sleeping bag and staggered outside to relieve herself. She hated this hideout, hated being forced by the Granite Gulch Police Department and the FBI to hurriedly leave the Rosewood Rooming House. Her place there hadn't been luxurious by any means, but at least she'd had a comfortable bed and civilized facilities at her disposal. Not this hole-in-the-ground living quarters without any running water.

She thought fleetingly of her half brother, Jesse Willard, and his thriving farm. The last time she'd talked to him, years ago, he'd tried to encourage her to move on. To stop grieving for her lost fiancé. Jesse didn't understand. That bitch had stolen the only man Regina could ever love, and she'd had to pay. No matter how the woman disguised herself, no matter how many times she changed her name, Regina recognized her... and made her pay.

Regina shook her head. She kept killing that woman, but the bitch refused to stay dead. So Regina had to keep killing her again and again. If she killed her enough times, eventually she would *stay* dead. Then she could relax, move away from this area and try to forget.

She blinked, then rubbed her eyes, trying to focus. How many times had it been altogether? She ticked them off on her fingers. "Seven," she said at last. She chuckled to herself. Yes, she'd been forced into hiding out in this shelter in the middle of nowhere, but not even the vaunted FBI had been able to stop her. She was on a mission, and no one would stop her until the bitch was dead. Permanently.

Holly packed swiftly. While her hands were performing that mindless task, she tried to make plans. *Where to go?* she thought. *New Mexico? Arizona?* Or should she just keep driving until she'd put thousands of miles between herself and the McCays? She'd never lived in the United States outside Texas, and a little niggling fear of the unknown made her heart skip a beat as she envisioned going to a completely strange place. Not just the difference between Houston and Fort Worth, but *completely* different. Yes, she'd visited South America as a young child with her missionary parents, but that was a long time ago—Texas had been her home ever since she'd started school.

Leaving again hadn't been an easy decision for Holly to make—she didn't want to leave. Not just for her own sake but for her boys, too, who had reached the age where they noticed changes in their lives. But the time had come to move on.

She wasn't really concerned about the Alphabet Killer, despite the fact that the killer was up to the *H*s now. All seven of the killer's victims had long dark hair, and while Holly's wig was dark, it was very short. Not that she was careless of her safety—she wasn't going to risk being the exception to the killer's rule.

But she wasn't running from the Alphabet Killer. She was running from the McCays. The McCays…and their attempts on her life.

She hadn't wanted to admit it at first. But when one near miss had led to a second, then a third, she'd been forced to look at the McCays with suspicious eyes. *Someone* wanted her dead. Who else could it be? She didn't have an enemy in the world. But she *was* the trustee for the twins' inheritance from Grant. Which meant she controlled the income earned on nearly twenty million dollars. Over and above the cash invested conservatively, the trust also owned stock in Grant's software company—now being run by others, but still doing well. So the trust had unlimited growth potential.

She'd always known Grant's parents—especially his mother—were cold and calculating. Grant had known it, too, although they'd never really discussed it—not when they were kids, and not after they were married. It was one of those things they'd just taken for granted. Was that why he hadn't left them anything in his will? Because he knew they were more interested in the fortune he'd earned from his breakthrough software design than they were in him or their grandsons?

She had no proof the McCays were trying to kill her, though. Nothing to take to the police except a growing certainty it couldn't be anyone else. Especially after the McCays tried to gain custody of the twins through the courts and had lied about Holly in their depositions—warning bells had gone off loud and clear. But even if she'd gone to the police, what would they have said? Those near misses could have been a coincidence. Accidents. The McCays were solid, middle-class, upstanding, churchgoing citizens. The salt of the earth. Or at least that was the image they projected. How could she even think of making a slanderous accusation against them...especially for such a heinous crime as attempted murder?

Which was why she'd packed up the bare necessities three weeks before Christmas, buckled her sons into their baby car seats and headed north toward the Dallas–Fort Worth metroplex with fierce determination. She hadn't really had a plan—plans could wait, she'd told herself—but she knew she had to put herself out of reach of her in-laws until she had time to think things through. She'd thought she could lose herself in Texas's second-largest metropolitan area.

But she wasn't a criminal on the lam, and she had no idea how to go about getting a fake ID. Not to mention she couldn't carry huge wads of cash with her in lieu of using her credit and debit cards. She had to withdraw money from the bank periodically—a bank account she'd opened with her real social security number and driver's license.

She'd moved a week after she'd opened the new bank account—as she'd moved every time she got the feeling the McCays were getting close. But she hadn't switched banks. She'd picked the Cattleman's Bank of Fort Worth precisely because it had hundreds of branches throughout the DFW area, including small branches in grocery stores. And Holly had used many of them to throw the McCays off the scent...assuming they were still trying to track her down. But she had to assume that. She didn't dare assume otherwise.

Which meant her time in tiny Rosewood, right next door to Granite Gulch, where Peg lived, had finally come to an end. Rosewood was so small she'd thought the McCays would never find her in this out-of-the-way place, since she was still paying cash for everything and varying which bank branches she was using to withdraw that cash.

She loved the small-town atmosphere here, and after she'd made friends with Peg at the Laundromat—*thank God Peg's washing machine broke down that day!*—she'd started to feel at home. So she'd convinced herself she was safe. But for the past three days she'd had... well...*the willies*, she told herself, for lack of a better term. A feeling she was being watched. Followed.

It *could* be the Alphabet Killer, she supposed. But she didn't think so. Either way was a disaster in the making, and she wasn't going to stick around to find out for sure one way or the other.

Holly stashed two suitcases into the rear of her SUV, then headed back to the rooming house for another load.

She held the door to her room open with one foot as she picked up a box of toys and books, then tried to scream and dropped the box when a tall blond man in a black Stetson loomed in the doorway.

A large hand covered her mouth, stifling her voice, and all Holly could think of in that instant was *No!* No, she wasn't going to be a victim. She wasn't going to let herself be raped or murdered or—

She tore at the hand covering her mouth, but the man plastered her against the wall inside her room and kicked the door shut behind him. Then just held her prisoner with his body as she desperately tried to free herself. She gave up trying to fight the hand that muzzled her and went for his eyes instead. But he ducked his head, placing his mouth against her ear as he said in a deep undertone, "Stop it, Holly! I'm not going to hurt you—I'm trying to save your life. Peg Merrill's my sister-in-law."

She froze. Her heart was still beating like a snare drum, but she stopped fighting at Peg's name. And when she did that, she realized the stranger wasn't using her immobility to his advantage. She tried to ask a question, but the hand over her mouth prevented her.

"If I take my hand away, are you going to scream?" he asked, still in that same deep undertone. Holly shook her head slightly and was surprised, yet not surprised, when he did just that—he removed his hand. But it hovered near her face, as if he'd clamp it back in place if she screamed.

She swallowed against the dry throat, which terror had induced, then whispered, "Who are you?"

"Chris Colton. And yes," he answered before she could ask, "Peg's really my sister-in-law."

"I don't understand. Why are you here? Why did you force your way into my room?"

An enigmatic expression crossed his face, and he looked as if he was of two minds about answering those questions. "If I let you go, are you going to run for it? Or are you going to give me a chance to explain?"

A tiny dart of humor speared through her, despite the dregs of terror that still clung to her body. "You'd catch me before I ran three steps," she said drily. "So I guess I have no choice but to listen to what you have to say."

He surprised her again by laughing softly, but "Smart woman" was all he said. He took a step backward, then another and another, slowly. As if he was expecting her to make a break for it. But Holly wasn't stupid. If he was there to kill her, she'd be dead already—her strength was no match for his. And if he was there to rape her, he'd never have let her go.

Besides, she'd felt the bulge of his gun in its shoulder holster when he held her pinioned against the wall, but he hadn't drawn his weapon and used it against her. This meant he was probably telling the truth. Probably.

"I don't understand," she said again. "If Peg sent you, why didn't she tell me she was going to? I was just there, and she didn't say a wor—"

"She didn't send me. Not exactly. And I know you were just at her house. I followed you there…and back. I've been following you for days."

"Why?" She managed to tamp down the sudden fear his revelation triggered. So she *wasn't* crazy. She *had* been followed.

He removed his Stetson as if he'd just realized he was still wearing it. Then ran his fingers through the hair the hat had flattened. "Because the McCays hired me to find you."

"What?" She barely breathed the word.

His face took on a grim cast. "I'm a private investigator, Holly. The McCays came to my office a week ago. They spun me a cock-and-bull story about you, which I almost swallowed hook, line and sinker. Almost." He looked as if he were going to add something to that statement, but didn't.

"Let me guess. I'm an abusive mother, and they want to rescue Ian and Jamie from my clutches."

"No."

A wry chuckle was forced out of her. "Well, that's a change. That's the story they told the court when they tried to wrest custody of my boys from me after Grant died." Curious, she asked, "So what was their story this time?"

Chris glanced down at the Stetson in his hand and ran his fingers along the brim. "You're the trustee for the boys' inheritance from their dad," he said when he raised his eyes to meet hers again. "You wanted to use the money on yourself instead of for the boys' benefit, and you took Ian and Jamie away from their loving grandparents so no one could call you to account. And you won't let the McCays even know where you are...where the boys are. Won't let them be a part of your children's lives."

Holly closed her eyes for a second, laughed again without humor and shook her head. "All of that is true, except for one thing," she admitted. "I *am* the sole trustee. And I *did* run with Ian and Jamie—three weeks before Christmas, did they mention that?" Chris nodded. "And I *haven't* told the McCays where we are... for a perfectly good reason. Because—"

"Because they're trying to kill you."

Stunned, Holly asked in a breathless whisper, "How did you know that?"

One corner of Chris's mouth twitched up into a half smile. "Because I'm damned good at what I do, Holly. Because the minute I found out you were friends with Peg, I knew the McCays were lying through their teeth, and I wanted to know why. I hate lies and I hate liars. But even more than that, I hate being taken for a sucker. So I did a little more digging...on them. And found out a hell of a lot more than they want the world to know."

"I can't believe you believe me."

"It's not so much a matter of believing *you*, it's

putting the facts together and believing the story they tell—no matter what that story is. No matter if the story seems incredible on the face of it."

Holly buried her face in her hands as emotion welled up in her. For months she'd had no one she could confide in about her suspicions. No one she could share her worry with. She hadn't even told Peg. And this man, this *stranger*, was telling her she'd been right all along.

When she finally raised her face to his, her eyes were dry. She wasn't going to cry about this, not now. She'd cried enough tears over the McCays, almost as many tears as she'd cried over Grant's death. Her lips tightened. "That means I'm doing the right thing taking the boys and leaving town."

Chris shook his head. "I didn't tell them I located you. And I won't."

"But don't you see? Even if you don't tell them where I am, if they hired you they know I'm in this area. And the next PI they hire might not… What I mean is, not everyone will suspect their motives. Not everyone will believe the truth."

Chris stared thoughtfully, then nodded. "You're right. But I can't let you run away again. Not knowing what I know. I'd never be able to forgive myself if…" He seemed to reach a decision. "I think the best thing would be for you and your boys to check out of this rooming house…but stay where I can keep an eye on you until we can set a trap for the McCays."

Holly shook her head vehemently. "I can't do that to you and your wife—put you in danger that way."

All expression was wiped from Chris's face in a heartbeat. "My wife is dead."

She gasped and covered her mouth with her hand.

"I'm so sorry," she whispered eventually. "I didn't know. You said Peg's your sister-in-law, and since you and she don't have the same name, I assumed..." Her words trailed off miserably.

"Peg never mentioned her younger sister, Laura?" Holly shook her head again. "I guess I shouldn't be surprised," Chris said. "Peg and Laura were particularly close. She took Laura's death hard." He didn't say it, but Holly could see Peg wasn't the only one who'd taken Laura's death hard. But that closed-off expression also told her this wasn't a topic of conversation Chris wanted to pursue.

Is that why Peg bonded with me so quickly? Holly wondered abstractedly. *Because she saw in me the little sister she'd lost?*

"So you're not putting my wife in danger," Chris said, drawing her attention back to the here and now. "Most of my family is in some kind of law enforcement, too, and I can recruit them to help me set a trap for the McCays. Of course, everyone's focused on capturing the Alphabet Killer right now, so the McCays aren't going to be a top priority. Especially since there's no concrete evidence against them. In the meantime, though, I want you and your boys in safekeeping."

"Ian and Jamie aren't in danger," she was quick to point out. "Just me."

"Are you so sure?" Chris's eyes in that moment were the hardest, coldest blue eyes she'd ever seen. "If the McCays are willing to kill you to gain custody, who's to say they wouldn't eventually arrange 'accidents' for the boys, too, once they had them in their control?"

"Their own grandchildren? I can't believe—"

Chris cut her off. "Believe it. Once you've taken the

first life, the next one is easier to justify in your mind. And the next." A bark of humorless laughter escaped him. "I should know. My father is Matthew Colton."

Holly's brows drew together in a frown. "I don't think I—"

"Matthew Colton, the original bull's-eye serial killer. He was infamous in his day. The Alphabet Killer is a copycat of sorts, marking her victims the way he did." His face hardened into a grim mask. "My father killed ten people twenty years ago. Including his last victim—my mother."

Chapter 3

"Oh, my God!"

Shock was obvious on Holly's face, followed quickly by the emotion Chris hated the most—pity. He'd had a bellyful of pity in his life—from the time he was eleven and became a quasi-orphan, right up through Laura's death almost two years ago. He didn't want pity and he didn't need it.

"My father killed nine men who reminded him of his hated brother, Big J Colton," he said brusquely, "before he killed my mother…whose only crime was that she loved him. So don't tell me the McCays couldn't possibly kill their innocent grandchildren."

"I…won't." The fear in Holly's eyes surprised Chris, because it wasn't fear of him. It wasn't even fear for herself as a target of the McCays. No, the fear was for her children. Then her face changed, and the fear morphed into fierce determination to protect her children at all costs, no matter what. If Chris had needed one more bit of proof Holly McCay was a good mother, he'd just received it.

"They're not getting anywhere near Ian and Jamie," Holly stated unequivocally. "What do you want me to do?"

He glanced away and thought for a moment, then nodded to himself. His eyes met Holly's. "I've got a house on the outskirts of Granite Gulch. No one lives there, but Peg looks after it for me, so it's not... abandoned." A wave of pain went through him and his right eye twitched as he remembered this was Laura's dream house, the one he'd built for her right before she died. The house she'd never had a chance to live in. The house he couldn't bear to occupy after her death. "It stands all by itself on several acres, and it's up on a ridge—you can easily spot someone coming almost a mile away. I can't think of a safer place for you and the boys to hide out."

"Just us?"

"And me. Until we can set a trap for the McCays, I don't want you out of my sight if I can help it."

"What about your job? You can't just—"

Chris's jaw set tightly. "I run my own business. I haven't taken a day off since Laura's funeral, so I think I can manage this. Besides, I do a lot of my work over the phone or on the computer. I can work from the office in the house. We designed the house—" *...with that in mind*, he started to say, but his throat closed before he could get the words out.

Holly didn't respond at first, just assessed him with an enigmatic expression on her face. The silence stretched from ten seconds to twenty, to thirty. Nearly a minute had passed before she said, "Okay. I appreciate the offer. And I'll accept it on my children's behalf. If it was just me...that would be a different story, but it's not."

A half hour later everything Holly and the twins had with them was loaded into her SUV, with the exception of the two fold-a-cribs she'd bought when she moved to Rosewood. Chris stashed those in the back of his truck, and Holly realized if she'd taken Ian and Jamie and run, she would have had to leave the twins' cribs behind—they just wouldn't fit.

"I'll follow you to Peg's," Chris said as he raised the hatch and clicked it firmly closed. "But first, we'd better stop in town and get some groceries. The utilities at the house are on—so we'll have water and electricity— but there's no food."

Holly nodded. "Sounds good."

"And while I'm at it, I'd better stop off and pack a suitcase, and pick up my laptop from my apartment. I live above the Double G Cakes and Pies."

"Oh, I love that place!" she exclaimed. "Mia—the woman who runs it—she always gives Ian and Jamie special cookies she makes just for them."

Chris smiled. "Sounds like Mia. She and my sister Annabel are best friends—they were foster sisters together." His smile faded, replaced by the closed expression that was becoming familiar to Holly, and she knew instinctively this was another topic of conversation he'd never intended to bring up. Foster care joined the growing list of subjects to avoid...unless Chris brought it up himself.

As they drove the short distance to Granite Gulch, Holly wondered about Chris. About his motives for doing this—protecting her boys and her. She also couldn't help wondering about his wife, Laura, and what had happened to her. Car accident? Some kind of illness, like cancer? Peg had never mentioned Laura that she could recall. But it wasn't just idle curiosity. She really wanted to know, because it was obvious Chris had been in love with his wife.

Holly glanced in the rearview mirror at the man in the truck behind her and sighed. If only Grant had loved her the way Chris had loved his wife. If only...

She couldn't help feeling a dart of envy comparing Chris to Grant. Not that Grant hadn't been a good man—he had been. So very different from his parents. No, the problem was that Grant had been her best friend growing up, and while he'd loved her, he hadn't been _in love_ with her. Not the way she'd been in love with him.

She'd grieved for Grant. Those first few months after his death she'd been devastated...but she hadn't been able to grieve for long. The McCays had seen to that.

Was that why I recovered from Grant's death so quickly? she asked herself now. _Because Grant's parents tried to gain custody of Ian and Jamie and that took all my energy and concentration? Because when that didn't work they tried to have me killed, forcing me to take my babies and flee?_

The first time a car unexpectedly swerved into her lane on the expressway just as she was approaching an overpass, Holly had dismissed it as merely poor driving on someone's part. The second similar attempt only two weeks later had raised her suspicions, especially since she thought she recognized the car. But the third try on her life had been the clincher—someone had deliberately attempted to run her down in the grocery store parking lot, and she'd escaped with her life only by diving between two parked cars as the vehicle in question sped away without stopping.

Holly glanced in the rearview mirror again. *Or is the reason I'm not still grieving because Grant never loved me the way I wanted him to love me? The way I loved him.*

She would never know. All she knew was that not quite a year after Grant's death she was ready to move on with her life...if the McCays would let her.

Holly buckled Ian into one car seat while Chris buckled Jamie into the other. She'd been surprised at first at how baby-knowledgeable Chris was, but she quickly realized she shouldn't be—Peg's kids adored their "Unca Chris," as Susan called him. Which meant even though she'd never met Chris at Peg's house in the three months the two women had been friends, he had to be a fairly frequent visitor.

Holly turned back to thank Peg just as the other woman came out of the house with a bag of dog food balanced on one hip, a bag of doggy treats perched precariously on top and a leashed Wally dancing joyously beside her.

"What the—" Chris began, but Peg cut him off.

"Holly's kids adore Wally, and he's attached to them, so that will help the kids acclimate faster. Besides, it won't hurt to have a guard dog out there, Chris. You know that. It's why you got Wally for Laura in the first place."

Chris's slow smile did something to Holly's heart. She wasn't sure what it meant, but she wouldn't have minded having that smile aimed at her.

"Thanks," Chris said, relieving Peg of the dog, the dog food and the doggy treats before planting a kiss on her cheek. "Come on, boy," he said, opening the door of his F-150 and letting Wally scramble up onto the front seat as Chris plopped the dog food on the floor.

Holly turned to Peg. "Thanks for watching the boys for me," she said softly. "I wasn't going to leave without telling you—please believe that."

Peg smiled and hugged her. "I do." She stepped back and her smile faded. "But you can't run forever, Holly. I know it's not easy, but sometimes you just have to face up to the truth and take a stand. Chris's idea is better any way you look at it. You owe it to your boys to have the McCays put away so y'all can stop running."

"I know."

The two women embraced once more, and Peg whispered in her ear, "Chris needs to do this, Holly. I can't explain, but he needs to do this. So just let him take care of you and your boys."

Chris drove at a sedate pace—unlike his usual hell-bent-for-leather style—watching Holly's SUV in his rearview mirror, making sure he didn't lose her. And as he drove he wondered about her. Not the facts and figures he'd uncovered in his investigation—he already knew far too much about her past, much more than most people would find out in a year of knowing her.

He knew where she'd grown up, what had happened

to her parents, where she'd gone to college and where she'd worked after graduation. He knew she'd been a stay-at-home mom when her husband had been side-swiped on the I-45 in Houston, triggering a massive pileup that had killed three people...but not the drunk who'd instigated the accident—a driver who'd been using a revoked license, and who now resided in the state prison. He knew how much Holly had received from her husband's insurance, and he knew how much her twins had inherited from their father in the trust the McCays had told him about—just about the only truth in their pack of lies.

But he didn't care about all that. What he wanted to know was what made her tick. She obviously loved her sons. Had she loved their father? His investigation hadn't uncovered any men in her life other than her now-deceased husband, which put her head and shoulders above most of the women he'd been hired to investigate. While the bulk of his work was doing background checks for a couple of major defense contractors in the Dallas–Fort Worth area, as well as extensive white-collar-crime investigation, no PI could completely avoid divorce work. Infidelities were profitable.

But the cases that eviscerated him were the non-custodial kidnappings. He'd had half a dozen of those cases in his career, three of which he'd taken pro bono, the same way he'd taken the McCays' case. What he wouldn't accept—could *never* accept—were people who deliberately separated children from the rest of their family for no real reason except selfishness. Not just parent and child, but also brothers and sisters.

His foster parents had done that. They'd deliberately

isolated him from most of his siblings growing up. They hadn't been able to keep Chris away from his twin sister, Annabel—Granite Gulch had only one high school, and they'd had classes together from day one.

But his foster parents had done their best to keep them apart anyway—even grounding him on the slightest of pretexts and piling him with a heap of after-school chores in addition to his homework—but Annabel had needed him. And beneath his laid-back exterior, Chris had always been something of a white knight. His twin had come first...even if it meant being perpetually grounded.

Chris had managed to reconnect with the rest of his siblings once he was an adult—all except his baby sister, Josie—but he could never get back those growing-up years he'd spent without his four brothers. Without those close familial bonds brothers often formed. That could have made a difference in all their lives, especially given their tragic family history.

That was why he'd taken those pro bono cases in the first place, one of which had come early in his career, when he'd been struggling to make ends meet. But he couldn't turn down a case involving children. Which was why he'd almost fallen for the McCays' sob story. Which was also why he was taking on the toughest case of his career to date—protecting Holly, Ian and Jamie McCay.

"Four bedrooms, Holly," Chris said as he shifted Ian into his left arm and unlocked the front door, then keyed in the code to disengage the alarm system. "Take your pick. Let me know which one you want for the twins, and I'll set up their fold-a-cribs. One of the bedrooms is—"

He broke off for a heartbeat, then attempted to finish his sentence, but Holly said quickly, "I want them with me." She cuddled Jamie, who was starting to fret. "I know all the baby books say it's a bad idea, but ever since...well, ever since we left Clear Lake City, Ian and Jamie have stayed in the same room with me. First in the motels and then in the Rosewood Rooming House. I'm afraid they'll be scared if I try to change that tonight, especially since this is a new place to them and all." She smiled down at the toddler in her arms. "Yes, Jamie, I know you're hungry. Give Mommy a few minutes, please. Okay, sweetie?"

"If that's what works," Chris said, "then it'd probably be best if you took the master bedroom. It's a lot bigger than the others, more room for both cribs."

"But that's *your* bedroom," she protested. "I don't want to put you out of—"

Chris shook his head. "I've never lived here. Never slept a night in that room. So you wouldn't be putting me out."

I did it again, Holly thought as that closed expression replaced Chris's smiling demeanor. She put Jamie down, and he clung to her leg. "I'm sorry." Her voice was quiet. "You're going out of your way to help us, and I...I keep saying the wrong thing."

Chris lowered Ian to the floor but kept a wary eye on him so the toddler didn't wander off. "Not your fault," he said gruffly. He herded Ian toward Holly with a gentle foot. "Why don't you give these two some lunch while I get everything unloaded? I'll bring in the groceries and the high chairs first."

* * *

Chris set up the fold-a-cribs in the master bedroom while Holly fed the twins. As he'd told Holly, the master bedroom held no memories for him, except…Laura had picked out the furniture. She'd picked out everything in the house…without him. Her dream house, she'd laughingly called it. But he'd been too busy to go with her, so she'd gone without him. She'd driven into Fort Worth with her sister, armed with the platinum credit card Chris had given her, and she'd furnished the house, room by room.

That was where she'd been exposed to viral meningitis. Somewhere in Fort Worth she'd come into contact with a carrier of the disease. Much later the Center for Disease Control had reported a mini outbreak of viral meningitis in Fort Worth—too late. Laura had never mentioned the subsequent symptoms she'd experienced to Chris—the severe headache, fever and neck stiffness—and he hadn't noticed. He'd been too busy to—

His cell phone rang abruptly, startling him out of his sad reverie. "Chris Colton," he answered, recognizing the phone number.

The voice of one of the administrative assistants in his Fort Worth office sounded in his ear. "Chris? It's Teri. Angus McCay just called. He wants to know the status on his case. I told him you'd call him. Do you need the number?"

"No, I've got it, thanks. Oh, and, Teri, I'll send an email, but can you let everyone in all three offices know I won't be in for the next few days? Something personal has come up I need to take care of. They can reach me by phone or email if it's urgent. And if any other client calls come in, have Zach or Jimmy deal with them."

"Sure thing, Chris."

He sensed the question Teri wanted to ask but wouldn't. His staff knew not to ask because that's the kind of manager he was—he kept his personal life and his business life completely separate. Chris disconnected, then thumbed through his phone book until he found the listing for Angus McCay and picked the office number. The phone rang only twice before it was answered.

"Angus McCay."

"Chris Colton here. You called me?"

Angus McCay cleared his throat. "I know you told us you'd let us know if you found Holly, Mr. Colton, but…it's been a week and we haven't heard from you. My wife…well, she wanted me to call you and see if you've made any progress."

"Not to worry, Mr. McCay," Chris assured him, his mind working swiftly. "I tracked Holly to Grand Prairie, but she gave me the slip." He deliberately named Grand Prairie because Holly *had* stayed there…just not recently. And Grand Prairie was southeast of Fort Worth, nowhere near Granite Gulch. "I'm hot on her trail, though. I think she might have moved northeast to Irving." Another place Holly really had stayed… briefly. "Just sit tight, and I'll let you know as soon as I have something concrete."

"It's not just our grandchildren at stake, you know. They still haven't caught the Alphabet Killer and… well…you see how it is. Holly's name begins with *H*."

Yeah, Chris thought. *Keep beating that drum. How stupid do you take me for?* "I don't think you have to worry about that, Mr. McCay. Both Grand Prairie and Irving are closer to Dallas than to Fort Worth, and the Alphabet Killer isn't striking anywhere near there."

"Okay, well…just remember, if you find Holly, we don't want you to do anything to scare her off. Just let us know and we'll fly up from Houston immediately. If we can just see that the boys are okay…if we can just talk to Holly…"

"You bet," Chris told him. "I'll keep you posted. And don't worry, Mr. McCay. Holly won't slip through my fingers next time." He disconnected just as a sound from the doorway made him swing around. Holly stood there, white as a ghost, a twin balanced on each hip.

Chapter 4

"You...you said you believed me about the McCays," Holly managed, despite the way her heart was pounding so hard she could barely breathe.

Chris tucked his phone back in his pocket. "I do."

"Then why... What were you telling my father-in-law? It sounded like you—"

He cut her off. "Just throwing him off the scent, Holly. I had to tell him something, and part of the truth is better than an outright lie—I *did* track you to Grand Prairie...after I'd already located you in Rosewood. And I wasn't lying...you *did* move on to Irving after you left Grand Prairie. But you only stayed there two weeks, too."

"How do know that?" Her voice was barely above a whisper.

One corner of his mouth curved upward in a half

smile. "I told you, I'm damned good at what I do. After Irving you moved to Mansfield, then Arlington. After Arlington you stayed almost a month in Lake Worth before you moved here."

He walked toward her as he said this, and she backed away on trembling legs, clutching Ian and Jamie as if they were talismans. *I was so careful,* she thought feverishly. *How could he know all that?*

She hadn't realized she'd spoken aloud until Chris gave her an "are you kidding me?" look and said, "You make a lousy criminal, Holly. But that's a compliment, not an insult."

When Holly bumped into the hallway wall outside the bedroom doorway, she realized she was trapped. But all Chris did was take Ian from her, hefting him under one arm like a football and gently swinging him until Ian laughed at the game. "Time for your nap, bud," Chris told him. "You and your brother." His blue eyes met Holly's brown ones, and there was a gentleness in his face. An honesty she couldn't help but believe. "I'm not going to hurt you, Holly. Ever. And I'd never do anything to hurt your sons."

Holly was so mentally exhausted and emotionally drained that after she read the twins a story, sang them two songs and tucked them up in their cribs, she lay down on the bed, telling herself she'd rest for just a moment. Then she'd unpack their suitcases, wash the lunch dishes, put away the dry-goods groceries she and Chris had bought and decide what to make for dinner. But before she realized it, she was out like a light.

At first her dreams were of happier times, when the twins were newborns and Grant was there. He'd been so proud and nervous at the same time, like most new fathers. Then her dreams segued into nightmares, starting with the devastating news of Grant's death...the lawyers trying to probate Grant's will and the McCays attempting to contest it...followed swiftly by the Mc-Cays trying to seize custody of the twins, along with control of the trust Grant had set up for his sons. A dazed and bereft Holly had been forced to fight, not only for custody and to carry out Grant's last wishes but for her good name, too.

That time in her life had been a waking nightmare. She'd won the preliminary battles in the courts and thought she was finally on firm ground...until those three close calls. Any one of them could have been an accident, but three? After the last one, when she'd shown up at the McCays' house shaken and trembling to pick up the twins, she'd sensed the McCays' surprise... that she was still alive. And she'd known in that instant they were trying to kill her.

In the way of dreams, Holly suddenly found herself at the Rosewood Rooming House with Chris. He was holding her, but not the way he had in real life. This time his strong arms were surrounding her in comforting fashion as he pressed her head against the solid wall of his oh-so-warm chest and promised her she was safe. "I won't let them hurt you," he said, referring to her in-laws. "And I won't let them get custody of Ian and Jamie."

The sense of relief she felt was incredible, and all out of proportion to her real life. Holly didn't subscribe to the theory that a woman couldn't take care of herself, that she needed a man to look after her. She was a software engineer, for goodness' sake! She'd supported herself after her missionary parents had been killed in one of their trips to South America—leaving very little in the way of life insurance—and had put herself through college. After graduation she'd held down a challenging job for NASA at the Johnson Space Center in Clear Lake City, Texas, before she'd taken maternity leave when the twins were born. She didn't need "rescuing" from her life…as a general rule.

But that was before the McCays had tried to kill her. The situation she found herself in now was so totally outside her experience, so much like one of the thrillers Grant had loved to read but that Holly had always avoided, that she recognized she couldn't do it all on her own. Single mother? Check. Guardian of her children's financial future? Check. Putting attempted murderers behind bars? Not so much.

Maybe that was why when Chris had held Holly in the shelter of his arms in her dream and promised she and the boys were safe, she'd believed him…because she *wanted* to believe him. Because she *needed* to believe him.

Then he'd kissed her.

No one had ever kissed her that way, with an intensity that shattered everything she'd thought she knew about men and women. Chris's kiss exploded through her body, as if she were gunpowder and he were a lighted match. He was hard everywhere she was soft, and it made her want to get closer…impossibly closer. Her nipples tightened and her insides melted as Chris tilted her head back and his lips trailed down, down, to brush against the incredibly sensitive hollow of her throat. Then lower.

Holly moaned in her sleep and curled onto her side,

pressing her legs together against the throbbing she felt there. And the dream suddenly vanished.

She woke to the mouthwatering aroma of baked chicken, Ian and Jamie's chorus of "Ma-ma-ma-ma-ma" as they stood and banged on the sides of their cribs to get her attention and the guilty memory of Chris's dream kiss. Not the kiss so much as her reaction to it, she acknowledged as a flush of warmth swept through her body. As if…

A tap on the door frame drew her attention, and there stood Chris in the doorway, almost as if she'd dreamed him into existence. Holly quickly hid her face with her hands and rubbed at her eyes, pretending she needed to wake up that way. She didn't—she just didn't want Chris to see her flaming cheeks.

"Dinner's ready" was all Chris said, and as he walked farther into the room, Holly scrambled off the bed. "I'll take Ian for you," he said, lifting the older of the twins—older by three minutes—out of his crib.

"How do you know that's Ian?" she asked, moving to grab Jamie. "They're identical. Most people can't tell the difference. Peg can, but it took her a week."

The intimate smile Chris gave her curled her toes. "Ian looks up when he sees me. Jamie looks away."

"That's it? That's how you can tell them apart?"

"Well…that and the fact that Ian's ears stick out just a little more than Jamie's, and Jamie's hair is just a shade lighter than Ian's."

Holly stopped short, glancing from the toddler in Chris's arms to the one in her own arms. "You're right," she said after a minute. "I never realized about the ears…but you're right."

"So how do you tell them apart? Motherly instinct?"

She adjusted Jamie to balance him against her hip and popped a kiss on his rosebud mouth. "I can't really tell you," she confessed. "I just know."

Chris nodded as if she'd given him the answer he expected. "Motherly instinct," he repeated, but this time it wasn't a question. He turned toward the doorway. "Come on, dinner will be getting cold."

"I was going to make dinner," she protested as she followed Chris into the kitchen, feeling guilty.

"You were fast asleep every time I came to check on you, and I didn't have the heart to wake you." Chris settled Ian in one of the two high chairs he'd pulled up beside the kitchen table and strapped him in. "Hang tight, buddy," he told the boy as Ian began banging on the tray and shouting, "Din-din-din-din-din!"

Jamie took up the chant as Holly got him settled. "Sorry," she told Chris over the boys' urgent demands. "I usually feed them a little earlier. I must have been more exhausted than I thought."

"Adrenaline will do that to you," Chris said as he grabbed two child-sized plates that were sitting in the microwave, added the baby cutlery she'd used at lunch from the rack on the drain board—*he must have washed the lunch dishes,* Holly realized with another little dart of guilt—and whisked the plates in front of Ian and Jamie. Baked chicken, cut into baby-sized bites, sat next to miniature mounds of mashed potatoes. Peas with a tiny dollop of melted butter rounded out the servings.

"Are you sure you're not a nanny in disguise?" Holly joked as the twins' eyes lit up and they dug in, soon making a mess out of feeding themselves. "How do you know—"

"Don't even *think* about finishing that sentence," Chris told her in a stern voice, but the twinkle in his eyes gave the lie to his tone. "I'm the second oldest of seven. That many kids in a family—you need a lot of hands to get all the work done. My twin sister, Annabel, and I used to help Mama with the younger kids, especially my baby sister, Josie."

He turned away to take the rest of the chicken out of the oven, but not before Holly saw a troubled expression slide over his face. *More land mines,* she warned herself. *He doesn't want to talk about his childhood.* That made sense given what he'd told her this morning—that his father was a notorious serial killer who'd killed Chris's mother, too.

She cast about in her mind for a safe topic of conversation as she filled a plate for herself from the chicken pan and the pots on the stove, and Chris filled Wally's bowl with fresh water. "I didn't realize you're a twin," she said as she seated herself at the table.

Chris started to respond, but Holly leaned over to Jamie, who was rolling his peas across his highchair tray and then smashing them flat with the tip of one chubby pointer finger. "You're going to eat those, mister," she told him in a no-nonsense voice. "So you just peel them up and pop them into your mouth." She waited until Jamie obediently scooped up two peas and ate them before she glanced up at Chris. "Sorry. It's a constant battle with boys this young. They want to feed themselves, but... What were you going to say?"

"I was just about to say that yeah, I'm a twin myself. Not identical, of course, but there *is* an unbreakable bond."

"I've seen that with Ian and Jamie already."

"Not surprised. It starts early."

"What does your sister do? Is she a PI like you?"

Chris shook his head. "She's a cop." He hesitated. "My brothers and I—we didn't want that for her. I know it's chauvinistic in this day and age, but this is Texas. We wanted her to be safe, you know? I had a big argument about it with her. And—" he had the grace to look ashamed "—none of us except Sam attended her graduation from the police academy. She graduated top of her class, too." He took his plate and settled in a chair at the other end of the table.

They ate in silence for a minute, then Chris said roughly, "I know how it sounds, but we've already lost one sister. Josie. We don't want to lose the only one we have left."

Treading cautiously, Holly asked, "What happened to Josie?"

"No one knows. We haven't heard from her in six years." His brows drew together in a troubled frown. "And even before that she practically refused to have anything to do with us for years." He thought for a moment. "I guess she was about twelve when she told the social worker she didn't want us visiting her anymore."

"How old were you?"

"Twenty. The summer before my junior year in college." He sighed. "But even before that she… When Trevor turned eighteen—Trevor's the oldest, three years older than me—when he turned eighteen, he tried to get custody of Josie, take her out of foster care. But she refused. We figured it had something to do with her foster sister, Lizzie. They were particularly close. And Lizzie says they were both attached to their foster parents."

He sighed again. "I also tried to get custody when I turned eighteen and graduated from high school. I'd have passed on college if that's what it took—scholarship be damned. But I didn't have any more luck than Trevor." He looked down at his plate, forked a bite of chicken and swirled it in the mashed potatoes, then ate it.

Holly pried peas off Jamie's tray, piled them on his plate and tapped an imperious finger. "Eat those, mister." She glanced over at Ian to make sure he was eating what was set before him without difficulty, then looked up at Chris. "What happened then?"

"Even with the scholarship it wasn't easy, but I managed. I worked to put myself through school, and when I graduated, I came back here to Granite Gulch. Laura was waiting for me—we'd been engaged since my junior year in college—but I told her I needed to try one more time with Josie...who turned me down flat."

That hurt him. Chris didn't have to say it; Holly just knew. "Josie didn't say why?"

"Nope. Basically her message was 'Leave me alone.'" He paused. "I don't blame her in one way. She was only three when our father murdered our mother—I doubt she even remembers her or us as a family."

But you do, Holly thought. *You remember...and it hurts you to remember.*

"So it only makes sense she didn't want to have anything to do with her brothers and sisters—we're not her family anymore. Then six years ago..." Chris began, but when he stopped, Holly raised her eyebrows in a question, so he continued. "Josie ran away six years ago. At least that's the best we can figure. I've been searching for her off and on ever since."

Now Holly thought she understood what Peg had

meant when she said Chris needed to do this, needed to shelter Holly and her boys from the McCays. Chris carried a load of guilt over his missing sister. *Probably some guilt over his mother, too.*

"You said there were seven of you, and that Trevor's the oldest. What does he do?"

"FBI profiler."

"Wow. Impressive."

Chris nodded, but Holly got the impression there were some unresolved issues between Chris and his older brother. *I wonder what that's about.* She wasn't going to ask, of course. But maybe he would volunteer something later on. "After Trevor it's you and Annabel, right? And Josie's the baby. Who else?"

"Ridge. He's two years younger than me."

"Unusual name."

Chris laughed. "It suits him. He's in search and rescue. He's big and bad and nobody messes with Ridge."

Kind of like you, Holly thought, but she kept it to herself. "And after Ridge?"

"Ethan. He's twenty-seven, and he is *intense*. He kind of keeps himself to himself, if you know what I mean." Holly nodded. "He's a rancher. His ranch is… oh, about ten miles from here. The isolation suits him, but he's going to have to get accustomed to having more people around—his wife, Lizzie, is expecting a baby any day now."

"Oh, that's nice. You'll be an uncle again." She counted up in her mind, then said, "One more. Another brother, right?"

"Yeah. Sam. He's a police detective, right here on the Granite Gulch police force, just like Annabel. He's twenty-five, and he just got engaged in January to the sweetest woman, Zoe. You'd like her."

"Wait. Zoe Robison? The librarian?"

Ian piped up, "Zo-ee, Zo-ee!" and Jamie copied him. Holly quickly looked over at her boys and realized they were pretty much done. They'd left a disaster that would need hosing down to clean up, but at least they'd managed to eat most of what was on their plates. What hadn't been eaten was now adorning them. She shuddered at the mashed potatoes Ian had massaged into his eyebrows.

"You know Zoe?" Chris asked.

Holly jumped up and grabbed the washcloth from the sink. "She runs the Mommy and Me reading program at the library," she explained as she wiped Jamie's hands and face, then did the same for Ian. "Ian and Jamie adore her, and yes, she's really sweet."

Chris waited until Jamie was clean, then he unstrapped the boy and lifted him out of the high chair, setting him on his feet. When Ian was ready, he got the same treatment.

"Leave this," Chris told Holly. "I'll clean up and put the dishes in the dishwasher."

"I should do it," she protested. "Ian and Jamie are the ones who made such a mess." She grimaced as she took in the condition of the floor, which had a few peas scattered beneath the high chairs—the ones Wally hadn't gobbled up—not to mention a couple of gooey globs that looked like mashed potatoes.

"You probably want to give the boys a bath before too long."

"You mean before they track the mess into the rest of the house?"

Chris grinned. "Yeah, that's exactly what I mean."

"You really don't mind cleaning up in here? I feel awful leaving this for you."

"Don't sweat it." He was already swiping a damp paper towel over the mashed potatoes and picking the remaining peas up off the floor as she spoke. Chris's cell phone rang at that moment, and he threw the peas into the garbage disposal before he checked the caller ID. "Annabel," he told Holly. "I should take this. Excuse me." He pressed a button. "Hey, Bella, what's up?"

He stiffened almost immediately, and Holly watched his lighthearted expression fade away as he listened to his sister on the other end. Two minutes passed, then three, before Chris said, "I'm sorry to hear it. What does Trevor say?" He made a sound of impatience, then nodded as if Annabel could see him. "Okay. I understand. Besides Trevor and Sam, who else knows?" He listened for a minute, then said, "Nothing I can do, but thanks for letting me know. Watch yourself, okay?"

He disconnected but didn't put the phone away. He hit speed dial, waited a few seconds, then said, "Peg? It's Chris. Have you been watching the local news?" Apparently the answer was no, because he added, "Turn it on. Now. Annabel just called me. They found another body with the bull's-eye marking. Yeah, number eight—Helena Tucker."

Chapter 5

Chris hung up with Peg, then glanced at Holly. She was kneeling on the floor, an arm around each twin, clutching them tightly. "Sorry," Chris said, thinking she was trying to keep the boys from hearing his side of the conversation. "I forgot there were little ears around." The face Holly raised to his was ashen, and guilty. "What?" he asked.

"It's terrible," she whispered. "I should be praying for that poor woman. But all I could think about when I heard her name was that I could stop worrying."

Chris shook his head. "You didn't really think you were in danger, did you? Yeah, your name begins with *H*, but hell—" He caught himself up short, remembering too late his vow to watch his language. "Heck," he amended, "you don't have long dark hair. Your hair isn't even really dark—I have the pictures to prove it."

"I know. I wasn't *really* worried, but…fear isn't always logical. It was just there in the back of my mind, you know? And the newspaper reported that the woman who's suspected of being the Alphabet Killer—I forget her name—"

"Regina Willard."

"Right. She once stayed at the Rosewood Rooming House, same as me."

"I know." Chris suddenly thought of something. "Before I forget, I wanted to tell you there's no internet service here at the house yet. And no cable. Water, gas, electricity and phone—yeah. I couldn't turn the water off—unless I wanted to let the landscaping shrivel up and die. Not to mention Peg needs water when she comes out here to take care of the place. And electricity and phone service are necessary for the alarm system. But no cable or internet landline. I called to get them turned on when we were at Peg's, but it'll be a few days."

"That's okay," Holly informed him. "I haven't watched TV since I left Clear Lake City. And I only browse the internet at the library anyway, so it's not a hardship to do without. But what about you?"

"I can survive without cable for a few days. And I've got mobile internet access for my laptop and smartphone—I need it for my PI business. So, I'm good."

Ian and Jamie both squirmed to get free at that moment, and Chris said, "Better get them their baths. Go on," he insisted. "It won't take me more than a few minutes to clean up in here. Then I have some work to catch up on. I'll be in the office."

A half hour later Holly ruefully fished her dark pixie-cut wig out of the tub in the master bathroom, where Ian had dunked it after he tugged it off her head. She rolled the wig in a towel to dry it as much as she could, then hung it on a hook over the shower. "Laugh," she told Ian in a mock-threatening tone as she lifted him out of the tub and wrapped his wriggling body in a towel. "You just wait until you grow up. I'm going to take delight in embarrassing you by telling your friends all the things you did to me.

"No, Jamie, we don't eat soap," she said, changing subjects, quickly removing the bar of soap from his vicinity. She scooped him out of the tub and wrapped him in a towel, too. She played peekaboo with both boys and their towels for a couple of minutes, then gathered them close as intense motherly love for her babies washed through her. "You're little monsters—you know that—but I love you madly," she told them. "And I wouldn't trade you for anything in the world."

Clean, Ian and Jamie looked like little angels, their golden curls fluffed into tiny halos. Holly brushed their barely damp hair, ruthlessly suppressing the curls, before using the brush on her own head when she caught sight of herself in the mirror. She wasn't vain about her appearance—well, not much—but she didn't want anyone seeing her with her hair a flattened mess. She refused to acknowledge who she meant by "anyone," but in the back of her mind lurked the memory of her dream that afternoon. The dream, and the kiss. Not to mention her erotic reaction to it.

Holly let the twins run naked into the bedroom, dabbing futilely at the large, damp patch on her pale blue T-shirt where Jamie had—deliberately, she was sure—splashed her with soapy bathwater. Then she followed her sons into the other room.

She dressed them in the pull-ups they still wore at night because they weren't *quite* potty trained yet, then in their nightclothes. "Come on," she told them, taking their hands in hers. "Let's go say good-night to Mr. Colton. Pretend you're really as angelic as you look so he won't mind sharing a house with us."

Chris leaned back in his leather desk chair and absently fondled Wally's head as the dog lay quietly beside him. "Look at this, boy," he murmured. "You think…?" *This* was a news article on his laptop's computer screen—a story about the daring capture of a fugitive on the FBI's Ten Most Wanted list. A dangerous man who was an alleged associate of a drug lord who'd been dead for six years—Desmond Carlton. The name Carlton was enough like Colton for the story to have caught Chris's eye, and he shook his head at a vague memory. Then he picked up his smartphone and hit speed dial.

"Hi, Chris," Annabel said when she answered. "What's up?"

"Carlton," he said abruptly. "Wasn't that the last name of Josie's foster parents?"

"Um…I think so. Yes, it was. Why?"

"I was just reading something on *Yahoo News* about a man who ran with Desmond Carlton six years ago."

"The guy who was on the Ten Most Wanted list? The one the FBI just captured?"

"Yeah, him."

"Why is that important? Other than someone else will be promoted to the list tomorrow, now that he's in prison where he belongs, the creep."

"I don't know," Chris said slowly. "But as I was

reading the story the name Carlton rang a bell. That, and the fact that Desmond Carlton has been dead for six years. Six years, Bella. Think about it."

"You don't mean... Josie? It's got to be a coincidence."

"I don't like coincidences. And I don't trust them. Especially two coincidences together." He thought a minute. "Do me a favor, will you? Find out what prison this guy is in. I might want to have a little chat with him."

Annabel's soft drawl took on a hard edge. "You don't want to ask Trevor? He's FBI. He could probably get in to see this perp whether or not he wants visitors." When Chris didn't respond, his sister said, "Are you still holding a grudge against Trevor? I thought you agreed it wasn't fair to him."

"Trevor's got enough on his plate right now," he pointed out, "what with trying to find Regina Willard. Especially now that she just added number eight to her victim list—the pressure to catch her has got to be intense."

"It's not just the FBI, you know," Annabel said drily. "The Granite Gulch Police Department is involved in this case, too."

Chris winced. His sister didn't say it, but it had been Annabel's solid police work that had identified Regina Willard as the Alphabet Killer. The woman hadn't been caught yet, though not for lack of trying on Annabel's part.

But the real reason Chris didn't want to ask for Trevor's help wasn't that his older brother was too busy—that had just been an excuse. Chris *was* still holding a grudge...but he wasn't going to admit it to Annabel. Okay, it was an old wound from his childhood that he should have gotten over long since—he knew that. The adult in him knew that. And yeah, it wasn't fair to Trevor—Annabel was right about that. And true, he and Trevor had finally reconnected years back…mostly.

But deep inside him resided that eleven-year-old boy who'd idolized his older brother, who'd felt betrayed when the family was split up and Trevor made no attempt to maintain the connection with him when they all went into foster care. Yeah, they'd seen each other a few times a year at the home of Josie's foster parents—court-mandated visits—but that wasn't the same thing at all. Chris had pretended it hadn't hurt…but it had. Badly. He was still trying to excise the scar tissue that had left on his psyche, but he wasn't there yet.

Then there was the whole Josie thing. When Trevor turned eighteen, he'd tried to get custody of Josie…or at least that was the story. But how hard had he tried, really? Chris didn't know, and the uncertainty of that ate at him. Josie would have been only seven back then. She'd turned Chris's offer down when *he* turned eighteen, but by that time it was already too late—she'd been ten, and had spent seven years with the Carltons. Maybe it was unreasonable, but Chris laid the blame for losing Josie squarely on Trevor's shoulders.

"But you're right," Annabel said, breaking into his thoughts. "Trevor's got enough to worry about. I'll see what I can find out."

"Thanks, Bella."

"No problem." Silence hummed between them, until Annabel said out of the blue, "I can't stop thinking about the day I saw her."

"Josie?"

"Mmm-hmm. I can't *swear* it was her, but—"

"But that gold charm you found clinches it," he finished for her.

"Yeah." She sighed. "Ridge and Lizzie believed it was her when they had their own Josie sightings."

"I know. At least she's alive. For the longest time I…" Chris's throat closed as he thought of how he'd imagined the worst. Young women disappeared all the time. Murdered. Their bodies disposed of in the most callous ways. It had killed him to imagine that was Josie's fate.

Annabel seemed to understand Chris couldn't talk about it, and she changed the subject. "Speaking of sightings, Mia told me she spotted you coming out of your apartment this morning carrying a suitcase and your laptop bag. You taking a trip? Something to do with your work?"

Chris hesitated, then remembered his heart-to-heart conversation with Annabel last month and his promise that he would take her seriously as a police officer going forward. She'd earned that right and then some. "No," he told her. "Remember that missing-person case I mentioned the other day? The one I was taking pro bono?"

"The widow who ran off with her twin sons? The one the in-laws are trying to track down?"

"Yeah, her. Turns out I was way off base."

His sister snorted. "Told you there was more to the story."

"Don't rub it in." Chris massaged the furrow he could feel forming between his eyebrows. "Anyway, long story short, I found her. But she had a damned good reason for running—her in-laws tried to kill her."

Annabel gasped. "Are you kidding me?"

"Nope. She's been living in the Rosewood Rooming House with her boys for the past three months, but she was just about to run again." He took a deep breath. "So I convinced her it would be safer for the three of them to live in my house for the time being...with me."

"Your house? You mean the one you built for Laura?"

"Yeah. I couldn't let her run, Bella. I wasn't going to tell the in-laws I found her, but I couldn't let her run. If she did and the in-laws hired someone else..." He knew he didn't have to draw his twin a picture.

"So you're living there with her?"

"And her sons," he was quick to point out. "Just until we can set a trap for her in-laws."

"We?"

"I was thinking Sam, you and me. Unless you don't want to." He knew when he said it what Annabel's answer would be. Set a trap for would-be murderers? If they pulled it off, it would be another professional coup for his sister.

"Count me in."

Annabel's enthusiastic response made Chris smile to himself. "I haven't asked Sam," he told her, "so don't say anything to him yet, okay? This all just happened this morning."

"No problem. Just let me know when and where. So, what's her name?"

"Holly. Holly McCay. And her boys are Ian and Jamie."

"Cute names. What's she like?"

Chris smiled again. Knowing his sister, he'd known

the question—or one very similar—was coming. "You'd like her. She's very down-to-earth. Very unassuming. And a good mother. You're not going to believe this, but Holly and Peg are friends," he said, knowing the message that would convey. "Other than Peg and me, you're the only one who knows where Holly is right now, and until we can prove anything against her in-laws, that's the way I want to keep it."

"Works for me. When do I get to meet her?"

Children's voices from the hallway outside his office alerted Chris that Holly and her boys were approaching, so he cut off his conversation with Annabel. "I'll let you know," he told her quickly and disconnected. He swung his chair around and stood up, but Wally was faster. The dog bounded across the room toward the hallway, tongue lolling out, tail wagging.

"Holly, I—" Chris began but stopped as if he'd been poleaxed when a blonde woman appeared in the doorway with Ian and Jamie. Long blond hair that owed nothing to artifice. Long blond hair that shimmered under the lights with a hundred different layered shades of gold. Long blond hair parted slightly off center, paired—unusually—with pale brown eyes. The eyes he'd seen before, but not with the blond hair. *Holy crap*, he thought as desire unexpectedly slashed through him, but all he said was, "What happened to the dark-haired wig?"

Holly laughed ruefully. "Ian thought it was funny to pull it off and dunk it in the tub."

He didn't mean to say it, but the words just popped out. "Your pictures don't do you justice."

She laughed again, but this time a slight tinge of

color stained her cheeks. "Thank you... I think." She stood there for a minute staring at Chris as if caught in the same trance as he was, and her not-quite-steady breathing drew attention to her breasts rising and falling beneath her damp T-shirt. But when the twins tugged free of her hold to play with Wally, the spell—or whatever it was—was broken. "We came to tell you good-night," she explained, the color in her cheeks deepening.

"Oh. Right," Chris said, forcing his eyes away from Holly and down to the toddlers and the dog. Their well-scrubbed cherubic faces were misleading, he knew—if they were like most boys, Holly's twins were no angels. But they were all boy, just as Wally was all dog. Boys and dogs went together like...well... like boys and dogs. And Chris had a sudden memory of his younger brothers Ridge and Ethan—four and two to Chris's six—and his dog back then, Bouncer, a golden retriever, just like Wally. It was a memory from his early years that didn't stab at his heart for once, a memory that made him smile for a change. He glanced at the clock on the wall and said, "Kind of early for bedtime, isn't it?"

"I start early," Holly explained. "I read them stories, then they get lullabies, and..." She smiled. "All of that can take an hour or more before they finally settle down and go to sleep."

He didn't know what made him make the offer, but he said, "How about I read them their bedtime stories?" When Holly looked doubtful, he added, "I'm a pretty good bedtime-story reader. Peg's daughter, Susan, would vouch for me if she was here."

Holly chuckled. "Okay," she agreed. "I wouldn't

mind a few minutes to myself for a change. Let me get the books. We have a ton of library books—I was going to return them on my way out of town today," she rushed to explain, as if she didn't want him to think of her as a library thief. "And we have some books I bought for the boys. I let them pick the books they want me to read."

She was back in no time, carrying a stack of books that Chris quickly relieved her of. "Their favorites are on top," Holly told him. "But I usually just spread the books out and they choose based on the cover."

"Fly," Jamie said. "Want fly."

"A Fly Went By?" Chris asked him, juggling the stack until he found the Mike McClintock title three books down from the top. He handed it to Jamie, who hugged it.

"You remember that book?" Holly asked, surprised.

"Hell—heck, yeah," he amended. "That was one of Josie's favorites. I read it to her so many times I think I have it memorized."

"Me, too." Holly smiled at Chris, a somehow intimate smile, and something he hadn't felt in forever tugged at his heart. Holly's smile made him realize there was more to life than merely putting one foot in front of the other. More to life than the work he'd thrown himself into with even more dedication after Laura's death. Except for his relationship with Peg, Joe and their kids, except for his relationship with his sister and brothers, his life revolved around his work. Work that gave meaning to a life that held little else.

But Holly's smile reminded him he was a man, first and foremost. A man who hadn't made love to a woman in close to two years, who hadn't even given it serious thought in all that time.

He was thinking of it now, though. He was definitely thinking of it now. In spades.

Chapter 6

Holly escaped to her bedroom, her cheeks burning. The intently male look Chris had given her the moment before was branded into her memory. *He wants you*, she told herself as she quickly stripped and stepped into the shower. *Just as you want him.*

The hot water pummeled her body, which had become hypersensitized merely from that one look from Chris, and felt like a man's caress. Which was *crazy*! She didn't react to a sexy man that way. Yes, she'd been physically attracted to Grant—far more than he'd been physically attracted to her, since Grant had looked on Holly more as a sister than anything else—but she'd been in love with Grant. She couldn't have carnal urges like this for a man she'd just met that morning... Only, she did. *Don't lie to yourself, Holly*, she warned. *You want him. Admit it.*

"Okay," she muttered, soaping her body and rinsing off quickly. "Okay, so I'm a normal woman with normal needs and it's been more than a year since I…"

Not just a year since she'd made love. It had been a lot longer than a year since a man had looked at her with that burning intensity in his eyes, his face. An expression that conveyed how unutterably desirable she was to him, and at the same time triggered those same needs in her.

Holly washed her hair just as quickly as she'd washed her body. *No one's* ever *looked at you like that*, she admitted to herself as she rinsed, and the memory made her nipples tighten into tiny buds that ached beneath the warm spray.

She wasn't afraid Chris would do anything she didn't want him to do…but that was the problem. She wanted him to do things to her she'd never imagined having a man do to her. And she wanted to do things to him she'd never believed in her heart women really wanted to do for men. And that was a *huge* problem.

She'd been nothing but Mommy for so long she'd thought she was immune to men. She'd thought wrong.

Chris knew Peg didn't allow her dogs on the furniture—not a dictum he would have made, but Wally wasn't really his dog, so he enforced the rule anyway. Since the twins wanted Wally close enough to pet while Chris read to them, he solved the dilemma by plopping down on the floor in his office with his back to the sofa. Wally lay across his legs and a boy sat on either side of him as he read. He'd finished *A Fly Went By* and had nearly reached the end of Dr. Seuss's *Green Eggs and Ham* when Holly returned.

Her long blond hair was damp and had been sleeked back away from a face that held not a vestige of makeup that he could see, not even lip gloss. But the minute she walked into the room the temperature rose to an uncomfortable level.

Holy crap, he thought as he read aloud the last two sentences, then closed the book and said, "The end."

He'd thought his sudden attraction to Holly had been nothing more than an aberration, the normal reaction of a man who'd gone too long without receiving an attractive woman's smile. He'd been way off base.

But there was something inherently…unsavory… about lusting after a woman when her eighteen-month-old sons were cuddled on either side of him, enthralled by his renditions of children's stories. So Chris tamped down his desire and smiled up at Holly without letting her see how much she affected him. "You're just in time," he told her. "We're done here."

Jamie scrambled to his feet, tripped over Wally's thumping tail and picked himself up again, patting Wally's backside as apology. "Sor-ry, Wally, sor-ry." Then he turned to his mother and demanded, "Ma-ma sing now."

"Later," she replied, bending over and picking him up, settling him against her hip. "Did you thank Mr. Colton for reading to you?"

Ian piped up, "Unca Cwis." He patted Chris's arm, and repeated, "Unca Cwis."

"Sorry," Chris said swiftly. "I told them to call me that. That's what Susan calls me, and I figured it was easier than saying 'Mr. Colton.'"

"Not a problem," Holly replied, then asked her boys, "Did you thank Uncle Chris?" A chorus of childish thank-yous followed her pointed question before she explained to Chris, "They don't have any real uncles. No aunts, either. Grant was an only child, and so was I." She sighed and added wistfully, "I always wanted a brother or a sister. So did Grant. I think that's one of the reasons we were such good friends growing up."

"You can have one of mine," Chris joked. "I've got plenty." He paused for a second. "Not Annabel. Not my twin. But you can have one of my brothers." He tilted his head to one side and thought about it for a moment, as if seriously considering his offer. "Not Sam, either. Or Ethan. They're too young—you don't want a younger brother. How about Ridge? He's twenty-nine, same age as you."

"Ridge, as in 'big and bad and nobody messes with Ridge'? That brother?"

"Yeah, him."

Holly shifted Jamie to her other hip. "I'm not sure I want a brother who will scare away all my dates," she teased, getting into the game. "I'll bet you heard that same line from Annabel. Am I right?"

Chris winced and held up both hands in mock surrender. "Guilty as charged," he admitted. "But it was for her own good. Honest. And I didn't scare away *all* her dates, just the ones who had something nefarious in mind."

"Mmm-hmm." She nodded. "I'll bet. What would Annabel say, though, if I asked her?"

He chuckled softly. "Funny you should ask me that. My sister just got engaged last month, so I guess I didn't scare them all away. Her engagement was kind of late in the game, though, especially since that's all my brothers and I wanted for her—that she find Mr. Right and settle down."

"Finding Mr. Right doesn't happen for all women." The suddenly serious way she said this made Chris wonder. "I should get these two down for the night. Come on, Ian. Say good-night to Mr.—to Uncle Chris, and let's go."

Ian patted Chris's arm to get his attention and in a plaintive tone asked, "Cawwy me?"

"Carry," Holly corrected automatically. "And you don't need to be carried, Ian. You're a big boy."

Before she could put Jamie down and make him walk, too, the same as Ian, Chris stood and swept Ian into his arms. Then he effortlessly lifted the toddler up onto his shoulder. "Hang on, buddy," he told Ian as the boy chortled with glee at being so high up.

"Me too, me too!" Jamie pleaded, holding his arms out to Chris, and Holly was so startled she almost dropped him. Jamie never voluntarily went to *anyone* other than her, so for him to want Chris to carry him was a shock.

"You don't have to," she protested in an undertone as Chris took Jamie from her arms.

"Fair's fair," Chris retorted, hefting Jamie onto his other shoulder. "Nobody wiggle," he told both boys. "And watch your heads as we go through the doorway."

Holly followed Chris through the hallway to the master bedroom, sighing a little at how easily he carried the twins. Ian and Jamie were off the charts for eighteen months, and it was getting harder and harder for her to carry one boy, much less two. But it wasn't just that. She also ruthlessly suppressed the little pang of motherly jealousy that her twins preferred Chris over her, even in something as simple as this. *If Chris was their father it would be different*, she reasoned. *I wouldn't be jealous. Would I?*

She wasn't quite sure, and that bothered her. She wanted so badly to be a good mother, wanted to raise strong, independent boys who would become strong, independent men. She didn't want to be one of those mothers who spoiled her children but kept them emotionally dependent on her, tied to her apron strings. *Not that you wear an apron*, she thought with a flash of humor. But that phrase perfectly described what she *didn't* want for her boys.

So this is a good thing for Ian and Jamie, she reasoned. A little masculine attention from a man she already knew would be a good role model…after knowing him for only a day. She stopped short at the realization that, yes, she'd known Chris for only a day. Not even an entire day at that.

Chris and the twins disappeared into the master bedroom, and she hurried after them. She was just in time to see Chris swing each boy down from his shoulders into his crib and was surprised he got them right. Jamie was in his crib, the one with baby pandas adorning the sheets, and Ian was in the crib with dolphins on the sheets. *He doesn't miss a thing*, she realized. *He notices…and he remembers.*

There was something very appealing in that revelation.

Chris had started down the hallway back to his office when he heard a warm, sweet contralto voice coming from the master bedroom, singing a lullaby he recognized with a sense of shock. And though he told himself not to, that he had no business intruding on Holly's private time with her children, he was drawn back to the doorway.

The room was dark, but the light was on in the master bathroom and the door was cracked open—a makeshift night-light for the twins. Chris could make out Wally's shape on the floor—the twins had begged to be allowed to have Wally sleep with them, and Chris hadn't been able to refuse. Neither had Holly. So Chris had used a folded-up blanket as a dog bed for Wally and had placed it meticulously equidistant between the two cribs.

But he wasn't really looking at the dog. And he wasn't really looking at the twins. All he really had eyes for was Holly, her back to him as she sang the haunting cowboy ballad he knew as "Utah Carl."

Chris closed his eyes, and in his mind he was four years old, listening to his mother, Saralee, singing that very same song to a two-year-old Ridge as she rocked him to sleep. She'd been almost nine months pregnant at the time—*that would have been Ethan*, he realized now—but despite her financial worries and her constant pregnancies, his mother had never let her children know her life was hard. The love she'd felt for each and all of them had shielded them from the knowledge of the trials she faced on a daily basis, not the least of which was loving Matthew Colton and standing by him through thick and thin.

There hadn't been a lot of money in the Colton household, but none of the children had known it at the time. There had always been enough money for the important things—school clothes, books, birthdays and Christmases. And Saralee had made sure all her children knew they were loved, from Trevor right down to baby Josie.

The ballad came to an end, but Holly barely skipped a beat, moving right into another song Chris also remembered from his childhood. A desolate ache for that long-ago time and for the mother he still mourned ripped through him, and his face contracted in pain. His eyes were damp when the song ended, and he quickly rubbed his fingers over his eyelids to remove that betraying moisture.

Then, before Holly could start another song, he slipped noiselessly away from the doorway. He went into his office and shut the door behind him. Firmly. As if he could shut the door on his memories the same way.

It was almost midnight and the house was shrouded in darkness when Holly turned over restlessly in bed. Ian and Jamie were fast asleep—she could hear their rhythmic breathing—and she envied them. If only she could sleep with that same innocent abandon. If only she could sleep believing all was right with the world.

"Shouldn't have had that nap this afternoon," she whispered to herself, although she knew it was a lie. It wasn't the nap preventing her from sleeping, it was her conscience.

Holly's missionary parents had raised her to know right from wrong. And to believe that actions have consequences. Which meant that sometimes—like now—her conscience uncomfortably reminded her that if she hadn't done what she'd done…maybe things would have been different. Maybe she wouldn't be running for her life.

Grant's death wasn't her fault. No way was she responsible for that. But the McCays? If she'd never gotten pregnant, if she'd never married Grant, then the McCays would have inherited Grant's wealth when he died, and they would have no reason to want her out of the picture.

"That's stupid," she told herself sternly. "You're not responsible because they're so mercenary they're willing to kill to get you out of the way."

But...

Friends to lovers was a popular theme in romance novels, but it didn't always work out that way in real life. Best friends Holly and Grant had attended the University of Texas at Austin together and had both earned software engineering degrees. Then Holly had landed that plum job at NASA, while Grant—always more adventuresome than she—went out on his own, starting his own software company.

They'd seen each other often, at least once a week. Holly had known about the women Grant was dating but had consoled herself that as long as he was playing the field she didn't really have to worry he was getting serious about any one woman, the same way he'd been in high school and college. And she'd done everything she could to remain a key part of his life.

One mistake on Grant's part on a night when he'd had too much to drink, and Holly had soon discovered to her secret joy she was pregnant. Grant had done the honorable thing and proposed when she'd told him. After all, he'd reasoned, they'd been best friends forever, so what better basis for a strong marriage? Especially since they'd eventually learned Holly was expecting not one but two babies.

I should have known better, Holly told herself now. Loving Grant secretly the way she had, she'd agreed to his proposal, hoping their babies would bring them together. Hoping that someday he'd realize he loved her, too, the way she loved him.

It hadn't happened. And while they'd both loved Ian and Jamie, their marriage had been...shaky... threatening to destroy their lifelong friendship. *My fault*, she acknowledged now. *I thought I could make Grant love me. But you can't* make *someone love you. Either they do, or they don't.*

Grant's breakthrough software design had hit the market at just the right time, and suddenly his company was raking in millions when Holly took a maternity leave of absence from her job. Holly had intended to return to work when the twins were three months old, but found she just couldn't leave them when the time came. And since Grant had certainly been able to afford it, Grant and Holly had decided she would be a stay-at-home mom until the boys were older.

Then Grant was killed in a car crash when the twins were six months old, leaving Holly mourning what had never come to be, and now never would.

Grant had left Holly comfortably well-off but had left the bulk of his estate in a trust for his sons—something Holly had known about and approved of when they'd both made their wills a month after the babies were born. No provision had been made for Grant's parents, who had first fought the will, then fought to gain custody of the twins from Holly so they could get their hands on the income from the trust. But Holly's in-laws hadn't been willing to wait for the court's final ruling...

Holly sighed and turned over again. Rehashing old

history in her mind was no way to fall asleep. She could never resolve the past. Couldn't change it, either. She just had to live with it, accept that she'd made mistakes and move on.

But thinking about moving on was dangerous, too, especially when the man she was interested in moving on with was Chris Colton. *So much emotional baggage*, Holly thought. *Holy cow, I thought* my *past was troubled.*

She started listing all the reasons getting involved with Chris was a bad, bad idea, but soon gave up... because she didn't care. Because the reasons *for* getting involved with him far outweighed the reasons not to, starting with the way he was with her boys. Not to mention the way he'd looked at her when he'd seen her without the wig for the first time...and her reaction.

Holly sighed again as she saw him in her mind's eye—so tall and impressively male, with muscles that rippled beneath the black T-shirt that fit him like a glove, the same way his jeans did. "Not helping," she muttered.

After ten more sleepless minutes she gave up. She tossed off the covers and rose from the bed, wrapped her robe around her and belted it tightly, then crept barefoot out of the bedroom and headed quietly for the kitchen. She'd tossed a box of her favorite herbal tea with oranges and lemons in their shopping cart this morning, and if that didn't help her sleep nothing would.

The tea bags and a mug were easy to find. Holly thought she might have to boil water in a pot—she didn't care for microwaved tea—but when she looked for a pot in the cabinet beside the stove, there was a brand-new teakettle. As she filled it with water and put it on the stove to boil, she couldn't help wondering about this house furnished with everything anyone could reasonably want...standing vacant. Uninhabited. Chris had told her Peg looked after it for him, so she wasn't surprised everything was spotless—as if the house's loving owners had merely stepped out and would return momentarily.

But it wasn't just that the house was well tended. Someone *had* loved this house once, even if Chris had never lived here. And it didn't take a genius to figure out that someone had to be Chris's deceased wife, Laura. But if Chris had never lived here, that meant Laura probably hadn't, either. And Holly's heart ached for the woman she never knew, the woman who had put so much time and effort into creating a home for the man she loved...and then died. A home her husband couldn't bear to live in without her...but couldn't bear to get rid of, either, because it had been *hers*.

Tears sprang to Holly's eyes as empathy and a kind of envy converged in her heart. *What would it be like to be loved that much?* she wondered with bittersweet intensity. And she knew in that instant she would sacrifice anything except Ian and Jamie to be loved like that.

The teakettle chose that moment to start whistling, and Holly dashed the tears from her eyes. Then she turned the flame off, grabbed a pot holder and poured hot water over the tea bag in her mug.

A deep voice from the doorway said, "Holly?" and she whirled around, almost dropping the teakettle in startled panic.

Chapter 7

Chris hadn't been to bed yet. After he'd left Holly singing her sons to sleep, he'd tried to do some work, but the memories evoked by Holly's lullabies were too sharp, too poignant. Though he tried to focus, his mind kept sliding back to his childhood. To his mother, of course. But also to his father.

Saralee had been a near-perfect mother, but Matthew hadn't been a bad father. Stern. Harsh on occasion. Busy, as a man would be trying to support such a large family on what a handyman could earn, and trying to keep the ramshackle Colton farmhouse from falling to pieces around them. But…he'd taken Chris fishing sometimes, had taught him how to ride a bike. Had even taught him how to handle a rifle and a shotgun and not blow his own damn fool head off.

Chris would also never forget the day he'd turned six

and Matthew had given him the best birthday present a boy could ever have—his golden retriever, Bouncer. Chris hadn't known then that Bouncer was the partial payoff Matthew had received for a job he'd done for a rancher who couldn't pay him in cash. Chris also hadn't known money was so tight for the Coltons that year that Saralee had despaired of where the money would come from for birthday presents for Chris and Annabel. All Chris knew back then was that Bouncer was *his*, and he'd loved that dog almost as much as he'd loved Saralee and Annabel. Almost as much as he'd loved Trevor.

Bouncer had been his constant companion for more than five years. Losing his dog had cut a gaping hole in Chris's heart. If he'd had Bouncer, the other losses—his mother, his father, his brothers and sisters—wouldn't have hit him so hard. But the foster parents who'd taken Chris into their home for the money the state paid them weren't willing to take on a dog as well—not without compensation. Bouncer had been sent to an animal shelter...and euthanized.

The boy he'd been had never recovered.

Now Chris stood in the kitchen, staring at the woman who'd opened the door to so many painful memories from his past he almost resented her for it. But then he realized she wasn't to blame—it wasn't her fault his father was a serial killer, had made Chris's mother his last victim and set in motion a chain of events no one could have predicted. And he couldn't blame Holly for being a good mother to her sons, either, for singing the bedtime songs Saralee had sung to her own children more than twenty years ago.

No, the only one to blame in all of this was Matthew Colton...whose murderous blood ran in Chris's veins.

"Sorry," he told Holly. "I didn't mean to startle you."

She shook her head. "You don't have to apologize. It's my own fault—I shouldn't be so jumpy. It's just that I wasn't paying attention, because I was thinking about—" She stopped abruptly.

"Thinking about the McCays?"

She shook her head again, then turned and put the teakettle down. "No. I was thinking about this house. About..." She hesitated. "About Laura. About how much you must have loved her. And I was thinking I would give anything to be loved that much."

Chris moved into the room until he stood right in front of Holly, staring down at her. So clean and wholesome. So sweet and desirable. "Yes, I loved Laura... but not enough," he said roughly. Holly's face took on a questioning mien, but all he said was "You don't want to know, Holly. But don't have any illusions about me. Laura wasn't a saint, but she was far and away too good for the likes of me."

The ache in Chris's heart grew until it threatened to overwhelm him. The urge to touch Holly, to kiss her, to lose himself in her arms was so great he almost did just that. And something in her soft brown eyes—a yearning empathy—told him she wouldn't stop him if he *did* try to kiss her. But if he touched her, it wouldn't end with kisses. It wouldn't end until he'd disillusioned her, until he'd proved to her she'd been wrong to trust him. Because he *would* hurt her...just as he'd hurt Laura. Not physically—he would never do that—but emotionally. And hurting Holly...hurting *any* woman ever again...would destroy him.

He took a step backward, putting distance between himself and temptation. "Don't look at me like that. And for God's sake, don't pity me." It hadn't been pity he'd seen in her eyes, but…

"Not pity," she told him quietly. "You're wrong if you think that. And you're wrong if you think anything your father did is a reflection on you, or that you could turn out like him," she added, unerringly going right to the heart of Chris's deepest fear. "Grant was a wonderful man—*nothing* like his parents. Should I not have loved Grant because his parents are the way they are?" Her voice dropped a notch. "Ian and Jamie are McCays, too. Should I blame them because their grandparents tried to kill me?"

Holly turned around and picked up her mug. She fished the tea bag out of it with a spoon, threw the tea bag in the trash, then turned back to Chris. "Think about it," she said. "Good night, Chris."

Chris stared at the doorway through which Holly had disappeared as he acknowledged she was right—his father's sins were his alone. Chris didn't need to atone for them. Just because a killer's blood ran through his veins didn't mean he was a killer. Chris had always known that deep down, but…but what? He'd let society's scorn for a serial killer's son color his perception of himself? He'd let the people of his hometown judge him for actions not his own?

Saralee's blood also ran through his veins, and she'd never hurt anyone. The people of Granite Gulch hadn't focused on that, though, just on what Matthew had done, and all the Colton children had paid the price to a greater or lesser extent. But Chris wasn't Saralee any more than he was Matthew. He was his own person.

His character had been forged by the life he'd lived, and the sense of right and wrong his mother had inculcated in him.

A few people in Granite Gulch outside his family had seen beyond the stigma he'd carried. Laura and Peg, of course. Peg's husband, Joe, who'd been Chris's best friend in high school. And when Chris had escaped Granite Gulch, when he'd gone to college in Arlington, no one had known who he was. No one had judged him except by his own actions. It had been a refreshing change, so refreshing he'd been tempted not to return to Granite Gulch after graduation.

But Laura had persuaded him to come back. Laura hadn't wanted to move to Fort Worth, even though that was where Chris had started his PI business, using connections he'd made in college. Laura had wanted to stay in Granite Gulch, near her parents and her sister. And because he'd loved her, Chris had compromised. He and Laura had lived in Granite Gulch and he'd commuted the forty miles each way to and from Fort Worth. But there'd been a price to pay for that compromise, a price Laura had increasingly resented. She'd never voiced that resentment to Chris…but deep down he'd known. He just hadn't been able to—

Chris stopped himself. He wasn't going there. Not tonight. Too many painful memories had already been dragged out into the light from the dark place Chris had stored them, and it was after midnight. He was going to have enough trouble sleeping without adding any more.

Holly woke to the smell of frying bacon. She hadn't had bacon in forever—it wasn't all that healthy for you, especially the kind sold in the United States—but she hadn't stopped Chris when he'd added a package to their grocery cart yesterday, because she secretly loved it. Bacon, eggs, toast and grits had been a Sunday-morning staple in her home growing up.

She glanced at the clock and realized it was early, just past six, which was why Ian and Jamie hadn't been what woke her up. If Holly slept past seven, the twins invariably woke her by banging on the sides of their cribs and calling "Ma-ma-ma-ma-ma!"

She dressed swiftly, brushed her teeth and washed her face, then decided to dispense with the wig. She wasn't planning to go anywhere, and besides, Chris had seen her without it. *And liked what he saw*, said a little voice in her head she tried to ignore.

Holly checked that the twins were still soundly sleeping before she headed for the kitchen, where she knew she'd find Chris. She'd thought about him last night as she'd drunk her tea, replaying that scene in the kitchen in her mind. Each time she'd thought of something different to say to him. Each time she'd wished she hadn't made it so obvious she was attracted to him. *But he was attracted to you, too*, her secret self reminded her now. And that gave her courage to face him without the shield of her twins.

"Good morning," she said as she walked into the sunny kitchen and saw the table set for two adults, with the two high chairs also set up.

Chris turned around from the stove. "Morning." He brought his attention back to his task and stirred something in a pot. "I should have asked you yesterday, but what do Ian and Jamie have for breakfast? I've got oatmeal here, do they eat that?"

Holly laughed. "They eat anything I'll let them eat, but they love oatmeal with a little milk."

"No sugar?"

She shook her head. "I'm trying to keep them from getting my sweet tooth," she confessed. "So no added sugar, no processed cereal except plain Cheerios."

"Good for you." He turned the stove off. "How do you feel about bacon and eggs?"

"I love them." She grimaced. "I shouldn't, I know. Nitrites and cholesterol."

Chris shook his head, his lips quirking into a grin as he leaned one jeans-clad hip against the counter. "Guess you haven't read the latest studies. The cholesterol in eggs is the good kind of cholesterol, not the bad. As for nitrites in bacon being bad for you, that myth has been debunked. The vast majority of the scientific studies suggest that not only are nitrates and nitrites not bad for you, but they may even be beneficial to your health."

"Really?" Holly could hardly believe it.

"Yeah. Doesn't mean you should eat them every day, but a couple times a week won't hurt you." He took a carton of eggs out of the fridge as he said this. "Bacon's already cooked—it's in the oven keeping warm. So how do you like your eggs?"

"I prefer them over easy, but salmonella is an issue." Her eyes sought his. "Or am I wrong about that, too?"

"No, it's a concern. I'm like you—I prefer them over easy, but I fry them hard for that reason."

"Then fry mine hard, too."

Chris's smile deepened, and all at once Holly couldn't breathe. She couldn't tear her eyes away from his face, either. Just like last night, sexual attraction tugged at

her. Chris was so uncompromisingly *male* standing
there in jeans and a white T-shirt, with a day's scruff
on his chin—he practically oozed testosterone. And yet,
he was comfortable in his masculinity. He didn't need to
thump his chest in the "me Tarzan, you Jane" approach
so many men thought made them seem more macho.
There was something particularly appealing about a
Texan who didn't think cooking was women's work.
Who didn't look on child rearing as women's work, too.

But it wasn't just that. What Holly couldn't reconcile in her mind was her reaction to him on a sexual
level. Just like last night, he made her think of things
she had no business thinking about. Of cool sheets and
hot kisses. Very hot kisses.

A plaintive wail floated into the kitchen, breaking
the spell. "That's Jamie," she managed from a throat
that had gone uncustomarily dry.

"I'll get breakfast on the table," Chris told her, turning back to the stove. "You go take care of your boys."

Evalinda McCay folded her lips together and stared
at her husband over the breakfast table. "I don't like
it, Angus."

"I told you what Mr. Colton said."

"Yes, but I don't like it. When we spoke with him
last week, he didn't think it would take very long. Now
it sounds as if he's not even *trying* to find Holly."

"It's not as if we're paying him by the hour, Eva,"
Angus McCay was quick to point out as he swallowed
the last of his coffee. "He's not even charging us at
all, except for expenses, so what's the complaint? Besides," he said, "*you* were the one who was so sure
he was the perfect PI for the job, what with his father

being a serial killer. And he didn't seem all that smart to me—he bought the story we told him."

"Maybe," Evalinda McCay said. "But now that I think of it, I wish we hadn't mentioned the Alphabet Killer angle. Too far-fetched. That might have made him suspicious."

"I don't think so. If Mr. Colton believes the idea that Holly was ever in danger from the Alphabet Killer is ludicrous, I'm sure he'd chalk it down to us being loving in-laws, overly concerned about Holly's safety." He cleared his throat. "Either way, it's no longer a concern now that the Alphabet Killer's eighth victim has been found—Helena what's-her-name."

"That's good," Evalinda McCay said. "Just be sure you don't mention anything about the Alphabet Killer the next time you talk to Mr. Colton."

"Yes, dear. Of course." Angus McCay winced inwardly. He wasn't about to tell his wife he'd brought up the Alphabet Killer only the day before, when he'd discussed the progress in the investigation with Chris Colton. It wasn't important, and she didn't need to know.

He wiped his mouth on his napkin and rose from the table. "I'd better be getting to the bank. I'll call you if I hear from Mr. Colton."

Chris put out two fires at work via phone and made a judgment call to trim the bill on the case of a man who'd been desperately searching for his teenage daughter—*it'll barely cover expenses*, his office manager had protested, but the man had cried when his daughter had finally been located. *It's not always about money*, Chris thought as he dashed off an email to his office manager. Business was booming, especially since so many companies were implementing preemployment background checks on their new hires, and employing firms like Chris's to do the work rather than relying on in-house human resource departments. He could afford to take the hit financially. He could still remember the way the man had wrung his hands when Chris had escorted the onetime runaway through her father's front door. Could still see the heartfelt tears in the man's eyes.

Happy endings didn't always happen in his line of work. The joy on that father's face when he was reunited with his missing daughter was priceless.

Chris rose and stretched, then moved to the other end of his L-shaped office, to the window there. He stared out into the fenced yard, where Holly, her twins and Wally were playing Wiffle ball. The twins were—understandably—not very good yet. But Wally chased down every ball that got past the boys and herded it back to them or carried it back in his mouth. Then, his tail wagging cheerfully, did it again and again.

Chris smiled, remembering playing ball with his younger brothers and Bouncer the same way. For the first time in a long time, thinking about Bouncer didn't hurt. "I must have been eight," he thought out loud. "Yeah, because Sam was about two, which meant Ridge was six and Ethan four." Stair steps, his father had dubbed them. "Stair steps," he whispered now, wondering how he'd forgotten that nickname. Trevor had been three years older, and somehow hadn't been included—only Chris, Ridge, Ethan and Sam. Annabel hadn't counted in his father's eyes; neither had a soon-to-be-born Josie.

Thinking of his father reminded Chris that this was his month to visit Matthew Colton in prison. His month to obtain the next clue to his mother's resting place. He didn't want to go. Unlike his brother Trevor, an FBI profiler who'd visited their father in prison regularly as part of his job, Chris had never gone, despite Matthew's requests some years back. From the time Matthew had been arrested for murder twenty years ago, from the time a trembling and tearful seven-year-old Ethan had confessed to an eleven-year-old Chris how he'd found their mother lying in her own blood, he'd had no desire to see his father ever again. But he couldn't *not* go. Not when everyone was counting on him for that next clue.

Chapter 8

Fifteen minutes passed before Chris went back to his laptop. Fifteen minutes spent watching Holly, the twins and Wally, torn between getting back to work and going out to join in the innocent play. But then he remembered that moment in the kitchen this morning with Holly, and the similar instances last night, and he told himself discretion was the better part of valor. The more time he spent in her company, the more he would want her. The more he wanted her, the more difficult it would be not to touch, not to taste. Not to run his fingers through the spun gold that was her hair and drown in those soft brown eyes. Not to carry her to his bed that had been empty and lonely for so long.

Just thinking about doing those things to Holly made him hard. Made him ache the way he hadn't ached for a woman since Laura. Not just an ache. More like a hunger, really. And he wondered about that. What was it about Holly that pierced the iron shell he'd built around his body...not to mention his heart?

It wasn't just that she was a good mother, as his mother had been, although that played into it, sure. And it wasn't just that she was quietly lovely in a whole-some, All-American, girl-next-door way, although that was part of it, too. At first he couldn't figure it out. Then it hit him. Holly trusted him. What had she said late last night? *You're wrong if you think anything your father did is a reflection on you, or that you could turn out like him...*

Very few women who knew about Chris's serial-killer father had ever looked beyond that fact enough to trust him. Really trust him. Laura had. Peg, too. And now Holly. Somehow she'd sensed that he didn't have it in him to kill as his father had killed. That whatever had been missing in Matthew wasn't missing in his son. She'd known Chris just a little over a day, and yet she trusted him with herself and her sons. Implicitly.

Which was another reason to keep his distance from Holly. Because even if she trusted him, he didn't trust himself.

When Chris finally dragged himself away from the window, he sat down and began Googling for more information related to the article he'd read last night on Yahoo, the one he'd discussed with Annabel. As he'd told his sister, he didn't believe in coincidences. Six years ago Josie had disappeared. At first every-one thought she'd run away because her boyfriend had dumped her. Then there'd been that period of time when Chris had feared Josie had been murdered, her body hidden in a remote location. But after the supposed sightings of Josie, he'd reverted back to thinking she'd run away for some reason. But what if she hadn't just run away? Could her disappearance have anything to do with the death of the drug lord with the same last name as her foster parents?

But the more he dug, the more questions he had… because he couldn't find *anything* on the death of Desmond Carlton. Not a single story. Not even a reference to Desmond Carlton in a related story *before* his death six years ago. The only mention of the man Chris could find anywhere was in the article from the day before.

That could mean only one thing. Someone—or a group of someones—had gone to a lot of trouble to erase Desmond Carlton's existence.

Chris picked up his smartphone and hit speed dial. "Brad?" he said when a voice answered. "It's Chris. I need you to run a trace for me. And this one's not going to be easy. I need you to track down any references you can find to a Desmond Carlton." He spelled the name carefully. "Or to a couple who may be related, Roy and Rhonda Carlton… Yeah, same last name. All I know about Desmond Carlton is he was a drug lord who was killed six years ago. As for Roy and Rhonda, they used to be foster parents, so there's got to be some kind of record of them with the state—criminal background checks, home inspections, the works. Oh, yeah, and they died in a car crash about five years ago."

He listened for a minute, then said, "No, there's no case to charge this to, but I'll clear it with payroll. Oh, and, Brad, when I said this one wasn't going to be easy, I meant it. You're not going to find anything on Desmond Carlton on the internet—I already looked.

You're going to have to hit the main libraries in Fort Worth and Dallas, see if you can turn something up the old-fashioned way. And if that doesn't work, try the offices of the *Star-Telegram* or the *Morning News*. I'm betting there will be articles in their morgues," he said, referring to the newspapers' private archives.

He listened for another minute, then laughed. "Yeah, that's why I called you. The younger guys wouldn't even know where to begin if they couldn't Google the name." His laugh trailed away. "Call me the minute you find out anything. And, Brad? Watch yourself, okay?... No, no, this isn't like the Winthrop case. But no one knows I'm looking for this info. Someone whitewashed the search engines, and until I know why...Yeah, exactly. Thanks, Brad."

Chris disconnected. His fingers flew over his laptop's keyboard and he pulled up the article he'd been reading the night before. He quickly skimmed through it again, noted the originating newspaper was the *Dallas Morning News* and jotted down the byline. "The guy must have dug deep to get as much as he got," he murmured to himself. "Good thing I told Brad to check those newspaper morgues—I'll bet a dollar to a doughnut that's where this guy found the link."

He thumbed through his smartphone's contacts until he found the number he wanted and hit the dial key. It rang three times before it was answered.

"Hey, Taylor, Chris Colton here...Yeah, long time." He shot the breeze with his old college buddy for a few minutes, then said, "I need to talk with one of your fellow reporters...No," he added drily at a question from the other end. "No, I'm not planning to give a scoop to a rival—any scoops I have go to you, you know that."

Chris rolled his eyes, glad Taylor couldn't see him. "I just need to ask a few questions about an article this guy wrote, so I need his direct line." He gave Taylor the reporter's name and jotted down the phone number he was given. "Thanks, Taylor, I owe you one."

Never one to let grass grow under his feet, Chris had no sooner hung up than he was dialing the new number. But all he got was the reporter's voice mail. He thought about it for a few seconds, and before the recorded message finished Chris decided not to leave a callback number and disconnected.

He drummed his fingers on his desk for a moment, then called Taylor back. "Hey, buddy, it's Chris again. I need another favor. Can you set up a one-on-one for me with your colleague?…Yeah, him. ASAP." After a few seconds he said, "No, nothing like that." Realizing he'd need to reveal a few more details to convince Taylor, but not wanting to say anything about the possible connection to Josie, he dangled a carrot. "I might know something about a perp in a story your colleague wrote that he would find very interesting." *It's not a lie*, Chris reminded himself. *If the two cases are connected...*

"Okay, thanks. Call me when you set something up. You've got my number."

Chris checked his work email again while he waited to hear back from Taylor, scrolling through quickly, skimming and scanning as was normal for him. Three cases had been successfully resolved during his brief absence from the office, and he answered with "Atta-boy!" messages, CCing the entire staff. It never hurt and cost him only a minute or two of his time. He paid all his staff well, especially his investigators—anyone who wasn't worth the salary Chris paid didn't last long at Colton Investigations. But money wasn't the best motivator—recognition was. Chris had learned that early on in his career. He'd just clicked Send on the last email when his cell phone rang.

"Hey, Taylor," he answered. After a minute he asked, "Where?" followed by "When?" He wrote swiftly. "Okay," he agreed. "I'll be there."

As soon as he hung up he hit speed dial. "Bella?" he said when his sister answered. "You're off today, aren't you? I need a big favor."

"I don't need a babysitter," Holly said furiously when Chris told her he was going out but that Annabel was coming over to watch her. "If that's what you think, you'd better think again."

"Not a babysitter," Chris explained patiently. "A bodyguard."

"Same thing."

"No, it's not." There was something implacable in his face, in his voice, and Holly knew she wasn't going to win this argument...unless she took her boys and stormed out of the house. Which would be a stupid "cutting off your nose to spite your face" kind of thing to do.

"Look," she began, but Chris stopped her.

"No, *you* look. Do I think the McCays will find you here while I'm gone? No. But am I willing to take that chance? No." His blue eyes had gone cold, but there was something fierce in their depths that reminded Holly of an eagle's basilisk stare. "*No one* is dying on my watch ever again, you got that? I made myself responsible for you—and you agreed to it." He

was breathing heavily now, as if he'd been running…
or as if deep-rooted emotions were taking their toll
on his body. "I've already lost—" He broke off, as if
the rest of that sentence would reveal more than he
wanted. "You agreed to let me protect you and your
sons, Holly," he said after a minute, a little calmer now.
"You have to let me do it my way."

"But—"

"No buts. My way, Holly."

She was going to keep arguing, but then she heard
Peg's voice in her mind. *Chris needs to do this, Holly.
I can't explain, but he needs to do this. So just let him
take care of you and your boys.*

She breathed deeply once, then again, and pushed
her independent spirit aside for now at the sudden
reminder. She wouldn't always knuckle under to
Chris—it wasn't her nature and it wouldn't be good
for him anyway. But in this instance, maybe he was
right. There was only a chance in a thousand something could happen to her or the boys while Chris was
gone, but that was a risk he wasn't willing to take. She
wasn't willing to risk it, either, not when it came to
Ian and Jamie.

"Okay." She held up one hand before he could say
anything. "Okay, this time. When are you going? And
when will your sister arrive?"

Chris glanced at his wristwatch. "Annabel will be
here in about fifteen minutes. I'm not leaving until
she gets here."

Holly let the tension drain out of her muscles. "I'd
better check on the boys—they've been quiet too long.
Then I'll make lunch."

* * *

Chris was long gone. They'd eaten lunch, after which Chris had left and Holly had taken the twins to the master bedroom for their nap. Then, with Wally at her heels, she returned to the family room, where Annabel was reading a magazine she'd brought with her, *Law Enforcement Technology.* Holly had given Annabel the silent treatment during lunch but realized with a touch of remorse it wasn't fair—Annabel was just doing her brother a favor, and giving up her free time to do it.

Before she could speak, though, Annabel said, "Your kids are really cute."

"Oh. Thanks." Holly chuckled, taking a seat at the other end of the sofa. Wally plopped himself at Holly's feet, and she reached down to ruffle his fur before saying, "You've only seen them after they're worn-out playing ball with Wally. Wait until you see them after their nap, when they're reenergized. The word *rambunctious* was created with Ian and Jamie in mind."

Annabel laughed. "Kids are like that. All kids. But women still keep having them anyway." A wistful expression crossed her face. "I wouldn't mind…" She didn't finish that sentence, just tossed her magazine to one side and asked, "How old are Ian and Jamie?"

"Eighteen months."

"Identical twins? They look like it, but have they been tested to know for sure?"

Holly nodded. "Identical. Even so, Chris can already tell them apart."

"Really." There was something in the way Annabel said that one word, something meaningful. Not a question, just an acknowledgment of what that said about Chris.

Holly nodded again. "He's incredibly observant." She started to say "for a man" but realized that wasn't true. Chris was incredibly observant, period.

"That's what makes him such a good PI," Annabel stated. Then she laughed softly. "Of course, that wasn't always such a great thing when I was in high school."

"Chris admitted he scared away a few of your boyfriends."

"That's an understatement!" Annabel's laughter softened into a reminiscent smile. "I tease him, I know, but he's a great brother in most ways. When we finally reconnected in high school—"

"Reconnected?" Holly's eyebrows drew together. "What do you mean, reconnected?"

Annabel looked surprised. "Didn't you know? We were all sent to different—" Then she stopped. "You *do* know about our father…and our mother…don't you?"

Holly nodded. "Chris told me the first time we met."

"Hmm. Doesn't sound like Chris. He doesn't tell many people."

"He was trying to make a point," Holly said. "I think he wanted to shock me."

"Now, that *does* sound like Chris," Annabel replied. Her expression turned somber. "And it's not like it's a secret—just about everyone in Granite Gulch knows." She was silent for a moment. "Well, if you know what happened, then I would have thought you'd know when our mother was killed and our father went to prison, the whole family was split up. We were all sent to different foster homes."

"Oh, Annabel…" Holly tried to imagine someone doing that to Ian and Jamie, and could hardly fathom it.

Annabel sighed, then continued. "That's what I meant when I said Chris and I reconnected in high school. We were eleven when we were separated. We didn't meet again until then."

Holly didn't know any way of expressing the pain that speared through her for the brother and sister who'd been so ruthlessly torn apart. All she could say was "Oh, Annabel" again.

"Chris and I were close growing up. I was a bit of a tomboy—do they even use that word anymore? But we did nearly everything together. He was always protective—not just toward me, but toward our younger brothers and sister, too. Our mother's death and the separation only exaggerated that trait in Chris. So when we reconnected in high school…" She shrugged. "There were some bullies who tried to pick on me because of…well, because of our serial-killer father. Chris helped me put a stop to it."

"It sounds like him." After she said it Holly was struck with the realization that she'd known Chris less than two days, but she already knew this much about him. It didn't seem possible…but it was true.

Holly still had questions about Chris, however, questions she didn't really want to ask him, and this seemed like the golden opportunity. She looked at Annabel and blurted out, "What was Laura like?"

Chris's sister thought for a moment. "Sweet. Pretty. And she had a gentleness about her that was very appealing, especially to a man like Chris." She hesitated, then added, "Chris was her world, and whatever he did

was right. Good in some ways, not so good in others."
Annabel looked as if she could say more, but wouldn't.

Holly digested this, then asked, "How did she die?"

"Viral meningitis."

"Oh." Holly stared blankly at Annabel. "I thought
that was treatable."

"It is…if you treat it in time. There was an outbreak
in Fort Worth, and somehow Laura was exposed. She
had all the classic symptoms—headache, stiff neck,
fever. But she never mentioned it to Chris. By the time
she called her sister, Peg—you know Peg, right?" Annabel said in an aside. "Isn't that what Chris said?"
Holly nodded and Annabel continued. "By the time
Peg rushed her to the doctor she was in a really bad
way. She was airlifted to Baylor Medical Center in
Fort Worth, but she didn't make it—she died en route."

A wave of empathy for Chris enveloped Holly, because she could relate. Grant had been airlifted from
the scene of the traffic accident that had taken his life,
but he hadn't made it to the hospital, either. "How horrible for Chris," she whispered.

"He took it hard," Annabel confirmed. "Especially
since he blamed himself."

"What do you mean? How could he— If Laura
didn't tell him she was feeling bad, how could he have
known?"

"That's something you're going to have to ask him,"
Annabel said with a guilty expression. "I probably
shouldn't have told you that much." She sighed suddenly. "But here's something maybe you should know,
something Peg could tell you but probably didn't. Laura
was four months pregnant when she died."

"Oh, my God." Holly covered her mouth with one

hand. Suddenly the statement Peg had made about Chris the last time she'd seen her friend made complete sense. "Peg told me—she said she couldn't really explain, but she said Chris needed to take care of the twins and me. And I should let him. This must have been what she meant."

"Probably." Annabel's blue eyes—so like her brother's—held Holly's gaze. "You haven't known Chris very long, so you might not understand. Chris has a very stern conscience. He would never admit it, but he fervently believes in atonement. He knows you can't change the past, no matter how much you might want to. But he *does* believe you can make up for it—if you're willing to pay the price. And he is."

Chapter 9

Chris drove the roughly seventy miles to Dallas in just over fifty minutes, with his foot on the accelerator of his F-150 and one eye on the rearview mirror, watching for the highway patrol. He'd gotten a couple of speeding tickets in his lifetime, but nothing that appeared on his driving record, and he wanted to keep it that way. Not enough to slow down—this was Texas after all—but enough to be semicautious.

He was pretty sure he remembered where the sports bar he was heading to was located, but he had his GPS on anyway, and he followed the directions. His tires squealed only slightly when he pulled into the parking lot, stopped the truck and got out.

Chris was accosted by a wall of television sets, all tuned to different sports channels, when he walked into the otherwise dimly lit sports bar. He glanced around, looking for the clothing Taylor had described the reporter would be wearing, but realized he didn't need that help after all. Taylor was standing at the bar with the other man, both of them nursing beers and munching on bar snacks, when Taylor spotted Chris and waved him over.

The introductions were made swiftly, after which Chris murmured to his friend, "Afraid of being scooped?"

Taylor laughed. "No, but whatever you have to say to Roger, I want to know. Just in case."

Chris ordered a longneck and a plate of nachos—he'd yet to meet a reporter who wasn't hungry, literally as well as figuratively—then said, "Let's get a booth. More privacy."

Chris sipped his beer as the other two men dug into the nachos, then put the bottle down in front of him and abruptly said to Roger, "What do you know about Desmond Carlton?"

Roger swallowed. "Uh-uh. That's not how this works. Taylor said you might have information for me related to the article I wrote on the man who was captured, one of the FBI's Ten Most Wanted."

Chris shook his head and moved his beer bottle infinitesimally. "Quid pro quo," he said. "Give and take. You tell me what you know, and I'll tell you what I know. *That's* how this works."

Roger glanced at Taylor, who said, "I vouch for him, Roger. He's never lied to me yet."

Roger nodded thoughtfully. "Okay," he told Chris. "What do you want to know?"

"Desmond Carlton."

Roger shook his head. "I don't know all that much. I'd been working on a story for a while, gathering whatever bits and pieces I could find on *all* the men on the FBI's Ten Most Wanted list." He grimaced. "Okay, so the angle was how long each man had been on the list, and why the FBI wasn't making progress in catching them."

Chris pursed his lips. "And?" he prompted.

"And then, boom! The FBI arrests one, and that angle kinda sorta went out the window. But my supervising editor said we could salvage at least part of the work I'd done by publishing what I'd uncovered on the guy, including his past history, the creeps he ran with, everything."

Chris took another sip of his beer. "So how did Desmond Carlton's name come into it?"

"He was collaterally associated with the perp the FBI arrested. But Carlton's been dead for six years. Now that this guy's finally been arrested, everybody associated with Carlton is either dead or behind bars. End of story."

Chris mulled this over for a minute. "Not quite," he told Roger. "Are you aware there's not a single mention of Desmond Carlton on any search engine?"

Roger's face betrayed him. "Yeah," he said slowly, "I didn't really focus on it, but now that you mention it, you're right."

"How did you find out the facts about him you included in your story?"

"The morgue had a few articles on Desmond Carlton," Roger said, confirming Chris's hunch. "Including one on his death six years ago. But remember," he was quick to justify himself, "Carlton wasn't the main focus of the story. So it never occurred to me…"

Taylor spoke up finally. "Are you saying someone

wiped Desmond Carlton's name out of every database?"
He glanced at Roger. "Now, *that's* a story."

"I don't know who, and I don't know why," Chris
admitted, "but yeah. Electronically Desmond Carlton is
a ghost." He slid his beer bottle back and forth between
his hands, considering what more—if anything—he
should reveal. Finally he reached a decision.

"Deep background, guys," he said, his voice rough.
His eyes met Roger's, then Taylor's. "Deal?"

Chris knew what he was asking. If Taylor and Roger
agreed, they could never quote him on what he was
about to disclose. They could only use his information
if they could confirm it with other sources, sources
willing to go on the record.

"Deal," said Taylor, and Roger echoed, "Deal."

Chris fixed his eyes on Roger. "In all your research,
did the name Josie Colton ever come up in connection
with Desmond Carlton in *any* way?"

Taylor blurted out, "Josie? You mean—" Chris
kicked Taylor under the table, and his friend fell silent.

Roger thought a minute. "Josie Colton?" He shook
his head regretfully. "Not that I recall, and I looked
under every rock I could find." Then he made the connection. "Wait a sec. Josie Colton. Wasn't the FBI looking at her for the Alphabet Killer murders?"

Chris held back his sudden spurt of anger. "Not anymore." He didn't trust himself to say anything else at
that moment.

Taylor, after one glance at Chris's suddenly closed
face, said, "That's right. They've pretty much narrowed
it down to Regina Willard, haven't they?"

Chris nodded, hoping that was the end of the questioning, but Roger said, "Colton, huh? Any relation of yours?"

"My youngest sister," he admitted reluctantly. But that was all he was going to say about Josie. No way was he going to mention her foster parents had the same last name as Desmond Carlton. No way was he going to reveal she'd been missing for six years, either—the same amount of time Desmond Carlton had been dead. If there was a connection…if Josie was somehow involved…

"You said you found an article in the morgue about Carlton's death," Chris said suddenly. "How did he die?"

"Shot to death. But there were no shell casings and someone even dug the bullets out of him, so there was very little to go on."

"Was anyone ever arrested for it?"

"Nope," Roger said. "The case is cold…not that anyone in the police department is losing sleep over it. Drug lord shot to death? A man who'd been a suspect in several murders but never arrested for any of them? The police probably figured whoever offed him was doing the public a favor taking him off the streets."

Taylor elbowed Roger in the ribs. "What?" Roger exclaimed. "I'm not saying anything other people haven't thought."

"Yeah," Taylor said. "But still…someone getting away with murder…it's not right. Whoever killed Desmond Carlton is probably still out there. And if he killed once, he could kill again. And the next time it might not be someone who deserved to die."

"Was there any mention of reprisals?" Chris asked.

"Could Carlton's murder have been the result of some kind of rivalry between drug cartels?"

"I never uncovered anything about that. Doesn't mean it wasn't drug related, but there was no mention of any kind of drug war in the newspapers in the months following Carlton's death. I couldn't find anything indicating he'd been killed in a coup within his own organization, either."

Which brings me right back to Josie and her possible involvement, Chris thought but didn't voice. He couldn't imagine his baby sister killing anyone—he'd never really bought into the idea that Josie might be the Alphabet Killer, but he'd sure been glad when the finger of suspicion had finally pointed away from her. He also couldn't imagine what connection Josie could have to a slain drug lord...except the coincidences of the time frame of her disappearance and her foster parents' last name. Coincidences he didn't trust.

Chris rubbed a hand over his jaw, then asked Roger one last question. "Are you planning any follow-up articles?"

"Nothing about Desmond Carlton, if that's what you're asking."

He smiled briefly. "Yeah, that's what I'm asking. Just wondered if you were holding anything back." *The way I am*, he finished in his mind.

"Nope, not this time. But—" Roger held up one hand, palm outward "—if I find anything from other sources that ties Josie Colton to Desmond Carlton's murder...all deals are off."

"Understood." Chris finished the dregs of his beer and stood. "Thanks, Roger. I owe you one."

"Hey, what about me?" Taylor asked in a mock-serious tone.

"I bought you the nachos," Chris said with a sudden grin. "We're even."

Evalinda McCay hummed to herself as she ruthlessly pruned the hydrangea bushes on either side of her front door. But she wasn't really giving as much attention to her gardening as she usually did; she was thinking about Holly. *Snip!* went the shears, slicing effortlessly through the branches the way she could easily have sliced through her daughter-in-law's throat.

I should have taken care of Holly myself, she acknowledged privately. She could have done it, too—no qualms assailed her about the course of action she'd decided on to get custody of the twins…and their all-too-tempting trust fund. Angus had protested at first, but he hadn't been difficult to persuade—she'd been unilaterally making their major decisions for all the years they'd been married…and even before then.

If I had killed Holly, she'd be dead now, and all that money would already be mine.

But Angus had insisted they insulate themselves, make it appear to be an accident. Even more, he'd shrunk from having a direct hand in eliminating Holly, as if that made it less of a sin somehow.

Evalinda wasn't worried about sin any more than she was worried about divine retribution. All she cared about was the money that would preserve their standing in the community. The income from the trust fund would eliminate their debt, would remove the sword of Damocles hanging over their heads and allow them to continue to live lavishly…the way she deserved.

It wasn't just the income from the trust she intended to have, however—the principal was also in her long-range plans, although she hadn't mentioned that to Angus yet. But first things first. Custody of the twins was the primary step. Everything else would follow from that. Which meant one way or another, Holly had to die. And soon.

That night, after the twins were in bed, Holly sought out Chris in his office. She tapped on the open door and said, "Knock, knock," before she realized he was on the phone. Chris swung around in his chair, cell phone to his ear, and held up a finger to indicate his call was almost finished. "Thanks, Sam," he said. "I appreciate it." Then he disconnected.

"Hey," he said to Holly. "What's up?"

"I wanted to talk to you about the McCays," she said, leaning against the doorjamb. "You said yesterday you wanted to set a trap for them, and I... Not that I'm not grateful for your hospitality," she rushed to add. "I am. It's a lovely house, and Ian and Jamie had a blast playing with Wally in the yard this morning." One corner of her mouth quirked into a half smile. "Peg was right to insist we bring him. He has helped the boys adjust to this new place better than anything I could have thought of."

"Boys and dogs," Chris said softly. "Nothing like the bond that develops between boys and dogs."

"Girls, too," Holly was quick to point out. "I had a dog myself growing up, a cocker spaniel I named Chocolate Bar because she was such a rich brown color. I called her Chox for short. I got her for Christmas in first grade. She died when I was fifteen and I wept buckets."

Chris's eyes crinkled at the corners for just a moment, and though he didn't say anything, Holly sensed there was a very sad story somewhere in Chris's past about a dog. She hurried to get back to her original subject. "Anyway," she said, "I wanted to discuss that trap you mentioned."

He leaned back in his chair with a creak of leather and indicated the sofa. "Have a seat," he said. "It just so happens I was talking with my brother about this when you walked in."

Holly sat. "You were?"

"Mmm-hmm. Sam agrees you can't keep running. He also agrees setting a trap for the McCays is the way to go, but we have to be careful about entrapment. Which means—"

"We can't entice them into committing an illegal act," Holly said before he could. "I understand."

A flash of admiration crossed Chris's face. "Exactly. We can do this, but we have to plan it carefully. And of course, Sam's concerned about using real bait."

"You mean me."

"Yeah. But I don't think we have a choice. You're the only way to draw them out into the open."

Holly nodded. "Makes sense."

"Sam's also worried about the twins. No matter what kind of trap we set, there's going to be some danger involved. He doesn't want the twins around when we spring the trap. I don't think you do, either."

"Of course not."

"So that means we need to stash them somewhere safe for the time being."

Holly stared blankly at Chris. "You mean…turn my children over to a stranger?"

Chris shook his head. "No," he said gently, and Holly realized despite his big, tough exterior, he really was a gentle man. "I'd never suggest that. But what about Peg? She'd do it for you, don't you think? The boys know her and her kids. And Peg told me you and she have traded off babysitting for the past three months."

"A few hours at a time," Holly said faintly as a sense of suffocation overwhelmed her. "And never overnight."

"If you've got a better idea, I'd like to hear it."

If she hadn't already been sitting down, she would have fallen, because her legs were suddenly weak and trembling. Leave her babies? Not just for a few hours, but for however long it took to set and spring a trap? She hadn't been able to go back to work after her maternity leave ended. How was she expected to spend nights away from them?

Holly's lips moved, but no words came out, and she forced herself to focus on Chris's face. "You want me to leave Ian and Jamie with Peg…indefinitely."

He shook his head again. "Not indefinitely. A few days, a week at the most."

Could she do it? She wasn't sure. But did she really have a choice? Chris and his brother were right—she couldn't keep on running. Not just because the McCays might eventually run her to ground, but also because the constant moving was too hard on Ian and Jamie, especially now that they were getting old enough to notice the change in their environment. She had to close that chapter in her life, and the only way to do it…the only *safe* way to do it…was to settle with the McCays once and for all. To get them arrested, tried and convicted. To get them locked away where they would no longer be a threat. Not to her, and not to her sons.

"Could I…could I at least talk to them every day?"

"Nobody's trying to stop you from being a good mother, Holly…except the McCays." That gentleness was back in Chris's voice. "But I don't want you to visit Ian and Jamie at Peg's, because once we set the trap the McCays will know where you are…and instead of going after the bait and trying to kill you, they could track you to Peg's house. Secretly. We'd have no way of knowing. And that would put the boys in danger. I know you don't want that."

"Of course not," Holly repeated.

"You can talk to Ian and Jamie several times a day, for however long you and they need. A week, max, I promise. Hard on you. Hard on them. But it'll be worth it if we catch the McCays in the act."

"Okay." She didn't want to do it, but Chris's points were irrefutable. She suddenly realized her palms were damp, and she rubbed them nervously on the sides of her jeans. "So when do we start?"

"As soon as I can coordinate things with Sam and Annabel—tomorrow or the next day. And I've got to get Jim Murray's blessing, too." She raised her brows in a question, and he added, "He's the Granite Gulch police chief. Sam and Annabel answer to him, so we can't do this without him giving it the green light. But I don't see Jim saying no."

"Can he be trusted?" Holly blurted out.

Chris smiled faintly. "He's honest as the day is long.

I've known him since I was a kid, and I would trust him to do the right thing. Always."

"Okay," she said again. She didn't say anything more, but she didn't leave, either. She knew she should—that would be the safe thing. The smart thing. But suddenly all she could think of was the kiss in her dream yesterday. The kiss that had devastated her with how much she wanted this man she barely knew. And then there was the kiss that wasn't. The almost-kiss in the kitchen last night. She'd seen it in his eyes—he'd wanted to kiss her. Why hadn't he?

Then she realized he was looking at her the same way he had last night, as if he was a little boy standing on the sidewalk outside a store window gazing long-ingly at something he wanted but knew he couldn't have because he couldn't afford it. As if—

"Go to bed, Holly," he told her, his voice suddenly harsh. But she couldn't seem to make her feet move. "This isn't what you want." Oh, but it was, it *was*.

So when her feet finally did move it wasn't to leave. Six steps was all it took to bring her right up to Chris, right up to his rock-hard body that exuded unbeliev-able warmth, just like her dream. She reached up and brushed a lock of hair from his forehead, then let her fingers trail down his temple, his cheek. The slight scruff of his unshaven chin made her shiver with sud-den longing, and her nipples tightened until they ached.

Then he pulled her flush against his body, and she wrapped her arms around his waist, holding on for dear life. She raised her face to his, her eyes mutely asking, and he kissed her.

Kissed? If she could think, she'd find a better word for what his lips were doing to hers, but every thought flew out of her head and all she could do was kiss him back. All she could do was match the hunger in him. The need. The frantic longing for something just out of reach, which they both knew could be theirs, if only...

She heard a whimper and realized it was coming from her throat. Heard a moan and realized that was hers, too. She couldn't seem to get close enough, even though he was holding her in his powerful embrace as if he would never let her go. *Don't let me go* reverberated in her brain, and if she'd had the breath she would have said the words out loud. But she couldn't, because he'd stolen her breath. Stolen her sanity.

He was hot and hard, but not where she wanted him to be—he was too tall...or she was too short. Then his hands grasped her hips and lifted her with unbelievable strength. She wrapped her arms around his neck and her legs around his hips, gasping with relief as she rocked up against the hardness she yearned for.

He was still kissing her and—oh, God!—just like her dream, she couldn't get enough of him. She was burning up from the inside out, and if he didn't make love to her in the next sixty seconds she would go crazy, she would—

A sudden wailing from the master bedroom brought everything to a crashing halt.

Chapter 10

Letting Holly go ranked right up there in the top ten most difficult things Chris had ever done, but he did it. He reluctantly let her slide down his body until her feet touched the floor. Compelled his lips to release hers. Forced his arms to set her free. Her breasts were rising and falling as if she was having the same difficulty he was having breathing, and there was a dazed expression in her eyes…one that quickly changed to mortification.

"I…I… That's Jamie," Holly stammered, practically running from the study.

Chris followed her, turning on the light in the hallway so she didn't have to feel her way in the darkness. She disappeared into the master bedroom before he could catch up, and when he turned the corner, she was already lifting a weeping Jamie from his crib.

"It's okay, sweetie," she soothed. "Mommy's here."

Ian, woken from a sound sleep by his brother's sobs, started fussing, his face crumpling as if he was going to cry, too. But Chris wouldn't let him. He lifted the boy out of the crib and propped him up against his shoulder. "Hey, buddy, don't you start." He chucked the boy under the chin. "Come on now. You're okay."

He glanced over at Holly cuddling Jamie in her arms, his face pressed against her shoulder as she rocked him back and forth. "Bad dream, you think?"

"Probably."

Holly's eyes wouldn't meet his, and disappointment slashed through him as he figured she was already regretting what they'd done. The best thing that had happened to him since Laura died…and Holly was regretting it.

Should have known better, he berated himself. *Should never have touched her. You knew that, so why…?*

He didn't want to address that question, but the answer refused to be silenced. He'd touched Holly… kissed her…caressed her…damn near made love to her…because he had to. Because the yearning in her eyes had aroused an ache in him he hadn't been able to suppress. Because the need to hold her had swept everything aside like a force of nature, the way a river in flood swept away everything in its path.

And now she wouldn't even look at him. As if she was ashamed.

That was the most hurtful thing of all.

Chris sat in his study a half hour later. Staring at his laptop, but not really seeing the web page he'd opened. Work, which had been his saving grace after Laura's death, couldn't hold his interest. He kept reliving the scene of Holly and him in this very room tonight. Only this time when he told her to go to bed and she refused to go…this time when she walked toward him and touched his face…this time when she raised her face to his asking for his kiss…this time he didn't touch her.

Which was what he should have done in the first place.

"Chris?"

He whirled around in his chair when a hesitant voice from the doorway said his name. Then he stood, needing to be on his feet to offer Holly the apology she deserved. In one way he wasn't sorry—he'd wanted to kiss her since the first time he'd seen her walking up the driveway of Peg's house, and now he had. And it had been like nothing he'd ever experienced in his life. But in another way he regretted it…because now he *knew* what it would be like with Holly…and he couldn't have it. Couldn't have *her*.

"I'm sorry."

"I'm sorry."

Chris spoke first, but Holly's apology was only a half second behind his. He shook his head. "You don't have anything to apologize for," he told her. "I should never have touched you."

Holly blinked, then her eyes creased at the corners. "I started it," she said quietly. "I'm not one of those women who blame the man for losing control when—" She broke off and breathed deeply. "You didn't do anything I didn't want you to do."

"That doesn't absolve me of blame." Chris tucked

his hands in his back pockets to keep himself from reaching for her. "You're under my protection, Holly. And you're feeling vulnerable—I knew that. I shouldn't have taken advantage."

A fierce expression swept over her face. "You shouldn't have taken *advantage*?" Her voice held that same fierceness. "What is this, the eighteen hundreds? If one of us took advantage of the other, it was me. *I* took advantage of *you*. I wanted you, and I—" She stopped, then continued bravely. "I wanted you, Chris. I've never wanted that way in my entire life, not even with Grant."

His brain tried to process her words, but they didn't jive with— "You ran out of the room," he grated. "You were mortified—no, don't deny it," he interjected when she tried to speak. "And in the bedroom you wouldn't even meet my eyes. You were *ashamed*."

"Not for the reason you apparently think," she said, a tinge of color in her cheeks. "When I heard Jamie crying, I…I didn't want to stop. Didn't want to go see what was wrong with him. *That's* why I was mortified," she explained. "Because I wanted you so much that for an instant I actually resented Jamie for interrupting." Her lips curved up slightly at the corners in a rueful smile. "I didn't want to be a mother at the moment, Chris. I just wanted to be a woman. A woman you wanted as much as I wanted you."

He could have sworn he didn't move, but suddenly he found himself standing right in front of Holly. "I wanted you," he said in his deepest voice. "I wanted you like I wanted my next breath." He raised a hand to her cheek and admitted, "I still do." He let that confession hang there for a couple of seconds before adding,

"And when Jamie cried?" His rueful smile matched hers. "I wished him in perdition."

Suddenly they were both laughing softly, and Chris lowered his forehead to Holly's. "That doesn't make us bad people," he told her, unutterably relieved she hadn't been ashamed of what they'd done after all. "It just means we're human."

"So I'm not a bad mother because I didn't immediately switch off the woman gene and switch on the mother gene?" she whispered, but in a tone that told him she was teasing.

"Hell—I mean, heck no," he teased back.

Holly touched her lips to his. "Glad to hear it," she murmured.

Desire zinged through his veins, but this time he had enough self-control not to follow through on it. "Don't start something we can't finish," he warned lightly.

"We can't?"

"Holly…" he began, then realized she was teasing again.

"It's going to happen, Chris," she told him, all teasing aside. "Not tonight. Maybe not even tomorrow night. But it's going to happen." Despite her brazen words, the little flags of color in her cheeks, the not-so-sure-of-herself expression in her eyes and the almost defiant way she said it told Chris this wasn't normal behavior for Holly. *She's probably never made the first move in her life*, he thought. And that turned him on no end. The idea that Holly—sweet, innocent Holly—wanted him that much was incredibly arousing.

But he wasn't taking any chances. Not tonight. "Go to bed, Holly," he told her, gently this time. "But I won't be upset if you dream about me, 'cause I'll be dreaming about you." He laughed deep in his throat, and it felt good to laugh, even though he knew he'd go to bed hard and aching and wake up the same way. "Oh, yeah, I'll be dreaming about you."

Holly woke before the twins again and lay there for a moment, enjoying the peace and quiet. Then she remembered how she'd brazenly told Chris last night they would eventually become lovers. Just *thinking* about it made her cheeks warm—she'd never been that bold with a man. Even when she'd made up her mind to do whatever she could to entice Grant into loving her, she'd never come right out and said it.

But then she'd never felt for Grant what she felt for Chris. Yes, she'd loved her husband, but…she'd never hungered for him. She'd never *craved*. And that was a revelation. She just wasn't sure what it meant.

She wasn't merely drawn to Chris physically, though. He tugged at her heart, too, now more than ever. Her conversation with Annabel yesterday afternoon had explained a lot about his behavior, and she believed she knew him better. But it wasn't just that. Watching him with her sons—could there exist a man more destined to be a father than Chris? He was a natural, his father instincts always on target. Like last night, for instance, when he'd stopped Ian from crying. How did he *know*? How did he unerringly know just what to do, what to say in every interaction with Ian and Jamie?

Holly turned over and tucked her hand beneath her cheek. Chris was a triple threat—hotter than sin, a perfect dad in the making and a man whose emotions ran so deep any woman would be drawn to him.

She sighed. Problem was…she was starting to fall

for him. Which had epic disaster written all over it, because she wasn't the kind of woman men fell in love with. Okay, yes, Chris wanted her. She was pretty enough, sexy enough, and other men had wanted her before. Not Grant, though. Except for the night Ian and Jamie had been conceived—and it had taken a few drinks more than he normally allowed himself before he'd seen her as a sexy, desirable woman—Grant's lovemaking had been...restrained. Good enough in its way, but...restrained. They'd tried hard to make a go of their marriage for the twins' sake. But Grant had never been in love with her...because she wasn't the lovable kind.

Chris told Holly at breakfast, "I called Peg this morning. She agreed to take Ian and Jamie for as long as you need."

She stopped supervising Jamie's attempts to feed himself and darted a dismayed look at him. "So soon?"

"The sooner we start, the sooner it will be over," he said patiently. "But actually, I have something I need to get out of the way first." She raised her eyebrows in a question and he hesitated, then realized there really wasn't any reason not to tell her. "I have to visit my father in prison."

"Visit your father?" The faint way she asked told him he'd surprised her.

"He's dying," he said abruptly. "Back in January he promised Sam that if each of his children visited him, he'd give us clues as to where he buried our mother."

"I don't understand."

Chris glanced at Ian and Jamie, but they were completely occupied with eating and weren't paying the least bit of attention to the adult conversation. "I told you what he did to our mother," he explained, masking his words for the twins' benefit. "But I never said that when he did it he took her away and buried her somewhere. Law enforcement searched at the time, but they never found her." Chris couldn't keep the hard edge out of his tone. "My brothers and I, and Annabel, too—we've been searching for years."

"But no luck," Holly stated.

"No luck," he agreed. "We've all been taking turns visiting my father since January. Annabel went last month. Now it's my turn." He breathed deeply, trying to tamp down his emotions, then added in a low voice, "We just want to give her a decent burial, Holly. Is that too much to ask?" She shook her head. "I haven't seen him in nearly twenty years. I never wanted to. But I can't pass up the chance to find out where my mother is."

"Of course you can't," she said stoutly. Her lovely brown eyes were filled with empathy. "I understand. When my parents were killed in South America—they were missionaries," she explained, and Chris didn't bother to tell her he already knew. "I...I was only a teenager. But I knew I had to bring their bodies home. It was a nightmare of frustration and paperwork, but I finally did it. They're buried together in a cemetery not far from their old church, so their close friends can visit their graves." She paused, then added softly, "Grant's buried right next to them."

Chris saw the tears in her eyes she was struggling to hold back. "Grant's parents—they wanted him buried in a more fashionable cemetery, but...he loved my parents and they loved him. I wanted them all together, you know?"

He cleared his throat. "Yeah, I do." The silence was broken when Ian accidentally knocked his sippy cup off his high-chair tray. The lid was securely fastened, so only a small amount of milk leaked onto the floor. But Holly jumped up, retrieved the cup, then grabbed a paper towel to wipe up the spilled milk.

After she rinsed off the cup and gave it back to Ian, she resumed her seat, and Chris said, "Anyway, I have to visit the prison today. I was thinking…if you wouldn't mind…I could take you and the twins to Peg's this morning. You could stay there until I come back to pick you up. I think you'll be safe there."

Holly's mouth twitched into a faint smile. "Let me guess—you already suggested this to Peg, right?" Chris had the grace to look abashed, and she chuckled. "Why am I not surprised?"

The independent woman in Holly knew she should be insulted, the same way she'd been insulted yesterday when she'd told Chris she didn't need a babysitter. Nevertheless there was something appealing about Chris's protectiveness that spoke to a more primitive aspect of her nature. Grant had never been protective of her—not that way. They'd grown up together, so he knew Holly could take care of herself. Still…she couldn't really fault Chris for wanting to make sure she and the boys were safe in his absence. Especially since he'd told her, *No one is dying on my watch ever again*…

She needed to ask Chris what he meant by that statement. Based on what Annabel had recounted about Laura, she had a pretty good idea it had something to do with his dead wife…and their unborn child.

But before she could ask him, Chris rose and put his breakfast dishes in the dishwasher. "I'll load the cribs and high chairs in the back of my truck. You'd better pack enough clothes and things for the twins to last a week. And maybe their favorite books and toys. Susan and Bobby have plenty, but those little bunnies the boys sleep with? Don't want to leave them behind." Then he was gone.

Matthew Colton looked smaller than Chris remembered. *Only to be expected*, he thought after the first shock of seeing his father sitting at the table, behind the glass separating the prisoners from the visitors. Chris had been eleven back then—nearly twenty years had passed. And his father was sick…dying. Which would account for his frail appearance that made him seem…a pathetic old man. *He murdered your mother*, Chris had to remind himself, steeling against the sudden wave of good memories. *Not to mention all the others he killed.*

And yet…there were a lot of worse fathers than Matthew Colton had been. How to reconcile the two pictures of Matthew? *Remember the bad times*, he told himself. *Remember Ethan finding Mama's body with the bull's-eye on her forehead. Remember your family being torn apart. Remember Bouncer being sent to the pound. That's all on him. That's all Matthew's doing.*

Chris sat at the table across from his father, removed his Stetson and placed it on the table in front of him, then ran a hand through his hair, which the Stetson had flattened. Then and only then did he pick up the phone. He had no idea what he would say, but Matthew spoke first.

"You look like your mother." If Matthew had stabbed him, Chris couldn't have been more surprised, but Matthew wasn't done. "Not your coloring, of course. Saralee's hair was long and dark, not blond." There was a wistful intonation to his words. "But you and Annabel look like her in every other way."

Chris cleared his throat against the wave of emotion that rose in him. "Yeah," he agreed. "Everyone who remembers her says we look like Mama." He'd thought he could do this, but now that he was here... "So you wanted to see each of us. And you bribed us here by promising a clue to where Mama's buried. Piss-poor clues, but then you knew that, didn't you?" Matthew's eyes turned crafty, and Chris nodded. "Okay, I'm here. You've got your pound of flesh from me. So what's my clue?"

"No 'Hello, Daddy'? No 'How are you doing, Daddy'? Just 'What's my clue?'"

Chris drew a deep breath and held it, holding his anger in at the same time. "What do you want from me?" When Matthew didn't respond, Chris reluctantly asked, "How are you doing?"

"I'm dying." The bald statement stood there while neither man spoke.

After a long, long time, Chris said the only thing that came to him. "I know."

Again there was silence between them, silence that was eventually broken by Matthew. "Twenty years, I've been locked away in this cage. Near twenty years, and the only one of you children to come see me was Trevor...and only because it was his job."

"What did you expect?" Chris couldn't keep the

bitter edge out of his words. "You really think any of us wanted to see you ever again?"

"Don't you sass me, boy," Matthew retorted with a spurt of anger, his free hand forming a fist. "I can still tan your hide, and don't you forget it!"

All at once Chris was eleven again, facing his father over a broken window caused by an errant baseball Annabel had thrown. Matthew yanking his belt out of its loops and fiercely demanding of his children, *Who did it? Who threw that ball?*

Chris had stepped forward immediately. Matthew wouldn't have hesitated to use the belt on eleven-year-old Annabel, and Chris was too protective of her—of all the younger children—to let her take the imminent whipping. But Annabel had piped up bravely, *I did it, Daddy.* So Matthew had whipped them both—Annabel for breaking the window, Chris for lying. For trying to take the blame, for trying to shield Annabel from Matthew's wrath.

Chris and Annabel had hidden out in their secret hideaway afterward, lying on their stomachs in the shade of a catalpa tree so as not to further exacerbate the wounds on their smarting bottoms. Annabel trying so hard to be as tough as Chris, fighting back tears. But Chris hadn't cried. Not then...and not at their mother's memorial service a few months later. He hadn't cried until Bouncer...

Then Chris's mind jumped to Laura's funeral, and he realized he hadn't cried then, either. He hadn't cried at the loss of the two most important women in his life. But he'd cried over Bouncer. He'd never thought about it before, but now he realized maybe the reason he hadn't cried for his mother and his wife was because some things went too deep for tears. Heart wounds, both of them. And one of them had been caused by the man sitting across from him.

"Whatever happened to your dog, boy?" Matthew asked abruptly. "Whatever happened to that golden retriever I gave you when you were six?"

Cold anger shook Chris. "He's dead."

"Well, hell, boy, 'course he is." Matthew smirked. "Dogs don't live as long as humans. I just wondered how he died, that's all."

Suddenly it was all too much for Chris. Suddenly the years rolled back, and he wanted to wipe that smirk off Matthew's face. Not just for Bouncer, euthanized despite Chris's tearful pleas to his foster parents, but for his mother, too. And for his brothers and sisters, orphaned yet not orphaned. Fighting the stigma of being Matthew Colton's child—a serial killer's child—to this day. He gripped the phone in a death grip and rasped, "Tell me where Mama's body is buried, Daddy. I'm begging you, damn it! Tell me!"

Chapter 11

The crafty expression returned to Matthew's face, and he shook his head. "Can't do that, boy. You get your one clue, just like the others." He waited for Chris to say something, but when Chris didn't speak, he offered, "Biff."

"Biff? That's it? Biff?"

Matthew nodded, a secretive smile forming. As if he knew what Chris was thinking. As if he knew that if Chris could have reached through the glass he would have put his hands around his father's throat and—

No! A tiny corner of Chris's brain forced him back to sanity. *You are not a killer*, he reminded himself, the words becoming his mantra. *You are not a killer. He's your father, but you are not him. And you are not a killer.*

He settled his Stetson on his head, shielding his eyes

from Matthew's searching gaze. "You are an evil man," Chris told his father evenly through the phone. "And yes, your blood flows through our veins. But Mama's blood flows through our veins, too. You killed her, but you can't kill her spirit—we're her legacy. She lives on in us."

He put the phone down and stood. Matthew was speaking—his lips were moving—but Chris didn't want to hear anything more his father had to say. He turned and walked toward the door…to freedom. Freedom his father would never know until the disease ravaging his body claimed him, and he left the prison in a hearse.

Chris would never return. Would never look on his father's face ever again, not even at his funeral…which Chris would not attend. But this visit had been necessary after all, and not just to receive his clue that was no more help than the clues the others had received. No, this visit brought closure. Chris hadn't realized he needed it, but now he finally acknowledged that the father he'd once known no longer existed. The stern father who—despite that sternness—had loved his wife and children had been a different man. This man—Matthew Colton, wife murderer and serial killer—wasn't the father of Chris's memory. Something had changed him. Twisted him. He was beyond the reach of even his children's pleading.

And knowing that, the shackles binding Chris to the past were finally broken. *I'm his son*, he acknowledged once again. *But I am not him.*

On the way back to town Chris passed the entrance to his brother Ethan's ranch. A sudden impulse to talk with Ethan made him brake sharply and swerve into the turn without signaling, earning him an angry honk from the truck behind him.

"Sorry," he muttered, glancing at his rearview mirror even though he knew the other driver couldn't hear him.

It wasn't just letting Ethan know the clue their father had given him that had made Chris turn, but also the desire to share that he finally understood Ethan's complete rejection of Matthew all these years. Ethan had been only seven to Chris's eleven when their father had murdered their mother—he didn't have the memories Chris had of the good times with their father. But that was all gone now, erased by the knowledge that the father he remembered and the man dying in prison were two different people.

Chris pulled up in front of the ranch house, parked and got out, leaving his hat on the seat and not bothering to lock his truck. *Ethan's probably out on the ranch somewhere, but Lizzie can tell me where he is.* His boots thudded as he mounted the wooden stairs and crossed the front porch, thinking about the last time he'd been out here. Ethan's ranch—Ethan and *Lizzie's* ranch, he reminded himself with a smile—had quickly become the Colton family gathering place. And soon there'd be another celebration, when Lizzie gave birth.

His smile faded as the never-to-be-forgotten sadness came to the fore. The loss of his own baby when Laura died wasn't the constant heartache it had been at first, but the pain would never go away completely. *His* baby would have been the first Colton of the next generation, not Ethan's. But that wasn't Ethan or Lizzie's fault. And he would love their baby the way he loved Susan and Bobby. The way he loved Ian and Jamie.

He stood stock-still for a moment. The way he loved Ian and Jamie?

You do, his shocked mind acknowledged. *You love them as if you were their fath—*

He chopped that thought off before he could finish it. "Don't go there," he muttered. "Don't."

He forced himself to move, to knock on the screen door. The front door was open, so he called through the screen, "Lizzie? Lizzie? It's Chris."

The only answer he got—a long, low moan—scared the hell out of him. "Lizzie!" He grabbed the handle on the screen door and pulled, but the latch was on and the door refused to budge. Another moan, and this time Chris wrenched at the screen door with all his might. With a creaking sound, the old wood gave way, the latch pulled free and Chris was inside. "Lizzie?" His gaze encompassed the neat living room, but he saw nothing, so he moved down the hallway, bellowing, "Lizzie, where the hell are you?"

"Kitchen— *Ohhh!*"

He found Lizzie there, her face drenched in sweat. She was bent over the back of a chair, gripping it tightly as the labor pain ebbed. His eyes took in everything, including the way her clothes were sopping wet and the panting sounds she was making as she breathed.

"Crap!" He lifted his sister-in-law gently into his arms and headed for the front door. *Hospital*, his frantic mind told him. "How far apart?"

"I...I couldn't time them," she gasped, "so I don't know. Four minutes maybe?"

"Your water broke already, so this didn't just start

a few minutes ago. Where the hell's Ethan?" He was already outside, maneuvering his way to his F-150 as fast as he could.

"He went into town. I didn't tell him… I've had false labor pains twice before and…and I didn't want to worry him again."

"Where's Joyce?" he asked, referring to the wife of Ethan's foreman, Bill Peabody.

"Joyce and Bill went to visit their kids. I never expected…"

He listened to her explanation with only half his attention. The rest was laser-focused on what he had to do. "Open the door, Lizzie," he told her when they reached the passenger side, and when she did, he kicked it wide-open with one booted foot. He placed her as carefully as he could on the passenger seat and fastened the seat belt around her, but when he went to close the door, she grabbed his arm.

"My things. Suitcase by the front door. Please!"

"Okay," he told her. "I'll get them. Don't go any-where."

Lizzie choked on a laugh. "Don't worry. Just hurry."

He found the suitcase right where she'd said it would be, then raced out, pulling the front door closed behind him. He wedged the suitcase behind his seat, sat down and belted himself in. As the engine roared to life he said, "Did you call Ethan?"

"I called him earlier, but…my water hadn't broken yet. He said he was on his way to get me."

Chris floored it, leaving a cloud of dust in their wake. The truck jounced and jolted until he got to the main road, and the minute he turned Lizzie clutched her stomach and started moaning again. "Crap!" he said again, glancing at his watch, then gave her his right hand, steering with the left. "Hold tight on to me," he said. "Scream if you want to—don't hold back. And aren't you supposed to be panting like a dog? Isn't that supposed to help?"

Between moans Lizzie laughed again the way he'd intended her to, but she didn't say anything, just gripped his hand in a death grip that—*holy crap!*—hurt.

When she finally let go, Chris surreptitiously wiggled his fingers to see if any bones were broken. When he figured they were still intact, he hit the Bluetooth button on his steering wheel as they barreled down the county highway.

He waded through the interminable questions the disembodied recorded voice asked him until he finally heard Ethan on the other end. "Ethan, it's Chris," he said, cutting his brother off. "I've got Lizzie and we're heading to the hospital." He darted a look at the clock on the dashboard. "I figure five to six minutes, tops." It would take longer...if he wasn't going ninety miles an hour. "Meet us there."

"Got it," Ethan replied. "Turning around now. Lizzie? Can you hear me?"

Chris glanced at Lizzie, then pointed to the speaker above his head. "Talk loud," he advised.

Lizzie laughed again. "I can hear you, Ethan," she shouted.

"Lizzie, honey, you hang in there, okay? I'll be with you before you know it."

"Okay."

"And, Lizzie?" The hesitation, Chris knew, was because he could hear every word Ethan said to her. "I love you, honey. You and the baby are the best things that ever happened to me, and I—"

"Yeah, yeah, yeah," Chris interrupted. "You love her, you need her, you can't live without her. Forget that crap and *drive*!"

He hit the disconnect button and glanced over at his sister-in-law, who was sitting there with tears in her eyes. "Now, don't *you* start," he told her in bracing tones.

"I love you, Chris," she blurted out as the tears overflowed. "I'm so lucky to have you as a brother-in-law." Then she caught her breath as another labor pain snared her in its grasp, and Chris could actually see the ripples go through her.

"Crap!" he said again and depressed the pedal until the speedometer hovered around a hundred. He offered Lizzie his right hand again, mentally girding himself against the pain he knew was forthcoming, but also knowing that whatever pain Lizzie inflicted on him was nothing compared to what she was going through. "Hold on tight."

Two hours later Chris was still in the hospital waiting room. Ethan had met them at Emergency and had lifted his pregnant wife out of Chris's truck even more gently than Chris had placed her in it. Chris had parked in the visitor's lot, retrieved Ethan's truck from where he'd left it half on the driveway and half on the sidewalk—smooth talking a policeman out of a ticket in the process—then headed for the Emergency entrance with Lizzie's suitcase in hand. He'd turned the suitcase over to the admitting clerk and had followed her instructions on finding the waiting room. Where he'd waited. And waited.

He'd called Peg and told her what was happening, asking her to pass along the news to Holly and explain why he was delayed getting back. Then he'd called Annabel and Sam, who were on duty and couldn't talk for long. But they'd both spared him a moment to say Jim Murray had approved them working with Chris and Holly on setting the trap for the McCays.

Chris had forgotten about that. Well, not exactly forgotten, but Lizzie's crisis had driven everything else out of his head in the heat of the moment. He'd quickly called Ridge and Trevor after that, but both calls had gone right to voice mail. He'd left a message, though, both about Lizzie and the clue he'd obtained during his trip to the prison today—Biff. Then he'd turned his mind to the problem of how best to set a trap for the McCays.

Lost in thought, he didn't see Ethan walk into the waiting room. Not until his brother stood right in front of him did Chris realize he was there. Ethan looked wiped out. Pale beneath his tan. But happy. Ecstatically happy, and relieved.

Chris stood up. "Lizzie okay?" Ethan swallowed hard, as if he wanted to speak but couldn't. Then he nodded, and Chris asked, "And the baby? Everything okay there?"

"Yeah." The rasped word was accompanied by a sudden smile that split Ethan's face. "A boy. Eight pounds, eleven ounces. Twenty-one inches."

"Wow, big baby. Must take after his dad." Chris grinned and wrapped his brother in a bear hug. "Congratulations, little brother. You did good."

Ethan returned the hug, and when the two men finally separated, Ethan dashed a hand against his eyes, swiping away the moisture. "Got something in my eye," he muttered, turning away.

"Same here," Chris said, following suit.

But then the brothers faced each other again, smiling to beat the band. Ethan shook his head. "I can never thank you enough, Chris."

"It was nothing."

"Don't give me that BS. I should never have left Lizzie this close to her due date, especially since Joyce and Bill weren't there. But she swore to me she'd be okay, and I was only going into town." His eyes took on an expression Chris remembered from their childhood, when the two youngest boys—Sam and Ethan—had looked up to their older "stair steps" and wanted to emulate them. And all four of them had looked up to Trevor, the oldest. "If not for you," Ethan continued in a grateful voice, "I don't know what Lizzie would have done."

Chris flexed his right hand and joked, "That's some woman you've got there. She almost broke my hand twice, so I figure she's tough enough to have worked out some other solution." Ethan laughed at that, and the emotional moment passed.

The brothers collapsed into two of the waiting-room chairs. Chris dug a hand into his pocket, pulled out Ethan's keys and handed them to him, saying, "Better give you these before I forget. Your truck's in the visitor's lot. Two rows down."

"Thanks."

After a moment Chris asked, "So you got a name picked out?"

"Lizzie and I had been toying with names ahead of time, but she and I talked just now and we're changing it. James Christopher Colton." Chris got that choked-up feeling again and couldn't have spoken even if he'd wanted to. "We figured a middle name would be okay. That way if you ever have a son and want to name him after yourself—" Ethan broke off as if he'd just re-membered Chris's baby that never was, and a stricken look filled his eyes. "Sorry," he said quickly. "I didn't think… I didn't mean to…"

Chris tapped Ethan's jaw with his closed fist, but lightly. "Yeah, I know you didn't mean anything by it. Don't sweat it. And tell Lizzie I'm purely honored."

The two men were silent for a few moments, then Ethan said gravely, "You know, I never wanted to marry. Never wanted to have kids. With a serial killer for a fa-ther, I…I didn't want to pass on the Colton name, or—" repugnance was in his voice "—Matthew's blood."

"I understand." This wasn't the time to get into what he'd planned to tell Ethan earlier, that Chris had com-pletely severed any emotional bond to the father he'd once known.

"But life doesn't always work out the way you plan," Ethan continued. "I never planned on Lizzie. I never planned on a baby. But Lizzie…well…"

"Yeah, yeah, yeah," Chris teased, trying to make light of another emotionally charged moment by using the same words he'd used in his truck on the way to the hospital. "You love her, you need her, you can't live without her."

"Yeah." The fervent way Ethan said the one word told Chris that—all joking aside—his brother adored his wife. And an ache speared through him. Not because he'd loved Laura and lost her, but because he hadn't loved her as much as Ethan loved Lizzie, as if all light and hope in life emanated from her.

"Lizzie and our baby—they're everything to me now. And I wouldn't change a thing even if I could. I thought I could cut myself off from life. Lizzie proved me wrong."

Simple words. Not particularly profound. Not even the kind of words that evoked a strong emotional reaction. And yet…there was something in those simple words that seemed to reverberate in Chris's mind. *I thought I could cut myself off from life.*

Wasn't that what he'd done? When Laura had died, and their baby with her, hadn't he tried to cut himself off from life, tried to build a fence around his heart? Hadn't he retreated—like Superman—into his fortress of solitude?

Those he already loved—his sisters and brothers, Peg and Joe and their kids—he couldn't stop loving *them*. But he'd walled himself off from loving another woman, because…

Because what you don't love you can't lose.

It sounded like a quotation from something. If it was, he couldn't place it, but it seemed singularly appropriate.

Only…he hadn't really been able to do it. Holly's boys had crept into his heart in just three short days. Identical twins be damned—he could tell them apart, and not by their tiny physical disparities. Ian, the outgoing one, with his "damn the torpedoes" outlook on life. Jamie, the shy one, with that "don't hurt me" look in his eyes. Holly's eyes.

That was when it hit him. Ian and Jamie weren't the only ones who'd slipped beneath his emotional fences. Holly had, too.

Chris stayed to keep his brother company at the hospital until Ethan went up to visit Lizzie again, in her room this time with the baby, dragging Chris along. Lizzie looked a thousand times better than the last time Chris had seen her, and baby James looked so much like Ethan it was almost comical. Chris knew you couldn't tell what color a newborn's eyes were going to be, but between Lizzie's green eyes and Ethan's hazel ones, he figured the odds were good his nephew's eyes would at least be hazel.

He kissed his sister-in-law's cheek and told her he'd back her in an arm wrestling competition anytime—making both Lizzie and Ethan laugh. He admired the baby, marveling that something so tiny could have such powerful lungs. "Just like you, Lizzie," he said, again making them laugh. Then he left the three of them to have some family time alone together and headed out.

It was after dark by the time Chris finally reached the Merrill house. His stomach was rumbling—he'd skipped lunch, and breakfast was a distant memory, but even if Peg asked him to stay for dinner he couldn't. He'd left Wally at his house, not realizing he'd be gone all day. Although Wally was outside in the fenced yard with a food bowl and a water dish, the food was probably long gone, and maybe the water, too.

Peg answered the door, Susan at her heels, and the minute he walked in Susan grabbed his knee. "Pick me up, Unca Chris." He obliged, heading for the family room with her propped on his left shoulder.

"Everything okay?" Peg asked, trailing behind him.

Chris waited until he reached the family room to make the announcement. "A boy," he told Joe and Peg. "James Christopher Colton. Mother and baby are doing great. Ethan I'm not so sure about—he looked pretty shaky to me."

The Merrills laughed. "Yeah, Peg wanted me in the delivery room when that one was born," Joe said, pointing at his daughter cuddled in Chris's arms. "But I nearly passed out. Remember, Peg?"

She snorted. "Yes, but I wasn't about to let you off the hook when Bobby was born." She didn't say it— *little pitchers have big ears*, he thought with an inward smile—but he knew Peg well enough to know what she was thinking. *If you're there for the conception, you damn well better be there for the delivery.*

Joe said something in reply, but Chris wasn't really listening because just then Holly walked into the room and took a seat near the twins. This was the first time he'd seen her since that morning, and now, after his startling revelation in the hospital…now he couldn't seem to look away. Her long blond hair was clipped neatly away from her face on one side—she'd ditched the dark-haired wig, and Chris couldn't be sorry. Not when she looked like this. He remembered the corn-silk feel of her hair between his fingers last night when he'd—

He put a clamp on that memory. But then he heard Holly saying in his mind, *It's going to happen, Chris. Not tonight. Maybe not even tomorrow night. But it's going to happen.*

Which was why he'd stopped off at the pharmacy in the hospital before he left. That package was hidden in the armrest of his truck, tucked there so Holly wouldn't see it and think he was assuming…well… what he was assuming.

"Staying for dinner?" Peg asked.

"What? Oh. No, we can't," Chris replied. "Wally's been home alone since this morning. Outside," he clarified. "But I'm sure he's as hungry as I am." He looked at Holly again. "You about ready to go?"

A stricken expression fleetingly crossed her face, then she pasted a smile in its place. She knelt between Ian and Jamie, who were arguing over who deserved the bigger truck, and tugged them into one last embrace. "Mommy has to go now. You be good for Ms. Peg and Mr. Joe, okay?"

"'Kay," Ian said, and Jamie echoed, "'Kay."

She kissed them both, then stood, stony-eyed, as if she refused to let herself cry in front of her sons. "Say goodbye to Uncle Chris."

Chris handed Susan to her father, then picked his way through the toys scattered across the rug. He leaned over, curled an arm around each boy and lifted them simultaneously, tickling their tummies with his fingers. "You be good for Ms. Peg and Mr. Joe," he reiterated and was rewarded with the same chorus of *'kays*, giggling ones this time.

He didn't know what made him do it—well, yes, he did—but he popped a kiss on Jamie's nose, then on Ian's, before he set them down. Then he grabbed Holly's hand and tugged her toward the doorway. "Come on," he muttered. "Let's get out of here before the waterworks begin."

They were already out the door before Holly gulped air and said, "I didn't think Ian and Jamie were going to cry. I've left them with Peg before, and they—"

"I wasn't talking about the twins. I was talking about you."

Chapter 12

"I wasn't going to cry," Holly insisted as Chris held the passenger door of his truck for her.

"Weren't you?" His voice held tenderness and understanding.

"Well…" She gave a little huff of semitearful laughter as she buckled her seat belt. "Not where the boys could see me anyway." Then she realized something. "Wait. My SUV is here."

"Yeah, I know. Give me the keys." When she did, he closed the door and left, but was back a minute later, climbing into the driver's seat. "I gave Joe your keys. I think it's best for now we leave your SUV here, rather than at my house."

He was already putting the truck into gear as he said it, and Holly asked, "Why?" Wanting an answer before they got too far away.

"Because I don't want the McCays to know you're at my house, not until we're ready to spring the trap. Do I think they suspect anything yet? No. Am I willing to risk it? No. I told Joe to park your SUV in their garage so no one can see the license plates." He glanced at her. "We're not that far away. If we need it, we can get it. But I don't think we will."

She didn't know why a little dart of panic went through her. She was so used to having the freedom of her own wheels—was that it?

"Besides," Chris said drily, breaking into her thoughts, "this way you can't sneak off to visit the twins when my back is turned."

That made her laugh for some reason. "I wouldn't do that," she protested. "I already agreed it would be safer—"

He reached across the seat and clasped her hand for a moment. "I know you did. But this way you won't be tempted." Then he let her hand go so he could shift gears, saying softly, "You're a good mother, Holly."

"I try to be."

"You remind me of my own mother."

When he said that, she remembered Chris had been eleven when his mother died. Old enough to have vivid memories of her. "What was she like?"

He didn't answer right away. Then he said slowly, "Beautiful…to me. Now when I look at old photos, I realize she wasn't really beautiful. Not classically beautiful. But if ever a woman's heart reflected in her face, hers did."

She gathered her courage and asked, "Why did your father kill her?"

At first she thought he wasn't going to answer at all.

Then he said, "No one can really answer that except him. She loved him through everything—the loss of his ranch, financial hardship, seven children. And for the longest time no one had a clue why he did it, because he refused to say. Not even when he was convicted of her murder. He finally told Ethan back in February—Ethan was the one who found her dead—that she figured out he was the bull's-eye serial killer.

"That's how my father used to mark all his victims," he explained, "with a red bull's-eye drawn on their foreheads." She heard him breathe deeply in the darkness. "She caught him in bloody clothes one day, which he tried to explain away. But then she found the permanent red marker in his pocket. And she saw something on the news the next day that made her put all the pieces together. She confronted him, told him what she knew and insisted he turn himself in. In a—I guess you could say a fit of rage…or fear…or both—he killed her. Before he knew what he was doing, he'd marked her forehead the way he'd marked his other victims."

"Oh, God," she whispered helplessly, her heart aching for him.

"Then he panicked," Chris continued, still in that deliberate way. "He realized he had to get rid of her body somehow, so he went to the garage…for a big trash bag."

She couldn't help her soft gasp of dismay. "Oh, Chris, no."

"Yeah…a trash bag. He killed her, and then he—Like she was garbage." This time she reached across the distance and touched his arm in empathy. He downshifted and turned a corner before adding, "He didn't know that in the few minutes he was gone, Ethan had come home from school—I told you Ethan found her. He was terrified. Imagine, you're seven years old and you find your mother's bloody, lifeless body."

"What did he do?"

"He ran to a neighbor's for help. But when they got back, the body was gone. Only the blood remained. But even though they never found Mama's body, Ethan's story of seeing her with the bull's-eye on her forehead led the police to finally arrest my—to finally arrest Matthew Colton, one of the most infamous serial killers in Texas history. Arrested. Tried. Convicted."

Holly hadn't missed the slight catch in Chris's voice or the way he'd changed *my father* to *Matthew Colton*. This morning he'd said he needed to visit his father in prison. *What happened between this morning and now?* she wondered. But she wasn't going to ask. If Chris wanted to tell her…that was a different story. If Chris *wanted* to tell her…he would.

Wally leaped to his feet and let out one bark of welcome when Chris pulled his truck into the driveway and parked. Chris grabbed the pharmacy bag from the armrest once Holly exited, and shoved it into his front pocket so she couldn't see it. Wally was eagerly wagging his tail and standing right by the front gate when Chris unlatched it and held the gate open for Holly, then closed it behind him so Wally couldn't escape. "Down, boy," he said when Wally threatened to jump on Holly in his exuberance at seeing them, but he wasn't surprised when Holly merely ruffled Wally's fur and let him shadow her footsteps to the front door.

Chris paused and picked up Wally's food bowl and water dish. "Empty. Just what I was afraid of." He unlocked the door, reached in and punched in the alarm code, then turned on the hall light before he let Holly enter.

"Are you really worried someone might have broken in?"

"No, but I couldn't take my gun to the prison with me today, so…" He caught the expression on her face. "I'm careful about gun safety, Holly," he said levelly. "I would never leave my gun where the twins could reach it, I promise. But in my line of work…a gun is practically a necessity." He flashed a grin at her. "Besides, this is Texas."

He didn't wait for her answer, just trod down the hallway toward the kitchen, flicking on the lights as he went. He filled the water dish, then he found the scoop in the dog food bag, filled the bowl and placed it beside the water Wally was already furiously lapping at. "Sorry, boy," he murmured, patting the dog's side. "Didn't expect to be gone this long."

Holly had followed Chris into the kitchen, and now she said, "You never explained what happened. What I mean is, Peg told me you were taking your sister-in-law to the hospital because she was having a baby, but…"

"Let me get dinner started," he replied, "and then I'll tell you."

A guilty expression crossed Holly's face. "No, it's my turn to make dinner," she said. "I can't let you do all the cooking—that wouldn't be fair." She bustled toward the fridge. "You talk while I cook."

"Whatever it is, make it quick, okay? I missed lunch and I'm starved."

Twenty-five minutes later Chris sat back at the kitchen table, replete. Holly's omelet and toast hadn't been fancy, but it had been good. Best of all it had been quick.

"I was terrified Lizzie was going to have that baby right there in the front seat of my truck," he confessed, finishing up his story. "But it all worked out."

Holly shook her head, a smile curving her lips. "I doubt you were terrified." Her admiring eyes conveyed her conviction that whatever happened, Chris would deal with it competently. And his male ego responded. *So maybe you did okay*, his ego seemed to be saying, puffing out its chest a little. *Maybe you deserved to have baby James named for you after all.*

But his ego wasn't the only male part of him responding to Holly. And it wasn't only food he'd been hungering for. Now that one appetite had been satisfied…

But that wasn't fair to Holly, no matter what she'd told him last night. She deserved candlelight and romantic music, flowers and fine wine. She deserved gentle wooing. Not some guy with a box of condoms crammed into his pocket.

Which reminded him…he *did* have a box of condoms crammed into his pocket. A box he suddenly and desperately wanted to use.

Holly's smile faded. But before he could say anything, she jumped up from the table, cleared away the dishes, his included, and stacked them in the sink, saying, "Probably shouldn't use the dishwasher if it's only going to be the two of us, since it will take several days to fill, and—"

"Holly." That was all he said. Just her name. But she froze at the sink. He found himself standing behind her somehow. Just as last night he could have sworn he never moved, but there he was, sliding his hands down her arms, gently turning her unresisting body to face him. And he knew she could see the aching need in him he couldn't possibly hide.

"I want you," he admitted, as if it wasn't obvious. "God knows I want you. But not like this. Not if you're afraid of me."

"I'm not afraid of you," she said quickly. "It's me. I'm afraid of me." She must have read in his expression that he didn't follow her, because she added quietly, "I want you, too, Chris. In fact, that's pretty near all I can think about whenever you're around." Her voice dropped to little more than a whisper. "And even when you're not."

"Then why afraid?" he asked, one hand coming up to cup her cheek, to rub his thumb against her lips. This close he could feel the tremor that ran through her. "I won't hurt you, Holly, I promise. I'd never hurt you." Then it occurred to him maybe she was worried about—

"I haven't slept around, in case you're wondering." He brushed a strand of hair away from her face, tucking it behind her ear. "There hasn't been anyone since Laura." He hesitated, of two minds about revealing more. But then he figured she had a right to know. "And there wasn't anyone before her, either."

Something about the way his confession was made touched Holly so deeply she couldn't respond at first.

"Thank you for telling me," she whispered finally, cradling his face between her hands for a moment. She let her hands drop to her sides, wanting to be as honest with Chris as he'd been with her. "Grant was... I'd loved him all my life, so I never…" Her throat closed and she couldn't continue.

"Holly." The aching need embodied in that one word shook her to the core. Then he kissed her, and it was even better than it had been last night. Passion had exploded between them the night before, but tonight… tonight there was tenderness mixed in with the passion. And wonder. Chris kissed her as if he couldn't believe she was there in his arms, but at the same time as if he couldn't bear to let her go.

He whispered her name again, and Holly thought she'd never heard so many suppressed emotions in a man's voice. Want was there, and need. Overlaid with a cherishing tone that told her this would be more than just sex for Chris. If she hadn't already figured out from his confession that he only slept with women he cared for deeply, she would have known it by his voice.

And that made her decision easy. Here. Now. Tonight. It wasn't just that she wanted to know what it would be like with a man who hadn't grown up with her, who didn't see her as more of a friend than a lover. She wanted to know what it would be like with *Chris*, with this man who haunted her dreams and tugged at her heart in ways she'd never felt before. Ways she'd never realized she *could* feel. She wanted to know if the reality of making love with him came anywhere close to matching her dreams. Because if it did, that would reveal something about herself she was eager—and a little nervous—to learn.

Chris reluctantly withdrew his lips from Holly's and gazed down into her face. If she'd been wearing that "don't hurt me" expression, the one so like Jamie's, which appeared on occasion when she wasn't aware, he would have let her go. But she wasn't. Her expression said she wanted him…and she wasn't afraid anymore.

"I need a shower." He pulled away from her a little and coaxed. "Come with me."

"Okay." He loved the little catch in her voice, and the not-quite-shy way she agreed. Then she looked puzzled and reached down to his jeans pocket. "What's this?"

Crap. He'd forgotten. But he wasn't going to lie to her. "Condoms," he admitted. Then hurried to add, "I wasn't assuming… Okay, maybe I *was* assuming… but only if you… I wanted to be prepared, and I… Just in case…"

He was floundering—he knew that. But then Holly put her fingers over his lips to cut off his jumbled phrases and smiled. A womanly smile. "Thank you for thinking of it," she murmured, kissing the corner of his mouth. Then she took his hand and led him from the kitchen…down the long hallway…into the master bedroom.

They undressed in the master bathroom. Chris shucked off his clothes in no time. But after one moment staring at his naked body—a stare his body responded to noticeably—Holly stalled with only her jeans removed.

"Don't go shy on me now," he said, moving to stand in front of her and reaching for the buttons on her blouse.

"It's not that. Not exactly." She put her hands over his, stopping him from undoing the buttons. "It's just that…well…I've had a baby. *Two* babies. And…well…"

He got it. "You think I care about a few stretch marks?" He laughed softly. "Holly, Holly, Holly," he chided. "You must not have much of an opinion of me if you think that."

"I don't, but I…"

He was already undressing her. Parting the unbuttoned edges of her blouse, reaching back and unerringly unclasping her bra, then helping her out of them both. Caressing the skin he'd bared. Including the ever-so-slight protrusion that was a reminder of the babies she'd carried, and the silvery, barely there stretch marks.

He slid his fingers beneath the elastic on her hips and slipped her underwear free, then down. When she was as completely naked as he was, he knelt and placed his unshaven cheek against her stomach, grasping her hips so she couldn't escape, rubbing until she shivered and her nipples tightened for him.

Then he stood. "Do you have any idea how beautiful you are?" he told her in his deepest voice, meaning every word. So she was obviously a mother. So what? So her body wasn't model perfect. Did she really think he cared? He wanted her like hell burning, and she was worried about these little imperfections? "So beautiful," he whispered, drawing her against his body and kissing her the way he'd dreamed of doing, with no barriers between them.

She was trembling all over when he finally let her go, and that turned him on big-time. But he needed that shower after the day he'd had. "Do you want to do something with your hair?" he asked. "So it doesn't get wet?"

She twisted her hair up, then used a clip to hold her hair in place.

Without another word he tugged her into the shower

with him. He soaped himself and rinsed off quickly but took his time washing her. Letting his fingers linger where he knew a woman loved to be touched. He'd made love to only one other woman in his life, but he knew the vulnerable places on a woman's body. Knew how to fulfill her, too—a man didn't have to be promiscuous to know that. All he needed was a little imagination and a strong desire to please.

He continued caressing her long after they were both clean, until she caught his hands and said, "Enough. I can't... I don't want..."

He captured her lips for a brief kiss. "Yeah," he growled when he let her go. "I don't want, either. I want to be inside you the first time. I want to feel you tight around me when you come." Primal, maybe. Direct. But the God's honest truth.

They barely managed to get the covers pulled down before they practically fell into bed together. Holly helped Chris roll on the condom—although *helped* wasn't quite the word that came to mind when her fingers touched his erection. But he held his breath and let her because she obviously wanted to. Because he knew it gave her pleasure to touch him this way.

That was his last coherent thought. As soon as the condom was in place he lost any claim to rationality he'd ever had. He felt like a heat-seeking missile, with Holly his only target. Despite the urge to thrust hard and deep, he eased into the damp warmth between her legs and she welcomed him with a soft moan of pleasure. Then another when he withdrew and returned. Again and again. Faster and faster. He pulled her thighs up around his hips to delve deeper, and she arched beneath him, gasping his name.

His lips found her nipples, first one, then the other, and she arched again and cried out, her fingernails digging into his shoulders as if she couldn't bear it. But he knew she could. "Yes," he groaned when she involuntarily tightened around him, and he knew she was close. So close. "Come for me, Holly. Yes, like that," he managed when he felt her internal throbbing, though he could barely breathe. Barely speak. "Like that. Oh, God, Holly, like that." Then with a flurry of thrusts he came, too.

In the few seconds before he lost consciousness, Chris tightened his arms around Holly, wanting to never let her go. *Needing* it. Needing her.

Chapter 13

Oh, my was all Holly could think of as she lay beneath Chris, both of them breathing heavily, his body still embedded in hers. *Oh, my. Oh. My.*

Her dreams hadn't even come close, because she'd had no idea. None. She gave a little hiccup that was half laughter, half tears, as she realized she and Grant hadn't… They'd never… Not even once. Not like this. For just a moment she grieved for Grant, because she wasn't sure she'd ever satisfied him the way she was absolutely certain she'd satisfied Chris. And she grieved for herself, too, for all the times she'd wondered what was wrong with her.

Chris grunted suddenly, as if he had temporarily blacked out and had just resurfaced. He tried to separate himself from her, but Holly tightened her legs, not wanting to lose this euphoric feeling, as if she was floating above herself.

"I'm too heavy," Chris muttered, but Holly's hands grasped his hips.

"Don't make me hurt you," she warned, only half kidding. "Move and die."

He laughed, a rumbling sound, then swiftly rolled them over so she was on top. "That's better," he said. "But, Holly..." His eyes teased hers. "You can't keep me prisoner forever."

"That's what you think." She deliberately contracted and relaxed her inner muscles around him. Once. Twice. Three times. And each time she felt him respond. "Have you ever heard of Kegel exercises?"

"What's that?"

"Something they teach women after they've had a baby. It helps restore pelvic floor muscle tone."

"Oh, great." He laughed under his breath. "I guess I really *am* your prisoner, 'cause I'm not risking damage down there." That made her laugh, too. "But, Holly, much as I'm enjoying this, I have to do something about the condom."

She'd forgotten about that, but he hadn't. She stopped Kegeling him, then squirmed until he was free. Chris jackknifed off the bed and disappeared into the bathroom. She heard the shower running for a minute, then he returned, a towel wrapped around his hips. His narrow hips. Above which his abs and chest muscles rippled in masculine perfection that until a few minutes ago she'd touched up close and personal.

Holly's fingers itched to touch him again, but instead she grabbed the top sheet and pulled it up to hide herself and her imperfections from his view. "Oh, hell no," he told her, throwing the towel on a chair and diving across the king-size bed. He wrestled the sheet away from her, then playfully held her down while he looked his fill.

Warmth in her cheeks informed her she was blushing, although she couldn't see it. But still he looked. And when his eyes finally connected with hers, he said softly, "Beautiful, Holly. You have absolutely nothing to be ashamed of."

She caught her breath at the very male, very intent expression on his face, and almost believed him. "I couldn't lose those last five pounds after the twins were born," she said faintly. "I tried so hard, too!"

"Where?" He settled between her legs, bearing most of his weight on his elbows. "Here?" He cupped her breasts, breasts that had never quite returned to their original size and shape after she'd breast-fed Ian and Jamie. His thumbs played over her nipples until they tightened unbearably. "You'll get no complaints from me here, Holly," he bantered. His big hands slid down to her waist, his thumbs stroking back and forth over her belly until she quivered. "Here? No, I don't think so." His husky voice, the look in his eyes, told her he wasn't kidding. Then those firm masculine hands curved over her hips. "Must be here, then," he suggested, as if he were serious, his long fingers lightly squeezing. He shook his head after a moment. "Wrong again."

She was melting and he knew it. That was all she could think of as his wicked blue eyes held hers. She'd just had the most incredible orgasm of her entire life, and already she wanted him again. And impossible as it seemed, he wanted her again, too—he was already hot and hard at the crux of her thighs, and she wiggled a little until she could feel him pressed up against exactly where she wanted him.

"Again?" he teased, emphasizing the last syllable.

She smiled at his playful tone and tried to make her tone just as light and playful. "Yes, please." She wasn't quite successful.

His eyes seemed to darken, and she shivered at the blatant desire that flared there. "Oh, I'm going to please you, Holly," he murmured, reaching for a condom on the nightstand, not waiting for her assistance. He fitted himself in place, then twined his fingers with hers. "I'm going to please you until you can't take any more," he whispered seductively. "And when I'm done, you'll know just how perfect you are." He smiled a very wolfish smile. "Hang on tight," he told her. "You may experience a little turbulence."

Holly's sudden laugh turned into a moan as he flexed his hips and thrust deep. Then withdrew and thrust again…slowly. Agonizingly slowly. Intense pleasure, sharp and urgent, knifed through her with each perfect thrust, until she clung to his hands and arched like a bow, crying his name.

"Still no word from Mr. Colton," Evalinda McCay reminded her husband as they dressed for bed…as if he needed the reminder.

"What do you expect me to do about it?"

The expression in her eyes bore no good for anyone. "How are we going to rid ourselves of Holly and get our hands on the twins and their trust fund if we can't locate her?"

"Mr. Colton promised us results," Angus protested weakly.

"One more day," she warned. "We'll give him one more day. Then I think we'll need to look for another detective."

"You really want to start all over? What if—"

"It was your idea to try to run her off the road the first two times," Evalinda reminded him contemptuously. "You were so sure that would work...but it didn't. Either time."

"Yes," he was quick to defend himself, "but at least Holly didn't suspect anything. It wasn't until you suggested running her down in the parking lot that she—"

Evalinda wouldn't let him finish. "Don't try to shift the blame for that fiasco onto me. *You* were the one who hired the men to kill her. If they hadn't been so incompetent..."

"You think it was easy finding someone who—"

"One more day," she repeated implacably, cutting him off, and he knew further argument was useless. Just as he'd fallen in with Evalinda's plans to murder Holly in the first place, he knew he would cave on this, too.

Chris woke at two in the morning when moonlight crept through the bedroom window. He thought about getting up and completely closing the top-down, bottom-up blinds that were lowered at the top. The way the blinds were drawn now gave the room's occupants privacy but still allowed them to see the night sky. That also meant, unfortunately, it let the moonlight in, and he'd always been a "pitch-black" sleeper. The blinds were completely drawn in the bedroom he was occupying. He just hadn't thought about it here in the master bedroom because he'd been too focused on the other things he was doing.

But he wasn't about to get up to close the blinds at this moment. Holly was sleeping cradled against him, her head pillowed on his shoulder. And he'd be damned before he woke her.

He and Holly had worn each other out earlier, but a certain part of his anatomy twitched to life at the reminder of everything they'd done tonight. Two spent condoms now resided in the wastebasket in the bathroom, but he hadn't been satisfied to leave it at that. They'd dozed after the second time but had woken before midnight. And as they'd cuddled and lazily caressed beneath the comforter, he'd told her in all seriousness, "I want to watch you come. Will you let me?"

She'd been adorable in her confusion, and he'd had a strong hunch no one had ever done that for her before. Holly had told Chris her husband was the only man she'd ever slept with, but that didn't mean other avenues had been completely closed. Apparently that had been the case, though. Equally apparent was the fact that Holly's husband had never put her needs first, which didn't surprise Chris. There were still a lot of men out there who never worried about pleasing a woman. Who thought she was responsible for her own orgasms, and if it happened, fine. If it didn't, oh well. He wasn't one of those men, but he knew some who were.

It had taken a little coaxing but eventually Holly had conceded. And then—*holy crap!*—her response had been off the charts. Hearing her...watching her... tasting her...had turned him on so hard he'd been tempted to use a third condom, but she'd pretty much passed out by then, so he'd refrained. But he'd promised himself next time they made love he'd start with that and see where it took them.

Next time? What makes you think there'll be a next time, hot shot? The thought hit him out of the blue, and he stopped to consider it. He'd come up with some ideas for trapping the McCays when he was at the hospital this afternoon waiting for Ethan and Lizzie's baby to be born, and they had to get going on that pretty damn quick. Now that Jim Murray had given them the go-ahead, he needed to coordinate with Annabel and Sam, who were supposed to stop by for breakfast tomorrow. If they were successful, in less than a week Holly wouldn't need his protection anymore. Which meant she'd be free to…return to her old life. Her old life outside Houston, more than three hundred miles away.

Devastation sliced through him—another shock. He didn't want Holly to leave; he wanted her to stay. And Ian and Jamie, too. He'd realized this afternoon that all three had crept under his emotional fences. He just hadn't recognized how firmly entrenched they already were in his life.

Not even a week, the rational side of him protested. *You haven't even known her a week.*

That didn't seem to matter—somehow he and Holly just clicked. Not only in bed, although he couldn't believe how perfectly matched they were, as if she were made for his earthy brand of loving. He had no doubt he'd pleased her, too—no way could she fake her response, especially the last time. But their sexual chemistry had its roots in something deeper. He wasn't sure what to call it, but a connection existed between them. An emotional connection.

He examined that word—*emotional*—and acknowledged that somehow it fit. Problem was, he wasn't sure exactly what it meant to him. Even worse, he wasn't sure what it meant to Holly.

The pealing of the doorbell woke them. Holly unwrapped herself from where she'd migrated in the night—splayed across Chris's chest—and pushed her tousled hair out of her eyes. She clutched the top sheet, wrapping it firmly around her. When she was finally able to focus, she glanced at the clock on the nightstand and realized it was already close to seven thirty.

She nudged Chris's shoulder—the one she'd been using as her personal pillow—and said urgently, "Wake up, Chris! Someone's at the door."

He awoke with a start, looking from Holly to the clock, and groaned. "It's Annabel and Sam," he informed her. He was out of bed in a flash, retrieving his jeans and shirt from where he'd left them hanging on the back of the bathroom door. "I forgot to tell you they're coming to breakfast," he said as he pulled his jeans on commando and zipped them up. His shirt was halfway on before he realized it was inside out. The doorbell pealed again and he ripped his shirt off, turned it right side out and tugged it on.

He ran a hand through his shaggy hair—and oh, how she hated that it fell right into place as if he'd brushed it—then added, "They're coming to have breakfast with you and me so we can make plans for catching the McCays in the act. I'll go let them in and take them into the kitchen. You can come in after you're dressed."

He was almost out the door when he turned back, snatched Holly up from the bed into his arms and kissed her senseless. He took his time about it, too. "Good morning," he whispered when he finally raised his head. His eyes were an intense blue, and Holly couldn't think of anything to compare them to. "Thank you for last night." Then his expression morphed from romantic hero to hard-as-nails PI. "And for God's sake, don't let Annabel see that satisfied look in your eyes—she's a bloodhound. Sam, too, but Annabel's a woman—she'll know exactly what put that look there." Then he was gone.

"About time," Annabel said when Chris finally opened the door barefoot. "I thought I was going to have to use my key."

Chris stared at her, perplexed. "When did I give you a key?"

"You didn't. I asked Peg, and she gave me a copy. She gave me the alarm code, too."

"What the—" He started to say *hell* but remembered just in time he was trying to break the swearing habit. He shepherded Sam and Annabel toward the kitchen while his guilty conscience gave him hell for all the times he'd said "crap" yesterday. *You're supposed to be cleaning up your language,* his conscience reminded him. Not just for Susan and Bobby, but for Ian and Jamie, too.

Annabel was still explaining about the key. "I asked Peg what her cleaning schedule was, what days of the week she came out here, and I told her I'd swing by regularly to check on her. I also told her I'd stop by every few days when she wasn't here, just to keep an eye on the place for you."

Chris was touched. "Thanks, Bella."

Annabel said gruffly, "Just part of my job—serve and protect," as if pretending she hadn't done anything out of the ordinary. When they walked into the kitchen, she glanced around, then said drily, "Nice breakfast."

"Coming right up," Chris told her. "You and Sam have a seat. I kind of overslept this morning." He quickly dumped food in the dog's dish and checked there was still water. Then he grabbed bowls from the cabinet, spoons from the drawer, and slapped them on the table. The gallon of milk from the fridge was followed by boxes of Cap'n Crunch and Cheerios from the pantry.

"Are you frigging kidding me?" Sam asked. "Cap'n Crunch?"

"Hey," Chris said, feigning hurt. "It's one of the basic food groups."

"I thought we'd at least be treated to your signature French toast," Annabel said.

"I was planning on it, but I told you, I overslept." Chris turned back to the counter to grab a couple of paper towels for napkins when he sensed rather than heard Holly walk into the kitchen. He swung around and barely managed to keep the betraying smile off his face. She was dressed as she normally was, in jeans and a cotton blouse—a deep, rich yellow this time. But now that he knew what she looked like *without* her clothes...

"Good morning," Holly said, smiling at Annabel. Then she turned to Sam. "I've already met Annabel, but you must be...Sam, right? Sam Colton?" She held out her hand. "Chris said you're a detective with the Granite Gulch Police Department. I'm Holly McCay."

As soon as Sam let her hand go, Holly glanced at

the table and said longingly, "Ooohhh, Cap'n Crunch. I haven't had Cap'n Crunch since I was little." Then she reached for the Cheerios box instead. "But I shouldn't."

Chris heard the regret in her voice. He poured Cap'n Crunch into a bowl and handed it to her. "Indulge. Once in a blue moon won't hurt you."

"Thanks." The smile she gave was one some women reserved for a gift of expensive jewelry, and Chris couldn't help returning her smile.

Out of the corner of Chris's eye he could see Annabel's head swivel from Holly to him and back again, and he could almost see her radar antenna quivering. *Crap!* He quickly amended the thought to *crud*, but it didn't come anywhere near expressing his fear that Annabel had somehow divined he and Holly had slept together. Just because he'd given her a bowl of Cap'n Crunch.

Chris tried to deflect Annabel's attention—and Sam's, too, for that matter, since Sam was giving him the once-over and doing the same to Holly—by saying, "Before I forget, I should tell you I went to the prison yesterday, and I got my clue." He snorted. "Biff."

"Biff?" Annabel measured Cheerios into a bowl and added milk. Then she handed the cereal box to Sam. "What's that supposed to mean?"

Chris turned the coffeemaker on, leaned back against the sink and crossed his arms. "Beats the heck out of me." He glanced at Sam. "Mean anything to you?"

His brother shook his head. "Doesn't seem to match the other clues. Texas. Hill. *B*. Peaches. Remember Trevor's theory that Matthew buried Mama on her parents' property in Bearson, Texas? That house sits on a hill, and there's a peach tree in the back yard. So all those clues fit. But Biff?"

"Sounds like a name," Holly volunteered.

"Yes, but…I can't think of anybody in the family by that name," Annabel replied. "Not even if it was a nickname." She turned to Chris. "Did you ask Trevor?"

He stiffened. He couldn't help it. "No," he said curtly. "Couldn't reach him yesterday. Left a message on his voice mail. And Ridge's, too." Annabel looked as if she were going to take him to task over his attitude toward Trevor, but he cut her off, warning, "Don't start, Bella. You can ask him if you want."

Which effectively ended that conversation. Chris's gaze moved from Annabel to Sam, who had his head down and his attention focused on his breakfast. Then Chris's gaze ended up on Holly. She was acting as if nothing was wrong, but she'd poured cereal into a bowl for him—his beloved Cap'n Crunch—and was adding milk. Just as if he were as young as her twins. Their eyes met, and for a moment they were alone in the room. "Eat your breakfast," she said eventually in a composed voice. Her "Mommy" voice, which she used with Ian and Jamie.

A smile tugged at the corners of his lips. "Yes, ma'am."

Sam and Annabel had left an hour ago, promising to start setting their end of things in motion. Holly was talking with her sons on the phone in the master bedroom. Wally at his feet, Chris was sitting in his office, brooding. Not over the plans they'd made about the McCays, but about his clue, Biff. And about Trevor.

A voice from the doorway said, "Want to tell me what that was all about?"

He swiveled around in his chair. He didn't ask "What do you mean?" because he knew. "Trevor and I have... issues."

"No! Really?" Holly said in a fake shocked tone. She moved into the room and took a seat on the sofa. Wally bounded over, tail wagging, and Holly scratched him behind his ears. "Want to talk about it?"

He did and he didn't. He knew what Holly would say. The same thing Annabel said—he wasn't being fair to Trevor. And he didn't want Holly to think he was holding on to a grudge like an eleven-year-old kid... although he was.

He sighed. "It's ancient history. And I know I should let it go. I *know* that. Annabel has told me often enough. But—"

"But you can't."

He shook his head.

"So what is it you can't let go?"

He didn't answer right away, tying to marshal his thoughts into some kind of order. Finally he said, "Trevor is three years older than me. I practically worshipped him as far back as I can remember. He could do anything in my eyes. And he was a great brother. I mean, he never seemed to mind when I tagged along after him, although three years is a pretty big gap in children's ages. He taught me to read when I was four. How to slide into second base when I was seven. How to throw a perfect spiral when I was nine, even though my hands weren't big enough to really hold the football right. He taught me so much..." The memories were all coming back to him, making his throat ache.

"So what happened?" The gentle, nonjudgmental way she asked the question told him she didn't want to know because she was curious. She wanted to give him the opportunity to talk about something he'd kept bottled up inside him for years.

"My father murdered my mother, that's what happened," he said flatly. "All seven of us were sent to separate foster homes. I was eleven. Trevor was fourteen." He swallowed the sudden lump in his throat that belonged to the eleven-year-old boy he'd been. "Trevor never made any attempt to stay in touch with me. I saw him a few times a year, but never at his instigation. Only during court-mandated visitation we all had with Josie at her foster parents' home. And when Josie decided she didn't want to see us anymore, that was it."

"Oh, Chris." Two little words that spoke volumes about Holly's tender heart.

"That's not all of it," he told her. "The story is that when Trevor turned eighteen he tried to get custody of Josie—the baby of our family. She was only seven at the time. But I always wondered just how hard he really tried before he headed off to college."

Holly's eyes closed as if she were holding back sudden tears, a conjecture that was confirmed when she opened her eyes again and they glistened. "What did Trevor say when you asked him?"

"I never asked him."

There was a long silence. Then softly, "Why not?"

Why hadn't he asked Trevor? When Chris had finally reconnected with all his brothers, why hadn't he asked Trevor why he'd abandoned him? Why hadn't he asked him about Josie?

"Because..." *Because why?* he asked himself. "Because a grown man doesn't ask another grown man those questions."

"Oh, Chris." The same two words she'd said before but this time was slightly different. Even though the maternal tenderness was there, even though he could hear how she ached for the lost and bewildered eleven-year-old boy he'd been as well as the man he was, there was also a note of something he couldn't quite put his finger on. Then it came to him. It was the same way all the women in his life had from time to time said, "Men!" As if the workings of the male mind were incomprehensible to women, and their feelings about it could be condensed down into one word that all other women automatically understood.

Despite the emotions churning inside him, something about it tickled his funny bone. "Stupid, huh?"

"Not stupid." She looked down at Wally at her feet and scratched his head again. "But if you never ask, you'll never know." She raised her eyes to his. "And I think you need to know, Chris, one way or the other. You need closure. Just like you need to know where your mother is so you can bring her home. So you can give her a decent burial. Just like you need to find out what happened to Josie. Closure. You'll never rest until you have it. One way or the other. Think about it."

She stood and snapped her fingers at Wally, who immediately rose. "Come on, boy," she said. "I think it's time to let you outside."

Chris stared at the door through which Holly had just left, thinking about what she'd said, and realized she was right in one way. But she was wrong, too. Because there was another reason he'd never asked his

brother why he'd abandoned him—he was afraid to
know the answer. Because the answer might be…that
Chris hadn't been worth the effort.

Chapter 14

After lunch Chris told Holly, "I need to take a ride out to my grandparents' place to check on something. It's about an hour from here, in Bearson. Come with me?"

It was worded as a question, but Holly knew it wasn't really. Chris didn't want to leave her alone in the house, not even with an alarm system and Wally to protect her. Thinking of the dog made her ask, "What about Wally?"

"We'll take him with us. He can run free to his heart's content out there—the house sits on a hill overlooking several acres."

"Okay."

"Need to call Ian and Jamie before we go?"

Holly was touched Chris had asked, but she shook her head. "I called them right before lunch. They're having a blast. And besides, Peg has my cell phone number. I hardly ever use it—"

"I know."

He knew because he'd been hired to find her. The reminder made her shiver, wondering what would have happened if the McCays had hired a different private investigator, one without the strong moral conscience that was such a large part of Chris's makeup. She sent up a little prayer of thanks that Chris *had* been the one who'd found her and the twins. And that he'd taken them under his protection.

"Well…anyway," she said, "Peg has my number if anything comes up, and she knows to call me."

"And we won't be that far away," he reminded her.

"Right." She smiled. "When did you want to leave? And is what I'm wearing okay?"

The wicked gleam in his eye as he looked her over sent warmth surging through every part of Holly's body, reminding her of last night. The way he wouldn't let her be shy with him. Especially the last time, when he'd coaxed her into letting him do unspeakable things to her body. Unspeakable things she wished he would do again. And again. But all he said was "If you've got boots, wear them. Otherwise you're fine. Five minutes okay?"

Chris had laid a blanket down in the back of his truck and had fastened Wally's leash to the side when Holly came out of the house, tugging the door closed behind her. "You want to lock this, Chris? And I don't know how to set the alarm."

He quickly hooked Wally's collar to the leash, then jumped down and headed to the house. "You should have reminded me to explain about the alarm the first day. All you do is this," he said, showing her, then making her repeat the six-digit code after him. He locked the door and resettled his black Stetson on his head. "You ready?"

They drove west, picking up US-380 and crossing over the southern tip of Lake Bridgeport, then through Runaway Bay. At Jacksboro they switched to TX-114. The truck ate up the miles—Holly smiled a little to herself and didn't say a word about the speed-limit signs they passed. But she trusted Chris and his driving, so she wasn't unduly worried they were going a good ten miles per hour over the limit.

He slowed as they drove through the little town of Jermyn, then resumed his earlier speed. "You seem to know the way," she said for something to say.

"I've been here before. We visited my mother's parents every couple of months when I was a kid. But after Matthew mur—after we went into foster care, no. And my mother's death was the death knell for my grandparents. They went downhill quickly after that, is what I heard, and I never saw them again. I didn't even know they were ailing—but that's probably why we had to go into foster care permanently—they weren't able to take care of us. They passed away a month apart."

He was silent for a moment. "My brothers and sisters and me—we own the place now. No one wants to live there, but no one can bear to sell the place because it's where Mama grew up. We all chip in to pay the taxes and the upkeep—well, not Josie but the rest of us. And we rent out the acreage to the farmer across the road, who keeps an eye on the house for us—vacant houses are easy targets for vandals and migrants—we gave him a fair reduction on the rent to do that."

He drew a deep breath. "And I've been here a few

times since I graduated from college. Not a lot, maybe once every two years, because—"

"Because what?" she asked when he didn't continue.

"Don't get me wrong, I don't believe in ghosts. But every time I go there, I feel…I don't know…sad, I guess. Thinking about my mother as a little girl there. Remembering the whole family visiting my grandparents there. They were good people, Holly, and my mother was their only child. It killed them—literally killed them—when she was murdered. I don't know how anyone ever survives the loss of a—"

When he broke off this time Holly knew what he'd been going to say. *The loss of a child.* Chris had lost a child. Not a child he'd held in his arms, but still…

She tried to imagine losing Ian or Jamie, and couldn't. She just *couldn't.* Chris's baby had died unborn, but that didn't mean he hadn't already loved it. She remembered how she'd felt when she'd been four months pregnant, and how Grant had felt, too. They'd already loved their baby-to-be—before they'd known there were two—but that was nothing compared to now. So she knew how devastated Chris's grandparents had been at the loss of their only child.

She reached across and placed a comforting hand on Chris's arm, letting him know she understood. Not just how his grandparents had felt, but how he felt, too.

Just before Loving they turned south on TX-16— Loving Highway, the sign read. And Holly wondered where the name had come from. Loving Highway was obviously named after the town of Loving, but how had the town gotten its name? *Must have been named after someone*, she figured. She didn't imagine Texas cattle barons being the sentimental kind.

Her curiosity piqued, she asked Chris. "You're right," he said. "Nothing to do with loving." He glanced at her and all of a sudden she couldn't breathe. Couldn't think. Could only remember how Chris had made her body sing last night. Her nipples reacted as if he'd caressed them, tightening until they ached. She crossed one arm over her breasts to hide her reaction from Chris, because she didn't want him to know.

Then he turned his eyes back to the road and said, "The town was named Loving because it was built on part of the Lost Valley Loving Ranch. And *that* was founded by a famous north Texas cattle drover, Oliver Loving."

"Thanks." Her body still humming with need, Holly turned away and gazed out the window. Very, very sorry she'd asked.

Regina Willard surreptitiously slid the wallet she'd just stolen from a woman in the drugstore into her purse, then walked out as if she hadn't a care in the world. *Women are such fools*, she thought contemptuously. Carrying their wallets in purses so full they couldn't be zipped or snapped closed. Then placing their opened purses in the child seat of a shopping cart...and wandering away. *She deserves to have her wallet stolen*, Regina rationalized. She wasn't a thief. She would cut up and discard the credit cards. And she would drop the money in the wallet into the collection box of the first church she came to.

No, she wasn't a thief. But she needed the driver's license. Now that the FBI and the Granite Gulch Po-

lice Department had trumpeted her name and photo
to the news media, she needed new identification so
she could get a job. One middle-aged woman looked
very like another in most people's minds. And besides,
driver's license photos were notoriously bad, often
looking nothing like the people they were supposed
to represent. So she wasn't worried about bearing only
a vague resemblance to the photo on the driver's license she'd just stolen. All she'd needed was new ID,
so she was set now. Next step, finding a job...unless
she spotted the woman who'd stolen her fiancé. Killing her would take precedence over anything else.

"This is it?" Holly asked as they drove up a long,
winding drive to an older farmhouse perched on the
top of a rise. "It's beautiful. Oh, I love those tall trees
planted all around the house."

"Folks did that a lot in the old days. Windbreaks,
they're called. Nowadays a lot of homeowners don't
want to be bothered with trees—too many leaves to
rake." He smiled as he parked the truck and they got
out. "Back then the trees did more than act as windbreaks. They provided much-needed shade at a time
when there was no air-conditioning. Which reminds
me," he told her with a slight grimace. "There's no central air. My grandparents had window units installed,
but..."

"I'll be fine. It's hot, but it's not that hot. When I was
a little girl, before I started school, my parents used to
take me on their missionary trips to South America.
No AC in an Amazon rain-forest jungle hut. I think
I'll survive."

They crossed the deep front porch, and Holly looked around curiously. Two wooden rockers resided on one side, a porch swing on the other. Chris saw where her attention was focused and said, "My grandparents called it a courting swing. But we kids didn't care about that." A reminiscent smile curved his lips. "We all tried to squeeze onto it when we younger—Trevor, me, Annabel, Ridge, Ethan and Sam. Five squirming boys and one long-legged girl with sharp elbows." He rubbed his ribs as if remembering all the times Annabel had dug her elbows into his ribs, but he was smiling, so Holly knew it was a good memory.

"No Josie?"

"She was just a baby." He laughed. "No way Mama would have trusted us with her on the porch swing." Then he seemed to recollect why he was here. He unlocked the door and pushed it open. "Come on. I want to see if I can find anything that might relate to Biff."

The curtains were drawn over all the windows in the front parlor, making the interior dim and gloomy even though the sun was shining brightly outside. So Chris flicked the switch, and the old-fashioned overhead light fixture came on. "We kept the electricity on," he explained. "The water, too. But we disconnected the propane and sold the stove and the refrigerator because we figured we didn't need them if no one was living here. Not that they were worth a lot—the fridge was almost twenty years old, and the stove was even older. But they were useful to someone, so…" He shrugged.

Holly looked around. "Who keeps the place clean?"

"The farmer who rents the land, his wife comes over once a month. She dusts—not that a lot of dust accumulates with no one living in the house—and she runs the vacuum over the floors. That's one of the reasons we kept the electricity on. We let her pick whatever she wants off the peach tree in the back, too, because otherwise it would just go to waste. She makes her own preserves and she bakes one heck of a peach cobbler."

He was silent for a moment. Then he admitted, "We probably should sell the place, but…as I told you, none of us can bear to let it go."

Holly was wandering around the room, picking up a knickknack here, a hand-crocheted doily there, then carefully replacing them. "I can understand in one way, but…someone put a lot of love into making this house a home with all these little personal touches. You shouldn't leave these things here where they can be stolen or vandalized."

Her eyes met his. "But it's not just that. You—I don't mean just you, but the rest of your family, too—should go through the furnishings and decide what you want for your own homes. These things should be used, Chris. Treasured…but used. Not left as some kind of shrine." She reverently touched the afghan folded and placed across the back of the sofa, crocheted in a light-ning pattern of royal blue and grass green, with a thin stripe of orange to add pizzazz. "If this were mine…"

She sighed, remembering her home in Clear Lake City, which had contained similar handmade treasures she'd inherited from both her grandmothers. Including three patchwork quilts and a yo-yo quilt. Not to men-tion the old-fashioned foot-pedal sewing machine she'd never used but had proudly displayed, which had come to her from her great-grandmother. When she'd run, she'd called a moving company to pack up everything and put it in storage, because even though she'd been terrified, she couldn't just abandon her heritage. *Having money comes in handy*, she thought. What would she have done if she hadn't been able to afford to put her belongings in storage?

You still would have run, she acknowledged. *It might have broken your heart to abandon everything, but you still would have run.*

An hour later, while Chris was searching the bedrooms, Holly came across a stack of old photo albums on a bookshelf in the corner of what she insisted on calling the parlor. *Because that's what it is*, she'd stubbornly told Chris.

She knelt in front of the bookcase and pulled out a half-dozen velour-covered photo albums. The deep blue velour was faded, but the silver lettering was still visible, and she figured she'd just uncovered a gold mine. "Look at this, Chris," she called. When he joined her, she handed the photo albums to him and stood, wiping off the knees of her jeans even though the floor wasn't really dusty.

Chris was already sitting on the sofa, turning the leaves of the first album, when Holly sat next to him. "Look," she exclaimed. "There are captions on the photos!"

The books appeared to be in chronological order. They went through the first one, but it was mostly pictures of Chris's mother as a baby, then as a toddler, all of them neatly labeled. There were a few pictures of a man and a woman Chris identified as his grandparents—which matched the first names in the spidery handwriting beneath the pictures—and some of people he admitted he had no idea who they were. "Todd and Nora," he read. "Todd and Nora who?"

"Doesn't matter. Neither one is Biff."

Holly touched Chris's arm to get his attention. "Would you explain about the clues? You said your clue was Biff, and Sam mentioned other clues that seemed to point here to your grandparents' house. But why is your father doing this to you? Why won't he just come right out and say where he buried your mother?"

"Because he's a twisted son of a bitch," Chris said roughly. "I think he's getting a kick out of torturing us. Like 'Ha-ha-ha, you think you can find her?'" His right hand, the one he'd been using to turn the pages of the photo album, formed a fist.

She didn't know why she did it, but she curled her left hand around Chris's fist, her fingers stroking gently until he unclenched his hand and twined his fingers with hers. "It hurts," he whispered. "Not just that we can't find her, but that he won't tell us. Won't tell me."

"Why does it hurt so much?"

Chris released her hand abruptly, stood and strode restlessly around the room. "All these years I never wanted to see my—to see Matthew. Never visited him in prison the way Trevor did, even when he asked to see us. Not that Trevor was visiting because he wanted to," he explained, "but because it was his job as an FBI profiler. He's the only one who ever visited Matthew until Matthew began this…blackmail scheme."

He drew a ragged breath. "Until I went to see him yesterday, though, I always believed… I don't know… I always believed that somewhere inside him was the father I remembered. Strict. Stern. Okay, yeah, harsh, too, sometimes. But a man who loved his children as best he could."

"But you don't believe that anymore."

He shook his head. "Yesterday I realized the father I remember no longer exists. If he ever did."

Holly tried to think of something to say, but all she came up with was "No one is all good or all bad. Do I think he's a twisted son of a bitch, as you called him? Maybe. And maybe he's using these clues to torture you, the way you think. But you said he's dying, and he knows it. You also said he asked to see you before—but that none of you did, except Trevor…and then only because it was his job. Isn't it possible Matthew wanted to see all his children one last time before he died? And in his sick, twisted mind, this was the only way he could think of to compel you all to visit him?"

She rose and walked to where Chris was, looking up at him, beseeching him to understand there was always another side to a story. "If he gave you halfway decent clues," she said softly, "you might solve the riddle before he provides the last clue. Which means the children who haven't yet visited him probably wouldn't have to."

The arrested expression on Chris's face told her he'd never considered this as a possibility. "You really think…?" he began.

"I don't know. But neither do you. Not for sure. Don't assume you know his motive. And don't erase what few good memories of him you have. Is he a serial killer? Yes. Did he murder your mother, who loved him? Yes. Am I glad he's in prison and can't do to anyone else what he did twenty years ago to all those other people? Of course. I despise what he did. But I also pity him from the bottom of my heart."

"You feel *sorry* for him?"

Holly nodded slowly, hoping she could make Chris understand. "Because he'll never know how wonderfully his children turned out. He'll never see the man I see when I look at you."

Chris didn't know what to say. He never knew what to say when someone gave him a personal compliment. *And why is that?* he wondered now. Insecurity left over from his childhood?

He was a damned good private investigator, he knew that. And he'd built Colton Investigations from nothing into the hugely successful business it was today with only his determination and willingness to work harder than anyone who worked for him—sometimes twelve- to fourteen-hour days. A thriving business with three—soon to be four—offices.

Self-confidence in the business arena didn't always translate into self-confidence in the personal arena, however. And he'd never quite convinced himself that his older brother hadn't abandoned him…because he wasn't worth hanging on to.

Laura loved you, he reminded himself. But it had never erased that sliver of self-doubt from his psyche.

Not that he'd dwelled on it a lot—he wasn't the kind to waste time in fruitless self-analysis, as a general rule. But yesterday's meeting with his father, the heart-to-heart with Ethan at the hospital and the conversation with Holly this morning about his issues with Trevor had all forced him to consider how the man he was had been impacted by everything that had happened in his life. Losing his mother and his family, not to mention Bouncer, his constant companion for five years. Growing up in a town where he could never escape the notoriety of being a serial killer's son. Foster parents who'd never been invested in him, who'd taken him in not out of the goodness of their hearts but for the money. The deaths of his wife and unborn child.

Pity party, Colton? he jeered mentally. *Suck it up, old son, suck it up. Don't dump this crap on Holly—she's got enough to handle right now.*

So instead of (a) telling Holly how much it meant that she saw him as a wonderful man, (b) kissing her and telling her the same thing, (c) kissing her until the pleading expression in her eyes became a plea that he make love to her until neither of them could walk or (d) telling Holly what he was thinking, he settled for (e). "Let's finish going through those photo albums," he said curtly. "There's got to be a Biff in one of them."

It was in the second photo album, containing pictures of Chris's mother around the time she was starting kindergarten, with dark hair in two pigtails when she was wearing jeans, and hanging in loose curls when she was wearing her Sunday best, that they spotted it.

"'Saralee and Biff,'" Chris read, not quite believing what he was seeing. Then he said blankly, "Biff was her dog."

Chapter 15

"She looks to be about five, wouldn't you say?" Holly asked, a trace of excitement in her voice. "He's just a puppy, but he kind of looks like Wally. Biff must be a golden retriever, too."

Chris turned the page, and there were more photos of his mother as a child, and the dog—no longer a puppy—who appeared to be her best friend. There were photos of Saralee with other girls, too, but Biff seemed to feature in most of them. Chris flipped through all the way to the end, then quickly opened the third photo album. There were fewer photos of Saralee here, as if she'd become self-conscious about having her picture taken when she grew into her teens. But there were still photos of her with Biff, and Chris felt a sudden ache in the region of his heart, an unexpected kinship with his long-dead mother he'd never felt before. "I never realized…"

"Girls and dogs," Holly reminded him. "I told you a strong bond can exist between a girl and her dog." She went through several pages, one by one, Saralee maturing with each page. They were almost to the end before they realized there were no more photos of Biff. Holly turned back to the previous page, and there was a photo of Saralee all dressed up, with a young man at her side, obviously her date for the evening. There were other teenagers in the background, and the caption read "Saralee and Jeff—Sweet Sixteen Birthday Party." Captured in the bottom right corner of the photo was Biff. Just one ear and his muzzle, but it was definitely him.

But on the following page and all the subsequent pages, Biff was noticeably absent. One picture caught Chris's attention, titled "Saralee and Luke—Junior Prom." He touched it, thinking how much Annabel resembled their mother when they were both that age. Annabel was a blonde and Saralee was a brunette, but their faces were nearly identical.

"Junior prom," Holly said softly. "She would have been seventeen." She was silent for a moment. "Biff must have died sometime between her sixteenth birthday and her junior prom. Seventeen."

"Yeah." Chris carefully went back through everything between the Sweet Sixteen and Junior Prom photos, but there was no picture indicating exactly when Biff had died, or where he might be buried. *Mama would have buried him in a special place*, he told himself, knowing it for the truth. Just as he would have buried Bouncer in a special place…if Bouncer hadn't been euthanized at the pound. If Chris had been allowed to bury his dog.

He couldn't help but wonder—if his mother really *was* buried somewhere here on her parents' land— if his father had buried her near her beloved dog. It didn't sound like the father who'd blackmailed his children into visiting him in prison. The father who'd grudgingly doled out meager clues to his wife's burial place. But it *did* sound like a man who'd once been in love with his wife. Who hadn't meant to kill her…and then felt remorse when he saw what he'd done. Who'd wanted to make amends in some way…even in something as simple as this.

Holly was right, he realized suddenly. *You can never really know another man's motivations. You might think you do, but…*

Chris didn't subscribe to the theory that to know all was to forgive all. His father had killed ten people. Not surprising he'd gotten the death penalty in a state where the death penalty was often imposed in capital murder cases, but behind the scenes political machinations had gotten those death sentences commuted to sentences of life in prison without the possibility of parole—to be served consecutively. Matthew would never get out of prison—except in a box. And Chris couldn't be sorry. Maybe his father had been sick, but if so, it was a sickness that could never be cured. No one else's loved one would ever die at Matthew's hand, and Chris was fine with that. Matthew was in prison— exactly where he belonged.

But…

Holly was right about that, too, he acknowledged. *No one is all good or all bad. Mama wouldn't have loved him if he was purely evil. And she* did *love him—I know she did.*

Which meant that Holly could be right and he could be wrong. Maybe his father *had* just wanted to see all his children one last time before he died. No matter what he had to do to make it happen.

Holly swung on the front porch swing while Chris strode around the outside of the house and the barn with an exuberant Wally at his heels. He'd told her he really didn't expect to find anything—it was twenty years ago, he'd stated flatly—but he had to look anyway.

Holly watched Chris from afar, her thoughts in turmoil. Every so often she pushed the swing with one booted foot to keep it moving. The hinges squeaked—*needs oiling*, she told herself—but it was still soothing to swing. And she needed something to soothe and calm her, because she realized she was in over her head.

Whatever this was with Chris had gone from zero to sixty in nothing flat. Last night—she couldn't get last night out of her mind. She'd never looked on sex as a recreational pastime. Sex with Grant had been an extension of her love for him, and even though it hadn't been…well…hadn't been anything like sex with Chris, she'd never in a million years have imagined she could react that way with a man she didn't love.

Three times in one night. The thought chased around and around in her mind, three orgasms that had shattered her image of herself. She'd almost convinced herself the first time had been a fluke…until the second time. Until Chris's fingers had intertwined with hers and he'd whispered in her ear, *I'm going to please you until you can't take any more. And when I'm done, you'll know just how perfect you are.*

Her response the second time had been as cataclysmic as the first, and she'd thought nothing could ever surpass either of them. She'd been wrong. Because the third time, when he'd said, *I want to watch you come. Will you let me?* she hadn't been able to refuse—she'd melted just *thinking* about it. She'd always been curious, but Grant had never wanted to do it, and she'd never pressed.

But Chris seemed to have no inhibitions. And he hadn't let her have them, either—that was what she couldn't get over, how utterly different she was when Chris was in her bed.

Best time ever, she acknowledged now. All because of a man who tugged at her heartstrings on so many levels. A solitary man who should never have been allowed to be such a loner—he was made for laughter and sweet loving. For children's hands trustingly clutching his, and a woman's tender smiles.

And sex. Holy cow, was he made for sex. All six foot two, hundred seventy-five pounds of solid muscle and bone, with an unerring knowledge of her body, as if she was made for him. As if he was made for her.

That thought brought her up short, and she dragged one foot on the ground to stop the swing. It wasn't possible. She'd known him for less than a week. "Not even a week," she muttered under her breath. But if she were honest with herself—something she tried very hard to be, always—it felt as if she'd known him forever, because she could usually tell what he was thinking, the way long-married couples seemed to be able to do.

Long-married couples? *What made you think of that?*

And sleeping with him? What was *that* all about? Not something she'd ever done before, sleep with a man she barely knew. Which begged the question— why *had* she slept with Chris?

She shied away from answering, because the question alone scared the hell out of her...much less the answer.

The drive home seemed to take longer than the drive out to the farm in Bearson, mainly because Chris and Holly didn't talk much. He glanced at her from time to time as she gazed out the window at the passing scenery—scrubland that wasn't much to look at.

Finally he couldn't take it any longer. "What are you thinking about?"

She turned and resettled herself against the truck door. "Last night."

"Before, during or after?"

She laughed as if she couldn't help it. "Why is it," she asked him, trying to look stern but failing miserably, "that you can always make me laugh, even when I don't want to?"

"Answer my question first." He cast her a wicked look before firmly fixing his gaze on the road. "Then I'll answer yours."

Laughter pealed out of her, and she shook her head. "Mine was a rhetorical question. I'm not expecting an answer."

"I am." And just like that he wanted her. His voice dropped, the husky sound taking on sexual overtones that at one time had come as natural to him as breathing. "Before, during or after?" He stole a sideways glance at her, and loved the way her cheeks betrayed what she was thinking, and guessed, "During."

"Yes." It was just a thread of a sound.

"If we hadn't been interrupted this morning…"

"Yes?"

His answer mattered to her. He didn't know how he knew, just that it did. So instead of teasing her—his first inclination because it was such fun to tease her—he confessed, "I wanted to see you in the light of day. Not with the sheets pulled up under your chin like they were this morning. But in all your glory."

"You…you shouldn't say things like that to me," she said faintly.

"Why not?" When she couldn't come up with an answer, he said, "Tell me you don't regret last night."

"Oh, no!" Those little flags of color were back in her cheeks, but she leaned over and placed a hand on his arm as if she thought he needed reassurance. He did…but he wasn't about to admit it. "I could never regret last night."

His ego liked hearing that. A lot. That was something else he wasn't going to admit, though, so all he said was "Me, neither." But he couldn't keep the sudden, lighthearted grin off his face.

The first thing Holly did when she got back to Chris's house was call Ian and Jamie, talking with them for almost half an hour while they babbled in their childish way about everything they'd done that day. Then Peg had gotten on the phone, filling her in on how the twins were doing. "They're fine today. No issues. And I wasn't going to tell you," Peg admitted, "but…"

"But what?" Sudden concern made her voice sharp.

"We did have a teensy scene at bedtime last night. Jamie wanted you, and when I told him you weren't there and weren't *going* to be there, he dissolved into tears and sobbed, 'Call-her-on-the-phone.'"

"Oh, Peg, why didn't you call me?" Guilt speared through Holly that she'd been having the time of her life with Chris while her baby needed her.

"I would have, Holly…if he'd continued crying. But Susan gave him her teddy bear to sleep with—you know the one that's bigger than she is?—in addition to his bunny, and he calmed down after that. It only took three bedtime stories and four lullabies and he was out like a light. We haven't had any issues today, although when I asked Ian and Jamie what they wanted for breakfast, they both said, 'Waffos!' So I—"

"You had toaster waffles in your freezer."

"Well, no, I didn't, but no big deal. I dragged out the waffle iron, mixed up a batch of waffle batter, and they were happy as clams."

"Oh, Peg," Holly repeated, but this time it wasn't a reproach of her friend. This time it was said in gratitude that Peg was doing all this for her. "Thank you so much! I can never repay you for—"

Her response was typical Peg—she snorted a very unladylike snort. "Don't talk to me about repayment, missy," she told Holly. Then her tone changed. "Besides…"

"Besides what?"

"Our tenth wedding anniversary is coming up at the end of next month, Joe and me."

She didn't come right out and ask, but Holly quickly volunteered, "I'd love to keep Susan and Bobby for you and Joe. You could go somewhere nice and romantic."

Peg chuckled in a suggestive way. "Nice and romantic is how we ended up with two children barely a year apart."

Holly was forced to smile. "You know what I mean."

"Yes, and we'll be happy to take you up on your offer…as soon as your in-laws are in jail." That reminder drove the smile from Holly's face. "I know it's only the first day," Peg continued, "but are you making any progress?"

"Not on the McCays," she admitted. "Annabel and Sam have some things to do before we can get started on that. But we may have uncovered something more on where Chris's mother might be buried."

Chris was in his office. He considered calling Annabel and his brothers to tell them what he'd found out about Biff this afternoon, but then chose to shoot one email with the details to all of them instead, saving himself time.

He'd brought all the photo albums back with him, and now he pulled the fourth one out, wondering what else he might uncover. He and Holly hadn't reviewed the last two photo albums after they'd figured out Biff had died near the end of album number three.

But he regretted his decision to keep looking as soon as he opened the fourth album. Because there on the very first page was a professionally taken picture of his mother and father in their wedding finery. So young. So obviously in love.

Two pages later he came across another picture of his parents, both smiling, with an infant. The caption, in what by now he'd figured was his grandmother's handwriting, read "Saralee, Matthew and Trevor."

There were more pictures of Trevor—some with their parents and some by himself—from infant to toddler. Then Chris came upon another professionally shot photo, with three-year-old Trevor looking somewhat self-conscious in a tiny suit, propping up two babies—one in blue and one in pink. And underneath that photo it said "Trevor, Chris and Annabel—our first granddaughter."

Chris turned the pages slowly. Soon Ridge made an appearance, followed by Ethan, then Sam. Josie still hadn't shown up by the time Chris came to the end of album four, so he switched to number five. And there was Josie. Baby Josie as he vividly remembered her. He and Annabel had been closer than most brothers and sisters—that bond of twins—and he'd been protective of her...when she wasn't nudging him with those sharp elbows of hers or trying to wrestle him over something. But Josie had been his baby sister. So tiny, so beautiful, with dark, wispy hair and a baby smile that fascinated him. He'd been eight when Josie was born, and he and Annabel had tried to do whatever they could to help their mother—who'd never really seemed to recover completely after Josie's birth. "Why didn't I remember that?" he whispered as the memory came back to him now, crisp and sharp.

Pictures of all seven children now, some that Chris could have sworn were taken at his grandparents' farm, and— Yes! There was a picture of six of them wedged tightly in the front porch swing, with his parents standing behind them, Josie lying in the crook of his mother's arm.

Then all at once the photos stopped. Halfway down

a page, two-thirds of the way through, the photos stopped. And Chris knew why.

Holly, with Wally at her heels, found Chris standing at the window in his office, staring out at nothing. She'd intended to pretend to knock, then ask him what he wanted for dinner. But when she saw him, silhouetted by the dying sun's angled rays through the window, it flashed across her mind that Chris could be alone even in a crowd.

"Chris?"

He swung around sharply, his right hand reaching for the gun in his shoulder holster in what she could tell was an instinctive move. "Holly," he acknowledged a heartbeat later, his hand dropping to his side. "Sorry. You took me by surprise."

Wally bounded across the room toward Chris, tail wagging, tongue hanging out. Sure of his reception in a way Holly envied. She would have liked to run to Chris, wrap her arms around him and let him know he wasn't alone. But she couldn't do that. Could she?

Chris squatted on his haunches, stroking Wally's head with both his hands. Scratching behind the ears where the dog couldn't reach, eliciting the doggy equivalent of a satisfied whimper. And in her mind Holly heard her own whimpers last night as Chris had caressed her body with those big hands of his—not once, not twice, but three times—then made her cry his name, a sound that still echoed in her consciousness.

Her heart kicked into overdrive, and in that instant she would have given anything to have Chris touch her that way again. Make love to her again. But instead of saying what she wanted to say, she glanced at the schoolhouse clock on the wall, drawing his attention to the fact that it was long past dinnertime. "It's getting late," she announced. "You must be hungry. Did you want me to make dinner for us?"

He raised his gaze from Wally and gave her his full attention. "I can cook," he said. His smile was a little crooked. "Pepper steak okay? You can help me chop the vegetables."

In the middle of slicing and dicing, Holly asked quietly, "You want to talk about it?"

Chris narrowly avoided slicing his own thumb when the knife he was using in a semiprofessional manner on the onions threatened to break free. "Not much to talk about."

He turned to the stove and dumped the contents of his chopping board into the cast-iron skillet he'd already used to sear the steak strips. As the onions began sizzling, he took Holly's neatly sliced bell peppers and dumped them into the skillet, too. "It's just... looking at old photos brought back...memories," he volunteered finally.

"Good memories?"

He nodded slowly. "And bad ones. They're a reminder—as if I really needed one—that we don't know where Josie is. But it's not just that. She was three when...when she went into foster care, and we were only allowed to see her a few times a year. She turned Trevor down, she turned me down, when we tried to get custody of her."

"You mentioned that before."

He added a little water to the skillet using the lid, then stirred the onions and peppers, making sure they cooked evenly. "Yeah, but the hardest part is not knowing anything about *who* she is, not just where she is. I remember her when she was little—she was the happiest baby. And so precocious. She walked early. Talked early. She loved coloring and finger painting—" He chuckled suddenly at a memory. "And oh, how she loved to finger paint, but what a mess she always made. Mama used to say Josie got more paint on herself than on the paper."

"That's one of the good memories, then."

"Yeah." He smiled slowly at Holly. "I'd forgotten all about that. Guess sometimes it does pay to talk about what's on your mind."

They smiled at each other for a minute, until Chris suddenly realized the veggies for his pepper steak were in danger of scorching. He turned back to the stove and stirred furiously, then added in the steak strips he'd seared earlier. Finally he turned off the burner.

"Who taught you to cook?" Holly asked as she got the plates from the cabinet.

"Taught myself when I was in college. I lived off campus with three friends, none of whom could cook. I couldn't stand eating frozen cardboard-like food heated up in the microwave the way they did, and I certainly couldn't afford to eat out all the time. So I checked out a basic cookbook from the library and started messing around. I got to liking it—not just eating decent-tasting food, but the actual process of cooking from scratch. It's relaxing. Once I started Colton Investigations, though, I rarely had time to cook except on the occasional weekend."

"This is really good," Holly said as she dug in.

"Cooking must be like riding a bike. You never really forget how to do it."

Chris forked a bite and chewed thoughtfully. "Not too shabby, if I do say so myself. Meat could have used a little time to marinate—I should have planned ahead and done that."

Holly shook her head at him, smiling. "It's delicious and you know it."

"Well…" Once again he didn't know how to respond to a personal compliment. No one who knew him professionally would believe it, he acknowledged. He was supremely confident as a PI. Not so much in his personal life.

Holly changed the subject back to Josie. "So you've been searching for your baby sister for six years, that's what you said."

"Off and on. Whenever I can."

"But no luck."

He almost agreed, then realized that wasn't quite true. The whole Desmond Carlton thing was setting off alarm bells in his mind, telling him there *should* be a connection there…he just hadn't been able to figure it out. "There *is* something new on Josie—at least I think there is. Remember when I asked Annabel to look after you and the boys the other afternoon?" Holly nodded. "I needed to meet with a reporter in Dallas about an article he wrote."

He went on to give her all the details. If he'd stopped to think about it, he might not have. Holly wasn't a PI. She wasn't even family. But he suddenly wanted to share this with her, knowing instinctively she could be trusted to keep everything to herself. Including…

"So you're worried Josie might have killed Desmond Carlton," Holly stated, going right to the heart of the matter, "and that's why she disappeared."

Chapter 16

"I never said that," Chris was quick to point out.

"You didn't have to say it. But you *are* worried."

"Maybe. Okay, yeah. I am."

"If she did—and that's a big leap, Chris—but if she did, did it ever occur to you it was probably in self-defense?"

He took a deep breath, trying to dispel the tightness in his chest. "It occurred to me."

"Josie was seventeen," Holly said gently. "If she's anything like Annabel—I know Josie has dark hair and Annabel's hair is blond, so I'm not talking about that, I mean her features—but if she resembles Annabel, then she's extremely attractive. She wouldn't be the first seventeen-year-old to be accosted...possibly assaulted...by an older man. Especially if that man was a frequent visitor to her home. If Desmond Carlton was related to her foster parents..."

"Doesn't make it any easier for me to think she killed him in self-defense," he said grimly. "It just reminds me I failed to keep my baby sister safe."

"Oh, Chris…" The hint of gentle chiding in Holly's voice reminded him of the way she talked to the twins sometimes, when they did something she didn't approve of. "You can't blame yourself for *everything*."

"I'm not—" he began, then realized she was right. "Okay, maybe I am," he conceded. "But…"

"But nothing. You tried to get custody of her. You *tried*. She turned you down. You can't *make* other people do the things you want them to do, no matter how much you love them." A stricken expression slashed across Holly's face, and though they'd been discussing Josie, Chris knew instantly she wasn't talking about his sister anymore. "No," she whispered. "No matter how hard you try, you can't make someone choose you. You can't."

Regina Willard shuffled her way up the aisle with the rest of the crowd exiting the movie theater. Her prey was right behind her. Ingrid Iverson—the name the bitch went by these days—had no idea she was being stalked, of course. Inside Regina was cackling with glee. But outside she appeared no different from the other movie patrons who'd just spent an hour and fifty minutes in the darkened theater.

The bitch was with a friend, but Regina wasn't deterred. She slowly made her way to her car while the two women stood talking for a couple of minutes Then the women waved at each other, got into their own cars and pulled out of the parking lot, one turning left, the other turning right.

Regina turned right, following her prey from a safe

distance. The woman drove a few miles over the limit. *Breaking the law*, she thought self-righteously as her foot depressed the accelerator to keep pace. *But what do you expect from a loose woman like her?*

She'd first spotted Ingrid Iverson a few weeks back, at the Granite Gulch Bar and Saloon. Regina hadn't recognized her at the time, though. Hadn't realized Ingrid was the bitch in disguise. But she *had* seen what a loose woman Ingrid was. Flaunting herself to the men in the bar in a tight-fitting, low-cut blouse and jeans that appeared to be spray painted on. Accepting offers from three different men to buy her drinks. Then letting one of the men sweet-talk her into a booth, where the two sat canoodling until after midnight.

Disgusting, Regina had thought at the time. *No modesty. No morals.*

But she hadn't recognized Ingrid as the bitch who'd stolen her fiancé until she'd spotted her in the movie theater tonight just as the lights were dimming. Then she'd had an epiphany.

Regina had killed the bitch only three nights ago. What name had she been using then? Helena Tucker, that was it. But she was already back. The days between sightings of the bitch were getting fewer and fewer, forcing Regina to take shortcuts. Risks. But she didn't mind, because she was on a mission—making *sure* the bitch stayed dead.

So Ingrid Iverson had to die. And Regina could rest…for a few days, anyway.

Angus McCay propped the phone against his shoulder, writing furiously. Then he put the pen down and gripped the phone in his right hand. "Thank you *very* much, Mr. Colton," he said, waving the notepad on which he'd written an address and a phone number, trying to catch his wife's attention. "What's that?... Oh. Oh, yes, we'll see if we can get a flight up to DFW first thing tomorrow."

He listened intently to the man on the other end. "Hold on while I write that down. Bridgeport Municipal Airport, you said. Do I have that right?" He jotted the name down on his notepad. "Appreciate the suggestion, Mr. Colton. Not likely any plane out of Houston's international airport flies into there, but Houston Hobby might. We'll check."

He listened again, then said, "No, no, we don't need you to pick us up at the airport. We'll rent a car. We'll fly into whichever airport we can get the earliest flight to—we'll let you know. What's that?...Come to your office in Granite Gulch first?"

Angus glanced at his wife, who was nodding vigorously. "Of course, Mr. Colton. We'll call you once we have our flight, let you know when you can expect us tomorrow. And thank you for everything. My wife and I are thrilled we'll finally be able to see our grandsons after all this time."

He hung up. "Why did you say to tell him we'll go to his office?" His face displayed his surprise. "I don't think that's—"

"Of course we won't go to his office." Evalinda McCay's expression was the long-suffering one Angus had seen many times. "That was just a ruse. We aren't even going to book a flight. Call Leonard," she ordered, referring to Leonard Otis, the man who'd been behind the wheel during the last of the three attempts on Holly's life. "Tell him to drive up there tonight with his partner and take care of the problem. Permanently."

Holly was lying on top of the comforter on the king-size bed in her room, crying softly to herself because she didn't want Chris to hear her. She'd retreated to the bedroom after they'd done the dishes, and she'd been in here alone for the past two hours. Chris hadn't followed her. Hadn't sought her out. Had he sensed her need to be alone? Or was there another reason?

She'd almost blurted out her most closely guarded secret at the dinner table...but she hadn't. She'd managed to change the subject while they finished eating and had steadfastly refused to think about it until the kitchen was spotless. But then...then she'd escaped.

She'd called Ian and Jamie, needing to talk to them one last time before they went to bed. And when Peg had gotten on the phone, Holly had been secretly relieved the twins *were* missing her, although she would never have said that to Peg.

But that wasn't the only reason she'd called. She'd also needed to reassure herself she wasn't a bad person because of what she'd done. That the ends justified the means. And while she'd been talking with the twins, she'd believed it.

When she'd finally hung up, though, her thoughts had inevitably returned to her dinner conversation with Chris. She'd been trying so hard to convince him he shouldn't feel guilty over Josie...but she was just as bad. The guilt she was carrying...the guilt she would *always* carry...could never be forgotten. Pushed to the back of her mind much of the time, but...always there. Waiting to sabotage her happiness.

Her heart was breaking. Not for Chris and what he was going through—although she wished with all her heart she could take his pain and heal him. And not for herself—she'd long since acknowledged she couldn't undo what she'd done and she just had to live with it. No matter how often her conscience gave her hell, she deserved it.

No, her heart was breaking for Grant...and her boys. Knowing she could never tell Ian and Jamie. She *couldn't*. Knowing, too, that wherever Grant was, he knew. Had he forgiven her? She would never know. Not in this lifetime.

A knock on the closed bedroom door startled her, and Chris's deep voice sounded on the other side. "Holly?"

She dashed the tears from her eyes and realized there was no way she could disguise the fact that she'd been crying. She darted toward the master bathroom, grabbed a clean washcloth from the shelf and ran it under cold water. She wrung the washcloth out and placed it like a cold compress against her red and swollen eyes.

"Holly?" he called again. "Are you awake?"

"Just a minute! I'm in the bathroom." Which she was, but not for the reason Chris would think.

She repeated her actions twice, then checked her appearance in the mirror. Passable. Maybe. She clutched the washcloth as she opened the door and pretended to be scrubbing her face, hoping the pink in her cheeks would make Chris think the remaining pink around her eyes was due to the same thing. "What's up?"

Chris stood in the doorway with a partially drunk

bottle of beer in one hand, an unopened wine cooler in the other—the wine coolers he'd bought that first day over Holly's not-very-insistent protests. But the first words out of his mouth were "You've been crying."

And what do you say to that? she asked herself. "Yes," she finally admitted. "But nothing to do with you, so don't add it to the load of guilt you're already carrying." Her tone was wry. "That load is already stacked way too high."

The worry in Chris's face over Holly crying morphed into something else, and for just a moment she couldn't figure it out. Then she recognized it—an expression she'd begun wearing herself shortly after she and Grant were married, whenever she forgot to disguise it. Remorse was a big part of it. And something else—a lack of forgiveness…for oneself.

"Why do you look that way?" she whispered, wanting desperately to know. Wanting Chris to confide in her. Wanting him to *trust* her…the way she already trusted him.

"I should never have touched you…" Holly barely suppressed a gasp, but then he continued, "Without telling you…"

"Telling me what?"

Chris glanced at the king-size bed behind her. "Not here," he said curtly. "Not where I…where we…"

"Then where?" She wasn't about to let him get this far without telling her everything.

"Let's go into the family room. I have something to tell you anyway." He handed her the wine cooler and smiled faintly. "And you might want Wally for moral support."

* * *

"I called Angus McCay," Chris said without preamble as soon as Holly settled on the sofa, with Wally at her feet, her wine cooler sitting unopened on a coaster on the end table beside her. Chris perched on the arm of the recliner, a few feet away, one booted foot swinging. He took a sip of his beer. "I told you I was going to, but I wanted you to be aware I actually spoke with him. Starting now we both need to be on high alert. Annabel and Sam will join us for breakfast again—and will stay with us all day tomorrow. So whatever the McCays intend to try, we'll have plenty of witnesses, and plenty of firepower."

"What about tonight?"

"In addition to Wally, this house is as safe as I could make it," Chris explained. "You know the little tinkling sound whenever the front and back doors are opened from the inside?" She nodded. "All the doors and windows are wired. Anything opened from the inside just warns you—that tinkling sound is the interior parent alarm, so parents know if a child is opening a window or a door. But the exterior alarm system is something completely different—it will give us ample warning in case someone tries to break in. I built the house knowing that Laura—" He broke off for a moment, and that remorseful expression returned.

He stared at the beer in his hand, then continued. "I knew Laura might be here alone at times, so I built in every fail-safe I possibly could. If the phone signal is lost, the alarm company calls the police. If someone cuts the electricity, the alarm has a battery backup it can run on for up to eight hours. And if the alarm switches to battery power, it goes off immediately—loud enough to wake anyone—and the alarm company is notified. You can override the alarm, in case the electricity goes out because of a storm or something like that, but you have to have the alarm code. Same thing for letting the alarm company know. There are special codes that tell them if something's wrong and you can't discuss it with them."

Holly started to ask when the battery had last been checked, but Chris forestalled her. "I checked it the day I brought you and the boys here, Holly." A muscle twitched in his cheek. "You think I would have let you stay here a single night without that safety feature?"

In her mind she heard Chris saying the other day, *No one is dying on my watch ever again, you got that? I made myself responsible for you...*

That was when she made the connection. Annabel telling her Chris blamed himself for Laura's death. Peg telling her Chris needed to take care of her and the twins.

"That's what you meant when you said you should never have touched me without telling me," she whispered. "It's something to do with Laura, isn't it?"

Chris stiffened, but he didn't look away. "Yes."

"Not that Laura was the only woman you ever slept with before me, because you told me that up front. It's something to do with her death."

His face could have been chiseled from granite. "Yes."

"Then..." Her throat closed as her heartbeat picked up. Whatever Chris told her was going to take their relationship to an entirely new level. One she wanted. But she would have to be as open with him as she was asking him to be with her. And that would take all the courage she had. "Then tell me whatever it is. Because

I want you to touch me." She breathed deeply. "I want you to touch me again, and if you can't until you tell me…then tell me."

He contemplated his beer, then took a swig. And Holly knew whatever it was wasn't easy for Chris to talk about. He wasn't much of a drinker—this was the first beer she'd seen him with in all the time she'd spent in his company—but apparently he needed a little something to loosen his tongue.

Abruptly he said, "Do you know what it's like growing up in a town like Granite Gulch? Not many secrets remain secret for long. And of course, when something bad happens in your family, it's an albatross around your neck forever."

Holly nodded her understanding. "Your father was a serial killer *and* he murdered your mother. Granite Gulch never let any of you forget it."

"Yeah." His eyes met hers. "So I always felt I had something to prove. From that time on I was driven—to excel. Not just to succeed, but to succeed spectacularly. Does that make sense?" She nodded again.

"I met Laura sophomore year in high school. I took one look at her and I knew I was going to marry her— it was that simple. Through the rest of high school and four years of college, I never really looked at another woman."

Envy unlike anything she'd ever known stabbed through her. Envy of a dead woman who'd had the unswerving love and devotion of a man like Chris, while she… "You loved her," Holly managed. "I know. And she loved you."

"Yes, Laura loved me, and I loved her. But not enough to temper my ambition. Not enough to make her my first priority…as I should have." He was silent for a moment, then dropped the bombshell. "And when she told me she wanted a baby, the first thing I thought of was that would at least give her something to do so she wouldn't always expect me to be home. She never complained, but I knew. I just never…" The expression of savage self-recrimination on his face tore a hole in Holly's heart.

"When she got sick, I wasn't here. I was at work. I was always at work. One office wasn't enough for me. Not even two. I was spreading myself too thin—I knew that—but I was driven to succeed…spectacularly. I was going to prove to everyone in Granite Gulch that I wasn't my father's son. Living here in Granite Gulch but having offices in Fort Worth and Dallas meant I had a hell of a commute every day. Something had to give…and that something was Laura. I loved her, but I didn't make time for her. I gave her *things*," he said bitterly, waving his free hand to encompass the beautiful house around them, "but not the one thing she wanted the most. Me."

He tilted the beer in his hand and drained the dregs, setting the empty bottle on the chair behind him. Then he faced her again and said, "That's the kind of man I am, Holly. My father's son. A cold, uncaring bastard."

She couldn't bear it. She left the sofa and moved swiftly to stand in front of him, cradling his face in her hands. "You may be his son, but that's not the kind of man you are," she said softly. "You think you're the only one who makes mistakes? Mistakes you can't ever make up for, no matter how much you regret them?" She brushed her lips over his and blinked back tears.

"I never told Grant…never told anyone…but I…I

trapped him into marriage." She swallowed hard.
"The McCays were right. I trapped him. I loved him
so much, I thought that made it right. I thought I could
make him love me."

Chris shook his head. "I don't follow you."

"I...seduced him one night when he'd had too much
to drink, but not so drunk he couldn't...couldn't per-
form. I just wanted him to *see* me for once. Not as his
best friend since forever, but as a woman. I thought..."

She gulped air. "I didn't... I wasn't deliberately trying to get pregnant... We did take...precautions. But
I was overjoyed when it happened. I thought...it's a
sign this was meant to be. That we were meant to be
together. I knew Grant would do the honorable thing
when I told him—that's the kind of man he was."

Her tears spilled over, trickling down her cheeks.
"Long before Ian and Jamie were born, I knew I'd made
a mistake. But I couldn't undo it. I couldn't even tell
Grant what I'd done. He went to his grave thinking it
was *his* mistake, thinking *he'd* taken advantage of *me*."

She bent her head and covered her face with her
hands, sobbing uncontrollably as remorse and regret
swirled through her. Then strong arms closed around
her, pulling her against a hard, male chest. "Every time
I look at Ian and Jamie," she choked out, her tears stain-
ing Chris's shirt, "every time I see Grant in them...I
think of how they were conceived. And I know I can
never make it up to them. No matter how good a mother
I am, I can never make it up to them."

"Shh," he soothed, his hand stroking her back in a
comforting fashion. "It's okay, Holly. You're human.
You made a mistake." She couldn't have spoken right
then even if she'd wanted to. "You love those boys,"

Chris continued as his arms tightened around her. "Anyone can see that. That's all that matters."

Her fingers clutched his arm, needing something solid to hold on to. Needing the human connection as she cried out her grief over what she'd done to one man in another man's arms. When her tears finally abated, she raised her face to his. "I didn't tell you that for me," she whispered, catching her breath on a sob. "I just wanted you to know you're not alone. Just wanted you to know you're not a cold, uncaring bastard. It's not your fault you didn't love Laura the way she wanted. The way she needed. Just as it wasn't Grant's fault he wasn't in love with me the way I was in love with him." Her eyes squeezed shut for a moment, then opened to face him honestly. "You're human, too, Chris. You made a mistake, just like me. But that doesn't mean you need to live in purgatory the rest of your life to atone for it."

They ended up back in the master bedroom. A part of Chris knew he'd kissed Holly as if his life depended on it, and she'd kissed him back. Then he'd swung her into his arms and carried her in here. But another part of him was taken completely by surprise. He wasn't the romantic kind. He was earthy. Direct. And his love-making had always reflected it. But somehow, Holly brought out the romantic in him, and at the moment he'd done it, carrying her into the bedroom had seemed like a good idea.

But he wasn't the only one having romantic ideas, and Holly surprised him. She dragged him into the master bathroom but prevented him from stepping into the shower when he stripped. "Uh-uh," she said, tugging his hand. "Whirlpool tub. When I was giving Ian and Jamie a bath in this tub, I couldn't help thinking it's big enough for two adults." She was already running the water, and when it was six inches deep, she asked, "How do you turn the jets on?"

He showed her, and with the water still running Holly put his hands on the top button of her blouse. Her suggestive "Help me" sent blood pulsing through his body—and one body part in particular.

When she was as naked as he was, he turned the water off, climbed into the whirlpool and helped her in after him. But when Chris would have sat down with his back to the tub, Holly stopped him. "I have this fantasy," she told him, a tiny smile on her lips. "Do you mind?"

Mind? He had no mind when she looked at him that way, when her voice curled through him as tangible as a caress. And the fantasies that came to Chris made his voice husky when he asked, "What did you have in mind?"

Chapter 17

Chris lay half-submerged in the whirlpool, his head pillowed on Holly's breasts, the water swirling around him. Holly's fantasy hadn't involved kinky sex—but then, neither had his. Her fantasy had turned out to be relatively tame compared to some he'd thought of. But how could he complain about fulfilling a fantasy that had him cradled in Holly's arms? A fantasy that involved breasts as tantalizing soft and smooth as hers beneath his head?

And oh, yeah, let's not forget what her hands are doing, he reminded himself blissfully. *Not to mention her legs.* Holly was amazingly limber.

Eventually, though, he couldn't take any more. "Holly," he warned.

"Me, too," she whispered.

They dried themselves quickly, and Chris was glad

to note Holly no longer seemed shy about letting him see her body. He looked his fill, which took his body from low gear to full throttle in less than a minute.

He knocked the box of condoms off the nightstand next to the bed in his haste. "Leave them," he told Holly when she made a move to retrieve the spilled contents. "I have enough for now." He opened his fist and let the handful he'd grabbed fall onto the nightstand. All except for one.

She gasped and he sucked in his breath when his fingers stroked over her tender flesh and found her ready. His voice was guttural when he said, "So damned ready for me, Holly. Do you know how much that turns me on?"

He captured her right hand and wrapped her fingers around his erection. "Take what you want." He almost went ballistic when she squeezed, then seated him in place, raising her hips as if to envelop him. She couldn't quite accomplish it—but he wasn't going to deny her or himself. His lips found hers as he slid into her tight sheath, swallowing her moan of pleasure. Her hips rose to meet his, taking him so deep he again experienced that sense of coming home he'd felt last night.

He soon found a rhythm that pleased Holly—if her little gasps meant anything. As for him, he loved riding her soft and slow, holding back and building her excitement to fever pitch. "Wait for it," he panted when her breathing quickened too soon. "Wait for it."

"Can't."

"Yes, you can." He slowed and she whimpered in frustration. He knew she'd been close, but that orgasm would have been a prairie grass fire—easily started, quickly over. He was aiming for an all-out conflagration, and he wouldn't be satisfied until she achieved it.

Deep and slow, deep and slow. Her fingernails digging into his shoulders, urging him to go faster. Sharp little fingernails that would have hurt—if he could feel anything other than Holly tight and wet around him, and oh so perfect. *Made for you*, he thought with that fraction of his brain that could still think.

But eventually his control cracked. His thrusts quickened. And Holly's body arched as she cried out his name and came. And came. And came. Her orgasm triggered his, and he let go with one last thrust and her name on his lips.

Wally's howl woke them both from a profound sleep. Holly was dazed and disoriented for a moment, but Chris wasn't. He was in and out of the bathroom before she knew it, tugging on his jeans and zipping them carefully. Wally's howls changed into urgent yips, as if he was trying to get at something. Chris's hands clasped Holly's arms and he pulled her close in the darkness to whisper in her ear, "Get dressed, but stay here. I'm going to check it out." Then he was gone.

"Oh, heck no," she muttered, scrambling into her clothes and tugging her boots on. "What kind of a wuss do you think I am?" She grabbed the first thing she could find that was big and could be used as a weapon. Then she ran after Chris.

She made it into the living room just in time to hear an engine roar as a car or truck accelerated away from the house down the long, winding driveway. A bare-chested Chris was crouched at one of the front windows, peering through the curtains. One hand was tightly clutching Wally's collar, holding him back. The other hand held a gun.

"Chris?" she hissed, and he whirled around.

"Damn it, I told you to stay in the bedroom."

"You're not the boss of me," she shot back without thinking. Then could have smacked herself for the less-than-adult response. She and Grant had used that phrase when they were kids, and it had become something of an inside joke when they were older. But Chris wasn't to know that.

The tense, worried expression on Chris's face rapidly changed to amusement. "I'm not the boss of you? What are we, in grade school?"

"Okay, that came out wrong. What I meant to say is you can't expect me to just obey you blindly."

"And what's that in your hand?"

Holly glanced down. "Oh. Well. I thought I might need a weapon."

"You were going to take on intruders with a Wiffle bat?"

"It belongs to the boys. I couldn't find anything else." She quickly put it down. "Forget about that." She pointed to the front door. "Was someone trying to break in? Is that why Wally was barking?"

Chris's expression went from amused to grim in a heartbeat. "Apparently so." He opened the front door, then turned on the porch light to see better before stepping outside. But there was nothing to see; whoever had been there was long gone.

"Burglars? Or do you think the McCays...?"

"Could have been your garden-variety burglar, but I doubt it. Too coincidental. But the two figures I saw moved way too quickly to be the McCays—late twenties, early thirties, I'd say." He turned to look at her, his face half in light, half in shadow. "You said the McCays tried to have you killed. Could have been the same goons. If it was them, they probably drove up from Houston—they had enough time."

"It probably *was* them." Holly shivered even though the evening was warm. "I know this is going to sound funny coming from their intended victim, but...they didn't seem all that competent when they tried to kill me before. What I mean is—"

"If they were halfway good, you'd already be dead?"

She laughed a little. "Something like that." Then another thought occurred to her. "The alarm didn't go off."

Chris came inside, closed the door and locked it with the two dead bolts. "They never got close enough to try the door or attempt to pick the lock. They took off as soon as Wally started howling."

He did something with his gun—*putting the safety on?* Holly wondered—then slid the weapon into the shoulder holster she hadn't noticed before was sitting on the floor by the window. He must have drawn his gun right away, as soon as he retrieved it from his bedroom, she reasoned, but he needed the other hand to hold on to Wally.

"Be right back," Chris told her, disappearing down the hallway. When he returned, his hands were empty.

He crouched down and scratched Wally's ears. "Good boy!" He praised the dog for several more seconds, getting his face washed in the process by an adoring Wally, then stood. "Let's continue this discussion in the kitchen. I want to give Wally a treat."

* * *

The clock in the kitchen said it was a quarter to four. Holly watched Wally gobble down the treat Chris gave him in one gulp, then plead for another. "Oh, hell, why not?" Chris said, suiting his actions to his words. "You deserve it." Then he glanced up sharply at Holly and stood. "Sorry."

"Sorry?" She wrinkled her brow in a question.

"I shouldn't have said *hell*. I should have said *heck*."

A smile slowly dawned along with understanding. "You're trying to clean up your language." Chris looked abashed, and she knew she was right. "I noticed it before, but I didn't really focus on it, if you know what I mean."

"Yeah." He put the bag of doggy treats back into the cabinet. "Peg mentioned the other day that Susan understands a lot of what she hears now. Peg also said she told Joe he needed to watch his language. She didn't say *I* did, too, but…"

The backs of Holly's eyes prickled suddenly, and she knew tears weren't far away. "You're such a good man, Chris," she whispered, moved by his attempt to do the right thing, to set a good example for the children around him, even in something as simple as this. "*Such* a good man."

That was the moment she fell in love with him.

No, that's not true, her inner self argued. *You've been falling in love with him since the first day. You're just now acknowledging it, that's all.*

She walked toward him, then placed her hands on his bare chest. She didn't realize her tears had overflowed their banks until Chris said, "You're crying again." Bewildered. His right hand came up to cup her cheek, his thumb brushing her tears away. "And this time I think it *does* have something to do with me. I just don't know why."

Holly choked back her tears as the laughter Chris could always evoke came to the fore. "Because..." She wasn't about to tell him her sudden revelation that she was in love with him, so she settled for "Because you're such a good man. The kind of man I want Ian and Jamie to grow to be someday."

Chris shook his head. "I'm no role model, Holly."

She cradled his hand against her cheek, smiling through the tears. "Think again."

Chris and Holly decided to try for a couple more hours of sleep before morning, although Holly made a sound of dismay when Chris brought his gun into the bedroom with them. "Just to be on the safe side," he assured her. "I don't think those men will be back. Not without a better plan." He placed the holstered gun on the nightstand...right next to the box of condoms she'd picked up and returned there last night.

He drew her into the curve of his shoulder. "You're safe here, Holly. I won't let anything happen to you."

"But what if the McCays don't fall for the trap we've set? What then?"

He smiled in the darkness. A grim smile he didn't let Holly see. "Those goons they sent? I'll call Angus McCay first thing in the morning, let him know they failed to kill you."

"How will you do that? You're not supposed to be staying here with me—at least that's what the McCays believe—so how would you know? And besides," she added, "you're not supposed to know the McCays want me dead, remember? So even if you know someone tried to break in, you wouldn't know they were anything other than burglars."

"Trust me, I'll come up with something believable." He laughed, but the humor was missing. "The McCays thought I was stupid enough to fall for their original story and not do a little digging on them. I won't do anything to disabuse their minds of that belief. But I'll get them up here in person." He kissed her temple, his voice softening. "See if I don't."

This time when Annabel and Sam arrived, Holly and Chris were dressed and ready for them. Chris was in the kitchen, putting together the fixings for his "signature French toast," as Annabel called it, and Holly was setting the table.

"I'll get it," she said when the doorbell rang.

Chris glanced at the clock as he whisked eggs in a bowl. "They're late." He looked at Holly. "Make sure it's them before you open the door."

Holly cast him an "are you kidding me, you think I need to be told that?" expression, but didn't say anything.

She glanced through the peephole and saw Chris's sister and brother on the porch. She swung the door open. "Hi, Annabel. Hi, Sam." Sam was in plainclothes; Annabel was in uniform. But they both looked…exhausted. Neither returned her cheerful greeting. And there was no answering smile on either face. "What's wrong?"

"Where's Chris?" Sam asked.

"He's in the kitchen making breakfast for you. French toast?" she faltered.

Sam headed straight for the kitchen, Annabel right

behind him. Holly clutched at Annabel's arm. "What's wrong?"

Annabel didn't stop, but she did say over her shoulder, "We found another woman murdered last night. Another copycat serial killing, with the red bull's-eye on her forehead."

"Oh, my God!" Holly covered her mouth with her hand, then quickly followed Chris's twin into the kitchen.

Sam was already telling Chris, "...and her name was Ingrid Iverson. Did you know her?"

Chris put down the bowl he was holding, turned off the fire beneath the skillet and shook his head. "Name doesn't ring a bell. But then the last few years new people have been moving into Granite Gulch. It's not like when we were kids."

Annabel said bluntly, "We're here, Chris, because we promised we would be. But we've been up all night." She glanced at her younger brother. "Sam won't admit it, but he's dead on his feet. I am, too."

"I'm okay," Sam insisted, but Holly saw the smudge-like circles of total exhaustion beneath his eyes. Beneath Annabel's, too.

"No, you're not." Chris's voice had that big-brother quality to it, mixed in with concern. And love. The kind of emotions most men hated to admit they felt toward a brother...even if they did.

Holly would have smiled if this wasn't so serious. Annabel and Sam were supposed to help them spring the trap for the McCays today. That was why they were here. And Chris had already set the plan in motion last night—the attempted break-in early this morning was proof the McCays were already taking the bait.

"I'm not letting either of you participate in this sting in the condition you're in now," Chris said unequivocally. "You're practically weaving on your feet." He thought for a moment. "The McCays sent men to kill Holly early this morning. Yeah," he confirmed when his siblings cast him alert looks that contradicted their exhausted faces.

Chris gave them a brief rundown of what had happened. "Their goons were here, but the McCays are still in Houston, so—"

Annabel interrupted him. "How do you know that?"

Chris smiled faintly. "Trust me, I have my sources. If they're coming in person—and I have a plan to get them here—they can't possibly arrive for a few hours. If they fly, we're talking three to four with all the hassle of flying nowadays. If they drive, at least four hours, maybe five or six even, depending on traffic. Either way, there's time for the two of you to get a few hours of shut-eye." He gestured toward the stove. "How about I make breakfast, then you can sack out." Chris was already heading out of the kitchen and down the hallway toward the bedrooms, Sam and Annabel following him. Holly brought up the rear.

"You can take my bedroom," Chris told Sam, opening a door. "And, Bella, you can have the other bedroom." Thinking she was being helpful, Holly opened the door to the bedroom across from the master bedroom. "Not that room!" Chris warned...too late.

A baby's room confronted Holly's eyes. Pale green with yellow-and-white trim, colorful decals decorating the walls. A baby crib held pride of place in the center of the room, a darling mobile of butterflies and flowers dangling above it. Exactly the kind of bedroom she'd decorated for the twins—times two—back in Clear Lake City.

Tears sprang to Holly's eyes as she realized this room had been lovingly created by Laura in joyous anticipation of her baby...her baby and Chris's. How much Laura had wanted her baby was clearly evident, even though she'd been only four months pregnant when she...

Holly blinked rapidly to hold back her tears and closed the door as quickly as she could. She turned, and when her eyes met Chris's across the hallway, she mouthed, *I'm sorry*. He shook his head slightly, as if telling her it was okay, he didn't want her to feel bad about her honest mistake. And though she knew he meant it, she hated seeing the shadow of sorrow cross his face.

"Must be this one," Annabel said in her calm voice, as if she hadn't witnessed the interchange between her brother and Holly—something Holly was sure Annabel had seen. "And you're right, Chris. I'm wiped out. A good breakfast and a couple hours of sleep, though, and I'll be good."

"Okay, okay," Sam finally conceded. "You've made your point. But I want a hot breakfast and a warm shower before I hit the hay."

Angus McCay hadn't had a decent night's sleep in months, and last night had been no exception. He'd managed to stave off his creditors, but robbing Peter to pay Paul only worked in the short run, and now the vultures were circling. If he and Evalinda didn't get their hands on the income from the trust Grant had set up for Ian and Jamie—and soon—the house

of cards Angus had built would come crashing down.
The fallout from that would be disastrous. Not to mention Evalinda would hold him personally responsible.

He and Evalinda had tried to overturn Grant's will
legally…to no avail. They'd tried to gain custody of the
twins legally, by painting Holly as an abusive mother…
but that had gone nowhere. Angus hadn't wanted to
resort to murder, he really hadn't. But Evalinda had
convinced him it was the only way.

The problem was, as Evalinda had been quick to
point out at four this morning, the men he could afford to hire weren't all that bright. Thugs willing to
commit murder, yes. But easily stymied. They'd called
him shortly after they'd been scared away—by a damn
dog—from the house where Chris Colton had told him
Holly was staying. But instead of lying in wait for
Holly to come out of the house in the daytime and killing her then, they'd been spooked. They hadn't turned
tail and run all the way back to Houston—not yet—but
they'd called Angus in a panic, looking for direction.

"Lie low," he'd instructed them. "I'll come up there."

He didn't want to. As Evalinda had stated last night,
it was far better for the two of them to stay in Houston,
establish an alibi there, than to head to Granite Gulch
to take care of Holly themselves. But it was beginning
to look as if they had no other choice.

And that was another thing. He wasn't sure he
could actually pull the trigger. *Squeamish*, Evalinda
had called him in that despising way she had when
he'd balked at killing Holly, back when Evalinda had
first raised the possibility. Eventually he'd caved…as
he always caved when Evalinda had her heart set on
something. This huge house in the best neighborhood,

which they really couldn't afford. The luxury cars that screamed "money," money they didn't really have. The expensive jewelry Evalinda just had to have, *because I deserve it*, she'd insisted.

This time, though, he wasn't going to cave. If Evalinda wanted Holly dead, she was going to have to do it herself. Sure, he'd help. But he wouldn't pull the trigger, and that was that.

Chapter 18

"Give me your keys," Chris told Sam as soon as breakfast was over. "I'll park your truck in the garage—make it look as if Holly's alone in the house." He glanced at Holly. "And as soon as I make one phone call, I'm driving over to the Merrills' to swap my truck for your SUV, so we can set the stage. I'll park your SUV right out front, so anyone who knows what you drive will know you're here."

Holly looked hopeful. "I can go with you and see Ian and Jamie?"

He shook his head and said gently, "Probably not a good idea. You wouldn't be able to stay long, and it might upset your sons more to have you come and go quickly than if you don't show up at all."

At her crestfallen expression he said even more gently, "Why don't you go call them now? I'll clean up in here."

He could tell she was disappointed, but she was putting a good face on it. "You cooked, I'll clean," she insisted. "Besides, it's still early. They might not be awake yet."

Chris was going to argue but thought better of it, since he was anxious to call Angus McCay. So while Sam and Annabel went to get some much-needed sleep, he moved Sam's truck, then headed for his office.

He hooked a recording device to his phone and dialed Angus McCay's home phone number. It rang five times before it was answered, and by the third ring he was saying, "Come on, be home!" under his breath.

"Hello?" A man answered and Chris had no difficulty recognizing Angus McCay's gruff voice.

"Mr. McCay? Chris Colton here."

"Oh. Oh, yes, Mr. Colton. I…I haven't had a chance to book a flight yet, so I can't tell you when my wife and I will be there. But soon, as soon as we can, because we can't wait to see our grandsons now that you've found them for us."

"About that," Chris said, smiling to himself. "I thought you should know your daughter-in-law called the police early this morning. Apparently someone tried to break into the house where she's staying. The police took her report, of course, but they have more important things to worry about than a break-in that never actually happened. You've probably seen the news by now—the Alphabet Killer claimed another victim last night. The FBI and the Granite Gulch police are all focused on that investigation."

"Sorry to hear—another victim, you say? No, I haven't read my newspaper yet this morning, so I didn't know." Angus cleared his throat. "Of course, it's terrible two men tried to break into Holly's house. Good thing her dog scared them off."

Bingo, Chris exulted inside. *Got you on tape, too.*

Angus kept talking. "If Holly was back home where she belonged, and Ian and Jamie, too, she wouldn't be alone at a time like this."

Chris rolled his eyes at the fake concern, but all he said was "Yes, sir. I totally agree with you. Holly and her sons need the kind of protection and support only a family can give." Spreading it on thick. "So when do you think you might get here? The thing is, an emergency cropped up in my Dallas office, and I'm going to have to drive over there—it'll probably take me all day to resolve. So I won't be able to meet you at my office in Granite Gulch today after all."

"Don't worry about a thing," Angus McCay reassured Chris. "You gave us the address last night. If we can get a flight, I'm sure we can find the place. As for your bill—"

"Not an issue. I can mail the bill to you after your daughter-in-law and your grandsons are safely back in Houston. Good luck convincing her that's where she belongs."

Chris hung up, laughing softly to himself. He disconnected the recording device and played back the conversation, nodding to himself as Angus McCay revealed three things that could be crucial at trial. First, Chris had never mentioned any details about the attempted break-in. But Angus McCay had revealed without prompting he knew it was two men. Second, he knew the men had been scared off by a dog. A dog he had no idea Holly had. Third, Angus McCay had admitted Chris had given him Holly's address last night. So he couldn't claim he didn't know where she was staying.

"What's so funny?" Holly asked from the doorway.

"Your father-in-law makes a lousy criminal," Chris joked. "Almost as bad as you."

Holly's face turned solemn, and Chris realized too late it wasn't a joke to her. "I had more difficulty accepting he was trying to kill me than I did about my mother-in-law," she said quietly. "She never liked me. Not when Grant and I were little, and not when we got married. But I never got that impression from my father-in-law. He…he's weak, though. His wife rules him. So if she decided I had to die, he'd go along."

She breathed deeply, letting the air out long and slow. "My parents were so different. Theirs was an equal partnership as far back as I can remember. Neither tried to dominate the other. Doesn't mean they didn't have their ups and downs. Doesn't mean they never argued. But the few times they couldn't reach an agreement, they agreed to disagree and left it at that. I promised myself that when I grew up I'd have a marriage like theirs."

He had to ask. "And did you? Was that what your marriage to Grant was like?"

She nodded slowly. "In a way. It wasn't like my parents' marriage, because Grant never— I mean, he loved me, but he was never *in* love with me. And that made things difficult at times."

She sighed softly. "But it wasn't like Grant's parents' marriage, either, thank God. I'm not a doormat kind of woman," she said, as if she were revealing a closely held secret. "Maybe you can't see that in me because you've only known me on the run. Terrified something will happen to me, but more because if something did, Ian and Jamie wouldn't have a mother. They've already lost their father. I can't let them lose their mother, too. If I didn't have them, I don't think I would have run. I would have stayed and fought it out with the McCays."

One corner of his mouth turned up in a half smile. "I know you're not a doormat kind of woman. Would a doormat have told me I'm not the boss of her?"

She smiled, but there was a touch of sadness to it. "That was an inside joke between Grant and me. If one of us tried to—oh, you know what I mean—the other would say that as a joking reminder. Then we'd laugh and things would be okay between us. But that was before we were married. When we were just friends."

More than anything in the world, he wanted to erase that sadness from her face. Wanted to banish it forever. Wanted to tell her how sweet she was, without being *too* sweet. Wanted to confess what a difference she and her sons had made in his life. Wanted her to know he couldn't imagine a more responsive lover—not just in the heat of passion, but the before and after, too. The way she fit so perfectly in his arms. The way she touched him so tenderly. The way she looked at him at times as if all light and hope in life emanated from him.

The way she loved him.

The realization hit him and knocked him for a loop. *She loves you.*

Hard on the heels of that thought came another, just as much of a body blow as the first. *And you love her.*

He opened his mouth to tell her, but the words wouldn't come. And before he could stop her, she turned away, saying, "I'm going to call Peg, see if Ian and Jamie are awake now." Then she was gone.

Chris stared at the doorway where Holly had stood, calling himself all kinds of a fool for not grabbing the chance to tell her how much he loved her. He started after her and was halfway across the office when his cell phone rang. He was going to ignore it at first, but when he glanced at the touch screen, he recognized the caller and cursed softly because he knew he had to take the call.

"Hey, Brad," he said when he answered his phone. "What's up?"

"Hey yourself. Just wanted to touch base with you about those names you asked me to track down. Desmond Carlton and Roy and Rhonda Carlton."

Chris quickly sat at his desk and pulled a pen and a pad of paper in front of him. "Okay, yeah, what have you got?"

"You were right. There's no mention of Desmond Carlton on any search engine I could find. Not that I didn't trust you, Chris, but it never hurts to double-check, you know? Desmond Carlton is a zero in cyberspace. A cipher. You'd think the guy didn't exist, unless..."

"Unless what?"

"Unless you peruse old police blotters and dig out old copies of newspapers. That's where I hit pay dirt. Desmond Carlton *was* a drug lord who was murdered six years ago—I located an article from that time. And get this—the obit on the guy lists he was survived by his brother and sister-in-law—"

"Roy and Rhonda Carlton?"

"Give the man a cigar. Also mentioned was a daughter, Julia. I haven't been able to track her down, but what I *could* find is that she was eighteen when her father bought the big one."

"She could have moved away. Gotten married. Changed her name some other way."

"Gee, thanks, why didn't I think of that?" Brad asked drily.

Chris chuckled. "Sorry. What else have you got?"

"Roy and Rhonda died five years ago in a car crash, just as you said."

"Was it really an accident?"

"Sure looks that way. Particularly gruesome one, but there never seemed to be a question it was anything other than an accident." Brad hesitated. "You know, when I dug into Roy and Rhonda, I came across a couple of names that—"

"Let me guess," Chris said laconically. "Josie Colton and Lizzie Connor, now Lizzie Colton. Right?"

"Yeah." Brad seemed relieved this wasn't news to Chris. "Lizzie's older than Josie, but both fostered with the Carltons from an early age. Josie until she was seventeen—when she up and vanished—Lizzie until the car accident. Apparently the Carltons considered her like their own daughter, and she was still with them even after the state was no longer paying for her foster care."

"Anything tying Desmond and Roy together other than they were brothers?"

"Nada. Roy was a straight arrow, and so was his wife. But Desmond?" Brad snorted his disgust. "Desmond had a rap sheet as long as my arm," he said. "But get this, Chris—no convictions. A dozen arrests, not a single conviction."

"That's got to be a mistake. A major drug dealer with no convictions?"

"No mistake. Not even a misdemeanor." Brad's

voice took on a cynical tone. "One thing after another. Problem with the chain of custody of the evidence? Case tossed out. Witness against him fails to show up at trial? Case tossed out. Oh, and I love this one. Evidence mysteriously disappears from the police lockup? Cased tossed out. The prosecutors were fit to be tied."

Chris cursed under his breath. "Either this guy was the luckiest SOB on the planet, or—"

"Or someone on the police force—maybe more than one—was helping him out."

"Right." Chris thought for a moment, trying to put all the puzzle pieces together. "Anything else?"

"Desmond Carlton's name came up in a murder investigation eleven years ago. He was never arrested, but he was brought in for questioning. A small-time drug dealer was murdered and word on the street was that Carlton had something to do with it. You know how that goes. But the police could never pin it conclusively on him, and the case went cold."

Eleven years ago. Something about that niggled at the corners of Chris's memory, as if it should mean something. *I was twenty,* he mused. *I'd just finished my sophomore year in college, but Laura and I weren't engaged yet. That was in the fall. So what happened eleven years ago?*

Try as he might he couldn't pull a thread loose, so he shelved the question, knowing that forcing your brain to remember rarely worked. But if you put it aside, the answer usually came when you least expected it.

"Is that all?" Chris asked.

"Pretty much."

"This is terrific stuff, Brad. No kidding. I knew you

were the right guy to put on this case, and you really came through for me. I won't forget it."

Chris took a moment to ask about Brad's wife and his three daughters, who were all in college and grad school. Then he disconnected and sat there, staring at the notes he'd jotted down on the pad of paper. "Eleven years," he'd written near the bottom, and circled it twice. It meant something. He didn't know what, but he knew it did.

The more he stared, the more convinced he became. Then he did something he would never have done a week ago…before Holly entered his life. He picked up his cell phone and hit speed dial. When the phone was answered, he said, "Trev? It's Chris. I know you're busy, but I need to ask you a quick question."

The urge to see her sons was so strong when Holly hung up the phone, she acknowledged Chris had been right. If she'd had her SUV, she wouldn't have been able to resist driving over to Peg's, even if only for a few minutes. And that could have been fatal. Not just for her, but for Ian and Jamie, too. Whoever had tried to break in during the wee hours of the morning could be lying in wait somewhere, watching for her SUV. She could be followed to Peg's house, and…

Chris had also been right about not going with him when he went to pick up her SUV. Ian and Jamie were doing okay. They missed her, but they were okay because Peg was making sure of it. It wouldn't be fair to Peg to flit in and out, getting the twins all wound up when their mother left.

One more day, she reminded herself. *Only one more day away from my babies.*

Holly wandered into the bathroom to brush her teeth, which she'd forgotten to do after breakfast. Her gaze fell on the whirlpool tub, and her memories of last night came rushing back. Not just what she and Chris had done in the tub. Not even what they'd done in the bed, although that qualified as one of those "just once in my life I want to" occasions she'd never forget. No, it was the moment they'd stood together in the kitchen, when she'd fallen in love with Chris, that she was thinking of now.

She stared at the mirror, but she wasn't seeing herself, she was seeing Chris in her mind's eye. So many different aspects of his character, but none more lovable than the "born to be a father" persona that came so naturally to him.

She wasn't looking for a father for her sons. She could never fall in love with a man who *wouldn't* be a good father, but that wasn't why she loved Chris. She loved him for the gentle, caring way he had, for the tenderness not far beneath the surface. She loved him for his straightforward approach to sex, and how he made her believe physical perfection was highly overrated. She loved him for the protectiveness he displayed, not just to her and her sons, but toward his sister and brother—his love for them ran so deep, but she wasn't sure he knew how deep it ran. She even loved him for his insecurities, for his self-doubt.

But most of all she loved Chris because he made her laugh. Despite the threat hanging over her head, despite her fear for herself and the twins, he made her laugh—she'd forgotten how much *fun* life could be. Nothing could ever be so bad that Chris couldn't find some humor in it, and she loved that about him. Gallows humor, maybe, but humor nevertheless.

"Now all you have to do is make Chris fall in love with you," she murmured to her reflection, "and you'll be in high cotton."

That was the problem in a nutshell. Holly had tried to make a man love her once and had failed spectacularly— she wasn't going down that road ever again. She'd even done something of which she would forever be ashamed in her quest for her love to be returned. Never again would she marry a man who didn't love her, heart and soul, unreservedly. No matter how much she loved him. No matter how tempted she might be.

"But if Chris *grows* to love you," Holly whispered to herself, "then…"

He was attracted to her. Okay, *more* than attracted. She was the first person he'd made love to since Laura, and that said a lot about how much he wanted her for herself. The question was, did he want her permanently? With all the baggage she brought with her?

"Not that Ian and Jamie are baggage," she corrected. "But we *are* a package deal."

She wouldn't use her sons, though. She wouldn't hold them out as an inducement to Chris to replace the child he'd lost—Chris had to love her for herself alone.

But if he did…she and the twins could make him so happy. Ian and Jamie were already attached to Chris— they could easily grow to love him, just as she did. They could be a family here. So much love had gone into this house—Holly could feel it. Not just the love Laura had for Chris, wanting to make a happy home for him and their baby. But the love Chris had for Laura, too. All the safety features he'd built in, to make his wife and child as safe as he could when he wasn't there.

Holly wouldn't be taking anything away from Laura—a part of Chris would always love Laura, just as a part of Holly would always love Grant. Holly didn't want to *replace* Laura in Chris's heart, she wanted to build her own place there...if he wanted it, too.

Love wasn't linear, it was exponential. And there was room in Holly's heart for the man she'd once loved...and the man she loved now.

She just prayed Chris would come to feel the same way.

"Eleven years ago?" Trevor asked Chris. "All I can think of is Josie telling the social worker she didn't want to see us anymore. I was a year out of college, just starting my career with the FBI. It was a knife to the gut, but Josie was adamant."

Chris snapped his fingers. "That's right. I'd forgotten exactly when that happened, but you're right."

"Is there anything else you needed?" Chris heard the exhaustion in Trevor's voice and figured he'd been up all night with the latest Alphabet Killer murder, same as Annabel and Sam. He'd been tempted to do as Holly had suggested—ask Trevor point-blank why he'd abandoned him when they all went into foster care. But his brother had enough to deal with right now. "Nothing urgent," Chris said. "Thanks for reminding me about Josie. Good luck on the case."

"Same to you."

"How'd you know I—"

Trevor cut him off. "I hadn't seen you around for a few days, so I asked Annabel. If anyone knew what

was going on with you, it'd be her. She mentioned she
and Sam were helping you set a trap to catch a couple
of attempted murderers in the act. I wish *we* were that
fortunate—catching our serial killer in the act," he
added drily. "So good luck."

"Thanks." Chris disconnected, then sat there for a
moment, mulling over what Trevor had said, carefully
fitting one more puzzle piece in place. Then he saw it,
the whole picture. And he could have kicked himself
it had taken him this long.

Chapter 19

"You had it all wrong," Chris murmured to himself. "Josie didn't kill Desmond Carlton, not even in self-defense. That's not what this was all about." Pieces of the puzzle were still missing—pieces only Josie could fill in—but he was pretty sure he knew the basic outline of what had happened.

Josie's strange behavior eleven years ago…at the same time that small-time drug dealer was murdered. She'd only been twelve—she couldn't possibly have had anything to do with it. And word on the street was that Desmond Carlton had killed the other man. What if Josie had witnessed the murder? Carlton had probably been a visitor in his brother's house—heck, the murder could even have taken place there for all he knew. And what if Carlton had threatened Josie somehow? Carlton could have killed her, but…he had a daughter himself, just a year older than Josie. What if he couldn't bring himself to kill Josie because of that, but had threatened her instead? *Keep quiet or I'll kill everyone you love.*

That made a heck of a lot of sense. Lizzie had given them all a clue back in February, when Josie had still been a suspect in the Alphabet Killer murders, but none of them had made the connection because they hadn't known about Desmond Carlton. Chris couldn't recall Lizzie's exact words, but the gist was that Lizzie and Josie had been extremely close, like sisters. Right up until Josie suddenly became distant and guarded at age twelve…eleven years ago.

Josie had never given Lizzie an explanation, Lizzie had told them, no matter how hard Lizzie had pressed Josie to open up to her. But Lizzie had also been adamant back in February that Josie wasn't the serial killer, long before there was concrete proof. That Josie didn't have it in her to kill at all.

Someone had killed Desmond Carlton six years ago, but not Josie. And someone—or some *organization*— had done their best to erase Carlton's name from existence. "Should have focused on that before," he berated himself. "Only one entity has that kind of power. That kind of clout." Conspiracy theories be damned, in this case there was only one answer—the federal government. That led directly to federal agencies that might have reason for secrecy of this nature, and only one came to mind. Witness Security, run by the US Marshals Service.

Which would mean Josie was in Witness Security, commonly known as Witness Protection by the general public. Which would also mean she hadn't run six years ago because she was guilty of something. And she hadn't cut off communication with her family when she was twelve because she no longer loved them, either. She'd been *afraid* for them...*because* she loved them. Carlton's threat wouldn't have worked otherwise.

Now Chris's mind was flowing freely from one conjecture to another, but conjectures that fit all the facts. What if six years ago Josie decided she was tired of living in fear, tired of living under Desmond Carlton's threats? What if she went to the police and told them what she'd witnessed? And what if they'd set up a sting to trap Carlton...a sting that went horribly wrong?

That matched what the reporter had said about Carlton's death. *There were no shell casings and someone even dug the bullets out of him, so there was very little to go on...* A botched sting would explain it. Or even a *deliberately* botched sting. Either way, they'd whisk Josie away into Witness Security afterward. Give her a new identity, just in case any of Desmond Carlton's associates decided they wanted revenge.

The more he thought about it, the stronger Chris's hunch became that Carlton's death might somehow be connected to why he had no convictions after twelve arrests. Why his murder had never been solved. Because someone didn't *want* it solved?

Maybe. But that wasn't the most important thing right now. Because all of Desmond Carlton's known associates were either dead or in prison. And if Chris's conjectures were true, Josie no longer needed to fear reprisals. Which meant...if she really *was* in Witness Security...she could finally come home to her family.

Annabel had told Chris where the man from the FBI's Ten Most Wanted list was currently incarcerated—the man who'd once run with Carlton. After this whole thing with the McCays was wrapped up, Chris was going to rope Trevor into paying the guy a visit with him. And get some answers.

Chris left, but not without telling Holly he was leaving. "I already took Wally outside, so he's good," Chris told her. "I'll be back long before the McCays can get here, but don't answer the door, just in case last night's goons return. Sam and Annabel are here—if Wally starts barking or the alarm goes off, they'll know what to do—so you don't need to worry about that. If the phone rings—"

"Don't answer it. Got it."

He shook his head. "*Do* answer it. We *want* the McCays to know you're here because we want to draw them here." He grinned suddenly. "Gotta bait the trap with something irresistible, and…" He looked her up and down, sending her pulse racing when he waggled his eyebrows at her and said in his most suggestive voice, "I can't think of anything more irresistible than you."

Then he kissed her as if he meant it, and her racing pulse went into overdrive. He muttered something Holly couldn't catch and reluctantly let her go, then grabbed his black Stetson from the hook by the front door and settled it firmly on his head. He turned with his hand on the door handle and said, "And stay away from the windows. I mean it, Holly," he added implacably when she started to speak. "You trusted me to keep you safe, and I will. I'm not chancing a marksman taking you out with a high-powered rifle."

He grinned again. "And before you say it, I *am* the boss of you when it comes to this."

* * *

The morning dragged for Holly. "Stay away from the windows," she grumbled under her breath. Problem was, there wasn't a single room in the house that didn't have at least one window, not even the bathrooms. She made the rounds of the house, Wally at her heels, and confirmed she was right.

The drapes were drawn in the living room and formal dining room—neither had been used since she'd been here—but could someone see her shadow if she got too near those large windows? The kitchen windows only had café curtains—they let in the sunlight beautifully, but she would be a sitting duck if someone took aim at her while she was in there. The family room wasn't any better than the living room, unless she crouched in the corner—something she wasn't about to do.

There were no drapes in the master bedroom, only those top-down, bottom-up shades, with a valance across the top and floor-length swags on either side. But those swags were decorative only—they wouldn't close. They looked pretty, but they wouldn't provide any additional coverage. The two guest bedrooms were occupied. And no way was she going into the baby's room, not for any money—she'd probably start crying for Chris and everything he'd lost.

Which left Chris's office. It had a window, but only one. And it was L-shaped. If she sat at his desk, no one would be able to see her.

She fetched a book from her bedroom, then settled down in Chris's desk chair to read. But for some reason the book couldn't hold her interest, so she glanced around the room. For the first time she realized that of all the rooms in the house, this was the only room that reflected Chris's personality. The rest of the house— even the master bedroom—had been furnished to a woman's taste. Laura's taste.

But this room was different. There were none of the little decorative touches here that were in the other rooms. Chris's office was beautifully furnished—desk, bookcases and credenza were all honey oak—but there was a solidity to the furniture and a lack of feminine knickknacks that bespoke a man's occupancy.

Holly nodded to herself, smiling a little. If she never saw Chris again after this was all over, if she returned to her life in Clear Lake City with Ian and Jamie, she would always remember Chris in this room. Sitting on the floor with Wally draped across his legs, Ian on one side, Jamie on the other, as he read them their bedtime stories. Sitting at this very desk, concentrating on his work. Standing in front of this desk and kissing her as if his life depended on it—their first kiss that had dev- astated her with how much she wanted him, and—oh, God—how much he'd wanted her. *Go to bed, Holly*, he'd told her in that deep rasp his voice made when he was hurting. *This isn't what you want.* Thinking of what was best for her and the hell with what he wanted.

"How could I not love him?" she asked herself.

Still smiling, but just a tad misty-eyed, Holly glanced down at the notepad sitting in the center of the desk. Cryptic notes jotted down in a distinctive scrawl that had to be Chris's—who else could it be? But she couldn't make heads or tails of it, although she was sure it meant something to Chris. Especially the two words circled near the bottom—*eleven years*.

She realized with a sudden start of guilt she had no

business reading anything on Chris's desk, and she hurriedly put the notepad down. She turned away, and that was when she saw the silver-framed photograph standing in a secluded corner of the desk. Not large—four by six, maybe—but the face, surrounded by wavy light brown hair parted on one side, was immediately recognizable. The resemblance to Peg was obvious, but even if it wasn't Holly would have known who this woman had to be. Annabel had described Laura to a T—sweet, pretty, with a gentle, almost shy smile.

Curious, even though Holly told herself not to be, she reached over and picked up the photograph, studying it minutely. Peg's features were here, but nowhere did she see what Peg had an abundance of. Grit. Determination. Character. Not Wonder Woman, but a woman who did what she had to do without complaint. Her love for those around her flowed from strength.

What had Annabel said about Laura? *Chris was her world, and whatever he did was right. Good in some ways, not so good in others.*

If this photograph was anything to go by, Laura wasn't much like her older sister. Not that sweetness and gentleness were traits to scoff at. And Laura was far prettier than Holly could ever hope to be. But there was something lacking in Laura's face Holly couldn't quite make out. Then it dawned on her—Laura wasn't a fighter. In Holly's place she could never have stood up to the McCays.

Maybe that was what Annabel had been trying to tell Holly the other day, that what Chris really needed was a strong woman. An independent woman. A woman who wouldn't always agree with him, who wouldn't let him immerse himself in his work, body and soul. Who would force him to have some balance in his life.

A woman like me.

The phone shrilled suddenly, and Holly almost dropped the framed photograph. Remembering that Chris had said to answer the phone if it rang, she snatched up the receiver. "Hello?" Nothing but dead air answered her. "Hello?"

Whoever it was disconnected without saying a word, and Holly shivered. Could it have been one of her in-laws? One of their henchmen? Or just a wrong number?

She hung up and carefully replaced the photo of Laura exactly where she'd found it. Then whirled and caught her breath when the bell-like alarm went off, indicating a door or window had been opened somewhere in the house.

"Holly?"

She breathed sharply when Chris called her name, only then realizing she'd been holding her breath until she knew who it was. She shook her head, impatient with herself because she should have known by the tinkling sound it wasn't someone trying to break into the house. "In here," she called back. "Your office."

Chris appeared in the doorway, so reassuringly big and male. "Hey," he said, juggling her keys in one hand. "Anything happen when I was gone?"

"Someone called just now. I answered, but they didn't say anything."

He smiled and nodded with satisfaction, as if this was just what he expected. "The McCays checking to make sure you're here."

"It could have been a wrong number, but—"

"But probably not," he finished for her. "I parked your SUV out front. They can't possibly miss it."

"So what do we do now?" she asked.

"We wait."

"What if they don't show up?"

He leaned his weight on one hip, his eyes narrowing as if debating whether or not to tell her something. Then he said, "They're already on their way. Driving, not flying."

"How do you know that?"

A faint smile touched his lips. "Because I sent a couple of men down there yesterday to shadow them."

She stared at him. "You did?"

"You think I'd have told the McCays yesterday where you were if I didn't have eyes on them? You think I'd have left you here today—even with Annabel and Sam—if I didn't know exactly where the McCays were at all times?" He laughed under his breath. "What kind of PI do you take me for, Holly?" He held up one hand when she started to speak, and joked, "No, don't answer that."

Holly's lips curved in a smile as she walked toward Chris. "But I want to answer the question," she said when she was close enough to touch him. Her fingers brushed a lock of hair from his forehead, then trailed lightly down, coming to rest on his shoulder. "I think you're incredible. Amazing. There aren't words to describe you. I thank my lucky stars the McCays hired you to find me, because I'd be in a world of hurt if it had been anyone else."

His slow smile rewarded her. "You'd have managed somehow," he said. "You're a fighter—no way would you ever surrender. I knew that from the minute I entered your room in the rooming house. That's what I lo—"

Chris stopped midsentence when the sound of bedroom doors opening down the hallway and questions asked and answered between Sam and Annabel suddenly intruded on their conversation.

Holly rarely cursed—it hadn't been acceptable in her home growing up as the daughter of missionaries. But if she *did* curse, she would have just then. She would have given anything to know what Chris had intended to say. Love? As in, "that's what I love most about you"?

But she couldn't bring herself to ask, especially since Chris had already turned toward his sister and brother. "Well, if it isn't Beauty and the Beast, finally awake," he drawled.

"Bite me." Sam obviously wasn't of a sunny disposition when he first woke up.

Annabel elbowed Sam. "What makes you think *you're* the Beast?"

Chris turned his head and his eyes met Holly's, a glint of humor in them. "And there you see why Ridge is a better choice than 'don't you dare call me beautiful' Annabel and 'don't call me a beast even though I am' Sam."

"I think I'm missing something here," Sam growled.

Holly laughed. "Let's have lunch and I'll explain."

Holly went to her bedroom after lunch to call her sons—"Keep away from the windows," Chris told her in no uncertain terms.

"I will."

Chris watched her go. Part of him wished they

hadn't been interrupted earlier, but another part was glad. He hadn't intended to say anything to Holly yet—not while she still needed his protection. He'd already had one tussle with his conscience over making love to Holly while he was guarding her—he didn't want her to think there was some kind of quid pro quo going on, that he expected sex in exchange for looking after her and her sons. And he'd had no intention of telling her how much he loved her until she was free to make a decision without the threat of murder hanging over her head.

But somehow, when Holly had smiled at him, when she'd touched him and told him he was incredible and, oh yeah, amazing, the words of love had almost come tumbling out despite his best efforts.

Annabel jabbed Chris in the ribs to get his attention, her tone caustic. "Wake up there."

"Ouch!" Chris rubbed his ribs. "Darn it, Bella," he complained. "You still have the sharpest elbows of anyone I've ever known, even if you *are* my favorite sister over thirty."

"I'm your *only* sister over thirty," she retorted.

"*Darn* it?" Sam raised his eyebrows in a question Chris wasn't about to answer.

He headed for his office, with Annabel and Sam right behind him. "Before we get caught up in the sting," he said as soon as they sat down, "I want to run something by you two."

He recounted his conversations with Trevor, Brad and the reporter for the *Dallas Morning News*. He reminded them of what Lizzie had said about Josie back in February. Then he gave them the conclusions he'd drawn. "Am I way off base here?" he asked. "Or does my theory fit all the facts as we know them?"

Sam glanced at Annabel, who nodded. "Your logic is sound," he told Chris. "But the only way to know for certain is to track Josie down and see what she says."

"Trevor might be able to help there," Annabel said. "If Josie really *is* in the Witness Security Program, the FBI is in a better position to approach the US Marshals Service. Let's see what he can shake loose."

Chris ruthlessly suppressed the tiny flare of jealousy triggered by Trevor's name. Annabel was right—Trevor was in a better position than Chris to take the investigation into Josie's disappearance to the next level. Yeah, Chris had been searching for his baby sister for years, but it really didn't matter who ultimately solved the mystery. Bringing Josie safely home was more important than his ego. "You're right," he told Annabel. "As soon as we wrap up this case, I'll talk to Trevor."

Holly walked into the office with a smile on her face, and Chris couldn't help it—his eyes softened at the sight of her. Then he caught Annabel watching him, and he quickly schooled his expression into one of pure professionalism. "Everything okay with the twins?"

"Fine, but Peg says they're starting to fret over the least little thing. Which means—"

"They're missing you something fierce." He and Holly shared a private smile.

"I shouldn't want them to," she confessed. "But I do. I want them to miss me." She glanced at Annabel. "Does that make me a bad mother?"

Annabel chuckled. "No, it makes you a perfectly normal mother."

Chris brought his mind back with an effort to the

reason they were all here, and said, "Let's get every-thing nailed down—who's going to do what. Planning ahead is half the battle."

Fifteen minutes later Chris had laid out his plan in detail. "Any questions?"

He glanced from Sam, who shook his head, to An-nabel, who did the same, and finally to Holly. "Got it," she said.

"My men tracking the McCays already called from the road. We'll know in advance almost to the minute when they'll arrive, so no worries there. My men will turn off before they get here—we don't want to spook the McCays, let them know they're being followed. I'll have them double back afterward, although I don't think we'll need them. But just in case…"

Just like the morning had, the afternoon dragged. Holly just wanted it *over*—she was unexpectedly calm about the upcoming confrontation with her in-laws, but she wanted it to be past tense.

Everyone, it seemed, had something to keep their minds distracted—except her. Sam read the morning newspaper he'd brought with him. Annabel had another police procedural textbook she soon became engrossed in. And Chris worked on his computer, answering a string of emails. Holly felt a twinge of guilt. Chris had a business to run after all. He'd made her case his top priority, but that didn't mean everything else came to a screeching halt. She wanted to ask him about the notes he'd left in the middle of the desk, but she didn't—for two reasons. She didn't want to interrupt him, and she didn't want him to think she'd been snooping. She wasn't sure which reason reigned supreme.

Holly sat on the floor stroking Wally, who lay in a contented heap at her side. And she wondered if Chris would let her take Wally back with her to Clear Lake City…assuming she went back. Assuming something didn't go wrong this afternoon. Assuming Chris didn't love her.

Chapter 20

At six minutes past three, Chris's cell phone rang, and he closed his laptop. He answered his cell phone, listened for several seconds, then said, "Thanks, Matt. Tell Andy the same from me…No, I think we've got it covered, but just in case, have Andy double back and park about a quarter mile before the driveway leading to the house. You can't see that part of the road from the house, so the McCays won't know you're there. If you don't hear from me in…oh…fifteen minutes, assume the worst and come to our rescue. But be careful—"

He broke off sharply, and Holly knew he could hear the same thing she did—the sound of a car pulling up in front of the house. "They're here. Gotta go."

Holly scrambled to her feet and wiped her suddenly sweaty palms on the sides of her jeans. Annabel and Sam were already moving purposefully to their assigned places—Sam to the coat closet near the front door and Annabel secreted behind the door in the kitchen.

The doorbell rang a minute later. Chris grabbed Holly's arm, pulling her back as she started to leave the office to answer the door. "We're right here," he reminded her." But worry etched furrows in his face. "If there was any other way, I—"

She put her fingers on his lips to stop him from completing that sentence. "I know," she said, her earlier calm returning. "But there isn't another way. And I won't let them get away with it this time."

The doorbell rang again, sounding somehow impatient, and Holly looked Chris directly in the face. "I love you," she said quietly. "If anything happens— I know you'll do your best, but… Anyway, I wanted you to know." She turned and walked out without waiting for a response, Wally at her heels.

Chris swore under his breath. Damn Holly for choosing that moment to tell him she loved him, when he couldn't do a thing about it. And damn her for walking out before he could tell her he loved her, too. That he couldn't imagine life without her. That there was no way—*no way*—she was dying on his watch.

Gun drawn, he double-checked the switches on the two hidden cameras in the living room, making sure the cameras were rolling—the different angles would ensure at least one would capture whatever the McCays tried to do. Then he did the same for the voice-activated recorder. The wireless microphones were already set up, just waiting to record every word the McCays said.

He pulled the door to the office nearly shut, listening intently. Time seemed to stretch out, and he could hear

Holly clearly as she opened the door and exclaimed, "Angus! Evalinda! How did you find— I mean, how lovely to see you."

Chris smiled grimly. Holly was playing it perfectly— acting surprised to see the McCays, but also acting as if she had no idea they were there to kill her. If the McCays were innocent, the first thing they'd ask was why Holly had run away with her sons six months ago. But they never asked...because they already knew the answer.

"Come into the living room," Holly invited.

This was the most dangerous moment, Chris knew. He'd theorized earlier that the McCays wouldn't just open fire the minute they saw Holly. That they'd make *sure* she was alone in the house before they started blasting. But theories were one thing. The woman he loved turning her back on her murderous in-laws as she led them into the living room was another thing entirely. He took comfort in the fact that Sam should be able to see everything from his vantage point in the closet, which was cracked open. And if one or both of the McCays reached for a gun...

"Where are the boys?" Angus asked.

Chris shifted slightly for a better viewing angle. *Nice job!* he told Holly in his mind as she seated the McCays on the living room sofa, directly in his line of sight—and right in the field of vision of each camera. She disappeared from his view, and he knew she was sitting in one of the armchairs across from her in-laws, exactly as planned.

"They're not here right now," Holly replied. "They have a playdate with friends—Susan and Bobby. Their mom and I take turns having playdates for the children." She laughed easily, as if she didn't have a care in the world. "It gives both of us a little free time to ourselves. And you know how it is with small children, Evalinda. Much as you love your children, sometimes you just need to be alone."

"So you're alone in the house?" Evalinda McCay asked sharply. Chris saw Mrs. McCay's hand reaching into her capacious purse, and he readied himself to launch.

"Yes, I'm alone. Except for Wally here." Chris couldn't see Holly, but he imagined she was patting the dog's head. "Why do you ask?"

Even if Chris hadn't seen the gun come out, Wally's sudden growl would have warned him.

"You should never have opposed us," Evalinda McCay said, as matter-of-factly as if she were discussing the weather.

"What are you— No, Wally," Holly said when Wally's growls deepened. "What do you think you're doing, Evalinda? I'm your daughter-in-law. The mother of your grandchildren. Why are you—"

Regret was evident in Angus McCay's voice when he explained, "I'm sorry, Holly. We didn't want to do this, but you left us no choice."

"Is it money? Do you need money?" Holly's voice held just the right panicked note. "I have Grant's insurance money. I'll be happy to share it with you, if you—"

Evalinda McCay laughed, but it was an ugly sound. "That pittance?"

"Not a pittance," Holly insisted. "Half a million dollars. If you had told me, I—"

"We want the money Grant put into a trust for Ian and Jamie," Evalinda McCay stated viciously. "That damned unbreakable trust. The only way to get our hands on that money is to get custody of the twins. And the only way *that's* going to happen is if you're out of the picture."

"You'd kill me for money?" Holly's disbelief sounded like the real thing.

"You turned Grant against us. You convinced him to leave us out of his will." Chris saw the evil smile that tugged at the corners of Mrs. McCay's mouth. "So killing you will be a pleasure, not just a necessity."

"I didn't!" Holly insisted. "Grant did that all on his own, I swear!"

Wally's growls were nearly ferocious now, and Chris imagined Holly was having difficulty holding the dog back. *Good boy!* he thought. *Protect Holly!*

"It doesn't matter either way," Evalinda McCay said. "But don't worry. We'll take good care of Ian and Jamie…for now. Everyone will be convinced—just as that stupid private investigator was convinced—that we're loving grandparents who only have our grandsons' best interests at heart." She sighed with mock regret. "You'll be the victim of a terrible home invasion. Thank goodness the twins weren't here when it happened! We'll play the grieving grandparents to the hilt, stepping in to care for our orphaned grandchildren." Evalinda McCay was obviously already getting into the role.

She stood suddenly. "Now get up. Slowly. I can make this easy, or hard. If you try to run…I'll have to shoot you quickly. The first bullet might not be fatal." The evil smile was back. "But I'll make sure you're dead before I leave, Holly. Count on it."

"Police! Freeze!" Annabel and Sam's voices rang out almost simultaneously, using the exact same words.

Chris burst through the library door, his one thought to get to Holly before Evalinda McCay fired. But Wally was there before him. With one last growl the dog pulled away from Holly's restraining hold and leaped for the hand holding the gun. His jaws closed on Evalinda McCay's wrist and jerked, so the bullet went wide.

"On the ground!" Sam ordered, wrestling a shocked Angus McCay down, then cuffing him with his hands behind his back.

Annabel was doing the same to Evalinda McCay, who was moaning in agony. She'd already dropped the gun and was holding her bleeding wrist, where Wally's teeth had broken the skin and nearly broken her bones.

"You're under arrest for attempted murder," Annabel intoned, then began reciting the Miranda warning to both McCays. "You have the right to remain silent. Anything you say can and will be used against you in a court of law…"

She reached the end and said, "Do you wish to talk to us now?"

"Go to hell!" snapped Evalinda McCay. "This is entrapment! And police brutality. My wrist is broken, and these cuffs are making it worse."

Annabel listened politely, then said, "We'll stop off at the hospital to have your wrist x-rayed. But you're still under arrest."

Long before the McCays had been cuffed, Chris had enfolded Holly in his arms, his gun still drawn. She was trembling—aftereffect, he knew—and his arms tightened. "It's okay," he told her.

"She was really going to kill me," Holly whispered as Annabel and Sam led the McCays away in handcuffs.

"Yeah, but you already knew that." Chris pulled back just long enough to holster his weapon, then his arms closed around her again.

Wally was bounding around the room in excitement, following the prisoners and, when the front door closed behind them, snuffling enthusiastically around Holly's and Chris's legs.

Holly extricated herself from Chris's arms and knelt to embrace the dog. "Good boy, Wally!" she praised. "I knew I could count on you."

Chris crouched down to ruffle Wally's fur in silent affirmation of the dog's heroic actions. "What about me?" he asked Holly.

Her unexpected smile warmed his heart. "I knew I could count on you, too."

He could have stayed like that forever, except he suddenly remembered something. "Oh, cra—crud," he amended, rising to his feet and whipping out his cell phone. He clicked quickly between screens and hit the callback button. "Matt? We're good here. Sam and Annabel put the McCays under arrest for attempted murder and are taking them to jail with a short detour to the hospital. You and Andy are done for the day, and there'll be a special bonus in your next paycheck— you've earned it. I'll talk to you both tomorrow."

Holly was still kneeling beside Wally, and after Chris disconnected, he helped her to her feet. "You and I have some talking to do," he told her.

"I still can't believe she was really going to kill me herself. I mean…it's one thing to want someone dead. Hiring someone to do it—that's worse. But killing someone yourself…looking them in the face and pulling the trigger…" She shivered. "That's so cold. I can't imagine hating someone enough to do that."

Chris drew Holly into his arms again, staring down into her face. "Forget that," he told her dismissively. "I have a bone to pick with you, and I'm not deferring this conversation until you have time to come to terms with what Mrs. McCay was going to do to you."

Holly shook her head, puzzled for a minute. Then her eyes widened in understanding. "You mean…?"

"Yes, I mean…" he replied. "You sure can pick your times, Miss Holly," he teased. "Dropping a bombshell on me, then walking out cool as you please to face down murderers."

Warm color rose in her cheeks. "I didn't mean to tell you— Well, yes, I did, but not— And anyway… You see, the thing is…"

"The thing is you love me."

It wasn't a question, but she answered it anyway. "Yes."

"If you'd waited half a second instead of rushing out, you'd have heard me say the same thing."

If anything her eyes grew even bigger. "You mean it?" she whispered. She clutched his arms. "Don't say it if you don't mean it. Please don't."

He tightened his hold on her. "I never say what I don't mean, Holly." He drew a deep breath. "I don't know how it happened, honest to God I don't, because I was determined it wouldn't. But it *did* happen. And now…"

A hint of a smile appeared in her eyes. "Is this where I say I love you and you say 'ditto'?" she teased, referring to an incredibly romantic movie more than twenty-five years old she'd seen on cable. "Because if that's the best you can do…" Her smile melted away, replaced by a touch of uncertainty. "I need the words, Chris—I think you understand why. So please…*please*…"

He tilted her face up to his with one hand and, with heartfelt conviction, said, "I love you. I need you. I can't live without you." He'd mocked Ethan—not once, but twice—with those same words the day Ethan and Lizzie's baby was born. But he'd never been more serious in his life. "If any of those statements match how you feel, Holly…please tell me. Because I'm dying here."

"I can't believe you even need to ask." She touched his lips. "I already told you in the office earlier."

"Tell me again."

She smiled tenderly. "I love you, Chris. I need you in my life. And I don't think I can live without you anymore, either."

He grinned as a weight lifted from his shoulders… and his heart. Even though he'd already figured it out on his own, even though she'd told him right before the McCays had arrived, he'd needed those words from her, too, and not uttered in the heat of the moment.

Then his grin faded and he said, "I don't just want you, Holly. I want Ian and Jamie, too. I want to be their father. Not that I want to replace their real father. From everything you've told me about Grant, he was a decent man and the twins are his legacy—I would never want them to forget him. But I love your sons, and I want the chance to be the kind of father I never had."

How was it possible to love Chris even more than she already loved him? Holly didn't know, but when he said things like this, she didn't have much choice. "The other day you said you were no role model. And I told you to think again. I knew then that I loved you. And I knew there couldn't possibly be a better role model for Ian and Jamie than you. You want to be their father? You can't want that more than I do—I would be honored to share them with you."

They kissed then. Not a passionate kiss, but a sacred pledge for the future.

"You don't read poetry, do you?" Holly asked when their lips finally parted.

"Not unless country-and-western lyrics count."

She laughed softly. "That wasn't exactly what I was referring to, but I'll keep it in mind." She cupped his cheek and said, "Robert Herrick wrote a sonnet hundreds of years ago that begins, 'How Love came in, I do not know.' That's how I feel. I don't know how it happened, just that it did. And I wouldn't change it for anything."

He chuckled. "Okay, so *now's* the time I say *ditto*."

"Chris…" she warned, but in teasing fashion so he'd know she wasn't serious. Much.

He shook his head at her. "I already told you I have no idea how it happened for me, but I wouldn't change it for anything, either." He drew a deep breath. "So, Miss Holly. If I were to get down on one knee and ask you to marry me, what would you say?"

Her heart sped up, then slowed down, but not back to normal. Not by a long shot. "Ask me and see," she murmured.

She thought he'd been joking, but when he gently pushed her into the armchair and knelt on one knee, she realized he was dead serious. *Yes, yes, yes!* her heart was already answering, but she waited.

"I know you loved Grant," he began. "But I also know you love me. I don't want to replace him in your heart, Holly. But I *do* want to build my own place there. Will you marry me?"

She was barely able to contain her gasp, because Chris was saying almost exactly the same thing she'd told herself yesterday. She didn't want to *replace* Laura, she just wanted to be the woman he loved *now*. Now…and in the future.

"I would be honored," she answered softly. She framed his face with her hands, the face that had become so incredibly dear to her in such a short time. "I would be honored to be your wife."

Chapter 21

Two weeks later the doorbell of Holly's Clear Lake City house rang at a quarter past six in the morning, waking her from a not-very-sound sleep. A jumble of dreams centering around Chris had woken her every few hours, and she was just dozing off again when she heard the chime.

She grabbed her robe and scrambled into it as she hurried to the front door, her only thought being *Please don't wake the twins!* Ian and Jamie had been fractious ever since the three of them had returned to Clear Lake City—apparently they were missing their life in Granite Gulch as much as she was—and she didn't want them to start off the day short of sleep.

The chime sounded again just as she reached the door, and she glanced through the peephole, intending to give whoever it was a piece of her mind for ringing the bell this early. Then she gasped and fumbled with the locks in her haste.

"Chris!" Holly threw herself at him, and his arms closed around her. "Oh, my God, what are you *doing* here?"

"I couldn't bear it without you a minute longer," he said when his lips finally let hers go. "I couldn't sleep because I was thinking of you, so I threw a few things in a bag, jumped in my truck and hit the road. Made good time, too."

"No speeding tickets?"

He grinned at her. "Not even one." His eyes softened as he gazed at her. "But if I *had* gotten one, it would have been worth it."

Two weeks' worth of yearning was obliterated in less than fifteen minutes. They snuggled in the aftermath, their hearts racing, both still having difficulty breathing.

"Wow," Holly said. Then, "Do that again."

Chris started laughing so hard he wheezed. "Give me five minutes—ten max—to recover, and you've got yourself a deal."

She joined Chris laughing helplessly. "I didn't mean *now*. Just *sometime*. Sometime soon."

He rolled her beneath him before she could protest. Then stroked his fingers over her still-hypersensitized flesh, making her breath catch in her throat. "Sometime soon can be now, Holly," he whispered seductively. "Just wait. I'll prove it to you."

And he did. All she could think of as her body took flight was that Chris was a man of his word. Then she couldn't think at all.

* * *

"When are you coming back to Granite Gulch?" Chris asked over the breakfast table an hour later. "I'm not trying to rush you—okay, yes, I am. The house just isn't the same without you and the twins."

"You're living in the house?"

He nodded. "I moved all my things out of my apartment the day you left. I also talked to Annabel and my brothers about the farmhouse in Bearson—what you said about not leaving it as some sort of shrine. So whenever you're ready, you can go through the farmhouse and pick out what you want for our home." A slow smile spread over her face, and Chris asked again, "So when are you moving back?"

"I've already listed this house for sale," she temporized.

"Yeah, I saw the sign on the front lawn."

"But I can't just move in with you," she began.

"The heck you can't." His voice was pure steel, his expression obdurate, but then he grinned suddenly. "Hey, did you hear that? I didn't even have to think about it, I just said *heck* instead of—" He broke off suddenly, glancing at Ian and Jamie, who weren't paying the least bit of attention to the conversation—they were eating their Cheerios with complete unconcern.

A lump came into Holly's throat. *How* she loved this man, especially at moments like this. But… "I can't just move in with you," she repeated. She tore her gaze away from Chris and looked at her boys, then back at him, praying he'd see what the problem was. "I don't want people to think—"

"That you're living in sin?" Chris waggled his eyebrows at her.

She flushed. "I know it's old-fashioned. And if it was just me, I wouldn't care, honest. But I don't want anything said that the twins might hear. They understand a lot more about what's going on around them, and I—"

Chris put his hand on hers. "You don't have to justify it to me, Holly. I told you two weeks ago, I love you. I need you. I can't live without you. I wasn't kidding. I asked you to marry me, and you said you would. So in my mind we were officially engaged the minute you consented to be my wife."

"Mine, too," Holly said softly.

"If it was up to me, we'd find a justice of the peace and make 'engagement' a thing of the past." She started to speak but he stopped her. "No, let me finish. I know weddings mean a lot to women. And I know you were denied a fancy wedding when you married Grant. I intend for this to be the last chance you have for the kind of wedding women dream of—so we'll do it right. Formal engagement party, formal wedding, and everything that entails."

Holly smiled at Chris through sudden tears. "Thank you for understanding."

"But once we're formally engaged, you're moving back to Granite Gulch, right?" The eagerness in his voice touched something deep inside her. She'd sworn she'd never again marry a man who didn't love her, heart and soul, but that would never be an issue with Chris. "I need you, Holly," he added in a low tone. "These past two weeks without you—life's too short. We both know that. So please don't—"

"I won't," she assured him. "They say suffering is

good for the soul. I don't know about you, but my soul has suffered enough."

He laughed softly. "Mine, too."

They stared at each other for endless seconds, then Holly cleared her throat. "So regarding an engagement party—would you believe I was going to call you about this today?—I was thinking next week would be good."

"We always go to Ethan and Lizzie's ranch for family celebrations now. I'd have to check with them."

Holly gave Chris her best "are you kidding me?" look.

"What?" he asked, obviously clueless.

"Lizzie just had a baby. Do you have any idea of the kind of work involved in a party like this? Even if it's potluck, the hostess—and the host, too—have a mountain of work both before and after. No way are we having our engagement party at their ranch."

"Then what do you suggest?"

"Peg offered to have it at her house, but I don't want to put that responsibility on her, either, any more than I want to do it to Lizzie. What about renting out the Granite Gulch Bar and Saloon for the afternoon? It's plenty big enough, it's right there on Main Street in the center of town and everyone would be free to enjoy themselves—no one would have to worry about the food or drinks or anything. And before you ask," she told him, "I already inquired. It wouldn't cost an arm and a leg, and besides, I have the money." She flushed a little. "My money, not money from the twins' trust."

Chris shook his head, a stubborn expression on his face. "We haven't talked about money, Holly, but I guess now's as good a time as any. I'm not a millionaire—not yet—but I'm not hurting, either. Your money is yours.

Whatever our family needs I'll provide. You want to be a stay-at-home mom until the twins are in school? Fine. I can afford it, no problem. I can afford to pay for our engagement party, too."

Holly lifted her chin, her eyes narrowing as she prepared to do battle. While she understood Chris's desire to provide for his family, to feel that he was taking care of them, there were a few things he needed to get straight before they went any further. She loved him with all her heart, but she couldn't be anything other than the independent woman she was. Not even for him.

She almost retorted that their marriage was going to be an equal partnership, with each of them pulling their own weight and all decisions made jointly, or else no deal. But then an idea occurred to her. "You're not the boss of me," she said softly. Hoping Chris would get the message.

The stubborn expression vanished and a lighthearted grin replaced it, followed by a reluctant chuckle. "Okay," he said after a minute. "We'll split the cost of the party fifty-fifty. But *I'm* buying the engagement ring. That's *not* up for negotiation."

In that moment Holly knew everything was going to be all right. Chris could always make her laugh… but she could always make him laugh, too. And that was just as important as love in building a relationship that would last a lifetime. There would be arguments in the future—of course there would be—but neither of them would ever go to bed angry with the other, because one of them would always make sure of it…with humor.

Epilogue

The engagement party was in full swing when Chris wandered over to one of the large coolers packed with ice and cold bottles of beer and cans of soft drinks. He helped himself, removed the bottle cap and let the ice-cold brew slide down his throat. It was only the end of May, but the day was hot and humid—typical north Texas weather—and even though the room was air-conditioned, the beer hit the spot.

Chris turned and watched Holly for a moment, the center of a small gaggle of women across the room, Annabel and Peg among them. Holly's dress was golden yellow—God, he loved her in yellow. Loved her in anything, really. But he loved her best when she was wearing nothing at all except the tender look of love she reserved for him alone. Their eyes met across the room, and there it was again—the expression that melted his heart every time he saw it.

"How did I ever get so lucky?" he asked himself quietly.

The rowdy song the band was playing came to an end, and the strains of a popular ballad soon filled the air. As Chris watched, Jesse Willard, Annabel's fiancé, walked up to her and touched her on the shoulder. The loving face Annabel turned to him was matched by the expression on Jesse's face, and a wave of happiness for his twin washed through him as the couple began to slow dance. All he and his brothers had ever wanted for Annabel was for her to find a good man to love her. She had that in Jesse. But Annabel was her own woman, the consummate professional police officer, finally doing the work she loved. Chris could understand that—he loved his work, too.

Peg was soon claimed by Joe for a dance, and Chris smiled. Peg and Joe were the best friends a man could ever have. Peg could have resented Holly on her sister's behalf—and he wouldn't have blamed her. But there was too much love in Peg for her to wish unhappiness on someone else. She deserved a steady-as-a-rock man like Joe to make her happy. And Joe, Chris knew, was counting his blessings, too.

Chris glanced away, and his gaze fell on his younger brothers. Ridge dancing with his high school sweetheart, Darcy, whom he'd finally reconnected with after all these years. Sam with Zoe, who was the best thing that had ever happened to him. And Ethan, with his arms wrapped tight around Lizzie, not really dancing, but swaying back and forth to the music.

"How did we all get so lucky?" Chris asked himself now.

Only Trevor was alone, and Chris's heart went out

to his older brother. At the same time he promised himself, *Soon. Holly's right. I have to ask Trevor why.*

Suddenly Holly was standing right in front of him. "Howdy, cowboy," she murmured. "You look familiar. Do I know you?"

Conscious that eyes were on them, Chris tamped down the urgent desire to kiss her until she was too dazed to tease him. Instead, he raised her left hand to his lips—the hand wearing the engagement ring that was his pledge to her—and kissed it. A romantic gesture he would have felt foolish making a few weeks ago. Before he'd known Holly.

"Okay, cowboy," she drawled, "you've made your point. I don't know who you are after all."

Chris laughed and feigned hurt. "And here I thought you'd be impressed with how romantic I could be."

Holly's soft brown eyes turned misty, and she whispered, "You're romantic enough for me, Chris, just the way you are. Every single day."

That deserved a kiss, and he didn't care how many people saw him do it. When he finally raised his head and took in the dazed expression in Holly's eyes, he couldn't help it—primitive masculine pride surged through him...particularly a certain body part.

"Don't you dare move," he warned Holly.

She laughed deep in her throat, but she knew what he was talking about so she stayed right where she was for a minute. Eventually he was able to release her without being too embarrassed, but he tugged her hand. "Come on," he told her roughly. "Let's go outside where no one can—"

That was when he spotted the dark-haired woman standing in the shadows across the room from them, near the door to the bar. A stranger, yet not a stranger. Incredulous, he whispered, "Josie?"

He dropped Holly's hand as if in a dream and took two steps toward the woman he instinctively knew was his baby sister. But when the woman saw him move toward her, she darted from the room like a frightened colt.

Chris gave chase. "Josie!" he called to the fleeing woman, who had already escaped through the front door. "Josie, wait! Don't run, Josie. You're safe, damn it! You're safe! It's all over!"

She must have heard him, because she stopped suddenly on the sidewalk, turned around and stared at him. But she was still poised to run. "It's over?"

Chris didn't stop running until he reached his sister, until he was sure he could prevent her from fleeing if she tried to take off again. "Josie," he whispered, still not quite believing she was really here. Then she was in his arms. "My God, it's really you."

Brother and sister finally stepped back, and all at once Holly was at Chris's side, her breath coming quickly. Then the rest of the family appeared—all crowding around Josie, hugging her repeatedly, exclaiming over her—their joy at finally being reunited with their baby sister mirroring Chris's.

Questions peppered the air. "Oh, Josie, we've been searching for you ever since you vanished."

"Where have you been? We've been worried sick."

"Why didn't you let us know you were alive?"

Chris held up his hands. "Hold it, everybody! One at a time."

Before anyone could ask a question, Josie looked at Chris, regret in her eyes. "I heard about Laura," she blurted out. "I wanted to call you when it happened and tell you how sorry I was. I really did, Chris. But I couldn't. I just *couldn't*. 'No phone calls,' they said. 'Let them think you're dead,' they said."

"Who said?" Trevor asked, getting his question in first. "Where have you been?"

"Witness Security. Six years. Ever since—"

"Desmond Carlton was killed," Chris said, cutting Josie off. When her eyes widened that he knew, he nodded, saying, "Yeah, I think I have most everything figured out." For the benefit of the rest of the family, he said, "Here's what I think happened. Correct me if I'm wrong, Josie." He laid out his theory of what had occurred eleven years ago, and then six years ago.

Josie interrupted him a couple of times to clarify a point, but when he was done, she said, "I can't believe you pieced that all together from what little you knew." Her eyes held admiration.

"Thank Lizzie and Trevor," he told Josie. "They're the ones who gave me the clues I needed." His gaze met Lizzie's, then Trevor's. Lizzie's eyes held nothing but joy, because she finally knew what had caused Josie to turn away from her friendship; Trevor's eyes held joy that Josie was found, tinged with…redemption? *Thanks, Trev*, Chris mouthed and knew Trevor had seen it by the slight nod he gave. Chris still didn't know why Trevor had abandoned him. But he no longer believed Trevor hadn't tried his damnedest to get custody of Josie when he turned eighteen. And that was a tremendous load off Chris's mind.

He turned back to Josie. "The most important thing in all of this is, everyone who was associated with Carlton six years ago is either dead or in prison—and will stay in prison for a long time. Which means it's all over as far as you're concerned. You don't have to hide anymore."

"You really mean it?" Josie couldn't seem to take it in at first.

Chris nodded. "And you're just in time. Holly and I are celebrating our engagement." He caught Holly's hand and raised it so Josie could see the ring.

"I know. That's why I came, because I...I wanted to be here with the family, even if I couldn't join in the celebration. Even if it meant risking being seen."

"You were spotted before," Chris told her. He glanced around the circle of his family. "Ridge saw you. So did Lizzie. And Annabel—"

"You left a gold heart charm in my house, didn't you?" Annabel interjected. "The one Mama gave you that's just like mine." When Josie nodded, Annabel asked, "Did you leave it on purpose?"

Josie nodded again. "I couldn't bear having you all think I was dead. No matter what my handlers in Witness Security told me."

Another flurry of questions ensued, and this time Holly intervened. "Let's take this back inside." She smiled at Josie and held out her hand, saying softly, "I'm Holly McCay, Chris's fiancée. I'm so glad you came to our engagement party. I can't think of anything that would make Chris happier than having you here. It's been tearing him up not knowing where you were. Not knowing if you were safe. Now he can really celebrate."

Chris disconnected and slid his smartphone into his pocket. He jumped guiltily, then whirled around when

Holly said behind him, "How are the boys doing with the babysitter?"

"How'd you know I was checking on them?"

She smiled the tender smile he loved. "Because I know *you*. Because that's the kind of man you are." She came to stand right in front of him and deliberately placed her hand on his heart, which immediately kicked up a notch at her touch. "You made yourself responsible for us that very first day," she said. "And thank God you did, because if you hadn't I never would have known you. Never would have loved you." Her voice dropped to a whisper. "And I never would have known what it was like to be loved the way you love me."

A lump came into his throat, and he wished he had Holly's way with words. Wished he could express what her love meant to him. But all he could do was touch her cheek with a hand that wasn't quite steady and say, "I don't want to lose you, Holly. Tell me that will never happen."

What you don't love you can't lose. He'd told himself that in the hospital right after Ethan and Lizzie's baby had been born. He'd lost so much in his life—Mama, Trevor, Josie, Laura, their baby—he hadn't wanted to risk loving again. Mama was dead, and so were Laura and their baby—he wouldn't see them again in this lifetime. But Josie had been miraculously restored to them. And if Chris ever got up the courage to ask Trevor one all-important question, maybe he'd finally find the older brother he'd once loved unreservedly—the brother who could do no wrong—in the man Trevor was now. Which meant it was still possible to find his mother and lay her to rest, the one remaining thing he desperately wanted to accomplish.

Holly seemed to understand what he meant when he said he didn't want to lose her, seemed to understand the lurking fear he refused to name but couldn't completely banish. "I can't promise not to die," she told him solemnly. "No one can promise that. But I *can* promise I'll love you, now and forever. Because love…enduring love…is a choice. And I choose you, Chris. I will always choose you."

The lump in his throat was back, but all he could think of to say was "Does this mean I get to be the boss of you sometimes?"

Her gurgle of laughter warmed the lonely place in his heart the way it had from the first time he'd heard it. The way it always would. "If I get to be the boss of you sometimes, too," she told him, her soft brown eyes alight with the laughter they would always bring to each other.

"Then I have nothing to worry about," he assured her, "because you already are that. Sometimes," he hastened to add, needing to be completely honest with her.

She laughed again, her twinkling eyes telling him she knew exactly the kind of man he was, flaws and all…and she loved him anyway. Then she kissed him, and in that instant he knew he was going to be all right. *They* were going to be all right.

Ethan had said it best. *I thought I could cut myself off from life.* Chris had thought that, too, but Holly had proved him wrong. You couldn't play it safe where life was concerned. Where love was concerned. You had to risk it all. You had to put your heart out there where it could get trampled, hoping and praying it wouldn't.

His heart *had* been trampled. There was no denying that. But Holly had healed him. She'd seen something in him worth loving, so she'd somehow mended the cracks. His heart wasn't good as new, it was *better*—because loving and losing and loving again had taught him never to take anything for granted, and he never would again. The really important things in life didn't entail proving a darn thing to anyone—except proving his love to those he cared about. It was a long list—something he finally acknowledged—and getting longer every day. Heading that list was Holly.

"Life is good," he murmured, drawing Holly back against him so they could look out at all his brothers and sisters together again…finally. And all his and Holly's friends also in attendance at their engagement party. Family. Good friends. Almost everything a man needed to make life worth living. Almost. Only one thing was missing from the picture—the one thing that was no longer missing from his life.

He curved his arms around Holly's waist, holding his future securely. "Life is good."

* * * * *

UNDER FIRE

CAROL ERICSON

To Marilyn, for all that you do.

Chapter One

The shell casings from the bullets pinged off the metal file cabinets. One landed inches from her nose and rolled one way and then the other, its gold plating winking at her under the fluorescent lights. The acrid smell of gunpowder tickled her nostrils. She smashed her nose against the linoleum to halt the sneeze threatening to explode and give away her position.

Someone grunted. Someone screamed. Again.

Ava held her breath as the rubber sole of a black shoe squeaked past her face. She followed its path until her gaze collided with Dr. Arnoff's.

From beneath the desk across from her, he put his finger to his lips. His thick glasses, one lens crushed, lay just out of his reach between the two desks. With his other finger, he pointed past her toward the lab.

Afraid to move even a centimeter, Ava blinked her eyes to indicate her understanding. If they could make their way to the lab behind the bulletproof glass and industrial-strength locks they might have a chance to survive this lunacy.

The shooter moved past the desks, firing another round from his automatic weapon. Glass shattered—not the bulletproof kind. A loud bump, followed by a crack and the door to the clinic, her domain, crashed open.

Greg bellowed, "No, no, no!"

Another round of fire and Greg's life ended in a thump and a gurgle.

Ava squeezed her eyes closed, and her lips mumbled silent words. *Keep going. Keep going.*

If the shooter kept walking through the clinic, he'd wind up on the other side in the waiting room. At this time of night, nobody was in the waiting room, which led to a door and a set of stairs to the outside.

Keep going.

He returned. His boots crunched through the glass. Then he howled like a wounded animal, and the hair on the back of Ava's neck stood at attention and quivered.

The footsteps stopped on the other side of the desk—her pathetic hiding place. In the sudden silence of the room, her heartbeat thundered. Surely he could hear it, too.

He kicked at a shard of glass, which skittered between the two desks.

Ava turned widened eyes on Dr. Arnoff and swallowed. She harbored no hopes that the doctor could take down the shooter. Although a big man, his fighting days were behind him. Their best hope was to make it to the lab and wait for help.

The black-booted foot stepped between the desks, smashing the other lens of Dr. Arnoff's glasses. A second later the shooter lifted the desk by one edge and hurled it against the wall as if it were a piece of furniture in a dollhouse.

Exposed, Dr. Arnoff scrambled for cover, his army crawl no match for the lethal weapon pointed at him. The bullets hit his body, making it jump and twitch.

Ava dug a fist against her mouth, and her teeth cut into her lips. The metallic taste of her blood mimicked the smell permeating the air.

Then her own cover disappeared, snatched away by some towering hulk. She didn't scream. She didn't beg. The gunman existed in a haze behind the weapon that he now had aimed at her head.

His gloved finger on the trigger of the assault rifle mesmerized her. She mumbled a prayer with parched lips. *Click.* She sucked in a breath. *Click.* She gritted her teeth. *Click.* He'd run out of ammo.

He reached into the pocket of his fatigues, and adrenaline surged through her body. She clambered over the discarded desk and launched herself at the lab door. With shaking hands she scrabbled for the badge around her neck and pressed it to the reader. The red light mocked her.

Her badge didn't allow her access to this lab. Her exclusion from the lab had been a source of irritation to her for almost two years. How could she forget that now?

She dropped to her knees and crawled to Dr. Arnoff's dead body. Her fingers trembled as she unclipped the badge from the pocket of his white coat.

Amid the clicking and clacking behind her, the gunman muttered to himself.

Expecting another round of shots at any second, Ava swiped Dr. Arnoff's badge across the reader. The green lights blinked in a row as if she'd just won a jackpot. She had.

She yanked open the heavy door and shoved it closed just as the shooter looked up from his task. Five seconds later, a volley of bullets thwacked the glass.

Knowing the gunman could lift a badge from any of the dead bodies around him just as she had, Ava slid three dead bolts across the door and took two steps back.

This windowless room, clicking and buzzing with machinery, computers and refrigeration, offered no escape, but it did contain a landline telephone. Maybe someone had been able to make a call to the police when the mayhem started, but no cavalry had arrived to the rescue yet.

After his first round, the crazed man outside her sanctuary had stopped shooting. He seemed to be searching the bodies of her fallen coworkers—looking for a badge, no doubt. He wouldn't find Dr. Arnoff's.

Ava pounced on the receiver of the telephone on the wall beside the door. Her heart skipped a beat. No dial tone. She tapped the phone over and over, but it remained dead.

Even if she had her cell phone, which remained in the pocket of her lab coat hanging on a hook in the clinic, it wouldn't do any good. Nobody could get reception in this underground building in the middle of the desert.

The lock clicked and she spun around. The shooter was leaning against the door, pressing a badge up to the reader. The lock on the handle responded, but the dead bolts held the door securely in place.

She'd resented being locked out of this lab, but now she couldn't be happier about those extra reinforcements.

He grabbed the handle and shook it while releasing another roar.

Ava covered her galloping heart with one hand as she studied the glittering eyes visible from the slits in the ski mask. What did he want? Drugs? Why murder all these people for drugs? Why come all the way out here to a high-level security facility to steal meds?

He gave up on the door and shook his head once. Then he reached up and yanked the ski mask from his head.

Ava gasped and stumbled back. She knew him. Simon.

He was one of her patients, one of the covert agents the lab treated and monitored.

Guess they hadn't monitored him closely enough.

"Simon?" She flattened her palm against the glass of the window. "Simon, put down your weapon. The police are on their way."

She had no idea if the police were on their way or not. The lab used its own security force, so she and her co-workers never had a reason to call in the police from the small town ten miles away in this New Mexico desert. Since the lab's security guards had made no attempt to stop Simon, she had a sick feeling Simon had already dealt with them.

"You need help, Simon. I can help you." She licked her lips. "Whatever you need me to say to the authorities, I'll say it. We can tell them it was your job, the stress."

His mouth twisted and he lunged at the window, jabbing the butt of his gun against the glass, which shivered under the assault.

Ava blinked and jerked back. She made a half turn and scanned the lab. If he somehow made it through the door and she got close enough to him, she could stick him with a needle full of tranquilizer that would drop him in his tracks. She could throw boiling water or a chemical mixture in his face.

He'd never let her get that close. He'd come through shooting, and she wouldn't have a chance against those bullets. None of the others had. She gulped back a sob.

The bullets started again. Simon had stepped away from the door and continued spraying bullets at the glass. That window hadn't been designed to withstand this kind of relentless barrage. She knew. She'd asked when she started working here, curious about the extra security of this room.

He knew it, too. Sweat beaded on Simon's ruddy face as he took a breather. He didn't even need to reload. He rolled his shoulders as if preparing for the long haul.

Then he resumed firing at the window.

Again, Ava searched the room, tilting her head back to examine the ceiling. Unfortunately, the ceiling was solid, except for one vent. She eyed the rectangular cover. Could she squeeze through there?

Simon took another break to examine the battered window, placing his weapon on the floor beside him.

She tried to catch his gaze, tried to make some human contact, but this person was just a shell of the Simon she had known. The sarcastic redhead who did killer impressions had disappeared, replaced by this creature with dead eyes.

Ava's breath hitched in her throat. Beyond Simon, a figure decked out in black riot gear loomed in the doorway of the clinic. Was it someone from security? The police?

Not wanting to alert Simon, she inched farther away from the window and kept her gaze glued to Simon's face.

The man at the door yelled, "Simon!"

How did he know who the shooter was? Had someone from the lab seen Simon before the rampage started and reported him?

Simon turned slowly.

"Give it up, Simon." The man raised his weapon. "We can get help, together."

Simon growled and swayed from side to side.

Would he go for his gun on the floor?

Taking a single step into the room, the man tried again. "Step away from your weapon, Simon. We'll figure this out."

Simon shouted, "They have to pay!"

Ava hugged herself as a chill snaked up her spine.

His animalistic sounds had frightened her, but his words struck cold fear into her heart. Pay for what? He'd gone insane, and they'd been responsible for him, for his well-being.

"Not Dr. Whitman. It's not her fault."

Ava threw out a hand and grasped the edge of a counter to steady herself. Her rescuer knew her name? His voice, bellowing from across the room, muffled by the mask on his face, still held a note of familiarity to her. He must be one of the security guards.

"It is." Simon stopped swaying. "It *is* her fault."

He dropped to the floor and jumped up, clutching his weapon. He raised it to his shoulder but it didn't get that far.

The man from across the room fired. Simon spun around and fell against the window, which finally cracked.

Ava clapped a hand over her mouth as she met Simon's blue stare. The film over his eyes cleared. They widened for a second and he gasped. Blood gurgled from his gaping mouth. He slid to the floor, out of her sight.

Every muscle in her body seized up and she couldn't move.

The security guard kept his weapon at his shoulder as he stalked across the room. When he reached the window of the lab, he pointed his gun at the floor, presumably at Simon.

Ava covered her ears, but the gunfire had finally ceased.

Slinging his weapon over his shoulder, the man gestured to the door. "Open up. It's okay now."

Would it ever be okay? She'd just watched a crazed gunman, one of her patients, mow down her coworkers and had barely escaped death herself.

She stumbled toward the door and reached for the first lock with stiff hands. It took her several tries before she could slide all the dead bolts. Then she pressed down on the handle to open the door.

The man, smelling of gunpowder and leather and power, stepped into the lab. "Are you okay, Dr. Whitman?"

She knew that voice but couldn't place it. Tilting her head, she cleared her throat. "I—I'm not physically hurt."

"Good." His head swiveled back and forth, taking in the small lab. "Are there any blue pills in this room?"

She took a step back from his overpowering presence. "Blue pills? What are you talking about?"

"The blue pills." He stepped around her and yanked open a drawer. "I need as many blue pills as you have in here—all of them."

"I don't know what you mean." She blinked and edged toward the door. Had she just gone from one kind of crazy to another? Maybe this man was Simon's accomplice and they were both after drugs.

He continued his search through the lab, repeating his request for blue pills, pulling out drawers and banging cupboard doors open.

A crash from another area of the building made them both jump, and he swore.

Taking her arm in his gloved hand, he said, "We need to get out of here unless you can tell me where to find some blue pills."

"I told you, I don't know about any blue pills, and there's no serum on hand either." Maybe he was after the vitamin boost the agents received quarterly.

He grunted. "Then let's go."

"Wait a minute." She shook him off. "H-he's dead, right? Simon's dead?"

The man nodded once.

"Then why do we have to leave? Maybe that noise was

the police breaking in here." Cold fear flooded her veins and she hugged her body. "Are there more? Is there another gunman?"

"He's the only one."

"Then I'd rather stay here and wait for the rest of your—" she waved a hand at him "—security force or the cops or whoever is on the way. That could be them."

He adjusted his bulletproof vest and took her arm again. "We don't want to wait for anyone."

Confusion clashed with anger at his peremptory tone and the way he kept grabbing her. She jerked her arm away from him and dug her heels into the floor. "Hold on. My entire department has just been murdered. I was almost killed. I'm not going anywhere. I don't even know who the hell you are."

"Sure you do." He reached up with one hand and yanked the ski mask from his head.

Her eyebrows shot up. Max Duvall. Another one of her patients, another agent—just like Simon.

"Y-you, you're…"

"That's right, and you're coming with me. Now." He scooped her up with one arm and threw her over his shoulder. "Whether you want to or not."

Chapter Two

Chapter Two

"Let me go!" She struggled and kicked her legs, but Dr. Ava Whitman was a tiny thing.

He could get her to go with him willingly if he sat down and explained the whole situation, but they didn't have time for that. That could be Tempest at the door right now. He couldn't even risk doing a more thorough search for the blue pills. He'd have to just take her at her word that there were none at the lab.

Maybe Dr. Whitman already knew the whole situation. Knew why Simon had gone postal. He couldn't trust anyone…not even pretty Dr. Whitman.

Clamping her thighs against his shoulder, he stepped over the dead bodies littering the floor. When he navigated around the final murder victim in his path at the door of the clinic, Dr. Whitman stopped struggling and slumped against his back. If she'd had her eyes open the whole way, she probably just got her fill of blood and guts.

He crossed through the waiting room and kicked open the door to the stairwell. He slid Dr. Whitman down his body so that she was facing him, his arm cinched around her waist.

"Will you come with me now? I need you to walk up

these stairs and out the side door. I have a car waiting there."

Through his vest, he could feel the wild beat of her heart as it banged against her chest. "Where are we going? Why can't we wait here for the police?"

"It's not safe." He grabbed her shoulders and squeezed. "Do you believe me?"

Her green eyes grew round, taking up half her face. She glanced past him at the clinic door and nodded. Then she grabbed the straps on his bulletproof vest. "My purse, my phone."

"Are they in the clinic?"

"Yes."

He shoved back through the door and pulled her along with him. He didn't quite trust that she wouldn't go running all over the lab searching for the security guards. Wouldn't do her any good anyway—Simon had killed them all.

She broke away from him and yanked her purse from a rack two feet from the body of a coworker. She dipped her hand in the pocket of her lab coat hanging on the rack and pulled out a phone.

Another crash erupted from somewhere in the building, and Dr. Whitman dropped her phone. It skittered and twirled across the floor, coming to a stop at the edge of a puddle of blood.

She gasped and hugged her purse to her chest.

The noise, closer than the previous one, sent a new wave of adrenaline coursing through his veins. "Let's go!"

Her feet seemed rooted to the floor, so he crossed the room in two steps and curled his fingers around her wrist, tugging her forward. "We need to leave."

Still holding on to Dr. Whitman, Max plucked her phone from the floor and headed toward the stairwell again. He half prodded, half carried Dr. Whitman upstairs, and when they reached the door to the outside, he inched it open, pressing his eye to the crack.

The car he'd stolen waited in the darkness. He pushed open the door of the building and a blast of air peppered with sand needled his face. He ducked and put an arm around Dr. Whitman as he hustled her to the vehicle.

She hesitated when he opened the passenger door. The wind whipped her hair across her face, hiding her expression.

It was probably one of shock. Or was it fear? "Get in, Dr. Whitman. They're here."

This time she didn't even ask for clarification. His words had her scrambling into the passenger seat.

He blew out a breath and lifted the bulletproof vest over his head. Would Simon have turned the gun on him after everything they'd gone through together? Sure he would've. That man in there who'd just committed mass murder bore no resemblance to the Simon he knew.

He threw the vest in the backseat and cranked on the engine. He floored the accelerator and went out the way he came in—through a downed chain-link fence.

He hit the desert highway and ten minutes later blew past the small town that served the needs of the lab. The lab didn't have any needs now.

After several minutes of silence, Dr. Whitman cleared her throat. "Are we going to the police now? Calling the CIA?"

"Neither."

Her fingers curled around the edge of the seat. "Where are we going?"

"I'm taking you home."

"Home?" She blinked her long lashes. "Whose home?"

Without turning his head, he raised one eyebrow. "Your

home. You have one, don't you? I know you don't live at the lab—at least not full-time."

"Albuquerque. I live in Albuquerque."

"I figured that. Once I drop you off, you're free to call whomever you like."

"But not now?"

"Not as long as I'm with you."

She bolted upright and wedged her hands against the dashboard. "Why? Don't you want to meet with the CIA? Your own agency? Tell them what happened back there?"

"What do *you* think happened back there?" He squinted into the blackness and hit his high beams.

"Simon Skinner lost it. He went on a murderous rampage and killed my coworkers, my friends." She stifled a sob with the back of her hand.

She showed real grief, but was the shock feigned? Extending his arms, he gripped the steering wheel. "How much do you know about the work you do at the lab?"

"That's a crazy question. It's my workplace. I've been there for almost two years."

"Your job is to treat and monitor a special set of patients, correct?"

"Since you're one of those patients, you should know." She dragged her fingers through her wavy, dark hair and clasped it at the nape of her neck.

One soft strand curled against her pale cheek. Whenever he'd seen her for appointments, her hair had been confined to a bun or ponytail. Now loosened and wild, it was as pretty as he'd imagined it would be.

"And the injections you gave us, the vitamin boost? Did you work on that formula?"

She jerked her head toward him and the rest of her curls tumbled across her shoulder. "No. Dr. Arnoff developed that before I arrived."

"Did he tell you what was in it?"

"Of course he did. I wouldn't inject my patients with some mystery substance."

"Were you allowed to test it yourself? Did you work in that lab?"

"N-no." She clasped her hands between her bouncing knees. "I wasn't allowed in the lab."

"Why not? You're a doctor, aren't you?"

"I…I'm… The lab requires top secret clearance. I have secret clearance only, but Dr. Arnoff showed me the formula, showed me the tests."

He slid a glance at her stiff frame and pale face. Was she still in shock over the events at the lab or was she lying?

"Now it's your turn."

His eyes locked onto hers in the darkness of the car. "What do you mean?"

"It's your turn to answer my questions. What were you doing at the lab? You weren't scheduled for another month or so. Why can't we call the police or the CIA, or Prospero, the agency you work for?"

"Prospero?"

She flicked her fingers in the air. "You don't have to pretend with me. Nobody ever told me the name of the covert ops agency we were supporting, but I heard whispers."

"What other whispers did you hear?" A muscle twitched in his jaw.

"Wait a minute." She smacked the dashboard with her palms. "I thought it was your turn to answer the questions. What were you doing there? Why can't we call the police?"

"You should be glad I was there or Skinner would've gotten to you, too."

Folding her arms across her stomach, she slumped in her seat, all signs of outrage gone. She made a squeaking noise like a mouse caught in a trap, and something like guilt needled the back of his neck.

He rolled his shoulders, trying to ease out the tension that had become his constant companion. "I was at the lab because I found out Skinner was going to be there. We can't call the police for obvious reasons. I'm deep undercover. I don't want to stand around and explain my presence to the cops."

"And your own agency? Prospero?"

"Yeah, Prospero." If Dr. Whitman wanted to believe he worked for Prospero, why disappoint her? The less she knew the better, and it sounded as if she didn't know much—or she was a really good liar. "I'll call them on my own. I wanted to get you out of there in case there was more danger on the way."

"You seemed convinced there was."

"We were in the middle of the desert, in the middle of the night at a top secret location with a bunch of dead bodies. I didn't think it was wise for either of us to stick around."

She leaned her head against the window. "What should I do when I get home?"

He drummed his thumbs against the steering wheel. If Tempest and Dr. Arnoff had kept Dr. Whitman in the dark, she should be safe. Tempest would do the cleanup and probably resume operations elsewhere—with or without Dr. Ava Whitman.

"Once I drop you off and hit the road, you can call the police." He frowned and squinted at the road. "Or do you have a different protocol to follow?"

She turned a pair of wide eyes on him. "For this situation? We had no protocol in place for an active shooter like that."

Maybe the whole bunch of them out there, including Dr. Arnoff, were clueless. No, not Arnoff. He had to have known what was going on, even if he didn't know the why.

"Then I guess it's the cops." Even though the local cops would never get to the whole truth. He pointed to the lights glowing up ahead. "We're heading into the city. Can you give me directions to your place? Is there someone at home?"

She hadn't touched her cell phone once since they escaped from the lab. Wouldn't she want to notify her husband? Boyfriend? Family?

"I live alone."

He supposed she'd want to be with someone, have someone comfort her. God knew, he wasn't capable. "Do you have any family nearby? Any friends to stay with?"

"I don't have any family…here. I'm kind of new to the area and I spend a lot of time at the lab, so I haven't had much time to cultivate friends."

Hadn't she told him she'd been working at the lab for two years? Two years wasn't enough time to make friends? Maybe she'd been taking some of her own medicine.

"When the police come, they may want to take you back to the scene. You'll probably have to lead them to the facility."

She gasped and grabbed his arm. "What do I tell them about you?"

He stiffened and glanced down at her hand gripping the material of his jacket. She dropped it.

Was she offering to cover for him? He figured she'd waste no time at all blabbing to the cops about the man who'd shot Skinner and then whisked her out of the lab. "Tell them the truth."

No law enforcement agency would ever be able to track him down anyway. Tempest had made sure of that.

"I can always tell them you were a stranger to me, that you wouldn't tell me your name." Her fingers twisted in her lap as she hunched forward in her seat.

She *was* offering to cover for him. Why would she do that, unless she knew more than she'd pretended to know?

"You'd lie for me?"

She jerked back and whipped her head around. "Lie? You're an agent with a government covert ops team. If I learned anything at the lab, it was how to keep secrets. I never revealed any of my patients' names to anyone, and I'm not about to start now."

"I appreciate the…concern." He lifted a shoulder. "Tell the cops whatever you like. I'll be long gone either way."

She tilted her chin toward the highway sign. "That's my exit in five miles."

"Then I'll deliver you safe and sound to your home, Dr. Whitman."

"You can call me Ava."

After riding in silence for a while, Ava dragged her purse from the floor of the car into her lap and hugged it to her chest. "What happened to Simon? He looked… dead inside."

"He snapped." His belly coiled into knots. If Simon could snap like that, he could snap, too.

"Did you know about his condition somehow?"

"I had an idea, and when I discovered he was heading out to New Mexico I put two and two together."

"Was it the stress of the assignments? I saw most of you four times a year, but of course you weren't allowed to discuss anything with me. You all seemed well-adjusted though."

Max snorted. "Yeah, I guess some would call that well-adjusted."

"You weren't? You're not? Can I do anything to help you?"

She touched his arm again, this time lightly, brushing her fingertips across the slick material of his jacket.

The human contact and the emotion behind it made him shiver. He clenched his teeth. "You can't do anything to help...Ava. You've done enough."

She snatched her hand back again and studied her fingernails. "This is the exit."

He steered the car toward the off-ramp and eased his foot off the accelerator. She continued giving him directions until they left the desert behind them and rolled into civilization.

He pulled in front of a small house with a light glowing somewhere inside.

She grabbed the door handle and swung open the door before the car even stopped.

"Hold on. I'll walk you up."

"I thought you were anxious to get rid of me."

He scratched the stubble on his chin. That hour-long drive had been the closest he'd come to normalcy in a long time. He didn't want to leave Ava, but he had to— for her own safety.

"I was anxious to get you away from the lab and back home. The police can pick it up from here."

If there was anything left of the lab when they got there. Tempest had to know by now that one of its agents had gone off the rails. The crashes and noises at the lab could've been Tempest.

"Well, here I am." She spread her arms.

He jingled the keys in his palm and felt for his handgun and other gear on his belt as he followed her to the front door.

She dragged her own keys from her purse and slid one into the dead bolt. It clicked and she opened the door.

Apprehension slithered down his spine, and he held out a hand. "Wait."

But it was too late.

Ava had stepped across the threshold and now faced two men training weapons on her.

And this time she wasn't behind bulletproof glass.

Chapter Three

Simon was back—in stereo. Ava caught a glimpse of two men with guns pointed at her for a split second before Max snatched her from behind, lifting her off her feet and jerking her to the side.

At the same instant, she heard a pop and squeezed her eyes closed. If the men had shot Max, she was finished.

An acrid smell invaded her nostrils and she opened her lids—and regretted it immediately. The black smoke pouring from her front door stung her eyes and burned her throat.

"Hold your breath. Close your eyes." Max lifted her and tucked her under one arm as if she were a rag doll.

She felt like a rag doll. The jolt of fear that had spiked her body when she saw the gunmen had dissipated into a curious out-of-body sensation. A creeping lethargy had invaded her limbs, which now dangled uselessly, occasionally banging against Max's body.

If she was lethargic, Max was anything but. His body felt like a well-oiled machine as he sprinted for the car, still clutching her under one arm. He loaded her into the front seat and seconds later the car lurched forward with a shrill squeal.

"Get your seat belt on."

Her hand dropped to the side of the seat, but her fingers wouldn't obey the commands of her fuzzy brain. At the next sharp turn, she fell to the side, her head bumping against the window.

A vise cinched her wrist. "Snap out of it, Ava! I need you."

How had Max known that those three little words amounted to a rallying cry for the former Dr. Ava Whitman?

She rubbed her stinging eyes. She sniffled and dragged a hand beneath her nose. She coughed. She grabbed her seat belt and snapped it into place.

Without taking his eyes from the road, Max asked, "You okay?"

She ran her hands down her arms as if wondering for the first time if she'd been shot. "I'm fine. Did they shoot at us? How did they miss…unless…?"

"I'm okay. They didn't get a shot off."

"I thought— What was all that smoke? The noise?"

"I was able to toss an exploding device at them before they could react. I don't think they were expecting you to have company."

"Let me get this straight." She covered her still-sensitive eyes with one hand. "Two men had guns pointed at us when we walked through the door and you were able to pull me out of harm's way and throw some smoke bomb into the house at the same time?"

"I had the advantage of surprise."

Her hand dropped to her throat. "Did you know someone would be there waiting? Because I was sure surprised to see them standing there."

"Let's just say I had a premonition."

She shook her head. "Superhuman."

Max jerked the steering wheel and the car veered to the right. "Why'd you say that?"

She tilted her head. Why the defensiveness?

"When I saw those guns, I thought we were both dead. Somehow you got us out of there alive. Did I ever thank you? Did I ever thank you for what you did at the lab?"

"Not necessary." He flexed his fingers.

"Are you going to tell me what those men were doing at my house? Are they with Simon? Did they come to finish the job he started?"

She held her breath. If she had a bunch of covert ops agents after her, what was her percentage of survival? Especially once Max Duvall left her side, and he would leave her side—they always did.

"I'm not sure, Ava."

The name sounded tentative on his lips for a man so sure of himself. Agent Max Duvall had always been her favorite patient and it had nothing to do with his dark good looks or his killer body—they all had those killer bodies.

Most of the agents were hard, unfriendly. Some wouldn't even reveal their names. Max always had a smile for her. Always asked about her welfare, made small talk. She looked forward to the quarterly visits by Max—and Simon.

Smashing a fist against her lips, she swallowed a sob. Simon had been friendly, too. He'd even admitted to her that he was engaged, although such personal communications from the agents were verboten. Where was Simon's fiancée now?

Did Max have a wife or a girlfriend sitting at home worried about him, too?

"Are you sure you're okay?"

She blinked and met Max's gaze. They were back on the desolate highway through the desert, and Max's eyes gleamed in the darkness. A trickle of fear dripped down her back. Maybe those men back at her house were there to save her from Max. Maybe Max and Simon were in league together.

"Are you afraid of me?" His low, soft voice floated toward her in the cramped space of the car.

"N-no." She pinned her aching shoulders back against the seat. "No, I'm not. You saved my life—twice. I'm just confused. I have crazy thoughts running through my head. Do you blame me?"

"Not at all."

"If you could tell me what's going on, I'd feel better— as much as I can after tonight's events. I deserve to know. Someone, something is out to extinguish my life. I need to know who or what so I can protect myself."

"I'll protect you."

"From what? For how long?" Her fingers dug into the hard muscle of his thigh. "You have to give me more, Max. You can't keep me in the dark and expect me to trust you. I can't trust like that—not anymore."

Tears blurred her vision, and she covered her face with her hands. Hadn't he just told her to snap out of it? If she wanted to prove that she deserved the hard truth, she'd have to buck up and quit with the waterworks.

"You're right, Ava, but I have a problem with trust, too. I don't have any."

"You don't think you can trust me?" Her voice squeaked on the last syllable.

"You worked in that lab."

"The lab that you visited four times a year. The lab that kept you safe. The lab that treated your injuries—both physical and mental. The lab that made sure you were at your peak performance levels so you could do your job, a job vital to the security of our country."

"Stop!" He slammed his palms against the steering wheel, and she shrank against her side of the car.

"That lab, that bastion of goodwill and patriotic fervor, turned me into a mindless, soulless machine." He jabbed a finger in her face. "You did that to me, and now you have as much to fear from me as you did from Simon. I'm a killer."

Chapter Four

Icy fingers gripped the back of Ava's neck and she hunched her shoulders, making herself small against the car door. She shot a side glance at Max. The glow from the car's display highlighted the sharp planes of his face, lending credence to his declaration that he was a machine. But a killer? He'd saved her—twice. Unless he'd saved her for some other nefarious purpose.

Her fingers curled around the door handle, and she tensed her muscles.

Her movement broke his trancelike stare out the windshield. Blinking, he peeled one hand from the steering wheel and ran it through his dark hair.

"I—I won't hurt you, Dr. Whitman."

She whispered, "Ava."

He cranked his head to the side, and the stark lines on his face softened. "Where can I take you…Ava?"

She jerked forward in her seat. She couldn't go home, as if she'd ever called that small bungalow teetering at the edge of the desert home.

But if Max thought he could launch a bombshell at her like that and then blithely drop her off somewhere, he needed to reprogram himself.

Had he really just blamed her for Simon's breakdown?

"Before you take me anywhere—" she pressed her palms against her bouncing knees "—you're going to explain yourself. How is any of this my fault?"

He squeezed his eyes closed briefly and pinched the bridge of his nose. "I shouldn't have yelled, but I don't know if I can trust you."

"Me?" She jabbed an index finger at her chest. "You don't know if you can trust me? You're the one who whisked me away from the lab, led me into an ambush and then threatened to kill me."

He sucked in a sharp breath. "That wasn't a threat. I don't make threats."

His words hung in the space between them, their meaning clear. This man would strike without warning and without mercy. The fact that she still sat beside him, living and breathing, attested to the fact that despite his misgivings he must trust her at least a little bit.

"You warned me that you were a killer, like Simon."

"What exactly do you think the agents of…Prospero do if not kill?"

"You kill when it's necessary. You kill to protect the country. You kill in self-defense."

"Is that what you think Simon was doing?"

She stuffed her hands beneath her thighs. "No, but that's what you were doing when you took him out."

He nodded once and his jaw hardened again. "I won't hurt you, Ava."

She swallowed. His repetition of the phrase sent a spiral of fear down her spine. Was he trying to convince her or convince himself?

"Tell me where I can drop you off, and you'll be fine. Friends? Family?"

"I told you, I don't have any friends or family in this area." She pushed the hair from her face in a sharp gesture, suddenly angry at him for forcing her to admit that pathetic truth.

"I can take you to an airport and get you on a plane to anywhere."

"No." She shook her head and her hair whipped across her face again. "Before I get on a plane to anywhere, I want you to explain yourself. What happened to Simon? Why did you blame me? Why did Simon attack the lab?"

"If you don't know, it's not safe for me to tell you."

"Bull." She jerked her thumb over her shoulder. "Those two men were waiting for me at my house. I wasn't safe back there, and I'm not safe now. What you tell is not going to make it any worse than it already is. And you know that."

Lights twinkled ahead, and she realized they'd circled back into the city after a detour on a desert highway so that he could make sure they hadn't been followed.

He pointed to a sign with an airplane on it. "I can take you straight to the airport and buy you a ticket back home to your family. You can contact the CIA and tell them what happened. The agency will help you."

"But the agency is not going to tell me what's going on. I want to know. I deserve to know after you accused me of being complicit in Simon's breakdown."

"You were."

She smacked her hands on the dashboard. "Stop saying that. This is what I mean. You can't throw around accusations like that without backing them up."

He aimed the car for the next exit and left the highway. "It's going to be morning soon. Let's get off the road, get some rest. I'll tell you everything, and then you're getting on that plane."

She sat quietly as Max followed the signs to the airport. He turned onto a boulevard lined with airport hotels and rolled into the parking lot of a midrange highrise, anonymous and nondescript.

He dragged a bag from the trunk of the car and left the keys with the valet parking attendant.

She hadn't realized how exhausted she was until they walked through the empty lobby of the hotel.

A front desk clerk jumped up from behind the counter. "Do you need a room?"

"Yeah." Max reached for the back pocket of his camouflage pants. Without the bulletproof vest, the black jacket and the ski mask, he looked almost normal. Could the hotel clerk feel the waves of tension vibrating off Max's body? Did he notice the tight set of Max's jaw? The way his dark eyes seemed to take in everything around him with a single glance? *Normal* was not a word she'd use to describe Max Duvall.

"Credit card?"

"We don't use one. Filed for bankruptcy not too long ago." Max offered up a tight smile along with a stack of bills. "We'll pay cash for one night."

The clerk's brow furrowed. "The problem is if you use anything from the minibar or watch a movie in the room, we have no way to charge you."

Max thumbed through the money and shoved it across the counter. "Add an extra hundred for incidentals."

The clerk's frown never left his face, but he seemed compelled to acquiesce to Max. She didn't blame him. Max was the type of man others obeyed.

Five minutes later, Max pushed open the door of their hotel room, holding it open for her.

She eyed the two double beds in the room and placed her purse on the floor next to one of them. If the clerk downstairs had found the request for two beds odd, he'd put on his best poker face. Maybe he'd figured their *bank-ruptcy* had put a strain on the marriage.

She perched on the edge of the bed, knees and feet primly together, watching Max pace the room like a jungle cat.

He stopped at the window and shifted to the side, leaning one shoulder against the glass.

"Do you want something from the minibar? Water, soft drink, something harder?"

She narrowed her eyes. She hadn't expected him to play host. Despite rescuing her from mortal danger, he hadn't seemed too concerned with her well-being. He'd gone through the motions and had acknowledged her shock and fear, but he'd done next to nothing to comfort her. Because he still didn't trust her.

"I'll have some water." She pushed up from the bed and hovered over the fridge on the console. "Do you want something?"

"Soda, something with caffeine."

The man didn't need caffeine. He needed a stiff drink, something to take off the hard edges.

She swung open the door of the pint-size fridge and plucked a bottle of water from the shelf. She pinched the neck of a wine bottle and held it up. "You sure you don't want some wine?"

"Just the soda, but I don't mind if you want to imbibe. You could probably use something to relax you."

"That's funny." She placed the wine on the credenza and grabbed a can of cola from the inside door of the fridge. "I was just thinking you needed something to relax *you.*"

"Relax?"

He blinked his eyes and looked momentarily lost, as if the idea of relaxation had never occurred to him.

"Never mind." She crossed the room and held out the can to him.

When he took it, his fingers brushed hers and she almost dropped the drink. That was the first time he'd touched her without grabbing, gripping and yanking. Although she'd touched him before, plenty of times.

Like all of the agents, his body was in prime condition—his muscles hard, his belly flat, barely concealed power humming beneath the smooth skin. As a medical professional, she'd always maintained her distance but she couldn't deny she'd looked forward to Max Duvall's appointment times.

But that was then.

She planted her feet on the carpet, widening her stance in front of him. "Are you going to tell me what this is all about now? Why did Simon go on a murderous rampage, why is someone out to get me, and why did you blame it all on me?"

He snapped the tab on his can and took a long pull from it, eyeing her above the rim. "Let's sit down. You must be exhausted."

"I am, but not too exhausted to hear the truth." She walked backward away from him and swiveled toward the bed, dropping onto the mattress. She had to hold herself upright because out of Max's tension-filled sphere, she did feel exhausted. She felt like collapsing on the bed and pulling the covers over her head.

He dragged a chair out from the desk by the window and sat down, stretching his long legs in front of him. It was the closest he'd come to a relaxed pose since he'd stormed into the lab in full riot gear.

"What do you know about the work at the lab?"

"Didn't we go through this already? We support a co-vert ops agency, Prospero, by monitoring and treating its agents. Part of the lab is responsible for developing vitamin formulas that enhance strength, alertness and even intelligence."

"But you're not part of that lab."

"N-no. I'm the people doctor, not the research doctor."

He slumped in his chair and took another gulp of his drink. "How do you know you support Prospero? Isn't that supposed to be classified information? After all, the general public knows nothing of Prospero…or other covert ops agencies under the umbrella of the CIA."

"We're not supposed to know, but like I said, people talk." She waved her hand in the air. "I've heard things around the lab."

"You heard wrong."

She choked on the sip of water she'd just swallowed. "I beg your pardon?"

"The rumor mill had the wrong info or it purposely spread the wrong info. You don't support Prospero. You support another covert ops team—Tempest."

"Oh." Clearing her throat, she shrugged. "One agency or the other. It doesn't make any difference to me. They must be related groups, since both of their names come from the Shakespeare play."

He nodded slowly and traced the edge of the can with his fingertip. "They are related, in a way."

"So what difference does it make whether we supported Prospero or Tempest?"

"I said the agencies were related, not the same. One is a force for good, and the other…" His hand wrapped around the can and his knuckles grew white as he squeezed it.

The knots in her stomach twisted with the aluminum. "Tempest is a force for evil? Is that what you mean?"

"Yes."

She jerked the hand holding the bottle and the water

sloshed against the plastic. "That's ridiculous. I wouldn't work for an agency like that. Would you? You're a Tempest agent. Are you telling me you all signed up for service knowing Tempest had bad intentions?"

"Not knowingly. Did you? How *did* you come to work at the lab?"

Unease churned in her gut and a flash of heat claimed her flesh from head to toe.

"What is it?" Max hunched forward, bracing his forearms against his thighs.

"Dr. Arnoff recruited me." She pressed her fingers to her warm cheeks. "He gave me the job because I had nowhere else to go."

"Why not, Ava?" His dark eyes burned into her very soul.

"I—I had lost my license to practice medicine. I was finished as a physician before I had even started. Dr. Arnoff gave me a chance. He gave me a chance to be a doctor again." Her voice broke and she took a gulp of water to wash down the tears.

"Why? What happened? You're a good doctor, Ava."

His gentle tone and kind words had the tears pricking the backs of her eyes.

She sniffed. "I'm not a doctor. I made a mistake. Someone betrayed me, but it was my own fault. I was too trusting, too stupid."

He opened his mouth and then snapped it shut. Running a hand through his thick, dark hair until it stood up, he heaved a sigh. "So, Arnoff took advantage of your situation, your desperation to get you to work for Tempest."

"And you? Simon? The others? How did Tempest recruit you?"

He dropped his lashes and held himself so still, she thought he'd fallen asleep for a few seconds. When he opened his eyes, he seemed very far away. "You're not the only one who has made mistakes, Ava."

"So, what is Tempest? What do they do? Wh-what have you done for them?"

A muscle twitched in his jaw, and he ran his knuckles across the dark stubble there. "Tempest is responsible for assassinations, kidnappings, tampering with elections around the world."

"I'm not naive, Max. A lot of covert ops groups are responsible for the same types of missions."

"Tempest is different. An agency like Prospero may commit acts of espionage and violence, but those acts promote a greater good—a safer world."

She crossed her arms and hunched her shoulders. "And what does Tempest promote?"

Max's dark eyes burned as he gazed past her, his nostrils flaring. He seemed to come to some decision as his gaze shifted back to her face, his eyes locking onto hers.

"Terror, chaos, destruction."

"No!" A sharp pain drilled the back of her skull and she bounded from the bed. "I don't believe you. That turns everything we did in that lab, all our efforts, into a big lie. My coworkers were good people. We were doing good work there. We were protecting agents who were protecting our country."

He lunged from his chair, slicing his hand through the air, and she stumbled backward as he loomed over her, his lean frame taut and menacing.

"Tempest agents do not protect this country. Tempest is loyal to no one country or group of nations. Tempest is loyal to itself and the shadowy figure that runs it."

Her knees shook so much she had to grip the edge of the credenza. Despite Max's sudden burst of fury, she didn't fear him. The man had saved her twice. But she did fear his words.

Maybe he was delusional. Maybe this was how Simon had started. Maybe she *should* fear Max Duvall.

"I don't understand." The words came out as a whisper even though that hadn't been her intent. She had no more control over her voice than she did the terror galloping throughout her body.

He ran both hands through his hair, digging his fingers into his scalp. "I don't see how I can be any plainer. Tempest is a deep undercover agency, so rogue the CIA is completely in the dark about its operations and methods. Tempest carries out assassinations and nation building all on its own, and these interests do not serve the US or world peace."

"Then what is their purpose?"

As if realizing his close proximity to her for the first time, Max shuffled back, retreating to the window, wedging a shoulder against the glass.

"I don't know. Tempest's overall goal is a mystery to me."

"If Tempest is so evil, why are you one of its agents? You said you were recruited, but why'd you stay? There's no way the agency could keep you in the dark, not...not like me."

She held her breath, bracing for another outburst. Instead, Max relaxed his rigid stance. His broad shoulders slumped and he massaged the back of his neck.

"You really have no idea, do you? You haven't figured it out yet."

A muscle beneath her eye jumped, and she smoothed her hands across her face. She sipped in a few short breaths, pushing back against the creeping dread invading her lungs.

"Why should I know? You haven't explained that part to me. You've made some crazy, wild accusations, throwing puzzle pieces at me, expecting me to fit them together when I haven't even processed the mass murder I just witnessed."

Her knees finally buckled and she grabbed for the credenza as she sank to the carpet.

Max's long stride ate up the distance between them, and he placed a steadying hand on her shoulder. "Are you okay? We should've saved this conversation for morning, after some sleep and some food."

When she didn't respond, he nudged her. "Can you stand up?"

She nodded, but the muscles in her legs refused to obey the commands from her brain.

He crouched beside her, slipping one arm across her back and one behind her thighs. She leaned into him and he lifted her from the floor and stood up in one motion.

He was careful to hold her body away from his as he carried her to the bed, but for her part she could've nestled in his arms forever. She wanted him to hold her and tell her this was all a joke.

He placed her on the bed with surprising gentleness. "Why don't you get some sleep, and we'll talk about this over breakfast?"

She grabbed a pillow and hugged it to her chest. "I wouldn't be able to sleep anyway. Tell me the truth. Tell me the whole ugly truth about what we were doing in that lab and why you stayed with Tempest."

He backed up and eased onto the edge of the bed across from hers. He blew out a long breath. "I stayed with Tempest even after I discovered their agenda because they wanted me to. Tempest controlled my mind and my body. They still do."

"No." Ava squeezed the pillow against her body, her fingers curling into soft foam.

"It's a form of brainwashing, Ava, but it goes beyond the brain. It's my body, too." He pushed up from the bed and plucked up a lamp with a metal rod from the base to the lightbulb. He unplugged it and removed the shade. Gripping it on either side with his hands, he bent it to a forty-five-degree angle. Then he held up the lamp by the lightbulb, which had to still be hot, and didn't even flinch.

Her eyes widened and her jaw dropped. "Dr. Arnoff's vitamin formula—stronger, faster, impervious to pain."

He released the bulb and the distorted lamp fell to the floor. He examined his hand. "So, he did tell you."

"That's what he was working on, but he told me it was years from completion."

He held up his reddened palm. "He completed it."

"What you're telling me—" she swung her legs over the side of the bed "—is crazy. You're saying that Dr. Arnoff's formula created some kind of superagent and that Tempest sent these agents out into the world to do its bidding?"

"Yes, but I told you it's more than physical." He tapped the side of his head. "Tempest messed with our minds, too."

She bunched the bedspread in her hands. "How? That didn't happen in our lab."

"No. That occurred in the debriefing unit in Germany where we went after every assignment."

She pinned her hands between her knees as her eyes darted to the hotel door. Max Duvall could be crazy. This could all be some elaborate hallucination, one that he'd shared with Simon Skinner. Then her gaze tracked to the metal rod of the lamp, which he'd folded as if it were a straw. So, he was crazy *and* strong—a bad combination.

"How did they do it? The brainwashing?"

He squeezed his eyes closed and massaged his temple with two fingers. "Mind control—it was mind control and they did it through a combination of drugs, hypnosis and sleep therapy."

"What is sleep therapy?"

"That's my name for it. The doctors would hook us up to machines, brain scans, and then sedate us. They said it was for deep relaxation and stress reduction, but…" He shook his head.

"But what?" She wiped her palms on the bedspread. The air in the room almost crackled with electricity.

"It didn't do that. It didn't relax us, at least not me and Simon. After those sessions, a jumble of memories and scenes assaulted my brain. I couldn't tell real from fake. The memories—they implanted them in my brain."

She gasped as a bolt of fear shot through her chest. "They wanted you to forget the assignments."

"But I couldn't." He shoved off the window and stalked across the room, pressing his palms against either side of his head. "Simon and I, we remembered. I don't know how many others did."

He really believed all of this, and he blamed her for administering the serum. Maybe the men at her house had been there to protect her from Max. The pressures of the job had driven them both off the deep end. Simon had snapped, and Max was nearing the same precipice.

"I-is that what drove Simon to commit violence? The implanted memories?"

"No." He pivoted and paced back to the window, a light sheen of sweat breaking out on his forehead. "The implanted memories were fine. It was the flashes of re-ality that tortured us."

If she kept pretending that she believed him, maybe

he'd drop her off at the airport without incident. She could make up family somewhere, a family that cared about her and worried about her well-being. A fake family.

"The reality of what he'd done for Tempest pushed Simon past the breaking point?"

"It's the serum." He turned again and swayed to the side. He thrust out an unsteady hand to regain his balance. "Simon tried to break the cycle, but you can't go cold turkey. I told him not to go cold turkey."

A spasm of pain distorted his handsome features, and Ava tensed her muscles to make a run at the door if necessary. "I'm not sure I understand, Max."

"The pills." He wiped a hand across his mouth and staggered. "I need the pills. I'll end up like Simon without them."

She braced her hands on her knees, ready to spring into action. The pills, again. He'd been going on about blue pills at the lab when he rescued her, too.

Max was talking gibberish now, his strong hands clenching and then unclenching, his gait unsteady, sweat dripping from his jaw.

"What pills?" She licked her lips. Her gaze flicked to the door. If she rolled off the other side of the bed, she could avoid Max, pitching and reeling in the middle of the room. Then she'd call 911. He needed help, but she didn't have the strength or the tools to subdue him if he decided to attack her.

"Pocket. The blue." Then he pitched forward and landed face-first on the floor.

Chapter Five

"Max!" She launched off the bed and crouched beside him. If he decided to grab her now, she wouldn't have a chance against his power.

His body twitched and he moaned. He *had* no power to grab her now. She could make a run for it and call hotel security. The hotel would call 911, and he could get help at the hospital from a doctor—a real doctor.

Max's dry lips parted, and he reached for her hand.

And if any part of his story was true? She knew the secrecy of that lab better than anyone. Those two men with the automatic weapons had been waiting at her house, for her. Max had saved her.

She curled her fingers around his and squeezed. "I'll be right back."

She ran to the bathroom and grabbed a hand towel. She held it under a stream of cool water and grabbed a bottle of the stuff on her way back to Max. She swept a pillow from the bed and sat on the floor beside his prone form.

He'd rolled to his back, so at least he wasn't unconscious.

Pressing two fingers against his neck, she checked his pulse—rapid but strong. She dabbed his face with the wet towel and eased a pillow beneath his head.

"Can you drink some water? Are you in any pain?" She held up the bottle.

"The pills." His voice rasped from his throat.

They were back to the pills? "What pills, Max?"

His hand dropped to his side, and she remembered what he'd said before he collapsed. His pocket.

She skimmed her hand across the rough material of one pocket and then the other, her fingers tracing the edges of a hard, square object. She dug her fingers into the pocket and pulled out a small tin of breath mints, but when she opened the lid no minty freshness greeted her.

Five round blue pills nestled together in the corner of the tin. She held up the container to his face. "These pills?"

His chin dipped to his chest, and she shook the pills into her palm.

He held up his index finger.

"Just one?"

He hissed, a sound that probably meant yes.

She picked up one pill between two fingers and placed it into his mouth. Then she held the water bottle up to his lips, while curling an arm around the back of his head to prop him up.

He swallowed the water and the pill disappeared. His spiky, dark lashes closed over his eyes and he melted against her arm. Her fingers burrowed into his thick, black hair as she dabbed his face with the towel.

His chest rose and fell, his breathing deeper and more regular. His face changed from a sickly pallor to his usual olive skin tone, and the trembling that had been racking his body ceased.

Whatever magic ingredient the little blue pill contained seemed to work. She peered at the remaining pills in the tin and sniffed them. Maybe he was a drug addict. Hallucinogens could bring on the paranoid thoughts.

His eyes flew open and he struggled to sit up.

"Whoa." Her arms slipped around his shoulders. "You just had a very scary incident. You need to lie back and relax."

"It passes quickly. I'm fine." He shrugged off her arm and sat up, leaning his back against the credenza. He chugged the rest of the water.

"Are you okay? I almost called 911."

"Don't—" he cinched her wrist with his thumb and middle finger "—ever call the police."

Her heart skipped a beat. She should've run when she had the chance.

His deep brown eyes widened and grew even darker. He dropped her wrist. "I'm sorry. I scared you."

She scooted away and rested her back against the bed, facing him. "And I'm sorry you're going through all this, but there's nothing I can do to help you. You need to see a doctor, and I—I'll go to my family and contact the CIA about what happened at the lab."

"You *are* a doctor." His eyes glittered through slits.

"Not exactly, and you know what I mean. You need to go to a doctor's office, get checked out."

"You mean a psychiatrist, don't you?"

"I mean…"

"You don't believe me. You're afraid of me. You think I'm crazy." He laughed, a harsh, stark sound with no humor in it.

"It's a crazy story, Max. My lab was just shot up and two men tried to kill me—or you."

"Both of us."

"Okay, maybe both of us, but I don't belong in the middle of all this."

"You're right." He rose from the floor, looking as strong and capable as ever. "Try to get some sleep. I'll take you to the airport tomorrow."

"And you?"

"I'll keep doing what I've been doing."

"Which is?"

"You don't belong in the middle of this, remember?" He tossed the pillow she'd tucked beneath him onto the bed and took a deep breath, the air in his lungs expanding his broad chest, his black T-shirt stretching across his muscles. "Would you like to take a shower? I need to take one, but you can go first."

"I would, but I can wait."

Still sitting on the floor, she'd stretched her legs in front of her.

Max stepped over her outstretched legs on the way to the bathroom and shut the door behind him.

Blowing out a long breath, Ava got to her feet and grabbed her purse. She could get a taxi to the airport before he even got out of the shower.

MAX BRACED HIS hands against the tile of the shower and dipped his head, as the warm water beat between his shoulder blades.

She'd be gone by the time he came out of the shower. And why shouldn't she be? She thought he was crazy. She didn't trust him. And she was right not to.

If she stayed, if she believed him, she could probably help him. She didn't seem to know about the pills, but she'd worked with Arnoff. She might know something about those blue pills that stood between him and a complete meltdown like Simon.

He'd warned Simon to keep taking the pills, but his

buddy was stubborn. He'd wanted nothing more to do with Tempest and its control over their lives.

Max faced the spray and sluiced the water through his hair. Maybe he'd made a mistake showing his hand to Tempest. As soon as he'd refused his last assignment, Foster had suspected he'd figured everything out—not everything. He and Simon hadn't realized quitting the serum would have such a profound effect on their bodies and minds.

He cranked off the water and grabbed a towel. At least he'd been able to save Dr. Whitman—Ava—from Simon. Stupid, stubborn bastard. Who was going to tell Simon's fiancée, Nina?

He dried off and wrapped the towel around his waist. A few hours' sleep would do him good, and then he'd reassess. He could contact Prospero, but he didn't know whom he could trust at this point. He didn't blame Ava one bit for hightailing it out of here.

He pushed open the bathroom door and stopped short.

Ava looked up from examining something in the palm of her hand. Her gaze scanned his body, and he made a grab for the towel slipping down his hips.

"You're still here."

"Did you expect me to take off?"

He pointedly stared at the purse hanging over her shoulder. "Yeah."

She held out her hand, his precious pills cupped in her palm. "What are these? They have a distinctive odor."

"They should." He adjusted the towel again and glanced over his shoulder at his clothes scattered across the bathroom floor. He couldn't risk leaving her alone with those pills another minute. She might just get it in her head to run with them. She probably thought he was a junkie.

Her body stiffened and she closed her hand around the blue beauties. "Why would you say that?"

"They're a milder form of the serum you inject in us four times a year." He cocked his head. "You really don't know that?"

The color drained from her face, emphasizing her large eyes, which widened. "Why would you be taking additional doses of the serum?"

"Weaker doses. To keep up. To be better, faster, stronger, smarter. Isn't that what the serum is all about?"

"Did you know what they were when you started taking them?"

"By the time the pills were introduced into our regimen, we didn't care what they were for. We needed them."

"They're addictive?" She swept the breath-mint tin from the credenza and funneled the pills into it from her cupped hand.

Max released the breath he'd been holding. "More than you could possibly know."

"Then tell me, Max. I deserve to know everything. I stayed." She shrugged the purse from her shoulder and tossed it onto the bed. "One little part of me believed your story. There was enough subterfuge in that lab to make me believe your wild accusations."

"Can I put my pants on first?" He hooked his fingers around the edge of the towel circling his hips.

Her eyes dropped to his hands, and the color came rushing back into her pale cheeks. "Of course. I'm not going anywhere."

He retreated to the bathroom and dropped the towel. Leaning close to the mirror, he plowed a hand through his damp hair. It needed a trim and he needed a shave, not that he'd given a damn about his appearance before Ava came onto the scene.

He pulled on his camos and returned to the bedroom.

Ava had moved to the chair and sat with her legs curled beneath her, a look of expectancy highlighting her face.

He'd memorized that face from his quarterly visits with her. Dr. Ava Whitman had been the one bright spot in the dark tunnel of Tempest. He believed with certainty that she had no idea what she'd been dosing them with. At first, he'd been incredulous that a doctor wouldn't know what was in a formula she was giving her patients, but her story made sense. Tempest sought out the most vulnerable. The agency used blackmail and coercion, and in Ava's case, hope, to recruit people.

Dr. Arnoff had kept her in the dark, had probably shut down her questions by reminding her that she wouldn't be working as a doctor if it weren't for the agency and then using the illegality of that work to keep her in line.

And she'd been good at her job. He had a hard time remembering the two missions he'd been on last year, but he could clearly recall Ava's soft touch and cheery tone as she checked his vitals and injected him with the serum that would destroy his life.

Ava cleared her throat. "If the blue pills are a weaker dose of the T-101 serum, why are you still taking them?"

"I have to."

"Because you're addicted? Why not just ride out the withdrawal?" She laced her fingers in her lap. "I can help you. I—I have some experience with that."

He raised his eyebrows. She had to be referring to a patient. "It's more than the addiction. I could ride that out. You saw Simon."

She drew in a quick breath and hunched forward. "Simon went over the edge. He lost it. The stress, the tension, maybe even the brainwashing—they all did him in."

"It's the…T-101, Ava. Is that what you called it? Without the serum, we self-destruct. Another agent, before Simon, before me, he committed suicide. Tempest put it down to post-traumatic stress disorder because this agent had killed a child by mistake on a raid. Now I wonder if that was even a mistake or his true assignment."

"Adam Belchik." She drew her knees to her chest, wrapping her arms around them.

"That's right. I thought he was before your time."

"He was, but I heard about him."

"He was the first to go off the meds, and he paid the price. He had a family, so he killed himself before he could harm them."

"Is that why you were jabbering about cold turkey? You can't quit cold turkey like Simon did, like Adam did. You have to keep lowering your dosage by continuing with the blue pills."

"That's it." He pointed to the tin on the credenza, the fine line keeping him from insanity and rage. "I find if I take one a day, I can maintain. I tried a half, and it didn't work."

"You have only five left." Her gaze darted to the credenza and back to his face.

"Four now. Four pills. Four days."

She uncurled her legs and almost fell out of the chair as she bolted from it. "That's crazy. What happens at the end of the four days?"

He lifted his shoulders. "I'll be subject to incidents like the one you just witnessed until they kill me or I snap... or Tempest gets to me first."

"And if they do?"

"They'll either kill me or I'll be their drone for the rest of my life."

She folded her arms across her stomach, clutching the material of her blouse at her sides. "There has to be another way. If we get more of the pills and you take smaller and smaller doses, maybe eventually you can break free. You tried taking a half, but it was too soon."

"Where would I get more pills? You said yourself you never saw them at the lab. They weren't administered at the lab. My quick search there revealed nothing."

She snapped her fingers. "Max, there has to be an antidote somewhere."

"Why would you think that? Tempest had no intention of ever reversing the damage they'd done to us."

"Maybe not to you, but Dr. Arnoff tested the T-101 on himself."

His heart slammed against his chest. "Are you sure?"

"I'm positive, or at least I'm positive that he told me he'd tried it on himself. He said he felt like a superhero—strong, invincible, sexually potent."

She reddened to the edge of her hairline and waved a hand in the air. "You know, that's what he said."

Sexual potency? It had been a long time since he'd been close enough to a woman in a normal situation to even think about sex.

He cleared his throat. "If he acted as his own guinea pig, he'd want something to counteract the effects in case things didn't go the way he planned."

"Exactly—an antidote."

"We could be jumping to conclusions." He dragged in a breath and let it out slowly in an attempt to temper his excitement. He'd learned to be cautious about good news. "Maybe Arnoff didn't develop an antidote. He could've dialed back by taking the blue pills—fewer and fewer of them until the cravings stopped and the physical effects dissipated."

"That could be, but it also means there must be more of those blue pills floating around." She dropped onto the bed. "What about the other agents? Can you all pool your resources and wean yourselves off of the serum?"

He cracked a smile and shook his head.

"What's so funny? That's the first real smile I've seen from you all night, and I wasn't even making a joke."

"I just got a visual of a bunch of Tempest agents sitting around a campfire sharing little pieces of their blue pills."

A smile hovered at her lips. "Not possible?"

"I don't even know who more than half of the agents are."

"I do."

His gaze locked onto hers. "You don't know all their names. You don't know where they live, and most of them are probably on assignment anyway."

She shook her finger at him. "You'd be surprised how many of them opened up to me."

"Not surprised at all." She'd obviously been a ray of sunshine for the other agents, too. "But we can't go knocking on their doors asking them to give up their meds. Unless they've already suspected something or had incidents like Simon and I did, they're not going to see the problem."

"I meant to ask you that." She fell back against the mattress and rolled to her side to face him, propping up her head with one hand. "What made you and Simon realize what was going on?"

"There were gaps, glitches in our response to the treatment. For me it was the memories. I recalled too much about my operations. The memories they tried to implant in my brain didn't jibe with my reality. On one assignment, Simon and I started comparing notes and then experimenting with the pills."

"Simon didn't show up for his last appointment with me. He never got his injection."

"He decided to make a clean break. He shrugged off the seizures even though I tried to warn him." He dropped his head in his hands, digging his fingers into his scalp. What would they tell Simon's fiancée?

The bed sank beside him, and he turned his head as Ava touched his back.

"You had to shoot Simon. He would've killed you. He would've killed me." The pressure of her hand between his shoulder blades increased. "Now, since you saved my life—twice—I'm going to save yours."

He wanted to believe her. He wanted to stretch out on the bed next to Ava and feel her soft touch on his forehead again.

"And how to you propose to do that, Dr. Whitman?"

Her hand dropped from his back. "Don't call me that. I told you, I never finished. I don't deserve the title."

"Ava."

"We're going to find that antidote or a million blue pills to get you through this." She yawned and covered her mouth with the back of her hand. "But first I'm going to sleep away the rest of what's left of this evening."

"And your family? I thought I was taking you to the airport tomorrow so you could fly out to be with your family."

"My family." She launched from his bed to hers, peeled back the covers and slipped beneath them. "I have no family."

Chapter Six

Ava buried her head beneath a pillow and ran her tongue along her teeth. She needed a toothbrush and a meal.

"Are you awake?"

Lifting one corner of the pillow, she peered out at Max sitting in front of a tablet computer at the table by the window. "What time is it?"

He flicked back the heavy drapes and a spear of sunlight sliced through the room. "It's around ten o'clock. You must be hungry. When was the last time you ate?"

"I had my dinner at the lab before...before everything went down."

"That was a long time ago."

"An eternity. A lifetime." She retreated beneath the pillow. How was she supposed to do this with Max? Why did her life always manage to get upended?

She heard his footsteps across the room and the crackle of plastic.

"I went down to the little store in the hotel and bought you a few things."

"A new life?"

The silence yawned from across the room and engulfed her. She tossed the pillow away from her and sat up.

Max stood in the center of the room, a plastic bag dangling at his side. "You don't need to do this, Ava. In fact, I'm going to take you to the airport right now. I'll pay for a ticket anywhere you want to go. Then you can call the CIA or whatever number the lab gave you in case of an emergency and you can forget about all of this."

She sighed. "I was trying to make a joke. I want to help you. I feel responsible for your predicament. If I hadn't been so anxious for a job, any job, I wouldn't have been injecting you and Simon and countless others with poison."

"Not your fault. They would've found someone else." He chucked the bag onto the foot of the bed. "Toothbrush, comb, deodorant, some other stuff. Take a shower. I have some stuff to get out of the car, and then I'll meet you in the restaurant downstairs for breakfast. You can let me know then what you want to do."

The door closed behind him and she stared at it for several seconds. A ticket to anywhere. A new start—again. How many new starts did one woman need?

She threw off the covers and grabbed the bag of toiletries. She didn't need a new start. She needed a finish. She needed to help Max Duvall.

Forty minutes later, freshly showered but wearing the same clothes from yesterday, Ava made her way down to the lobby. She spotted Max immediately. Did everyone else notice the aura of power and menace around him or did she just have that special switch that flicked on when danger sent out its Siren's call?

He glanced up from his newspaper and watched her approach with an unwavering gaze, as if willing her to his side. He didn't have to throw out any lures. She was all in.

He rose to his feet when she reached the table and pulled out her chair. "Do you feel better after your shower?"

Sitting down, she flicked the collar of her blouse. "I'd feel even better if I had some clean clothes to step into."

"I wouldn't recommend going back to your house for a while."

"Ever?" She turned her coffee cup over and nodded at the waitress bearing a coffeepot.

"When this all blows over."

"When will that be?" After the waitress came by with the coffee, Ava poured a steady stream of cream into her cup, watching the milky swirls fan out in the dark liquid.

"When the CIA or Prospero gets a handle on Tempest and puts a stop to its clandestine operations."

The spoon hovered over her cup. "In other words, I'd better get used to these clothes."

"Buy new ones."

"Is that what you do?" She took in the dark blue T-shirt, very similar to the black T-shirt he'd been wearing last night. He'd swapped the camouflage pants for a pair of faded jeans.

"I've been carrying my clothes—and everything else— with me for the past month. I have one bag for my clothes and a second one for my…tools."

She slurped a sip of coffee, wondering how best to ask him about his tools, when the waitress came back and saved her from doing something stupid.

They both asked for omelets, but Max added a bowl of oatmeal and some fresh fruit to his order.

She folded her hands on the table and tilted her head. "When was the last time you ate?"

"It's been a while." He brought the coffee cup to his lips and stared at her over the rim. "Airport?"

She gripped her hands together and sucked in a breath. She let it out on one word. "No."

"Are you sure?"

"I have some ideas, Max."

The waitress placed Max's oatmeal between them, and

he dumped some brown sugar and raisins into the bowl. "I'm listening."

The maple smell of the brown sugar rose on the steam, creating a homey feel completely at odds with their conversation.

"I know where Dr. Arnoff lives—lived." She pushed her cup out of the way and tapped a spot on the table. "The lab is here and Albuquerque is this way. He lives in a suburb, a high-end suburb. We can start with his house and see if he has anything there, any of those blue pills. I know he keeps a work laptop at home."

"Is he married? Does he have a family?"

"He is married, but his children are adults. One lives overseas and the other one is in Boston."

"You think his wife, his widow, is going to invite us into her home so we can snoop around in her dead husband's personal effects?" He plunged his spoon into the oatmeal.

"You're a spy, aren't you? We either break in or gain entrance through some kind of subterfuge."

He raised an eyebrow. "I repeat. You do not have to do any of this. You can hop on a plane and put this behind you."

"No, I can't." Whatever happened, she'd never forget Max Duvall. She'd always wonder if he made it or not, and if he didn't make it she'd always blame herself.

He left his spoon in the bowl and pushed it to the corner of the table. "You mentioned you had no family. Do you have friends you can stay with?"

"Out of the blue like this?" She spread her hands. "No."

"If anything happened to you…"

She pressed her fingers against his forearm, and his corded muscle twitched beneath her touch. "I'll be with you. For better or worse, you still have T-101 pulsing through your system. You're practically indestructible."

"I may be, but you're not." He covered her hand with his own, his touch rough, awkward but sincere. "You can give me directions to Arnoff's and I'll go there on my own."

"What am I supposed to do? Where am I supposed to go?"

They broke apart when the waitress delivered their food. "You had the Denver and you had the spinach? Ketchup? Salsa?"

"Both, please." Ava flicked the napkin into her lap.

When the waitress returned with their condiments, Max spooned some salsa onto his plate and took up the conversation without missing a beat. "You can stay here."

"Stay here?"

"I'd come back after going to Arnoff's in case nothing panned out there. You could help me find a few other agents and be on your way." He sawed off an edge of his omelet with his fork. "Once you decide where you want to go."

"I'd need to call the CIA or rather the emergency number I have."

"You have an emergency number?"

"I thought I told you that." She stabbed a potato and dragged it through the puddle of ketchup on her plate. Then she remembered the blood all over the lab and placed the tines of her fork on the edge of her plate.

"You told me you planned to call the CIA."

"Yeah, the emergency number."

"You know for a fact that the emergency number goes to the CIA?"

"I just assumed it did." She wrapped her hands around her cup, still warm from the coffee the waitress had topped off. "D-do you think it's the number for someone at Tempest?"

"Could be." The blood-red ketchup didn't seem to bother him as he squirted another circle of it on the side of his plate.

Her hands tightened around the mug. "I can't call that number. Those men at my house could've been from Tempest."

"They *were* from Tempest." He tapped her plate with his knife. "Eat your breakfast."

She spooned the ketchup from her plate into a napkin. "So, who am I supposed to call? The number for the CIA isn't exactly in the phone book."

"You should call Prospero—once I'm out of the picture."

"You don't trust Prospero but you expect me to?"

"You're not an agent formerly working with Tempest. Prospero has no reason not to trust you."

"Really? Because you trusted me immediately?"

"I can't trust anyone, Ava."

"Maybe I can't either."

"You can trust me."

"As long as you keep taking the reduced dosage of T-101 in those pills."

He glanced up from his plate, his dark eyes narrowing to slits. "I'm glad you recognize that. Don't forget it."

His tone made her a little breathless. What would she do if Max turned into Simon? She'd have to be long gone before that ever happened. He'd make himself long gone before that ever happened.

She finished her omelet and put her hand over her cup when the waitress swung by to offer refills.

Max pushed his plate away and crumpled up a napkin next to it. "Do you have Arnoff's address?"

"Yes. When are you going out there?"

"I think it's best if I wait until night."

"In case Mrs. Arnoff isn't cooperative?"

His hand jerked and the water in the glass he'd been holding sloshed and the ice tinkled. "I wouldn't hurt Dr. Arnoff's wife."

Her cheeks burned. "I didn't mean that at all. I just… I mean in case you have to break in or something."

His shallow breath deepened and he seemed to unclench his jaw. "I won't hurt her. I won't do that."

She didn't want to probe too deeply into whether or not he'd hurt civilians for Tempest. Whatever he'd done for the agency, it disturbed him profoundly.

"She must know by now her husband's dead. Maybe she's not even home." She patted the newspaper on the chair between them. "I suppose there's nothing in the paper about the mayhem at the lab."

"No journalists even know about the lab, do they? Do the police in that area make a habit of patrolling around the lab?"

"No. We had our own security force. No police."

"They knew it was there?"

"They knew it was a top secret government entity. The lab's security force had given the local cops instructions to keep their distance."

"Then maybe nothing's been discovered yet. Did family members ever drop by?"

"I…"

"Other employees' family members."

She pursed her lips. She hadn't been about to tell him she had no family again. Guess she'd already beaten that particular dead horse. "I was going to say, I never saw any family members there. A lot of the lab employees didn't even reside in New Mexico. They lived elsewhere and had come out here for the assignment. I got the impression most left their families behind."

"Except Dr. Arnoff."

"He was the head of the lab, so he was a permanent fixture."

"Did he tend to work long hours? Sleep at the lab?"

"He did."

"Then his wife may not even know he's dead."

"Perhaps not. You're not going to tell her, are you?"

He held up his hands. "Not me, and I doubt if she'd take kindly to a stranger snooping around and asking questions."

She sat forward in her chair, hunching over the table. "That's why I need to go with you. I'm sure she remembers me. We met a few times. I can get us into the house by telling her Dr. Arnoff sent me to collect something. Once we're in the house, you can do your spy thing."

"As you delicately pointed out before, I can get into the house and she'll never know I was there."

"But my way might be easier."

"I think you'd be safer here at the hotel."

Folding her arms, she sat back in her chair while Max left some money on the check tray. He didn't plan to leave until dark, so she still had some time to work on him. "What are your plans in the meantime?"

"Shopping."

"A little retail therapy? I never would've guessed you were the sort."

He waved his finger up and down to take in her wrinkled blouse. "I was thinking of you. Do you want to pick up a few clothes here?"

"That would be great, but you don't have to come along."

"Humor me."

FOR THE NEXT few hours, she humored him. She picked up some jeans and T-shirts, a comfortable pair of ankle boots and some sneakers. She added some underwear and a few more toiletries. Max picked out a small carry-on suitcase for the plane trip he was convinced she'd be taking. She let him believe that.

He paid cash for everything from a seemingly endless supply of money even when she offered to use her credit card, which he refused and told her to put away.

She wasn't going to allow him to pay for everything, so when he ducked into a sandwich shop to get some drinks she headed toward an ATM.

Placing the edge of her card at the slot, her hand wavered. It had to be okay to use her card just once. The machine piled up the bills for her to snatch. She tucked them into her purse and returned to the front of the sandwich shop.

Max approached her, carrying two drinks in front of him. "Are you going to get that other pair of shoes?"

"No, I decided against it. I don't want to spend any more of your money." She held out her own cash to him. "And I really want to pay you back."

Max reached out and squeezed her shoulder. "Don't worry about it. I appreciate the gesture, but you keep the cash just in case." He handed her a soda and picked up her shopping bags. "I don't know about you, but I need a nap after last night's activities."

She could use a nap, too, but sleeping in the same room as Max was awkward—at least for her. He seemed all business now, definitely not as friendly as when he was her patient. But he hadn't known the extent of his enslavement to Tempest at that point and that she'd been injecting him with poison. He had no reason to be friendly to her.

He'd parked his car in the parking structure below

the mall, and they took the elevator into the bowels of the garage.

As they approached the blue sedan, she turned to him suddenly. "Where'd you get this car? Why do you have all that cash?"

He clicked the remote and put a finger to his lips. "I still have some secrets."

She eyed the car as he opened the trunk and swung her bags inside. It didn't look like a spy's car unless it had special, hidden gadgets.

"Does this thing have an ejection seat or turn into a hovercraft?"

He opened the passenger door for her and cocked his head. "I don't think it can even do eighty miles an hour."

The car went sixty on the highway on the way back to the hotel. Max rolled into the hotel's parking garage, and they returned to the room.

He pulled the drapes closed on the gray day and stretched out on the bed with his tablet propped up on his knees.

She pointed at the computer. "I thought you were going to sleep."

"I am. I'm actually reading a book. Even though it's a good one, I should be drifting off any minute—and you should, too."

She sat on the edge of the bed and toed off her shoes. Then she fell backward, her knees bent and her feet still planted on the floor, and stared at the ceiling.

She should've never taken the job offer from Dr. Arnoff. It had seemed too good to be true—a chance to practice medicine without the medical license. Now she was paying for her lies. She always did.

"Do you generally sleep with your legs hanging off the bed?"

"I'm almost too tired to move."

"Shopping does that to me, too."

"I don't think it was the shopping." She hoisted herself up on her elbows. "I think it's more the threats on my life and the fact that my job was a sham."

"Sorry."

She studied his face. Was he being sarcastic?

He stared back at her, his dark eyes serious, not a hint of sarcasm. Had he lost that ability, too?

No, he meant it. His life was in the toilet and he still had empathy for her. Guess the T-101 hadn't worked that great on him if it had been designed to erase human emotions. Max kept a tight rein on his feelings, but he definitely had them.

"Thanks. I'm sorry, too. Sorry that you're going through this. Sorry that I was a party to it."

He dropped his gaze to his book. "Let's try to get some sleep."

Folding her legs on the bed, she rolled to her side and closed her eyes. If Max thought he was leaving her here when he went to Dr. Arnoff's, he had another think coming.

This agent, this damaged man, was her only hope of returning to a life with any semblance of normalcy—not that she'd ever had that before.

THIS TIME SHE woke up first. She scooted to the edge of the mattress and peered through the gloom at Max fast asleep on the other bed, the tablet rising and falling on his chest with every deep breath.

Even in repose, sleeping on his back, he looked primed and ready. Could he ever really relax?

She rolled to the other side of the bed and slipped off

the edge. Tiptoeing around the room, she gathered a few of her new purchases and retreated to the bathroom.

She peeled off the clothes she'd dressed in yesterday morning, never dreaming she was heading into a nightmare, one worse than the previous nightmare she'd already lived through.

Did the nightmares ever end?

She brushed her teeth and washed her face. She dabbed on some moisturizer and added a little makeup. She didn't want to scare Mrs. Arnoff before she could talk her way into the house.

She padded on bare feet back into the room, her dirty clothes tucked under one arm, her shoes hanging from her fingertips.

"I was getting used to those slacks and blouse."

She jumped and dropped a shoe.

In the darkness of the room, Max was watching her from the bed, a pillow wedged beneath his neck.

She swept the shoe from the floor and stacked the armful of clothes on top of the suitcase Max had bought, still believing she would hop on a plane to somewhere.

"If I never see these slacks again, it will be too soon. I could toss them down the trash chute and be perfectly happy." She scraped at a spot on the navy blue pant leg. "Th-there are spots of blood on them that I never noticed before."

"You can send them to the dry cleaner while you wait for me." He swung his legs from the bed, raising his arms above his head in a long stretch.

"Yeah, about that." She busied her hands folding the clothes. "I'm going with you."

"No." He dropped his arms and shoved off the bed. "I have no idea what I'm going to find at Arnoff's house."

"You're probably going to find Mrs. Arnoff." She wedged

her hands on her hips. "She knows me. She'll let me in the house. She'll let me go through her husband's things if I tell her he sent me. She'll give me his computer."

"Unless she knows he's dead somehow."

"I don't think she will. You said yourself that news of the lab won't leak out until everything's cleaned up. And if she does—" she shrugged "—I'll make up another story to get us inside based on what she thinks she knows."

"Why are you so hell-bent on coming along? You don't owe me anything. I believe you that you knew nothing about the T-101 and Tempest's true mission."

"I'm not volunteering out of a sense of guilt." Clearly, she needed to use a new justification. "I don't want you to leave me here alone. You're the only person who can help me now, the only one I can turn to."

His nostrils flared. "Are you really afraid to stay here by yourself?"

"I'd feel better if I came along with you." She waved a hand at the window. "I don't know what's out there. I don't know who's out there, and I'm certainly not prepared to meet them if they come after me."

He crossed to the window and pressed his forehead against the glass as if assessing the danger below. "I think you'd be fine here, but if you're not comfortable, you can come with me."

Ava released a measured breath, not quite a sigh. "I would feel more comfortable, and I think I can get us into the house."

He held up his hand. "We'll see when we get there. I'm going to brush my teeth and get some gear together."

It was exactly that gear she was counting on to keep her safe. She'd played on Max's natural protective instincts to get him to agree to let her come along, but it hadn't been a total ruse. What would she do here alone? What would she do if someone came after her?

For now she'd stick to Max and his gear.

While he got ready, she turned on the TV, not that she expected to see any news about the lab. Tempest or the CIA would clamp down on that story. When she and Max parted ways, could she trust the CIA? Tempest had presumably been operating, unchecked, right under the nose of the agency.

Max slung a bag across his chest, gripping the strap with one hand. "Are you ready?"

She'd think about whom to trust when she and Max parted once they reached that point. She hadn't been lying to him. Right now, he was all she had.

She tossed the remote control on the bed. "Ready."

They took the elevator to the second floor and then jogged down the stairwell, their shoes slapping against the metal steps.

Max pushed through the fire door and she followed him across a short hallway to a side exit that led to the parking structure.

The parking lot had cleared out some since they'd returned to the hotel from shopping, and it looked as if they'd missed the dinner crowd leaving for their restaurants.

Max unlocked the car and hoisted his bag into the backseat.

She scrambled into the passenger side of the car before he could change his mind.

They snapped their seat belts in unison and Max slipped the key into the ignition. It clicked.

"What the…?" His fingers hovered over the dangling keys.

Ava's nostrils flared. "What's that smell?"

"Ava, get out!" He yanked off his seat belt as she stared at him with her mouth agape.

He popped the release for her and then nudged her shoulder. "Get out of the car now and run for the exit!"

He reached into the backseat and a surge of adrenaline pulsed through her veins. She snagged her bag from the floor of the car and shoved at the door. It fell open and she stumbled out of the car.

"Get to the stairwell." Max sprinted behind the car, the black bag banging against his hip.

She didn't know why the hell they were running, but when Max Duvall yelled "run" in that tone of voice, she obeyed.

He crowded behind her, urging her to move faster.

Just when she smacked her palms against the cold metal of the stairwell door, an explosion rocked her off her feet, driving her against the door.

As Max smashed against her back, she jerked her head over her shoulder—just in time to see their ride go up in flames.

Chapter Seven

Max cranked his head around, squinting through the black, acrid smoke billowing from his stolen car. No collateral damage. *Please, God, no civilians.*

He peeled himself away from Ava, flattened against the stairwell door. "Are you okay?"

She nodded, covering her ears with her hands.

The noise from the explosion hadn't affected him. He still had enough T-101 coursing through his bloodstream to make him immune to such things.

"Did you see anyone else up here when we went to the car?"

"What?"

He put his lips close to her ear, which had to be ringing. "Any other people. Was anyone else on this level?"

"I didn't see anyone."

"Let's get out of here." He reached around her and pressed the door handle down. The door swung open, and he had to catch Ava around the waist as she tripped.

They'd been discovered. How?

Footsteps echoed in the stairwell, and Max pulled the gun from its shoulder holster and held it against his chest, beneath his jacket.

A man and two women, faces white, eyes wide, met

them on the next landing. The man gripped the handrail. "What happened?"

"A car on level four is on fire."

"Fire?" One of the women grabbed the man's arm. "That sounded like an explosion."

Max shrugged. "I don't know. Maybe the flames reached the gas tank. We called 911."

As if on cue sirens called in the distance.

Ava put her hand out. "I wouldn't go up there. It's dangerous. Let the firemen handle it."

The man asked, "Nobody's up there? Nobody in the car?"

"No." Max grabbed Ava's hand and tugged her downstairs. He whispered in her ear. "When we get to the hotel room, throw your things in that suitcase. We're out of here."

Back in the room, Ava moved like a robot, but at least she moved like a fast robot. She swept the items she'd bought that afternoon into the new bag without one question on her lips. Despite the quick movements, she had a dazed expression on her face. That would change to fear soon enough when the shock wore off.

By the time they returned to the garage, the fire department had cordoned off every level except the first. In the confusion, people had abandoned their cars in the circular driveway. Max scanned the cars lined up, waiting for the valet.

"This one." He propelled Ava toward an older SUV with its hatchback open. He threw his bags in the back and pried her suitcase from her fingers and tossed it in after his.

With his hand against the small of her back he maneuvered her to the passenger side of the car. She stalled and for a minute he thought he was going to have to pick her up and drop her on the seat.

Then she placed one foot on the running board and he helped her inside.

Glancing around him at the chaos, he strode to the other side of the car, turned the keys dangling from the ignition and rolled away from the curb.

He paused to let another fire engine careen into the garage, and then he floored the accelerator and whipped around the corner.

Ava kept her eyes glued to the street in front of them as he dodged between cars, glancing at his rearview and side mirrors at every turn.

Tempest had tracked them down. He'd figured someone had been monitoring the cameras at the lab, and chances were his car had been made. He should've ditched it at the first possible opportunity instead of shopping with Ava.

He'd let his guard down.

As he zigzagged around the city making sure to lose any possible tail, Ava maintained a stony silence on her side of the car. His eyes darted to the side once or twice to make sure she was still breathing.

At the end of his circuitous route, he took one more look at his mirrors and headed for the freeway on-ramp. They still had a date with Dr. Arnoff's widow.

Ten minutes later, Ava shifted in her seat and expelled a long breath.

"Are you okay?"

"It's my fault."

He swiped a hand in the air between them. "Don't be ridiculous. It was my idea to go shopping. We probably should've just stayed in the room and left the car in the parking lot."

"No." She hiccuped and then covered her mouth with her fingers. "I led them to us by using my ATM card."

His gut rolled. "You used your ATM card?"

She nodded, covering her face with her hands. "I'm sorry. I didn't think. I didn't realize."

"When? At the mall when I was getting drinks?" He opened and closed his hands on the steering wheel. He shouldn't have left her alone for a second.

"Yes. I—I just wanted to pay you back. I guess it never occurred to me that they could track me that way." She dragged her fingers through her long, chestnut-brown hair and sighed. "That's not true. I had a moment right when I stuck the card in the slot, a moment of panic."

"Why didn't you tell me?"

"I convinced myself it meant nothing. It was too scary to contemplate that someone would be tracking me."

A muscle ticked in his jaw. He couldn't expect Ava to have the same instincts that he did. He should've warned her against using her cards. Obviously, she didn't understand the significance of the large amounts of cash he carried with him. Or she understood the importance for him but not herself. It probably was a form of denial.

Hunching his shoulders, he braced his hands against the steering wheel and extended his arms. "Don't worry about it now. It's a done deal."

"Your car…"

"Not mine."

"Stolen like this one?"

"Yes."

She blew out a ragged breath. "How did they find the car? How did they know what you were driving?"

"They probably have it on video from the cameras at the lab. I tried to take out as many cameras as I saw on my way into the lab, but I'm sure there were others hidden from view. Once you used your card at the mall, they knew where to look. They could've trained a satellite on the area."

"They're relentless, aren't they?"

"That's one word for it."

"And they have the advantage because they know who we are, and they're just some nameless, faceless assassins to us."

"Maybe, maybe not." He slowed the stolen SUV until the car behind them passed on the left and sped out of sight.

"Do you think you might know the man or men after us?"

"I might and you might if Tempest is sending its agents to take care of us."

She pinned her hands between her bouncing knees. "I can't imagine even one of my patients trying to kill me."

"Have you forgotten Simon already? Your patients, as you call them, are programmed to do just that. Tempest will tell lies to get them to do the job. Keep your eyes open for a familiar face."

"Ugh." She wrapped her arms around herself. "Where are we going now?"

"Dr. Arnoff's house, as planned."

She whipped her head around to face him. "Won't Tempest figure we'll be heading there?"

He squinted into the rearview mirror at a pair of headlights behind them and then let out a breath when the car turned off. "Tempest doesn't know what I know. They don't know if I've gone off the rails like Simon or if I've put any of the puzzle pieces together yet. That car bomb was meant to kill me or warn me."

"Uh, it blew up that car. I think the message was pretty clear."

He held up a finger. "Ah, but it didn't ignite right away. It's not like Tempest to make a mistake like that. As soon as I turned on the ignition, I sensed the danger. They had to know I'd figure it out."

"And if you hadn't?"

He shrugged. "We'd both be dead."

Her body stiffened and he silently cursed his insensitivity. She wasn't like him—cold, unfeeling.

"Sorry." His hand shot out and covered hers, clutching her thigh. His fingertips brushed her soft skin, and he felt her tremble. He slid his hand from hers and rested it on the console between them.

"Anyway, Tempest might not realize I need to search Arnoff's house. They know I know he's dead—end of story."

"And if they *are* at his house?"

"We'll take every precaution. Going to Arnoff's is worth the risk."

"If you say so. They'd probably figure us for a couple of lunatics going to Arnoff's after that car bomb, so we just might be safe."

"I can drop you off on the way, Ava." He wiped one palm on his jeans. "I can still take you to the airport."

"Then what? I go underground? Go into the witness protection program for spies?"

"I told you. Prospero can help you. You get on a plane to anywhere and call Prospero once you reach your destination. I can give you a contact number."

"You implied earlier that you couldn't trust Prospero."

"I can't trust anyone, but once you separate from me, you should be okay. You can tell them whatever you want. Just don't tell them you believed me. Tell them I'm insane. Tell them I held you against your will."

"What about you?"

"I'll figure it out."

"You'll figure it out a lot faster with me by your side. I may not be a real doctor, but I'm familiar with formulas, especially this one. If there's an antidote out there, I'm going to recognize it faster than you will."

"I appreciate the offer, but…"

She pounded the dashboard. "You keep getting this crazy idea that I'm doing this for your benefit. Don't you get it? I don't have anywhere else to go. You're it. You're my protector whether you want to be or not."

He wanted to be. The thought came out of nowhere and slammed against his chest. Just as quickly, he stuffed it away.

Skimming his palms along the steering wheel, he said, "It's going to be dangerous. I can't guarantee your safety."

"You've done a pretty good job of it so far." She jabbed a finger at the windshield. "Two more exits."

"Do me a favor when we get there."

She crossed her arms and gave him a wary look. "What?"

"Follow my lead."

"I've been doing that ever since you dragged me out of the lab."

"Any complaints?"

"I'm alive, aren't I?"

So far they both were and he intended to keep it that way.

Following her directions, he maneuvered the car through a well-heeled neighborhood. Looked like being employed as a mad scientist had its rewards.

Ava pulled a slip of paper from the pocket of her hoodie and peered at it. "Have we hit Hopi Drive yet?"

"Nope."

"It should be coming up."

"I'm not driving up and parking in front of the house. I'll drive by first and tuck the car away somewhere."

"Good idea, considering it's stolen."

"Any complaints?"

"Considering our car had been…disabled, none at all."

She directed him to Dr. Arnoff's house, and he slowed the car down to a crawl as he passed in front of it. Lights burned somewhere in the house and a late-model Mercedes crouched in the driveway.

"Do you know if that's Arnoff's car?"

"It's his wife's. He drives a Caddy and as far as I know it's still at the lab."

He wheeled around the corner, made a U-turn and parked at the curb. "I'm going to leave the doors unlocked and the key in the ignition. If anything happens in there, make a run for it. Take the car and don't look back."

Her tongue darted from her mouth and swept across her lower lip. "I'd wait for you."

"That might not be an option."

He cracked the door and she put a hand on his arm. "Are you really expecting trouble?"

"I always expect trouble."

She slid from the car and dropped to the ground on silent sneakers and then pushed the door closed. *Good.* He didn't have to tell her to be quiet. She was a fast learner.

"I hope nobody steals the car."

A dog barked in the distance and another howled an answer. Max put a finger to his lips.

He held out his hand behind him and she took it. Then he hunched over and crossed the street, pulling Ava close in his wake. Might as well not make it easy for someone watching to distinguish two figures in the night, even though they planned to knock on the front door.

When they reached the other side of the street, Max

followed the hedges bordering the sidewalk, the shoulder of his jacket brushing the stiff leaves.

He tucked Ava behind him as he edged around the corner, glancing up and down the block. Lights dotted the houses along the quiet residential neighborhood, but everyone must've turned in early for the night.

He kept to the available shadows and Ava stuck close to him, the flowery perfume she'd gotten at the department store tickling his nostrils.

They made their way up the driveway, skirting the luxury car. The porch light created a yellow crescent, encompassing the porch and a flower bed under the window. The fragrance from the colorful blooms matched the scent wafting from Ava.

Funny how smells could distinguish a place and time. Whatever happened, the particular smell of those flowers would always remind him of this night with Ava. No drug could take that away from him.

She whispered, "Are we going to knock? Unless she's already heard about the lab, she won't be surprised to see me."

"Go ahead."

Max turned and faced the street as she rang the doorbell. A footfall from inside the house had Ava standing up straight and plastering a smile on her face.

A muffled voice reached them through the heavy door. "Who is it?"

"Mrs. Arnoff, it's Ava Whitman—from the lab?"

A chain scraped and the door eased open. Mrs. Arnoff, a robe wrapped around her body, peered at them. "I thought that was you. Is everything okay at the lab?"

Mrs. Arnoff didn't know.

Ava widened her smile until her cheeks hurt. "Everything's fine. Dr. Arnoff is hard at work and sent me over to pick up a few things for him."

The door swung open. "I've been trying to call him for two days. He didn't mention that he was spending the night at the lab this time."

"You know how it gets there sometimes—crazy and our cell phone reception is nonexistent."

"He usually does get out to call me though." Her gaze shifted to Max. "Come on in."

Ava waved her hand at Max. "This is...Mike, my friend."

"Hello, Mike." Mrs. Arnoff offered her hand to Max. "I'm glad to see Ava has made some friends."

Ava winced. So, Dr. Arnoff had told his wife about her pathetic social existence.

"Ava and I have been friends for a while." Max draped his arm across her shoulder.

For a man with no emotions, he sure seemed to be getting into this role.

Mrs. Arnoff gestured to a half-full wineglass on the coffee table in front of the muted TV. "Would you like some wine? Something else?"

Ava folded her hands in front of her, trying not to twist her fingers. "No, thank you, Mrs. Arnoff."

"Lillian—please call me Lillian. I feel like I know you even though we've met just a few times. Charles talks about you a lot."

"Really?" Ava coughed. "Dr. Arnoff is brilliant. I'm so lucky to be working with him."

"Well, the feelings are mutual." Mrs. Arnoff shook her finger and Ava realized Lillian was slightly drunk.

That could make things easier.

"What did my husband want? It's just like him to send a woman to fetch for him."

Max stepped close to Ava and nudged the side of her hip. "His laptop. Isn't that what you told me, Ava? And samples, some kind of samples."

Ava nodded, the stupid smile still on her face, a breath trapped in her lungs. Max had just decided to go for it.

Lillian's brow furrowed and she tucked strands from her gray bob behind her ear. "His laptop's in his office, but I'm not sure what samples you mean. He doesn't keep any of his lab work at home."

"Let me grab the laptop first." Ava pivoted toward the hallway. "His office?"

"I'll show you."

Max cleared his throat. "Do you mind if I use your restroom?"

Ava shot him a glance beneath her lashes. Did he think he'd find the T-101 pills in the medicine cabinet?

"Right across from the office, Mike." She patted Ava's hand. "Follow us."

Lillian weaved toward the hallway and Ava got the crazy idea that if they shared a bottle of wine with her, she might just pass out.

When they reached the first two rooms in the hallway, Lillian pushed at the door on the right. "Bathroom in here."

Then she reached into the room across from the bathroom and flicked on a light. "He usually leaves his laptop on the corner of his desk. Did his computer go down at the lab or something?"

"He didn't tell me, Lillian. I just obey orders. He asks me to pick up his laptop—" she snapped her fingers "—I pick up his laptop."

"And samples?"

Ava scooped up the laptop from the desk and hugged

it to her chest. "He meant the blue pills. You know, the blue pills?"

Lillian tilted her head. "He doesn't tell me much about his work. Can you email him or something and ask him where they are?"

"I-it was an afterthought. Maybe they're not very important."

Lillian led her out of the office and winked before she turned off the light. "Maybe if we forget about it, Charles will come home to get them himself."

They stepped into the hallway, and Max came from the opposite end.

"Hope you don't mind. There was no hand soap in this bathroom, so I found another."

"That's fine."

As Lillian headed back to the living room, Ava squeezed Max's hand and he shook his head. No blue pills in the medicine cabinets, but at least they got the laptop.

"Are you sure you don't want some wine?" She grabbed her glass and gulped down the remainder of the burgundy liquid. "God knows, my husband's never home anymore to join me."

"Ava, why don't you have a glass with her? If you don't mind, Lillian, I'll just take a quick look in the garage since Ava mentioned he sometimes works out there."

Mrs. Arnoff blinked her eyes. "He does?"

"Yes, yes, he did say something about storing some work in the garage." Ava swept past Lillian and grabbed a glass from the wet bar in the corner. "I'd love to join you."

The boozy smile erased the confusion from Lillian's face. "Wonderful. It's an outstanding year for this particular cab."

She almost knocked the bottle over and Ava grabbed it. "Allow me."

Max had disappeared through the door to the attached garage, and Ava poured a generous amount of wine into Lillian's glass and a splash in her own.

She clinked her glass with Lillian's. "Here's to Dr. Arnoff."

"Wherever he is." Lillian took a long pull from her glass.

The knock on the front door startled them both.

Lillian put her glass down and brushed her fingers together. "Looks like we're going to have a party tonight without Charles."

She took a halting step toward the front door as Ava glanced at the garage. If that was the police reporting Dr. Arnoff's death, she'd better do some quick thinking and she could use Max's help.

Mrs. Arnoff was halfway to the front door when Max came barreling into the room. "Don't answer that."

"What?" Lillian stumbled to a stop.

"You shouldn't answer your door when you're home alone at night."

"But I'm not alone." Lillian spread her arms to take in the two of them and proceeded to the door.

"Wait." Max held up his hand.

A man yelled from the porch. "Mrs. Arnoff? It's the cable company. Several people in your area have been reporting outages."

Ava's heart thumped and she stepped back, glancing at the TV, still flickering with images. Lillian must have a great cable provider if they came out at this time of night.

Mrs. Arnoff reached the door and placed her hand on the knob while leaning toward the peephole. She called out, "I think my TV's fine." She glanced over her shoulder at Ava. "Don't you think so?"

Max charged forward and grabbed the laptop. Then he

took Ava's arm and whispered in her ear. "We need to get out of here. She just announced our presence."

"We still need to check, ma'am," the voice on the porch insisted.

Lillian took the chain off the door and Max yanked Ava toward the sliding door in the back.

As soon as Max slid open the back door, a crackling sound rang behind them and Lillian fell back into the room—missing half her head.

Chapter Eight

Ava didn't have time to react. Didn't have time to let loose with the scream gathering in her lungs.

Max yanked her out the back door and sped across the patio toward the fence on the side. She moved mechanically, still in shock. His voice grated in a harsh whisper. "I don't know if they saw us or not, but they'll know someone was there. Even if they didn't hear Lillian speaking to you, they'll notice the second wineglass."

They reached the fence and Max bent over and cupped his hands to hoist her up.

She wedged one sneakered foot in his hands and grabbed the top of the stuccoed fence. She pulled herself up and over, landing in some dirt on the other side. "Slip the laptop over."

She stepped onto a sprinkler cover and reached up with trembling hands. The hard edge of the laptop met her grasping fingers and she eased it over the wall and hugged it to her chest. "Got it."

Two seconds later, Max vaulted over the fence, landing beside her. "Any vicious beasts in residence?"

She gulped. "Not yet."

She followed his lead across the backyard, hunching forward and keeping to the shadows, her knees trembling with each step. The next fence presented a bigger problem, as spiky hedges bordered the entire length.

She huffed out a breath, as fear clawed through her chest. "How are we going to get over that fence?"

"Don't worry. We got this. The hedges are stiff enough to use as a ledge."

Before she could respond, he took the laptop from her and his hands encircled her waist. He lifted her off the ground, high into the air. "Find a stable point to get a foothold."

With her legs dangling in the air, she tapped her foot against the dense hedge until she found a stationary spot. "I think I'm good here."

"Is there a place to put your hands?"

She groped along the edge of the bush, ignoring the sharp pain from the nettles, and found the rounded top of the stucco fence that separated the two houses. "Yeah."

"Are they coming?"

Glancing across the yard, she shook her head. "I don't see anything coming this way."

He released her and she put her weight on her hands, her feet lightly dancing over the hedge until she could swing her legs over the fence. She let herself drop to the ground.

Her panting merged with the panting coming from behind her and she spun around and nearly tripped over a furry, four-legged creature.

Before she could warn Max, he dropped down beside her with the laptop tucked beneath one arm. The dog backed up, lifted his nose and let out a howl.

"Shh." Ava dropped to her knees and placed her hands on either side of the mutt's head and rubbed his ears. "You don't need to do that."

The howl ended and the little dog pranced around their feet in excitement.

Max nudged her back with his knee. "Let's get going before he changes his mind."

Rising to her feet, Ava chucked the pup under the chin, reluctant to leave the one spot of normalcy in the entire evening. "You're a good boy."

They dashed across the yard with the dog at their heels, but at least he'd decided they were friends instead of foes.

The fence on the other side, leading to the street where Max had parked the car, posed less of an obstacle than the other fence, and they both hopped over easily, landing on the sidewalk across from the stolen SUV.

Ava took a step toward the curb, but Max had other ideas. He grabbed her wrist and pulled her back.

"Hold on." He nudged her behind his back as he ventured into the street, looking both ways. "Stay with me."

She practically stepped on his heels as she jogged across the street in his wake.

When they reached the car, he cupped his hands at the window to peer inside. He nodded and carefully opened the door.

She did the same on her side and let out a long breath when she collapsed on the passenger seat. She twisted around and placed the laptop on the floor of the backseat.

Max started the car and then manually turned off the headlights that came on automatically. He put the car in Reverse and backed up, avoiding Dr. Arnoff's street.

It didn't do any good.

JUST WHEN HE reached the next cross street, a car, its headlights blinding them, came roaring around the corner.

Max didn't miss a beat. The Tempest agents must've gone out to the street, listening to every sound in the night—the howl of the dog and the engine of the car. He continued his reverse turn around the block, and when the other car turned down the same block, Max punched the accelerator and sped past the car in the other direction.

His eyes darted to the side mirror. The driver of the other car hadn't bothered turning around. He'd taken off after them in Reverse. That gave him and Ava an advantage.

Max clenched the steering wheel. Now if he only had a high-performance car instead of this clunky SUV. They were fast approaching the end of the block, and he'd have to make a hard right turn or end up in someone's living room.

He glanced at Ava's white face. "Hang on."

The other car was almost abreast of them. Max eased off the accelerator and jerked the steering wheel to the right. The tires squealed but stayed on the road—for the most part.

Cranking her head around, Ava peered between the two front seats and out the back window. "They made the turn. Now they're facing the right direction."

"That's good. Now they can go even faster."

"How is that good? They're going to catch up to us."

"I noticed something on that first road we turned on just off the freeway. I was cursing this SUV a few seconds ago, but I think its wide body is just what we need."

"If you say so. Are they going to start shooting into this car?"

"If they get the chance." With the other car roaring closely behind them, Max kept floating to the left to keep them from drawing up next to them. But he had plans to take them to a wider stretch, as long as they didn't start taking potshots at the back of the SUV.

He careened around the next corner toward the freeway, keeping the SUV in the middle of the road so the other driver couldn't see what was on the horizon.

When Max neared the dip in the road that he'd noticed before, he slowed the SUV until the other car was almost at their bumper. Then he pulled to the right and slammed on the brakes.

The black sedan screamed past them and hit the dip going almost seventy. The front end of the car flew into the air, its spinning wheels leaving the asphalt. It seemed to float for a second and then crashed to earth with the shrill sound of twisting metal. Max saw a single wheel go airborne before he headed down another street for the freeway.

A siren wailed in the distance and Ava pressed her hands to her heart. "Someone had already called the police."

"Too bad there are no witnesses to the crash since we'll be long gone. I wonder if the cops are going to discover Mrs. Arnoff's body?"

Ava pinned her hands between her knees. "I'm slowing you down, aren't I? They wouldn't have tracked us down if I hadn't used my ATM card like an idiot."

"Don't keep beating yourself up about that. You're a civilian. Your mind doesn't work like mine. I should've known Tempest would pay a visit to Mrs. Arnoff—just didn't realize they'd show up so soon and kill her."

"You did know they'd pay her a visit, but in the end it was worth the risk, wasn't it?" She jerked her thumb at the backseat. "We got Arnoff's laptop."

"That's another thing. I never would've known about that laptop, Ava."

She sighed and tilted her head back. "What now?"

"We need to take a look at Arnoff's computer, see if he has any information about an antidote or the location of more blue pills."

"Even looking at his notes on the serum will help us, help me. I just might be able to figure out a way to neutralize the drug's effects."

"And I need to warn the other Tempest agents."

He could feel her gaze searching his face.

"Why do you need to do that?"

"Tempest is planning something big. All of my assignments have been leading to something big. If Simon hadn't gone off the rails like he did, I'd still be working for Tempest, still be on the inside."

"You still wouldn't have gotten all the names of the other agents. Tempest kept you apart, right?"

"That's right, unless we worked an assignment together like Simon and I did. My guess is Tempest won't be putting any agents together anymore. Anyway, I'm hoping to get the other agents' names from Arnoff's laptop, unless you have their names."

"I just knew a few names, usually first names only. Most of my patients didn't want to get personal."

He slid a quick glance her way. He'd wanted to get personal with her even though she'd known them by their numbers. "They may have given you phony names anyway."

"Did you and Simon discuss your memory lapses and suspicions when you had that assignment together?"

"Not then, but we became aware of each other. Later he found me in Brussels. I don't know how he found me and I don't know how he knew I was having the same experiences he was having, unless it was something he noticed during that joint assignment."

"Did you ever ask him?"

"Of course I did. He wouldn't tell me. I don't know if it was for his safety or mine."

"Or someone else's."

He raised an eyebrow. "You think he had someone on the inside?"

She shrugged. "Where are we going?"

"We're going to drive for a while and find a place to spend the night. Then we're going to delve into the private world of Dr. Charles Arnoff."

He bypassed the lights of Albuquerque and headed toward a small town on its outskirts. He'd need to swap this car for another. He had the cash to buy a used car and avoid the danger of getting pulled over for auto theft.

Ava tapped on the window. "How about that place? Not too small, not too big."

"Why don't we want a small motel?"

"Too few people checking in, so we'd be more memorable."

"And why not too big?"

"Too crowded, so we wouldn't be able to keep track of the other guests coming and going." She tilted her head. "Was that a test?"

"If you're going to help me out for a little while longer, I need to prepare you better."

"But you did tell me not to use my cards. I wasn't listening to the subtext of your words."

"You shouldn't have to listen for subtext—this is life and death. I'm going to spell it out for you from now on."

From now on? He took the next turn a little too fast. Ava could help him figure out what was on Arnoff's computer, and then she needed to get out of here—away from him.

He swiped the back of his hand across the beads of sweat on his upper lip.

"The pills?" She hunched forward in her seat, her brow furrowed.

"Yeah, I could use another, but I'm going to try to hold out."

"You're not going to hold out as long as you did yesterday. That's just dangerous."

"It'll be dangerous when I run out of the meds, too."

"That's not going to happen."

He swung into the parking lot of the midsize motel. The night clerk was talking to another guest when they walked into the lobby.

Max sized up the other man with a glance—tourist looking to escape his room filled with the wife and kids.

Although he had some cards with an alternate ID, Max repeated his bankruptcy story and the clerk was only too happy to take cash.

"The luck's with you tonight. We have two rooms left and both have a king-size bed."

"Great." He'd be spending the night on the floor.

Max handed over the cash and the clerk slid two key cards across the counter. "Enjoy your stay."

Ava tapped her card against her chin. "Free Wi-Fi?"

"Yes, ma'am."

They left the clerk and the guest to their conversation and headed for the side door that led to their room. Steam rose from the outdoor pool and Jacuzzi to their right, and heads bobbed above the gurgling water.

Max rolled his shoulders. "That looks inviting about now."

"Tell me about it." Ava rubbed her head.

He stopped and placed his hands on her shoulders. "Are you okay? That was a wild car ride and you must've gotten jostled around. I'm sorry I didn't even ask if you were hurt."

Her lashes fluttered as her chest rose and fell quickly.

The pulse in her throat beat out her scent, and it was as intoxicating as the bougainvillea creeping along the gate surrounding the pool.

"I—I'm fine. I didn't think we were going to get out of there alive."

He gave her shoulders a squeeze before releasing them. "Too bad they heard Mrs. Arnoff talking to us before she opened the door. We could've gotten away and they would've never known we were there."

"Too bad Lillian opened the door at all. She'd still be alive."

"No, she wouldn't be, Ava." He turned back to the lit pathway, and she followed him silently.

He told her he was going to be truthful, and that meant making sure she knew the tenacity of the enemy they faced. Tempest came to do a job and Mrs. Arnoff's death was the goal of that job. Finding him and Ava there had just been a bonus.

They reached their room, and Max opened the door for Ava, pushing it wide. The big bed dominated the space, but Max did his best to ignore it.

He dropped his bag in the corner. "You must be starving. I noticed a pizza place a few doors down. I'm sure they deliver here."

"That sounds fine." She parked the laptop on the credenza next to the TV and placed her suitcase next to his duffel. "Should we start in with the laptop?"

"Let's get some food in first. It might take some work to get around Dr. Arnoff's security." He reached into the front pocket of his jeans and shook the tin back and forth, tumbling the pills inside. "Besides, I've got four pills left. We have plenty of time."

She rolled her eyes at him. "Is that your attempt at humor?"

"Not very funny, huh?" He tossed the tin onto the nightstand.

"Don't give up your day job."

"Now, *that's* funny." He yanked open the single drawer of the nightstand and pulled out a telephone book. "Pizza, pizza. Here it is. We're on Cochise Road, right?"

She perched on the edge of the bed, reached across him and plucked up the notepad next to the phone. "Yep, Cochise Road."

He held the receiver of the phone to his ear. "What do you want? The works?"

"Excluding anchovies and pineapple." She wrinkled her nose, looking adorable, and *adorable* wasn't a word he used often—ever.

He ordered the pizza and then pulled some change from his pocket. He jingled it in his palm. "I saw a vending machine out by the pool. Do you want something to drink?"

"Diet anything."

His gaze swept her lithe frame from head to toe. "Because you look like you need to diet."

"When you're short, you always need to watch what you consume."

"You're the doctor."

"Not really."

Her solemn voice and downturned lips had him taking two steps toward her and brushing her jawline with his fingertips. "You were the best damned doctor I ever had."

"I was injecting you with poison, and I didn't even know it. Some doctor."

"You had a great bedside manner when you were doing it." He tugged on one wavy lock of her dark brown hair, and she flashed him a quick smile from her tremulous lips.

"Lock the door behind me and don't open it for anyone. The pizza's not going to get here that fast."

"Got it."

He stood outside the door of the motel room until he heard the dead bolt and the chain. Then he followed the path back to the gated pool with a whistle on his lips.

He hadn't felt this hopeful in a long time—not since he and Simon had figured out what Tempest was doing to its agents. He finally had someone on his side—someone who offered real help, not a hothead like Simon.

What had Ava done to lose her chance at a medical license? He couldn't imagine her doing something illegal, although she hadn't been squeamish about stealing cars and lying to Lillian Arnoff. In fact, she'd adapted to life on the run more quickly than he would've imagined.

He braced a hand against the soda machine outside the pool gate and studied the selections. A woman's low laugh bubbled from the hot tub, followed by a soft squeal and a sigh.

He closed his eyes. He'd like to try to make Ava sigh like that—a sigh of contentment instead of one of exhaustion or fear.

His lids flew open, and he fed some coins in the slot and punched the button for a diet soda and then repeated the process for a root beer. He'd try to get a good night's sleep tonight and pop one of the precious pills in the morning.

Gripping a cold can in each hand, he glanced over his shoulder at the steam rising from the hot tub, the heads so close together now as to be indistinguishable. Lucky bastard.

When he returned to the room, he tapped on the door with the edge of one can. "It's me."

She slipped the chain from the door and opened it.

"I hope you looked out that peephole before opening the door."

"I did, although that didn't help Mrs. Arnoff, did it?"

"Mrs. Arnoff was a fool—and drunk. A bad combination."

She took her soda from his hand. "She paid a high price for a few glasses of wine."

"She paid a high price for being married to Dr. Arnoff." He slammed the door behind him and threw the chain in place again. "And you're paying a high price for working with the man."

"Maybe Dr. Arnoff didn't realize how Tempest was using its agents. Maybe he truly thought you were a force for good."

"Then why all the secrecy? Why keep you out of the loop?"

"That's easy." She popped the tab on her can and bubbles sprayed from the lid. "What he was doing was completely unethical. T-101 hadn't been properly tested or vetted or reviewed or approved by the FDA. It was a dream situation for Dr. Arnoff. Tempest was funding an illegal lab for him, a lab where he had complete control."

"And unwitting guinea pigs at his disposal."

Ava wandered to the laptop on the credenza. "I powered it up while you were gone. It's password-protected and there's not much life left on the battery."

"We're going to have to crack that password." A pulse pounded in his temple, making his eye twitch.

"And we're going to have to get a new power cord."

"How much juice does it have left?" He rubbed his eye with his fist.

"About an hour, and I just might be able to figure out that password."

"How are you going to do that?" He dropped into the

one chair in the room, stationed by the sliding door that led to a small patio.

A rosy pink blush rushed across her cheeks. "I went through Dr. Arnoff's desk once at the lab."

"Really?" He cocked one eyebrow at her. Definitely not as sweet as she appeared.

She spread out her hands. "It was because of the lab. He was so secretive, I decided to do a little digging of my own."

"You obviously didn't dig very far if you didn't find out the real purpose behind T-101."

"No, I never did get that far, but I did discover a bunch of his passwords. There's a good reason why cyber security people advise against writing down your passwords."

He pointed at the computer. "Have you tried any of them yet? Do you even remember them?"

"I remember some of them. I'd just tried a few when you knocked on the door, but I was afraid of draining the battery."

Another knock sounded on the door, and Max held up one finger. "Hang on."

He squinted through the peephole while grabbing the door handle. "It's pizza time."

Still, he felt for his weapon tucked into his holster before opening the door. Anyone could impersonate a pizza delivery guy, just like anyone could impersonate a cable repairman.

The pizza guy held the box in front of him. "Pizza?"

"That's us. How much do I owe you?"

"That's fifteen ninety-five."

Max traded a twenty for the pizza. "Keep it. Thanks."

"Thank you."

Max locked up again and put the pizza on the credenza next to the laptop. "Do you want to try again?"

"My mind is in a fog right now, and I don't want to waste the battery trying out twenty different passwords. I'd rather wait for that power cord."

He tapped the box. "Sit down and have a slice or two before you faint from hunger." Or was he the only one ravenous?

Ava looked around the room. "Our seating options are limited, aren't they?"

"You can have the chair. I'll take the bed."

"Just don't leave any crumbs in there."

He could've said something about crumbs in the bed and whether or not he'd kick her out for the offense, but he refrained. She obviously hadn't considered the sleeping arrangements yet.

He dropped two pieces of pizza on one of the paper plates provided by the pizzeria and handed it to Ava. "Looks good."

Then he filled up his own plate and reclined on the bed against a couple of pillows. The cool pillow felt soothing against the back of his head, which had started throbbing, along with his temple, in the past ten minutes.

Had to be hunger. He tore into a slice of pizza with his teeth. The flavor of the spicy pepperoni filled his mouth, and he wiped his chin with a napkin.

Ava took a small bite from the tip of the triangle and dabbed her lips. "Mmm, that hit the spot."

He waved his pizza at her. "You *are* going to eat more, right?"

"Of course." Her gaze slid to the computer on the credenza. "I'm dying to find out what's on there."

"It's almost eleven o'clock, Ava. We're not going to find a power cord at this time of night. We can pick up a cord first thing tomorrow."

"You have a point." She leaned forward and closed the lid of the laptop. Then she collapsed back in the chair and took a big bite of her pizza.

"Are you going to tell me how Tempest recruited you?"

He dropped his crust on the plate and brushed his fingers together, trying to buy time.

"The short answer?"

"Do you have any other kind?"

"I was a Green Beret, and I disobeyed orders. Tempest saved me from a court-martial."

"D-did you do something wrong? Something illegal?"

"I saved four men in my unit." His mouth twisted. "But I still disobeyed orders. They were bad orders."

"Tempest must've been on the lookout for guys like you."

"Yep."

"Where's your family? Do they know you're going through this?"

"That's another thing Tempest looks out for—I have no family."

"Parents, siblings?"

"I was an only child and my parents died in an embassy bombing in Africa. My dad was with the State Department."

"I'm sorry."

"That's why I enlisted." He rose from the bed and placed two more pizza slices on his plate. "I didn't tell you my sob story to ruin your appetite. Eat up."

She nibbled at the edges of her second piece of pizza. "Did you go into the service with the intention of saving the world or just avenging the deaths of your parents?"

"Does it matter? It led me to the same place."

"I never knew all this about you when you were my patient."

"It's not something I'm going to blurt out to a medical doctor."

"Stop calling me that." She took a fast gulp of soda and her eyes watered.

"You know it's coming, don't you, Ava?"

She looked up from wiping her eyes with a napkin. "What?"

"How did Dr. Arnoff recruit you? I showed you mine, and now you definitely have to show me yours."

The pink tide rushed into her cheeks once again.

He hadn't meant that as a sexual reference, but if she'd taken it that way then maybe this attraction he felt for her wasn't one-sided.

She tossed the napkin onto her plate and folded her hands in her lap. "While I was still in medical school, a clinical student, my brother thought it was a good idea to use my credentials to steal meds and write prescriptions."

"Addict?"

"Yes, just like our father before him."

"How did his actions impact you? I can see reprimanding you for carelessness or poor judgment, but you didn't steal the stuff."

The knuckles of her laced fingers turned white, and she clamped her lower lip between her teeth.

"Did you?"

"I didn't steal anything…but they thought I did."

"Because you let them believe it." He rolled the can between his palms. "You took the fall for your brother."

"I had to. He was facing his third strike." Her chin jutted forward, and her lips thinned out to a straight line. "He has an illness, and he was not going to be let off with a slap on the wrist and a treatment plan."

"So, you allowed him to ruin your career and everything you'd worked for?"

"It's complicated." She rose from the chair and wedged her shoulder against the sliding glass door. "Our parents were a mess. Mom crashed her car into a tree while driving drunk and Dad dealt with the loss of his drinking partner by ingesting even more drugs before OD'ing. Even before they died, I'd always taken care of Cody. I guess I didn't do a very good job."

"Because raising a child is not the job for another child." He plumped the pillows behind him and massaged his temples. "Where is your brother now?"

She traced a pattern on the window with her fingertip. "He's in Utah, working at one of the ski resorts near Salt Lake as a snowboard instructor. I think he's tending bar until all the lifts are open up there."

"Did he even feel a shred of guilt letting you take the fall? Did he ever make any kind of restitution?"

"Sure he did." A half smile curved her lip. "He hooked me up with Dr. Arnoff."

A shaft of pain flashed behind his eyes, and he squeezed them shut.

"Are you okay?"

"Slight headache." He pinched the bridge of his nose. "Your brother knew Dr. Arnoff?"

"He'd met him on a hike in the Grand Canyon." She turned to face him, leaning her back against the glass of the door. "Cody didn't tell me at the time, but he and Dr. Arnoff had shared some hallucinogens."

His eyes flew open, his brows jumping. "Dr. Arnoff was into psychedelics?"

"Dr. Arnoff was into experimentation. Anyway, when Cody told Dr. Arnoff about me, the doctor said he might have a job for me at his lab. The rest—" she spread her hands "—is history."

"That's gotta be the weirdest job referral ever."

"Yeah, and look where it got me." She pushed off the door and folded her plate in half. "All kinds of alarms were going off in my head after I spoke to Dr. Arnoff, but I ignored every last one of them. I just wanted to see patients, treat people. I allowed that desire to override my common sense."

"I get it, Ava."

"You would." She buzzed around the napkins and packets of cheese, ending her confessional.

He did get it—and her. No wonder Tempest had targeted them both.

He forced his heavy limbs off the bed and helped her clean up. "Do you want the rest of the pizza?"

"We can have it for breakfast."

"My kinda girl."

He just wished he didn't mean that so literally. He'd always looked forward to seeing Ava at the clinic, and spending this time with her under dire conditions had strengthened that attraction even more for some crazy reason.

He coughed. "Do you want to use the bathroom first?"

"Sure."

While Ava was in the bathroom, he dropped a couple of pillows on the floor and found an extra blanket in the closet. He'd set up a serviceable place to sleep by the time she finished brushing her teeth.

She exited the bathroom with a hitch in her step. "What's that?"

"My bed for the night."

Her gaze shifted to the real bed. "You can have the bed. You were just complaining about a headache. You take it. That blanket isn't even going to cover your feet."

"I've slept on a lot worse."

"I'm sure you have, Max, but that's not the point." She

stuffed her clothes in her suitcase and perched on the edge of the bed in the long cotton T-shirt she'd bought for a nightgown. "If you won't trade, then just join me. This bed is big enough for the two of us."

His pulse thudded thickly in his throat. "I don't want to crowd you."

"I don't take up a lot of room, and I wouldn't be able to sleep knowing you were on the hard floor."

"It's not that bad." He tapped his foot on the blanket.

"Max."

"Okay, you don't have to twist my arm. Pick your side and I'll hit the bathroom."

After he brushed his teeth, he braced his hands on the sink and leaned into the mirror. He had no intention of making a move on Ava, but sleeping next to her just might drive him crazier than the lack of T-101. With any luck, she'd be sound asleep by the time he made it back to the bedroom.

He stripped to his boxers and then considered putting his T-shirt back on. He could always sleep on top of the covers with that blanket he'd found in the closet.

He turned off the light and eased open the door to the room. He could barely discern Ava's small frame on the far side of the bed, lying on her side, the covers pulled up to her nose.

The lamp on his side of the bed still burned, and he crept across the carpeted floor and placed his folded clothes on top of his bag. On his way to the bed, he snatched up the blanket and pillows from the floor and settled on top of the covers, wrapping the blanket around his body.

Ava couldn't be sleeping over there with that shallow breathing, but her pretense was probably a good thing.

He closed his eyes and tried to block out the images

that always marched across his mind at night. He had no
way of knowing which ones were real or fake anyway.

A sliver of pain lanced his temple. He'd hoped to put
off taking a pill until morning, since that would mean
progress.

A bead of sweat rolled down his face, and he licked
his dry lips. He'd left the tin of pills on the nightstand
and tried to raise his arm to reach them, but the familiar
numbness invaded his limbs.

The pictures in his head flashed like a slide show across
his vision, and his hands curled into fists. The blood. The
carnage. The destruction.

A strangled cry rose from his throat. A surge of adrenaline reanimated him. He clawed the blanket from his body.

He had to make them stop. He reached for the form
next to him and sank his fingers into the soft skin.

Chapter Nine

Max's hand grabbed the back of her neck. Already on alert, she twisted away from him and shouted his name.

She tumbled from the bed and landed on the floor with a thud.

The thrashing and moaning continued from the bed, so she crawled on the floor around the foot of it. He'd tossed the blue pills on the nightstand.

She reached up from the floor and plucked the tin from the bedside table. She popped it open and pinched one of the pills between her thumb and forefinger.

She turned her attention to Max, his limbs flailing, frightening, guttural sounds emanating from his lips. The same sounds Simon had been making.

She let out a long breath and hopped onto the bed. "Max. Max, listen to me."

His head thrashed to the side, and she straddled his body, clutching the pill.

"Max, it's Ava. I'm going to put this pill beneath your tongue. You'll be fine in a few minutes."

Did his dark eyes gleam with understanding from the pain etched across his face?

She slipped her fingers inside his mouth and tucked the pill beneath his tongue, covering his lips with one hand.

He bucked beneath her, his hands cinching her around the waist. Another minute. "C'mon, Max. You can do it. It's me. It's reality. You're coming back."

His frame lost its rigidity. He pulled in a couple of long breaths. He blinked and swallowed. "Ava."

Despite the raspy edge, it was the sweetest sound she'd ever heard. Leaning forward, she cupped his jaw with her hand. "That's right. It's Ava. I'm here."

The hands around her waist tightened before they dropped.

His spiky, dark lashes shuttered his eyes, and he dragged the back of his hand across his mouth. "Did I...did I hurt you?"

Her heart pounded. "Absolutely not. I wasn't in any danger at all."

He cursed and shifted her off his body. "I could've killed you."

Lying next to him, she didn't move one muscle. "I don't believe that, Max."

He sat up and shook his head, his chest heaving with every breath. "I should've taken another pill when we ate. I had no right to push my luck—not with you here."

"It's a good thing I was here. I was able to do something for you this time."

"I haven't done anything for you except drag you into a mess of epic proportions."

"You've saved me so many times, I'm beginning to lose count, and you didn't drag me into anything. I walked into this mess with my eyes wide open. I posed as a doctor and worked for a man I already knew to be unethical."

He rolled out of bed—away from her—and stumbled toward the credenza. He grabbed a bottle of water and chugged the contents.

"Now, I'm going to spend the rest of the night on the

floor, and if you had an ounce of sense, you'd sneak out of here while I'm asleep."

For the first time in a long time, something made perfect sense to her. She whipped back the covers on the bed and patted the mattress. "You need a good night's sleep now more than ever, and the floor is not going to cut it."

He hesitated halfway to the bed, folding his arms over the sculpted chest she couldn't help noticing.

"I mean it, Duvall. Doctor's orders, even if they're from a fake doctor. Get back to bed and relax. You have a small dosage of T-101 running through your veins. No chance of another seizure now."

He snorted. "Is that what you're calling it?"

But at least he was moving toward the bed—and her.

He crawled in beside her and she let out a pent-up breath. "Feeling better?"

"Anything's better than what I just went through." He held his hands in front of him and flexed his fingers. "I could've hurt you."

"You didn't."

He turned away from her and shifted to his side.

Did he think he could get rid of her that easily?

She rolled to her side facing his back and stroked the hair away from his forehead. "It's going to be okay, Max. You're going to be okay."

And she would be okay as long as she had this damaged man to protect her. Then she would return the favor—she was going to fix Max Duvall.

THE WARM SKIN felt smooth beneath her fingertips. Ava moved in closer and rested her cheek against Max's broad back as she brushed her knuckles across the hard plates of muscle on his chest.

She'd examined his beautiful body, scars and all, at

the clinic before, but never in such an intimate way. She uncurled her hand and ran her palm up to his shoulder.

He sighed and halfway rolled onto his back, flinging his arm to the side where it rested across her hip.

She took his hand in hers and smoothed her fingertips over the rough spots where his fingers met his palm. They had to make this right. He could keep lowering his dosage, but an antidote would counteract the drug's effects in his system. Arnoff had to have one somewhere.

"What time is it?"

His gruff voice startled her, and she dropped his hand. "Sorry."

He shifted completely to his back and stretched his arms over his head. "For what?"

She held up her hands, spreading her fingers. "For mauling you in your sleep."

He hitched up to his elbows. "If that was mauling, I'm all for it."

"How are you feeling?"

"Okay." He ran his tongue over his teeth. "Dry mouth, slight headache, but I still have my sanity—thanks to you."

"All I did was give you a pill." She tugged the hem of her T-shirt over her thighs.

"That's all I needed."

"You need that antidote."

"Yeah, that too."

She sat up and tilted her chin toward Dr. Arnoff's laptop. "And we just might find the clues to that antidote in there."

"I'm claiming the shower first, and then I'll go out and pick up some breakfast. Bagels, coffee?"

"Anything like that." Max had just put an end to her visions of lolling in bed with him while they discussed strategy. Who was she kidding? If he wanted her, he could've had her. She'd had her hands all over him. Wasn't that obvious enough for him?

The slam of the bathroom door put a punctuation mark on her foolish imaginings.

She scooted off the bed and flipped the lid on the laptop. Sleep had recharged her brain if not the battery, and she had recalled several different letter, number and character combinations that Arnoff had written down using his wife's name. She'd give those a try and then wait for the power cord.

She powered on the computer, checking the battery life. Looked as though they had about an hour—an hour to save a life.

She wrote down each password as she tried it and then squealed when she entered the fifth combination.

Max charged out of the bathroom, sluicing his long hair back from his face, his jeans hanging low on his hips. "Are you okay out here?"

"More than okay. I got the password."

"I'm impressed, especially after the night you just had."

The night she'd just had was her best in recent memory. "I recalled that he'd written down his wife's name using different letters, numbers and characters. It just took a few tries, but we're still going to need that power cord."

"We can at least make a start." He rubbed his knuckles across the dark stubble on his chin. "I was thinking in the shower, Ava."

Her gaze flicked to his flat belly and back to his face. "I'm listening."

"If we can't locate any more blue pills or an antidote in the next few days, I want you gone."

She tapped the computer's keyboard. "We're going to find something, Max. Dr. Arnoff may have been unethical, but he was brilliant. He wouldn't have developed a drug like T-101 without an escape plan."

"You find that escape plan while I go round up some breakfast." He pulled a T-shirt over his head, strapped on his shoulder holster and shrugged into a jacket. He turned at the door. "Lock up behind me and don't answer for anyone."

She padded to the door after it closed and put the locks and chain in place. Then she picked up the pad of paper with the hotel logo on it and dragged the chair in front of the computer on the credenza.

She wrote down the names of all the folders on the desktop, arranged them in alphabetical order and double clicked on the first one.

She was into the third folder by the time Max returned with breakfast. She opened the door wide as he walked through with coffee in each hand and a white bag pinned to his side with his elbow.

"Nothing fancy—just a couple of bagels with some cream cheese and coffee. I did throw some sugars and creams in the bag."

She pointed to the coffee cups. "Are these the same?"

"Plain old black coffee."

"Fine with me once I douse it with cream."

She popped the lid on her coffee and dumped in three little containers of cream. "I'm systematically going through the files on the desktop. I haven't even opened the hard drive yet to see what's on there."

"Discover anything so far?" He ripped into the bag and twisted two halves of a bagel apart.

"Nothing, but I'm only on the third of seven folders."

"I'll help you as soon as I devour this bagel. In fact—" he reached out and hooked a finger beneath the sleeve of her nightshirt "—why don't you take a shower and get dressed and let me take over folder duty."

Her cheeks burned as she glanced down at the hem of her T-shirt where it hit her midthigh. "I completely forgot."

"I know. You couldn't wait to delve into that computer." He licked some cream cheese from his thumb. "What am I looking for?"

"Formulas, calculations, numbers, any reference to T-101."

"Agents' names."

"Yeah, that too." She shoved the laptop in his direction. "I'll make myself presentable."

He grunted and started tapping at the keyboard, which was not the response she'd been fishing for.

Max didn't play those games. He dealt in black and white, not subtleties.

She dug through her suitcase for clean clothes and retreated to the bathroom. This morning she washed her hair and scrubbed her body to remove all traces of Max that still clung to her from spending the night in the same bed with him. If someone had told her a month ago that she and Max Duvall would sleep in the same bed and actually sleep, she would've sent them to have their head examined.

She toweled off her hair and scrunched up her waves with some mousse on her hands. She pulled on the same jeans from yesterday, a white camisole and a blue V-neck sweater over it. She stroked on a little makeup and even added a swipe of lipstick. Just because Max didn't actually voice his compliments, it didn't mean he didn't notice.

She stepped from the bathroom and folded her nightshirt on top of her suitcase. "Find anything?"

"I'm not as methodical as you, but I may have located

some of the other agents. I entered the names I knew in the search engine, and they pop up in a few places."

"While I understand your desire to warn the other agents, it's more important right now for you to get an antidote flowing through your veins." She hooked her thumbs in the front pockets of her jeans and sauntered to the credenza.

He lifted one shoulder. "I didn't know what to enter in the search field for a formula or antidote. I entered what I knew."

"Okay, then." She leaned over his shoulder and peered at the screen. "What came up?"

He jabbed his finger at the display. "They come up in a database in some program, but I'm not sure how to launch it. It's not some static file. It updates automatically."

"Let me see if it looks familiar." She wedged her hip on the arm of his chair, hunching forward. "Okay, I think we can open it with this database program."

She clicked on a menu and selected the icon for the program. It launched a map of the world and she opened the file with the agents' names Max had found from inside the program.

Red dots began flashing on the screen. A man's face would appear and then zoom to a different area of the map.

She held her breath as the dots populated the map, and Max swore softly.

"It's some kind of locator for the agents."

When the last dot found its home, Ava expelled a long breath. "Are you on here?"

"I didn't see myself." He poked at the middle of New Mexico. "And there's nothing coming up in our location."

"How is this program tracking agents?"

"I'm not sure. I'm just relieved Tempest didn't inject

some kind of tracker beneath my skin. I'd been worried about that."

"Have you gotten rid of anything issued by Tempest?"

"A few things, most notably my phone. Tempest could've easily put a tracking device in our phones. We're supposed to carry them with us at all times. They have a hotline to Tempest and not much else." He flicked a finger at the map somewhere south of them. "But this is what I'm interested in. This looks like the agent closest to us—somewhere in Central America."

"Wait. Click on the red dot so we can see who it is."

Max clicked on the dot, and a head shot appeared on the screen with a name.

"You know him?"

"That's Malcolm Snyder, or at least that's the name he gave me. He's very quiet, almost shy. Are you going to try to track him down?"

"My goal is to get to all of them, help all of them break free."

She laid her hand over his on the mouse. "You need to break free first, Max. You can't save every Tempest agent unless you save yourself."

"I know that, which is why we'll keep looking through Arnoff's files. We may have to venture onto the next big town so we can buy a power cord for the laptop. I don't think the local hardware store is going to have one."

"Looks like we have another half hour or so." She tugged on his arm. "Let me get on there. If we're not following my system, I might as well start searching for some common formulas."

They switched places, and he pulled another bagel from the bag. "Do you want one?"

"You take it." As the laptop's battery drained, she started typing more furiously. Every action seemed like a race against time—if not the battery, then the blue pills. What would happen to Max when he ran out? To save his life, he might have to throw himself on Tempest's mercy. He wouldn't allow himself to go down the same road as Simon—possibly hurting other people, possibly hurting her.

She glanced over her shoulder at him lounging across the bed, biting into a bagel and watching a football game on TV. Would he take himself out rather than submitting to Tempest again? She shivered and slurped a sip of lukewarm coffee.

She entered another chemical from Dr. Arnoff's original T-101 formula and clicked on Search. Three files popped up and she sucked in a breath.

"I got a hit here."

He muted the TV and joined her at the credenza.

"This chemical is in the original formula." She opened the first file and the formula for T-101 was laid out on the screen. Her pulse rate ticked up. "We're onto something."

"You're onto something. That looks like gobbledygook to me."

"Very important gobbledygook." She minimized the file and opened the next one. Her gaze darted down the screen, and she squealed and grabbed Max's arm. "I think this is it. I think this is the formula for the antidote."

He squinted at the letters and numbers against the white background. "What's that going to do for us?"

"Max—" she bounced in the seat "—this is the antidote. You can take one dose of this and it will counter effect the T-101 in your body—no blue pills, no more shots. You're done."

He scratched the sexy stubble on his chin. "It's just a formula on a computer. How do we actually get the antidote?"

She shoved back from the credenza as a low-battery message flashed across the screen. "We make it."

"You can make—" his finger circled the air in front of the computer screen "—that."

"I know how to mix a formula. I know what these chemicals are. I was allowed to do that work with Dr. Arnoff, and I've done it before in other labs."

"Yeah, but you had an actual lab. Where are you going to cook up that stuff now? In the sink at the Desert Sun Motel?"

She jumped up from the chair and paced the floor. "I know who can find me a lab—and those chemicals."

His voice rose. "Really? Who?"

"My brother."

Chapter Ten

Max folded his arms, his rising excitement extinguished by Ava's words, which acted like a splash of cold water. "Your brother? The guy who completely screwed up your life?"

"My brother the druggie. My brother, who has dabbled in the production of meth and probably knows about every meth lab in the southwestern corner of the United States."

"A meth lab? You're going to cook up a batch of T-101 antidote in a meth lab?"

"Exactly."

"You can't trust your brother, and you can't trust anyone who cooks meth." Hadn't she learned that lesson about trust the hard way? He balled his fists against his sides. Obviously not, since she was still here with him.

"Who said anything about trust?" She waved her fingers in the air as if she was sprinkling fairy dust. "We rent the lab, cook up our own batch of drugs and leave it the way we found it."

"You said your brother's in Utah?"

"That's right. I know he'll help us. Cody owes me."

Max dragged a hand through his hair. "That Tempest agent we located on the computer is in the other direction—south."

She stopped pacing and marched toward him. She grabbed his arms with surprising force. "Unless that other agent has a storehouse of blue pills that he can share, it's pointless to warn him. We need to stabilize you first. I don't care about any Tempest agent right now except Max Duvall."

With her flushed cheeks and bright eyes, Ava looked ready to take on the world—for him. He reached out and brushed his thumb across her smooth cheek. "Why *do* you care, Ava? Am I another homeless dog to save? Another broken family member?"

Her words came out on a whisper, her warm, sweet breath caressing his throat. "You saved me. You're protecting me, and I'm going to do the same for you. Right now, you're all I have, a-and I think I'm all you have."

His thumb traced her bottom lip. "You are."

She met his gaze steadily and something passed between them—a pact, a bond. At that moment, he knew he'd do anything to protect this woman. He'd already killed for her...and he'd die for her. But not yet.

"Can you reach your brother?"

She blinked and nodded. "Yes. Should I call him now or track him down when we get to Utah? I know which resort he's working at."

"You know your brother best. Is he going to bolt if he knows you're on your way?"

"No, but I'm afraid to use my cell phone. Once I used my ATM card and they tracked us down, it got me thinking about other methods they could use to get to us. You said yourself, the program on Dr. Arnoff's laptop is probably tracking the agents through their cell phones."

He kissed her mouth because he couldn't help himself anymore and then chucked her beneath the chin. "I'm going to turn you into a covert ops agent yet. Dump your cell phone, pick up one of those temporary ones or use mine and then call your brother."

Stepping back from him, she said, "I'll get a phone at the same place where we buy a power cord for Arnoff's computer."

"We have at least a ten-hour drive ahead of us, so let's get going."

"What are we going to do about that SUV? Even if nobody saw us careening through Dr. Arnoff's neighborhood last night, the owner has definitely reported the car stolen."

"I have a bottomless pit of cash and a few fake ID's that I haven't even used yet. I'm going to purchase a car at a used-car lot, so we can drive to Utah in relative safety."

"That would be a first." Ava pivoted away from him and started shoving clothes into her bag, her long hair creating a veil over her face.

He eyed her stiff shoulders. He shouldn't have kissed her. No, the kiss was okay, but he shouldn't have made light of it after. If he'd never kissed her in the first place, he wouldn't have had to shrug it off.

Damn it. Being a robot had been a hell of a lot easier than dealing with these human emotions.

He strode across the room toward her, and she made a surprised half turn at his approach. He pulled her into his arms and planted a kiss on her parted lips.

Running his hands through her hair, he tilted her head and deepened the kiss.

One hand still clutching a T-shirt, she wrapped her arms around his waist and pressed her body against his.

The pressure of her soft breasts and intoxicating scent lit a fire in his belly. He hadn't felt this way in a long time, if ever. Tempest had tried to steal those memories from him, as well, and had mostly succeeded. Had he ever loved a woman? Did he even know how?

Was it fair to use Ava as his guinea pig?

He pulled away and dropped a kiss on her forehead, her cheek and her nose, ignoring the stab of guilt that twisted in his gut at her confused expression. "We'd better go trade that SUV for something legal."

"Good idea."

He turned and she grabbed his hand. "Max?"

"Yeah?" Her deep green eyes drew his gaze like a magnet.

"I don't regret that kiss. Do you?"

"No."

With that single word, her face brightened and he left it at that. She didn't need to know about the confusing emotions warring in his brain right now.

Ava was a big girl and had been making her own choices for years. He couldn't help it if they'd all been bad.

AVA LEANED AGAINST the headrest of the compact car as Max drove it off the used-car lot. That had been easier than she expected, but then, Max did have a boatload of cash and a few alternate identities.

He should just use one of those to get out of the country—after she injected him with some T-101 antidote. Maybe he could get an extra ID for her, and they could ride off into the sunset together.

She bit the inside of her cheek, trying hard not to draw blood. What *would* she do once she got Max stabilized? He was a man who flew solo. He'd let her help him, and then he'd let her go. She could tell by the way he kept fighting his attraction to her.

And he *was* attracted to her, just as she was to him. All she could do right now was help. She owed him that.

"Drives like a dream." He tapped the steering wheel.

"A three-thousand-dollar dream with ninety thousand miles on it?" She rolled her eyes. "Let's just hope it can get us up to Salt Lake without incident."

He tapped the GPS that the dealer had thrown in with the deal. "Once we get the name and address of the resort where Cody's working, we can enter it and be on our way. Are you sure you don't want to use my phone to call him?"

"I'll wait until I get one of my own. Cody's not going anywhere. The ski season hasn't officially started yet."

He handed her the GPS. "Do you want to find the next midsize town? Someplace with a decent electronics store for the power cord? You can pick up a throwaway phone anywhere."

"Like I said, I'm in no hurry." She patted her gurgling tummy. "I'm more interested in finding some food."

"You should've had one of those bagels. How about a quick drive-through so we can get on the road?"

"Find me a breakfast burrito and I'll be happy."

"There are usually a few fast-food places around the freeway, so I'll keep going that way."

One block before the freeway on-ramp, Ava tapped the window. "That'll do."

Max pulled into the drive-through, ordered a burrito for her and a couple of coffees, and they were on the freeway five minutes later.

After Ava polished off her breakfast, she reached for the laptop in the backseat. "Do you think the battery's dead?"

"Not sure. What are you going to look for?"

She opened the computer and tried to power it on, but the battery had died. "I just wanted to check out the formula again. We should probably buy a thumb drive so we can copy the formula and print it out somewhere. If something happens to this computer, we'll be lost."

"Who knows? Tempest may even have a kill switch to Arnoff's laptop. If it leaves his possession, they may be able to shut it down remotely."

"They can do that?" Her fingers curled around the sides of the computer, her palms suddenly sweaty.

"Tempest employs top-notch people. You said it yourself—Dr. Arnoff was brilliant."

"He was. Too bad he used that brilliance for a terrible cause."

"He paid for it."

She rubbed the goose bumps on her arms. "As did everyone in the lab, whether they knew about the true purpose of T-101 or not."

"I'm sorry."

Turning her head toward the window, she blinked back tears. Max's sincerity ran deep. Maybe because he was in danger of losing his emotions, he relished them more than the average man.

There was no way she'd let him morph into Simon. She'd mix up a batch of that antidote if she had to hijack a hospital to do it.

A few hours later, they started seeing signs of civilization. Max pulled off the freeway, and they spotted an outdoor mall with several stores.

Max said, "We're in luck. We can get computer accessories in that electronics store on the corner."

"And find a place to work in one of the restaurants on the other side."

They bought a power cord that fit Dr. Arnoff's computer, a thumb drive and two temporary cell phones.

Ava nodded toward a coffeehouse at the edge of the mall. "If you're not too hungry, we can get a snack in there and plug in the laptop. That's probably the only place with an outlet for us to use."

"That's okay with me."

They settled into a corner table next to a woman tapping away at her keyboard, and Max held up the plug. "Can I use the outlet beneath your table?"

The woman glanced up from her computer. "Sure."

Leaning back, Max plugged in Arnoff's laptop.

While Ava powered it up, he pointed to the counter. "Sandwich and coffee?"

"Just a latte for me."

The laptop woke up, and Ava dipped into the plastic bag on Max's chair and unwrapped the thumb drive. She inserted it into the USB port and navigated to the file containing the antidote formula. By the time she'd dragged the file to the external drive, Max had returned with her latte.

"They're microwaving my sandwich. Did you copy it over?"

"I did." She leaned back in her chair, wrapping her hands around the large coffee mug, inhaling the milky sweet aroma of her drink. "Now I can relax a little. You really had me on edge with that comment about a kill switch."

"Like I said—Tempest has experts in every field." He tapped the back of the computer's cover. "Are you going to print it out, as well?"

"I think that's a good idea. Did you notice a copy place in this shopping center?"

"I didn't see one, but I'm sure we'll find a printer we can use in this town." He looked at his watch. "Now we just have eight hours until we get to Salt Lake. Are you going to call Cody now?"

"I'll turn on my cell long enough to copy his number from my contacts into this temporary phone and call him from the car when we can get some privacy." She scrolled through her contacts and punched Cody's number into the new phone.

The barista called from behind the counter. "Sir, your sandwich is ready."

As Max carried his sandwich back to the table, Ava pressed the button to turn off her cell phone and asked, "Who *is* behind Tempest, Max? Do you even know?"

"I know." His lips formed a firm line, and she raised her eyebrows.

"Does he have a name?"

"He has a code name—Caliban."

She snapped her fingers. "I get it. Caliban was the monstrous little character in *The Tempest.*"

"Yeah, emphasis on *monstrous.*" He picked up one-half of his sandwich and paused. "If I'd been more well-read, maybe I would've figured out the allusion. I didn't read that play in school. Then I found out the Caliban character tried to kill Prospero, and the code name suddenly made sense."

"Have you ever met Caliban?"

"No, but I know he's former military—special ops."

"Do you think someone turned him?" She blew on her coffee and took a sip.

"Someone or something, but he must've been off in the first place. You don't flip a switch like that and become a bad guy overnight. He definitely used his time in the military to make contacts. Tempest is a worldwide organization. It has no boundaries or loyalties—only to itself and its agenda."

"How do you know all this and the other agents don't?"

"I told you, Ava. The T-101 never worked right on me, or Simon. I don't know who else. I have to believe there are others. So, we suspected something was not right. I did some investigating while I was still in the fold. That's why I warned Simon to hang tough, but he couldn't do it."

"Does anyone else know anything about this? The CIA? Prospero?"

"God, I hope not." He broke his sandwich in half and prodded the crumbs on his plate with the tip of his finger. "The implications that the CIA or Prospero knows what Tempest is up to is too chilling to contemplate."

She narrowed her eyes. "But you've contemplated it."

"That's why I haven't contacted either agency. I'm not willing to take the risk." He took a bite of his sandwich and wiped his fingers on a napkin. Then he spun the laptop around to face him. "Have you checked the agent tracking program?"

"No. We're not going after anyone, Max. We need to work on this antidote. As it is, Cody is going to have to come up with the chemicals for the formula, even if he can find me a lab."

"We may not have far to go." He turned the laptop sideways on the table and flicked the screen. "It looks like this agent has come up from Mexico to Texas. It'll be easier to reach him now that he's in the States."

"After—" she closed the lid on the laptop "—we shoot you up with antidote."

"The sooner the better." He tapped her phone. "When you make that call to Cody, put him on Speaker."

"You don't trust me?"

"I don't trust him. Do you blame me?"

"Not at all." She popped the last bite of his sandwich in her mouth and dabbed her lips with a napkin. "In that case, I'd better make the call from the car. I don't want the cops coming down on me now as I discuss meth labs with my brother."

Max brought the plate and cups back to the counter and rapped his knuckles on the wood. "Is there someplace nearby where we can print a file from a thumb drive?"

"There's a twenty-four-hour copy shop about a mile down this street."

"Thanks."

When they got back to the car, Ava pulled the phone from her purse. "I'm not sure he's going to pick up a call from an unknown number."

"Leave a message."

She punched the speed-dial number for her brother and pressed the speaker button on the side. As she suspected, the phone rang four times and then voice mail picked up.

"Hey, man, I'm probably shredding. Leave me a message."

"Hi, Cody. It's me, Ava. Give me a call ASAP. I need a favor."

Max cocked an eyebrow. "Do you think telling him you need a favor is the best way to get him to call back?"

"*The* best way." She winked. "I told you he feels guilty about what happened before. I never ask him for favors, so he'll jump at the chance."

"Is he going to balk at the request?" He started the car and maneuvered out of the shopping center's parking lot.

"Coming from me? Maybe. Coming from anyone else? Just another day in the life of Cody Whitman."

Max parked in front of the copy shop, and Ava patted the side pocket of her purse where she'd stashed the thumb drive. "Got it."

The clerk behind the counter directed them to a computer in the corner. "You can use that one. It'll scan your media first, and if there's a problem, you won't be able to continue."

Max waved. "I'm sure it's fine, thanks."

Ava inserted the thumb drive and printed out a copy of the file with the formula. When she took it off the printer, she folded it and stuffed it in her purse. "Okay, that's two backups."

On the way back to the car, her phone rang. "Cody?"

"Yep. What's up, Ava?"

"Hang on just a minute."

Max unlocked the car and they both slid inside. Then Ava put the phone on Speaker. "I need your help, Cody."

"I figured that from your message. Anything. You know I'm good for it."

Ava rolled her eyes at Max. "You're at Snow Haven, right? I'm on my way up to Salt Lake, and I need a lab."

"Yeah, yeah. Snow Haven." He coughed. "A lab? Aren't you still working for Dr. Arnoff?"

"It's a long story. I'll tell you later, but right now I need a place to work."

"I'd like to help you out, but how am I supposed to find you a lab?"

"Don't yank my chain, Cody. If you're not using, you know who is."

"Whoa, whoa. We are *not* discussing this over the phone."

"All right. We'll discuss it up there. I should be in town around ten o'clock tonight."

"Should I pick you up at the airport?"

"I'm driving in."

He whistled. "I don't even know what's going on with you right now, but I'm not sure I want to get involved."

"You don't have a choice, little bro." She looked at Max and shrugged. "Why are you so jumpy?"

"I didn't want to tell you, didn't want to worry you, but there's some weird stuff going on up here."

Ava's pulse picked up speed. "What are you talking about?"

"At work the other day, one of the other snowboard instructors told me someone was sniffing around looking for me—didn't sound like anyone I knew and he didn't give her a name."

"Maybe it was someone looking for lessons."

"I don't think so."

"Why are you so sure? You're in a tourist resort. It could be anyone asking about you."

"Two days later, I came home late from a party and someone had broken into my place and trashed it."

"What?"

"Yeah, and the weird thing is I think whoever trashed it was still there...waiting for me."

"What makes you say that?" Her hand gripped the small phone so tightly it almost popped out of her grasp.

"I just felt it, so I didn't go inside. Turned right around and headed for my buddy's place."

"Did you call the police?"

"I don't want to draw attention to myself here. My friend and I just went in and cleaned up later and then I got some new locks."

She blew out a breath. "Be careful, Cody. I'll call you when I get in tonight."

After she ended the call, Ava cupped the phone between two hands and twisted her head to the side to look at Max. "What do you think of all that?"

"I think Tempest tracked him down."

...

Chapter Eleven

Ava's eyes widened, but her grim mouth told him she'd already suspected the same.

"It makes sense. Tempest wouldn't have any trouble tracking down your brother, especially if he's already in the system." He closed his hand around hers to soften his words.

"I don't know about that, Max. I never put Cody's name on any paperwork. Dr. Arnoff knew about him, of course, but I didn't have him listed with HR. If they did track him down, d-do you think they'll hurt him?"

"They might…ah…try to get him to talk if they think he knows your whereabouts."

Her right eye twitched, and he smoothed his hand across her brow.

He said, "If they're watching him and he goes about his business, maybe they'll leave him alone."

"But not if he goes about his business finding me a lab."

He squeezed her hands. "Tempest is good but not that good, Ava. They still don't know how much we know, what we're after. They only know I've pieced together parts of their scheme and what they've been doing to the agents. They have no idea we're looking for a lab to mix up an antidote. They may not even know about the antidote."

"I'm pretty sure Dr. Arnoff didn't go blabbing to his superiors about testing the T-101 on himself, so maybe he never mentioned the antidote." Her fingers twisted beneath his hold. "I just don't want to drag Cody into this."

He got that. He hadn't wanted to drag Ava into this either, but Tempest had already done its part to make sure she was up to her neck in it. "We can turn around right now, find some other lab, abandon the whole project."

"No." She pinned her shoulders to the back of the seat. "This is your only chance, Max. We have to see it through."

"It's up to you."

"Snow Haven it is."

They crossed through a corner of Colorado, and the temperatures dropped as the elevation rose. Ava offered to drive, and they switched places.

They drove through another fast-food place for dinner, and Max vowed to wine and dine Ava once they got to Snow Haven. It sounded like a perfect place to relax and sink into luxury, but it wouldn't turn out to be much of a haven for them with Ava cooking up potions in a meth lab while they looked over their shoulders.

Maybe they'd both jumped to conclusions. Given Cody's lifestyle, it could've been anyone going through his stuff—maybe even the cops.

"We still have a few hours. You can take a nap if you like." She patted the GPS stuck to the windshield. "I can get there."

"We should've asked your brother for a hotel recommendation."

"Aren't we going straight to his place? I was going to call when we got to town to get his address."

"I don't want to go rushing up to his apartment, especially if it's been compromised. Let's get a feel for the place first."

"Cody's probably tending bar tonight anyway. I didn't even ask him."

He peeled the GPS from the glass and tapped it. "I think this will list hotels and restaurants, too. We can look something up when we get to Snow Haven."

"I wonder if they have any snow yet. Do you ski?"

"Yeah. Do you?"

"That's an expensive sport, and my family didn't exactly have money."

"How did Cody learn to snowboard?"

"Cody's been playing pretty much since he graduated from high school—snowboarding, surfing, mountain climbing. He's done it all."

"How'd he afford that lifestyle?"

"Don't ask." She pursed her lips and stared at the highway.

Max closed his eyes, but he'd never mastered the trick of sleeping in a moving car or plane or bus. He never got tired though. He was wound too tight to relax. Tempest must've thought he was prime material for their spy games.

"Are you okay to drive the rest of the way? I can't sleep anyway."

"I'm good." Her brow furrowed. "You need to get some rest."

"You mean because it's almost time for Mr. Hyde to come out?"

"I'm just wondering if you could hold out for a little longer if you practiced meditation or deep breathing or something like that."

He lifted his shoulders and let them drop. "Never tried it."

"My point exactly."

He slumped in his seat and closed his eyes again. "I'll start working on it right now."

A few seconds later, Ava was poking his arm. "We're here."

He blinked and rubbed the back of his stiff neck. "Where?"

"In Snow Haven, and it's not snowing."

"You're kidding." He pressed his forehead against the cold window, as the outline of stark trees rushed by in the dark. "I actually fell asleep."

She scrunched up her face. "It wasn't a very deep sleep—lots of mumbling and twitching."

"That must've been attractive. Any drooling?"

She giggled. "Not that I noticed."

He wiped his chin with the back of his hand anyway and dug the GPS out of the cup holder. He tapped the display for places of interest and selected hotels.

Several popped up and he scrolled through the list. "How about the Snow Haven Lodge and Resort."

"Sounds expensive."

"Tempest is footing the bill."

Her jaw dropped. "Is that where you got all this cash?"

"They owed me—big-time."

"Let's do it. It's not like you're going to return any leftover funds to Tempest, is it?"

"Not unless they pry them from my cold, dead hands."

Ava sucked in a breath and punched his shoulder. "Don't even joke about that."

Hadn't she figured out yet that he didn't have much of a sense of humor? He rubbed his arm. "Ouch."

"There's more where that came from if you insist on tempting the fates with that kind of talk."

Ava Whitman could be a fierce little thing.

He selected the Snow Haven Lodge and Resort, and the GPS told them to take the exit in two miles.

He yawned and shook his head. "I don't think I could take your brother tonight anyway. I need a good night's sleep, a meal and a shower first."

She tilted her head. "You don't think you could take Cody? I can't imagine you'd have anything to fear from him."

"Fear?" He snorted. "I'd be hard-pressed not to clock him for the way he treated you."

"Really?" Her voice squeaked.

"You've never had anyone look out for your interests?"

"I wouldn't say *never*. One of my professors in med school took me under her wing." She shook her hair back from her face. "Of course, she abandoned me when she discovered what I'd done."

"What Cody did. Didn't you ever tell her the truth?"

"I've never told anyone that truth, except Dr. Arnoff, who'd already heard the story from Cody. And you."

"Like I said, that brother of yours will be lucky if I don't knock his block off."

"Please, don't. We need his connections."

A little smile hovered around her lips as she took the exit, so he knew she kind of liked the idea of someone knocking her brother's block off for what he'd done to her.

A few miles in, Max pointed to an alpine structure set back from the road. "There it is. I'm hoping they have a vacancy since the season hasn't officially kicked off."

She pulled the tired little beat-up car up to the valet station and popped the trunk.

As she took the ticket from the valet, she asked, "Are there rooms available?"

"Yes, ma'am. We won't fill up for another month unless the snow comes early."

The bellhop pulled the duffel from the trunk first, staggering under its weight. Max made a grab for the strap and hoisted it over his shoulder. "I'll get this one. It has some sensitive equipment."

They approached the front desk with the bellhop wheeling the rest of their belongings behind them.

Max booked one of the suites. This way they'd have two different rooms for sleeping without actually asking for two separate beds. He didn't know if he could handle another night lying next to Ava. He couldn't trust himself to keep his hands to himself.

The clerk slid two key cards toward them. "You're going to appreciate this suite. It has a fireplace and a wonderful view of the mountain."

Ava smiled brightly. "Perfect."

The bellhop trailed them to their room, and Max slipped him a tip after he'd unloaded their bags.

Ava wandered to the window and pulled back the drapes. "We could see the skiers from here if there were any."

"Are you hungry?" He shoved his bag in the closet.

"Not after driving all day and that icky fast food. Are you?"

"No, but I could use some water or a can of soda. Should we brave the minibar?"

"It's all courtesy of Tempest, right?"

He flung back the door beneath the flat-screen TV and opened the minibar. "Soda? Juice? Wine?"

"If you don't mind, I'll have some wine."

"Why should I mind?"

"I just figured you didn't drink. That's what you used to tell me during your checkups."

"I don't drink, but I don't mind if you do."

"We never recommended abstinence—from drinking. Did Tempest have some sort of rule against it? Not all of my agent patients were teetotalers."

"Red or white?" He held up two half bottles of wine.

"I'll take the red. It wasn't in the fridge, was it?"

"Next to it." He twisted off the lid and poured the ruby liquid into a glass. "My reasons for not imbibing aren't medical. I just never wanted to feel impaired in any way on the job."

"And you were always on the job, weren't you?" She strolled to him and took the wineglass from his hand.

"Twenty-four seven."

"When's the last time you had a vacation?" She ran her fingertip along the rim of the glass before taking a sip.

"I can't even remember." He snapped the tab on his soda and gulped back the fizzy drink. "That was the point of the Tempest agents on T-101. We didn't need vacations. We're superhuman."

She dropped to the love seat in front of the fireplace and toed off her shoes. "I suppose I should call Cody and let him know we're here."

"Tell him we'll meet him for breakfast."

She put her phone on Speaker again and called her brother.

When he answered, he shouted across the line over raucous background noise. "Ava? What is this number, anyway? Not your usual."

"Never mind. I'm here at the Snow Haven Lodge and Resort. Do you want to come by here for breakfast tomorrow morning? Ten? I know you're not an early riser."

A shrill whistle pierced through the noise. "The Snow

Haven Lodge and Resort? Dr. Arnoff must be paying you well."

"Can you get over here at ten?"

"I'll be there. Enjoy your fancy digs."

She pushed up from the love seat and plugged her phone into the charger. Then she placed her wineglass on the mantel and fiddled with the switch on the side of the fireplace.

"I think that ignites the pilot." He strode to the fireplace and picked up a box of long matches. "Turn it to the right, and I'll light the fire."

A little blue flame flickered beneath the logs and he struck a match and lit the kindling. The blaze raced along the log and then shot up into an orange fire.

"I like that." He grabbed his can and sat on the floor before the fire, leaning against the love seat Ava had just vacated and resting his forearms on his bent knees.

She took a sip of her wine and gazed into the fire. "This feels good—almost normal."

"Have a seat." He patted the cushion behind him.

Cupping the bowl of her glass with one hand, she took a few steps toward the love seat and lowered herself to the edge.

The soft denim of the jeans encasing her legs brushed his arm. She stretched her feet out to the fire and wiggled her polished toes.

"How's the wine?"

"It's good. It's been a while since I've had a drink, too, except those few sips with Lillian Arnoff." She swirled the wine in her glass and took a gulp. "I can feel it sort of meandering through my veins, relaxing each muscle set as it warms it."

He twisted his head around to look at her. "Are you tipsy already?"

A slow smile curved her lips, which looked as red as the wine in her glass. "I don't think so, but I sure feel relaxed."

"Good. You've had a rough few days."

She sat forward suddenly, her hand dropping to his shoulder. "No, you've had a rough few days—a rough few months and maybe even a rough few years."

Tears gleamed in her green eyes. Maybe that wine hadn't been such a good idea after all.

He patted her hand. "I'm okay, Ava."

She slid off the love seat and joined him on the floor, stretching her legs out next to his. "What are you going to do once you get the antidote?"

"*If* I get the antidote, I'm going to try to reach out to the other agents. Tempest will have a tough time carrying out its plans without its mind-controlled agents doing the dirty work."

"Once we have the proof for the CIA or even Prospero, those agencies can take care of Tempest. You don't have to be a one-man show anymore." She yawned, and her head dropped to his shoulder.

"I'm not a one-man show." He snaked his arm around her shoulders. "I have you."

"Mmm." She snuggled against him. "Pill. Don't forget your pill."

Ava's breathing deepened, and Max let out a pent-up breath. Her exhaustion just saved him from battling his attraction to her. The suite, the view, the fireplace had all made him forget for just a minute who and what he was.

He disentangled his arm from Ava's shoulders. She stirred. He swept her up in his arms and carried her into the bedroom. He dipped and stripped back the covers on the bed with one hand. Then he placed her on the cool sheet and tucked the other sheet and the blanket around her chin.

She murmured, "Max?"

"Shh. Go to sleep."

He fished the breath-mint tin from his pocket and plucked out one of the blue pills. He swallowed the pill with the rest of his soda and then stretched out on the couch by the window.

He'd just protected himself and Ava from another one of his spells, but if Ava couldn't cook up that antidote he'd have to take more drastic measures to protect her.

He'd have to leave her.

AVA FLUNG HER arm out to the side, clutching a handful of sheet. Her lids flew open and she squinted against the light filtering through the drapes.

She ran her tongue along her teeth in her dry mouth. Had she gotten drunk and passed out? No wonder Max hadn't spent the night with her.

Max. A spiral of fear curled down her spine. Had he taken his pill last night or did he try to tough it out again?

She scrambled from the bed, still wearing the clothes from yesterday. "Max?"

She shot out of the bedroom and plowed right into his chest.

"Whoa." He grabbed her around the waist to steady her. "Are you okay?"

Brushing the hair from her face, she studied his clear, dark eyes and the smile hovering around his mouth. "I was worried about you."

He cocked his head. "Me? I'm not the one who went comatose after one glass of wine."

"I—I mean, I didn't know…"

"I took a pill before I went to sleep." He dropped his

hands from her waist. "In fact, you reminded me right before you passed out."

She poked his hard stomach. "I didn't pass out. At least, I don't think I did."

"You were wiped out after that drive. Anyone would've fallen asleep after a glass of wine."

"At least it was one glass instead of the ten it took to put my mom under the table." She dropped her lashes. "You didn't have to sleep in the sitting room. I think we proved the other night that a king-size bed is big enough for the two of us."

His eyes flickered. "I didn't want to disturb you."

"No...incidents last night?"

"If you mean did I start gnashing my teeth and breaking out in a cold sweat, the answer is no. The pill worked just like it always does."

"Glad to hear it, but now you have just two left, so I need to get to work. Cody's meeting us at the restaurant at ten."

"No, he's not."

"Oh my God, did he call or something? Is he backing out?"

"I didn't talk to Cody, but I don't want him coming over here on his own. He might be followed. We still don't know who broke into his place and why or if they're still here."

"Should I have him meet us somewhere else?"

"Tell me where he is, and we'll pick him up so I can make sure he's not being tailed, and we can stop for breakfast somewhere else."

She ducked around Max and snatched her phone from the charger. "I'll call him right now."

When her brother answered the phone, he sounded half-asleep.

"Change of plans, Cody. My friend and I are going to pick you up. Is there someplace for breakfast around there?"

"Tons of places in the town of Snow Haven."

"Give me your address and wait outside for us. We'll be there at ten."

Cody rattled off his address and asked, "Who's your friend? Is she hot?"

"He is hot—very hot."

She ended the call and turned to face Max, who had looked up from his tablet. "I think you just disappointed Cody. Is he going to be a no-show now?"

"He'll be more curious than ever."

Forty-five minutes later, they were on the road to Cody's. Ava had shoved Dr. Arnoff's laptop into her bag and had the printed-out formula folded up and stuffed in her pocket. They'd put the thumb drive in the hotel safe, along with stacks of cash from Max's bag.

Max followed the directions from the GPS, and when they pulled onto Cody's street Ava tipped her chin toward her brother, dressed in jeans and a red flannel shirt, his hair scraggly. "That's him."

Max rolled the car to a stop at the curb, and Cody bent over and peered into the car. When he saw her, he broke into a smile, wreathed by a scruffy brown beard.

Max popped the locks on the car and Cody climbed into the backseat. "Hey, Ava, good to see ya."

"Cody, this is Max. Max, my brother, Cody."

Max looked into the rearview mirror and nodded.

"How you doing, man?" Cody settled against the backseat. "There's a breakfast place called Holly's about a half a mile up and to the left. So, what's this all about?"

"I'll tell you when we get to Holly's."

Assured they hadn't been followed from Cody's place,

Max parked the car in a metered lot a half a block from the restaurant.

On the walk, Cody peppered her with questions about her job and Dr. Arnoff, which she avoided and deflected. Since Cody was a master of both, he didn't pressure her for answers.

They snagged a table in the back of the restaurant, near the kitchen. Cody and Max ordered full breakfasts with the works while she stuck with blueberry pancakes.

They traded comments about the weather and the drive and Cody's job until he planted his elbows on either side of his plate. "Are you going to tell me about this favor you want me to do, Ava?"

Max pointed his fork at Cody. "And don't forget, you owe her for destroying her career."

Cody's eyes bugged out. "You told him about all that, Ava? Are you crazy?"

"He had to know. It's all tied to what I need from you now."

"Spit it out."

"Are you still using, Cody?"

He glanced over his shoulder. "If by 'using' you mean addled, dazed and confused—no. I use a little for recreational purposes, mostly weed these days."

She sighed. "With our family background and your own past addictions, I don't understand why you risk it."

"It is what it is, Ava." He shoveled more food into his mouth.

"Do you have a dealer in Snow Haven?"

As he wiped his mouth with his napkin, his murky green eyes narrowed. "Who wants to know?"

She shoved her plate away from her and her fork clattered to the table. "If I wanted to turn you in, I would've done so a long time ago."

Cody leveled a finger at Max. "You're not a cop, are you?"

"Do I look like a cop?" He glared at Cody's finger, and Cody dropped his hand.

"No, but you could be one of those undercover guys."

"I'm not. Look, we don't give a damn about your drug use, or at least I don't. We need a lab, and we need it yesterday."

Cody's brows disappeared under the messy curls across his forehead. "You mentioned a lab before. What is this all about, Ava?"

"I know you've been involved in the production of meth, Cody." She held up her hands. "Don't even bother lying to me."

"And you want me to secure a meth lab for you?"

"Exactly." She slid a piece of paper across the table. "And it needs to be stocked with these chemicals."

He glanced at the list before pocketing it. "Why do you need all this?"

She folded her arms. "You have your secrets, and I have mine. You don't need to know. I need a place to work, and I need those specific chemicals."

"What about Dr. Arnoff? Don't you already have a lab where you work?"

"That lab is no longer feasible." Max took a sip from his coffee cup, watching Cody over the rim.

Cody balled up his napkin and tossed it onto his plate. "Are you in some kind of trouble, Ava? Is this guy taking advantage of you?"

Ava held her breath as her gaze darted to Max's clenched jaw.

"You have some nerve saying that after what you put her through."

Cody flinched. "I know I'm a jerk, but that doesn't

mean I want my sister to get mixed up with anyone else who's going to hurt her."

Max's dark eyes got even darker. "I'm not going to hurt your sister."

Ava waved her hands between them. "Hey, I'm right here at the table. You don't have to talk about me like I'm not."

The waitress broke the tension with her coffeepot. "Refills?"

When the waitress left, Ava turned to Cody. "All you have to know is that Max and I are helping each other. I wouldn't be here right now without him."

"Okay, I believe you. So, I'm supposed to find you a lab, no questions asked."

"Last time I checked, cooking meth was illegal. We're the ones who won't ask any questions." Max wrapped his strong hands around his coffee cup.

Cody swallowed, his Adam's apple bobbing in his throat. "Deal. I have an option in mind, but just so you know, it won't be my lab and it won't come cheap. I don't cook the stuff."

"I don't care, but your sister does. For her sake, you should think about cleaning up your act."

Before Cody irritated Max any more, Ava tapped his water glass. "Tell me about the break-in. Was anything stolen?"

"Not that I could tell, but then, I don't have much stuff. I had my phone with me. I have a roommate and none of his stuff was taken either. The place was tossed. That's why I figured it might be the cops."

"The cops are going to break into your place without a search warrant and go through your stuff?" Max shook his head. "I don't think so."

"You sure you're not a cop?"

"I'm sure, but I don't think the police operate that way."

Cody snorted. "You don't know the cops like I do."

"I'm sure nobody knows the cops like you do, Cody." Ava rolled her eyes. "How soon are you going to know about the lab?"

"Today." Cody scratched his beard. "He'll want to be paid. You good for that?"

"I am, but he'd better not try to gouge me." Max's voice had rolled into a growl.

"He won't, he won't. He's a good guy."

Ava made a noise in the back of her throat and her brother had the grace to turn red.

"I mean, for a guy who cooks meth."

Ava waved her hand in the air for the waitress. "Don't come to our hotel to see us. Give me a call on that number when you have something."

Max added, "And watch your back."

Cody's hand collided with his water glass. "Why do I need to watch my back?"

"Someone broke into your place, right?" Max lifted one shoulder. "I don't think it was the cops."

"Are you telling me that break-in had something to do with this lab business?"

Ava reached across the table and encircled Cody's wrist with her fingers. "Maybe. Just do me a favor and be careful."

"You too, Ava." He grabbed her hand. "You deserve to be happy. And safe—you've never been safe."

She slid a glance to Max tossing some bills on the check tray and whispered, "I'm safe now."

Max handed the money to the waitress. "Cody, can you get back to your place from here?"

"I get it. You don't want us to be seen together." He winked. "Done deal, man. Ava, I'll be in touch."

He leaned across the table and tugged her hair, and then he scooted out of the booth.

Max slumped in his seat. "He's a character. You two are nothing alike, except…"

"Except what?"

"Hard to explain." His hands formed a circle. "A certain naiveté about the world, I guess."

"I'm not naive anymore, Max. I've seen too much."

"Sure you are, and that's part of your charm. You're able to hold on to the good even among waves of bad. It's a gift."

"You don't have to dress it up."

"I'm not." He tapped the table. "Let's get back to the hotel. I was looking at the spa services, and a massage sounds pretty good about now, doesn't it?"

"Sounds like heaven."

He opened the door for her and they stepped onto the sidewalk.

Max stopped in front of a kiosk and grabbed a local paper, perusing the front page while Ava scanned the notices pinned to the bulletin board.

Out of the corner of her eye, she noticed a man pivot suddenly and hunch forward to look in a shop window.

As she studied his profile, beneath the baseball cap pulled low over his forehead, her heart jumped. She grabbed Max's wrist. "I recognize that man to your left in front of the T-shirt shop."

Max didn't move a muscle, but his frame stiffened. "Who is he?"

"He's a Tempest agent."

Chapter Twelve

Max didn't turn around despite the adrenaline pumping through his veins—the adrenaline and the T-101, but that Tempest agent shopping for T-shirts would have even more T-101 pumping through his veins.

He dug into his pocket and pulled out some change and a pen. He shoved the coins in the slot for the paper and put his lips close to Ava's ear. "Take this pen. We're going to split up, so I can draw him away from you. If he comes after you and he gets close, flip off the lid to this pen and jab him. It's not ink… It's poison."

She sucked in a quick breath but she took the pen from him and curled her fingers around it. "What about you?"

He gave a slight nod to his right. "I'm going to lure him into that public restroom by the bus stop. I have my weapon."

"He'll have a weapon, too."

"He will." He nudged her hip. "Head down the street like you're shopping. Go into one of those shops. He may follow you, but he's not going to shoot you down in broad daylight in the middle of a store."

"What if he has a knife or a poison pen of his own?"

"Like I said, Ava, if he gets close, stick him first."

Cupping her cheek with one hand, he kissed her mouth. "Goodbye, Ava."

He looked both ways before crossing the street, taking in the man with the baseball cap. He never would've known the guy was from Tempest.

When he reached the other side of the street, he glanced over to make sure Ava was on her way.

He window-shopped along the way to the bathroom, releasing a long sigh when the Tempest agent crossed the street to follow him. At least Ava was safe—for now. If he didn't come out of this encounter alive, she'd have the good sense to contact the CIA, or maybe she'd have the good sense to leave the country. Would Caliban want to leave any loose ends? He didn't think so.

The man was shortening the distance between them, but he wouldn't shoot him on the street, even with a silencer. The streets weren't crowded, but there were enough people to deter him.

He tensed his muscles and headed into the bathroom. The door had been taken off its hinges, but a divider wall separated the entrance from the urinals and stalls.

He slid his gun from his shoulder holster beneath his jacket and approached a urinal, turning to face the entrance.

The thought had crossed his mind that this agent might be someone like him and Simon. Even if he had the opportunity, could he just start shooting as soon as the guy walked in?

He didn't have to worry about that.

The agent emerged from behind the divider, his gun drawn.

Max immediately raised his own weapon. He recognized him now—the agent that was positioned in Central America on Arnoff's locator. So, he couldn't have been the same person who broke into Cody's apartment. He couldn't have made it here that quickly.

Snyder stretched his lips in what passed as a smile for a Tempest agent. "I should've known you'd be ready for me, Duvall. I'd considered tossing an explosive device in here, but that would've caused a scene. You know how much Caliban detests scenes."

"Yeah, he's a real low-key guy." He trained his aim right between Snyder's eyes. "Looks like we have a stand-off here."

"Not really. I don't care if I die for Tempest. You do. That gives me the upper hand. I start shooting, you start shooting, we both end up dead. And without you to protect her, Dr. Whitman will be next."

A quick, hot rage thumped through his system. He'd never allow that to happen. "Dr. Whitman already knows too much, and she'll know what to do once I'm gone."

"I don't think so."

"You're a drone, Snyder. Don't you care? You're a dispensable pawn to Tempest and your hero Caliban. You're drugged. You're a machine. I can help you."

"I don't want help. I've committed great acts of heroism for Tempest. We will rule the world one day."

"Is that what Caliban is after? He wants to rule the world?" Max tightened his finger on the trigger. Snyder had an automatic and would cut him down as he was getting his own shot off. But he *would* get the shot off.

"Caliban is a madman, like many before him. He'll never rule the world. He'll just succeed in murdering a lot of people and causing strife among countries."

"And that, Duvall, is the first step."

Snyder had lied. If he didn't care about dying, he would've pulled the trigger already.

"Come back to the fold, Duvall. You're too valuable

an agent for Tempest to lose. Get back on the program.
I know you have to be hurting right now. We can shoot
you up with the juice and make it all better."

So that was Snyder's motive, to get him back to Tempest. If he pretended that was what he wanted, he could
buy more time.

Max rubbed his temple. "It's hell coming down off
the stuff."

Snyder's voice turned silky smooth. "You don't have to.
The lab where Dr. Whitman worked, where we used to get
our shots, has been destroyed. She destroyed it. She's our
enemy now."

Was that the lie Tempest was spreading among its agents?
It was designed to make Ava enemy number one, which
would be laughable if it weren't life-and-death.

Max cleared his throat. "Where are we getting our
shots now?"

Snyder hesitated, his eyes flickering. Tempest agents
didn't do well when they had to make decisions like this
on their own.

Straightening his spine, Snyder said, "Germany. We're
going to Germany now, where the other testing takes place."

The other brainwashing, but Max was supposed to be
a good little agent and not state the obvious.

"I don't know, man. It's hard."

"Come back, Duvall. We need you. The cause needs
you."

Maybe if he went with Snyder, Tempest would forget
about Ava, or he could convince them she knew nothing,
was no threat.

"You'd take me to Germany now?"

"Yes. If I had orders to kill you, I would've done it
before I walked into this bathroom."

He believed that. "And Dr. Whitman? We just leave

Dr. Whitman? She really doesn't know anything. Hell, *I* don't know anything."

"Yes. We leave her here." Snyder shifted his gaze to the wall and back.

He was lying.

Max's muscles coiled. He'd take the shot and then die for it. Die for Ava. It would be the most human action he'd taken in a long time. He'd go out a man, not a machine.

His gaze focused on a point right between Snyder's eyebrows.

Max sensed a whisper behind the divider and then Ava emerged from behind it. In a flash, she lunged at Snyder and plunged the pen into the side of his neck. He dropped like a brick, his automatic weapon slipping from his hands.

It all happened so fast, Max still had his weapon pointing at thin air.

Ava grabbed a paper towel, wiped off the pen and tossed it in the trash. "Let's get out of here before the lunchtime bus service starts and someone actually comes into this bathroom."

"We can't leave him here with this weapon. The drug you just injected him with mimics a heart attack."

"Do your thing. I'll watch out for witnesses."

While Ava hovered near the door, he crouched beside Snyder's body and started breaking down his weapon. He threw some pieces into the trash can. The rest he'd toss into the Dumpster around the corner.

When he had the two longest pieces of Snyder's gun in his hands and his own weapon tucked back into its holster, he joined Ava at the door.

"Let's slip around the back. Do you see any cameras around here? I checked when I headed inside, but I didn't have much time."

They scanned the outside of the small dilapidated building and Max didn't detect anything. He grabbed Ava's hand and pulled her to the back of the bathroom. Then he leaned into the Dumpster and buried the two pieces of metal beneath a mountain of trash.

He wiped his hands on the thighs of his jeans. "Let's do a little window-shopping on our way back to the car." He took her hand again and they strolled down the sidewalk like a couple of tourists, except Ava's skin had an unnatural pallor and her hand was shaking in his.

When they got to the car, she folded her frame in half and covered her face with her hands. Her shoulders shook and heaving sobs racked her body.

Although he wanted to take her in his arms, he wanted to get out of the area more, so he let her cry alone until he pulled the car into a turnout for a view point.

When he threw the car into Park and turned off the engine, he reached for her, running his hand along her back. "I'm sorry, Ava. I'm sorry you had to kill a man. You shouldn't have followed me, but you saved my life."

She rolled her head to the side, looking at him through wet lashes. "I don't care about killing him, Max. He was evil. I was just so afraid I wouldn't get there in time. And when I heard the last part of your conversation, when I heard him lie about letting me go, I knew you were going to shoot him. I knew you were going to die."

"Ava." He pulled her upper body across the console and she rested her head against his chest as he stroked her hair back from her moist face.

"I never expected you to come to my aid like that. The pen was for your own protection. You shouldn't have put yourself in danger. Snyder would've been only too happy to shoot you dead if he'd seen you before you pulled that ninja move."

"I know, but I had to take the chance. You've taken so many chances for me."

He kissed the top of her head. "I appreciate it more than I can express. I'm just sorry it came to that. I never wanted to put you in a position like that."

She wiped her nose on his shirt. "Desperate times, desperate measures. Speaking of desperate, I need to check on Cody. He left the restaurant ahead of us. What if Snyder harmed him?"

"Call him."

She placed the call, holding the phone against her ear. "Yeah, yeah, I don't expect you to have anything yet. I'm just calling to see if you're okay."

She paused and nodded to Max. "Just checking. Everything's fine and we still need that lab and the chemicals."

She ended the call and dropped her phone in the cup holder. "He's okay. I didn't want to tell him what happened. He doesn't need to know any more than he already does."

"Do you think he'll suspect anything when he finds out a man died of a heart attack in the bus station bathroom minutes after we met for breakfast?"

"Cody pays very little attention to anything that doesn't involve Cody."

"Are you sure you're okay?" He threaded his fingers through hers.

"I'm fine. I'll be fine."

"Let's get back to the hotel, monitor the news and relax." He started the engine and pulled back into the stream of traffic.

"Maybe we can schedule those massages at the same time." Grabbing the back of her neck, she tilted her head from side to side as if to get the process started.

"I mentioned the massage for you, not me."

She jerked her head toward him. "Why not? You're the one Snyder was holding at gunpoint. You need it more than I do."

"I can't." He hunched his shoulders. "I don't really like massages."

Was there any good way to tell Ava that he didn't like to be touched? Except by her.

"I understand." She placed her hand on his thigh and he didn't even flinch under the gentle pressure.

He didn't need to explain. She got it. She got him.

He pulled in front of the hotel and left the car for the valet. As they walked into the lobby, he whispered in her ear. "I'm taking it as a good sign that there are no police here to greet us."

"Nobody saw what went down. That bus stop was deserted. I think it's mainly used during ski season as a shuttle stop and at lunchtime."

They got into the elevator with another couple, and Ava stopped talking. As soon as the couple got off, she turned to him as if she'd never stopped. "There weren't any cameras there either. What are the police going to find when they check his ID?"

"A man who has a convenient next of kin only too happy to take care of all the details."

When the elevator reached their floor, she straddled the doors holding them open. "Do *you* have convenient next of kin?"

"Absolutely."

"What about Simon Skinner? He had a fiancée—Nina. He talked about her all the time."

He corrected her. "He *had* a fiancée. They'd split up. She left him."

"So, Tempest won't even notify her?"

"No, but I wanted to notify her. It doesn't seem right. She'll never know what happened to Simon."

"It doesn't, but don't you think Tempest is going to be monitoring her now? They might suspect that you'll contact her."

He unlocked the door to their suite and pushed it open. "You're probably right."

"Like I said before, you need to worry about yourself right now. Look at Snyder. You were all ready to rush off to warn him and he was on his way to capture or kill you." She swayed on her feet and he caught her around the waist.

"You're not fine, Ava. You just killed a man."

"I-it was self-defense." A tremble rolled through her slight frame.

"And totally justified. I know that, but it doesn't make it any easier. Even if you took him out while he was pointing a gun right at your head, you'd still feel traumatized. Anyone with any human emotions would feel the same way. That's why Tempest had Dr. Arnoff create T-101—to develop agents without those human emotions. Killing machines."

She looked into his eyes. "That's not you. They couldn't do it to you."

"I've done my share…"

"Shh." She placed two fingers against his lips. "That wasn't you, and then you fought it. You're still fighting it…and you're going to win."

He kissed her fingertips. "Only with your help."

"It's the least I can do after you saved me from Simon and then those two assassins at my house, even after I'd been responsible for your predicament."

"I thought we were over the blame game. You didn't know what you were doing."

"And neither did you when you were working for Tempest."

"Then we're both guilt-free and can move on." He stuck out his hand. "Agreed?"

"Agreed." She shook his hand, and he rubbed his thumb across her smooth skin.

"I meant it about that massage. You look all wound up."

"And what are you going to do while I'm getting pampered?"

"Work." He walked to Dr. Arnoff's laptop on the desk by the window and turned it on. "I'm curious if that agent-locator program shows Snyder here in Snow Haven."

"That would be one way to make sure it's accurate. You're off that grid, so we can't check the accuracy that way."

Max drew his eyebrows over his nose. "So, how did Snyder find me? How'd he know to head to Snow Haven, Utah?"

Ava stopped digging through her suitcase and looked up. "I thought we determined that they'd tracked us down through Cody."

"Maybe someone on Tempest's orders initiated the break-in at Cody's place, but that was no Tempest agent or he would've shown up on the locator."

"Tempest found Cody and sent an agent here to follow up. He didn't show up on the locator because he wasn't here yet."

"The agent knew we were here one day after we arrived. How'd they get that info from Cody's apartment? They couldn't have."

"You said you got rid of your cell phone. That's how they'd been tracking you before. They must've just gotten lucky this time."

"Yeah, lucky." He navigated to the agent-locator program and pulled up the map. "Son of a... Ava, look at this."

She stood rooted to the floor, clutching a T-shirt to her chest. "I'm almost afraid to see."

"You're the kind of woman who wants to know what you're up against, right?" He didn't want to heap any more bad news onto her already fragile psyche, but they were partners in this thing and he needed her up to speed.

She squared her shoulders and joined him at the desk. "What are we looking at?"

"The locator map." He jabbed his finger at the display. "It shows Snyder here in Utah."

"Okay, so we know it works. That's a good thing, right?"

"Look at the other dots." He trailed his finger across the map from east to west. "You notice anything about the location of these agents?"

"One's on the West Coast and one's on the East Coast. So what?"

"Yesterday, this one was in Southeast Asia and this one was in France. They're converging on us, Ava."

Chapter Thirteen

His words sucked the air from her lungs and she grabbed for the desk with one hand. "Snyder must've told them we were here."

"Impossible." He exited the program. "These agents were already on their way before Snyder even made contact with us. Tempest always knew we were headed to Snow Haven."

She licked her lips. "How? How could they be so sure just because Cody was here? Tempest can't possibly know what we have planned and how Cody can help us. Caliban may not even be aware of the antidote."

Max shoved the laptop and then landed his fist on the desk beside it. "It's the laptop. It's reciprocal. While the program tracks the agents, Tempest can track Dr. Arnoff. They found us at Arnoff's house. They knew Arnoff was dead, and they killed his wife. Once the laptop went on the move, they had to know it was us."

She stepped back from the desk on wobbly legs. "We thought it was such a great find at the time, and it ended up betraying us."

"It's not human, Ava, and it *was* a great find. You discovered the formula for the T-101 antidote. Now you have the antidote printed out and on a thumb drive. It's time to get rid of the laptop."

"If we just destroy it, they'll have no reason to believe we left Utah."

"Exactly, which is why we have to do something other than destroy it."

"Which is?"

"Send it on a trip."

"How are we going to do that?" She clutched her hands in front of her. Everything was moving too fast.

"Think about it." He tapped his temple. "We're in a tourist area, in an upscale resort. People are flying in and out of Snow Haven all the time."

"Are you crazy?" She took a turn around the room, scooping a hand through her hair. "Nobody is going to take a laptop from us. TSA agents even warn people against it at the airports."

"Did I say we were going to ask?" He spread his hands. "I'm going to get into the hotel luggage area and slip it into someone's bag, after deleting everything on it except the locator program, which won't make sense to anyone else anyway."

"How are we going to do that?"

"There's no *we* this time. You go off and get your massage, and I'll get rid of the laptop." He strode toward her, cupped the side of her head in his large hand and smoothed a thumb between her eyebrows. "Don't worry about it. This sort of thing is a piece of cake for me. This laptop will be on its way to Boston or Atlanta or San Diego in no time, and those agents will have to adjust their travel plans."

To forget about everything for an hour or two and leave this in Max's capable hands sounded too good to pass up. Besides, those Tempest agents were still thousands of miles away, weren't they?

She took a deep breath and blew it out, ruffling the edges of his long hair. "Okay, but what if you get caught?"

He folded his arms and raised one eyebrow. "Really?"

"Okay, okay, piece of cake."

"Get on the phone and see if you can get an appointment right now. I'll start deleting stuff from the laptop."

The spa had an available appointment for a full body massage in twenty minutes and she took it.

She peered over Max's shoulder as he dragged files into the trash can and then emptied the trash. "It's a ninety-minute massage. Will the deed be done by then?"

"Yep. You just relax and enjoy, knowing we're sending those Tempest agents on a wild-goose chase."

"Not sure I'll be able to relax."

"Sure you will. I've got this, Ava."

She believed him. She trusted him. He'd been ready to take a bullet for her in that bathroom or even return to Tempest. She'd had to prove that he hadn't misplaced his trust even though sticking that man—Malcolm Snyder—in the neck with the pen had been just about the most frightening action she'd ever taken. She'd had to stuff down every memory of Snyder, every feeling she'd ever had about him, and go on autopilot.

That was how the T-101 worked. It put those agents on autopilot to allow them to do their jobs without question.

She shivered and pulled on a clean T-shirt. She didn't blame Max one bit for wanting off the stuff.

"I'm going to head down to the spa now. Should I just meet you back up here?"

"Hang on." He clicked the mouse without looking up. "I'm going to walk you there."

She wrinkled her nose. "I thought you said we were safe for now, no Tempest agents in the immediate vicinity."

He dragged one more file to the trash can and looked

up with a half smile on his face. "I just want to walk you down."

"I thought you wanted to let me in on the whole truth and nothing but the truth?"

He shoved a card key in his back pocket and placed his hand on her lower back. "I think we're safe right now, but nothing is one hundred percent."

"Okay, I can accept that."

They took the elevator down to the basement floor, one level below the lobby, and Max walked her to the door of the spa. He touched his lips to hers. "Enjoy yourself."

Ava checked in, relaxed in the waiting room with a cup of tea and some aromatherapy and then followed her masseuse to one of the back rooms. When the masseuse left her, she undressed and slipped beneath the sheet on the table.

She closed her eyes, the hushed atmosphere of the spa already working its magic and the gentle New Age music soothing her nerves. What if she told the masseuse that she'd just killed a man in a bus station bathroom? The Hippocratic oath she'd taken never seemed further out of reach.

The masseuse returned to the room, and they exchanged very few words as she started working on her back.

The masseuse cooed. "You have a lot of tension in your shoulders and neck. I'm going to work on those knots."

Lady, you have no idea.

Ava responded with an unintelligible murmur as the masseuse dug her thumbs into her flesh.

Ninety minutes later, kneaded, pinched and pounded, Ava rose from the table a new woman. She paid with Tempest's cash and left a generous tip.

Back in the real world, she hoped Max had gotten rid of that laptop without getting detained by hotel security.

She hoped someone had discovered Snyder in the bathroom and had already ruled his death a heart attack. And she hoped her brother had come through with a usable lab and the chemicals she'd need to mix up a batch of T-101 antidote. Was that asking too much?

She could feel the tension creeping back into her shoulders already. Maybe the spa could give her a daily appointment—she'd need it.

Stepping from the spa, she spotted Max lounging against the wall down the hallway past the gym. The stress that had been clawing its way back into her muscles melted away.

Maybe she just needed a daily appointment with Max.

When she approached, he pushed off the wall. "I don't even have to ask how it was. You look…relaxed."

"I'll be more relaxed once you tell me how things went on your end." Despite herself, she scooped in a breath and held it.

"Arnoff's laptop is safely on its way to Florida."

"Where it will get plenty of fun in the sun." She touched his arm. "Do you think it'll work?"

"It bought us a little time, although we don't know who's here checking up on your brother."

"Maybe that was a simple break-in. God knows, Cody attracts his share of trouble without even trying."

"I doubt it, but at least we know the person here working for Tempest is not one of the T-101 agents. They're all being tracked with that program. I might have some trouble handling another T-101 robot, but not anyone else."

"That massage made me incredibly hungry. Did you eat lunch yet?"

They continued past the gym and he pointed at the weight machines behind the glass. "I could use some lunch, and then I'm going to work out. If I can't take advantage of the spa here, I'm going to at least use the gym."

"Sandwiches in the lobby restaurant?"

He took her arm and propelled her down the hallway. "If you don't think you'll float away."

She covered a yawn with her hand. "Do I look like I'm floating?"

"Yep, and I'm glad to see it. I told you I'd take care of the computer."

She pressed the elevator button. "What about Snyder?"

"It just so happens that I overheard a couple of the bell-hops talking about a man found in the men's room at the bus stop—an apparent heart attack victim."

She held up her crossed fingers. "Let's hope the coro-ner concurs with the initial finding."

"Believe me, Snyder's next of kin will make sure that they relate a history of heart disease. Tempest protects and conceals the deaths of its agents. You haven't heard any-thing about what happened in New Mexico, have you?"

"Not a word."

They sat down at the restaurant and she ordered a salad while Max stuck with a French dip sandwich. Just as she was about to dig into her salad, her cell phone buzzed in her pocket.

She pulled it out and smiled. "It's Cody. He says he's working on it."

"That's vague, but I'll take it."

"That's a lot from Cody. He's really trying to com-municate."

"Let's hope he can nail this down for us."

She crunched through her vegetables to avoid the ques-tion on her lips. What would happen if Cody couldn't find them a lab? The formula and instructions for the antidote wouldn't do her any good without the chemicals to cook it and a lab to cook it in.

Since Max had taken a huge bite of his sandwich, she had to assume he didn't want to discuss it either.

He had two blue pills left, and he had to take one tonight. That didn't leave them a lot of time until…

She grabbed her soda and slurped through the straw. "If you don't mind, I'm going to let you hit the gym on your own. I'm going to take a nap. That massage made me feel like a limp noodle."

"That's okay. I'm not a very social gym rat. I'd rather listen to music than talk."

She traced a bead of moisture on the outside of her glass. "I suppose talking's a girl thing, huh?"

He crossed one finger over the other and held them in front of his face. "My mother taught me never to stereotype girls."

"Smart woman, your mom."

"Yeah. Smart and a little bit reckless." He clinked his glass with hers. "Like someone else I know."

"I'm not reckless. I just always end up in the wrong place at the wrong time."

"Like in the men's room at the bus stop with a poison pen clutched in your hand."

"Okay, maybe a little reckless."

Max paid the bill and Ava took a soda to go. When they returned to the room, Max retreated to the bathroom and changed into some basketball shorts and a tank.

"Just to be on the safe side, when I'm gone lock the dead bolt and don't answer the door. I'm not going to send you room service or a special note or anything else. If it's the housekeeping staff, it can wait. Okay?"

"Okay, but your words keep belying your assertion that we're safe."

"Ava." He sat next to her on the bed. "We're not going to be safe until this is over. You know that, right?"

She dipped her chin to her chest. "I do, but sometimes I just need to hang on to the illusion. Do you know what I mean?"

He curled a lock of her hair around his finger. "I know exactly what you mean. We can pretend everything's normal once in a while."

She parted her lips because she really, really wanted him to kiss her—and not one of those soft, gentle kisses he'd been bestowing on her as if she'd crack beneath any pressure from his lips. She wanted a real kiss—a hot, full-bodied, gasping-for-air kind of kiss.

He released her hair and stood up, reaching for his tablet on the bedside table. "You're welcome to go through my library and read something if that'll help you fall asleep."

"I'm not sure I'll need help. I'm pretty exhausted."

"You have reason to be." He peeled his card key from the credenza and pointed it at her. "Lock the dead bolt behind me."

She bounded from the bed when he closed the door, knowing he'd be waiting to hear the dead bolt. After she flicked it into place, she smiled as she heard his footsteps retreat down the hallway.

So, no hot kiss. Maybe she wouldn't get one until this was all over. He'd get so carried away when she shot him up with the antidote, he'd crush her into his strong arms and kiss her silly.

She snorted. She'd better hang on to that daydream because that was all it was. And did she really want a gratitude kiss?

She grabbed his tablet and fluffed a pillow behind her.

Actually, she'd take anything he had to offer, motivated by anything.

She clicked the tablet, and his current book popped up. She scanned the text—one of Homer's epic poems. Didn't he say he wasn't well-read? Maybe after missing the Caliban reference, he decided to get well-read—or he was using this as a sleep aid.

She clicked back to the book list and noted some history, some true crime and a fantasy series. Max Duvall would probably never cease to surprise her.

She started in on the fantasy because she needed a little escape from this world. After reading about ten pages, she realized the fantasy world was no better than the real world—at least her real world.

She clicked the remote for the TV and crossed her legs at the ankles, tapping her feet together. She stopped the channel surfing at a reality dating show. Now, *this* was a fantasy she could get into.

By the time the show ended, Max was at the door. She peeked through the peephole and flipped back the dead bolt. "Wow, did you lift every weight in there?"

He pushed a damp lock of hair from his eyes, and his biceps bulged. "Yeah, sorry. I need a shower. Any news from Cody?"

"Nothing yet, but I think that woman should choose the dog trainer for the next date."

His brows shot up. "What?"

She flicked her fingers at the TV. "I got very engrossed in that show. Now I'm going to have to follow it and see who she picks."

"I thought you were supposed to take a nap."

She muted the TV. "I didn't feel that tired, but honestly vegging in front of the TV is pretty relaxing."

"Don't do much of that?"

"Not usually." She ran her gaze up and down his body, trying not to get hung up on a particular part of it. "How was the gym?"

"Good. I've lost some strength."

"That's good?" She covered her mouth. "Oh, the T-101 is having less of an effect on your body."

"Seems like it." He jerked his thumb over his shoulder. "I'm going to take a shower. You can indulge in more reality TV if you like."

"Funny thing about reality TV."

He cranked his head over his shoulder when he got to the door of the bathroom. "What's that?"

"It's so much more fake than real life, I don't know why they call it reality TV."

"Probably to make it seem like your own life is incredibly boring."

"Those reality TV people don't know my life."

"Right." He shut the door behind him.

She skimmed through the rest of the channels and left the TV on the local news. Maybe there would be some more information about Snyder. She hoped by the time his so-called next of kin came to Snow Haven to pick up the body, Tempest would be tracking them to Florida.

Max emerged from the bathroom with a towel around his waist. "I forgot to bring some clean clothes in with me."

She'd seen it all before, but the first time she'd seen him half-naked she still thought he was a crazy person. Now he was everything to her.

She clamped her hands over her waist, stilling the butterflies. She didn't want to feel that way. Red flags and danger signs were waving and flashing in front of her eyes.

He stopped on his way to his bag and turned. "Are you okay, Ava?"

"Yeah, I'm fine."

He crossed the room and put the back of his hand against her forehead. "You looked pale. The whole incident in the bathroom rattled you more than you probably even realize. You could even experience some post-traumatic stress."

She'd been more upset about her unrequited feelings for Max than about killing a man. What did that say about her? She'd never admit that to Max.

"I'm just anxious."

He stroked her hair. "Understandable."

Her phone rang and she jumped to grab it from the nightstand. When she saw Cody's name on the display, she punched the speaker button.

"What do you have for us, Cody?"

"Nothing. I got nothing for you, Ava. There is no lab."

Chapter Fourteen

Her legs turned to rubber and she sank to the bed. "What
are you talking about? You know people. There has to be
someone in the area cooking meth."

"I'm not getting any hits, Ava. I'm sorry." He cleared
his throat. "On the plus side, I got the other stuff you
needed."

"What am I supposed to do, Cody, cook it up in the
hotel bathroom?"

"I don't know what to tell you. The only possibility I
have is out of town. He'll be back next week. I can probably set you up then."

She gripped the phone with two hands. "We don't have
until next week. We don't have two days."

"I'll keep working on it, Ava. Maybe something will
come through. These guys are cagey."

"Obviously. That's why we gave you all that money."
Tears had filled her eyes and she dashed them away. "You
owe me, Cody. You ruined my life, my career. I protected
you, and now you owe me."

"I know that. I'll keep looking, Ava."

When she ended the call, she chucked the phone across
the room and fell back on the bed, the tears running into
her ears.

Max had stood silent and still like a statue during her conversation with Cody. Now the mattress dipped as he sat down beside her.

He wiped away her tears with the back of his hand. "It's okay, Ava. Don't cry."

She hoisted herself up on her elbows. "How can you say that? You know what it means, Max. You have two pills left—one for tonight and one for tomorrow. After that, you're cut off."

"Maybe I'll find more. That's where I was when I met up with you. I had no hope for an antidote then. I'm back to my original position."

"No, you're not." She tossed her hair back from her face. "You had five pills when you rescued me from Simon."

"If I had never gone to that lab to chase after Simon, I'd still have two pills today—and you'd be dead." He lay down next to her and captured her hand. "I'd say I'm in a lot better position now."

She sniffled. "What will you do, Max? How can I help you?"

One corner of his mouth lifted and he kissed her fingers. "You've already helped me, Ava. Nothing more is necessary. Nothing more is required. We have a new goal now—get you to a secure location."

"Max." She twined her arms around his neck and pulled his head close to hers, pressing her forehead against his. "I don't want to lose you. Stay with me. I'll help you ride it out."

He wrapped one arm around her waist, and his other hand skimmed up her spine and cupped the back of her head.

Slanting his mouth across hers, he whispered her name against her lips.

The towel had come loose from his waist, and she trailed her hand down the warm, smooth skin of his back. Her fingers dug into the hard muscle of his buttocks, and she moved in closer to him, drawing him closer to her.

He deepened the kiss, thrusting his tongue inside her mouth, lighting a fire in her belly, curling her toes. Here it was at last—the hot kiss she'd longed for, but now it meant goodbye.

He yanked off his towel and tossed it over his shoulder onto the floor.

Her eyes still closed, she let her hands create the visual as they roamed over his naked body, skimming the hard muscle and the flat planes, caressing the smooth skin.

He ended the kiss, leaving her panting and disoriented. Her lashes fluttered and her gaze met his dark eyes, alight with passion and desire. The look from those eyes melted her core.

Then she drank in what her hands had been exploring, and the beauty of his form took her breath away. Pure muscle cut through his lean frame. The nicks and scars on his body relieved it of perfection but added a layer of sexiness and danger that fueled her attraction.

On impulse, she ducked her head and planted her lips against the chiseled slabs of muscle on his chest. Her tongue toyed with one brown nipple, and she felt his erection plow into her belly.

With one hand, she reached down between his thighs and encircled his hard, tight flesh with her fingers.

A groan escaped his lips as he thrust into her hand. His fingers curled around the hem of her T-shirt. "Why are you still dressed?"

Before she could form a coherent answer, he had tugged the shirt from her body and over her head. It joined the towel on the floor. He slipped one hand into the cup of her bra, kneading her breast, swollen and aching with want.

His thumb trailed across her nipple, and she sucked her lower lip between her teeth to keep from screaming. He unclasped her bra and cupped both of her breasts in his hands. Dipping his head, he encircled one nipple with his tongue and then sucked it into his mouth.

"Oh." She dragged her fingers through his thick hair, her nails digging into his scalp. She hitched her leg over his hip to get even closer to him, and the head of his erection skimmed her bare belly.

She needed more of that.

She struggled with the buttons of her jeans with trembling fingers until Max drew back from her.

"Need some help with that?"

"If it means you have to stop doing what you were doing to my left breast, I think I got this."

He chuckled and unbuttoned her fly with deft fingers. "I have plenty of time to return to that luscious left breast."

At the mention of time, her heart jumped and she yanked off her jeans and her panties in one stroke. They had precious little of that and she intended to make every second count.

She kicked her pants to the floor and rolled onto her side again where Max awaited her. Wrapping his arms around her, he pulled her body against his. They met along every line, bare skin touching bare skin, fusing together in heat and passion.

With their arms entwined around each other, Max bent his head and captured her lips again. She invited him inside, their tongues dueling and exploring.

His heart beat against her chest, strong and steady while hers galloped and skipped. She stroked him from his broad shoulders to the curve of his buttocks, reveling in the raw power tingling beneath her fingers.

He cupped her derriere with one hand, the calluses on his palm tickling her tender skin. He caressed her flesh and fit her pelvis to his as his erection prodded her impatiently.

When he broke away from her, he planted a path of kisses from her chin, down her throat and between her breasts. Then he cinched her around the waist and rolled her onto her back.

Missing the contact already, she reached for him, dragging her nails lightly across his six-pack.

He shivered, and then rising to his knees, he positioned himself between her legs, his body proud and masculine on display before her. If just the sight of him turned her to jelly, how would she be able to hold herself together once he entered her?

She'd have to wait to find out, since Max had other ideas.

Slipping his hands beneath her bottom, he lifted her hips. He leaned forward, kissed each breast, flicked his tongue down her belly and nibbled the soft flesh of her inner thighs.

She thrashed her head from side to side. "You're going to drive me crazy."

He rested his head against her leg, his hair tickling her. "Do you know how long I've waited to drive you crazy like this?"

She rolled her eyes toward the ceiling. "Ever since I saved your life in the bathroom?"

"Nope, before that." His tongue darted from his mouth, flicking against the sensitive skin between her legs.

She sucked in a sharp breath. "Ever since I saved your life at the Desert Sun Motel?"

"Before that." He teased her again with his tongue.

She squirmed, her hips bouncing from the bed. "Ever since I saved your life that first night in Albuquerque?"

He raised his brows. "Do you think this is gratitude I feel for you right now?"

"Mmm, this feels a lot better than gratitude."

"I'm glad you recognize that." He trailed his tongue up the inside of her thigh and brushed it across her throbbing outer lips.

She closed her eyes and let out a long sigh, even though her muscles had coiled in anticipation of a sweet release. "So, how long have you been waiting to drive me crazy?"

"Ever since you first had me strip to my skivvies in your examination room."

Her lids flew open. "Really?"

"Oh, yeah. You couldn't tell by my—" he coughed "—reaction to you?"

She giggled, the heat rising to her cheeks. "I thought your heart rate was a little elevated."

He snorted. "It wasn't my heart rate that was elevated, sweetheart. Now it's payback."

He ran his thumb along the outside of her moist flesh and then used his tongue and lips to drive her crazy.

All at once, everything came unraveled and she cried out as her orgasm jolted through her body. This was no smooth wave of pleasure. Instead her ecstasy clawed at her over and over, driving her to new heights. Max rode it out with her, shoving his fingers inside her, prolonging her release as she tightened around him.

When she lay spent, her breathing ragged and her chest heaving, he straddled her. Was the T-101 responsible for that erection? If so, she gave a silent, guilty thanks to Dr. Arnoff.

And then the guilt and the fear and the desperation all

dissipated like feathers in a strong gust of wind as Max thrust into her. She closed around his thick girth as if he was a part of her.

He was a part of her. Whatever happened to him, to them, he'd always exist deep in her pores.

Each time he pulled out, even though it was for a nano-second, she ached for his return. He plowed into her, over and over, as if he couldn't get enough, couldn't get close enough.

Her sensitive flesh, still tingling from her orgasm, re-sponded to the close contact of Max's body, the tension building in her muscles again. She clawed at his buttocks, wanting more of him, needing more of him.

When he paused to capture her lips with his own, she shattered beneath him, her orgasm sending rivers of tin-gles throughout her body. She thrust her hips forward to engulf him and the motion acted like a trigger.

His frame stiffened as he plunged deep into her core. Then he howled like a wild, untamed beast and she trem-bled beneath him.

His release racked his body until sweat dripped from the ends of his hair, and his legs, still straddling her, trem-bled. He held himself above her, wedging his arms on ei-ther side of her shoulders. Then he lowered himself and kissed her mouth.

He growled. "I could do that all over again."

She dabbed her tongue against his salty shoulder. "Is that the T-101 talking?"

Grinning, he pulled out and rolled to her side. "Is that why you instructed your brother to fail on the lab?"

"Max." She drew her brows over her nose, and he tweaked it.

"I'm just kidding. You have to excuse my sense of humor. It's been AWOL for a few years." He smoothed the back of his hand across her cheek. "Let's just enjoy the time we have left."

Blinking back the sudden tears that flooded her eyes, she shifted to her side and smoothed her hand along the hard line of his hip. "I can do that."

"Glad to hear it." He rolled onto his back and pulled her close, molding her against his side. "You think we can find that reality dating show again?"

She twisted around and felt for the remote control on the bedside table. "Not sure about that show, but I'm sure we can find something that has more drama than our lives."

She aimed the remote at the TV and clicked the power button.

The hotel phone on the nightstand jangled and the hand Max had been circling on her belly froze.

They both stared at the phone as it rang again.

Ava swallowed. "I-it could just be housekeeping."

"Don't answer it."

They watched the phone ring three more times, Ava holding her breath until it stopped.

Max's entire demeanor had shifted from the passionate, considerate lover to the wound-up spy on the run, his jaw tight and his fists curled. She wanted to smash the phone with her own fist.

"Maybe we should call the front desk and see if it was housekeeping."

Max leveled a finger at the phone. "Whoever it was left a message."

She jerked her head to the side and eyed the blinking red light on the phone with trepidation. "That's good. Maybe they just want to drop off towels."

Max sat up and reached across her. He pulled the phone

onto the bed. He punched the message and the speaker buttons in succession.

The automated voice droned. "You have one new message. To listen, press two."

He punched the two button. A rasping breath burst over the line, followed by a man's harsh voice. "Max, it's Adrian Bessler. I'm a Tempest agent and I need help."

Chapter Fifteen

Max put his finger to his lips as Ava started talking, her voice rising with each word.

The agent—Bessler—coughed and cleared his throat. "This isn't a trap, I swear. I know what happened to Skinner. I know what's happening to you. It's happening to me, too. We can help each other. I'll tell you more, but you have to meet me. I'm afraid to talk on this phone. I'll keep it for a while longer to wait for your call, and then I'm throwing it away. Hurry." He recited his phone number and then the message ended.

Max stared at the phone in his hands. "It's too convenient."

"I know Adrian Bessler, Max, and he didn't show up on the agent-locator program. I never thought to count those red dots on the map to verify if all the agents were accounted for, but I know Bessler's name wasn't among them."

"That doesn't mean anything." He slammed the phone in its cradle and Ava jumped. He closed his eyes. "I'm sorry."

"It's okay." She rubbed the back of his hand with her fingers. "I realize it all could be a ruse, but he wasn't on that map."

"That could all be by design. Maybe Tempest figured since you were with me and had treated all the agents that you would've noticed Bessler's absence on the map, making this call more believable."

"But what if it's the truth?" She curled her fingers around his hand and squeezed. "You said yourself that you wanted to track down the other agents and warn them. Now you don't have to. One has come to you."

He pinched the bridge of his nose, squeezing his eyes closed. "I'd have to be very careful meeting him."

"Of course, and I'll be there, too."

"Forget it."

She squeezed his hand tighter. "I thought we were partners. I, at least, will know what Adrian Bessler looks like. That'll give us an advantage. You'll be walking in blind. He could be anyone—and that's dangerous."

"You could describe him to me. I'll tell him to wear something specific for the meeting."

She opened her eyes wide. "Didn't I ever tell you I'm really bad at describing other people? Besides, he could tell you he'll be wearing a red baseball cap and then blindside you. With me, there will be no blindsiding."

He shoved the phone to the foot of the bed and took Ava into his arms again. Her silky, soft skin soothed him. "I don't want you in harm's way, my love."

She sipped in a small, quick breath and he mentally gave himself a good swift kick. He hadn't meant to mention anything about love, but after the incredible connection they'd just shared, the words had come to his lips naturally.

"If you don't want me in harm's way, then don't leave me—ever." She nuzzled his neck and pressed her lips against the pulse beating in his throat. "Call him back.

Let's meet him and see what he has to say. We can use all the allies we can possibly get on our side."

With her soft breasts pressed against his chest and her wavy hair tickling his chin, he couldn't refuse her anything.

He sat up and reached for the phone. He put it back on Speaker and punched in the number Bessler had left.

The agent picked up on the first ring. "Yeah?"

"Bessler, I got your message."

"Duvall?" Bessler released a long, ragged sigh.

"Start talking."

"I'm in the same boat as you, man. The juice stopped working on me or something. I started remembering things, terrible things I'd done."

Max flinched and Ava ran her hand down his back.

"How did you find me? Why are you off the grid?"

"I knew you were with Dr. Whitman. I knew Dr. Whitman had a brother in Snow Haven. She told me herself that he was headed there to be a snowboard instructor. And I'm off the grid because I chucked my phone, just like you."

Max glanced at Ava and she pressed three fingers to her lips and nodded.

"I tracked her brother down, broke into his place to see if I could find out anything about Dr. Whitman. But I didn't know I'd be running straight into a Tempest trap."

"What does that mean?"

"You took him out, didn't you? The agent in the bathroom. I knew it was you as soon as I heard the circumstances. If he had seen me here, I'd be dead. I may still be dead. I can't talk any more, Duvall."

"We meet in broad daylight, tomorrow."

"In public."

"Exactly. There's an ice-skating rink in the center of town. Be there at noon in a green scarf and cap."

"And how will I know you?"

"I'll be in a green scarf and cap, too." Max drummed his fingers on the receiver. "And I have one more question for you."

"Yeah?"

"How many blue pills do you have left?"

"Not nearly enough, man, not nearly enough."

When the call ended, Ava took the phone and placed it back on the nightstand. "He sounds legitimate, doesn't he?"

"He said all the right things."

"His story makes sense, Max. I did tell him about Cody because Adrian is a snowboarder, too. He must've heard about the massacre at the lab and somehow knew I escaped. He ditched his phone to go off the grid and then figured he might find us here. It all adds up."

"I repeat—too convenient."

She stretched out on the bed, raising her arms above her head and grasping the headboard. "I believe him."

He dusted his hands together. "If you believe Agent Adrian Bessler, so do I."

"Really? That was easy."

"We'll find out if he's legit one way or the other tomorrow, and I'm not gonna lie, I care more about getting back to you than I do about Bessler because you look totally irresistible like this." He ran the flat of one hand down from her neck to her belly, and she shimmied beneath his touch.

The worry lines around her mouth and eyes dissolved, and the knots in his own gut loosened just a little. He had no idea if Bessler would try to kill him or if he'd have to take out Bessler.

It didn't matter right now. Regardless of what Bessler had to offer, he had limited time with Ava and he wasn't going to waste another minute of it discussing Tempest.

Or how he'd have to leave her in two days to protect her from the inevitable rage that would take over his mind and body.

She wiggled her toes. "We still need to eat dinner, but I'm all for room service in bed."

"With reality TV?" He flipped open the room service menu.

"What else?"

They ordered cheeseburgers and French fries and chocolate cake and spent the evening in bed eating and talking and laughing. And he'd never felt so alive.

Then he popped a blue pill, leaving one in the tin, and made love to Ava again as if it was his last night on earth.

MAX STOOD IN front of a mirror in the hotel's ski shop and wrapped the scarf around his neck. "Why did I pick green?"

"Probably because it stands out in the crowd." She adjusted the ends of his scarf and patted his chest.

"It stands out in the crowd because nobody wears it." The matching hat Ava held in her hands brought out the emerald color of her eyes, and he knew why he'd chosen the color—he'd been thinking about her eyes.

He took the hat from her and pulled it onto his head. "Bessler will definitely be able to pick me out."

"And you him, but wait for the signal from me first. If I see him at the skating rink and he's not wearing green, that's a sure sign he's planning to ambush you."

"He could just be the lure with someone else waiting there to ambush me. That's why you stay out of sight and keep your distance from me."

"Got it."

He swept the cap from his head and yanked the scarf from his neck. "I guess these will do."

He paid for the hat and scarf and took Ava's hand as they walked out of the store. "Are you hungry? You hardly touched your breakfast."

"I'm too nervous to eat. I hope…" She lifted her shoulders and then dropped them.

"You hope what?" He brought her hand to his lips and kissed each knuckle, one by one.

"I don't know. I just hope Adrian has a plan, that he's discovered something we haven't." Her green eyes sparkled with tears. "You have one pill left, Max."

"I know that, Ava."

She rounded on him and dug her fingers into his shoulder. "What do you plan to do when it's gone?"

"I'm not going to subject you to another Simon. I'm not going to subject anyone to that."

She bit her lip and one tear trembled on the edge of her long lashes. "We can get you help."

"A padded cell?" He shook his head. "T-101 is not exactly an FDA-approved drug. No doctor is going to know what to do with me, and they won't have a chance to even experiment. Tempest wouldn't allow that."

"What about the CIA? Prospero?"

"I told you, Ava." He caught the tear on the end of his thumb. "I don't know who I can trust, except you. I trust you."

She stared past him bleakly, her eyes dead. "I love you, Max."

The words rushed over him in a warm wave, and he closed his eyes to savor every sensation those words inspired. With Ava's faith in him, he'd achieved a monumental goal. Caring for her, loving her had made him human— more human than any antidote.

He kissed her right there in the hallway outside the ski

shop. "I love you, too, Dr. Whitman. Now let's get some coffee or hot chocolate and get ready to skate."

In the coffee shop, Max planted his elbows on the little table between them, hunching forward. "What do you remember about Bessler?"

"He's husky, blond, usually has a buzz cut." She skimmed her finger through the mountain of whipped cream floating on her cocoa and sucked it into her mouth.

He dragged his gaze away from her lips. He had to stay focused on this meeting with Bessler. "I don't mean his physical appearance. What was he like? Seems like he was one of the talkers if he told you he was a snowboarder and you mentioned your brother to him."

"He was nice, young." She snapped her fingers. "He was like you and Simon—friendly, talkative. A lot of the guys were reticent, didn't have much to say for themselves."

"So, you think Bessler could be on the up-and-up because he was friendly?"

"It kind of makes sense, or at least it's a positive sign. You three were not affected by the T-101 as much as the others." She sipped her hot chocolate and ended up with a fluff of whipped cream on her nose.

He reached over and dabbed it off. "Would you stop doing all that with the whipped cream?"

"Doing what?" She rubbed the back of her hand across the tip of her nose, her eyes widening.

"I'm supposed to be running through my plan for meeting Bessler and you're flicking whipped cream all over your body."

Her lips twitched into a smile. "You need to get your mind out of the gutter."

"It's not the gutter I'm imagining." He drew a line with his fingertip from her slender throat down to the V of her sweater. "It's a big bed with tousled covers and tousled hair and lots of whipped cream."

She swallowed and whispered, "Maybe if everything goes well with Bessler, we'll have time to live out that fantasy."

It always came back to that. She had to stop dreaming. He had one blue pill left, one pill between him and sure madness. And he planned to be as far away from Ava as possible when that madness descended.

"Hmm, don't know about that." He rolled his eyes to the ceiling.

"Wh-what? I have faith."

"I don't know if I want whipped cream or warm fudge and strawberries—maybe both, maybe all three."

Blinking her eyes, she smiled through her sniffles. "Once we get out of this mess, you can have me any way you want me."

He smacked the table. "You just pumped up my motivation tenfold."

She tapped her phone. "It's time. It's eleven forty-five."

"So it is."

They left their cups on a tray and made their way to the front of the hotel for the lunchtime shuttle into town. A few other guests from the hotel joined them, and then the driver hopped in.

He looked in his rearview mirror and called out, "This shuttle is going into town, makes one stop and then turns around."

The driver cranked the doors shut, and the bus lurched forward.

Max closed his eyes, trying to visualize his meeting with Bessler, but instead of a green scarf, all he saw was a pair of sparkling green eyes, and the thought kept pounding his brain that this could be his last day with Ava.

Even if Bessler hadn't called to lure him out and kill him, the other agent probably didn't have much to offer and he hadn't had Ava to help him. Bessler had called out for help—not much chance he could solve the problem.

The shuttle turned the corner and threw Ava against his shoulder. She stayed put, and Max draped his arm across the back of her seat and drummed his fingers on her collarbone.

She'd put on a good face today, but she'd been tense and had seemed on the verge of tears a couple of times. He'd take the coward's way out and slip away in the middle of the night. Ironic for a man who'd been searching for human emotion for the past two years only to escape from it in the end.

She pointed past his shoulder at the yellow tape tied to a post near the restrooms and waving in the breeze. "The bathroom isn't cordoned off, so it's obviously not a crime scene."

"Obviously. I heard a man dropped dead of a heart attack in there."

"This time it will be different." She laced her fingers through his and kissed the back of his hand.

He put his lips close to her ear. "Remember, we part company when we get off the shuttle. Head to the skating rink via the main drag, and I'll slip through the back-streets."

She nodded.

"If you don't see Bessler at all or you see him and he's not wearing green, just send me the text we agreed upon."

"No green."

"I'm gonna make a spy out of you yet." He pinched her soft earlobe. "We give him fifteen minutes to show. Then you return to the restaurant where we had lunch with Cody."

"Holly's. If he's there and wearing green, I'll text you *green*."

"And the most important part of the plan?"

"I stay out of Bessler's sight, keep out of the open and stick with other people."

"You got it." The bus rumbled to a stop and the doors, front and back, creaked open.

"Have a great day, folks. The shuttles are still running on a reduced schedule, so we'll just have five more runs with the last one at two o'clock, and then we start up again for dinner at five."

Ava stood up first. She leaned over and kissed him on the lips. "Good luck."

She was the only luck he needed.

He brushed a knuckle across her cheek. "Be careful."

He watched her hop off the bus and tag along behind a couple on their way to the main street.

"Sir, are you getting off or going back to the hotel?"

"Just looking for my hat." He plucked it from his lap and pulled it over his head. "Found it."

He jumped onto the sidewalk, still wet from the rain the night before, but not icy. He slipped around the corner of the bathroom, wondering if the Tempest cleanup crew had ever found Snyder's weapon.

With his muscles tense and all his senses on high alert, he navigated the backstreets of Snow Haven, which was neither snowy nor a haven for anything but traps. Total fail on that name.

He reached an alley between two buildings that led to the town square at the end of the main street. On one end of that square was the ice-skating rink, which abutted the end of a ski run. That town run hadn't yet opened for the season, and brown patches and clumps of trees dotted the side of the hill.

Reaching the end of the alley, he poked his head out and looked down the sidewalk both ways. The crowds of people that would usually clog the streets during the full ski season were thinned out, but enough people milled around the shops and restaurants to give him some cover.

He let out a breath and leaned against the wall, pulling his phone from his jacket pocket where he cupped it in his palm. A chill seeped through his veins as his adrenaline merged with the T-101 still pumping through his system.

He recognized the feeling. He welcomed it.

The phone buzzed in his hand and he glanced at the display. He read the one word aloud as if to connect him with Ava. "'Green.'"

Game time.

Squaring his shoulders, he pushed off the wall and stepped onto the sidewalk, his gaze sweeping the town square. He joined a clutch of people heading for the skating rink as he hunched his shoulders and pulled his scarf around his face.

He spotted Bessler immediately hanging over the side of the rink, watching the skaters, his green scarf tucked into a black jacket. What else did he have tucked in there?

Max waited in line at the booth and then paid to rent a pair of ice skates and for an afternoon of ice-skating. He picked out a pair of skates and slung them over his shoulder.

Bessler had raised his head and was staring across the rink. He'd been made, but did Bessler have to be so obvious? Ava was right. The other agent was young and green—another good reason for the chosen color.

Max stalked toward the skating rink, waiting for Bessler to make his move. The agent clumped toward the opening of the circular rink and glided onto the ice. At least the guy could ice-skate.

Max edged around to a less populated rim and gripped the wooden railing that circled the ice. He smiled and waved to a little girl, hanging on to her mother's hand and wobbling across the ice. Maybe her mother would have him arrested before he could even talk to Bessler.

Bessler skimmed around the ice, even doing a few turns and jumps. Then he started making wide circles around the perimeter of the rink, stopping every few laps to watch the rest of the action.

He neared Max and then bent over to adjust his laces. He came to a stop a few feet away from Max.

Max leaned forward and waved again. "How'd you know where we were staying?"

Bessler replied to the ice, his head still bent. "I bugged Dr. Whitman's brother's place. I heard him on the phone. Tempest doesn't know about Cody Whitman. They tracked you here some other way. Do you still have your Tempest phone?"

"Of course not." Max didn't want to reveal too much to Bessler just yet, so he didn't need to know about Arnoff's computer. "What do you know?"

"I know they're pumping us full of juice to brainwash us, to create some superagent, but it's not working on me, at least not completely. I heard Skinner went nuts and shot up the lab but Dr. Whitman escaped. I know she's with you."

"She's not with me anymore." Max laughed and waved at his imaginary daughter. "You're doing great, sweet-heart."

"Cut it out, Duvall." Bessler untied his laces again. "I heard a lot more from Cody Whitman than where you two were staying. He's trying to find a lab for you. Why?"

Max whistled between his teeth. He had to admit the guy had skills. "How do I know this isn't a setup?"

"If it were, you'd be dead by now."

"Or you would. Don't flatter yourself, kid." A woman barreled into the side of the rink, almost tripping over Bessler.

Catching her arm, Max said, "Be careful."

"I don't think this is my thing." She laughed and then skated off.

Max leaned back and looked over his shoulder. "Besides, I don't think Tempest wants to kill me. Snyder already had his chance."

"Snyder?" Bessler finished tying his skate and brushed ice chips from his snow pants.

"The guy in the bathroom."

"Why does Dr. Whitman need the lab, Duvall? Can she create more of the juice? A weaker strain like the blue pills? Because that's one thing I do know. We can't quit cold turkey or we'll wind up like Skinner—and I have no intention of winding up like Skinner."

Bessler rose from his crouch and then his blue eyes widened as he clapped the side of his neck.

Max dropped to the ground and hugged the ice rink's barrier. He didn't need to see it—he'd heard it.

Bessler crashed to the ice.

Chapter Sixteen

Adrian Bessler fell to the ice and Ava stifled a scream when Max disappeared behind the ice rink's barrier. They'd both been hit.

She dropped the cup of hot chocolate she'd been drinking on the ground and rushed toward the ice rink, her heart pounding, her mouth dry.

A few people had stopped next to Bessler, but nobody had panicked yet. Did they think he'd just fallen? Wasn't there any blood? And why had nobody gone to Max's aid on the other side of the barrier?

She ran onto the ice, her booted feet slipping beneath her. Five feet away from Bessler, she fell, her hands hitting the cold, solid surface. Sobbing, she crawled toward the fallen agent on her hands and knees.

He looked as though he was sleeping. There was no blood on the ice, no gaping wound in his head.

"Is he your husband? I think he might've fallen and hit his head. He's out."

Ava gazed past the woman's blurry face to the place where Max had just been standing. Had nobody on the other side of the wall seen him go down?

As she dragged herself toward Bessler's inert form,

attracting more and more attention, Max's head popped up on the other side of the barrier.

"What the hell are you doing?"

She nearly collapsed to the ice in relief. "I—I thought…"

"Doesn't matter what you thought. Stand up and do it quickly. I'm going to yank you over this wall."

The eyes of the woman attending to Bessler bulged from their sockets as they ping-ponged between her and Max.

An attendant in a blue parka started skating toward them.

"Wait!" Ava grabbed the lapels of Bessler's jacket. "His pills."

The Good Samaritan sat back on her heels. "Oh, does he have a heart condition?"

"Yes, yes."

Max growled. "Let's go."

Ignoring his command, Ava unzipped Bessler's jacket and patted his pocket, her hands tracing over his weapon. In a tiny inner zippered pocket, she felt the outlines of a pill bottle. With trembling fingers, she unzipped the pocket and snatched the pill bottle.

"You need to get off that ice—now."

The attendant skated up. "What happened? Does he need an ambulance?"

"He might have had a heart attack." The woman pointed to Ava, now crawling across the ice toward Max behind the wall. "His wife was looking for his pills."

"Ma'am?"

Ava twisted her head over her shoulder. "I'm not his wife. I've never seen this man before in my life."

When she reached the barrier, Max leaned over and pulled her over the wall. She landed on top of him.

"Stupid, stupid thing to do." He pinned her against the

wall, clamping his hands on her shoulders. "Stay down and keep to the wall."

Bending forward, they edged along the wooden barrier, as the buzz on the ice grew. Was Bessler dead? Why had he gone down? "Max…"

"Shh. We're going out the front way. I think they hit him from behind the rink, from the mountainside."

He whipped off his hat and shed his scarf. "Take off that jacket in case they saw you."

She shrugged off her jacket, shoving the pill bottle in the front pocket of her jeans.

Max grabbed her hand and pulled her behind the rental booth. "We can't sit around and wait for the shuttle. I saw some taxis by the ski rental shop back toward the bus stop."

They weaved up and down a few streets, sidling along the walls of buildings, joining groups of pedestrians on the sidewalk. They meandered through the ski shop and exited on the other side.

Max hailed the first taxi he saw. He bundled Ava into the backseat and said, "Snow Haven Lodge and Resort."

Bessler's bottle was radiating heat in her pocket and it took all her self-control not to dig it out and discover its contents.

When the taxi reached the hotel, they marched through the lobby without speaking one word. Finally, when Max slammed the door of their suite behind him, she pulled out the bottle.

He took a turn around the room, raking a hand through his hair. "What were you thinking? You were supposed to stay out of sight—no matter what."

"I thought you'd been hit. I saw Bessler go down and almost at the same time you went down, too."

"Doesn't matter."

"It does matter. Nothing else matters." She flipped off the lid of the bottle and peered inside. Her heart did a somersault in her chest. "Look, Max."

He stopped pacing and pivoted. "What?"

She dumped the blue pills into her palm and held out her hand. "Two of them. We have two more days together."

Her smile faded as she studied his face, his jaw hardening, the lines deepening. "I-it's two more days, Max."

His harsh laugh frightened her.

"Is that how I'm supposed to measure out my days left on earth? By counting little blue pills?"

She closed her hand around the pills and dropped her lashes. "These represent two days we didn't have before."

"It doesn't make any difference, Ava. Are we going to lure other Tempest agents here, get them killed and steal their stash?"

Anger flashed across her chest. "That's not how it happened. I'm sorry for Adrian, but he found us. I just took advantage of a terrible situation. Does that make me selfish? Then, yes, call me selfish for wanting to spend another two days with the man I love, the man I can't live without."

He reached her in two long steps and crushed her against his body. He buried his face in her hair. "You have to, Ava. You have to go on without me."

She clung to him, tears stinging her eyes. "I have the formula for the antidote, Max. I can save you."

"And what lab, what hospital is going to allow you to mix it up?" He drew back from her, cupping her face in his large hands, strands of her hair still clinging to his beard.

"A lab at the CIA or Prospero. They're the good guys. They'll help you."

"They've also put their trust in Tempest. Don't you think Tempest has already put out the word? Rogue agents, armed and dangerous. If the CIA doesn't kill me first, they'll send me back to Tempest to deprogram. I'm an intelligence asset. They can't allow me to walk the streets spouting crazy conspiracy theories."

"And Prospero?"

Furrows creased his brow. "I don't know. They're a wild card. Why did Tempest's leader choose that name and moniker of Caliban for himself?"

"You said it yourself. Tempest is the dark side of Prospero. Where Prospero is a force for good, Tempest is a force for evil."

"That's just it. Is Tempest the flip side of Prospero? Two sides of the same coin? I can't take that chance. I'm not going to end up in Tempest's clutches again."

"Caliban doesn't want to kill you, does he?"

He released her and fell across the bed, toeing off his shoes. "Do you know what happened to Bessler?"

"No." She sat on the foot of the bed. "He wasn't shot. There was no blood."

"Someone shot him in the neck with a tranquilizer dart."

"Do you think he's dead?"

"I don't know, but the same type of attack was planned for me and I know my dose wouldn't have been lethal. I would've wound up in the hospital, and my helpful brother or doctor or even wife would've come to collect me, bearing all the necessary ID and paperwork to airlift me to a facility of their choosing."

"They're diabolical."

"To say the least." He punched a pillow. "Tempest wants me back, but I'm not playing along. Before I'd go back to my so-called life at Tempest, I'd rather..."

Her nose tingled and she gulped back a sob. He'd rather kill himself. And what could she do to stop him? He didn't want to be around her once the withdrawal from the T-101 turned him into a raging machine.

She shivered as she recalled Simon Skinner's dead eyes through the glass at the lab. She never wanted to look into Max's deep, dark eyes and see that look. Better to remember the warmth kindling there as he made love to her.

She'd have that memory forever, and she'd never let it go.

Opening her hand, she stretched it out toward him. "We still have three more days. Let me have those three last days with you."

He pinched the two pills between his thumb and forefinger, took the tin from his pocket and dropped them inside to join the other. "We'll make these three days feel like an eternity."

She scooted between his legs and rested against his chest, feeling at home against the steady beat of his heart. "Let's start now."

He stroked her hair. "God, I was so terrified when I saw you on the ice, I didn't even ask if you were okay. *Are* you okay?"

"I'll probably have a couple of bruises on my knees. I'm sorry that I tore out there like an idiot, but you disappeared right after I saw Adrian collapse. I thought they'd gotten to you, too."

"I have no doubt they planned to nail both of us, but I think they wanted to get me first. Bessler stood up suddenly and that's when he was hit. I knew immediately what had happened, so I dropped."

She ran a hand along his belly. "I'm glad I did go out there. I remembered he'd said something about not having enough blue pills, so I figured he must've had a couple. And he did."

"Poor kid. I kind of have to believe now that he was on the up-and-up, unless Caliban plans to kill him to tie up a loose end."

"What else did he say before he was hit?"

"I'd forgotten all about what he said, but it was interesting." He toyed with her fingers. "He's the one who broke into your brother's place, and he bugged it. That's how he knew we were staying here, and he knew your brother was trying to secure a lab for us."

"That's two pieces of good news." She balanced her chin on his chest. "Maybe Tempest doesn't know about Cody. They tracked us here through Dr. Arnoff's computer, and so far they don't know we're holed up here."

"And the second thing?"

"That my brother was actually trying to find a lab for us."

"You doubted that?"

"He's my brother. I know him too well." She shifted to Max's side and twined her leg through his. "Did you tell Bessler why we needed the lab?"

"No. I didn't trust him until the moment he got shot with the dart. I still don't trust him, but he figured you might be mixing up a batch of weak T-101 to get us through the withdrawals."

"Adrian was sharp. He removed himself from Tempest's tracking system and managed to find us faster than Tempest did." She sighed. "What a waste."

"At this rate, Tempest isn't going to have any agents left to do its dirty work."

"He'll recruit more, won't he? Caliban. This whole thing—" she fashioned a big circle in the air with her hands "—is bigger than you and me. It's not just about developing an antidote to T-101. It's about stopping Caliban."

"We have to find out who he is before anyone can stop him."

"Do you really believe the CIA and Prospero are in league with him? It seems to me they're the two agencies that *can* stop him."

He ruffled her hair. "That's for you to find out, Ava. You're going to see this thing through. I have faith in you."

She clenched her teeth and pushed the dark feelings aside. When she and Max were lying here together, so close both physically and mentally, she could forget that they had just three more days together before he left her. And she'd never see him again.

He must've sensed her funk because he curled his toes against her feet and nuzzled her neck. "We picked at breakfast and skipped lunch completely. Are you down with another feast in bed?"

"I could go for that." She twisted her fingers together. "What's going to happen to Bessler?"

"If he's still alive, Tempest probably has him. If he's dead, the cleanup crew will take care of all the details."

"I'd like to think he's alive. Tempest can have him for now, but when I produce that antidote we'll get him back." She sat up, her heart galloping. "That's it, Max."

"Hmm?" He looked up from the room service menu and she snatched it from his hands.

"Tempest can have you back, too. Eventually, I'll have that formula ready to go and we'll save all of the Tempest agents, including you."

One side of his mouth quirked up in a half smile. "How will you ever find me again?"

She blinked. "I'll find you, Max. Wherever you are in the world, whatever you're doing, I'll find you."

"I almost believe you when you talk like that." He rubbed his hand up her arm, and she shook him off impatiently.

"Tell me you'll think about it. We may even get the antidote to you before Tempest can send you out in the field again."

"I'll think about it." He shook open the menu again and ran his finger down a row of items. "Cheeseburgers were good, but I could go for some pasta."

She stared at him over the edge of the menu and held her breath. It wouldn't do any good to shout at this immovable piece of granite. She'd work on him gradually. Hell, she wasn't above using her body to convince him. She'd give him such a mind-blowing experience in bed tonight, he'd agree to anything.

"You're smiling." He tapped her with the corner of the menu. "I see you like the idea of pasta."

"Let me see that thing." She held out her hand for the menu. "Do they have any whipped cream, hot fudge and strawberries?"

He raised an eyebrow at her. "I don't know what the strawberries would be like this time of year, but I'm sure they can scrape up some hot fudge and whipped cream."

"Purrrfect." She arched her back and tousled her hair.

He grabbed her around the waist and pulled her into his arms. "You're damned sexy, Dr. Whitman."

She wouldn't even correct him this time. He could call her Dr. Whitman until his dying day, as long as he delayed his dying day by turning himself over to Tempest.

Closing her eyes, she lifted her face for his kiss. When it didn't come, she opened one eye to find Max searching her face.

She thrust out her bottom lip. "What happened to that kiss?"

"You are so beautiful." His fingers dabbled lightly over her nose and mouth. "I'm imprinting you on my memory."

"You're already imprinted here in my heart." She tapped her chest, tight with emotion.

He tossed the menu over his shoulder. "It's a little early for dinner anyway. I think I want my dessert first—forget the whipped cream."

Just when they got comfortable under the covers, her phone rang. As always these days, the sound caused a shaft of fear to plow through her heart.

She rolled to the side and swept it from the nightstand. She met Max's eyes over the glowing display and peeled her tongue from the roof of her mouth. "It's Cody."

"Answer it."

"What's up, Cody? Are you okay?"

"Besides a string of crazy things happening in Snow Haven ever since you and that cyborg showed up, I'm fine. And you're gonna be fine, too."

"Why? What happened?"

"I got you a lab."

Chapter Seventeen

"Where? How? What?" She bounced on the bed. "I love you. You're the best brother in the world."

"Wow, before I was the scourge of mankind for mixing you up in my illegal activities. Now I'm freakin' hero material."

"Cut to the chase, Cody." Max threw off the covers and swung his legs over the side of the bed.

"You could've told me I was on Speaker, Ava." Cody coughed. "Hey, man, I totally meant that cyborg comment as a compliment."

Max grunted. "Whatever. Spill."

"That one guy I knew who was out of town got back to me when he heard about the money involved. He knows I'm no snitch."

"Which is coming in very handy right now." Ava's voice squeaked. She could barely contain her excitement. "Go on."

"Anyway, he has a place that he abandoned because the DEA was onto him."

Max interrupted. "Does the DEA know about this place?"

"No. My friend abandoned the place when the DEA started tailing him. Nobody knows about the lab except him and his partner, and now us."

Max asked, "Where's his partner?"

"Uh, dude's in jail."

"Great." Ava nibbled the side of her thumb. "Where is this place, Cody? Is it ready to go?"

"I already have the key and the code and someone's delivering all the chemicals you need as we speak. I gave the guy your money already, including the dude who got the chemicals, and I kept my cut. You said I could keep a percentage, right?"

"We did." Max walked to the window and peered through the blinds. "How are we going to get the key from you? I don't want you near the hotel right now."

"I don't think I'm being followed. Haven't noticed anything since the break-in."

"Humor the cyborg."

Cody choked. "A friend of mine works at the Haven Brewery in town. Her name's Dina. I'll leave it with her—no questions asked."

"Got it." Max grabbed the hotel pad of paper by the phone. "Now, where is this lab?"

Cody gave them detailed directions to a place south of Salt Lake City, along with the code for the door. "You have to follow these directions exactly because you'll never find the place using your GPS or a map. As far as I can tell, it's in the middle of nowhere."

"That's exactly what we're looking for." Ava took a twirl around the room. "Cody?"

"Yeah?"

"Have I ever told you you're the best brother in the world?"

"Yeah, like five minutes ago. Look, I don't know what you two are up to, but be careful. And, cyborg?"

"Are you talking to me?" Max rolled his eyes at Ava.

"Don't let anything bad happen to my sister. She's all I got."

"I won't." Max joined her at the foot of the bed and curled his arm around her shoulders, pulling her close. "She's all I got, too."

When Cody hung up, Ava jumped into Max's arms, wrapping her legs around his waist. "He came through. I can't believe it. He came through."

"Are you sure you want to do this?" He smoothed her hair back from her face. "It's going to be dangerous."

She wrinkled her nose. "How? I've been working in labs for the past ten years of my life. I know my way around a lab."

"Adrian Bessler had your brother bugged. How do we know Tempest hasn't done the same?"

"You said yourself, Tempest tracked us here from Arnoff's computer. Tempest doesn't know about Cody. He's off their radar."

"He was, but nothing remains a secret from Tempest for long."

"Then we'd better get moving." She wriggled out of his arms. "I've got a batch of T-101 antidote to cook up."

"Before we start packing up—" he shook his tin of pills "—I'm going to pop one of these for what I hope is my last time."

A half an hour later, they'd packed their bags and Ava stood at the door looking back into the room.

Max nudged her. "Are you ready?"

"I just want to remember where I spent one of the happiest nights of my life."

He kissed her ear. "I'm going to give you plenty of those, Dr. Whitman."

With the car packed up, they drove into town and

parked in a public lot. Max hesitated before opening the door.

"What's wrong?"

"Every time we come into this town, something bad happens."

Before she opened her door, she blew him a kiss. "Our luck just changed."

The crowds on the streets of Snow Haven were thicker at night than during the day, the restaurants bustling with people eagerly awaiting the first snowfall.

The Haven Brewery had a line out the door, and Max shouldered his way through, dragging her along in his wake.

They hung on the end of the bar, and Ava tapped the wrist of a waitress picking up a tray of drinks. "Is Dina here tonight?"

She pointed to a pretty blonde behind the bar, filling a pitcher of beer. "Dina! Customer over here wants to see you."

Ava thanked the waitress, and when Dina finished topping off the pitcher, she wiped her hands on a bar towel and approached them.

"Let's see, you want the Haven pale ale and you want the Haven IPA, right?" She winked.

Ava nodded, suppressing a smile. Cody couldn't resist going all secret agent on them.

When Dina slid the beers toward them, she slipped a key beneath Ava's mug.

Ava took a sip of beer through the foam, the malty taste filling her mouth. "This is good."

Max eyed her over the rim of his mug. "Do you really think you should be tipsy in the lab?"

"It's one beer."

"One very big beer, and I've already seen how you handle your booze, and it ain't pretty."

She punched his rock-hard biceps and took another tiny sip of beer. Her ears perked up when she heard the man next to them mention the ice-skating rink.

She glanced at Max, but she could tell by the hard lines of his face that he was already focused on the conversation.

"Yeah, it was weird. The guy went down like a sack of potatoes. I guess he tripped or something, but he wasn't getting up."

Max sidled closer to the man and said, "I was there watching my daughter skate. We left when he was still down. What happened to him? Did he die?"

The man took a gulp of his beer and wiped the foam from his upper lip. "No, no, that was the other guy in the bus station bathroom. That guy dropped dead from a heart attack, I heard. This guy was okay."

"Really?" Ava gripped the handle of her mug so hard, she half expected it to explode in her hand. "You mean he got up and skated away?"

"Nah, some guy, a family member I guess, came to his rescue and got him up."

Max traced a bead of moisture on the outside of his glass. "The attendant was going to call 911. Did the ambulance take him away?"

"Nope. His brother, or whatever, took him away before the ambulance got there." He elbowed his friend in the ribs. "Some brother. If it was me, I'd want to go to the hospital. That guy was out cold, from the looks of it."

"Yeah, me too." Max shoved his glass away from him. "We gotta go, honey. Olive will be happy to hear the man at the rink was okay."

Ava waved to Dina and pushed back from the bar.

Max paid for the drinks, leaving Dina a hundred-dollar tip.

When they hit the sidewalk, Max cursed and took her arm, hustling her toward the parking lot.

"What's wrong, Max? I know you think being in Tempest's clutches is the worst thing ever, but at least Adrian's alive."

"Being a Tempest drone is not being alive, Ava."

She puffed out a breath, happy for the hundredth time that Cody had secured the lab. Max would've never gone for her plan to return to Tempest only to be rescued by the antidote later, no matter how much whipped cream and hot fudge were involved.

He beeped the remote for their little car. "It's not just being under the spell of Tempest again. Tempest has Bessler and they'll be privy to any information he has—including info about Cody and maybe even the bug Bessler put in his place. Do you know if Cody was home when he called us?"

Max's words had instilled a cold fear throughout her body. "I think so. We need to warn him."

"I don't want you to call him. If Tempest does know about him, he'll be tracked."

She pressed a fist to her lips and then clapped her hands. "Dina! I'll give a message to him via Dina. She's already proven herself to be discreet."

"I'll drive you around the front of the bar and wait for you in the street."

He exited the parking lot and pulled the car in front of the bar, double-parking.

Ava ran into the bar, threading her way through the crowd. She gestured to Dina to join her at the end of the bar.

"Hey, thanks for the tip."

"Do you want another?"

The girl's heavily lined eyes widened. "Sure."

"I need to get a message to Cody but I can't call him on his phone. I don't want you to call him with this message either. Can you get him to come down here and talk to him in person?"

She smiled a slow, seductive smile. "I can get Cody to do anything I want."

"Too much information." Ava held up her hand. "When he gets here, tell him to leave town immediately and throw his phone away. Tell him it's life-and-death."

Dina's jaw dropped. "Seriously?"

"Seriously."

"I'll do it, of course."

"Thanks." Ava slipped her another hundred-dollar bill, courtesy of Max's stash. "Maybe you should join him."

She ran back to the car, still double-parked, and jumped in. "Done."

"We need to get out to that lab as soon as possible."

They left town just as a light snow began dusting the treetops. Max maneuvered the car down the mountain and they sped past Salt Lake City, heading south.

Ava clutched the piece of paper with the directions to the lab in her lap, crinkling the corners. "We're turning off in about four miles. What's the odometer reading?"

He poked a finger at the control panel. "I just reset it. I'll keep my eye on it, not that it looks like there are going to be a lot of options for turning off in the next five miles."

Darkness had descended and the snow had turned to slush.

Ava turned up the heat and folded her arms across her body. "Too warm for you?"

"It's fine." He flipped down the vent. "We don't have to

go through with this, Ava. We can drive on by and spend our last few days together someplace warm and safe."

"It's right within our reach." Her fingers danced along his forearm. "I'm not afraid."

"I know you're not. That's what scares me."

He took the turnoff and she continued to guide him by reading the directions from the notepaper. "I hope you have a flashlight in your bag of tricks because it's dark out here."

"What would you expect from a covert meth lab?" He scratched his chin. "Where did your brother get all those chemicals?"

"Don't ask." She turned in her seat. "You're not going to snitch him off, are you? I mean, about the meth lab and the drugs."

"I don't like the idea of someone out here making and selling illegal drugs, but I think under the circumstances I can let it pass." He shrugged. "Besides, the guy's out of business and his partner's in prison, right?"

"For now."

"That's all I have—right now."

He turned the car down what looked like an abandoned road, and a few buildings crouched together in a semicircle.

He cut the headlights. "Looks like there was a little light industry here at one point that never got off the ground."

She waved the paper. "It's the building on the left. It should have a keypad for the code he gave us and a padlock on the sliding door."

Max wheeled the car behind the building and parked. He dragged his bag out of the trunk and fished through it for a flashlight. He aimed the beam at the ground. "Stay close."

She hooked her finger in his belt loop and followed him around to the front of the building. As he shined the light on the keypad, she punched in the code with stiff fingers. Something clicked and she whispered, "That's a good sign."

Max inserted the key in the lock and sprang it open. He pocketed the lock. Then he yanked on the sliding door, and after a brief resistance, it slid open.

They stepped inside what felt like a cavernous space, and Max shut the door behind them.

Ava felt for the switch next to the door, and when she flipped it, white light bathed the room. She let out a long breath as she took in the gleaming stainless-steel surfaces and the neat placement of the lab equipment.

Max dropped his bag on the floor. "Wow, our meth cooker was a neat freak."

"It's perfect." She flexed her fingers. "I can do this, Max."

"Get to it." He gestured around the room. "I'm going to take care of security."

He watched Ava for a few minutes as she washed her hands, pulled on a pair of gloves and positioned a pair of safety goggles over her face. How the hell did he get so lucky to have this incredible, brave woman on his side?

He withdrew his weapon and loaded a second one. He placed it on the counter near Ava. "This one's for you. All you have to do is point and shoot."

She tapped a metal drum on the floor. "Can you crank this open for me?"

"Should I put on some gloves?"

"Yes, and some goggles. The fumes can sting your eyes."

"And you're going to be injecting me with this stuff?"

"It's better than the other stuff I'd been injecting you with for almost two years."

He opened the spigot on the drum for her. "Is this chemical flammable?"

She pointed across the room. "That stuff is. Why?"

He winked. "You do your thing, and I'll do mine."

While Ava continued to measure, pour, stir and heat, he secured the lab with a few booby traps using the equipment from his duffel. Tempest agents were always prepared.

If Tempest had their hands on Bessler, it was only a matter of time before they got information from him on Cody, including audio from the bug Bessler had set up in Cody's apartment. They should have some time on their side, since Bessler had been completely out of it.

Once Max outfitted the room, he slid open the front door. "I'm going to move the car away from the building. Be right back."

She said something unintelligible but didn't look up from her work, so he figured it wasn't important. Once outside, he surveyed the building and couldn't detect any light coming from it.

He moved the car another twenty feet from the structure, lining it up with a boarded window in the back—their escape hatch.

He returned to the lab and punched in the code to lock the door. He sat on a table facing the door. The building had no windows, so he couldn't see anyone coming but he could hear them.

"How are you doing over there?"

"It's coming along. Say what you will about Dr. Arnoff, but the man was a genius."

"Yeah, like a mad scientist."

"This formula is beautifully simple."

"I'll take your word for it. Let's just hope after all this hoopla, the damned stuff works."

"Count on it."

He let her work in peace, his muscles aching with the tension of the wait. Different noises came from the various equipment Ava was using, and then Max heard a low droning sound.

Tilting his head, he moved closer to Ava's work space. "What is that?"

She flipped the switch of some vibrating machine and the buzzing merged with the low drone.

He drew his finger across his throat, and she stopped the machine. "What?"

"Do you hear that noise? Is that something you're doing?"

She spread her gloved hands. "No."

Suddenly the drone turned into a roar, and the building shook.

Max clutched his weapon and tilted his head back to look at the ceiling, which seemed to be vibrating.

A voice boomed over a loudspeaker above them. "Give it up, Duvall. Come out with your hands up or we'll destroy that lab and everything…and everyone in it."

Chapter Eighteen

Ava dropped something on the floor and it shattered.

His heart jumped. "You okay?"

"Yeah. What do we do?"

"I'm not surrendering to Tempest, not now, not ever." He kept his weapon trained on the ceiling. "Get your stuff together. We're out of here."

"How are we going to escape? There's a helicopter up there, and I'm pretty sure they have weapons—lots of them. Besides, I…"

He held up his hand. "I know you're not ready yet, Ava, but I don't want to hear it. You have to abandon the antidote. Put down the test tube and pick up the gun I gave you."

The voice came through the bullhorn again. "We want to hear what you have to say, Duvall. Call the hotline. We'll pick up from the chopper."

Max reached for his phone, and Ava jerked her head up from pulling off her gloves. "What are you doing?"

"Buying time. I need to set our escape in motion, but I need you to pick up that gun and crouch down in the corner by the front door. Keep your goggles on."

He punched in the number for the Tempest hotline,

the line they used when they got into trouble. He'd never had to use it yet.

They must've patched the line through to the helicopter because someone picked up on the first ring and it was the same voice from the loudspeaker.

"That's better, Duvall."

"Who is this? Foster?"

"Does it matter? I'm Tempest. I'm authorized to speak for Caliban."

"What do you want from me?" Max put the phone on Speaker and then crept to the boarded-up window in the back of the building, past Ava's work area, where she'd been minutes away from saving his life.

The anonymous voice continued. "We don't want to kill you, Duvall. You're a valuable asset. Caliban thinks you're the most valuable agent we have. Give yourself up to us and we'll make sure Dr. Whitman gets out of here alive."

Liars. He checked the wires he'd set up earlier and glanced at Ava huddled in the corner, one hand shoved into the pocket of her jacket, the other clutching a gun.

"Is Dr. Whitman listening?"

"Yes."

"Dr. Whitman, you can take Dr. Arnoff's place. He neglected to tell us about that antidote. We'll allow you to mix up that antidote and more closely monitor our agents, including Max."

Max headed for the front of the building, with only one ear listening to the lies spewing from the phone. He checked his wiring there and lit a fuse hanging from the ceiling. There was no turning back now.

Max gave Ava a thumbs-up sign and muted the phone. He joined her in the corner and whispered, "Stay put but get ready to move through the back of the building once it blows."

Her eyes widened. "Blows?"

He put his finger to his lips and unmuted the phone.

Ava rose from her crouch and shouted into the phone in Max's hand. "Where's Agent Bessler?"

"He's safe and sound, Dr. Whitman. We treated him and he'll be fine."

"You mean he'll be a drone for Tempest."

"It's what our agents do, Dr. Whitman. Dr. Arnoff understood that and used the opportunity to conduct experiments that would've never been allowed in the medical community. You can do the same."

Max held up the phone and nodded.

Ava yelled, "No, thanks!"

Max punched in a three-digit number on his cell phone and the back of the building exploded outward, rocking the structure.

He grabbed Ava's hand. "Let's go!"

They ran toward the gaping hole in the wall in a crouch while machine gun fire sounded from above.

He pulled Ava close. "When we hit the opening, I'm going to lunge forward and I'm taking you with me. Get ready."

They stumbled through the gap, and Max launched himself forward just as the building behind them exploded. The force propelled them closer to the car, the heat intense on his back, the ends of his hair singeing.

The helicopter above them screamed and whined, and he twisted his head around to see it lurch onto its side, its spinning blades glancing the roof of the burning building.

Max dragged himself up from the ground and Ava popped up beside him.

She clambered into the driver's side and crawled across

the console to the passenger seat, dropping her weapon on the floor, and he gunned the engine before he was even sitting in the driver's seat.

Another explosion burst into the night sky as the chopper plowed through the roof of the building.

Max hit the accelerator as burning debris fell around them.

Ava turned around in her seat to watch the lab collapse. From his rearview mirror, Max witnessed a ball of fire rolling toward the sky.

Not until he reached the road that connected to the main highway did he let out a long, smoky breath.

He rubbed a patch of soot from Ava's white cheek. "Are you all right? Not hurt?"

She covered her face with her hands and said through parted fingers, "When you said you were securing the building, I didn't know that meant you were booby-trapping it."

"I figured the less you knew the better. You had other things to concentrate on. I didn't want to scare you or distract you."

"How'd you know they'd be coming by helicopter? How'd you know they'd be coming at all?"

"I didn't know about the helicopter, but car or helicopter, that explosion would stop either one. And once I heard they had Bessler, I figured it was only a matter of time before they found that lab. They'd debrief Bessler or shoot him up with truth serum or torture him, but one way or another they were going to find out everything he knew about us, including that bug he put in your brother's apartment."

She ran her hands through her hair, showering bits of debris into her lap. "I hope Dina got to Cody and he made it out of Snow Haven safely."

"Once you get to a secure location, you can call him. Tempest is not done with you, but once we part company

I'm sending you to Prospero. You can tell them our story. You can show them the formula for the antidote. They'll take care of you, whether they believe you or not."

"You still don't trust Prospero? You won't come with me?"

"Even if I had the time, which I don't, I wouldn't turn myself over to Prospero, but you should be okay."

"And who says you don't have the time?"

He grabbed her hand and circled his thumb in her palm. "We're not going to find another lab and get our hands on those chemicals in three days, Ava. It was a good try and we were close. I appreciate everything you did. I more than appreciate you. I love you. Always know that."

He steeled himself for more tears. It was a bittersweet victory that he was human enough now to be undone by Ava's tears.

She laughed.

He whipped his head around, but she continued to laugh, her eyes sparkling in the darkness of the car. Maybe the stress and tension had finally driven her off the deep end.

"I guess the idea of a doomed man falling in love could be funny and I'd rather see laughter than tears from you, but are you sure you're okay?"

"You're not a doomed man, Max."

"Three pills, three days."

She plunged her hand in the pocket of her jacket. She pulled it out and opened it wide, cupping a glass vial in her palm.

"Do you want to reconsider telling me you love me? This is the T-101 antidote, and you have a lifetime with me ahead of you."

Epilogue

Prospero's chief, Jack Coburn, cleared his throat over the phone. "We've been suspicious about Tempest's actions for a while, Duvall, so I'm inclined to believe your story."

Ava came up behind Max, sitting on the edge of the hotel bed, and draped her arms around his shoulders.

He captured her hand and pressed a kiss against her palm. "Do you know who Caliban is?"

"No, but we'd like to find out."

"I take it the CIA doesn't know either."

"Caliban reports to the director, just like I do, but Tempest has always been more secretive about its organization and actions."

"Now you know why."

"I repeat my offer for both you and Ms. Whitman. You can come in from the field and we'll protect you."

"It's not that I don't trust you, Coburn."

Jack Coburn interrupted him. "But you don't trust me. I understand, but to stop Tempest we need to know more about its operations. We want to debrief you."

"I get that, but we'll have to do it over a secure connection and from a safe distance. We will take you up on the offer of the new identities though, and Ava will turn over the formula for the T-101 antidote."

"That's a deal. Be careful out there and we'll keep you posted as we move forward with this investigation."

"What's next?"

"Nina Moore, Agent Skinner's fiancée. We have reason to believe she's being watched."

"Whatever you do, take care of her."

"We're on it, Duvall. You need to disappear now."

Max ended the call and reclined on the bed, pulling her down next to him. "We're done with Tempest—for now. We'll let Prospero handle them. You know, I think that's what Caliban wanted all along—some kind of face-off between Tempest and Prospero."

"Well, it looks like he's going to get his wish." She waved a hand around the hotel room. "Do we need to disappear any more than this?"

"Prospero will send us a couple of new identities. We can go even further underground."

She caressed his strong face, which had lost its hardness since he'd taken the antidote. "Can underground include a tropical paradise somewhere?"

"Absolutely." He kissed her mouth. "But we're not joining your brother and Dina in Hawaii, if that's what you're thinking."

"Hawaii?" She snapped her fingers. "We can go more exotic than Hawaii, can't we?"

"We can go wherever you want, Dr. Whitman."

She slipped her hand beneath his T-shirt and swirled her fingernails over his hard belly. "Now that you have your life back, are you sure you want to spend it with me?"

"If you can handle a cyborg for the rest of your life."

"Cyborg?" She snuggled next to his side and rested her head against his chest. "You're all man, Max Duvall, and you're all mine—forever."

LET'S TALK
Romance

For exclusive extracts, competitions
and special offers, find us online:

... experience all the excitement of a
gripping thriller, with an intense romance
... at its heart. Beautifully true-to-life
women and strong, fearless men face
danger and desire ... a killer combination.